After the Ball

David P. Penhallow

Rice Street Press
Lihue, Kauai, Hawaii

Printed by in Hong Kong by Magnum Offset Printing.

Second printing 2007.

Published by Rice Street Press
P.O. Box 148
Lihue, Kauai, Hawaii 96766

Library of Congress Catalog No.:99-96072

ISBN:0967414709

Edited by Donna Stewart, Rainbow Consulting, Kauai, Hawaii

Design and production by Barefoot Design Studio, Kauai, Hawaii

Cover by Laka Morton

TO MOTHER AND MARION

ACKNOWLEDGMENTS

This writer did not do it alone and I have many to thank: To God first, who hopefully forgives my lapses in gratitude, when my ego thinks that this novel is his work.

To my angels, Marian Benham, Pat Palama, Leslie Fritz, Ed Goka, and Candy Bahouth who supported, read, commented, and corrected a manuscript in its "baby" inception.

To my special angel, Jan Oshiro, who spent hours at Borders listening to Percy's tales and always cheering this author on, when at times it read so much like dross and she never let on and to Rob Sanford for his generious spirit.

To the others who gave their time, assistance, patience and creative suggestions during the many years of writing and rewriting. They were: Grace Guslander, Robert Schleck, Michael Scott, Beryl Moir, Andy Bushnell, Charles Penhallow, Theanne Specht, Linda Soltysik, Wil Welsh, Nancy Budd, Mary Judd, June Stark, Deedee Wilhelm, Chris Faye, Berry Wakefield, Mary Wilson, Rich Budnick and Julie McLeod.

All of my friends at Borders Lihue Kauai.

Shannon and John Tullius (Maui Writers Conference) and my mentors, Elizabeth Engstrom, Don McQuinn, John Saul and Bryce Courtenay.

M.J.Smith, Managing Editor, for permission to use *The Honolulu Advertiser* excerpts.

Booklines, for their kindness and disrribution.

DeSoto Brown (Bishop Museum), Margaret Lovett (Kauai Museum) and Carol Colbath (Bess Press) for their expertise and historic photographs from their collections.

Dick Lyday (Heritage Graphics) for seeing that this book became a physical reality.

The late Alice Faye for the hours of bliss at the movies.

Best Foods mayonnaise heaped on rice, tuna, eggs, tomatoes, stew, or by the spoonfuls. Heaven on earth.

And finally a special and grateful mahalo to Donna Stewart and Tom Niblick for their dedication, wisdom, talent, and friendship given so many times when in the dark of night, I thought this novel would never see the light of day. They made it possible.

This novel is a fiction but could not have happened without the wonderful, warm, humorous, sad, passionate people who have played a role in the continuing movie of my life...I will always love them.

"Ah, but a man's reach should exceed his grasp, or what's a heaven for?"
Robert Browning.

Prologue

I was cursed.

I was cursed the day I was born. I didn't know who cursed me or what the curse was, but from the way my life unfolded, while I was sucking my thumb, wetting my bed, observing my family, I knew somebody had cursed me. I had prayed every night since I was five years old, when I understood the ways of witches and curses, asking God to tell me what the curse was.

In the year 1941, God answered my prayers.

Until then, nobody paid any attention to me. In my child's head, I figured that was part of the curse.

In our living room, Daddy sat in his rattan chair reading the evening paper. He was on his third bourbon and Coke. Mother sat across from him, crossed-legged, correcting her third grade students' spelling papers with a blue Esterbrook pen and a jar of red ink. She had settled on a couch she covered in a floral print of red anthuriums. The couch was her pride and joy.

Mother had matched Daddy drink for drink.

My sister Marigold, spread-eagled across a piano bench, was wearing cardboard Roy Rogers cowboy boots and flipping through a Superman comic book. She made ugly, yucky sucking sounds in her throat. She was getting over a cold.

Grandma had gone to bed complaining of a gassy stomach. She told Mother the Brussels sprouts Hatsuko served at dinner were raw. They made her "bilious."

I told Grandma the Brussels sprouts made her fart. She slapped my head and steamed like a battleship for her bedroom, poop-da-pooping all the way.

Mother instructed me to ignore Grandma's gas because "She couldn't help it. Act as if it never happened. That's what gentlemen do."

I told Mother Grandma's gas was hard to ignore because her poops were louder than a thunderstorm. Mother warned me one more remark like that and she'd wash my mouth out with a bar of soap. At seven years old, I had acquired a real taste for Mother's green Palmolive bath soap that Mary Pickford advertised in *Life* magazine.

That night, standing in the doorway of our living room, I admired the room Mother called "katish!" Katish meant "swell." She decorated the room with the help of the "most katish" interior decorator in all the Hawaiian Islands.

The room was over-stuffed with Victorian furniture inherited from both sets of

my grandparents and a modern rattan couch and two chairs she bought at
Grossman and Moody's. Mother told me she had paid Greta Golmer hundreds of
dollars for the Grossman and Moody furniture. Mother had used up two months of
her teaching salary to make the living room pass inspection for our relatives who
lived on the slopes of Diamond Head.

I stood brooding in the doorway as my family continued to ignore me. I
grabbed my "peepee" and pretended I had to go to the bathroom. I fancied my
mother would look up and say, "Percy, do you have to go?"

Mother sipped her drink.

I jumped up and down, moaning as if I had to go real bad.

Daddy yawned.

I sang Grandma's favorite song loudly, hoping that Grandma would storm out
of her bedroom poop-da-pooping to the waltz.

> *"After the ball is over.*
> *After the break of dawn,"*

Marigold discarded one comic book and picked up another. Daddy walked to
the bar, made another drink, and sat down again. Mother dipped her pen into the
inkpot and slashed more red marks on her students' papers.

I sang louder, hoping Mr. McLaine, our old neighbor across the street would
hear me.

> *"After the dancers leaving,*
> *After the song is gone"*

My family continued to act like the silent gargoyles that watched over Paris
on top of Notre Dame Cathedral. Grandma showed them to me in her French picture book. Marigold stopped making sucking sounds and blew a wad of snot out of
her nose. She wiped the gunk away with her arm.

Our living room turned into an Egyptian tomb filled with dead mummies. I
thought to myself, "Maybe I'm not really here. Maybe I'm adopted. Maybe an
ugly witch left me on the doorstep of our house because nobody wanted me
because I am a cursed child."

I would have offered Grandma all my allowance to hear her poop-da-pooping,
it was so quiet. I sang louder so our rich neighbors on top of the hill would phone
Daddy to tell me to shut up.

> *"Many the hearts are breaking*
> *If you should leave them all.*
> *Many the hearts that are breaking*
> *After the ball."*

The phone didn't ring. The living room turned into a battle of wills.

I twirled into the room, humming. My arms flapped like wings, fingers flying
up to the ceiling, and fingers flying down to the carpet. Up and down, up and
down, around the room, I soared like an eagle. In a great dramatic flourish, I hit
Daddy's drink off the table. It fell on the beige carpet.

The Egyptian tomb burst open and the pharaoh roared, "GOD DAMNIT, PERCY!" Daddy rose off his throne and commanded, "STOP IT RIGHT NOW!"

I froze! Daddy's eyes were on fire. He ordered me to pick up his glass. I dropped to the floor and gathered the ice back into his glass as fast as I could. I rubbed with one hand to keep the bourbon and Coke from spreading into a lake. It was too late. The stain had shaped into Lake Michigan. I gave up rubbing, stood up and gave Daddy back his empty glass.

I chirped, "Here's your glass, Daddy, good as new."

"Good and empty," he snorted. Daddy grabbed the glass out of my hand and strode to the bar to make himself a martini. He complained to Mother, "DEIDRA, WE'VE GOT TO DO SOMETHING WITH THIS BOY."

Marigold put down her comic book and said in a voice that was as prickly as a porcupine, "Daddy, Percy is a big fat pig. He can't help it. Fat pigs can only act like big fat pigs!" Daddy and Marigold smiled into each other's eyes. My bacon always fried on their stoves.

I put my hands on my hips and said, "I am not a big fat pig, Marigold. You're the big fat pig."

Mother, waving her blue pen at us, ordered, "STOP THAT. BOTH OF YOU. RIGHT NOW."

Marigold and I turned our backs on each other.

Mother sighed and followed Daddy to the bar. "Dick, Percy is still a little boy. He'll grow out of this. Go back and read your newspaper and forget about it. Miss Marigold, I don't want to hear another word out of you tonight. I've had a very tiring day. Mind me tonight, Marigold." Mother faced me. "Percy, did you know you have been very VERY annoying?"

My eyes were focused on the carpet where the stain had now spread into Lake Erie and Lake Michigan. As everyone was trying to ignore it, I murmured, "Yes, I know."

Mother took my face in her hands and raised it up to hers, "Are you paying attention to me?"

I nodded.

"Are you sorry?"

A tear fell out of my left eye. "I'm sorry."

"Good. Apologize to your father."

"I'm sorry, Daddy." He grunted from behind the sports page.

Mother sat down on her precious couch again. As she picked up the pen, she called to our maid who was cleaning up in the kitchen, "Hatsuko, come in here please."

Hatsuko, wearing a blue and white kimono, wiping her hands on a dishtowel, rushed in. "Yes?"

"Hatsuko, take Percy into the kitchen. Give him a glass of milk and a cookie. Then put him to bed."

Daddy slammed down his newspaper, demanding, "Why in the hell are you doing that for, Deidra? He'll wet his bed again."

Picking up her drink, Mother replied. "Percy's been very good this week, Dick. In fact, this whole month he hasn't wet his bed once."

Standing next to Hatsuko, I interjected, "I haven't, Daddy. Really, I haven't. Mother, I wish you wouldn't mention it out so loud. Mr. McLaine across the street will hear you, and especially not in front of Marigold. She tells everybody at school I wet my bed."

"Everybody knows you're a big baby, Percy," Marigold taunted me by swinging her legs at me. "Don't they, Daddy?"

Mother waved her pen at Marigold. "Stop that, Marigold."

Marigold pouted and stuck her lower lip out by a mile. She always pouted when Mother scolded her. Daddy never said a bad word to my sister because she wasn't cursed.

Daddy looked up. I thought he was going to say how proud he was of me for not wetting my bed for a whole month. "Percy, only babies wet their beds and you're not a baby any more. Are you, Percy?"

"No, I'm not, Daddy."

"Will you do me a favor?"

"I will, Daddy."

"Take off your mother's lipstick."

"Sure, Daddy."

I rubbed my mouth hard with my two hands. "I did it, Daddy." A red gash now streaked across my mouth.

Mother relaxed and said, "Say goodnight to everyone, Percy."

I walked over to Daddy and held out my left hand. Left-handed people are cursed.

Daddy didn't hug me. Daddy didn't hug me because he thought my curse would rub off on him and he'd be left-handed too. We touched our left hands. Shaking hands with Daddy was a two-finger up-and-down exercise. Daddy also didn't want my "Ruby Red" lipstick on his Brooks Brothers white shirt. Looking down at my nails as our fingers touched, Daddy's eyes spoke that he was about to ask me to take off Mother's pink nail polish, "Deliciously Exotic." He said nothing.

I walked over to Mother and reached over for a goodnight kiss.

Oops! I spilled the open jar of red ink on her dress, and the ink ran onto her beautiful new couch.

Hatsuko rushed to Mother. "I help!"

Mother, holding back a scream, waved her away. "No, Hatsuko, take the boy. Take him away now, Hatsuko. Into the kitchen. Anywhere.

"Marigold, run to the bathroom and bring me some towels. Hurry it up, Marigold. Marigold, don't sit there. Go now," Mother ordered.

Hatsuko handed the dishtowel to Mother. "Please, Hatsuko, take Percy out of here. Please."

Marigold rose from the piano bench and stared at Mother. Hate glowed in her eyes. "Can't you teach Percy to clean up his own mess?"

Mother jumped up, dripping red ink onto the carpet, "NOW, MARIGOLD!"

Marigold ran out of the living room screaming, "Percy is a pig. Percy is a big FAT pig. Mother is an ugly witch."

Daddy hid behind the newspaper. As Hatsuko took my hand and walked me into exile, I overheard Daddy say from behind his paper, "See, Deidra."

I turned around and saw that Mother looked miserable because the red ink had ruined her couch and dripped on the carpet. Mother snapped back at Daddy, "Leave me alone, Dick."

A screaming fight was about to begin...again.

In the kitchen, Hatsuko brought down two glass cookie jars and set them on the kitchen table. "Percy, what do you want? Oatmeal cookies or chocolate ones?"

"Oatmeal cookies, please, Hatsuko. They're my favorite." I sighed. "When I get upset, I have to eat something."

I pulled a cookie out of the jar. "If I don't eat, I'll fart just like Grandma does. Right now I want to throw up - but only after I eat this cookie." Chewing on the cookie, I reached in the jar for another one. I stuffed two more cookies into my mouth. I placed my free hand on my forehead to feel if I had a fever.

"Hatsuko?"

"Yes, Percy?" She handed me a napkin to wipe my mouth.

"I think I have a slight fever," I continued. "Hatsuko, I got their attention tonight, didn't I?" I heaved a sigh, resting my head on my hands. "Do you think someday my father will like me as much as he likes Marigold?"

I bit my tongue as I chewed. "Ouuuuuuch. Hatsuko, why am I cursed? Do you know who cursed me, like the witch cursed the princess in *Sleeping Beauty*?"

Hatsuko smoothed down my cowlick and cooed, "You're not cursed, Percy. You were born special and I'm very proud of you. You got more talent than any of those movie stars in our movie magazines. Someday, you'll be as big a star as Nelson Eddy and Jeanette MacDonald, and then your father will be very proud of you."

She screwed the lid back on the cookie jar and placed it high up on a shelf, then my best friend came and gave me a kiss on my cowlick and led to me to bed.

As Hatsuko tucked the covers all around me, I said with all the love that churned in my tiny heart, "Hatsuko, you don't talk like a Japanese mama-san. You talk like Ginger Rogers and I love you almost best of all the people in the whole wide world. Please don't leave me."

She gave me a kiss in the center of my forehead. "Percy, someday I'm gonna marry a man who looks like a movie star, but until then you are my best boyfriend. I'll never leave you even if I marry Gary Cooper. And if I do, we'll all live together in Hollywood."

"Please promise me that because you are the only one who can protect me from the curse and all bad witches in the world," I pleaded.

"Percy, you are not cursed and there are no bad witches. Witches are only in storybooks. Anyway, only bad people are cursed and have bad things happen to them."

That night I wet my bed.

1

Opening Credits

In November of 1940, I longed to be the most wonderful, talented, brightest movie star on the 20th Century Fox lot. I wanted to look, dance, and sing like Alice Faye, the golden-haired movie queen of the Fox musicals. In order to forget witches and curses, I imagined life to be a Technicolor song and dance movie. I sang at breakfast, danced to school and walked into a black and white movie as soon as the school bell rang. There were problems: I wasn't living in a Technicolor musical. I was fat and I couldn't dance if my life depended on it. Because I thought I was cursed and didn't know what the curse was, my life began to unravel like a spool of film that had broken away from its projector and rolled wildly across the island on which I lived.

There were other problems. I was a boy. My father wanted me to play football. My mother didn't want anything my father wanted. My sister wanted me out - out of her hair, out of the house - OUT OF HER LIFE!

I wanted to be Alice Faye.

Every morning looking into a mirror, I saw a fat sissy boy. To the outside world, I sensed that being fat and a sissy didn't make me lovable - especially to my father. I was a figure of ridicule. Adding two and two together, I figured that any boy who was fat and a sissy and wanted to be Alice Faye had to have the biggest curse in the world placed on him. I knew I should want to be Clark Gable flying a plane over the Amazon River - that's what all the boys in my first grade class wanted to be, but I longed to be Alice Faye, crooning love songs to Tyrone Power in a Hollywood musical.

I wasn't always fat.

In fact, when I was born, I was considered puny. I was sickly and bedridden. I have memories of mustard plastered to my chest and the smell of camphor steaming next to me. On long days, to forget the smell of illness, I daydreamed of Sharp Ears the Whale, Babar the Elephant, and was drawn into the radio dish-soap operas of Ma Perkins' lumber yard and Helen Trent's love life after age 35.

At five, I discovered Best Foods mayonnaise. It was love at first swallow. Best Foods mayonnaise became my passion. I heaped it on tuna, rice, eggs, tomatoes, and stew. I ate it alone by the spoonfuls.

Home from elementary school, I'd sneak into the kitchen, open the icebox door, grab a loaf of Love's white bread and a jar of mayonnaise. With a large tablespoon, I'd slather mayonnaise thickly on two slices of the soft white bread. After putting the bread and mayo back into the icebox, I'd tiptoe out the kitchen door. I'd sit on the dirt by the side of my house and wolf down my passion. Overnight, I became well, fat and round. I turned into Mr. Doughboy.

Gertrude and Agnes were my make-believe friends. I drew them first on a blank sheet of paper when I was five. They started out as stick figures that I soon rounded out with colored crayons. Within weeks, the funny faces I drew began to talk. Soon, Agnes and Gertrude sat on either side of me, real as life, and gossiped as I ate mayonnaise sandwiches by the side of the house. We became best friends.

Gertrude was as skinny as a light pole and had a thick head of curly black hair.

Agnes was a sun-bleached blonde. She had straight hair with braids that hung down on either side of her head. She looked like Hitler's fat first cousin. I sat next to Agnes because she made me look skinny.

Agnes and Gertrude had different opinions on how I should act and became my critics. Agnes was the bad me and challenged me to eat a hundred mayonnaise sandwiches a day. Gertrude hated mayonnaise. At least once a day, I could count on Gertrude telling me how disappointed she was in the way I had behaved in school. Gertrude was the me who held his nose high in the air and Agnes was the me that wet his pants.

When Gertrude told me I was eating too many mayonnaise sandwiches, I answered that mayonnaise sandwiches helped the tears slide "kerplunk" into my belly; therefore, my belly held a bucketful of tears. I learned that by storing tears in my belly, I could laugh away the teasing I got at school. I was considered a good sport.

Gertrude and Agnes cried for me.

Along with Agnes and Gertrude, I had a world of secrets. Not only did I store tears in my belly, but all the secrets I heard. Because of all the secrets and tears floating in my stomach, my belly became huge. Daddy said my belly had grown stupendous because it was filled with second helpings.

The first big secret in my belly was the appearance of Agnes and Gertrude. I never told anyone about them - not even Hatsuko. Gertrude and Agnes were the only ones who knew that I hated my name Percy. That was a real big secret because I didn't want to hurt Mother's feelings.

PERCY! Percy sounded like a sissy name. I hated the way it looked on paper. I hated the name most of all because Percy fit me. I had been born a sissy and that was the reason my parents gave me that terrible name. I couldn't find anyone in the family named Percy in the five generations of my family, on either side, who had lived in Hawaii.

At six, I was tormented with the nickname of "Fat Percy."

FAT PERCY. It stuck like an ugly leech. When people called me Percy, their eyes always added "fat." I first heard "Fat Percy" yelled on a sunny Sunday morning, while I was swimming off Waikiki Beach. I was wearing a blue wool swimsuit that itched like a hundred prickly pimples. I was floating belly-up on the waves at Waikiki, bobbing up and down and pretending to be a mammoth blue whale ready to spout. My first, second and third cousins were on the beach, arms around each other, pointing at me and hollering, "Look at Mr. Blubber."

Everybody on the beach heard them and looked at me.

My cousins yelled again, "Look at Fat Percy - thar he blows."

Agnes and Gertrude, swimming with me, yelled, "Put your head underwater and they'll go away." We put our heads underwater and I held my breath for three whole seconds. When I came up for air, my cousins were still yelling.

Agnes and Gertrude whispered, "Don't show them that they bother you. Laugh."

I laughed.

"Laugh again."

I laughed louder. I yelled, "Do you want to see me spout?"

"Yea." The cousins jumped up and down, screaming for everyone to watch a big fat whale spout. I spit water out of my mouth as far as I could up into the air and then flapped my legs like a whale's tail.

When I started playing the fat whale, my cousins stopped yelling and became bored. I had played their teasing game and when I did, they lost interest in yelling at me. Lesson here - play their game and they will go away because you are no fun to tease anymore. I loved acting like a whale because whales are kind animals and don't mind being fat.

At seven, all I needed was to wear a Best Foods mayonnaise blue wrapper to make myself look like a walking advertisement. Gertrude said it was because I was mayonnaise white all over - a full head of blonde hair, round like a bottle and lots of white skin. She said I even waddled around like one - a little fat bottle that walked from side to side on two little fat legs. I had a touch of color - yellow teeth when I didn't brush first thing in the morning.

I laughed all the time to make people like me.

I lived on Oahu, the third largest and the busiest island in the Hawaiian chain. The islands of Hawaii were a territory of the United States, statehood being a vague dream. My home, 1909 Kapaka Drive, was at the bottom of a cone-shaped hill that rose from the middle of a valley. The valley had once been a dormant volcano. Centuries of rain and wind eroded the volcano into a lush valley that reached toward the city of Honolulu. By 1920, the tropical forests and taro fields that once filled the valley were replaced by rows and rows of homes designed by architects who were influenced by the cottages that stood on the sand dunes in Cape Cod.

Our hill was the only volcanic intrusion in the middle of the valley. It stuck out like a dunce's cap. The valley is called Manoa and the dunce's cap, Rocky Hill. Rocky Hill's inhabitants attached their single wall homes precariously to the hillside. The very rich lived at the top.

Our hill was hexed because it was dangerous for an average automobile driver to maneuver his chug-a-lug up and down the dunce's cap. In a rainstorm, driving up the hill was death defying because the road was so slippery, and in any weather, driving down could end up with a driver having a cracked head like Humpty Dumpty.

Heroic drivers who made it to the top of the hill would stop at the summit and shift their cars into first gear. Taking a deep breath, thinking it might be their last, they'd gaze out at a spectacular view of Honolulu and Pearl Harbor, pray, release their hand brakes, and fly down the roller-coaster hill. Most drivers made it and the ones that didn't ended up in Queen's Hospital.

We lived in the third house at the bottom of the hill, near Vancouver Street.

It was exciting living at the bottom of Rocky Hill because there was a terrible car crash nearly every month. These accidents were caused by either a speedster who didn't swerve his steering wheel fast enough to make the curve at the bottom or a numbskull who forgot to put on her hand brake.

I loved the smash-ups as long as the car didn't end up in our kitchen.

Rich people who lived on top of the hill built driveways that plunged down to a garage. We lived at the bottom of the hill so our driveway meandered upwards. On more than one occasion, a neighbor's Packard smashed through our backyard hedge and into our house because the rich dodo forgot to put on his hand brake to keep the car from charging down the hill like a raging bull.

My distant cousin Bessie, a real battle-ax and our hillside blabbermouth, became the star of the neighborhood automobile crashes. Daddy told me Cousin Bessie caused more car accidents than anyone on Oahu because she was crazy. Daddy also warned me Cousin Bessie was a bitch because he was sure she rode a broom on full moon nights around our house, and I'd better watch out for her.

Mother ordered me not to call Cousin Bessie a bitch no matter what Daddy said. Mother told me bitch was another word for witch. Mother confided that Cousin Bessie had lost money in the 1929 Crash and people who lose lots of money have mental breakdowns. I groaned, "I don't feel sorry for her because she's a mean old witch. She told me she's going to turn me into a pillar of salt because I talk too much and next time she says something mean to me, I'm going to tell her Daddy says she is a real bitch."

My mother thumped me on my head and reminded me that my sassy mouth was getting me into lots of trouble. She ordered me, on a threat of a spanking, to be nice to everybody including Cousin Bessie. Otherwise, Cousin Bessie would not merely turn me into a pillar of salt but a rock that couldn't speak.

Hatsuko told me Cousin Bessie's mental breakdown occurred before I was born. Legend had it, on the day she lost her money, Cousin Bessie ran up and down our hill stark naked, screaming to a full moon and wishing death on her stockbroker. Daddy said mental breakdowns galloped like a herd of cattle through Mother's side of the family and that, on full moon nights, he made it a rule to stay away from Mother's sisters and all our cousins once removed. Daddy reminded me his side of the family was littered with saints.

Gertrude told me that if I had any sense, I'd listen to my mother and keep out of Cousin Bessie's way because someday Cousin Bessie, she predicted, was going to get me into lots of trouble. "Gossips find a way of getting little people into trouble, and when you're not looking, Cousin Bessie will do something terrible to you - probably boil you up in a soup full of dead toads and turnips."

Cousin Bessie's spectacular accident happened on a Saturday morning, in September, 1940. After the accident, I became famous at school for being a big mouth storyteller. It was at "show and tell" time that I told Cousin Bessie's story. I called the story "Cousin Bessie Make Die Dead Her Mother." *Make* (ma-kay) means dead in Hawaiian.

At show and tell time, I held up an old spark plug for my prop to tell the story, but Cousin Bessie's story was so gruesome that it didn't matter what I held in my hand. The story as I told it to my second grade class went as follows.

"Saturday morning, my Cousin Bessie was chugging up her steep drive to pick up Darlene, her big, smelly, eighteen-year-old Persian cat. Everyone in our neighborhood hates Darlene. I hate Darlene. Darlene was going to be de-wormed. Darlene has worms that stick out her behind - this long."

I stretched my hands as far apart as they would go.

"Cousin Bessie NEEEEEVER leaves her phone unanswered. That's a fact because I've seen her run from our house to hers whenever she hears her phone ring. Boy, can she run fast for an old lady. On Saturday morning, Cousin Bessie drove out of her garage and up her driveway. Her phone rang. She stopped her Cadillac perpendicular - straight up and down in the middle of her driveway and ran into the house. Cousin Bessie left her five-year-old 'Pumpkin,' baby grand-daughter Pamela, in the front seat, and her old mother Nana, drooling in the back seat. Nana drooled like this."

I drooled for the class.

"Our neighborhood hates Pamey as much as they hate Darlene because Pumpkin and the cat are both brats."

Here, I made up the rest of the story. "Nana in the back seat said to Pamey, 'Pamey dear, please sit down.' Pamey stuck out her tongue."

I stuck out my tongue. I said in my old-lady voice, "Baby, don't you dare touch that brake!"

In a high voice, I laughed like "The Shadow," "Ha. Ha. Ha." Back in my nor-mal voice, I continued, "Then Pamey released the brake and Nana screamed for help. Cousin Bessie's car ran down the drive out-of-control and jumped over a lava wall that is as high as the one in China and into Cross-Eyed Mama's backyard."

I took a breath, then continued, "Down below, Cross-Eyed Mama was eating her Wheaties when she heard the crash. She ran out and found Cousin Bessie's car sitting in the middle of her lily pond. Pamey was jumping up and down in the front seat screaming for help. Cross-Eyed Mama found Nana in the back seat clutching her heart, dead as a squished cockroach. I saw dead old squished-up Nana in the back seat and I wasn't afraid - not even one little bit."

I made a face to show the class how dead old Nana looked.

Everyone screamed, "OOOOOOOOO, disgusting!"

"No more," Wigay Wix, my favorite classmate friend, pleaded. I finished the story and got an A.

The part of the story I didn't tell was that when I heard Cousin Bessie's car land in the lily pond, I was home playing dress up. I was wearing one of Mother's favorite evening gowns, a black velvet with rhinestones all around the neck. In her gown, I ran through the hedge to Cross-Eyed Mama's house, reaching the smashed-up car as Pamey was screaming for help. I saw Nana in the back seat clutching her bazooms. Her face really looked as if she'd been given the biggest

Christmas present in her whole life.

I told Cross-Eyed Mama, standing next to the car, "Imagine, one minute Nana thought she was going bye-bye with Cousin Bessie, and the next minute she went off to visit God. I'll bet you a nickel she didn't know that was going to happen."

Cross-Eyed Mama kept staring into the car, speechless. Someone in Cross-Eyed Mama's house phoned for an ambulance.

I picked up my skirt, circled Cross-eyed Mama and continued to ramble, "I never know what's going to happen next on our hill. I'm going to have to wear clean underwear all the time because one can never know when God is going to invite me up to heaven for a tuna sandwich."

Someone grabbed Pamey out of the car.

Cross-Eyed Mama looked as if she had just gotten out of bed because she was still in her bra and panties and had sleep in her eyes. She looked real colorful because she wore pink hair curlers in her hair and showed off her bright, blue veins that crisscrossed like a tic-tac-toe game on big, fat elephant legs.

I said in a loud voice that she better get dressed because the ambulance men were about to come around the corner, and the way she looked right now, God wasn't going to invite her up to visit Nana in heaven.

"And furthermore," I said, swirling my dress around like a Honolulu debutante and pointing at her panties, "You've got a big hole in your underwear." Thinking I had done Cross-Eyed Mama a big favor by pointing out the hole, I added, "I'd be very happy to loan you this dress before the ambulance men come."

It was like I had put Cross-Eyed Mama's thumb into an electrical socket. She shook all over, looked down at the hole in her panties and blushed beet red. She turned suddenly into a colorful fireworks display. Cross-Eyed Mama, who was bigger than all the giant ladies in a Tarzan movie put together, picked me up with one arm and tossed me over the hedge. As she threw me, she yelled that I was never to come back to her house again because good little boys never mention the unmentionables.

I added "panties" to the word "fart" on the list of words I shouldn't say in front of grown-ups. I told Agnes it was getting hard to understand grown-ups when they ignored what was in plain sight for everyone to see or pretended not to hear sounds that were louder than a thunder clap. I figured that grown-ups live in a bigger world of make-believe than I did.

Soon after my show and tell story, Cousin Bessie received a phone call from the Punahou School president. Her accident had become really famous after my story had reached the principal of the school. By the time the principal heard the story, Cousin Bessie had killed her mother and her cat by driving her Cadillac over them three times. I was overjoyed to learn that the president of the school said that my teasing cousins were suffering terrible nightmares from my story.

Cursed people can give other people headaches.

Cousin Bessie phoned Daddy at work. When Daddy came home, he took his hairbrush, pulled down my pants and whacked me three times, hard. He yelled as he spanked, "Where did you get your mouth from?"

I screamed and answered that I was adopted. I was so mad at Daddy because the night before, I told him all about Cousin Bessie's accident and Cross-Eyed

Mama's panties and Daddy laughed as if I had told him the biggest joke in the whole world.

After the spanking, Daddy got madder because I was wearing Marigold's sun suit that had yellow sunflowers printed on it. "Take off that God damn dress. And where in the hell did you find that dress?"

"I traded the football you gave me with Marigold for this dress."

"Take it off."

Pulling off the dress, I screamed to Daddy that what I told him was the real truth and I shouldn't get a spanking for telling the truth. I stomped to my room and cried to Agnes and Gertrude in the closet. As I sat down, I realized that Daddy made me poop in my pants.

Pamey, Cousin Bessie's granddaughter, the little girl who had released the brake and sent Nana to heaven, had to go to a mind doctor. Hatsuko overheard Cross-Eyed Mama and Cousin Bessie telling Mother to send me to the same mind doctor with Pamey.

At prayer time, after reciting "if I should die before I wake, I pray the Lord my soul to take," and blessing everyone I could think of, I'd add, "Dear God, please, I'm not ready to go to heaven yet because I can't go to heaven until I find out why I am cursed and who did it. Anyway, my bags aren't packed and my underwear is dirty. And please, God, buy another house on top of our hill for Mother and Daddy because I don't want to die like Nana did in the back seat of a car. And God, if you have any pull with Daddy, let him smile at me once in awhile, and please, God, whoever put the curse on me, tell them to take it back because I don't like Daddy spanking me for telling the truth."

I joined my cousins in nightmares. I dreamt that Cousin Bessie's car crashed into my bedroom and Daddy screamed that it was my fault. I had on Marigold's sun suit. The nightmare ended with me pooping in my pants.

What I didn't know was that God had just taught me a big lesson. The lesson was that people in my world would die suddenly, without reason, and it's best *not* to know, in the coming tomorrows, what was about to thunder down my hill.

I read books by the time I was four years old. I loved reading as much as I did the everyday excitement that came charging down our hill. Actually, I loved reading more. Reading books, I learned about heroes, goblins, witches, and curses that filled dark forests and castles in a storybook world and real life.

I learned to read by sounding out words. I read first and second grade books before I entered kindergarten because Mother gave me books about Dick, Jane and Spot. Spot's ball was colored red - a color I learned to hate.

My great-grandmother, my poopy Grandma who lived with us, told me from the very day I started to understand words written on a page that every intelligent boy must read the newspaper every day, that is, if he wanted to grow up and be as smart as Abraham Lincoln.

At seven, I read *The Honolulu Advertiser*, the city's morning daily paper. The newspaper was thrown with a thump against our front door at six o'clock in the morning. Though I didn't understand all the pages of newsprint, I read and understood the headlines and looked at the photographs. I drooled over pictures of Hollywood movie stars and scanned the passenger lists of the Matsonia, Lurline and Mariposa. Walking down the gangplank on the Lurline was the most glamorous thing a person could do in 1941 Hawaii.

In the Sunday editions of the newspaper, I'd seek out the women's section with the lavish spreads on the weddings performed at Central Union Church. The wedding veils, each week, got longer and longer...and longer. Best of all, on the next page were the write-ups of the new movies that had opened on Friday.

Thursday's food section gave me the latest price of a quart of Best Foods mayonnaise, canned Coral tuna fish and Dairymen's chocolate ice cream. If Hatsuko had served tuna salad and chocolate sundaes at breakfast, lunch and dinner, I would have thought I was living in heaven.

I never read the funnies because I didn't think they were very funny. I preferred reading comic books. Comic books had complete stories of exciting adventures in them. "Is it a bird? Is it a plane? NO - IT'S.... Superman." Superman was my favorite of all the comic books. Batman ran a close second. Both heroes wore tiny shorts. My two most favorite villains were in the Batman comic book, the evil white-faced devil, The Joker, and the squatty Penguin.

The sports section I ignored. That pleased Daddy because I didn't mess up those pages. I did enjoy reading about the vivid personalities like the Joes - Louis and DiMaggio. Other football players, basketball players, baseball players, and prizefighters were not interesting or heroic to me.

Amelia Earhart, the woman pilot, was heroic. She had disappeared mysteriously in her plane somewhere in the middle of the Pacific Ocean. Amelia Earhart was never found. She was cursed. All heroes, Gertrude told me, were cursed because heroes are born different from other people.

Other than reading the newspaper, I adored flipping through the pages of my Aunt Momi's movie magazines, especially *Photoplay*. That magazine had glossy photos and stories about gorgeous and handsome movie stars living in Hollywood. I placed movie stars next to Best Foods mayonnaise on my shelf of those things I loved most.

From the age of five, because of Hatsuko's love for movies, I followed the careers of Lana Turner, Clark Gable, Rita Hayworth, Cary Grant, Hedy LaMarr, and Ann Sheridan. Beauties, I adored.

Hatsuko idolized Ann Sheridan. Annie was a Warner Brothers' gum-chewing, smart-mouth talking movie star who usually portrayed a waitress flipping hamburgers in a sleazy New York dump.

Hatsuko, who had beautiful, shiny, thick, jet-black hair, wanted to be a strawberry blonde and have round eyes like Annie. Ann Sheridan was dubbed the "oomph girl" by her fans. Hatsuko and I would have given anything to have an ounce of Annie's "oomph."

I thought all movie stars and the King of England were God's chosen people because they never peed or pooped. I never once saw a picture of the King of England sitting on the pot or a movie star taking a doodoo or making *shishi* (urinating) into a toilet.

President Roosevelt, I was sure, must have peed because he was like a father to me, and fathers always peed. My father peed all the time and everywhere. One night after a big party, my father peed in my mother's closet and on all her dresses because he thought he was in the bathroom.

A word that jumped out at me when I first started to read, a word I fully comprehended with all its meaning, a word written in brazen letters that seared itself into my brain, was LOOK!

I looked at everything from *The Advertiser* to my books and my neighbors' antics. At the same time, to forget the curse I thought a witch had given me at birth, I lived inside myself in a vivid, imaginary world. I also found eating a ton of mayonnaise sandwiches helped when thinking about scary things around me, but the spoonfuls of mayonnaise were never enough to keep me from being jumpy and thinking that something was around the corner waiting for me. I was nervous because I read in the headlines that my home was in danger and a war loomed beyond the surf at Waikiki Beach. A war that was about to erupt like a volcano between the United States and Japan...and Germany.

Once, when I had my father's attention, I asked, "Daddy, what's a war like?"

Daddy answered that a war is a dangerous and horrible thing. "People die in wars like Nana did next door. I don't want a war to happen to us here in Hawaii.

Right now, son, that s.o.b. President Roosevelt is leading us into a big war - that is, if he can. And if a war *does* happen, it will happen right here in our own backyard."

I looked at Daddy and, trying to be as smart as Marigold, said, "President Roosevelt is Fala's father. Fala's father would never get us in a war." Fala was President Roosevelt's Scotty dog. Daddy grimaced.

I immediately said, "Daddy, President Roosevelt can't be a bad man if he owns a dog. All people who have dogs are good people. People who own cats you have to watch out for, because cats belong to bitches like Cousin Bessie."

Daddy always laughed when I said bitch, meaning a witch.

I tried to pretend to Daddy that I was as smart as Marigold and understood everything he said to me, which I didn't. I did understand when Daddy told me to shut up and go to the bathroom.

I wasn't worried about Daddy's war because I was thinking about Cousin Bessie's car killing me and making me disappear up into heaven with Nana. After all, it was Cousin Bessie who drove a car and lived in my backyard. But reading the headlines in *The Advertiser* about the evil Mr. Hitler and the evil Mr. Tojo killing people in far off places, I knew something bad was going to happen to us because the newspaper told me so. I prayed every night that God would take Hitler and Tojo for a ride in Cousin Bessie's car and make them disappear like He did Nana.

Every morning, I'd wake at the sound of the newspaper hitting the front door, and race out of bed to read the newspaper first. I hoped each day because, according to Grandma, in the newspaper I would find the answers to all my questions. I never did. I only found more troubles piling up and up out beyond the blue horizon.

As I continued to read *The Advertiser* in the next year, I and some of the people in my life were going to fall into the black hole of Calcutta - my daddy's expression. I, at least, would know the curse that had been placed on my head.

The Honolulu Advertiser

84 Years Your Morning Newspaper – Established on July 2, 1856

LORRIN P. THURSTON - President and General Manager
RAYMOND COLL - Editor
RAY COLL, JR. - New Editor
JAN JABULKA - Business Manager

READ THE SPECIAL 6 A.M. EDITION OF THE ADVERTISER
FOR ALL THE NEWS OF WAR DEVELOPMENTS WHILE THEY ARE NEWS
The Honolulu Advertiser - December 7, 1940

JIMMY FIDLER IN HOLLYWOOD, HONOLULU, U.S.A. AUGUST 25
Dear Staff, I've written of Ginger Rogers' unfortunate visit to Hawaii and

how she lost friends by her failure to give the press and the crowd at the dock even so much as a smile, so it's only fair to Hollywood that I retell the very different behavior of another star, Shirley Temple.

She did correctly everything that Ginger did badly. She gave autographs, posed for pictures, proved herself to be as sweet and natural as our little girl and yours.

Advertisement: **PIGGLY WIGGLY - HOME OWNED - HOME OPERATED**
Prices Effective, Thursday, Friday, and Saturday, Dec. 5,6,7

Silex Coffee	27 cents a pound
Sugar	47 cents a pound
Leg of Lamb	28 cents a pound
Pard dog food	25 cents for 3 tins
	$3.75 by the case of 48 tins
Best Foods Mayonnaise	32 cents a quart

NAZIS HASTEN CONSTRUCTION OF U-BOAT FLEET

KGU - RADIO STATION
5:55 a.m.	Japanese Program
12:00 a.m.	Ma Perkins
6:00 p.m.	Lone Ranger

PAWAA THEATER - Phone 91700
ANDY HARDY MEETS DEBUTANTE
- Mickey Rooney's social debut in New York.

MOVIE ACTOR ERROL FLYNN DUE ON PAN AMERICAN CLIPPER TODAY

3

Honolulu, 1940

As Christmas of 1940 approached, my dog Uku ran away. *Uku* in Hawaiian means flea. He lived up to his name. He was a *poi* dog (mixed) and to me the most beautiful creature in the world. We slept every night in my bed, nose to nose. Marigold said Uku ran away because he couldn't stand my "pukey" breath. Mother was thrilled he had disappeared because I quit scratching fleabites at dinnertime.

In 1940 Hawaii, Hatsuko and I tasted our first chocolate soda at the Alexander Young Hotel coffee shop. The hotel stood tall on Bishop Street. My mother was visiting with a neighbor-island relative who was staying on its fourth floor. Mother treated Hatsuko and me to our sodas because we had to wait for her downstairs in the lobby as she visited with Uncle George. Anyone staying in a room on the fourth floor had to be very rich. Uncle George was very rich. He was the most powerful politician in Hawaii and was Mother's lawyer.

Mother's parting remarks to Hatsuko were, "I'll be down in a minute." I groaned. My mother's minutes always turned into hours when she was drinking with any of our visiting relatives.

When Hatsuko and I finished our two chocolate sodas, I became restless. I suggested a ride up and down the Young Hotel's elevator a hundred times. The elevator was one of the great novelties in downtown Honolulu. I thought riding the elevator was as good as having your picture taken on Waikiki Beach with Diamond Head in the background. After our tenth ride (ninety more to go), up - up - up from the lobby and down - down -down from the roof garden, the elevator operator became irritated.

Hatsuko and I wouldn't get out. I kept ordering: "Roof garden, my man."

The operator glowered.

I told Hatsuko in a loud voice that the elevator man was the spitting image of Peter Lorre, the sinister German actor. "YUK!" I said. "He's got the same fat killer eyes."

That did it! The black-haired gnome gave me a killer look and demanded, "Eh, who you going see, fat boy?"

I pulled up my chins and answered like a lord of the manor, "We're here to see Miss Jeanette MacDonald and Mr. Nelson Eddy - that's who, my boy."

"Eh, no shit me," he snarled. His eyes bugged out at us. "You tink I look like one dummy? Get da hell out of my elevator!" He shoved us out.

Dizzy from elevator riding, Hatsuko and I plunked down on an old couch, hidden behind two potted palms. An hour passed. Another hour of waiting began.

All of a sudden Mother scurried out of the elevator. She didn't see us at first until she heard raucous laughter from behind the potted palms. I was performing my Tarzan act, impersonating Tarzan, Jane, and Cheetah the monkey for Hatsuko and three brightly made-up ladies who had cigarettes dangling out of their mouths. I had become the "starh" of the Young Hotel lobby.

When Mother saw me behind the palms, I had my shirt off and was squeaking like a monkey. I hung onto a palm leaf and was picking my nose. Mother yanked me into a corner, shook me and whispered, "Simmer down, young man." I wiggled around like a monkey trying to get away from her.

"Right now, Percy! I mean it. Put your shirt on."

Mother called Hatsuko over and told her to take me home immediately by bus. Her visit with Uncle George was taking longer than she thought. They were discussing important family matters.

I rolled my eyes to the ceiling and imitated Cousin Bessie, "Isn't the old bastard drunk yet? Uncle George should have passed out hours ago."

"Percy, where do you hear such things?" Mother said, yanking me and buttoning up my shirt.

"From you."

Mother slapped my hand. "You have never heard such things from me. And don't you tell anyone you do."

I confessed, "I heard it from Cousin Bessie that Uncle George was an old bastard and a drunk and a disgrace to the family, even if he was the richest son-of-a-bitch in the islands and the best lawyer in town."

"Percy!"

"I'm only repeating what I heard. What is a bastard, Mother?"

She put her hand over my mouth, "Percy, Uncle George is a nice man. You mustn't talk that way about him. He's having lots of troubles. Uncle George is an adult and you don't speak about adults that way, and he's very good to me. You must be respectful to your elders. When you become an adult, I'll tell you what bastard means. Until then, you mind your manners. When you're older, Percy, you can talk any way you like. But if you insist on speaking the way you do, nobody, and I mean nobody, will want you around. Do you hear me?"

Mother smothered my mouth with her hand before I could answer. After I nodded, she took her hand away. I could hardly wait to be a grown-up because I hated being smothered to death and having my mouth washed out with soap for speaking the truth.

Mother turned to Hatsuko, "Hatsuko, see that he behaves himself and that he doesn't do any more theatrics. Make him go to the bathroom before he gets on the bus." Turning to me, she warned, "We don't want any accidents, do we, Percy?"

Opening her purse, Mother took money out and said, "Here's some money, Hatsuko. Take him home." Mother turned, flounced her dress, shook her head, and stepped back into the elevator with old sourpuss Peter Lorre. The elevator door closed. She rode up to the fourth floor and joined Uncle George for another drink.

I grabbed Hatsuko's hand and quizzed, "How much did she give you?" Opening her hand, I shrieked, "Twenty dollars! Twenty whole dollars. That's a fortune. I bet she didn't know she gave us that much. Let's go shopping before we catch the bus home. We have enough money to buy me anything I want at Kress's." I was going to faint with excitement.

"Hatsuko," I said, jumping up and down, tugging on her hand, "We're on our own with all that money. Do you know what that means? It means I can buy all the toys I want today."

Hatsuko's face flooded with fear. "Percy, remember what your mother told me to do?"

"No."

"Yes, you do, Percy. She told me to take you straight home."

I pulled on her arm, pleading, "She'll never remember. She always forgets. Mother will never know. I promise, Hatsuko. I can keep secrets."

I had read in *The Honolulu Advertiser* that all the stores in town had started decorating for Christmas. Kissing and smooching Hatsuko's hand, imitating Charles Boyer, the French actor, I said in a seductive voice, "My darling, Liberty House has put up their Christmas tree, and it must be the most beautiful tree in zee planet. (The word planet I learned from the Superman comics.) Watcha think, babee?"

Hatsuko could never resist my Charles Boyer imitation. We ran over to Liberty House, a block over on Fort Street. Liberty House was the spiffiest department store in Hawaii, and when we walked in, we saw it was decorated for Christmas. The store had turned into a magical forest at the North Pole. Holding hands, Hatsuko and I gawked up at the Christmas tree that stood miles high in the department store's entrance. This year's tree looked sad because its branches drooped to the floor. The branches were weighted down with gobs of bright balls in all sizes and shapes and tons of silver tinsel. The Christmas tree made me feel sad, so I kissed its branches.

Taking in a deep whiff, the Christmas tree smelled like the forest it came from. Hatsuko said the fragrance of pine needles smells just like snow. I plucked a couple of needles off the tree and stuck them up my nose so I could smell snow all the way home.

With pine needles sticking out my nose, I ran around the store with Hatsuko, chattering about everything we saw. We flew up and down the staircases and explored every department. Out of breath, we ran back downstairs, taking two steps at a time, and once again looked up at the Christmas tree.

Then I turned to Hatsuko and with our eyes, we telegraphed each other: "SEEN IT! DONE IT! LET'S GO TO KRESS'S."

We rushed out into the street and zooooooomed as fast as we could up to Kress Store. I loved Kress Store. I especially loved its stink. It smelled of broken crayons, cheap perfume and spilled Coca Colas. Kress's, downtown, was the biggest and grandest five-and-dime store in the whole world.

I once told Cousin Bessie, when I asked her for one of her old dresses, that Kress Store was the best store in all Hawaii. Cousin Bessie snorted that Kress Store sold only junk and she wouldn't be caught dead in it. I told her she must be dead because I saw her in Kress's buying two bottles of red nail polish last Saturday. She slapped my head and told me I was acting fresh again, and she wasn't ever going to give me any of her dresses. Cousin Bessie kicked me out of her house...again. I was sad for a whole day because I had my eye on her old red taffeta evening gown.

Maybe Kress Store was everything Cousin Bessie said it was - cheap, junk, and Japanese-made, but it fit into my budget and taste. My weekly allowance was fifteen cents a week to stay out of Daddy's way. Hatsuko loved Kress Store as much as I did because it fit into her budget. Mother paid her twenty dollars a month.

Everyone in Hawaii really adored Kress Store, from the Dillinghams living on Diamond Head to the Hashimotos living in a camp house on a sugar plantation.

Daddy said the rich loved bargains as much as poor people do - maybe more. One night Daddy, paying his bills at the dining room table, told me rich people always try to get something for nothing and they were known to be the last to pay their bills, and that's why they are so rich. "And don't kid yourself, Percy. The rich shop at Kress Store all the time."

I questioned Daddy, "Is that why you're not rich, because you pay your bills on time and buy your pants at Liberty House?" Before he could answer me, I said, "Do you think, Daddy, the real reason you're not rich is because you're always buying liquor and cigarettes at Day's and not buying lots of toys for me at Kress's?"

Daddy told me to shut up, get out of the dining room, and go to the bathroom, because I was being sassy again and needed a bowel movement.

I stood in front of the children's counter at Kress's, transfixed as I fingered all the toys in front of me. Hatsuko watched and was anxious to get me on the bus before I could spend Mother's twenty dollars. Hatsuko realized Mother had made a mistake - Mother had given Hatsuko her weekly food money.

I pleaded with Hatsuko in my icky sweet voice to please buy me a small Japanese wooden boat fitted with tiny, tiny masts. I told her the boat would float like a dream in my bathtub. Hatsuko shook her head and nudged me forward, looking for the exit and holding Mother's twenty-dollar bill tight in her fist.

I ignored Hatsuko and wandered down the aisles, humming to myself as my fingers ran along the glass counters. I was trying to think of a way to get Hatsuko to hand over Mother's money. I rounded the corner of the children's counter and spied the Christmas displays.

I stopped and rested my nose on the counter. A miniature German creche that displayed Mary, Joseph, and farm animals gazing down at a smiling Jesus lying in bits of real hay immediately dazzled me. I tried to reeeeeeach over the counter and touch the baby Jesus. Baby Jesus was the size of a thimble - a little ivory white doll. The doll looked so real, I could see baby Jesus burp. I jumped up and down trying to reach for Jesus, but I couldn't finger Him.

After much pleading, Hatsuko lifted me up and let me touch the ivory doll. The doll felt smooth, cool and round. I rolled Jesus around with my fingers and pleaded with Hatsuko to let me buy Jesus. "Please. Please. Please. Pleeeeeeese!

You have a fortune in your fist, Hatsuko. I want to take Jesus home and put Jesus on Uku's pillow." I kept pleading with Hatsuko. "PLEASE, HATSUKO. Mother will like Jesus better than she did Uku. Jesus doesn't have fleas."

"No can, Percy." Hatsuko spoke pidgin English when she was nervous. "Jesus no like leave his mama. You can do that? You take Jesus away from his mama?" she asked.

I hung my head, looking at the floor, thinking, "No, Hatsuko. Still. Maybe. Maybe his mother won't miss Him, in fact, I know she won't." I started to count on my fingers, "Look, His mama got a donkey, a rooster, two cows, and Joseph to keep her company. Six."

"Five," corrected Hatsuko. "I think your mama miss you lots if you sleep somewhere else. If your mama go away, she miss you and you miss her. Yes, Percy?"

Looking up at Hatsuko, I replied, "I hope so." Blinking my eyes, I wondered, "Would you miss me, Hatsuko?"

"Yes, Percy. I miss you lots." Hatsuko grabbed my hand and led me quickly out of the store before I could ask her to buy me everything I saw. Back out on Fort Street, I stopped her in the middle of the sidewalk and made her look at me.

"Hatsuko, this is serious."

Hatsuko cringed because she thought I was going to ask for Mother's money and go back into Kress's. "Why serious, Percy?"

I squinted into the afternoon sun and pleaded, "Hatsuko, promise me. Promise me, promise me, promise me that you will never leave me. You're the only one who can protect me from doing something bad all the time."

Kissing my cheek, relieved I hadn't asked for the twenty dollars, she cooed while stroking my head, "I will never leave you, Percy. You in my heart always. Promise."

Holding out my hand, I demanded, "Good. Now give me the twenty dollars."

"Percy, you should be ashamed of yourself."

Smiling like an angel, I admitted, "Yes, I am very ashamed of myself, but Daddy says it never hurts to ask."

"Percy-san, my answer is no."

Walking down the street, taking Hatsuko's hand again, I said, "Boy, I could have had a lot of fun with Mother's twenty dollars. But let's go home, babee."

Hatsuko looked at her watch, "Percy, we bettah get home before your mama get home."

It was five in the afternoon. We walked hand in hand as I passed fascinating people of many colors. People of Honolulu were as exotic and different as Hedy Lamarr's name. Japanese women had lacquered jet-black hair fashioned into large pompadours. They walked like geisha girls, wearing high wooden *geta* (clogs), clack - clack - clack - clacking their way through the crowds. I walked behind them trying to copy their mincing walk.

They carried their belongings wrapped in dark purple silk bundles. Hatsuko carried a black purse held with a strap around her arm. I wanted Hatsuko's purse. The Japanese ladies' kimonos were designed in red, blue and black patterns. Their long sleeves flapped in the wind like sails. Hatsuko wore a plain blue, cotton dress that buttoned down the front.

While I was drooling over an open box of chocolates in a See's candy store window, Hatsuko whispered into my ear, "Percy, man follow me. He keep looking at me. He plenty drunk. Go fast."

Not listening, I dawdled, looking into other store windows while scraping my shoes on the sidewalk.

Slim Chinese women passed around me, dressed in brocaded gowns of green, orange and blue. They had an advantage to reach the bus first because they had slits all the way up the sides of their dresses and could walk fast. A ton of creamy, naked skin was flashed when they walked fast. Local men passing the Chinese ladies looked down, praying to see oodles more of the ladies' golden skin. God heard the men because miracles happened all the time. Powerful gusts of wind blew down from the mountains, separated the flaps of the dresses and everyone saw the Chinese ladies' black underwear. When those miracles happened, the Chinese lilies smiled.

I stopped and lifted my pant leg. No one looked.

"Percy, man right behind us. Hurry up. We go. Let's get on the bus *wiki wiki* (quickly). Put down your pants. Pick up your feet and go now," Hatsuko urged.

I continued mincing along like a geisha girl.

"Stop daydreaming, Percy, and walk straight."

I wasn't paying any attention to Hatsuko. I was spellbound now, watching several plump Chinese ladies coming toward me. Their little feet were stubs, bound up in cloth. I couldn't imagine how they kept their balance. They teeter-tottered like lady seesaws. As soon as I got home, I planned to take bandages and bind my feet into stubs to see if I could walk like a seesaw. The tiny-feet ladies elbowed me in the ribs to get me out of their way. Their faces were painted white and they wore lots of clunky jade jewelry on their fingers. They had as much jewelry on their fingers as the Christmas tree in Liberty House had ornaments.

Hatsuko said Chinese ladies were the smartest women on the street and no one could cheat them. I once overheard Hatsuko tell a girlfriend on the phone that the Chinese seesaws dispensed Chinese herbs for love, health and "prick" erections and were considered by the Japanese and Filipino men to be miracle workers of God and Honolulu.

Hatsuko grabbed my hand and muttered, "Walk faster - bus stop over there. You see policeman? Soldier-man still follow me. He making me scared."

I continued to walk in my fantasyland, oblivious to what Hatsuko was saying. I kept ogling the human flowers of all races on the streets of Honolulu. Some women wore leis and this wasn't even May Day. One or two ladies had tropical flowers stuck behind their ear. One tall, distinguished Hawaiian lady, who walked with a cane, had arranged white cattleya orchids all over her head. She was the biggest wonder of the day, a walking garden of Babylon.

Hatsuko kept pushing me along saying, "Honolulu bad place. Too many soldiers. No feel safe anymore." She kept looking in back of us and finally gave a sigh of relief after she couldn't see the man following us anymore. "I think we lost drunk soldier."

"What are you talking about, Hatsuko? I don't see any drunky soldier. Don't you see the magic around us? Downtown is just like the city of Oz. I think only good witches live here. Bad witches live on our street."

Indeed, Honolulu of 1940 was a magical city. The streets were lined with tall coconut trees and beautiful ladies of paradise strutted around as if they were walking in the garden of Eden. The men in the garden didn't belong because they wore brown suits, drab as the dirt in my backyard. Once in awhile, a turquoise pheasant feather hatband on a man's hat would catch my eye, but it was the women who were the jewels. Women of Hawaii, I thought, were the most beautiful creatures on God's earth. They were as beautiful as my dog, Uku. I wanted to march in their parade, my head smothered in white orchids, wearing a Chinese lavender gown that was slit up to my navel, and singing "Ah, Sweet Mystery of Life" like Jeanette MacDonald did in the movies.

We reached the bus stop. Hatsuko was perspiring. She breathed another sigh of relief because she was sure that the soldier was no longer following her. To be really sure, she asked me to look around the corner to see if he was behind us.

I looked around and said, "I don't see anyone, Hatsuko. I think you're dreaming." I stepped off the curb and peered down both sides of the street to make out if the bus was coming.

Hatsuko yelped behind me. The drunken soldier, wearing a liquor-stained uniform, surprised her from behind. He had been hiding in a bush. The soldier began dragging Hatsuko down the street. She tried to pull away from him, but he was too big, too ugly, too drunk, and too strong.

He yelled at her as he pulled, "Come here, you yellow Jap. I saw you look at me. You come drink with me." Hatsuko was about to fall to pieces and couldn't utter a word as he was dragging her away from me.

I waved at people to help us. They ignored me. Women dressed in hats, gloves, pinched into tight girdles, kept walking by us. They looked embarrassed because they kept their heads down and wouldn't look at me. Society matrons of Honolulu were treating Hatsuko and the soldier as if they were having a boyfriend-and-girlfriend fight and it was none of their business.

Worse yet, it was shocking behavior, a Japanese girl and *haole* (white skinned or Caucasian) soldier were out in public, fighting. Outcasts, as far as these sallow-faced shoppers were concerned, because, as Hatsuko told me later, different nationalities didn't mix. Especially, haoles didn't marry Japanese and Japanese didn't marry haoles in 1940. If they did, the ladies on top of our hill, founding members of the Honolulu Humane Society, would have wanted to drown the haole in the toilet like they did their unwanted kittens. For both the haole and Japanese cultures, it was the ultimate disgrace if ever they married and had babies.

The soldier, round-eyed, red-faced, puffing out of breath, kept pulling as he yelled, "Drink with me, Jap."

Hatsuko, finding her voice, cried out, "Please. Please. Go away. Please I no like drink with you. I don't know you. Percy, help me."

I grabbed Hatsuko's hand and tried to pull her towards me. A tug of war began. The soldier was on one side, Hatsuko and I were on the other. He continued to make loud grunting sounds and squealed like a pig, "You come here, Jap."

He was stronger than both Hatsuko and I together and I knew we were losing.

So I dropped Hatsuko's hand and ran around to the soldier and screamed into his ear, "Let her go, you big fat, smelly pig. She's my illegitimate daughter. You are a fiend, and I'm going to report you to President Roosevelt."

He was so surprised at what I had yelled, Hatsuko was surprised at what I had yelled, I was even more surprised at what I yelled that we all froze still as if we were playing the game "statues." After a few seconds, the soldier let Hatsuko go. He apologized to me, with his stinking gin breath, that he caused trouble for my illegitimate daughter and staggered down the street.

I yelled after him, "Hatsuko is not a Jap. She is a Japanese and don't you forget that." Putting my hands on my hips, I screamed louder, "You are a stupid hussy," a line I remembered from a Bette Davis movie.

Our bus arrived immediately. We jumped on. Walking to the back seat, Hatsuko and I held onto each other and sobbed. After we sat down, Hatsuko composed herself and asked me what made me say that I was her illegitimate daughter.

"It's the only thing that came into my mind."

Hatsuko looked puzzled. I took her hand as I remembered and said, "Last week when we saw *The Old Maid* with Bette Davis, you told me that Bette Davis's daughter was illegitimate because Bette didn't have a husband. But you said Bette Davis loved her daughter a lot more than if she really had a real father. Well, I love you a lot, so I guess you're my illegitimate daughter."

Hatsuko laughed out loud. She looked into my eyes and said, "Percy, we have a lot of secrets to keep now, don't we?"

"Yes, I guess we do."

Hatsuko continued, "First, let's not tell your mother that we walked around Honolulu."

"I think that's a very good idea, Hatsuko."

"And let's not tell your mother about the soldier. She might not let me take you to the movies any more."

"I wouldn't want that."

Taking both my hands and squeezing them, she continued, "Percy, you were very brave today. You saved my life. You were a hero. Your father would have been proud of you, but we won't tell him about this, will we?"

Looking down at her hands, I said quietly, "He'd never believe me, anyway. I only told that soldier hussy bastard what I thought of him."

Hatsuko confided in a soft, quiet voice, "Percy, I'm going to tell you another secret. Bastard means the same thing as illegitimate. It's a child without a father."

I clapped my hands, "Oh, that's a good secret, Hatsuko. Thank you. Boy, won't Mother be surprised when I'm grown-up that I already know the meaning of bastard."

Hatsuko's voice got softer, "I'm an illegitimate child, Percy."

I yelled out so everyone on the bus heard me, "That's great you're a bastard. You must have been really loved. I wish I had been a bastard. Maybe I was. Sometimes I wish I was like you, Hatsuko, and never had a father. I'll never call Uncle George a bastard again, because he's not the lovable type. I'm going to have to correct Cousin Bessie when she uses that word. From now on, I'm just going to call only the people I love bastards. Hatsuko, I'm so glad you're a bastard. And that soldier certainly wasn't a bastard. I should have called him a pink panty fart."

Wishing she was off the bus, Hatsuko asked, "Percy, promise me something else?"

"Oh, anything, Hatsuko. Anything for you."

She whispered in my ear, "Let's keep the word bastard our own special word. Just between us. Not ever say it out loud again. Just say it in your head. That's how you really keep secrets and tell people you love them."

Kissing her on the cheek, I promised, "I will, Hatsuko. So every time I see someone doing something nice, or that I love, I'm going to say in my mind, isn't he a wonderful bastard."

I paused. "Hatsuko, I love having secret words for my stomach." I smiled to myself because I now had some good secrets and words to store in my stomach instead of all the bad stuff.

I had to tinkle. I was going to try to hold it till I got home and I wasn't going to worry Hatsuko that I had to pee and was about to wet my pants. She had been through enough for one day. There were times when I wished I still wore diapers.

I could hardly wait to tell the secret word "bastard" to Agnes and Gertrude. Agnes, Miss Sassy-pants, would probably tell me that she knew that word long before I was born.

Sitting next to Hatsuko as the bus took us home, I felt happy, protected and secure. I was so sure that day, as sure of anything real in my seven-year-old life up to then, that my Hatsuko would always love me till the day I joined Nana in heaven. Hatsuko will always be my favorite bastard because I knew she would always get me home and keep me safe from curses.

I asked one more question, "Hatsuko, did you ever know your father?"

"I met him once or twice. He lives most of the time now in Japan."

"I bet he doesn't know he has a daughter who looks like a movie star."

Hatsuko squeezed my arm and smiled, "And he doesn't know that my best friend is going to be one and is now a big hero."

I sat in the back of the bus, aching to tinkle, feeling good about myself, and watching the city of Honolulu go by. More than ever I wanted to be a movie star because movie stars never tinkled.

After we got off the bus, I wet my pants when we walked by Cross-Eyed Mama's house. Her waterfall tinkling into her lily pond made me tinkle too. Cross-Eyed Mama, the Amazon witch, must have cursed me.

*Shirley Temple visiting Hawaii, 1937. Courtesy of Bishop Museum
Archives, Honolulu, HI.*

4

Movie Stars, Ships, and Baltimore Cousins

Every morning, waking up in Hawaii, a new adventure began. I lived on an island in the middle of the Pacific Ocean, with different looking people "mashed" together, and I never knew what strange things were about to happen around my house or what new, exotic person was arriving on the Lurline.

Hatsuko and I screamed ourselves hoarse seeing movie star Dorothy Lamour in real live Technicolor. I was very disappointed that Dottie had left her sarong in Hollywood. I read in Jimmy Fidler's gossip column in *The Honolulu Advertiser* that Dottie said Hawaii was her most favorite vacation spot in the whole wide world.

On a hot Saturday afternoon, Hatsuko and I were scrunched in the middle of a crowd of screaming fans outside the Waikiki Theater, hoping to see Dorothy Lamour. Standing on the steps of the theater, Dottie looked very Hollywood and every inch a movie star, from the way she blew kisses at us to how she casually wore dark glasses on top of her white turban hat. Hatsuko told me to wave to Dottie because she could tell that Dottie was waving at me. I waved and then yelled above the crowd, "I love your sarong, Dottie. I have one just like it." She blew a kiss straight into my face.

I loved Dottie Lamour.

Hatsuko and I swooned when we saw Shirley Temple in the flesh. Shirley was covered in leis up to her neck. She clasped her parents' hands as they waited to ride the elevator in the lobby of the Royal Hawaiian Hotel. Prompted by Hatsuko to speak out, I called, "Hi, Shirley - I love you, Shirley. Look this way, Shirley. Look at me, Shirley. Hellllloooooo, Shirley Temple. Hello! Hello. I love you, Shirley! It's me, Shirley. It's me, Peeeercy! I'm going to be the biggest star in Hollywood. I'm going to be just like you, maybe even bigger."

I turned to Hatsuko, "Wave, Hatsuko. She doesn't hear us."

Hatsuko waved her arms at Shirley like she was fanning a fire that broke out on top of Shirley Temple's head. I pointed to Hatsuko waving and then yelled to Shirley, "Hatsuko is your biggest fan, Shirley."

Shirley stood motionless next to her parents. Her eyes never left her mother's face. Hatsuko said in a loud voice, "She's stuck up, Percy."

Shirley didn't flick an eyelash. Shirley's parents, standing on either side of her, held her to them like two Brinks guards protecting an armored truck. The elevator door opened, the Temples walked in, turned around, faced out, looked straight ahead, and before the attendant could close the door, Shirley Temple, the movie star, stepped out of the elevator, looked me straight in the face and stuck out her tongue. She wheeled around in her Mary Janes, walked back in the elevator as the door closed, and the Temples rose up to their room on the second floor.

I stuck my tongue out at the elevator door. Shirley Temple's Technicolor pink little tongue is my lingering memory of Hollywood's little movie star. I hated Shirley Temple and thereafter vowed to love only movie stars who wore sarongs. Movie stars in bathing suits were far nicer than the movie stars who look like midgets, dress in pink ruffles and who stick out their tongues at me.

Saturday afternoons, Hatsuko and I strolled along the long, red velvet carpet in the lobby of the Royal Hawaiian Hotel, pretending we were movie stars who had just arrived from Hollywood on the Lurline. I carried Mother's Japanese umbrella and twirled it while we made our promenade.

As we strolled, I searched for movie stars checking into the hotel, coming out of the bathroom or buying a tube of toothpaste in the gift shop. Sometimes I'd go in the men's bathroom, kneel down and look under the stalls to see if Tyrone Power was sitting in one of them. I never found Tyrone doing number two, but then again movie stars never went to the bathroom, but I did surprise a lot of old men.

Everyone looked at us as we paraded through the lobby because we were dazzling - a tub of mayonnaise wearing short pants, twirling an umbrella, and holding hands with Madame Butterfly who acted like she was Ann Sheridan, the oomph girl. We'd make-believe on those afternoons that we were in the midst of a Hollywood premier and pretended to chat about Hollywood gossip, the success of my movies, hundred dollar gowns, and Hatsuko's marriage to Tyrone Power, all the while waving to our adoring fans who walked by us, gaping. We'd play-act as we walked toward the beach that we were drinking champagne out of crystal goblets.

Midway down the lobby, we'd stop at a faucet that poured the free ice cold pineapple juice and pretend it was champagne. The pineapple juice was there for the pleasure of the houseguests. A FOR GUESTS ONLY sign hung over the faucet. I drank a dozen paper cups of free pineapple juice every Saturday afternoon. I had a plan if we were caught and rehearsed it with Hatsuko. I planned to tell the hotel people that we were visiting Cousin Jeanette and Cousin Nelson from MGM, "don't you know," and we were here to sign them up for a movie starring me. Luckily, the pimply-faced assistant manager never asked or kicked us out of the hotel. I told Hatsuko I knew why. I explained it, opening my eyes as wide as Shirley Temple's, filling up my eighth cup of pineapple juice, that no one bothered us because we looked and acted like real movie stars. Hatsuko was disappointed that, on those Saturday afternoons during our promenade, no one ever asked me for my autograph. If someone had, I planned to draw a picture of Shirley Temple sticking out her tongue right below my signature.

Mother and I met arriving ocean liners that sailed into Honolulu harbor from Maui, Kauai, the Big Island, and the Mainland. The ships usually docked at the crack of dawn at piers 12, 13 and 14. Marigold liked to sleep late and Daddy played golf on weekends, so they never came with us.

Mother wouldn't meet a ship by herself because she was afraid that a gangster would stick her up. Mother was a scaredy cat because she had seen too many Jimmy Cagney stick-em-up movies and believed hoodlums lurked under the piers, waiting to rob and kill helpless women. For some unknown reason, Mother thought a fat, little sissy would protect her from all the dangerous John Dillingers of Hawaii. Agnes and Gertrude giggled.

Mother would wake me at five, as Marigold in the bunk above me pulled the covers over her head and told us to go away. After Mother dressed me, I'd grab for my smelly, small baby "blankey," still sleepy-eyed, and pile into the back seat of the car. I'd curl up puppy dog fashion and try to go back to sleep. I'd wake up because Mother honked her way down Beretania Street to keep the bad guys away from our car. I'd stick my nose out the back window, puppy-dog fashion, to smell the fresh morning rain on the pavement. It was hard to see anything because the glare of the street lights made the wet roads into rivers of blinding silver.

Arriving at the dock, we'd slam the car door and sprint for the pier as if we were racing Jesse Owens in the Olympics. Mother made me run in back of her and called out, "Run, Percy. Don't be a slow poke. Pick up your feet. Run for your life." Mother always ran fast because she felt something terrible was coming behind her.

I'd wave to the Hawaiian lei sellers huddled against the cement walls of the pier as we wizzzzzzed past them. We ran so fast, the ladies always yelled out, "Eh, here comes da track stars or da Halley's comet?"

I'd yell to them, "My mother is the tail. I'm the star." They'd hoot, holler and whistle, cheering us to run faster.

The leis made the air around the pier smell sweet with the fragrance of carnations, ginger, and plumeria, a perfume that greeted every visitor who arrived on or departed from our Hawaiian shores.

The most memorable of all the arrivals in September of 1940 were two old maid cousins from Maryland who wore brown felt hats with pheasant tail feathers sticking out from their brims. The cousins were sisters, two years apart. In one week, Nelda wore blue on Monday, Wednesday and Friday. Louisa, whose nose hooked like parrot's beak, wore brown on Tuesday, Thursday, and Saturday. The following week, they alternated colors and jewelry. On Sundays in their Maryland home, they stayed home, played cribbage and ate cottage cheese for dinner, wearing gray bathrobes.

The sisters fought with each other over politics, food and relatives. They were the tweedy sort of ladies that a farmer would find frolicking in a stack of hay on a New England spring morning or swimming nude in Thoreau's icy pond with Katherine Hepburn. Both sisters, Nelda and Louisa, had sharp tongues. Mother told me that people from the East Coast didn't mince words and cousins Nelda and Louisa didn't with me. They referred to me as their "aboriginal cousin." Needless to say, they didn't take to my conversations about movie stars who lived in what they referred to as "that awful town" called Hollywood, and they couldn't understand how a little boy got so fat. They did understand the fat part after seeing me eat mounds of egg salad topped with splats of mayonnaise.

The sisters forcibly made me eat fried liver smothered in onions and crispy bacon. It was their favorite meal because they felt it was filled with all kinds of goodness. They talked to me feverishly about liver all the time and told me to eat it everyday because liver was good for my tired blood. I told the cousins, "I never knew my blood was that tired or that sleepy or that repulsive." I told Nelda that looking at liver on my plate reminded me of her purple tongue. Nelda slapped my head.

The cousins told Mother that she must send me back with them to the East Coast to be educated properly. I told them straight out that going to movies had educated me better than anyone living in any old Baltimore City and my blood loved mayonnaise and I wasn't ever tired and I definitely wasn't leaving my mother. Eventually, I learned to stomach liver without thinking about Cousin Nelda's tongue and loved my cousins when they didn't have an old-fashioned cocktail in their hands. The sisters drank lots of old-fashioneds before dinner, and when they were on their second old-fashioned, they growled mean to me like people from New York City. Everyone in the neighborhood called them "good sports," because they drank and smoked cigarettes like Daddy and Mother did.

The cousins stayed a month, sleeping in Grandma's bedroom. Grandma moved out and stayed in a hotel with Marigold. I was stuck with the cousins and ate liver with them at lunchtime, always whining that they wouldn't let me smother Nelda's tongue with mayonnaise.

After two days with me, the cousins presented a long handwritten list of improper things that I shouldn't do. The words "you should not" were used a lot by the sisters from east of the Mississippi when talking to me. Behind their backs, and to Agnes and Gertrude alone, I called them "The Cousins Should Nots." They were determined to train me like a monkey in the circus.

Nelda and Louisa would sit me down on the living room couch, when they could catch me, and read out in their high Eleanor Roosevelt voices their list of the "should nots." At the top of their list was that I should not curl my hair with bobby pins. Both of them intimated that if I followed their list of "should not rules" based, so they told me, on the golden rules of a Puritan relative, they would leave me a great fortune in their will.

I told them Daddy said that their pinhead Puritan relative with his golden rules puked his way over on the Mayflower and they were safe in keeping their fortune intact because I was not about to give up putting bobby pins in my hair or eating mayonnaise on everything. Eating mayonnaise was found at the top of their "should not" list. Their fortune really went out of my reach the day I greeted them at breakfast wearing one of Mother's tattered old nightgowns.

The sisters didn't know how to laugh except when they had an old-fashioned in their hands. Nelda and Louisa wouldn't have been caught dead sitting by the side of my house eating a mayonnaise sandwich with Agnes and Gertrude and me. These East Coasters told me their fun was digging clams on the banks of the Chesapeake River in a blizzard.

These dames, as Daddy called them, to the end of their visit remained as tough and as durable as a winter in Maine. Whenever I was around them, I never dared to pee in my pants. I didn't realize it, but in a year's time, these two old birds would play a very important part in my life. They would help me break the curse.

Honolulu in 1940 was a beautiful city, filled with beautiful people. It was an exotic port of call where the famous and not-so-famous came to visit. Most of all, in the autumn of 1940, my family, who lived at the bottom of a hill, was a family together. Hatsuko cooked in the kitchen. Agnes and Gertrude slept in my bed. Marigold tickled me. My great-grandmother, my mother and father talked of the good old days. And even though my father didn't fancy me in Mother's dresses, he was home every night to carve our roasts at dinner. Once in awhile, I glimpsed he loved me.

What I didn't know was that on the day my mother visited with Uncle George at the Alexander Young Hotel, while Hatsuko and I window shopped at Kress's, twenty days before Christmas, my family was about to break apart. But while Nelda and Louisa visited us, looking from the outside, we seemed a perfect family.

I thought we were perfect because my family ate dinner every night together and slept in our beds at night. I checked every night the sleeping sounds of my family. It was as if Paul Whiteman was on the radio at the St. Francis Hotel in San Francisco but was playing his band in our house. Daddy snored the loudest. He sounded like a bassoon. Marigold's was a snoring tone behind Daddy. Mother was a flute. Grandma poop-poop-da-pooped even in her sleep.

The disappearance of Uku was the first sign of the curse. Every afternoon, I whistled for Uku to come home, but he never did. I prayed while walking home from school that Uku would suddenly appear running down the street, jump into my arms and lick me all over. I had planned what I'd do when he returned. At first, I'd pretend to be mad by looking him square in the eyes and scold him, shaking my finger at his nose. Then I'd growl like a dog, telling him what a bad dog he had been by leaving me. After that, I would give him my biggest smile, scratch his behind, pick out a flea, hold him, hug him, and tell him I loved him better than anything I knew because he was my favorite, favorite dog of all times. I would then lean down next to his head and whisper gently into his ear to please never go away from me again.

I loved Uku, who never came home. I loved all the bastards in my life. I hated curses.

5

My Favorite Bastards

I loved Hatsuko and she adored me. She adored me fat and round and I found her cuddly, lovable and Japanese. She was a Buddhist and burned incense in her room. After eating a mayonnaise sandwich with anything on it, I'd whisper into Hatsuko's ear that she was my sunshine and that meant she was my favorite bastard. She'd blush, pinch my tummy, and give me a kiss and remind me that bastard was our secret word.

She cooked only for me, and she made no bones about it to Daddy. That riled my father. After scraping mayonnaise off his plate, he'd roar, "Can't you remember, Hatsuko, that I hate mayonnaise, and I pay the bills around here."

Hatsuko was never afraid of my father's complaints. When he screamed at her, she'd give him back her wide-eyed Ann Sheridan look, put her hands on her hips, and look at him as if he was an idiot, answering, "I know you pay the bills and so does Percy's mama." Daddy waged losing battles with Hatsuko over her cooking. He would tell Mother, after a fight, that he never met a Japanese person like Hatsuko in his whole life. One more smart aleck remark out of her mouth and he was going to fire her. Daddy never did because Mother smoothed the waters, reminding him, "Who are we going to find to take care of Percy?"

Daddy couldn't think of one person.

At age seven, I was never far from Hatsuko's side or her kitchen. Her kitchen was my safe haven. I always kept fingers poised in the air ready to swipe into anything in sight that looked like food, preferably gobs of chocolate frosting left over in a bowl. At four in the afternoon, before the dessert was made, Hatsuko and I would settle down at the kitchen table with a glass of milk and a dozen graham crackers smeared with peanut butter and mayonnaise and we would chat about movies, movie stars and "what's for dinner." I'd whine to Hatsuko every afternoon that I wanted creamed tuna for dinner. I hungered for it every day because, as I told Hatsuko, her creamed tuna looked like cooked mayonnaise.

At 4:30 Hatsuko gave me my bath. She'd take off my clothes and lower me with a loud "kerplunk" into our Japanese sunken green-tiled bathtub. On the tile walls above the bathtub were painted red, black, and yellow striped Hawaiian fish that swam through an underwater tropical forest. Our Japanese bathtub inspired Hatsuko to make my bath time into a movie event.

Once, my bath-taking turned into a Cecil B. DeMille movie. We had recently seen DeMille's decadent Roman movie epic, *The Sign of the Cross,* where actress Claudette Colbert acted as an evil Roman empress. In one memorable scene, Claudette bathed in a sunken tub filled with donkey's milk. It was considered a racy scene because everyone saw in a flick of an eyelash Claudette's "chichis" (breasts). Hatsuko tried to copy the DeMille bathing scene by pouring stinky white bath powder into the tub. When the water turned creamy white, we oohed as if magic had occurred. As Hatsuko soaped me in the sudsy, white water, she told me the story of the movie over and over again - lions eating Christians, how handsome actor Frederic March acted as a Roman soldier and what an evil, vicious Roman princess Claudette played.

I started impersonating the evil Claudette for Hatsuko by first arching an eyebrow, then hissing like a snake, and finally standing up and showing my chichis. I ended the performance by "whooshing" soapy suds all over Hatsuko, yelling, "Death to the Christians. Lions, eat those Christians. I'm going to serve Christians up in a mayonnaise sandwich."

After getting completely soaked a couple of times while telling the story of that movie, Hatsuko changed the movie to *Heidi* that starred "stick out the tongue" Shirley Temple. I told Hatsuko I wanted to learn to yodel like everyone did in *Heidi.* When Hatsuko soaped my privates, I learned to yodel, "Oh delayyyy-eeeeeee-ooooooow." Hatsuko stuffed cotton in her ears whenever she bathed me.

Hatsuko gave me a choice of the bubble bath each bath time: rosemary, lavender, carnation, or purple hyacinth to match the movie we were going to perform that night. I mostly chose hyacinth because the name sounded funny. HYACINNNNNTH! For weeks, I ran around the house yelling HYACINNNNNTH!

I once caught Daddy and Mother using my hyacinth bubble bath powder. They were in the tub fooling around in the suds. I asked them what movie they were going to play and what scent of mine were they were using? They laughed and imitated me, crying out together, "HYACINNNNNTH." Daddy threw suds at me and told me to go see Hatsuko.

Hatsuko told me Mother and Daddy were playing a grown-up game. It was the only time that I remember seeing my parents having fun together. Taking a bath with Hatsuko bathing me, play acting, and seeing my parents in the bathtub having fun are some of my happiest childhood memories.

Hatsuko was an inch over five feet tall, twenty years old and smelled of washing starch. She had a glowing skin of yellow and little brown freckles all over her face. Unlike my old Cousin Bessie's skin that hung down from her arms like old wash cloths on a clothesline, Hatsuko's skin stuck to her.

She believed, with all her heart, that someday I would become a star at 20th Century Fox, earning thousands of dollars and driving a shiny black Dusenberg to Hollywood premiers. In her eyes, my stardom was indelibly written in the stars. It was Hatsuko telling me stories of Hollywood that made me want to become a movie star.

My favorite treasured gift from Hatsuko arrived on my seventh birthday. She gave me a bottle of Vitalis hair tonic. It was the same hair tonic that Nelson Eddy advertised in *Life* magazine. Vitalis set Nelson's hair into a grand cow pie that was as high as Marie Antoinette's wig. When Hatsuko applied Vitalis on my head, it stung like Listerine mouthwash. I screamed. Hearing me scream, Marigold prayed that Vitalis was turning me bald. Hatsuko, stars twinkling in her eyes, was convinced that Vitalis, no matter how it stung my head, was about to bring out my star power like it did for Nelson Eddy.

I believed everything Hatsuko told me.

Before I left for school, she and I would stand in front of a mirror with my black Ace comb poised as we decided on which hairstyle I was to wear that day. After Hatsuko made up my mind, she would pour Vitalis liberally over my head and force my hair into an outlandish mass of swirling, golden curls. Every morning, I looked into the mirror and saw the same fat Harpo Marx staring back at me. Loaded with blonde curls all over my head, dressed in short pants, after Hatsuko patted my "tushy," I tottered off to school. Every morning, I walked to school feeling like a movie star, because Hatsuko adored every curl on my head.

At school, I had become a star because I sang popular songs at all the Friday morning assemblies. I rehearsed the songs of the day in the bathtub with Hatsuko coaching me. My greatest triumph was singing Victor Herbert's "Ah, Sweet Mystery of Life, At Last I Found Thee." I sang that song, flinging my head from side to side like Jeanette MacDonald did in the movies. I once performed that song spontaneously in the middle of the lobby of the Royal Hawaiian Hotel. After I finished singing it, someone gave me a penny.

Hatsuko told me that movie stars waved and smiled at everyone they met on the streets because that was the way to become popular and that I should live each day as if I starred in an MGM musical. She made me feel that nothing bad could ever happen to me as long as she was at my side. Hatsuko was my good fairy and I knew she would protect me from curses and my sister beating me up.

I told Hatsuko as Thanksgiving of 1940 approached that we really had to work hard because I had been asked to sing "Silent Night" under the Christmas tree in front of the whole "dang" school. "It's going to be a really big thing, Hatsuko." The performance date had been set for the last day of school before Christmas vacation began. I knew the offer came because I had the best singing teacher in the world, Hatsuko, who was the "bestest friend" I ever had and who had made me a star at school last May.

Before school let out for the summer the year before, I had been cast as the Prince in *Snow White and the Seven Dwarfs*. I sang all the parts except for the dwarfs and the witch. Wigay Wix, the nicest and prettiest girl in our class, was cast as the princess, a part she hated. Nobody wanted to act in the production because everyone in our class was shy, that is, except for Booby the Bully, who tried out for all the dwarf parts, and me. The wicked witch part went straight away to Peggy Leilani Potz because she was the ugliest girl in our class. Peggy hated me because I was Wigay's friend and Peggy asked me to be hers.

I memorized all Wigay's lines and songs in case she got nervous and threw up. Hatsuko coached me letter perfect in both parts. I bragged to Hatsuko as the performance date drew near that real stardom was around the corner. During the performance, in front of an audience, Wigay did throw up and after being sick, hid under a table all through Acts I and II. If there had been an Act III, Wigay would have gone home. I sang and spoke all the princess's and prince's lines and sang "Someday My Prince Will Come" - to myself. That was a big treat. When the curtain came down, the audience gave me a standing ovation. I became a star.

I bowed and told the audience at my curtain call speech that I was so MOOOOOVED by their applause, and I thanked them for coming. Hatsuko, standing up in the front row, clapped louder than anyone else did. I continued my curtain call speech by introducing Hatsuko as the coach to a new Hollywood star. After the curtain call, she gave me red roses she stole from Cousin Bessie's garden. Hatsuko told me within earshot of everyone that I was the greatest new Hollywood star in the world and made me sign her autograph book three times.

Mother and Wigay's parents left at intermission. Daddy never attended any of my performances because I overheard him tell Mother that he was afraid to come to see me act because he feared that he'd find me performing in one of Marigold's dresses.

The seven dwarfs and the wicked witch, seeing that I had hogged all the attention, hated me. Grumpy gave me a kick in my rear end as I was taking my third bow. I told Agnes and Gertrude a kick in the rear is the price one pays for fame. Princess Wigay, after much coaxing by me, came out from under the table and took a bow with me. Wigay, as we walked off stage, told me that she loved me because I had saved her life and added that I was her hero. She kissed me right on my lips as princesses do. It was the first time I had been called a hero and kissed on the lips by a pretty girl. Wigay's kiss made me feel so nervous, I ran home because I had almost peed in my pants.

Hatsuko's instincts regarding toilet training were infallible. She told me she could have written a dictionary on the subject. When I reached age two, one of her techniques was to place me on my toilet seat at the precise moment my mother would be maneuvering her Ford down our narrow driveway. Mother's mind always zoomed twenty minutes ahead of her watch, a family trait, and thus she had a hard time paying attention to her driving. Thinking about a fight with Daddy, she'd careen our car into the kitchen wall once a week. Mother ran up a huge bill at Lemm's Service Station.

When I heard the sound of Mother's car smashing into our kitchen wall, the revving of the car tires trying to extricate the car from the wall, metal leaving wood, is when I pooped. Hearing me poop, Hatsuko would cheer. It was toilet training at its best.

Once I learned, I never missed hitting my target and Mother never stopped crashing into the kitchen wall. From the age of two to seven, when my mother drove down our driveway, I'd run for the bathroom to make a dump. Daddy didn't dump much and complained to Mother that her weekly car accidents and high bills at Liberty House were stopping him up and driving him crazy and into the poor house. Daddy drank gallons of Milk of Magnesia before going to work. I felt sorry for Daddy because he didn't have Hatsuko's toilet training when he was a little boy.

Hatsuko lived in a little room off the garage. I never entered her quarters. It was her inner sanctum. I never knew how her room was furnished, what pictures she hung on the walls or if she had a bathtub. In that sense, Hatsuko was a mystery. I also never met any of her relatives but she did tell me she had a sister on the other side of the island. Her sister never visited us. What I did know was that her sister, Rose, was separated from Hatsuko from the age of two. They had different mothers. Rose was raised on the island of Molokai and Hatsuko raised on Oahu. Hatsuko's mother had died young and her father remarried. Because Hatsuko was not getting along with her stepmother, she went to work for a haole family in Waikiki from the age of eight. She started out as a kitchen helper. It was from the haole family that she learned English and all about Hollywood. The mother of the haole family was a mystery writer who was well known on Hollywood and Vine.

Hatsuko never told me if she had attended school, who her friends were, or what was her favorite color. I never once asked her if she was sad. When I walked into her kitchen every morning, breakfast was cooking on the stove, and she'd drop everything and hug me with all her might. It was as if we hadn't seen each other - forever. She'd hold me to her, kiss the top of my head, smooth down my cowlick - and ask me if I had "shishi-ed." I always answered "yes" even if I hadn't because I wanted to see her smile. Hatsuko was my total sunshine.

My mother and Hatsuko had two things in common. They both were bad drivers and they both loved me. My mother taught Hatsuko how to drive our car by driving down our driveway. Hatsuko never hit our kitchen wall, just the mailbox and a coconut tree.

Mother was my other love. Mother descended from a missionary family that came around the Horn to Hawaii in 1836. She was nicknamed "Pumpkin" when she was born because Mother was round, orange-haired and, even as a baby, as much fun as a Halloween party. When Mother became a teenager, everyone stopped calling her Pumpkin because she turned slim and blonde.

When Mother grew up in Berkeley, California, she was as fat as a butterball. Making me feel better when I told her about being teased at school for being fat, Mother recounted stories about being taunted by her sisters and classmates because she looked like an enormous elephant. Mother said she stood out like a round watermelon growing up in a patch of slim, beanstalk sisters. Once, so hurt by her classmates' stinging catcalls, Mother covered herself from head to toe in poison ivy. Itchy red welts rose like blisters all over her skin, making her eyes into puffy balloons. Mother stayed out of school for three whole weeks. Because Hawaii didn't have poison ivy, poison oak or snakes on any of the islands, I prayed to God to send poison ivy over in gunnysacks on the next Lurline. I planned to plant it all around my house so I could stay out of school whenever I got tired of being teased.

I had a bad first day in kindergarten. I came running home from school crying because Booby the Bully said I looked like a big, fat cow pie. Mother consoled me by saying that I would grow out of being fat and told me one of her fat childhood stories.

The story went that after many terrible weeks of teasing at Miss Ramson's, before school and after breakfast, Mother climbed to the top of her steep garage roof and hid. Perched on the roof like a frozen crowing rooster, Mother kept still as a stone statue all day. Mother determinedly sat on the roof without saying a word for the entire day, looking down as everyone searched for her. Her mother, Granny, spent a frantic day looking for her Pumpkin around the neighborhood, and then, in the late afternoon, my grandmother looked up and found Pumpkin sitting on top of their garage, motionless as a weathervane. No amount of pleading would bring Pumpkin down and everyone, including Grandpa, was too chicken to climb up a ladder and fetch her.

Granny, in desperation, called the Berkeley fire station to retrieve her baby. Mother said that night her mother read her the story of *The Ugly Duckling*. Her mother swore on a stack of Bibles that one day, Mother would turn into a beautiful swan. That promise was kept. Mother swore that I, too, would become a handsome prince someday and I just had to be patient. Inside my head I knew that no matter what Mother said, I was never going to become a handsome prince because Mother wasn't a cursed person like I was.

I didn't know it then, but Mother was cursed, too.

At thirteen, Mother lost her baby fat and turned athletic. In high school, she became the captain of the basketball team, the tennis team, the horseback riding team, and she was the star swimmer for her school. Because she loved children and coaching sports, Mother became a schoolteacher. She taught third grade at Punahou School, the first private school west of Colorado and established in 1841. Because Mother taught at Punahou, Marigold and I were awarded free tuition and were able to attend this exclusive school that otherwise would have been too costly for Daddy's small salary.

I thought my mother was heroic because she could fight Daddy with words and win. Mother was a tigress when driving her chariot down on Beretania Street. She drove like General Sherman galloped his horse through Georgia during the Civil War, never taking prisoners. Mother galloped past red lights. Her driving so terrified Daddy that when he sat in the passenger seat, he closed his eyes, all the while keeping his hand on the door handle in case a lamppost blasted through the windshield. When Daddy drove our car like a sea captain steering his ship careful-ly through calm waters, he stopped at red lights. As he waited for the light to turn green, Mother called Daddy a sissy. One thing I can say for my mother's driving, she always made the curve at the bottom of our hill, gunning the accelerator at top speed.

I thought Mother was Eleanor Roosevelt, Charlie Chaplin, and Joan of Arc all rolled up into one large energetic package that I loved. Charlie Chaplin? Observing Mother since the time I could remember things, I noticed she had the little tramp's courage to defy the obstacles that life put in her way. She was a woman who, unlike most of her middle-class haole girlfriends, worked for a liv-ing. Mother had financial freedom that most women in Hawaii didn't understand. She had her own checking account. Mother was an oddity to Daddy's man friends because they thought wives should be kept at home, working like slaves without a checking account to draw on or having a thought beyond the gossip of the day.

Mother told Daddy she wasn't about to become a wife who was solely depen-dent upon her husband's whims or judgments. She also wasn't about to keep her mouth shut about things she believed in and she certainly wasn't going to live her life playing bridge on Wednesdays and attending "girlie lunches" at the Halekulani Hotel on Fridays.

Mother started teaching full time as soon as she hired Hatsuko. Over games of cribbage and martinis, Daddy complained that women in Hawaii didn't have a serious brain in their heads and he could prove it. Mother, thinking he was talking about her, answered Daddy, saying he was wrong because it was the women in Hawaii who were left vast fortunes by tycoon husbands, men who had died in their primes, who were now running businesses in 1940 Hawaii. Daddy, annoyed that Mother disagreed with him, swore and said what was wrong with Hawaii today was that there was too much female interference in what should be men's business and that Mother should keep her stupid remarks to herself. Whenever Daddy drank a martini and not his usual bourbon and Coke, I knew he was upset with Mother. Mother's best friends were people who didn't take themselves too seriously.

Eleanor Roosevelt? Mother had President Roosevelt's wife's crinkled kind eyes and smiled with a mouth full of teeth. Joan of Arc? Joan of Arc, I read about in Grandma's French books. She was a fighter and a believer in God. Joan of Arc had no patience with fools or a weak king sitting on a throne, and would burn at a stake for what she believed in. Mother was willing to burn at any stake if she thought she was right. When my mother made up her mind about anything, there was no changing it...even if she was dead wrong. She had not changed from the day when she was a little girl who sat on a garage roof, and she still couldn't be coaxed by my father or anyone to do anything she didn't like or believe in.

Mother was a goddess whom I worshipped from afar because she didn't like to be kissed that much. She spoke and laughed in a baritone voice that tough Barbara Stanwyck, a movie actress, used when she slapped Clark Gable's face. When Mother laughed her HAAAAAAAAAAAAAAAAA's, the sound came from her toes. Mother's voice became lower the more she smoked her two packages of Lucky Strikes a day. More than once, when Mother answered the phone, a stranger thought Daddy was on the line.

Mother was the new woman of the thirties that I saw portrayed in the movies. She wasn't the Clara Bow of the twenties, the silent movie flapper girl; Mother was the Irene Dunne of the thirties, a smart-talking independent woman who took on Cary Grant.

She loved me - that I never doubted. She was never upset that I played with dollhouses, collected toy cars, ran around playing cowboys and Indians, and adored wearing her dresses as much as she did. Mother stuck up for my weirdness against Daddy and said I was only going through a fat, silly phase that all children go through. She added that with a little time, I would turn into a tiger.

Mother was a storyteller. It was through her stories told from the time I was out of the crib that I learned about magic spells, monsters, heroes, witches, good fairies, and curses. Sitting on my bed at night, before I fell asleep, she'd weave fantastic tales that were better than having her read from any of the Oz books. Her own made-up stories were the most treasured moments of my child night-world. Nights when Mother and Daddy weren't attending a cocktail party, Mother would come into our bedroom, tuck Marigold and me in, make us comfy, shut off the lights, and say in her low voice, "Shall I tell a story tonight?"

"OOOOOOOH!" Marigold and I would scream.

Every night when her story began, an evening rain hit softly against the window screens. Mother's stories, the rain and the darkness of the room opened wide our imaginations. Before Mother began her story, she'd make us say our prayers and after the "amens," she would tell us how much she loved us even if we had been very bad that day. Mother, Marigold, and I always kissed and made up at story time. After we said we were truly sorry and would never do it again, her story would begin.

She'd start out in a husky Barbara Stanwyck whisper, "Once upon a time in a dense, dark - dark - dark forest, there lived a wild ugly beast who ruled a forest of many colors. His name was Hunkacha."

Whenever I heard Hunkacha's name, I'd sigh and snuggle down under the covers, letting only my hair and eyes peep out above the blanket. Mother, after hearing my sigh, would continue, speaking softly. "In the middle of the forest, there lived two children named Little Johnny and Patty. And isn't it funny - these two children were about the same ages as you two."

Marigold and I would scream hysterically whenever Mother put children in her stories who were our ages.

"These children lived with their very old father in a little thatched hut under a big, wide oak tree. Their old father was a very wise man and had a long white beard, as long as a river. The ancient father told Patty and Little Johnny that in this forest, the most beautiful, lustrous blue pearls were hidden at the bottom of a dark, cold blue lake. These pearls held all the secrets of life to protect the children from evil monsters and to help them leave the forest and find their fortune. These magical pearls would also make them very wise. These blue pearls once belonged to Patty and Little Johnny and were a gift from an angel called Husskelson.

"The blue pearls were stolen from Little Johnny and Patty when they were little by Hunkacha, the evil monster, because Hunkacha didn't want Patty and Little Johnny to leave the forest. He didn't want them to become wiser, wealthier and healthier than he was. He was jealous of the two children. So while stealing the pearls, Hunkacha cast a spell on Patty and Little Johnny, so that, without the pearls, they could never leave the forest to find all the good things that awaited them beyond the trees.

"Mean old Hunkacha slept in a dark cave on the other side of the forest, right beside the lake where he guarded the pearls night and day. They still lay shining like a thousand diamonds on the muddy bottom. The old father said that Patty and Little Johnny were at the perfect age to enter the dark forest to bring back the blue pearls.

"Remember," Mother explained in the middle of the story, "these pearls were more precious than a room full of gold and jewels because they held the secrets of life that would protect Little Johnny and Patty forever."

Mother acted the father by speaking in an old person's shaky voice, "I'm going to give each one of you something that will help you fight and kill Hunkacha and bring back the pearls. The first thing you must remember is that you must help each other on the journey, otherwise, you will not be able to bring back the blue pearls and Hunkacha will keep you his prisoners for life in this forest or eat you up for supper.'

"The old father gave his children gifts to help bring back the treasures. He presented Patty with a harmonica made of gold. When Patty played it, the sweetest tune in the whole world spun forth. He then bestowed on Little Johnny a golden reed that could blow the biggest spitballs in any fairy country. With a big breath, Johnny could blow a spitball as straight as an arrow or stay under water using the reed to breathe.

"Little Johnny complained to his father that Patty always got better presents than he did because he liked the gold harmonica best. The old father scolded Little Johnny and said that each gift was especially for them. The harmonica and golden reed were to help each of them, in their own way, to find and bring back the blue pearls. Then the old father gave them two tuna sandwiches to eat on their path."

For me, that was the best part of the story.

"The father waved them off as they started their journey into the forest of many colors, which in the beginning was colored red. Their father warned Little Johnny and Patty that Hunkacha was a cunning beast, so they must keep their wits about them. So hand in hand, Little Johnny and Patty entered into the red forest to start their journey. Their father stopped the children as they were about to step into the forest, and warned, 'You must remember one thing - no matter what happens to you in the magical forest, you must always tell the truth - no matter what temptations or dangers come your way. Do you hear me, children?' They nodded and waved one more final farewell to their father. This last warning was going to be very hard for Little Johnny because Little Johnny hardly ever told the truth in his whole life."

Mother stopped the story because our eyes had shut. Drifting off, I mumbled to Mother to please continue the story tomorrow night but I had had such a tiring day that I couldn't keep my eyes open. I pleaded with Mother to tell me if Little Johnny and Patty found the pearls and killed Hunkacha. Mother promised she would tell me tomorrow night, but right now I must go to sleep. As my eyes closed and as Mother's voice faded away, it was her perfume, An Evening In Paris, I remembered best. Her smell is a strong childhood memory I have of her. She was the one I loved best.

During that year, as Mother told of Little Johnny and Patty's adventures into Hunkacha's forest of many colors, Daddy never joined us at story time. Because Mother's story was so scary, I began to watch and look round corners for Hunkacha to jump out of a bush and scare me to death, especially when walking outside on dark nights without shadows.

The other bastards in my life who were special were Daddy, Marigold and Grandma. Each one of them scared me to death. They sometimes scared me as much as Hunkacha did.

6

Daddy

Daddy, I feared. He made me poop in my pants.

My father was a shipping agent for Castle and Cooke, one of the Big Five companies in Hawaii. He never once told me what he shipped, except once he yelled he was going to ship me to China.

Daddy's great-grandfather had arrived on a whaling bark in 1842, a few years after Mother's preacher great-grandparents began spreading the word of Jesus on Maui. Daddy had a jowly face with large pouches under his eyes. He reminded me of the hound dog that chased Eliza over the ice fields in *Uncle Tom's Cabin*. He had broad shoulders that gave him a square look. He was of average height and lurched - chunk - chunk - chunk when he walked. I thought of Daddy while watching a Pathe Newsreel at the Pawaa Theater. My father walked like a German tank jerking itself over the Maginot Line.

My daddy, though just under five-foot-eight-inches, was a man to be reckoned with by family, foes and friends. He had a fierce countenance even when he smiled. Because of his small stature, as compared to his six-foot-one-inch cronies, Daddy bullied his way through life. Daddy never wanted to be called a sissy like his son, but I once saw him cry and carry on - after a couple of drinks - talking about his dead mother. He had a "poochy" belly.

His brother, Uncle Bob, told me Daddy was a sickly child and had to stay out of high school for a whole year. He never graduated with his class because he was plagued with a terrible sinus infection and spent a year in a Maui sanatorium breathing in cold, dry air. At the sanatorium, he caught tuberculosis.

During this sick period, he painted watercolors, and during his last year in high school, having recovered from TB, Daddy took the lead in the senior class play. He played Prospero in Shakespeare's *The Tempest*. After graduating from high school, Daddy turned to manly sports at the University of Hawaii and became a he-man. Throughout his life, even on his good days, he never was without a sinus headache.

Daddy was the eldest of four brothers and had been spoiled rotten by his grandmother. After his father died, no one in the family made a major life decision, including marriages, without the blessings of Daddy.

Daddy drank his bourbon with Coca-Cola or martinis straight up, and smoked three packs of Lucky Strikes a day. He played around with hulking men who were called in middle age by their old college nicknames: Bip, Dutch, Slurpie, Fat, Frenchie, and Kanaka. His football friends called him Dickie Boy. His teammates were all members of a famous football squad called "The Wonder Team." That team brought glory to the University of Hawaii in the mid-1920s. Each man wore and displayed a small eighteen-carat gold football as a reminder of their glorious moment in the sun. Now as they entered the 1940s, their gold fobs had tarnished, but the teammates met religiously on Sunday afternoons (Hatsuko's day off) in our living room to remind themselves of their glory days on the football field.

On these Sunday afternoons when the wonder team met, hunkered down in Mother's rattan chairs, they replayed over and over again their football games of long ago. As afternoon shadows deepened into dusk and the teammates' inebriation became stronger, conversations turned into grunts. "Dickie Boy, remember that touchdown?"

I stopped conversations when it was my turn to pass around a dish of peanuts. To get into the spirit of the afternoon, I wore lipstick, a sarong, and clomped around in Mother's high heels. Daddy shuddered when I put the peanuts in his hand. The football team always thanked me kindly as I served them. I overheard Kanaka, Daddy's best friend, tell my father that every boy wanted to look like Bette Davis. The other athletes agreed and sounded sincere, as if they meant it. They didn't want Daddy to beat their brains out.

Daddy knew better. He knew his friends were being kind because they had sons who wore football pads and dirty jock straps to bed. Daddy, on the other hand, had a freaky son who passed hors d'oeuvres on Sunday afternoons singing Jeanette MacDonald's "Rosemarie."

"Rosemarie" was Daddy's favorite song. I sang it every Sunday afternoon for him. Singing his favorite song didn't please Daddy because sometime during the afternoon I told his best male friends that I hated football, showing off at the same time the red nail polish on my fingers. Trying to be one of the guys, I advised Bip and Kanaka that when I grew up, I was going to be a cheerleader for the University of Hawaii and that when I went to bed, I washed my face with Ivory soap. I told them that Hatsuko, my best friend, advised me that Ivory soap and a glass of Welch's grape juice just before bedtime would keep even old broken-down football stars handsome and regular.

I said that because, looking into their bleary faces, I saw that their eyes had turned puffy and red from decades of drink. I added, tightening up my sarong, that they sure didn't look like the same people I saw in the photograph on Daddy's bureau, dressed in spiffy green and white football uniforms. Not letting well enough alone, I added they looked as beat-up as an old junk car.

Daddy groaned, shooshing me away with his cigarette, and ordered, "Go see your mother." I heard Kanaka tell Daddy as I sashayed into the kitchen, "He'll grow out of it, Dick. He's one in a million."

My father responded to Kanaka, "If you think he's so one in a million, you take him home. I'll throw in a case of Ivory soap and a case of Best Foods mayonnaise for the taker."

There were no takers.

My sister Marigold, who sat at my daddy's feet on those Sunday afternoons, was a big football fan. When she grew up, she told Daddy, she wanted to play tackle for the University of Hawaii.

Daddy and his old football heroes drank any kind of liquor I put in their hands. By their third drink, their faces melted. Their skin became yellow candles dripping wax down their cheeks and they looked like men who were about to cry. By their fourth drink, there was no animation in their talk.

Thinking back on those days, I knew Daddy and his friends had given up on birthday parties, the Easter bunny, and Santa Claus long ago. Drinking gins with beer chasers didn't turn Daddy or his friends heroic or younger. The childhood magic had gone out of their eyes. Remembering old football games only made their pain of the present stronger. What these men tried to forget and what the mirror told them every morning as they shaved - life had passed them by and what they needed was Percy's Ivory soap. These middle-aged men were looking for something to revive the glory world of their youth. Little did they know that there was something for them that was just around the corner to revive their zest in life and that something was going to be a war.

There was always a bright moment, on these long, dreary Sunday afternoons when Daddy drank with his friends. At five in the afternoon, he turned on the radio to the "Jack Benny Show." Wives and children were then allowed to join the men in the living room. We gathered around them, sitting on the floor, as Don Wilson, the fat announcer, began the show crying out, "J- E- L-L- O presents THE JACK BENNY SHOW!" Everyone in our house became alive as the sounds of Mary Livingston's "Oh, Jaaaaack," Rochester's "What's up, Boss?" and Phil Harris's "Hi, Jackson!" floated over the airwaves from California into our living room.

"Oh hi, Mary, Rochester, Phil." A long pause. We'd shriek with laughter because in our imaginations we saw the Jack Benny look. "Oh, Rochester - OH, ROCHESTER, get the Maxwell (his car)," Benny would order.

I'd squiggle on the floor, hardly able to contain myself, waiting to hear the "Chugga, chugga, wheeze, bang, bang, ugga, ugga," magic of Mel Blanc's sound effects when Jack's car arrived on the radio waves. The Maxwell car with Rochester, his chauffeur, at the wheel, drove Jack down to his bank, where he kept all his money. Jack's bank vault was located down in a drippy dungeon protected by snapping alligators. Jack Benny was known as the stingiest and funniest man on radio and the worst musician. When Jack started to play his violin, Phil Harris ran for cover. Mary Livingston, his sassy wife, told Jack that she would rather hear the sounds of his fingernails scratching down a blackboard than hear him play his Stradivarius violin.

"Oh, Marrrry, you don't mean that," he'd retort.

Jack Benny and his friends brought laughter into our home. Those half-hours with Jack Benny were the only moments I remember during my childhood when Daddy, Mother, Marigold, and I joined together with Daddy's friends and forgot where we were, who we were, the house we lived in, and that I was a fat, sissy boy and cursed.

Jack Benny was an important part of my family. He was as close to a spiritual epiphany as I ever experienced with my daddy. Jack Benny was my church because he made me laugh.

God Bless Jack Benny!

The Sunday radio programs continued on into the evening as my dad and his cohorts became dangerous to be around. As the hours dragged on, their talk of long-ago football victories faded into exaggerated, slovenly, drunken talk, and by seven o'clock, Daddy and Kanaka were ready to fistfight with each other. Fantasy had become truth and truth was found at the bottoms of Daddy and Kanaka's bourbon and Coke glasses.

On these Sunday afternoons, the sexes separated. Wives, new and old, girl-friends, new and old, were exiled to the kitchen to fix drinks for the men and feed the kids. Munching on potato chips, drinking their bourbons straight or gins with tonic (more gin than tonic), the ladies gossiped about husbands, boyfriends, and their "best friends" who were back home in bed with the flu.

I listened, unnoticed, as the ladies gossiped, and after three drinks, the kitchen gang turned into a backbiting free-for-all. Heaven help the person home in bed who had become Topic A because she wasn't around to defend herself. Whenever someone breathed, "Please, I am telling you this in the strictest of confidence," all the ears perked up, and it was a certainty that by noon the next day, every "secret" word uttered in the kitchen would have been spread in all kitchens of Honolulu. I expected to see it headlined in Monday morning's *Advertiser*.

Confidences on Sundays were never sacred. I added to the scandalous telling. After school on Monday afternoons, I repeated everything I heard to Cousin Bessie. After three Mondays of great gossip telling, she gave me her red taffeta evening gown.

For most middle-class haole women in Hawaii in 1940, there were few diver-sions. They could partake in gossip, handle the kids, volunteer at the Daughters of Hawaii or the Outdoor Circle, or drink. Many ladies drank a half a bottle of gin before noon.

We, the children of the men drinking in the living room and the women gos-siping in the kitchen, were stashed away in my bedroom. Except for a call to listen to the Jack Benny program or to pass the drinks or peanuts, we were told to stay put in my room and be quiet. We obeyed because while out of sight of our dad-dies, we couldn't get a licking. Wearing a Dorothy Lamour sarong on Sundays, I never got a licking.

Mother warned us kids in the bedroom, "Do not disturb your fathers on any condition."

I was perfectly content to stay put as long as I had a radio and could listen to "The Shadow," who fought the evil in the world. I knew, as everyone else did, The Shadow was really Lamont Cranston and only the lovely Margo Lane knew his real identity. I'd shiver as The Shadow's voice began, "Who knows what evil lurks in the hearts of men - only The Shadow knows."

"OOOOOOOH," we'd scream. I'd jump off the bed, run, and turn off the lights to make everyone scream louder. I pretended I was The Shadow and observed, listened and remembered all that went on around me on those Sunday afternoons, and no one noticed. Adults never believed that a fat seven-year-old sissy who wore a sarong would remember anything said in front of him.

I remembered everything.

One incident sticks in my memory of when my father and I did communicate. Mother decided I was to become a pianist. Hatsuko went along with Mother's inspiration and wasn't about to disagree with my mother on anything. Over coffee, they plotted. What they didn't observe was that I had teeny-weeny hands and a wandering mind. I could have told them that God spoke to me before I was born, declaring that I was not to be a piano player, but the earth goddesses just couldn't see it. I told them, while they drank their coffee, that I didn't want to play the piano; I wanted to sing and dance like Ginger Rogers in an ostrich feather dress.

Mother, not to be deterred, argued and wore down my father into buying a piano on time, along with a year's piano lessons with Mrs. Love. Mrs. Love was a kindly lady who taught piano to talented and untalented students at Punahou School. Teaching me to run scales on a piano, Mrs. Love almost went mad but learned the patience of Job. What made up my father's mind about paying for the piano lessons was that Marigold decided that she was going to be the Artur Rubinstein of the Wild West. She was itching to play a rinky-dink piano in a saloon where John Wayne drank whiskey. She wanted to join me in piano lessons to further that career. Daddy bought a spinet piano at Thayer's Music Store.

Mother ordered me to practice on the piano for an hour every day. I was to practice because Daddy had paid good money, which was hard to come by, for the piano and the lessons with "that Mrs. Love." Daddy called her "that Mrs. Love." A piano recital for parents had been planned the week after Thanksgiving and I was on the program to perform a short piece.

One afternoon, I was ordered by Mother to practice my piece for the recital. Marigold was playing baseball out on the street. Daddy was home sick with a sinus headache and had been assigned by Mother to watch me run the scales and learn a simple song about a train running up and down a hill for the recital. I wanted to be outside playing with Marigold and began banging the piano keys in all the wrong ways, trying to get the train up the hill.

I ran my fingers on my right hand up the piano - F - A - C - E - but my baby finger was too short and I kept missing the E key. My off-key playing went on for ten minutes. Up the scale I went, always missing the E key. My mind wandered back and forth from the piano keys to the icebox and the Best Foods mayonnaise bottle sitting on a shelf. I yearned for a mayonnaise sandwich to make my stomach stop growling. I started missing the A, the C and, of course, the E keys. My stomach kept groaning in protest.

Daddy sat in his chair near me, stoic, tired, sick, head throbbing, and trying to read the evening paper. After I missed the E key for the tenth time, he slammed down the newspaper and commanded, "God damn it, Percy, enough. You're driving me crazy."

"I'm driving myself crazy, too, Daddy. I can't stand myself."

Taking my hands off the piano, I put my head on my chest and sighed. I placed the tired, swollen, useless red hands under my fanny. Daddy rose from his chair and told me to move over. He sat next to me. I looked at his hands resting on his lap. His hands looked as if they could play the piano really good because his fingers were long and thin. He pulled my hands out from under me and inspected the small, stubby fingers and said, "Too bad you couldn't have been a stronger fellow, Percy."

"I was cursed, Daddy."

He said softly, "Maybe if I had been stronger, you would have been stronger. You almost died twice just after you were born. I was worried that you wouldn't live."

"Did you worry about me, Daddy? I'm glad to hear that. I'm sorry you have your headaches. Mother says she's never had a headache in her life." I looked at his hands now holding mine.

"Percy, your mother is a strong woman. You have a lot of her in you. When I was young, I was sick all the time. My brothers were healthier than I was, but they did what I told them to do because I was the eldest. Don't tell your uncles but I was much smarter than they were. After I got well, I became strong. So strong, I could win any fight with any of my brothers. Pretty soon, Percy, I got the girls to love me. When you are small like we are, we have to be smarter, stronger than anybody else, especially since there are a lot of tall fellows around in this world who want to bully you. Tall fellows will take away your girls...if you let 'em. Remember that, Percy."

Daddy, still looking at my fingers, continued, "Percy, do you think someday you might want to play football?"

Taking my hands away from Daddy, I confessed, "To tell you the truth, I don't. I'd like to play football for you, but I'm just not interested. The only time I wanted to play football was when I saw Ronald Reagan die in the Warner Brothers' movie *Knute Rockne*. The Gipper was a great football player and he died good. I cried when The Gipper died and that's the only time I ever wanted to play football because I wanted to die like Ronald Reagan did in the movies."

I paused, looking into my father's face. "Do you like me, Daddy?" I asked.

Daddy took my hands into his again and replied, "You're my son."

I squeezed his hands. "Thank you, Daddy. I'm going to ask God tonight to take all your headaches away."

He reached his arm around me and pulled me to him, asking, "Would you like me to help you with your piano playing?"

"I would."

My father took both my hands and put them on the piano keys. "Now listen to what I have to say, Percy, and take your time. Pay attention. You don't have to be in a hurry. Think, always think, what you are doing. I've been watching you. You're not concentrating. Your mind is racing elsewhere."

Daddy looked stern again.

I nodded and started to play the scales again and still missed the key of E.

"Damnit, Percy," he bellowed. "Think. F - A - C - E. FACE. Try it again."

His yelling made me nervous. I tried and tried and tried, but every time I kept missing the right keys. Pretty soon, I couldn't concentrate on piano playing and pleasing Daddy at the same time.

After my tenth try and still missing the key of E, Daddy was at his wit's end and he screamed, "YOU ARE A STUPID LITTLE SISSY. YOU'LL NEVER BE ABLE TO LEARN ANYTHING! I GIVE UP ON YOU." He took his hands and slammed them down on mine as my hands rested lifeless on the piano.

I cried out in pain and got up and yelled into his face, "I HATE YOU. I

HATE YOU! I HATE YOU! I'LL HATE YOU THE REST OF MY LIFE AND I WILL NEVER EVER PLAY THIS STUPID PIANO AGAIN - EVER."

I stalked out of the living room, never to touch the keys of a piano again. Outside, Marigold heard me screaming and rushed into the living room, carrying a baseball bat. She dropped the bat on the floor, sat on the piano bench next to our father, and started to play the scales perfectly. Marigold's train always went up the hill, and I thought at that moment my daddy would never protect me from the curse.

I never discussed the incident with anyone - not even Hatsuko - but that moment in time was never forgotten. When Daddy came home from work the next day, he found me prancing around his house in Mother's high heels with a banana tied to my head, singing as loud as I could a Betty Grable song, "Down Argentina Way."

I ignored Daddy for a week. I ignored the piano in the living room. For seven days, the piano and Daddy didn't exist. Before Thanksgiving, I changed my act from Betty Grable to the twittering, excitable Brazilian movie actress, Carmen Miranda. She also appeared in musicals at 20th Century Fox. I now tied a bowl of fresh fruit on top of my head.

A few weeks after that incident, my daddy didn't come home - forever.

The Royal Hawaiian Hotel and the Moana Hotel dominated Waikiki in the 1930s and 1940s. Photo courtsey of Bishop Museum Archives, Honolulu.

7

Marigold

Daddy loved my sister, Marigold.

Marigold was older, taller, smarter, and stronger than I was. There wasn't a puny bone or soft muscle in her body. I was scared of her. No, to tell the truth, I was *very* scared of her. Agnes and Gertrude were scared of her, too. Only Hatsuko had her number and Marigold knew it. Marigold obeyed everything Hatsuko told her to do.

Marigold was older by four years and a smaller version of Daddy. Because she was quick in adding figures and got straight A's at school, my father, my mother and all the relatives in Hawaii thought she was going to turn out to be the next Albert Einstein. I, in turn, who barely added two and two together, was treated as the reigning Dumbo, a fat, stupid elephant who charged around our house in high heels, avoiding Marigold.

Marigold was given her name because at birth she had a halo of yellow-orange hair that reminded my parents of my mother's Aunt Mari, who lived on the island of Kauai. Aunt Mari, at 65, was so mean she made Cousin Bessie look like a saint. The Kauai aunt wore her red hair pulled back into a severe bun and had a tight, pulled-back face to match. Photographs of this sinister terror that were hanging on our wall made her look as if she was always facing a hurricane. Daddy said that the bun and her face were wound up as tight as her sphincter muscle. I asked Daddy what a sphincter muscle was. He said I sat on it.

Aunt Mari had a fiery temper which my sister inherited. Marigold's hair changed to a dark chestnut brown at the age of three and lost the Aunt Mari hurricane look.

I never understood why my parents named Marigold after that aunt. Maybe they thought, according to Gertrude, she would leave Marigold lots of money after she joined Nana in heaven. I told Hatsuko that parents should take their time naming their children because we turn into the person we are named for. I was the perfect Percy person and Marigold, who wasn't sweet like the flower, was sure to turn into a mean, old Aunt Mari when she got old.

Marigold hated her name, too. She wanted to be called Billy the Kid, Jesse James, or any of the outlaws from the legendary West. After seeing the movie *Stagecoach*, Marigold wanted to change her name to John Wayne. Mother wouldn't hear of it.

Knowing Mother loved showing off Marigold's beautiful curls, in a fit of temper, Marigold cut her hair. We were all asleep on the eve of her eleventh birthday. At midnight, Marigold sliced off all her chestnut curls with Daddy's carving knife. The next morning, as I was eating a cheese and mayonnaise omelet, Marigold arrived at breakfast sporting bangs cut at uneven lengths. I spit out my omelet and gagged when I saw her. I told her a fat rat in the attic must have gnawed her hair while she was sleeping.

Marigold hated rats and she ran around the table and punched me on the arm hard, like John Wayne. Standing next to me and holding two imaginary guns at her hips, Marigold declared she had an important announcement to make. She had Mother's attention and she had mine because she had one arm locked tight around my neck.

She drawled slowly like a western cowboy, "My name is RANDY; forget John Wayne. Any questions, parrrrdners?"

I raised my hand.

"Put your hand down, Percy, and don't talk."

I never followed directions and blurted out, "I'm going to call you Rancid Randy from now on." Hatsuko called food that had gone bad "rancid." Marigold gave me a Rancid Randy smack on top of my head.

"Owww! That hurt! Where'd that name come from? Randy sounds pretty stupid to me. I liked John Wayne better or even Dale Evans or Tonto. Randy, yuck!" I argued. Agnes said that the reason everyone said I was so dumb was because I never learned to shut up.

Marigold held my neck tighter.

I yelled, "Let me go. I want to eat my omelet."

Marigold decided since it was her birthday, I deserved another thump on the head and she pinched my arm for good luck.

Mother cried out, "Marigold, stop that. Leave your brother alone. Oh, Marigold, how could you make such a mess of your beautiful hair?"

I copied Mother, "Oh, Marigold, how could you make such a mess of your beautiful hair? Listen to Mother and leave me alone."

Marigold released her hold around my neck.

"Marigold?" I ventured stupidly, as she stalked away.

"Yes?" Turning and giving me a mean Marigold look, she warned, "This better be good, twerp."

"It is. Happy Birthday!" I reached under the table and brought out a water gun and squirted her like Gene Autry did in the movies and yelled, "Bang. Bang. You're dead."

She yelped like a coyote and made a leap for my throat and gun, yelling, "I'm gonna kill you."

Luckily, Daddy walked into the dining room and caught her. "Give your daddy a big birthday kiss, honey."

They kissed. After they kissed, they hugged. Daddy looked down at her hair, smiled and cooed like a lovebird, "Honey, I love your haircut."

"Oh, Dick," Mother said, shaking her head.

Marigold looked up at Daddy and smiled a million sunbeams. She turned to

Mother and gave her her best "Oh, Mother how could you be so stupid" look.

Mother cast her eyes down at the tablecloth, sighed, looked up, smiled, and said, "Happy Birthday, Marigold. After breakfast, we're going to open up all your birthday presents in the living room."

Marigold shuffled slowly over to Mother and kissed her dutifully on the cheek. Walking back to her seat, Marigold gave me one of her sappy smiles, her eyes saying she didn't give a fig that I hated her haircut. Another look said she was going to get lots of presents after she had finished eating her scrambled eggs and I wasn't going to get a thing - spoiled brat.

Sitting in her chair, picking up her fork, she snarled under her breath, "After breakfast and after I open my presents, I'm gonna beat you up for good, you runty, little brother." I kept my finger on the trigger of the water gun and kept pointing it at her belly button.

I never did find out where the name Randy came from and told Hatsuko Marigold must have heard it in a bad dream. I tried to pry it out of her after breakfast by singing "Happy Birthday" twenty times but she wouldn't tell me.

In the days that followed, to my peril, I called her Marigold, not Randy, and when she wasn't looking, I'd shoot her with my water gun and run as fast as I could into Hatsuko's arms. As Hatsuko held her away from me, Marigold yelled that I was a brat and she was going to drown me in the bathtub.

One afternoon, I hid behind a bush, spying on my sister as she walked home from school with a new boyfriend. Marigold, walking next to Mr. Handsome, was trying to impress him with her new Randy personality and at the same time making big goo-goo eyes at him. I got all excited because I had her. Hiding in the bush, I yelled at the top of my lungs: "MARIGOLD LIKES JIMMY. MARIGOLD HAS FUNNY HAIR. RANCID RANDY IS A ROTTEN PEANUT. JIMMY LIKES MARIGOLD. MARIGOLD SMELLS RANCID. JIMMY IS DOG POOP."

They looked around to see where the voice was coming from and saw my blubbery figure hiding in the bush. Together, snarling like mad dogs, teeth showing, they charged me. From the look in their eyes, I was pretty sure they were going to tear me apart limb from limb. I ran as fast as I could into the house and yelled for Hatsuko to protect me.

A week after that, Marigold dropped the Randy name because she fell in puppy love with dog-poop Jimmy. He told Marigold he didn't want his parents to learn that he had goo-goo eyes for a girl called Randy, so Marigold became a girl again.

By her eleventh birthday, Marigold had perfected Daddy's walking lurch and had her own fierce John Wayne stance when she wanted to make me do something I didn't want to do for her. When playing with Jimmy after school, Marigold's costume was a pair of blue jeans, a plaid shirt, a ten-gallon cowboy hat, and a toy gun. Only Hatsuko could pry her away from her six-shooter and jeans at bath time. The cowboy hat never left her head unless Daddy was home, she was at school or playing with Jimmy around his parents' house. Otherwise, she wore the stinky old cowboy hat while taking a dump, beating me up, and in bed.

When we bathed together in the sunken bathtub, which wasn't often, her cowboy hat dominated her small bony body and me. Not to be outdone by Marigold's cowboy hat, I wore a fruit basket tied on top of my head. We always ended up fighting in the bath because someone hogged the soap that was shaped like Goofy. Splashing soapy water all around us, we'd make a lake on our parents' bathroom floor. Looking at the big puddle we had made, we'd exclaim to each other that was the lake where Hunkacha hid the blue pearls.

One day, Aunt Momi, Mother's sister, looked at us in the bathtub after a soapy fight, raised the gin drink in her hand, and said, "Jolljamit, if you two aren't Jesse James and Carmen Miranda. I wonder where you two came from? You two are jolljamit unique."

Pointing to the puddle on the floor, we yelled at Aunt Momi to watch her step because she was about to step right on Hunkacha's blue pearls lying in his lake. Marigold and I sometimes played while in our bath together that we were Little Johnny and Patty swimming in Hunkacha's blue lake, trying to rescue the blue pearls.

In my heart, I knew that my sister, Marigold, would protect me from the curse, that is, if she put her mind to it and wasn't always trying to tickle me to death.

8

Grandma

Grandma rounded out the bastards who lived on Rocky Hill. Grandma, according to Daddy, was my deceased paternal great-grandfather's wife. I didn't understand what that meant; I just knew Grandma was old. Daddy told me that Grandma's husband had been a sea captain and was dead and Grandma had nowhere to live because her son, Daddy's father, had died too. I told my father Grandma must be a very dangerous person to have around because everyone died.

Grandma's husband had mastered a ship from Hawaii to the Mainland in the late nineteenth century. My impression of Great-Grandpa came from the photograph on Grandma's bureau next to her koa wood four-poster bed - both pieces of furniture that Grandma said were from their cabin on their sailing ship. In the old, brown, faded photograph standing on the bureau, the Captain had been a tall, bearded, handsome man with the eyes of a gray fox. Gazing at his photo whenever Grandma was out of her room, I wondered what he would have done to this fat, little pygmy great-grandson? Gertrude sniffed that because I was such a sissy, he would have made me walk the plank into the shark-infested waters just like they did in Errol Flynn's pirate movies.

A family legend had it that when Grandma was a young bride, just married, she stowed away in the Captain's cabin as he set sail out of Boston for a two-year tour around the world. Grandma, not about to be left alone on shore, hid under the Captain's bed until after the ship had sailed out on the high seas. From that day forward, for better or worse, she never left the Captain's ship, except when she was forcibly put ashore on the beaches of Waikiki to give birth to my grandfather.

Grandma was a tiny woman. She was two inches under five feet and wore her hair swept up in a Charles Gibson style that gave her height and authority. Every day, she slipped on pointed black shoes with two-inch, square heels that made clumping sounds as she strode the decks of our house. She wore a long, black dress with satin petticoats that rustled underneath the gown. It was her uniform. A black lace ruche circled her neck to hide unseemly turkey wattles, and she held her head as high as a figurehead mounted on the bow of a ship. A dark purple amethyst pin, with small seed pearls encircling the stone, held the ruche in place. The purple amethyst was Grandma's only color.

Since the day the Captain died, Grandma took her mourning seriously. Her appearance never changed. Grandma wearing her black dress was as reliable as a

Hawaiian sunrise in front of our house. Her moods were as changeable as the weather at sea. Some days she was a thunderstorm, other days she was an arctic field, and on good days, she was a clear, sunny, blue sky. We prayed for her good days. When Grandma entered a room, I raised my finger to check her weather.

She spoiled my father and sister outrageously. Neither one could do any wrong in her eyes. They were her angels and the most important passengers on her ship as she sailed through life in our house. She liked to dress my sister in sailor's clothes that she bought on sale at Liberty House. Mother hated Grandma's interference with Marigold's dress and upbringing, but Grandma ignored Mother's entreaties and, in turn, treated Mother as her first mate. I was Grandma's cabin boy whom she wanted to shackle in irons and stow below in the brig out of sight, especially when her sailing friends were around and I would traipse around the house wearing Cousin Bessie's red satin evening gown.

When the Captain died, Grandma moved into my grandfather's home on Maui. She ran her son's household like she did ours - as the captain of their Wailuku sugar plantation manager's home. My grandmother, Daddy's mother, was also relegated to the role of first mate. God must have whispered to Grandma on the high seas that He wanted her to take charge of all the men in her life, and taking charge meant a whipping if any of her boys sassed her back. Grandma herded, disciplined, and guided her four grandsons as if they were sailors swabbing the deck of her Captain's ship. A black leather riding-crop was the instrument of authority. She used the whip liberally on her grandsons' backsides but never on Marigold or me.

I kept watching for the whip to make an appearance, especially when I told Grandma she had farted. I was safe because Grandma knew that Hatsuko would have poisoned her soup and forced her to eat raw Brussels sprouts for the rest of her life if she touched one strand of my golden curls. When I look back, the only difference between Grandma and the performance of Charles Laughton as the tyrannical Captain Bligh in MGM's *Mutiny on the Bounty* was that Grandma wore a dress.

After her son, my grandfather, died making love to a younger second wife, Grandma moved lock, stock and barrel into our home. When Hatsuko told me the story of Grandpa's death, I told Hatsuko I never knew that kissing could be so strenuous.

Daddy was her favorite grandson. Her other three grandsons, and especially their wives, breathed huge sighs of relief that she didn't book passage into their homes. After she moved into our guestroom, Grandma, once a staunch teetotaler, started to drink lots of brandy on the sly. She told me that living with us had made her lonely for her Captain and all the close friends who passed away and went to heaven with Nana. She hid the empty brandy bottles from my mother in her shower and kept the full ones in the closet behind her black dresses. When Grandma was out driving with Daddy and Marigold, I'd make a quick run around her room, inspecting her closet and shower, and reported back to Hatsuko and Mother how many bottles of brandy Grandma had drunk that week. My observation of Grandma at the dinner table was that her drinking didn't make her into a happier person - usually after having a few snorts under her belt, her weather turned foul.

I loved Grandma's breath because it smelled like lavender flowers.

Grandma was a Miss Nosyparker. I told Gertrude and Agnes that I inherited my nosiness from Grandma. When we were out of the house, Grandma would steam open all the letters she found in the post box, hunt through our closets for secrets, and once I caught her rummaging through my box of junk jewelry. It was Cousin Bessie who taught Grandma how to steam open letters.

Mother caught on to Grandma's wily tricks and hid all her important letters in her bureau drawers. Once when Mother's favorite sister was visiting and gossiping within earshot of Grandma in the next room, Mother whispered to Aunt Momi that she had a letter from Ida in Paris and couldn't remember where she put it.

Grandma, who told all of us that she was hard of hearing, hollered from the next room as if she was standing in a crow's nest spotting a whale on the horizon, "It's in your third drawer under your underwear." Grandma hated Aunt Ida, her son's second wife, because Grandma blamed her for kissing her darling son to death.

I liked Grandma best on Saturday mornings when she would sit Marigold and me down and talk of days at sea with the Captain. She'd start by saying, "Children, my Captain was the bravest man I ever knew. He stood six-foot-five."

Looking down at my tiny feet, I interrupted her and said, "Grandma, why did Daddy and I have to inherit your small side of the family and not the Captain's tall side?"

Grandma thumped me on the head and continued to talk, pretending not to hear me. "There wasn't a man sailing the seas that didn't respect him. It was when he broke his leg in that damn storm - that's when he had to retire from the sea, and retiring killed him, children - right inside his mind - flat out. He just shut down. You'd have loved him, Marigold. It was living on land that killed him. I remember hitting seas that had waves taller than mountains. Fifty-footers. Green water pouring over the bow, making us all think that at any moment we'd be down in Davy Jones' locker.

"I'd be on deck with him with all the green water around us, up to our waists in muck, and he'd yell to me, 'Damn it, Eliza, go below.' I wouldn't go because I was as good as any sailor on that ship and if a wave was going to get us, I wanted to go overboard with the Captain. I knew the names of every man on board our ship, their weaknesses and their strengths. I even memorized the names of the riggings and every sail. I knew that ship as well as the Captain did, you bet. I knew what to do in a storm. When he'd yell for the men to bring in the sails, I'd yell right along with him. Then, because I was a damn woman, he'd lash me to a mast so I wouldn't go overboard with a wave.

"Once that great writer Jack London and his beautiful wife, Charmiane, were our passengers in a hurricane. That drunken old flirt said he'd write about me - but that old fool never did. Jack London was just full of hot air and his stinking grog. That Jack London could put it away. He drank like a fish. He was a bad influence on my Captain. My Captain liked his drink but I watched him like a hawk. Old Jack London wasn't as tough as he made himself out to be. His wife, Charmiane, now she was tough like me and a good sailor too. She never got seasick but that old Jack, that big he-man, puked up all his meals."

Letting out a big breath of lavender flowers, she paused, looked us straight in the eye and warned, "Now, you two kids don't go smoking and drinking on me. It'll stunt your growth." I told Agnes that Grandma knew what she was talking about because it was her brandy drinking that caused Grandma to be so short.

"Marigold," Grandma said, rustling my sister's hair, "you'd make a fine sailor. I just know it. You're tough like me!"

Raising my hand, I asked, "What about me, Grandma?"

Taking off her pince-nez glasses, squaring her shoulders back, thumping her two fingers on my head, Grandma answered, "Percy, the Captain would feed you to the sharks, boy. You'd make a hearty meal for them sharks. Boy, you wouldn't last a minute at sea and you'd be like that old Jack London and puke up your breakfast." After making that declaration, she threw her head back and laughed and laughed like an old salt - showing a gold tooth, caught her breath in short gulps, and....

Grandma, trying to talk above the sound of her fart, continued to lecture me. "Percy, you're getting too old to wear your mother's dresses, and I'm going to stop buying sailor's things for Marigold. You're both growing up and need to leave those things behind you. Are you listening to me, Percy?"

I wasn't. Marigold pinched me to make me pay attention to what Grandma was saying because I was far away, daydreaming of big waves and hungry sharks eating me up in the ocean. I hadn't heard a word Grandma said, so I mumbled "yea, yea" to make her think I was and went back to daydreaming about waves that were as tall as buildings and sharks' fins that circled me in the water.

Marigold pinched me again, saying, "Grandma's talking to you."

I nodded, "Yes, Grandma, whatever you say, but I don't want to be eaten up by sharks."

Grandma smacked me atop my head, "Pay attention, boy. You ain't got the sense you were born with."

I loved her lavender breath.

Grandma was part French and told me stories about France after school. Because of Grandma, I loved reading and hearing about the French people, the French kings, Notre Dame Cathedral, Joan of Arc, and Marie Antoinette. I thought the French revolution, as Grandma told it, was far more exciting than our little tea party in Boston.

Grandma and I had two things in common - we loved France and pooped gas. I pooped gas as loud and as much as Grandma did. Mother told me that only old people pooped that much. I told Mother I was born ancient in the gas department. Grandma and I were kindred spirits, but she loved Marigold more.

While watching Grandma's wobbly head move back and forth when she talked to me of her Captain's ship on Saturday mornings and seeing her hands shake when she picked up a drinking glass at dinner, and smelling the caked pink powder that covered the wrinkles on her face, I also understood that my grandma was too old to help me keep the curse away from my door.

The curse was beginning to loom larger as everyone in our house was acting too nice and nobody was anybody they pretended to be.

9

Everyone Turned Nice

A week before Thanksgiving, I knew that I was living in the shadow of the curse because everyone turned nice. Nobody, not even Grandma, slapped me on the head when I chewed with my mouth open. Even Marigold, red-eyed, wasn't pinching me under the breakfast table, but in a fit of unexplained temper, she gave me my cap gun back. She screamed, throwing the cap gun at me, that she didn't want anything that belonged to Daddy. Grandma gazed at me across the dinner table like I was her favorite grandchild, tears welling up in her eyes, and between slurps of soup, she mumbled, "You poor boy. You poor boy."

The biggest clue something was wrong was that Daddy wasn't sleeping in his bed anymore. Agnes told me the reason Daddy wasn't sleeping in his bed was that he was still angry with me for telling him that I hated him for life. Agnes chattered on that my father was so mad that he was going to ship me out on one of his Castle and Cooke freighters and shanghai me to China to play a piano in an opium den just like the ones I saw in a Charlie Chan movie.

Gertrude put in her two cents, muttering, "Something is up, Percy, and it ain't what Agnes is telling you. It's far worse." I answered my imaginary friends with my face under the pillow, mumbling, "It's the curse. The curse is coming to get me."

Other funny things happened around the house. Hatsuko became dreamy-eyed when she bathed me and we weren't going to movies any more. Mother stopped telling stories at bedtime. She said she was too tired from correcting her papers and when I asked about Daddy, she told me the reason Daddy wasn't coming home was because he was working hard at the office "to keep your mayonnaise in our icebox."

As all of this uneasiness grew around me, a big ache started to grow in my stomach. Before Thanksgiving, our house became quieter and quieter, so quiet that Mother, Marigold, Grandma, and Hatsuko quit answering any of my questions. Everyone turned nice.

One night, at three o'clock in the morning, while raiding the icebox to make a mayonnaise sandwich, I discovered Hatsuko had a terrible secret. Looking out the kitchen window, I saw a sailor coming out of her room, wearing his white uniform, buttoning up his shirt, walking down our driveway. I knew in an instant why everyone in our house was nice and quit answering my questions. They didn't want me to know that Hatsuko had a boyfriend. As the man drove away in a beat-up Ford, I called for Agnes and Gertrude.

Gertrude immediately spouted that Hatsuko didn't love me anymore and loved someone else because I was too fat and too ugly to love. Agnes whispered into my other ear that crazy Gertrude was loony as a coot and that Hatsuko loved me fat and I was having a bad dream. Gertrude snorted, "Maybe so. Maybe so. But don't count on it. It looks pretty bad to me. Keep quiet, Percy. Don't say anything and don't ask questions; maybe the sailor is a bad dream just like Agnes told us, and will go away. Anyway, tomorrow at breakfast, see if Hatsuko tells you about the sailor. Go back to bed."

I listened to Gertrude and closed the icebox door quietly and didn't make a mayonnaise sandwich that night. Back in bed, I knew Agnes had to be right and I was only having a bad dream because Hatsuko had promised me a thousand times that she'd never leave me.

The next morning, Hatsuko had dark, purple circles under her eyes. She yawned in my face before she kissed me. After her kiss, I didn't see the sun rise in her eyes. I kept looking for my sun in her brown eyes but it wasn't there. That morning I didn't smell her washing starch; she now smelled of a man's after-shave lotion, the same smell Daddy put on his face before he went to work.

After the night I saw the sailor walk out of Hatsuko's room, my life grew peculiar and never returned to how I had known it before. I couldn't explain the peculiarity to myself, to Agnes, to Gertrude, or to God at prayer time because after I discovered Hatsuko's secret, I looked at people differently. I told Gertrude, nobody in our house was anybody they pretended to be. Every night, thereafter, I would wake up at midnight and watch for the man wearing a sailor suit to walk down our driveway. Those nights were long and without sleep, and the few nights the sailor didn't appear, the next morning Hatsuko smelled of washing starch again.

Three nights of watching for the sailor out the kitchen window at midnight, my heart choking my throat, tears streaming down my cheeks, purple circles growing dark under my eyes, I realized that Gertrude was right. Hatsuko had a boyfriend. On the nights he didn't walk down the driveway, I prayed to God he was driving Cousin Bessie's car and he and Cousin Bessie had crashed over the Pali or Daddy had shipped him out to a Chinese opium den.

Hatsuko's having a sailor boyfriend broke my heart for the first time in my life - just like Bette Davis's heart smashed to pieces in *The Old Maid*. Hatsuko had betrayed me. I hinted to Mother, Marigold and Grandma that a sailor was walking around our house at midnight. They answered that I was imagining things and having funny dreams. Hearing them, I realized that Hatsuko was keeping her secret from my family, too. I'd keep her secret too because of Daddy. If Daddy found out about the sailor, he would ship Hatsuko with the sailor out to that opium den in China.

Every night, Hatsuko's secret punched me in the stomach as Gertrude snorted through her teeth, "Nobody is to be trusted in this world, Percy." I hated it when Gertrude acted like Miss Smarty-Pants because her snotty voice implied that she was right and Agnes was wrong. Gertrude kept repeating over and over again, "Hatsuko is leaving you. Hatsuko is leaving you." I knew her words were going to come true because in my storybooks, bad things happen to cursed people.

I decided to punish Hatsuko by pretending that she didn't exist and to never again sit around the kitchen table and talk about Jeanette MacDonald's love life.

Eight-year-old Cynthia and her six-year-old brother Vinnie lived next door. I decided they were going to be my new best friends and take Hatsuko's place in my heart. I hardly knew them because Cross-Eyed Mama, the elephant-legs Amazon who was their mother, kept them away from me. I made up my mind that if Hatsuko had a new friend, I'd have new friends too, and I wasn't going to hold it against Cynthia and Vinnie that old Cross-Eyed Mama was their mother.

When I came home from school, instead of heading for Hatsuko's kitchen, I ran next door. I told Cynthia and Vinnie that I wanted to be their best friend and said loudly, hoping Hatsuko could hear me, "Let's play together. Let's be friends. I hate friends who talk about movie stars all the time. They're not my friends any more and you are my friends."

Cynthia was blonde, sweet looking, and as soon as we met, she said she would show me for two pennies her "dazzling" birthmark. Only after she got my pennies, which I stole from Mother's purse, would she lift up her skirt, pull down her panties and give me a peek.

Her birthmark was a long, golden tail that grew right above the crack in her behind. Black Beauty, the horse, any horse for that matter, would have been proud to have such a beautiful tail. Inspecting the tail carefully, I wondered why Cross-Eyed Mama didn't braid the birthmark because it had grown so long. Stretching the tail out into the air with my fingers, I observed that at its present length, the tail would surely get in the away of Cynthia making doodoo in the toilet. I advised Cynthia to wipe carefully. After Cynthia showed me her tail and I got my penny's worth, the ice was broken, and Cynthia and I became friends immediately. I learned that by showing anything personal about yourself, hidden under your clothes, you make friends easily.

I loved secrets - even if I had to pay for them.

Vinnie was the pride and joy of his father. I was jealous of the fact that his father loved him like a rare jewel. Vinnie had bright red hair, wore thick eyeglasses and short pants with suspenders, and looked and acted like a weenie Teddy Roosevelt. His father looked like a grown-up Teddy Roosevelt. Both Vinnie and his father charged up their driveway on weekends, pretending it was San Juan Hill.

Vinnie wee-weed in his pants more than I did. I liked that. His wee-weeing made me feel like a grown-up because grown-ups hardly ever wee-weed. The only games he wanted to play were cops and robbers and kick ball. In two days, I mastered both games. My daddy would have been proud that I was playing boy games and that I became so good at them.

On my second boring afternoon playing with my new friends, who were not imaginative children because they didn't know the difference between Cary Grant and Mae West, I came up with a brilliant idea.

Agnes thought so. I wasn't speaking to Gertrude.

I came up with the idea that Cynthia, Vinnie, and I would act out the fairy tale "Rapunzel." Rapunzel was a beautiful maiden who was known in fairytale land for her long, golden hair. The beautiful princess was a prisoner in a tower watched over by a mean old witch. The only way to enter the tower, which had no doors, was to climb up Rapunzel's long hair when she let it down. A handsome prince riding by saw the beautiful princess and rescued Rapunzel by climbing up her hair, strand by strand, and killing the old witch on the way up. Rapunzel and the prince lived happily ever after.

Cynthia was the perfect princess because of her beautiful birthmark and I cast myself as the handsome prince. I wanted to play the princess but I didn't have Cynthia's outstanding birthmark. Vinnie was cast as the mean, ugly old witch, as I told him all witches I knew or heard about had red hair. My Aunt Mari did.

Cynthia and Vinnie lived in Cross-Eyed Mama's two-story house. It was the perfect setting to act out our play. I crowned myself the director and star, and instructed in a prince-like fashion that Cynthia run upstairs, take down her panties and stick her butt out the bedroom window as soon as I called "go." I also instructed her to fluff out the tail so it would fly in the wind for all the fairies in the fairy kingdom to see. I explained that as soon as I saw her butt out the window, tail flying in the wind, I'd pretend to climb up and rescue her.

Cynthia yelled that she loved being a princess but wasn't that eager to stick her fanny out the window for Cousin Bessie and all the other neighbors to ogle when they drove by her house. After all, being a practical, eight-year-old girl, she was charging two cents for the privilege.

I reached deep into my pocket, pulled out two pennies, held them high in the air and waved them at her. Cynthia flew downstairs, and in one swoop, grabbed them, rushed upstairs, and stuck her naked butt out the window even before I could yell "go." I commanded her to stick her big fanny back inside and wait for my call.

"Don't be so anxious," I yelled.

As Cynthia pulled her behind inside the window, I checked on Vinnie to see if he was in place. He was. He was wee-weeing like bad witches do in the bushes.

I put my finger up in the air to check which way the wind was blowing and hoped for a strong gust to send Cynthia's tail flying like a streamer. Agnes, my weather girl, reported that strong trade winds were gusting today. I was ready. I cupped my hands like a megaphone, Cecil B. DeMille fashion, like the photograph of the director I had seen in *Photoplay* magazine, and yelled, "GO, CYNTHIA!"

At the sound of my voice, two ripe, pink, plump "melons" appeared out the window and the trade winds miraculously raised up Cynthia's magnificent birthmark and floated it into the air in a long, yellow, beautiful streamer.

Looking up at the naked fanny sticking out the window, a hairy birthmark flying in the wind, I remembered reading in *Photoplay* that actors would do anything for two cents. I was in ecstasy. My first attempt putting on a play was a smash. I yelled and pointed at everyone driving by Cynthia's house to look at her tail flowing in the wind. Cynthia's pink behind glowed in the sunlight.

With my hands on my heart, I called up to Cynthia's behind, "Oh, princess, dear sweet princess, let your tail down so I can climb up and rescue you."

Cynthia yelled from inside the house, "Oh, prince, my tail is out as far as it can go but there's an ugly, old witch hiding in the bush who is keeping me a prisoner up here and who wants to kill you."

Putting my hands on my hips, I roared, "Never fear, dear princess, I will kill the red-headed witch and climb your tail and rescue you."

"OHHHHH," Cynthia screamed, "the witch in the bushes. Kill him!"

Vinnie, hiding in a hibiscus hedge, was making mean witch sounds as he was peeing in his pants.

I yelled up to Cynthia, "I'll take care of the witch, but stick your behind out further so your tail can really fly. I want everyone on Waikiki Beach to see you, too."

At that moment, as Cynthia was maneuvering her fanny further out the window, Cross-Eyed Mama drove up the driveway. Shocked, seeing her daughter's rear end wiggling in the second-story window, Cross-Eyed Mama smashed the Packard into the mailbox.

I fled for home. Running through the hedge, I was still wearing Cynthia's mother's kitchen tablecloth as a cape. Hearing Cross-Eyed Mama getting out of her car and yelling to Cynthia to stick her fanny back into the house, I knew it was too late to return the tablecloth. I knew I was going to be in the "soup" with Cross-Eyed Mama.

Cynthia, a true blue-blooded princess, never squealed. She told her mother her fanny needed an airing. Cross-Eyed Mama knew better. The next day, looking over the hedge, Cynthia's mother spied her tablecloth hanging on our clothesline. From that day forward, she never liked me and told her children to keep far away from me. Whenever I came in sight, she always kept her crossed eyes on me. I had a hard time knowing what to do, what to say, or where to hide, because I could never tell if she was looking at me or at her nose.

Green with jealousy, I announced to Hatsuko, folding the tablecloth, "Cynthia and Vinnie are my best friends." With that, I pretended to close the door on our friendship.

Afternoons, playing in my living room when Crossed-Eyed Mama was out doing church work, Cynthia, Vinnie and I would dance and sing "Beer Barrel Polka" at the top of our lungs, accompanying the Andrews sisters on our wind-up RCA record player in our living room. I sang it loudly, hoping Hatsuko would think I was having the best time of my life with my new best friends. We'd run around Mother's living room in a frenzy, carried away by the jiving music, sweating buckets, and dancing to the beat of the Andrews Sisters' "Don't Sit Under the Apple Tree." We'd swing our arms up and kick our legs into furniture, turning Mother's living room into a shambles. Hatsuko had to clean up the room up as soon as we finished dancing around because she didn't want me to get a spanking from Daddy or Mother.

I was creating a mess to make Hatsuko's days longer and harder.

Bored with Maxine, Laverne, and Patty (the Andrews Sisters), I'd shout, "Let's conga!" To demonstrate the conga, I kicked my leg high up in the air, knocking over an end table with ashtrays on it. I told Cynthia and Vinnie that Betty Grable, the movie actress, kicked her leg the same way I did, and they copied me in kicking over the rest of the end tables in the living room. "Kicking tables, Cynthia, is the best part of the dance," I yelled above the music.

With Cynthia leading, we'd sing, "One, two, three, La Conga." Kick. Over went another table. "One, two, three, La Conga." Kick. We'd dance in circles, following the patterns of the rose vines on our Persian carpet, a wedding present from Aunt Mari. We'd conga into other rooms of the house, creating bigger disasters as we kicked furniture from room to room. I was going nutty to help me forget that my stomach hurt and that the person I loved most next to Mother had betrayed me.

Grandma, sipping brandy in her bedroom, screamed to us as we danced through the house, "I want to take a nap. One more sound out of you and your little friends and I'm coming out with my whip, and you'll wish I hadn't. You remember my whip, Percy? It's hanging on my bedpost and you know what I do with it to bad children who annoy me. I mean it."

We screeched to an abrupt halt as I described Grandma's whip to Cynthia and Vinnie and how she used it. "I have red welts all over my back after Grandma whips me. Honestly. I have purple scars on my back to prove it."

Because I scared Cynthia and Vinnie by telling made-up tales of Grandma's whip, we'd tiptoe into my bedroom, shut the door quietly and cut out Cynthia's Lana Turner paper dolls for the rest of the afternoon. Lana Turner was a luscious movie star at MGM who wore tight yellow sweaters before she was sixteen. In seconds, we'd mess up my room with piles of scrap paper and spilled paste that we scattered all over the floor - more work for Hatsuko to clean up.

I was determined to make Hatsuko hurt as much as I was hurting.

After Cynthia and Vinnie left for home before Cross-Eyed Mama returned, I'd run around telling the walls, loud enough for Hatsuko to hear while she cooked dinner, that Cynthia and Vinnie were more fun to play with than Hatsuko ever was. "I don't want to be a movie star any more. I'm going to be a great movie director and control everybody in my life. People will have wished they had been nice to me," I yelled.

Not hearing a voice from the kitchen talking back, I'd yell louder, "I want to be a gunfighter. A killer. I hate sailors." I didn't mean a word of what I was saying, except that I hated the sailor who took Hatsuko away from me. I tore up my *Popeye the Sailor* comic books in protest.

Cynthia and Vinnie were never my best friends. They could never be because I hardly knew them, and they didn't know me or love me like Hatsuko did. With them, I had to pretend to be someone else - a gunfighter, do boy things, play like they wanted to play, and to keep who I really was inside of me, a prisoner. The best times we had together were when Cynthia asked us to help her cut out dresses for her paper dolls. I was learning to live inside me and never share that person to anyone. I never shared Agnes and Gertrude. With Cynthia and Vinnie and those I played with at school, I knew that if I didn't pretend to like their interests, I wouldn't be invited to their birthday parties. There was another thing that could never, ever, make Cynthia and Vinnie my new best friends: like all my friends at school, they were totally dumb about movies and movie stars.

Cross-Eyed Mama was a staunch Baptist and told her children that movies were the works of the devil and that anyone who went to a movie was riding in an elevator down to hell. Their mother's real name was Nanette and like the song, their mama had a lot of no-no's on her lips. Cynthia told me Cross-Eyed Mama had informed everyone in her church that the devil lived next door to her and the devil was a little boy who wore a dress and went to the movies.

I told Cynthia and Vinnie to tell their mother that I had given up wearing dresses and never went to movies anymore so we could play together. They didn't lie because with the people in my house going cuckoo and Hatsuko about to abandon me, Mother's dresses were undisturbed in her closet and nobody took me to the movies anymore. I did suggest to Cynthia to tell her mother that her birthmark was the sign of the devil. I hoped that Cross-Eyed Mama would let one devil play with another.

On afternoons when I couldn't play with Cynthia and Vinnie because their mother was home, I'd wander aimlessly around the house. With nothing to do, I'd lie down on my bed, put my hand on my heart because it hurt, and search for the words to say to my best friend cooking in the kitchen. I wanted to tell Hatsuko to poison her sailor's after-shave. I kept looking for ways to make the world right again. I wanted my heart not to feel like it pumped rocks. I wanted life to go back to where it had been before I saw that terrible sailor walk down our driveway at midnight. I wanted to join the Navy, become an admiral and run the sailor out on a plank like Errol Flynn did in the movies, and then kick him overboard to the sharks.

My curse up to that time had been a little plaything in my imagination - a fairy story. Now, I knew the curse was real.

Nobody was anybody who they pretended to be, but Hunkacha was real and ready to eat me up in the dark shadows of the night.

Myrna Loy, publicity still from MGM.

The Last Supper

I carried *The Honolulu Advertiser* to school for current events the morning that Daddy promised Mother he'd come home for dinner.

The Honolulu Advertiser

LITTLE BIT OF HISTORY OF HAWAII'S BACKGROUND

All of the six flowers that form flower perfumes in the world can or do grow in Hawaii - lavender, the orange blossom, rose, jasmine, violet, acacia, and tuberose.

Coffee was being produced in Hawaii in 1817. Over 8,000,000 pounds are now produced annually.

In the summer of 1886 an exhibition of electric lights was given in Honolulu. The palace grounds were illuminated. Five years later, current was made available for public use by the Hawaiian Electric Company.

In 1892, the Macadamia nut was introduced to Hawaii from Australia as a shade tree. Since 1922, it has been cultivated as a crop.

Polo was played on the island of Oahu in 1880. Golf became a popular sport in 1901.

Advertisement: **AMERICAN HAWAII MOTORS** on Hotel & Alakea Streets. - Dodge Distributors
    Used 1928 Dodge Convertible Coupe $60
    Dodge Kingway Business Coupe $965
Advertisement: **VITALIS** - Helps Keep You Healthy and Handsome.

MATSONIA - brought Brig. General Joseph H. Rudolph to assume command of the 1st bombardment at Hickam Field in replacement of Brig. General Walter H. Frank. He has his gracious wife with him....

WAIKIKI THEATER Phone 9967   Shows tonight at 6:30   9:30
    Laughter and Love   **DOWN ARGENTINA WAY** - Starring Betty Grable, Don Ameche, Carmen Miranda and Charlotte Greenwood.

TERRITORY OF HAWAII POPULATION JUMPS 14 PER CENT
The Census Bureau reported tonight that Hawaii's 1940 population is 423,330 persons, an increase of 14.0 per cent from 1930

The morning I gave my current events report, I was no longer living in the MGM musical world that Hatsuko had created for me. I was no longer dancing to school; I was waddling like a fat hippopotamus. I didn't smile or wave at anyone anymore. I had turned into Mr. Grumpy.

I was bored with Cynthia and Vinnie in a week as I missed talking about movie stars with Hatsuko. I was so unhappy with myself, there were days I forgot to play with Agnes and Gertrude while eating mayonnaise sandwiches. Going to school, I carried my books as if they had the weight of the world. I tied them together with one of Daddy's old whipping belts to remind me what a bad boy I had become. In a paper sack, I carried two large tuna fish sandwiches for lunch that Hatsuko wrapped in last year's Christmas wrappings - Santa Claus riding on a sleigh.

Hatsuko added Hershey Kisses inside the sack signaling how much she loved me. The Kisses, I knew, were bought out of her own salary. Every day at breakfast, Hatsuko asked me what was wrong. I looked past her and never answered because I didn't know what to say. I wanted to tell her how much the Hershey Kisses meant to me but the words stuck in my throat. She kept on putting Kisses in my lunch even though I wasn't speaking to her and continued her kindness without asking any kindness in return.

I turned into a spoiled, sulky, sullen little boy and when I was forced to speak to ask for something to eat, I spoke to Hatsuko as if we had just met. I couldn't tell her that I knew about her sailor boyfriend, even though every night as I watched him come out of her room, Gertrude told me to do so. I was too frightened that I'd hear her say that she loved the sailor more than she loved me. For that reason, I mumbled in the afternoons that I was no longer her little baby and began to bathe myself. I didn't want her or anyone to touch me any more.

I talked gruff like Daddy when I told her, "I'm seven years old, Hatsuko, going on eight. I'm grown up now. I'm going to act like a grown-up and take my bath by myself. Go away." I shut the bathroom door in her face, locked the door and took my bath alone. I spoke those words on an afternoon after she had smelled of her sailor at breakfast.

The week after I discovered Hatsuko's sailor, my home was as quiet as a Monday afternoon when people put ginger flowers by a tombstone at Oahu Cemetery. Marigold skulked around the house hiding her face under her ten-gallon hat. When I asked her what's the matter, she told me to shut up because she was planning an assassination. I told her she couldn't assassinate me because I was writing J. Edgar Hoover at the FBI for a bulletproof vest and a machine gun and I was planning my own assassination. Grandma napped all morning and in the late afternoons drank up all her brandy. I continued to check the empties in her shower.

I wasn't noticing the dramas going on in my home because I was all over miserable that Hatsuko had a new best friend. I ignored that my father had left our house for good. I thought he was away because he was still mad at me. I wanted to tell Daddy to come home and that I really didn't mean it when I said I hated him for life. I just had hated him for three days. It was the piano I hated for life.

The day Mother cut her hair off was the night when Daddy left our house forever. It was the night Hatsuko broiled lamb chops from New Zealand and Grandma cried at the dinner table. Eating lamb chops at our house was as big a treat as eating an artichoke from Salinas, California. Both were outrageously expensive and rare and in our house considered treats for special occasions.

We ate lamb chops maybe twice a year. Daddy loved eating any kind of lamb, whether it was a chop, a leg, or cubed in a spicy hot Indian curry. That night, because Daddy promised to be home for supper, Mother planned a special lamb chop celebration, hoping Daddy would want to stay home with us forever and not work late every night. Mother told me to pretend that this dinner was as special as a Thanksgiving dinner. She made me promise to behave myself and act the proper gentleman and "please not to upset Daddy" by opening my mouth and saying something that would annoy him. Mother ordered Hatsuko to "pull out the stops" and make sure there wasn't a smidgen of mayonnaise in sight.

Mother arrived home late, but in time for the 6:30 dinner. We were all seated at the table waiting for her. She made a grand entrance, pointing to her hair. Mother had shorn it off like they clip sheep in New Zealand.

Her cut hair bewildered me because Mother prided herself on her long, straight, blond hair. When she unfurled her hair at bedtime, it hung down like a golden waterfall to her waist. Mother's hair rivaled Rapunzel's hair and Cynthia's birthmark. All Mother's sisters were envious of her long hair since childhood because their hair was curly and colored doo-doo brown. Everyone said Mother's hair was her best feature. The first day Mother faced a classroom as a second grade teacher, she wanted to look older, so she fashioned her long hair into a spinster-like pug on the back of her head, just like mean old Aunt Mari did. She used long mammoth hairpins to keep it in place. Her big hair bun on the back of her head gave her the staid, solid look of a schoolteacher she wanted. The bun was the most familiar feel of her since the time I was a baby. Her bun smelled like flowers and tickled my nose when she burped me over her shoulder.

The afternoon of the lamb dinner, after school, wanting a new modern look to please Daddy, Mother ordered her beautician Nancy Yoshimoto to cut her long hair off. Mother said Nancy cried, saying she couldn't do it, but when Mother offered a ten-dollar bill, the scissors came out and chop-chop, off went the hair. Then, Nancy gave Mother a Japanese permanent. A Japanese permanent is when an operator plasters tight spit curls all over a lady's head, making the lady look bald. In Nancy Yoshimoto's hair salon, even when the curls were dried and let loose, the lady still looked bald because the curls remained stuck to her head.

When Mother came out from under Nancy's dryer, she looked bald and ordinary. She looked like the rest of her sisters except her hair was blonde. Mother had hoped that a new Myrna Loy hairdo would make her look the perfect wife in Daddy's eyes and keep him at home.

Myrna Loy was Mother's favorite movie actress. Myrna was famous for being the faithful, wisecracking wife in the MGM *Thin Man* series. She had short, wavy red hair and her hairstyle was considered the *in* thing in 1940.

As Mother stood in the dining room, waiting for Daddy's approval, Daddy and Marigold held their noses, pointing to her hair. My father, shaking a fork at Mother, told her immediately how much he hated the look and told her that he wished she had never done it. Making a terrible face, Daddy continued to rage, "What in heaven's name possessed you, Deidra? You must have gone crazy. Go look at yourself in the mirror and see what a mess you've made of yourself."

Marigold, holding her nose, happy to get back at Mother for criticizing her rat-chewed haircut, sniffed, "Pee-u, Mother. Your hair cut stinks." Grandma got into the act, stroking her hands upward into her thick white hair, and gloated, "You look common, Deidra. If that's your intent, well, you've succeeded. You look like a cheap floozy on Hotel Street."

I forgave Grandma on the spot for calling Mother a cheap floozy because Grandma drank a lot of brandies that afternoon. When Grandma became red-eyed and crinkled her nose like a bunny rabbit, she never made sense. I was mad at Marigold and Daddy because they didn't have any excuses to be mean.

I sent Superman rays at Marigold.

Mother sat down, picked up a napkin, spread it on her lap, and smiled at Daddy and Marigold like they had said the most pleasant compliments. It was the way I imagined she acted at Miss Ransom's when her classmates teased her by calling her fat. Mother told me she learned never to let anyone get her goat.

Holding back tears, she said like she meant it, "I think I look like Myrna Loy."

"Myrna who?" Daddy pretended to be ignorant of the movie star.

I prayed that Daddy would change the subject because Mother's lips were beginning to quiver. I told Agnes later in bed, "I bet when Mother heard Daddy and Marigold teasing her, she wished she could have covered herself with poison oak and gone to bed for three weeks."

Mother turned to me, "Percy, what do you think of my hair?"

"You look katish." Resting my head on the table, I gazed up at her, looking at her hair as if I'd put her hair under a microscope, and asked, "Why are you and Marigold cutting your hair off? Do you have cooties? Miss Storey said that if we get cooties in our hair, we'd have to shave our heads. Do you and Marigold have things crawling around in your hair?"

Mother laughed, "Percy, I don't have cooties, dear. I cut off my hair because I wanted to look pretty for your father."

Marigold kicked my leg under the table.

Rubbing my leg, I continued, "Mother, Marigold has bugs in her hair. I've seen them and I know she has ants in her pants because she picks her behind all the time."

Marigold kicked me again but missed. She hit Mother's ankle.

I laughed that the joke was on Marigold because she missed me. Marigold, furious that she missed, gave me her dirty Batman look.

Mother ignored Marigold's kick.

Putting my napkin firmly on my lap, trying to be a gentleman for Daddy while attempting to kick Marigold at the same time, I looked down at the table-cloth and said, "Well, I like Mother's hair. Mother's hair looks better than katish. Mother is prettier than Myrna Loy is; in fact, Mother is the prettiest woman in Hawaii. And if Marigold doesn't think so, it's because Marigold is a dumb, ugly bunny who lets rats chew her hair off."

Marigold made another attempt to kick me but missed again because I was ready for her kick and quickly held my legs under the chair.

Mother patted my hand. "Thank you, Percy. I think I look katish too, no matter what your sister and father think of my hair."

Inside my stomach, I hated the permanent and missed her pug.

Mother not only looked funny, but she wasn't acting normal anymore. Her lipstick was too red and she had covered black smudges on her face with pounds of pink powder. Lately, I noticed she was trying too hard to please Daddy all the time. I wished she could have given her permanent back to Myrna Loy.

Sitting straight up in her chair as if riding a horse, Mother ignored Marigold and Daddy, who were whispering about her hair under their breaths. Wearing a new dress from Liberty House, which she told me not to wear with the threat of a spanking, Mother paid no attention to Marigold and Daddy's whispering by talking around them. She was determined to make the lamb chop dinner a happy evening for my father. Mother had warned me the night before to use my good table manners, chew my food slowly, speak only when spoken to, and wipe my mouth with a napkin, not with my shirt sleeve.

Mother, as if to remind me of the conversation we had the night before, patted my hand and said, "We don't want to upset Daddy tonight, do we, Percy? Tonight, you're going to eat like a little gentleman, aren't you?" There was a sound of urgency was in her voice.

Mother took pride in setting a beautiful table. Her rosewood dining room table, an inherited treasure, came around the Horn in 1830 with her great-grand-parents from Maine. Tonight we had on the table matching Wedgwood china, Venetian crystal, silver from Shrives, and Belgian lace napkins rounded into silver napkin holders with someone else's initials engraved on them. Mother borrowed the settings from Cousin Bessie. Mother asked Daddy two or three times what he thought of the fancy table decorations.

Daddy ignored Mother's dinner table signals to make this evening pleasant and continued to whisper to Marigold about things we couldn't hear. He turned to Grandma and said in a loud voice that Aunt Elizabeth, the sister-in-law he hated, set the best table in the family and that was because "Lizzy stole all the good china from Papa's house." He blathered on to Grandma about her investments and Grandma, after two seconds of his stock and bond lecture, closed her eyes and nodded her head on her chins.

When Daddy stopped talking, Grandma opened her eyes again, lifted her chins, and pinched Daddy on the cheek and told him to take good care of her investments. "All I care about, Dick, is that my dividend checks arrive on time. You take care of the rest." Grandma needed lots of money to buy brandy.

Daddy turned back to Marigold and questioned her on current events, leaving

Mother and me out of the conversation. When Daddy started to talk about Japan's rising military strength, I raised my hand. Seeing my hand up, Daddy furrowed his eyebrows and tried to stare my hand down as he continued to talk, man to man, to my sister. I ignored Daddy's stare and kept my hand up. Daddy buttoned and unbuttoned his coat as he kept ignoring my hand. Trying to concentrate on his current-events lecture to Marigold, and not my fingers making hula-hula motions at him, he pulled his tie up to his neck and choked himself. Seeing he wasn't going to look at me, I began to swirl my hand round and round up in the air as if I was lassoing a cow.

Exasperated, Daddy finally looked at me and growled, "Percy, can't you see I'm talking to your sister? I'll talk to you later."

I put my hand down in my lap.

Daddy's chair was closest to the kitchen and he kept looking at his watch, then at the kitchen door, then he made a furtive glance at the front door as if he wanted to make an escape. He kept telling Marigold that he hated this fuss over him. Daddy never looked at Mother.

A fight was itching to begin.

When Daddy took in a breath and stopped talking, Marigold turned and gave Mother her best dirty look and said to Mother that she had spoiled Daddy's evening home by going modern and making a fuss. Marigold scolded Mother that her father liked old-fashioned girls - like Mother used to be.

Daddy blushed.

I huddled next to Mother to protect myself because if I said anything, Marigold would reach over and pinch me. Marigold said under her breath that I was upsetting Daddy, too. Looking at everybody being so miserable at the dinner table, I knew this family was cursed.

Daddy laid his pocket watch on the table and groused, "For God's sake, what's holding up dinner, Deidra?" He looked around for our elusive silver dinner bell as he spoke.

"Damn it, where's that confounded bell?" he demanded.

I knew where it was. Hatsuko hid it. The bell rested peacefully at the bottom of a Chinese vase. Hatsuko hated the bell because she said it made her feel like a slave and not a person. Daddy, when he had it in his hand, rang it every five minutes for her to come out of the kitchen to answer some stupid question. Whenever a dinner bell was sitting on the table, as long as Daddy rang it, Hatsuko never answered.

Daddy, frustrated that dinner was still not on the table, bellowed to the kitchen door, "Hatsuko, for God's sake, we're ready."

Hatsuko burst into the room like Aladdin's genie with our meal served on silver trays. To my surprise, Hatsuko wore a starched white uniform with white buttons running up and down its front. Another loan from Cousin Bessie. I gritted my teeth, wondering if her sailor friend buttoned up her dress. GRRRR, I mumbled under my breath. I preferred Hatsuko in her kimono.

Everything and everybody was changing around our house too fast. I hated these changes. I wanted everything to go back to normal, before the Navy landed in Hatsuko's bedroom and Mother cut her hair. BOOOOO, I wanted to shout out to the world. BOOOOOO was my word to scare away the curse.

Touching the back of her head, feeling for her lost hair, Mother sighed and told Hatsuko to serve Daddy first. Daddy surveyed the platters of food on Hatsuko's tray and sniffed the lamb chops. I never once heard Daddy compliment or appreciate the hard work Hatsuko did to get our dinner on the dinner table. I told Gertrude that Daddy took his anger out on Hatsuko because she loved me more than she loved Daddy.

I knew, more than anyone living in the house how hard she worked each day. With a wave of a magic wand, with grit and sweat, Hatsuko cooked magnificent meals every day. She cooked these splendid dinners after feeding us breakfast, serving Grandma's lunch on a tray, boiling our clothes, ironing the linen, cleaning the entire house which included bed making, running the errands for Mother, and humoring a movie-struck baby. Now she had to clean up the house all over again because a sulky, moody kid, who knew how hard she worked, was intent on making her life miserable. It was to Hatsuko's sainthood that no matter how badly I mistreated her, or how rude and demanding Grandma was, or how often my father barked unreasonable orders, my Hatsuko, wearing a flower in her hair, graced us each night with her sweet smile.

We dined that evening like I imagined the Dillinghams did on Diamond Head, spooning mashed potatoes and vegetables out of polished silver trays. The trays were wedding presents from an aunt who still ate dinners served by a battery of servants in a home that had as many bathrooms as bedrooms.

I knew I was never going to be a rich person because I could never serve myself food from silver dishes to my plate. I spilled everything on the floor, on Mother's heirloom tablecloth, or on my lap. I ended up on these formally served dinners with most of the food on the floor and starved like those Armenian children Mother told me about in a country that I couldn't find on the map. My father screamed in frustration the moment I picked up a spoon to transfer food to my plate and spilled. Brown gravy was always the biggest challenge. That night, I created a huge mud puddle on the tablecloth.

"Damnit, Deidra, can't the boy serve himself yet like a man?" When Daddy said that to Mother, he was rubbing a wet napkin onto his Brooks Brothers shirt, trying to remove a gravy spot.

"He's doing his best, Dick. You make him nervous." Mother, taking the gravy ladle out of my hand, said to Daddy, "We're trying to have a nice time tonight, Dick - or didn't you notice?"

Grandma got into the act and commanded like a captain at the helm of a ship, "Sit up straight, Percy. Be like your father - like Marigold. Don't hunch over like that. If you have good table manners, you'll be able to eat with kings. Good table manners are a sign of good breeding. Heavens, boy, don't spill, and chew your food with your mouth closed. Marigold, have you ever seen such a dreadful sight?"

Marigold spat out a piece of lamb gristle and nodded to Grandma.

Grandma continued, "You don't concentrate, Percy. You have a weak brain. How many times have I told you to chew, chew, chew your food with your mouth shut?"

As Grandma talked, my mind had wandered up to a little moth that was flitting around a light bulb, about to die.

"Percy, pay attention." Grandma had turned into her Captain Bligh role and spoke louder, "I think it would be a good idea, instead of running around with those hooligans from next door, you come to my room and learn to become a gentleman."

I saw her whipping sailors in front of my eyes. As Grandma talked, Daddy kept rubbing at the stain on his shirt, hoping we weren't noticing.

Grandma slapped her hand on the table, and barked, "Wake up, Percy. What are you thinking about?"

Daddy and I jumped up in our chairs like little boys. I blurted out, "I was thinking about Daddy's gravy stain and your black riding whip hanging on your four-poster bed waiting to beat my weak brains out of my head."

A gloom settled over the room.

"Deidra," Daddy broke the silence, still rubbing the gravy stains. "I have to go back to the office tonight to work on a report."

Mother banged her fork down on the plate and yelled, "That's the third time this week, Dick. You're never home anymore. Can't you stay home for one night with me and the children?"

Daddy slapped his fork down on the table and yelled back at Mother, "For God's sake, Deidra, who's going to pay for that piano in there? A piano not being used except by Marigold. Marigold has all the gumption in this family and the stick-to-itiveness. I never hear you give her any credit for that. All I hear about is what Percy is doing. Hell, I'll tell you what he's not doing, he's not playing that goddamned piano." Daddy pointed his spoon to the piano in the living room and then at me.

Daddy was not about to let up and now spoke in a low, menacing voice to Mother, "Mrs. Love has made a fortune on us. Those piano lessons at Punahou are exorbitant. She's charging me prices that only a Cooke and a Dillingham can pay."

Finished rubbing the stain, he groaned, "And I saw the bill for art classes at the Academy of Arts. When did that happen? Are you wearing a new dress from Liberty House? That's the third new dress this month. Just who in the damn-hell do you think we are? Damn it, can't you see I work hard and all I see around here is everybody spending money like I'm Mr. Got-Rocks?"

Mother calmly spoke back to Daddy, "I'm glad you've noticed something tonight, Dick. You haven't noticed much lately. You don't seem to notice that I work hard all day, too, and forget that I, too, pay the bills around here. You seem to forget that very conveniently. I work hard to support my kids, put food on the table, and never once do I hear you give me credit for that. They'd never be able to go to Punahou if I didn't teach there. Did you ever think once - just once - I could have had a hard day, too? It's because of you and your temper that Percy is not taking piano lessons from Mrs. Love. And for God's sake, quit swearing around the house. Marigold is beginning to think swearing is cute and she's swearing all over the place."

Picking up her fork and shaking it at him, she continued, "And Dick, I don't think I can stand much more of this bickering." Mother took in a breath and pushed away her plate. She hadn't eaten her lamb chop.

I put my hands over my ears as she started to speak again.

"I am proud of both my kids. I am very proud of Marigold. Marigold is bright, not only because of her father, but because she also has a smart mother too. And Percy is talented because...."

Mother stopped. I thought she was going to cry because she couldn't speak anymore. I always knew the name of Percy was cursed because when people say the name, they sometimes stop talking.

I turned smugly to Marigold and said under my breath, "I'm saving Daddy lots of money because I'm not taking piano lessons and you are. You're driving Daddy into the poor house."

Daddy heard me. He laid his fork down on his plate and looked at me. I wanted to crawl under the table because he looked like he was going to pop like a balloon. Perspiration bubbled on my forehead. Our dining room had turned into a Jimmy Cagney movie - the death house at Sing Sing. A convict was about to be executed and a canary was about to sing.

I put my head down on the table and waited for Daddy's ax to cut my head off. Looking down at the floor, waiting for the ax, I counted all the string beans I had spilled.

In a slow, low, menacing voice, Daddy pointedly said, "Percy is a quitter. A big quitter. He's never once saved me a cent. Percy only wastes my money. Everyone in this house wastes my money. Deidra, look how much money you spent on yourself tonight. You're ruining me by going behind my back and spending money buying dresses and the lamb chops that we don't need. Deidra, you're a Jesus Christ Judas. You are going to send me to the poor house." He paused and said, "I've got a headache."

"A Jesus Christ Judas. I can't believe you said that, Dick. That just doesn't make any sense. No sense at all, and so untrue. You've given me a headache and I don't have headaches. Let's change the subject and eat our dinner and try to have a pleasant evening tonight - what's left of it," Mother retorted. She picked up her fork and sweetly said to Marigold, trying to bring our house back into order, "How was your day at school, Marigold?"

Marigold muttered angrily back at Mother, but only looked at Daddy, "Okay."

Grandma's eyes flashed red flames as she slurred her words and lashed out at Mother, spewing daggers, "Deidra, a wife's place is to keep her man happy and to keep her mouth shut. You should know better than to argue about important matters at the dinner table - especially in front of your children. It's bad for their digestion and their little minds. My mother told me that the night before I married - a wise thing."

Grandma belched. She continued without taking notice of her gas, "The first commandment of a marriage is that your husband is always right and the wife is the person in the home to keep the peace in the family. That was good advice, Deidra. A husband is always right and has the last word. Like your hair - Deidra, you're hell bent on becoming a modern day Jezebel."

Stung by Grandma and Daddy's words, Mother stood up from her place and spit out what she had been holding back since dinner began. "First, I'm called a

Judas and now I'm a Jezebel. You two have made me into a biblical back-stabbing vixen. Grandma, I can't believe for one minute that you ever followed an ounce of your mother's advice by the way you treated the Captain and because you're too pigheaded and too opinionated to listen to anybody. You're just like your big bully grandson sitting over there, whom I don't listen to any more because half the time he doesn't know what he's talking about. Especially about any of the things around his home - including his children. How could he know what's going around here? He's never home."

Grandma started to cry. Daddy looked at his gold watch as if he had timed Mother's speech.

Mother's voice started to rise, "Tell me, Grandma, when did the Lord above tell you and that man sitting next to you that you and your family are so doggoned perfect? Well, He didn't. And let me tell you that you're not - none of us are. I am not a Judas or a Jezebel. And when you think about it, Grandma, it was kind of me to take you into my home, whether you think so or not. I've cared for you as best as I can, but in payment, I only get complaints about the food, about my children, and about my hair. I have supported my husband in everything he's ever wanted to do and frankly, to tell you the truth, I didn't want to cut off my hair. I loved my long hair, but I thought my husband would like it short because he hasn't liked much about me for a long time and he has made that very plain this evening. Haven't you, Dick? I have made a mistake. A big mistake. This dinner is a big mistake. But I am a wife who does her best for her husband, her husband's grand- mother and her children, and I resent both you and Dick calling me names."

Mother paused. She was out of breath.

Daddy blurted out so Mother would stop talking, "That's enough, Deidra."

"Yes, that's enough," Mother sighed and sat down.

In shock, Marigold gasped, "Mother, how could you talk to Grandma and Daddy like that? That's sacrilegious."

Grandma rose from her chair, spouting like a whale, weaving side to side. She stared straight at Marigold, poop-da-pooed, and sobbed into her handkerchief. Grandma had a lot of Bette Davis in her.

Then Grandma pooped again and wailed like an air raid siren, "I've never been talked to in such a manner in my whole life. You have a cruel tongue, Deidra. My Captain never ever raised his voice once to me and he loved me till the day he died. You have no idea what it's like to be old, discarded, and without a husband, and have to live on crumbs in a house where you are not wanted. I'm going to my room and never coming out. I'm leaving this house tonight, Dick, and never com- ing back to a house where I'm not wanted."

Mother groaned, got up from her chair and walked over to Grandma. She put her arm around the old lady and said, "I'm sorry, Grandma, for what I said. It's my nerves. I apologize. Please stay with us. You know you can live here as long as you like. We love you. Stay for dessert anyway. Hatsuko's made something very special tonight - just for you. It would please Dick if you stayed. I'm very sorry, Grandma, for what I just said."

Grandma sat down like a sack of potatoes. Grandma had a sweet tooth and wasn't about to pass up dessert. Dramatically, she wrung out her handkerchief and snuffled, "I'll do it for Dick - just this once more."

Daddy and Marigold glowered fiercely at Mother as if she had struck
Grandma in the face with Grandma's whip. Grandma was a faker. A faker recognizes other fakers. Grandma wasn't ever going to leave us or die.

Not to be upstaged by Grandma's performance, I decided to change
Grandma's "Bette Davis atmosphere" and turn everybody happy again. I was also
starving. I jumped up and slammed my hands on the table and said, as sunny as a
chipmunk, "Tonight, I'm going to clear the dishes, just for Daddy. This is Daddy's
special night."

Everybody at the table looked at me - dumbstruck. Nobody said anything so I
put my hands up in the air and yelled, "Yea, for me."

Grandma stopped crying. Marigold groaned. Mother, perplexed, said, "Percy,
what a little man you are. Don't you think so, Dick?" Mother looked pleased as
punch that I was turning into a "mother's little helper."

Daddy, stung by Mother's words, spoke two words, "Good, son." I stuffed the
words into my stomach to stop its churning.

Wiping my mouth with my napkin - all gentlemen did that in the movies - I
excused myself from the table. I picked up my plate and Mother's and shuffled
toward the kitchen, doing a Stepin Fetchit number. Stepin Fetchit was my favorite
black character in the movies because he made me laugh. He could do stupid
things and get away with it. As I shuffled off, I mumbled, "I'm gonna take care of
my massa tonight. My massa is a good man and I'm ready to slave for him. I'm
even gonna wash his feet tonight."

I smiled back at my family like a black saint as their eyes did pinwheels at my
sudden performance. Dishes piled crookedly on each other, I dribbled gravy on the
floor as I walked into the kitchen. As soon I shut the kitchen door, I flung Cousin
Bessie's heirlooms into the sink and turned into a whirling dervish. I searched for
any leftover food on the kitchen table. Finding it, I smashed the food into my
mouth as quickly as I could. In three seconds, I ate five times the amount of food
that I hadn't been able to eat at the dinner table. It calmed the wrestling match in
my stomach.

As I did this, I told Hatsuko I knew how all the starving Armenian children
must have felt when they got upset. On my way back out of the kitchen, I swiped
the leftovers in the silver trays. Hatsuko sat on the kitchen counter and applauded
my performance. Carefully wiping mashed potatoes off my face, I bowed to
Hatsuko, and reentered the dining room, playing the new saint of Kapaka Street
again. I shuffled around the table, picking up the rest of the plates. I said to
Grandma, patting her on the head, "What a good Missy youse been tonight and,
honey, because youse ate all youse good food like a good girl, I gonna see you get
dessert. Now honey, youse just dry those tears because you got a big surprise coming."

When I played the fool, I could say anything to anybody because nobody took
fools seriously.

Looking into Daddy's eyes, I declared, "And next year, boss, I wants my freedom. I wants to get out of herah because President Lincoln done promised me my
freedom."

Daddy was about to snap my head off, but I held up my hand in front of his face and continued, "I stills wash youse feet, massa, and I'm happy to clear youse dish because youse has been so good to me and so kind. Youse just like a big Jesus to me." Frustrated, not knowing what to say or do with my stupid performance, Daddy looked like he would have nailed me to the cross with Jesus.

I gave Marigold a wide berth because her pinchy pinchy fingers were out for action, ready to tickle me under the arms, with the hope that I'd drop the plates and make a mess like I usually did. "Massa Marigold, youse trying to be a little devil, youse is. Youse reach out and hand me youse plate because I don't trust youse pinchy little hands. They look like little crabs to me and youse want me to drop my plates. That youse do." I grabbed her plate and ran into the kitchen.

It took three runs to clear the table, and each time Hatsuko had food waiting for me. After I finished taking all the plates off the table, Hatsuko placed a chocolate Kiss in my mouth. I kissed Hatsuko on the cheek because tonight she didn't smell of her sailor's after-shave. With a familiar pat of her hand on my fanny, she pushed me out into the dining room while she prepared to serve dessert. I returned to my seat and wore a big angelic smile on my face and a satisfied big fat belly. My belly was so full of food now that it had burst the first two buttons off my pants.

As I sat down, Mother and Daddy told me what a thoughtful little boy I had been. For a few minutes, I wore a tarnished halo and the mood at the table had changed to talking about the weather.

Marigold socked my leg because she never bought the act. The week before, she had followed me into the kitchen and caught me gnawing on a leftover chicken leg. She knew exactly what had just happened behind the kitchen door. But Marigold and I never snitched on each other. There were times when I threatened to tell Mother something bad that she did, but I only threatened because I was sure if I had snitched, Marigold would have given me a black eye or murdered me in my bed.

When the dessert was served, the storm clouds cleared and Grandma forgot she was going to pack her bags. Chocolate cake and vanilla ice cream always put our family back into a good mood.

After licking my spoon and finishing off the vanilla ice cream, I raised my hand and offered an opinion, "Daddy, when I grow up I want to be a black slave."

"Why, Percy?"

"In the movies, black slaves are always happy because they sing and dance at work and make everybody happy and everybody loves them. It looks to me that by being a black slave you can always have a good time, and everybody loves you. Daddy, I want everybody to love me like they do the black slaves. I wouldn't ever want to be a white slave because the Emperor Nero fed them to the lions. I saw that in the movies. No, I am certain that I want to be a black slave if I could."

Daddy, puzzled, said, "That's a very odd thing to say, Percy. You wouldn't want to be a black slave, Percy, because their masters treated them cruelly and they weren't free. They lived a very hard life because they were whipped and treated like dogs."

"Just like Grandma whipped you. But then, Daddy, if the slaves were treated like dogs, they could sleep in a bed like Uku did. Daddy, maybe - now this is just a thought - maybe I could have a slave all my own, someone all to myself, someone who would never ever leave me for someone else. That would make my life swell." I was talking, man to man, to my daddy.

"No, Percy, a man has to have his freedom. You can't keep a man around if he doesn't want to stay where he is and is unhappy. A man has to feel free to come and go. That's important to a man. A man has to be free, Percy."

When Daddy finished telling me a man has to be free, he folded his napkin into his napkin ring and looked like he had lost his best friend. My father looked so unhappy that I wanted to get up and wash his feet.

Lately, when he was home, Daddy's routine after dinner was to pick up his briefcase, kiss Mother on the cheek, wave goodbye, and leave the house for his office. Some nights he didn't come home until after midnight. I knew the exact time he came home because I would be at the kitchen window, watching for the sailor to come out of Hatsuko's room. Mother would have gone to sleep after she had corrected spelling papers and watched the clock. On those nights when Daddy worked late at his office, Marigold, "Miss Straight A Student," studied, dividing factors into something and memorizing poems out loud for her English class. When Marigold memorized her poems, she was very boring. Grandma would have scuttled back to her bedroom for a slug of brandy to wash down Hatsuko's dessert.

I, alone on the lanai, spent hours listening to the radio, playing with Agnes and Gertrude and drawing pictures of wishing wells. All my wishing wells had sailors drowning in them and calling for help. I never had to do homework, because I told Mother I had finished my homework by the time school ended. I lied. When Daddy crept into the house, the lights were out and everyone was asleep but...me.

That evening, our last supper with Daddy, when we ate lamb chops and Mother cut her hair, that night, Mother broke Daddy's routine before he left for the office. "Dick," Mother said, reaching for the missing pug on the back of her head.

Daddy didn't answer when she spoke because his mind was elsewhere.

She called again, "Dick, I'm going with you tonight. While you're at the office, you can drop me off at a movie. I want to do something fun tonight. You can pick me up after you finish work. I'm tired and not thinking right."

Daddy didn't reply because he was talking to Marigold about the Nazis invading Norway, Hitler's army in the Sudetenland, Neville Chamberlain, England's Prime Minister who was preaching peace, and Japan's aggressive moves in China. He ended his talk, confiding to Marigold that he couldn't afford Hatsuko's salary anymore and how extravagant Mother had been to serve lamb chops at dinner. He emphasized his last words for Mother to overhear, saying, "We have got to cut corners around here, because a war is coming right around the corner."

Mother interrupted, "Did you hear me, Dick?"

Daddy let out his breath and sighed, "Yes, I heard you. Get your purse and let's go."

Little did Daddy realize that by taking Mother with him to work that night, a war was about to explode around a corner that he didn't expect.

Hawaii Theatre, around 1940, Honolulu. Courtesy of Bishop Museum Archives, Honolulu, HI.

11

The Invisible Man

When Mother returned the night of our lamb chop dinner, she arrived home alone and Daddy never slept in his bed again. I missed his snoring.

Daddy became invisible. With Daddy gone, Mother took me to the movies after school. We went to scary movies, the scarier the better. One afternoon at the Varsity Theatre, Mother whispered to me to please get up off the floor. I had hidden under the theater seat because ugly wart-faced Charles Laughton, the actor in *The Hunchback of Notre Dame,* played like he was Hunkacha and was scaring me. He lurked like a crazed beast, in and out of the dark streets of Paris, searching for the beautiful, creamy-skinned Irish actress, Maureen O'Hara. In a fit of anger, he threw boiling hot oil from the top of the Notre Dame cathedral onto his enemies below. I was glad Marigold didn't see that movie because it would have given her new ideas to torture me.

On those afternoons, Mother was determined that we were going to be scared to death. After Daddy became invisible, we saw every ghoulish movie that played in Honolulu.

My fights with Marigold became intense. I carried a ton of bumps on my head, and she carried teeth marks on her arms like a thousand pearl bracelets. We looked like the walking wounded.

Marigold was in a bad mood from the time she woke up to the time she went to bed. Before dinner, she'd leap around the dining room table like a wild Indian, saying she was going to live with Daddy, and every morning, she'd scream while sitting on the toilet, that she hated everybody. After school, before Mother was home, Marigold would burst through the front door breathing fire like a Hawaiian volcano goddess, looking for a victim. I'd hide in my closet with Agnes and Gertrude until Mother came home.

As soon as Mother and I came back from seeing the scary movies, our phone rang. I overheard her tell Cousin Bessie and other relatives not to listen to rumors and to keep their noses out of her business. Mother couldn't stand the notion that her relatives had enrolled her into the Hawaiian gossip mill. Mother believed "her business" would work out and she didn't want any interference from outsiders. She believed it when she told us that Daddy had gone away temporarily.

Within a couple of days after Daddy left, Mother found that every one of her friends and sisters knew that my father had girlfriends on the side, long before

Mother caught him red-handed in his office. Aunt Momi, her middle sister, had given hints about other ladies before Daddy left, but Mother wasn't listening. Mother wouldn't hear anything negative said about my father, but deep down somewhere inside of herself, she had been concerned enough to cut off her hair.

Aunt Momi, my eccentric aunt, was a beauty-parlor-dyed Titian-haired beauty who likened herself to Clara Bow, the "IT" girl of the silent movie days. This aunt had a raunchy sense of humor, and after three drinks, she told dirty jokes that I repeated at school. I thought a "pussy" was a cat.

Aunt Momi was a big movie fan and drank "sidecar" cocktails with Dorothy McKail, a movie star who stayed at the Royal Hawaiian Hotel. After three martinis, my aunt called Daddy "Dickie the Ripper," and after her fourth drink, he became "Little Dickie-poo." My father loathed Aunt Momi after her fourth drink because she swore at him. After a fifth martini, she'd wiggle her pinkie at Mother and sing "Little Bo Peepie has lost her sheepie."

After Daddy left, Aunt Momi became an important person in my life and one whom I found was capable of fighting curses and old dragons.

When Daddy lived with us, Aunt Momi, when visiting from Kauai, was the last guest to leave what she called Mother's "boring Saturday night cocktail parties." During the middle of these parties, she'd pull Mother aside and ask in a gravelly voice, "Look, kiddo, what the hell is going on around here? Give it to me straight. Something's going on." Aunt Momi already knew the straight; as she told Mother later, my father had propositioned Aunt Momi's best girlfriend at a funeral. Mother would push Aunt Momi out of the house when she became too nosy, replying, "Nothing. Go back to Kauai." Aunt Momi told Mother there was the talk around the town about her marriage and our house was as "fake" as a Shirley Temple movie because no one was speaking from their gut and everyone was acting too icky sweet.

Aunt Momi would say to Mother, "Jesus-K-Christ, Deidra, don't you and Dick talk to each other? Living around here must be like living in an ice palace for Republicans. I mean everybody in this house is frozen stiff. I'd hate to think if the sun came out. You'd all melt. Then what?"

Mother would tell Aunt Momi she didn't know what she was talking about and what does our house have to do with living in an ice palace for Republicans and all that sunshine nonsense. Mother wasn't political.

After one cocktail party, after Daddy had left, Aunt Momi, sober, called on Mother to continue her lecture from the night before. "All I heard about last night were that the sugar prices were down, Kona winds are rusting our cars, Roosevelt's bullshit fireside chats and Hawaii's going to hell with that Roosevelt, and Eleanor Roosevelt's buckteeth. Who gives a shit about Eleanor's buckteeth and screw that Fala. Egads, Deidra - you're making their dog a topic of conversation when there's much more important things to talk about, don't you think? As a matter of fact, where was Dick last night?"

I hid in the living room behind a curtain listening to them. I was starting my spy career.

"Talk to me. I don't give a shit about the Roosevelts. Actually, I like the Roosevelts. I voted for them. Talk to me, Deidra." Aunt Momi kept pressing

Mother to tell her where Daddy was.

Mother took a cigarette out of Aunt Momi's purse and lit it. She promised Aunt Momi that everything was fine. "There's nothing to talk about. Dick and I are fine, fine, fine. Don't let Dick hear that you voted for Roosevelt - he hates his guts."

Ignoring Mother's protests, Aunt Momi sat next to Mother and pressed on, "Come on, Deidra. The truth."

There was a pause. Mother lit another cigarette while she still had one smoking in the ashtray, crossed her legs, looked at her sister, and said, "Dick's living at the YMCA. I kicked him out of the house."

Everyone knew Daddy lived at the YMCA before Aunt Momi knew. The chatter around Honolulu was that our family had split. Mother ignored the chatter and spoke in public as if the most important things in her life were Eleanor Roosevelt's buckteeth and Fala's fleas.

Mother divorced Daddy with Uncle George's help. Aunt Momi, when on her sixth drink, now called Daddy Adolph Hitler. Mother confessed to Aunt Momi that she had been unhappy with Daddy since her honeymoon.

I confessed to Mother that before Daddy left us, I told him I thought President Roosevelt was better than God was. Daddy replied, going out the front door, that any son who thought that and wore his mother's dresses was going to grow up to be a Democrat.

I told Mother the real reason Daddy had left was because I told him I hated him and that I was going to grow up to be a Democrat, and that someone like Hunkacha cursed me and maybe she should send me away to China so Daddy would come back.

Mother only laughed and said I was talking silly. I knew better because I knew I only messed things up for everybody around me - without even trying.

My family had broken apart but my country, the United States of America, remained as steady and firm as the coconut tree waving in front of my house. I loved America. My country was my big family. I felt I belonged to the United States of America even if Hawaii wasn't a state.

I stood like a patriot and pledged allegiance to my flag at school everyday.With my hand on my heart, I'd yell louder than anybody else, saying, "with liberty and justice for all." When I looked at my picture book on America, I loved looking at the wart on President Lincoln's face, his monument, bald-headed Benjamin Franklin flying a kite, Thomas Jefferson in a wig signing the Declaration of Independence. I wanted all of them to be my fathers.

I loved my land of the free and my flag of the red, white and blue that flew over an island where people of many colors marched to Hawaiian songs. We had our own flag that spoke to me of a Hawaiian kingdom of long ago and we said what we thought at political rallies and were not shot at by Gestapo agents for raising our hands to go to the bathroom.

I lived in a country where the father of our country, George Washington, never told a lie. He never told a lie because he had a father who never told a lie, and probably his father had a father who never told a lie. A lie was a terrible thing because it wasn't the truth. President Washington's father didn't spank George Washington even though he wasn't perfect and confessed to chopping down a cherry tree. George Washington's father praised him for telling the truth and that helped George Washington become the first President of the United States. That's what my first grade teacher, Miss Storey, told me when we celebrated George Washington's birthday on the 22nd of February.

My father wasn't George Washington. I wished he was, but my father didn't live at home anymore - and I was beginning to tell big lies like my father. I lied to Cousin Bessie every time she called our house. I told her I was fine, my mother was fine, Marigold was fine, Grandma was fine, Hatsuko was fine, and the biggest lie of all, my daddy was sleeping in his bed.

Before Thanksgiving, everyone knew I lied because the whole world read in *The Honolulu Advertiser* that Mother filed for divorce. The cat was out of the bag. Cousin Bessie told me Daddy was sleeping at the YMCA before Mother did

Once the divorce became a fact, Grandma retreated to her room, not talking to anyone, especially not to my mother. Grandma talked all day to the photograph of her dead Captain on the bureau, saying, "What has this world come to?" When Grandma checked her bearings, sticking her nose out the bedroom door, asking Hatsuko for food on a tray, and inquiring if Daddy had called, she smelled different. She smelled old and musty. Her lavender scent had disappeared.

Mother sent Marigold to visit her godmother Aunt Mari on Kauai. I, left behind, ate my meals at six-thirty sharp at the dining room table with Hatsuko. Hatsuko and I spoke, but never about movies or my father.

The windows of our house, once open to the warm gentle trades that floated down from Manoa Valley, were shut tight to keep the wind and busybodies out. Only a handful of trusted friends and advisors, Mother's favorite dragons, were allowed to make pilgrimages into our house. Muffled conversations, crying and wailing and lots of carrying on took place in our living room. It was as if Bette Davis had come to visit. The room filled up on those afternoons with thick smoke that was exhaled from the lady dragons.

Once, when the dragons were waiting for Mother to come home from school, I listened to bits and pieces of conversation inside the living room. "The beast. I never liked him. She was much too good for him. Good riddance to bad rubbish, that's what I say. But then again, dear, she wasn't a saint. She's put on a lot of weight or didn't you notice, and that dreadful hair. Deidra's doing the right thing; after all, he didn't give her much of a choice. Flaunting that common person right in front of her eyes. What he did was unforgivable. But then again, dear, we don't divorce in our family."

Curious as Cousin Bessie and Grandma, wearing Mother's new dress from Liberty House, I placed an empty water glass against the outside of our living room wall to hear their conversations, a spy technique I learned from a Bob Hope movie. After awhile they lowered their voices and I couldn't hear anything through the water glass, so I skipped into the living room to see what the dragons were up to. Because they had closed the curtains, our living room was as dark as a cave that hid smoking dragons in King Arthur's time. Nothing was going to stop me from learning what these puffing dragons were snorting about my daddy. Standing

at the entrance of the living room, dressed to kill in Mother's Liberty House fanciest dress, holding a frayed Betty Grable paper doll in my right hand, I spoke like a
ray of sunshine, "Hi!"

They were so engrossed in dissecting Mother and Daddy that they didn't
notice me at first. To get their attention, I waved the paper doll at them and said,
"What's up?"

Startled by seeing me and getting caught talking about Mother, their eyes
snapped to me in unison, as if they were Mussolini reviewing his troops. Dragon
One, inhaling on her Lucky Strike, gave me the once over as if she was smelling
her doo-doo. "That's a lovely frock, darling."

I replied, "Just a rag."

Dragon One continued, exhaling smoke from her nose, "Percy, don't you
think little boys should be seen and not heard?"

I looked at her and imitated her smoking a cigarette, replying, "No."

Dragon Two French-inhaled her Camel, pulling smoke through her nose and
"whooshing" it out her mouth, and snorted, "I didn't know little boys played with
paper dolls."

I scratched my head and thought for a minute. "This little boy does."

Dragon Three, having the shakes so badly that her ashes from her Chesterfield
cigarette scattered over our carpet, making snow on the old bourbon and Coke
stain, asked, "Did you wet your dress, Percy?"

"No," I answered truthfully, "I spilled the water in the glass that I used outside
to listen to you."

"Did you hear anything?" Dragon One asked nervously.

I paused. "Yes."

They paused, waiting for me to continue. I paused. They paused. They looked
at me. I looked back at them. After a long moment of silence, they each reached
for another cigarette, waiting for me to leave or say something more.

I cleared my throat. They cleared their throats.

I broke the silence. "By popular request, and by the management of this
house, I will do a hula for you!"

The dragons' lips puckered as if they were sucking lemons.

"Lovely Hula Hands?" I continued eagerly.

Dragon Two dropped her pack of cigarettes on the rug.

"Miss Brandt taught me this ancient hula at the Academy of Arts last week."

Dragon One tapped her foot, pulled her dress up to her knees, and asked, "Did
you go number two today, Percy?"

"No, I didn't, did you?" She gasped and choked on her cigarette smoke.
Dragon Three coughed so hard, her face turned purple.

Dragon Two pointed. All three dragons looked down at my shoes. I had on
Mother's San Francisco fancy Frank Moore, black high heels, each on the wrong
foot. I had such a hard time telling my left from right and my right from left. I
jumped out of Mother's shoes and hid them behind my back. I looked straight into
Dragon One's eyes and said, "What have you done with my daddy?"

I heard their girdles snap.

Dragon One, exhaling her smoke, scolded, "Percy, that is not for little boys to know. Little boys don't go around pestering grown-ups, and we don't want to see your hula."

Mother walked in behind me, and in her low Barbara Stanwyck voice, ended my performance. "Percy, I see you have been entertaining my friends. I'll tell you what happened to your father later, but right now Hatsuko's fixed you a bologna and cheese sandwich with lots of mayonnaise. You look a little tired, dear, and starved." Turning me away from the dragons, she said gently, "Go on your way."

"Will you promise to tell me what happened to Daddy? I think - I think I might have said something to make him leave us," I begged.

"Percy, you had nothing to do with your father leaving, and I promise you I'll tell you where Daddy is. Now please, be a good boy and go eat your sandwich." Mother turned and smiled at the dragons.

I blurted, "Cousin Bessie says he's staying at the YMCA."

"Go eat," Mother replied.

I took the bribe, but before I left, I said to the dragons, "Just for your information, ladies, Cousin Bessie says I dance better than Hilo Hattie and sing better than Kate Smith. Next time you come, I'm going to charge you ten cents for me to entertain you. It's my going price and I wish you'd quit talking about Mother and Daddy when they aren't here." Waddling off to the kitchen, I had a better understanding of why St. George killed dragons.

That night Mother forgot to tell me what happened to Daddy.

The pilgrimages dwindled down within two weeks. When the last dragon departed, smoking her last Camel cigarette, Hatsuko opened up the windows for Mother and once again the trade winds blew and cleared away the stale smoke. I watched the cigarette smoke circle out the screen door and float up lazily into the Hawaiian sky and disappear. Just like my daddy did. He disappeared from sight just like Claude Rains disappeared in the *Invisible Man!*

I came home from school every afternoon hoping to see a glass of whiskey floating in mid-air or the smoke from his Lucky Strike lingering in the living room. I searched from room to room for him, hoping for his puff of smoke, his gruff voice, or his glass of bourbon and Coke. I wanted to tell Daddy that I didn't mean what I said when I told him I hated him for life. I looked and looked, but it was in vain. Daddy ran away like Uku did. There were no good-byes, no tears, no leis, no manly shake of hands, and there was no body lying in a coffin - Daddy was just gone. Poof!

Divorce was not a topic discussed with children in 1940.

Every time I eat a lamb chop, I think of that night I played the fool for my father.

12

Nobody Lives on My Street Anymore

I heard the name "Golden" hissed in our house when Aunt Momi ground a cigarette into an ashtray and muttered, "Golden, that bitch." Aunt Momi told a dragon, while I hid behind a curtain, that after our lamb chop dinner and seeing a movie, Mother surprised Daddy as he was lying on top of a desk with Miss Golden. I thought that was an odd place for them to sleep. When I told Hatsuko that piece of news, she told me that Daddy and Miss Golden were sharing a Hershey Kiss.

Miss Golden was Daddy's secretary. I knew without being told that Miss Golden, other than me, was one of the reasons my father left us. She was his secretary who sat cross-legged behind a small mahogany desk near Daddy's office. She had lots of curly orange hair piled up in masses on top of her head and stunk of jasmine perfume. Miss Golden wore purple lipstick and grew fingernails as long as eagle's claws. Whenever I visited Daddy at his office, Miss Golden handed me a piece of chewy chocolate. Cousin Bessie told me Miss Golden was fired from Castle and Cooke.

In 1940 my parents divorced. Cousin Bessie confided to me that Daddy was now dancing with lots of ladies on the rooftop of the Alexander Young Hotel.

Feeling blue, Mother confided to Cousin Bessie that Aunt Mari wasn't speaking to her. Mother had received letters from the old witch on Kauai saying that Mother was never to marry again and was to concentrate on raising her children. She wrote that divorce was considered a disgrace to women who had descended from preachers who came around the Horn in a leaky sailing ship. God-fearing women stayed married and that was that. Mother's sisters, except the eldest who had been dropped at birth, thought she had guts, but Mother was out of Aunt Mari's will.

When Marigold returned from her visit with Aunt Mari, the divorce was final and she wasn't speaking to us. I asked Marigold if Aunt Mari cut out her tongue. She showed me her tongue. Aunt Mari hadn't. I was really disappointed seeing her pink tongue was intact.

Dinner was served at six-thirty again.

Thanksgiving holiday came and went. I thought our Thanksgiving dinner was the best ever because Hatsuko ate dinner with us and we served ourselves in the kitchen. It was the first Thanksgiving dinner that I didn't land most of my dinner on the floor. Marigold sat in Daddy's place. Grandma was on her right. Mother was next to me and Hatsuko ate turkey beside me. I loved Hatsuko because at Thanksgiving, she smelled of washing starch again. I kept my fingers crossed under the table that the sailor had drowned at sea.

Marigold and I each ate a drumstick. Daddy usually coveted one of them.

Grandma hardly ate. I could see she was thinking about Daddy. She grimaced all through dinner as if her ship was plowing through rough seas. Grandma now brought her brandy glass and brandy bottle to the dinner table. With Daddy gone, there was no reason for secrets. Grandma and Marigold stared spitballs at Mother between courses and whispered to each other how much they missed him. By their mean looks, it was clear that they blamed Mother for Daddy not sitting at the head of the table. Mother picked at her food and overheard everything.

Before we ate dessert, Mother told me that Daddy was alive and had rented a studio at the Seaside Inn in Waikiki. After we finished dinner, Grandma announced that she was moving out and going to share Daddy's cabin in Waikiki.

Grandma left two days later. She packed her three black suitcases plastered all over with colorful labels from the hotels she and the Captain had stayed in when they toured the world. She threw away the empty brandy bottles that were piled up in her shower. I wanted to pipe her off that morning as she clumped down our front steps like a four-star admiral, looking fierce. Mother, Marigold and I marched behind her like obedient deck hands, each carrying a suitcase. Our heads were dutifully bowed as we walked her out of the house. Daddy, standing beside his car, looked as if he hadn't taken a shower. The pouches under his eyes were bigger and his business suit was wrinkled and had gravy stains on it.

Daddy never stepped inside our house again.

Marigold ran in front of us, dropped the suitcase, and leaped into his arms. Grandma, when she arrived beside the car, stood looking at Daddy holding Marigold, and blinked back tears. Grandma, chin out, lips pursed, got into the car with Mother's help, and sat bolt upright in the front seat. She looked straight in front of her as if she was sitting on the bow of a ship searching for dangerous ice-bergs. Not a muscle on her face twitched. She reminded me of the pictures she showed me of fierce carved figureheads on the sailing ships. Sitting in Daddy's car, waiting for him to drive away, Grandma was steeled to conquer new worlds - worlds Mother and I would never inhabit. She hadn't spoken one word to us that morning. Grandma had thrown us to the sharks.

Mother walked over to Marigold, without a word or look at Daddy, and pried her gently from her father's arms. Leading Marigold back up the steps to our house, we all turned and looked down at Daddy and Grandma sitting in the car. Three abandoned sailors were standing alone, marooned on a desert island.

We waved Daddy and Grandma off as the car lurched into first gear and drove away. Grandma looked back at Marigold as Daddy shifted into second gear. It was a nod - a knowing look - a look that blamed Mother for the whole darn mess. Mother was Blackbeard the Pirate.

Grandma scuttled Marigold that morning. Grandma told Marigold everyday of her child life that she was a special creature and that "Grandma will never, ever, ever leave you, darling. Grandma will always be by your side, Marigold. Through thick and thin. We're stuck together forever. We're a team, child."

Those words of promise were whispered into Marigold's ears, as Hatsuko had whispered her words of promise into mine. Grandma vowed to Marigold that she would never leave her from the moment Marigold understood love. When Daddy drove off with Grandma, Marigold had been torpedoed for the second time.

After Daddy's car rounded the corner, Marigold and Mother turned and walked back into our empty house. They separated and went into their bedrooms and closed their doors.

I headed for the icebox and made myself a thick mayonnaise sandwich. With my sandwich in my hands, I sat on the steps of our front porch with Agnes and Gertrude sitting on either side of me. I took a bite out of the sandwich and started to cry. I knew that I was the cause of this whole darn mess. I was a sissy. I wore Mother's dresses and didn't like Daddy's football. I never tried to be what anybody wanted me to be, and I never listened to anyone. I made a list of the things that I lacked and came up with that I was not as smart or as courageous as Marigold, and Hatsuko, my best friend, loved a sailor more than she loved me. I hadn't become the movie star I promised Hatsuko I'd be. I had spoiled it for everyone - for Mother, for Marigold, for Hatsuko, and for me.

Someday, and, this I was certain, I'd come home from school and "poof"- our house would be empty and everybody would have turned invisible. That was going to happen. I just knew it. I was going to be abandoned by everyone. I was a big fat blob who had a terrible personality. I looked down the empty street and thought of Uku. I called out, "Uku, Uku, Uku!" Our street stayed empty. Only the blue exhaust of Daddy's car lingered in the air. Gertrude said that Uku wasn't ever coming home and to quit feeling sorry for myself. Agnes consoled me, saying, "Uku's in a hospital with the flu and he just hasn't gotten well yet."

I took a bite out of my sandwich. My belly was growing larger with all the tears and secrets inside it. I felt I was about to burst. I was going to cause the biggest explosion that anybody ever heard - better than when Krakatoa erupted. I finished eating the sandwich and let out another call for Uku.

I walked back into the house and slathered more mayonnaise on bread. I knew I had to do something to keep me from being left alone. I had to make certain that no one would turn invisible on me again. I didn't know how. I couldn't have a slave. Daddy said so.

I was cursed. There's no hope for cursed people.

Coming back out on the porch, munching on another mayonnaise sandwich, I looked around and saw that I lived on an empty street. I felt sick in my stomach. I felt soggy all over as if someone had poured gallons of water into my body.

Gertrude became exasperated, threw up her hands, and said I was squealing like a spoiled, baby pig. She started to lecture me. Her words came right out of Barbara Stanwyck's movie, *Stella Dallas*. "Snap out of it, kid." At the end of the movie *Stella Dallas*, Barbara Stanwyck stood in the rain, looking at her daughter inside a house as she was being married. Barbara Stanwyck was an outsider and she had to live the rest of her life on a lonely, empty street.

Someone opened a window. I looked across the street at Mr. McLaine's house. Two eyes were staring back at me.

Robert Taylor as Armand and Greta Garbo as Camille in "Camille," by MGM. (Supporting actors Laura Hope Crews and Rex O'Malley.) From J. D. Eames, 1975, The MGM Story. Crown Publishers, Inc., New York, NY.

13

Betsy

Betsy moved into our house the day I lied to Santa Claus. Santa had arrived on the Lurline.

The Honolulu Advertiser

SANTA CLAUS HERE TODAY
St. Nick to disembark at Pier 12 at 11 a.m., all children invited.

BAREFOOT FOOTBALL CHAMPIONSHIPS AT HONOLULU STADIUM
2 P.M. Sunday - December 8 St. Anthony VS St. Agnes
Admission: Adults - 25 Cents Children - no charge
Two previous games ended in tie scores

KANSAN OFFERS BOMBS TO HIT HITLER
E. Haldenmen Julius (Publisher) today sent a letter to Prime Minister Winston Churchill offering to pay for a ton of bombs to be dropped on Chancellor Adolph Hitler's Berchtesgaden retreat, plus $100 for gasoline.

"If any money was left over, " he said, "it could go for a big dinner for the bomber crew."

HISTORIC CATHEDRAL IS LEVELED AS NAZI BOMBS FALL IN COVENTRY - ENGLAND

C.B. BALDWIN HOST IN LIHUE, KAUAI (FROM THE GARDEN ISLAND NEWSPAPER.) Mr. And Mrs. Cedric B. Baldwin entertained at a poi supper Friday night honoring former Senator and Mrs. Ralph O. Brewster of Maine, who were their guests.

Advertisement: **THE LIBERTY HOUSE** - Gifts that sing of a Happier Christmas. Toy Shop, 3rd Floor. **BINGO BEDS** - Children from 18 months to 4 years gain muscular control and eye-coordination through pounding pegs squarely. $1.25

When Daddy and Grandma left our house, I started to wet my bed again. Gertrude warned me that Santa didn't fill stockings of boys who wet their beds. I tried everything to stop. I quit drinking water two hours before prayer time and stood in front of the toilet peeing at least ten times after dinner. I even sat down and had a serious talk with my peepee but my peepee wouldn't cooperate. I tried every suggestion that Mother and Hatsuko gave me to turn off my faucet, but at four a.m., a big yellow stain soiled my sheets. I was a hopeless case.

Santa made his home on the third floor at The Liberty House in 1940. Every Christmas, a fat Santa sat on a huge chair decorated in silver tinsel in the toy department, right next to the counter that sold Tootsie Toy cars. The way Santa faced his chair, there was no way for a child to avoid him. As much as I adored Santa Claus, I was deathly afraid to sit on his lap this year. I was afraid because last year, he asked me if I had been a good boy and I lied. I told him I had been the best little boy in the whole wide world.

That was a big lie. I lied because Agnes made me lie. This year, I knew he had checked his North Pole files on my lies and found out what a bad boy I had been last year and the year before that. With all the bad things I had done this past year, I was sure one of Santa's elves was going to put me in irons and ship me off on the Lurline to serve time in Alcatraz where Humphrey Bogart lived.

I was a thief, too. I stole a box of gold stars from Mr. Murray's Five and Dime store on Beretania Street. I wanted a box of gold stars so badly, I ached as I looked at them sitting on the counter. The boxes of stars were staring me in the face, waiting for me to stuff them in my pocket when no one was looking. I wanted the gold stars because every Friday my teacher, Miss Storey, licked them onto student's papers that she found perfect for that week. I was never perfect so I never had a star. Without gold stars, I considered myself stupid. Each week, I tried to be creative and make my schoolwork perfect. My school papers were messy, colorful, and as unreadable as a German secret code. Miss Storey shook her head, trying to make sense of my homework, and told me that deciphering hieroglyphics on an Egyptian tomb was duck soup compared to my scribbling.

"Percy," Miss Storey scolded, tapping a pencil on my head, "you have a mind that's not quite with us all the time. Where does it go to?" I couldn't answer her because I wondered that myself sometimes. I had a gypsy mind that had lots of fun, ran in circles but it never earned me any stars - blue, pink, silver, or gold. I wanted stars of any color to prove to Mother and Hatsuko that inside me shimmered a bright light and that I was smart like Marigold and Daddy.

In Murray's Five and Dime, Agnes told me that if I stole a box of gold stars, I could lick them onto my stupid Egyptian-looking papers and make myself look smart to the world. Agnes hissed into my ear, "With your own box of stars, you can come home from school, parade your papers around as if you were in a Judy Garland musical, and your mother and Hatsuko will think you're smarter than Marigold." While Agnes chattered into my ear, she kept looking around for something else to steal.

In my other ear, Gertrude said she was ashamed of me as I slipped a box of stars into my pocket when Mr. Murray was talking to Mother. Before we left, Mr. Murray, who lived on our hill, told me what a nice boy I was and gave me a bag of gumdrops and a blue pencil. He made me feel so bad that I never licked those stolen stars on anything except Mother's toilet paper. Walking out of the store, Gertrude had to have the last word and had the knack for making me feel like a criminal, warning, "Percy, now that you've become a thief, someday, mark my words, you're going to end up in an electric chair."

Feeling guilty, I hid the box of stars inside an old, discarded, ripped-up teddy bear. I found the forgotten box of stars a year later when a Japanese Zero shot bullets at me. You would think a person who was cursed wouldn't tempt fate.

Gertrude told me Santa knew a criminal on sight because criminals had shifty eyes. Gertrude cautioned me that one look into my eyes and Santa would know that I had made career out of lying, stealing and wetting my bed. I walked around the house practicing, keeping my eyes wide open so I wouldn't look shifty when I sat on Santa's lap. Worst of all, Gertrude snapped that Santa knows that I am a rotten bad boy because I broke the fifth commandment - "You told your father you hated him."

On the second day when Santa sat on his chair at Liberty House, wouldn't you just know it, Mother took me to see him. She needed a girdle. I told Mother to shop for her girdle while I visited with Santa by myself. The reason I told her that I didn't want her with me was because I wanted to tell Santa a secret - what to bring her for Christmas.

Mother believed me.

I was heading like a speeding train down into Hell. I lied because I didn't want Mother to hear Santa spill the beans that she harbored a criminal in her house and she should keep me on bread and water without mayonnaise for the rest of my life. I made sure Mother made her way into the girdle shop before I walked up to the third floor to sit on Santa's lap. Agnes and Gertrude watched me from the lingerie department.

Once on Santa's lap, one fatty sitting on another fatty, shaking with fright, I told him everything I wanted for Christmas in one quick breath before he could tell me what a bad boy I had been. I told him I wanted Daddy, Grandma and Uku back home, and then I told him that he had bad breath. I was surprised that he smoked cigarettes just like Mother and Daddy did. Up to then, I thought Santa Claus was a holy person. I considered Santa one of the special people who never peed or smoked, just like Jesus. I added in my next breath, as he coughed, that he should buy my Mother a new blue dress because yesterday I had ripped her favorite cocktail dress dancing the tango outside in her rose bushes.

Santa, after hearing my requests, paused, removed the eyeglasses from his nose, wiped them with a handkerchief, and took my hand. I thought to myself, "Here it comes. I'm off to prison." Santa surprised me and said kindly as a Santa is supposed to do, "Other than having your father, your grandma, and your dog back, and a new dress for your mother, what would you like?"

I was so taken by surprise by his question that I answered him, demonstrating with lots of hand flounces, "Oh, something simple. Lots of sparkles on it and a big bow at the neck and a bow in the back, right around here to match the front." I patted Santa's back all the while, demonstrating what the dress looked like. I continued, "High heels to match. A dress that Loretta Young would wear drinking a chocolate soda on Hollywood and Vine."

Santa put the glasses back on his face, patted my head, and asked, "Have you been a good boy this year?"

Now this had to be it! I gulped, quivering, because now I was sure Santa was going to call the police and send me to Alcatraz. Closing my eyes, I squeaked out an answer, and lied, "I have been the best little boy in the world."

"That's good," Santa replied, then took me off his lap and called, "Next!"

Walking out of the store, with Mother carrying a new girdle in a package, I felt strangely funny. Santa didn't know me.

Mother took in a boarder. The boarder rented Grandma's room for twenty dollars a month. She slept on the Captain's four-poster bed and her rent kept Hatsuko cooking our meals and a bottle of mayonnaise in the icebox. Betsy was a freshman at the University of Hawaii and cute as a button. She had just turned eighteen and was from Maui. She called herself a country bumpkin. I called her a hick to her face. Anyone from Maui had to be a hick.

Betsy was a romantic because she read *Modern Romance* magazines. She loved reading the magazine because she said all the love stories ended happily. Hatsuko said that was bunk. Hatsuko knew what she was talking about because I could tell Hatsuko was having a firsthand experience at a broken romance. Gertrude and Agnes observed that Hatsuko's romantic life ain't going too well because no one was walking out of her bedroom any more. I leaped around the house, singing "Brother, Can You Spare A Dime," because Hatsuko was mine again. Agnes, my expert on romance, told me sailors were not to be trusted because they wore tight pants.

Betsy believed everything I told her. When I lied that I had been to Hollywood and met Clark Gable, she swooned. Betsy was boyishly slim, had tiny chichis, was five-foot-two, and wore her brown hair in a pageboy like Ruby Keeler did. She was what "da big boys" at Punahou School called "a babe." What made her real cute was that she had a nose that turned up into the air. Her nose looked like she smelled a sweet flower all the time. I sighed when she first walked into our house because she looked like a 20th Century Fox movie starlet. I could forgive anyone for being a hick if they looked like a movie star.

On Saturday nights, Betsy sported a handsome part-Hawaiian boyfriend on her arm. He worked as a lineman for the Hawaiian Telephone Company. Marigold and I thought Jack was "the cat's pajamas" because he owned a motor scooter. He called it a putt-putt. It was a two-wheeler that made putt-putting sounds like Grandma poop poop POOP da pooped around the house.

At our pleadings as we almost ripped off his shirt, Jack would ride us around the neighborhood in turns on the back of his putt-putt. With my arms around his waist and a white scarf tied around my neck, I looked like the Red Baron, according to Gertrude. Jack would rip me full speed down Vancouver Street, turn around, and then zoom up as fast as he could, up and down our Rocky Hill. I'd scream all the way. Hatsuko said I looked like Isadora Duncan, the dancer, with my scarf flying in the air.

Riding on Jack's putt-putt was the bravest act of my life. It was death-defying because if I didn't hold onto Jack with all my might, I'd fall off and die. I'd splatter my head on the ground like a broken egg. I told Jack what I was thinking and he laughed as if I'd told him a funny joke. I told him I was serious. "It was no yolk" to me. He laughed harder at my "yolk" joke, giving himself a stomachache.

I thought, after riding a couple of times with Jack, that dying might be a plan I had been looking for to take the curse away. If I died, my death would solve everything. I wouldn't be cursed anymore and Daddy would come home. Grandma would sail back into our house and be the captain of our ship, and Mother and Marigold would be happy again, eating lamb chops. Riding on Jack's motor scooter, I began a preoccupation with death. I told Agnes and Gertrude that by letting go of Jack's back, I'd die quickly, as fast as I could snap a finger. I'd hit the ground so hard and so fast that I'd die on the spot and wouldn't feel a thing.

I wasn't afraid to die. I already knew about Mr. Death because I almost "kicked the bucket" twice from pneumonia before I was three. I remembered back to long nights under a tent trying to breathe in air. I recalled heaving in air with all my might as yellow goop kept piling up inside my lungs. I thought I was going to suffocate. Many times during those weeks of illness, my lungs as full as my piggy bank, I heard angels singing. Mother and Hatsuko, each hour, would warm my chest with love in the form of a mustard plaster. They were the ones who brought me back to life.

The nights held the worst memories. After midnight, my lungs became so sticky that I couldn't sleep. I couldn't call for help because I was out of breath and I didn't want to wake anyone. I'd lie still in bed and look up at the ceiling. The bathroom light would make fluttering patterns above me - ducks and chickens talking to one another. I was afraid to close my eyes and waited for the sun to rise to sleep.

Lying under the covers, I could hear Mother, Daddy and Marigold breathing softly. Their breathing made living seem so easy. On those nights, hearing them in the next room, I held tight to the sheets to keep something inside of me from floating up to join the ducks and the chickens on the ceiling. That's when I started to think about the curses in storybooks, but I knew a witch could never steal me away and throw me into an oven as long as Mother and Hatsuko were nearby.

Dying, splitting my head open, falling off Jack's motor scooter, seemed like a breeze compared to breathing with goop in my lungs. My death from falling off Jack's motor scooter became a movie I played in my imagination.

While I was in the midst of my death plan and her sailor had disappeared, Hatsuko and I saw Greta Garbo die in the movie *Camille*. Her death looked really great because handsome Robert Taylor mooned all over her as she said, coughing blood into a handkerchief, "Armand, I vant to be alone." She got her wish right away and died. I told Hatsuko, coming out of the movie, that if I was dying to please call Robert Taylor, long distance, and have him come to my house and moon over me. One thing troubled me though; I didn't think I could cough into a handkerchief with blood gushing out my mouth as pretty as Greta Garbo did it. I'd work on that.

Munching loudly like a cow chewing walnuts as she ate a Hershey bar, Hatsuko wept buckets as Garbo died in the movie. I thought if Hatsuko wept buckets over Garbo dying, what would she do when I died falling off Jack's putt-putt? She'd make a flood for sure and Noah would have to build another ark. As we got on the bus to go home, I asked Hatsuko that if I died, I would appreciate it if she didn't eat a Hershey bar until after they put me in the ground.

I got to love my death plan because I saw myself as the star of the funeral. I was the center of attraction in my coffin. I made my funeral into an MGM spectacle. I daydreamed about my funeral during school hours, in the bathtub, and lying on the grass with Agnes and Gertrude and looking up into clouds imagining that I was playing a harp in heaven. I gave up drawing wishing wells and drew funerals.

My funeral fantasy always opened up with a Busby Berkley spectacular dance number. Thousands of scantily dressed chorines danced on coffins, as a soulful ballad was sung by extras as they dug my grave near Hollywood and Vine. The opening number was performed with the biggest line-up of Hollywood stars, living and dead, praising me. Jean Harlow led the pack. She was dressed in a black negligee that blew in the wind, showing off her white chichis. All my funerals were lavish spectacles and shot in Technicolor.

Christmas approached.

My super-colossal funeral daydream came after I filled up on chocolate sodas at Bensen-Smith Drug Store with my father and Marigold. It was the first time I had seen Daddy since he took Grandma away. While driving us downtown, he told Marigold and me that he wanted to tell us why he left our home. I don't remember what he said, I only remember that I drank three chocolate sodas in a row. I drank the sodas as fast as I could, wanting to tell Daddy that I didn't hate him for life. I didn't open my mouth because I was afraid he was going to tell me that the reason he left our house was because of me. After Daddy brought us home, I dreamed the best funeral I had ever imagined. It was a major movie in my mind.

MY BEST FUNERAL: PRODUCED, DIRECTED, AND STARRING PERCY

CAMERA READY - TAKE ONE - ACTION:

After the credits rolled with PERCY, PERCY, PERCY written in large, bold letters, the funeral opened. The usual dance number began, but this time the chorines danced the Charleston on the coffins. They wore sparkly, black spangles and had wiggly worms on their white shorts. The chorines, in blond wigs, jumped off the coffins, wrapped their arms around each other, kicked up their legs, and sang, "We've Got A Crush on You - Percy-Pie."

After they finished their number and ran out crying, Ginger Rogers and her mother, Lela, led the congregation in belting out, "We're In the Money." Lela Rogers was a pushy Hollywood mother that I read about in Jimmy Fidler's column.

Stars in the front row were Robert Taylor gushing tears, Shirley Temple with her mouth shut, Dorothy Lamour wearing a sarong, Cary Grant and Randolph Scott in white bathing suits and holding hands, Rod LaRue cracking his whip, Gary Cooper plucking his eyebrows, Charlie Chaplin dressed as the tramp and eating a shoe, John Wayne with a cigarette hanging out of his mouth, the Marx Brothers setting fire to a lady, and Rita Hayworth showing her legs.

My relatives, wearing Adrian gowns, even the men, were forced to sit in the back pews because the church was so crowded. Adrian designed everyone's clothes at the funeral. He was known to dress Joan Crawford in football pads at MGM. Louis B. Mayer, the big daddy of the MGM studios, was the usher who kept my relatives from killing themselves because they were so crazy when they couldn't find seats. They stood in back weeping, tearing out their hair and pointing to my coffin. They wore green make-up because they were so jealous that I knew so many famous Hollywood people who sat in the front row. My cousins passed around rolls of toilet paper to wipe the tears from their eyes. Cousin Bessie carried on the loudest and disturbed everybody. Mother slapped her face and told her to quit showing off.

Hatsuko, dressed in a gold lame kimono, blew a gold whistle to start the relatives goose-stepping down the aisle in high heels to view my body. All the men wore high heels. They marched like Nazi soldiers to the commanding voice of Nelson Eddy singing, "Give me some men, some stout hearted men." As my relatives reached the coffin, they became whirling dervishes, heads rolling all around, and sang with Nelson and got really carried away. They circled around my coffin, singing hallelujah over my body. Agnes and Gertrude were in the coffin, singing hallelujah with them.

My corpse was beautiful, but put together with paste because my body had broken apart like Humpty Dumpty when I fell off Jack's scooter. Max Factor made up my face to look like Greta Garbo. My body lay in state on a magnificent platform and was dressed like a knight in golden armor. Gertrude insisted I looked like the *Man in the Iron Mask* character but without the mask. Prince Charming said I eclipsed Snow White in my magnificence.

Everyone wailed, tearing off their dresses, screaming, "Oh, Percy, PERRRRCY, what a brave boy he was and he even smiled when he fell off Jack's putt-putt." I overheard Cousin Bessie, still smarting from Mother's slap, whispering to Rita Hayworth, "It took three weeks for the City of Honolulu to clean up his brains off our street because his brains were so massive. I had to call the Board of Health because they smelled so awful. The smell was so strong it cured my cat of worms. My dear, you should have seen his guts, they were bigger than his brains. Bigger than King Kong."

Cousin Bessie climbed into my coffin, stood, turned to Mother so everyone could hear her and screamed, "Percy should be buried next to my darling Nana."

I pushed her out of the coffin and yelled, "NO! NO! GET OUT!"

Now standing in front of the coffin, Mother, my angel-defender, screamed back, wiping a tear from her eye, "NO, YOU OLD WITCH. YOU MEAN OLD WITCH, YOU HEARD HIM. GET OUT. YOU PUT THE CURSE ON HIM. IT WAS YOU THAT CURSED HIM."

Cousin Bessie jumped out of the coffin, wet her pants and fled screaming, taking Hunkacha with her. All the movie stars applauded.

Neither Daddy nor Grandma was at the funeral. I peeked. Marigold was. I found her weeping in the front row, sitting next to John Wayne, asking God to forgive her for hitting me on the head all the time. I prayed to God, in a humble prince-like way, to forgive her. God had a hard time making up his mind what to do, but I pleaded really hard. God made up His mind. There was a crack of thunder and Marigold turned into an angel and immediately married John Wayne.

As the daydream ended, before the closing credits were shown in my head and the words THE END appeared on my screen, a lavender cloud came out of the ceiling with Aunt Momi floating down, holding a wand. She peered into my coffin, waved the wand, and gasped, "The fat frog has turned into a handsome prince. Dying does wonders, jolljamit." Aunt Momi told Mother, taking some of Mother's toilet paper to wipe her tears away, "That's who he really was all the time - a handsome, slim prince, not a fat, ugly toad."

Mother broke into my daydream and called me in for dinner.

Gertrude and Agnes got sick and tired of my death daydreams and started calling me a baby. One afternoon, Gertrude pointed to a photograph in *Life* magazine. The photograph was of an abandoned Chinese baby boy sitting squat in the middle of a bombed-out street in Shanghai, alone and blackened by war. The baby was wailing for his mother, who was not in the picture. He cried as if a Japanese soldier had stuck a thousand bamboo sticks into his body. His mother must have died. A burned-out street, bomb craters, and smoking buildings were his playground.

Gertrude told me that death meant being alone - alone on earth without your mother or alone somewhere out in the sky - but ALONE. Death wasn't an MGM movie with kicking chorines and Rita Hayworth all around you. Death was ugly, lonely, lasting because once you died, there was no turning back.

"Listen, kiddo," said Gertrude, trying to sound like Aunt Momi and scaring me, "you'd better be sure you want to die because after you're dead, there may be no mayonnaise sandwiches, no Mother or Hatsuko to protect you. Death means going it alone or it means being abandoned like that baby in the picture without its mother. No kidding, kiddo, dying is the wrong way to go. Stay alive as long as you can because at least you know what you have - an egg salad sandwich for lunch, a roof over your head to keep the rain away, a mother, a friend, and a warm bed to snuggle in. Look for another way to get rid of the curse because I don't want to die with you. And anyway, being cursed is no big deal. Look around you, it seems that everyone in this world is a little bit cursed some of the time."

Gertrude's words confused me but the photograph of the little Chinese boy in *Life* magazine didn't. It scared me. It scared me so much that I changed my thoughts about dying. I decided to live forever so I could find out who cursed me and kill them. Cousin Bessie was a top contender. That picture told me without words that children can be abandoned, mothers are killed and death looked pretty awful, and Daddy said a war was coming right around our corner.

I packed some of my imaginary bags in a hurry and left those MGM daydreams behind and became a person who wanted to live forever. I threw the *Life* magazine into the garbage can. I now held onto an emotion that became my new companion and was as close to me as Agnes and Gertrude were. The companion's name was fear.

Gertrude, jumping up and down in my head, kept nagging me to find the curse, kill it, and make something of myself so she and I would live forever. Agnes, sitting in the dirt and buffing her nails, told me she didn't give a fig about this fear thing or that silly old curse. "Life is to be lived and that's that. Put the curse away."

I got on my knees in my bedroom and prayed to God to give me another plan to kill the curse, but in the meantime, please let something nice happen to me.

Then Hatsuko's sailor returned, walking down the driveway. God wasn't listening. Then I realized God had answered my prayers. He had brought an angel into my house. Her name was Betsy. She had come to stay in Grandma's bedroom.

It was Betsy who brought Alice Faye, the movie star, into my life. Alice Faye, on the screen, promised to take the curse away. I started a plan, a journey that Agnes said was sure to work. A plan, I thought, that would protect me from curses and witches and make me be remembered, loved and never abandoned for all eternity. Anyway, it was better than dying.

14

Alice Faye, the Movie Star

Betty Grable had legs. Alice Faye had a flat stomach. Alice Faye was more durable than Betty Grable because she sang like an angel, wore black ostrich feather hats, chewed gum, and looked rich. Alice hung diamonds as big as robin's eggs around her neck. Every week, an Alice Faye movie played in Honolulu. Betsy and I went gaga when *The Honolulu Advertiser* had pictures of Alice Faye.

The Honolulu Advertiser

Advertisement: **NESBITT BOTTLING CO. LTD.** Phone: 67674 Clayton St. **BOTTLERS AND DISTRIBUTERS OF NESBITT'S CALIFORNIA.** An orange drink to your content. Five cents for a Big Bottle. Pure Beverage - Made with Real Orange Juice...for flavor.

LOCAL ACADEMY OF ARTS HAS VARIED CULTURAL INTERESTS FOR EVERYONE
by Marvell Allison Hart

The existence of the Honolulu Academy of Arts, that familiar low, white building occupying the block on Beretania Street facing Thomas Square, must provide a pleasant surprise for the cultured visitors to Hawaii. It is the only art museum in the Islands. The Director, Mr. Edgar Craig Schenck, has been with the Academy since 1935. The staff assisting him, which in 1927 numbered only six, today has increased to 14 to meet the ever growing demand in the several fields of the museum's activities. Whereas in 1930, 14,817 people passed through the galleries, in 1940, the number increased to 96,399. The Academy of Arts was founded in 1922 by Mrs. Charles M. Cooke and incorporated under the name "Honolulu Museum of Art.

TOMORROW NIGHT - FIRST VUE 10:15
WAIKIKI Theater   Phone 9967

"The woman whose beauty had the world and its most famous men at her feet...yet who longed to love one man so madly nothing else in the world could matter."

Darryl F. Zanuck's **LILLIAN RUSSELL** with Alice Faye, Henry Fonda, Don Ameche, Edward Arnold, Warren William, Leo Carrillo - Songs old: "After the Ball is Over" "Rosie, You Are My Posie" "The Band Played On" and other Lillian Russell hits. A 20th Century-Fox Picture

HONOLULU PIG STEALING CASE IS CHARGED WITH A FAKE SQUEAL. THE PIG AND THIEF WERE IMPOSTERS.

Betsy became the focus of my attention. I had been formally banned by Cross-Eyed Mama from playing with Cynthia and Vinnie. I had dressed him up as Mae West and sent him home to get his mother's jewelry box. Cross-Eyed Mama bumped into Vinnie as he was walking out the kitchen door wearing her ruby necklace. After that, Cynthia and Vinnie were warned they'd be placed on a diet of bread and water for weeks if they so much as spoke a word to me. Cross-Eyed Mama now kept them locked in their bedrooms whenever she shopped or played the church organ.

I began to follow Betsy around the house as soon as she walked in the front door. Hatsuko had been exiled because she smelled of the sailor's after-shave again.

I loved to spy on Betsy on the afternoons when she and Jack smooched on the couch in the parlor. I dressed up as Mata Hari, the World War I spy, and lurked behind doors like a secret agent. I mascaraed my eyes to look like a raccoon and wore a black scarf around my face so the lovers wouldn't see me. I always carried a pad and pencil in my hand. Hiding behind a potted plant, I wrote up every kiss they smacked and printed as fast as I could every "lovey-dovey" word they uttered to each other.

Betsy caught me behind the palm taking notes and forced a deal on me. If I would quit spying on her and cease leering at her through Daddy's binoculars as she dressed, she'd tell me on Saturday mornings about all the new films she and Jack previewed on Friday nights at the Waikiki Theater. For a movie-struck kid who loved movies as much as he did mayonnaise, that was a terrific bargain, even for a spy.

Gertrude, disgusted, said I'd never make a great Mata Hari because great spies never took bribes. All great spies never squealed on each other, kept their allegiance to their country and, if caught spying, were happy to be shot to death in front of a firing squad. I told Gertrude that I may not be a great spy but I was a good spy because I knew about my neighbors' drunken parties, their fights at breakfast, babies born at Kapiolani Maternity Hospital, and what the crazy people on our hill did at night.

Hatsuko was sick. She had an upset tummy all the time. She stayed in her room for days and never went to the movies. Betsy and Mother took turns cooking. Mother was a terrible cook because she was always in a hurry. The only dish she knew how to make was something mysterious baked in a casserole crunched with potato chips. To eat it, I pretended I was feasting on mayonnaise.

Mother took a second job teaching English to Japanese ladies. She took the job "to make ends meet" and was away from home on Monday evenings and Saturday mornings. Mother gave me permission to go to the movies by myself on the weekends. I had convinced her that I was old enough to ride a bus by myself because Joan Crawford danced the Charleston at age eight, Hitler shoveled snow at age six and George Washington, the Father of our Country, took out his father's garbage at seven. Percy, going on eight, could take the bus by himself. Mother laughed and let me go to the movies alone.

Twenty cents stuffed in my pocket, riding the bus in bare feet, on Saturday and Sunday afternoons, I went to the movies. I was scared at first, but in a couple of Saturdays, I became a familiar sight riding the bus to Waikiki. I began to think myself big stuff because I didn't know any other seven-year-old who went to the movies all by himself. I'd prance up to the bus, hop on, and pretend I was King Arthur's horse in search of a new movie.

The Waikiki Theater became my church. Sitting in the front row, I worshiped God for two hours. In His church, I forgot that I was fat, cursed and without a father. It was in the movies that I learned what God did to other people. Movies were more religious to me than coloring Bible pictures at Central Union Church's Sunday school. The only thing I liked doing in Sunday school was coloring Adam's fig leaf different colors. Bette Davis, Greta Garbo, and Katherine Hepburn taught me more about what a woman did to a man than hearing Miss Jones, my Sunday school teacher, read to me that Delilah gave Samson a haircut.

Waikiki Theater, my movie temple, had whitewashed walls on its sides that held back a Tarzan-like jungle of papiermache coconut, banana and papaya trees. Bright, nail-polish red crepe-paper bougainvillea splashed over the white walls, looking like a frozen flock of red butterflies. I worshipped my God on those matinee afternoons in His Garden of Eden.

A massive Robert Morton organ was centered on the floor below the movie screen. My God had to have music. When the organ played, all the keys lit up like a multi-colored Christmas tree. Mr. Sautelle, the organist, looked like St. Peter and acted like the crazy Mad Hatter when he played the ivory keys and his feet pumped the pedals. He was God's head angel. Mr. Sautelle played an hour before God dimmed the house lights and announced the movie had started with a newsreel. Mr. Sautelle took requests. I ran down the aisle with other barefooted children to whisper into his ear my favorite song. I always requested a Bobby Breen tune.

At that moment, Bobby Breen was a twelve-year-old RKO singing movie hero of mine. He sang falsetto and had recently starred in a singing/adventure movie set in the Islands titled *Hawaii Calls*. The film was shot on Oahu and Maui.

Hatsuko was furious that Hollywood hadn't called me to star in the movie. Before the movie was shot, across the front page of *The Honolulu Advertiser* splashed a large photograph of Bobby in a white suit, arriving on the Lurline. I was so depressed looking at the photograph that I ate half a bottle of mayonnaise in one afternoon. Hatsuko tore out the picture and thumbtacked it above my bed. She said it was to inspire me to become as famous as Bobby. Instead, the photograph made me think bad thoughts of drowning him in a sea of sharks with Hatsuko's sailor. I wanted to be the photograph and sign it - "To Bobby. Wish you were ME. I hope you make it big someday like ME. Percy." I was jealous of Bobby Breen.

Betsy was late coming to breakfast to keep our bargain. I had finished eating scrambled eggs, crisp bacon, a waffle, and had shoved my orange juice aside. I roamed from chair to chair and looked out the window, trying to keep my mind occupied. Hatsuko was out of bed, cooking breakfast, but seemed in an awful rush. She had cleared my plate and didn't even ask if I wanted any more scrambled eggs.

Going back into the kitchen, she ordered, "Drink your orange juice if you want hair on your chest." I yelled back to her that I didn't want to look like King Kong. I hated Hatsuko's orange juice. She filled it every morning with cod-liver oil. It was a hand-me-down recipe from her father in Japan. I told her it was really invented by Tojo to kill little fat, white boys. I pleaded with Hatsuko I'd even give up being another Bobby Breen if she'd just let me off the cod-liver oil for at least one morning a week.

The ship's clock struck eight bells.

I wanted to throw the orange juice into Marigold's face when she walked into breakfast. A dangerous thought. I was bored waiting for Betsy. Marigold slid into her seat happy as a lark because she was going to be with Daddy all day. I hadn't been invited to go along because they were attending wrestling matches, and wrestling matches, according to Marigold, were only for grown-up people.

Hatsuko placed a bowl of Wheaties in front of my sister. She ate the cereal in three seconds and then picked up the funnies without looking at me or saying a polite "good morning." I was itching to throw the orange juice all over her head. My hands trembled on the glass, ready to make the toss. Hatsuko peeked through the kitchen door, saw what was going through my head and commanded, "Drink."

I drank the poison. Hatsuko saved my life again.

Marigold started humming like an annoying bee. I made a Frankenstein monster face at her to make her stop humming. She kept on humming. I moaned and made monster sounds. "GRRRRRR!" She sang a song I hated, "I'm an old cowhand, from the Rio Grande."

I yelled at her, "BOOOOOO! I HATE THAT SONG."

She pushed her face further into the funnies. I stuck out my tongue at the newspaper. I drooled on the table. She shook her newspaper as if she was getting rid of a fly and ground her teeth.

Betsy was still sleeping in Grandma's bed.

I WAS BECOMING ANNOYED WITH EVERYONE.

I kicked the dining room table leg in loud beats. Kick! Kick! Kick!

Marigold put down the paper and commanded like a general, "Percy, stop kicking. Can't you see I'm reading the funnies? I can't concentrate with you making faces, drooling on the table and kicking the table! NOW STOP IT!" She went back to reading the comics and again sang the song I hated.

I kicked the table again.

"PERCY." She put down the newspaper again and gave me killer eyes and warned, "You're annoying me. You know what happens to you when you annoy me." She wiggled her fingers, making them into crab-like pincers.

"What?" I asked innocently.

"Death!"

I picked a goober out of my nose and kicked the table leg again.

"You're disgusting. Wipe your nose. One more kick and you'll wish you never lived because I'm going to tickle you to death. I'll make you suffer like you've never suffered before."

I hated her tickling fingers. I put my head down, and this time I tapped the table leg but just slightly. My foot hardly made a sound.

But Marigold heard it. She put her paper down and got up slowly like an awakened mummy. She was serious. I was in trouble because Hatsuko had slammed the kitchen door and gone to her room. My bodyguard had deserted me.

I raised my hands and sputtered, "I didn't do it. I didn't do it! Promise. I was just kidding. I surrender. I surrender. I surrender. Promise I won't do it again. Please don't tickle me. Please. Marigold, I quit. I quit. I promise. Promise. Promise."

"Promise?" Marigold snarled.

"Promise!" I said meekly, but my fingers were crossed under the table. "Marigold?" I said as she sat down again, "Betsy's not out yet."

"I know that." Marigold made kissing sounds with her lips, imitating what she thought Betsy and Jack did the night before. Marigold was an awful kisser for an old person. Her kisses sounded the way cowboy movie star Tom Mix kissed his horse, Tony, on the lips. But her "smmmmmmmmmmmmmicks" brought Betsy out of her bedroom.

Betsy staggered into the dining room. She didn't look a bit like the starlet this morning because her nose drooped toward the floor. She plopped down into her seat and gasped, "COFFEE - BLACK."

I went into the kitchen, brought out the pot and poured her coffee.

Marigold made one more kissing sound - smick - smick, as Betsy took a sip of the coffee and took the front page of *The Advertiser* away from Marigold.

"Oh, that was you, Marigold. I thought a bullfrog was mating in the dining room," Betsy said.

I shrieked with laughter and rolled all over the dining room floor at Betsy's joke. Marigold ran around the table and pinched me on my arm while she hit my head. I stood up, sat down, stuck out my lower lip, and pouted. Marigold and Betsy laughed, thinking Marigold had silenced me good. They both started to read the newspaper again.

THEY WEREN'T PAYING ATTENTION TO ME so I began an attack on Betsy. "Welllll, Betsy!" I leered, twitching my eyebrows up and down like Groucho Marx.

"Well what, Percy?" A voice came from behind the newspaper.

"What did you and Jack do last night?"

Putting down the funnies, Marigold got into the act. "Yea, what did you and Jack do last night?"

Betsy had little experience with brats before she came to our house. Her only experience with brats had been watching bulls snort at sweet-tempered cows in her father's dairy pasture. When she first arrived at our home, she didn't have a clue on how to protect herself from experienced gun fighters who dueled to the death every morning at breakfast. I thanked God a new victim to terrorize had arrived because our own battles had become stale and I lost most of them. I figured now that Betsy was in Grandma's room, the heat was off. Betsy, to my disappointment, became a fast learner. Within days, she caught on how to protect herself by bribing us with rides on Jack's putt-putt. We surrendered easily.

Once, eavesdropping in my Mata Hari outfit, I overheard Betsy talk on the phone with her mother on Maui. She told her mother that Marigold and I were the most horrible children she had ever met and made her want to get out of our house as soon as she could afford to, get married to Jack and never have babies. If Jack didn't ask her to marry him soon, she was going to become a nun.

So much for Betsy's sincerity. Nobody was anybody whom they pretended to be.

Taking a big gulp of black coffee, Betsy put the newspaper down and smiled at us. "Well, good morning, you two. You want to know all the details of what Jack and I did last night?"

We jumped to the bait and responded, "YES!"

"You really want to know?" After she dropped that bomb to silence us, she paused, sipped her coffee, and looked at us, smug as Uku chewing on a bone, and continued. "Will you two be good if I tell you and leave me alone today? I have a terrible headache." She popped two aspirins into her mouth. She took another pause to let the aspirins take hold in her head. The silence gave us time to think what to reply because we had a hard time being good.

I finally said, "Yes," as I crisscrossed my feet and fingers under the table. My feet and fingers crossed meant to me that I wasn't lying when I was really lying. Crossed feet and fingers took away the lie.

Marigold, who lived her life like a true-blue honest John Wayne cowboy, uttered under her breath, "Maybe."

Satisfied we were under control, Betsy took another gulp of black coffee and another aspirin and said, "Jack and I saw the most romantic movie I have ever seen in my whole life last night."

"Ohhhhhhhhhhhh," I wailed. Betsy was heaven's angel and worth waiting for.

"Is that all?" Marigold jumped up and stalked bowlegged out of the house to find Jimmy to play a game of two-man baseball before Daddy arrived. Marigold thought that only John Wayne, Gene Autry and Roy Rogers movies playing at the Palace Theatre on Beretania Street were worth seeing. Those movies were for he-men. Romantic movies were mushy ones for silly girls. The Waikiki Theater, as far as Marigold was concerned, showed only mushy movies for sissies.

I was a sissy and a mushy movie fan. As Marigold slammed the front door, I yelled out to her, "Say hello to Daddy for me." I turned to Betsy and mooned like a sissy, "Tell me, what was the rooomantic movie about?"

Sipping her coffee, looking dreamy eyed, Betsy gazed out the window. "It was really romantic romantic, Percy. I cried at the end when Alice Faye and Henry

Fonda kissed."

"Okay, you cried. Now tell me, what was the movie about?" I said, drumming my fingers on the table.

"Alice Faye - she was the star and played a famous actress called Lillian Russell." Looking dreamy-eyed again, she went on, "Lillian Russell was really talented and all the rich, powerful men in the world adored her and gave her thousands of dollars worth of diamonds hidden in huge baskets of flowers in her dressing room every night after she sang. She always had men around who loved her because she was the most beautiful, rich, talented, and famous woman in the whole world."

Taking another sip of her coffee, she looked out into space and dreamed about the diamond bracelets in baskets of flowers. Looking at her, I bet she wished Jack was rich and famous and was able to give her "oodles" of diamonds. All I ever saw Jack give her was a grungy bracelet made out of castor beans. When she showed off the bracelet to me, I commented, "That's what you get for dating a poor man - a bean bracelet from a man who's working at the Hawaiian Telephone Company."

After trying on the bracelet, I advised her, "Betsy, you can do better than Jack, even if he has a putt-putt. Date a man who drives a Packard and that way you won't get your hair wet all the time going to movies."

Betsy grabbed the bracelet off my arm and sniffed, "Percy, you wouldn't know true love even if it smacked you on your head." That was true. I had been smacked on my head a lot of times and it never felt like true love - it just hurt.

After Betsy finished her coffee, she got up, wiped her mouth with a napkin, took another aspirin, and went back to bed for the day.

I was left alone.

Lillian Russell, the movie Betsy cried over, didn't sound that promising, but a movie is a movie is a movie. I rode the bus that afternoon and headed for the matinee at the Waikiki Theater. After seeing the movie, I was hooked on Alice Faye. I was certain she was going to help drive the curse away from my home.

15

Lillian Russell

I was hooked on Alice Faye. I almost wasn't hooked because an amazon nearly killed me inside the Waikiki Theater.

I arrived late as Mr. Sautelle ended his organ recital. The electric rainbow encircling the screen began to dim. It was God's signal that the movie was about to begin. As the strands of the rainbow grayed, the theater darkened. I sat on the aisle in the second row, my favorite seat. When it became night in the theater, a flock of fake, fleecy, white clouds floated across the blue velvet ceiling above me.

I looked up at my theater heaven and spoke to God, "Hi God! How are you today? I like it here better than being with Marigold and Daddy, even if they didn't ask me. If dying is going to the movies, God, take me up to St. Peter's gate. But if there are no movies in heaven, forget it, God, because I want to stay here and that's the truth. I hope in Heaven, God - please, please have movies, chocolate ice cream, Best Foods mayonnaise, and tuna sandwiches every day for all your angels and good little boys. I'm trying to be good, God, and please forget about the harp playing business for me because I can't play the piano. Harp playing looks very boring."

I waited to hear God speak back to me. He did. The screen flickered and a black and white rooster standing on a globe crowed, and Pathe News was on the march. Hitler greeted Mussolini as he stepped off a plane.

"Cock-a-doodle-doo." I entered God's "pearly gates."

I had to pee. I hated it when that urge hit me in the movies. Today, it made me mad because if I went to the bathroom, I'd miss the cartoon. I ran up the aisle as fast as I could, already leaking, but I made it just in time to unbutton my pants and spill into the urinal. At other matinees with Hatsuko, I held it because the movie was too exciting to leave, despite the pressure that was building down by my peepee. In those matinees, I wet my pants, especially if the movie had Abbott and Costello in it. I'd walk behind Hatsuko, sticking to her like peanut butter, to hide my stain when we exited into the bright sunlight. Now, I was by myself, so I couldn't take any chances.

A regiment of local high school beauties, dressed in white slacks with royal Hawaiian red sashes wrapped around their waists, ushered at the Waikiki Theater. I thought these Hawaiian girls had the most perfect job on earth, better than being

President Roosevelt, because they got to see MGM movies free.

I was scared of these beauties because they acted like soldiers who dug fox-holes at Schofield Barracks. They looked tough, muscular, mean, even though most of them were as pretty as Dorothy Lamour. I did admire the way they snapped theatre tickets out of your hand like the military police at Pearl Harbor. Heaven help the stragglers who came in late because these girls could give them the worst "stink eye" in Hawaii.

After I peed and came out of the bathroom, a huge line-up of latecomers milled around the lobby. The girls were scurrying around trying to handle them and were giving everyone the stink eye. Agnes whispered that this was my chance to do something good for God and to show the Consolidated Amusement Company that I could be a future usher. I would have done anything - even drink cod liver oil straight - to be an usher at the Waikiki Theater for life and see MGM movies free. I would have given up mayonnaise for a day for the job and here before me was my chance.

I found a pencil flashlight lying on the floor near one of the entrance doors. I picked it up and found next to me a sweet, elderly Japanese couple waiting to be seated. I went up to them acting as if I was starring in *Hitler's Children* with mean movie actress, Bonita Granville. Flexing my muscles, trying to act like one of the tough usherette beauties, I waved the flashlight at the couple. I told them gruffly in a George Sanders German Gestapo accent, "Vell, may I help you? Vhy are you late, mien herrs? Don't you know you are going to be a big nuisance? Now, we are going to have to disturb all the good people who came on time. Shame on you. Follow me."

They marched meekly behind me to one of the entrance doors. I turned around and spoke to them like an army general bucking up his soldiers, "Now, before we go in, let's pretend we are in an Errol Flynn movie. Crouch down so no one can see us coming in. Let's pretend we're guerillas hiding from the Nazis. No noise - not one peep." I put my finger to my lips and uttered a long "SHHHHHH!"

I beckoned them to follow me and we entered the darkened theater. The old couple crouched so low their noses almost touched the carpet. Down the aisle, we crept. I waved the pencil flashlight all over the theater, shining it into everyone's eyes, looking for seats. Stalking down to the fifth row, I saw the previews were about to begin. I loved the previews of coming attractions better than the cartoons. I stopped at the row. It was filled except for two empty seats smack in the middle.

I ordered the man on the aisle seat to tell everyone to move down and fill up the empty seats. He protested.

I told him, "Look behind me." When he did, I told him it was Jeanette MacDonald and Nelson Eddy in from Hollywood. Luckily for me, it was dark. I snarled in a loud voice, "Move it or I'll report you to the governor and he will send you to Oahu prison for life." The whole row got up in unison and filled in the empty seats. As the two elderly folks, red with embarrassment, sat down, a hot hand grabbed the back of my shirt and dragged me up the aisle.

Lokilani was the general in charge of the ushers. She was the biggest "tita" I had ever seen in my whole life. A tita is a local tough girl who beats up on boys and especially fat, little white boys.

Out in the lobby, I had to think fast because I could see I was in danger of not seeing the movie. Agnes and Gertrude had deserted my head and fled to the powder room to sit on the john. I looked up at Lokilani. She had arms and breasts as big as my stomach. She slapped my head and yelled, "Eh brah, what you tink you doing in there? Dats my job. You one big fat haole nuisance. I'm gonna kick your ass out of here."

Figuring I was about to die, I gave her my sweetest smile, and said, "Miss, I was only trying to help you because you were all so busy in here and because my uncle wanted me to seat Jeanette MacDonald and Nelson Eddy in their seats." I repeated, "I was just trying to help you and you were so busy."

Lokilani had flames coming out of her ears like a blowtorch. Luckily for me, she hadn't seen the Japanese couple closely enough to know that I was lying. Even so, I thought she was going to punch me with her big Popeye arms. I stammered, blinking my eyes, waiting for the fatal blow, "I'm very sorry if I caused you any trouble, Miss. May I go back to join Jeanette and Nelson?"

I started to slither away. She grabbed me again, squinted her eyes into slits and barked like a mad German Shepherd dog, "You sure dats dem?"

I crossed my fingers and said meekly, "Do I look like a person who would lie to a nice person like you?" I took a big chance saying that because her arms were over me like she was going to chop off my head. I fell down on my knees to pray before she could hit me. After all, this was God's church, and she couldn't kill me if I was praying.

I looked up at her and pleaded, repeating, "Do I look like a person who would lie to you? You look like the nicest person in the world." My eyes began to blink out of control. My eyes always went haywire when I lied BIG.

"You sure dats the trut?" Lokilani barked, punching me on my head like a hammer hitting a nail.

"Yes. And quit hitting me," I screamed. I got up off my knees, rubbing my head, and said I was sure, and she could call up my uncle, Governor Poindexter, if she thought I was lying. As soon as I mentioned Governor Poindexter, Lokilani's eyes blinked faster than mine because she believed me. According to local beliefs, all white people were related, rich and missionaries. Seeing that I might be part of the enemy, Lokilani turned to one of her lieutenants and growled, "Couldn't you just kill this fat haole?"

I pulled out of my pants my last box of jujubes as a peace offering. From that moment on, Lokilani and I became friends. At Sunday school, Jesus taught me the way to win people over is to feed them Love's bread and tuna fish sandwiches when they got cranky. Eating food, I observed, always made cranky people smile, even Marigold.

Lokilani escorted me back to my seat. A smelly old man now sat in my aisle seat. He stank of stale beer. I stepped on his toes as hard as I could as I wiggled past him, signaling that he was sitting in my seat. As I sat down, hoping Loki would hear me, I said, "Hi, Uncle Nelson and Auntie Jeanette." After hearing that, Loki seemed satisfied and walked back up the aisle now that Mr. Haole Nuisance was out of her way.

As I looked up at the screen, the old stinky man next to me put his hand on my knee and said, "Hi, kid. Wanna drink? Which am I, Nelson or Jeanette?"

I told him right off, "Don't touch me again, stinkpot. I almost got killed and I just peed in my pants." He clutched his paper bag to his chest and fled to the back of the theater to bother someone else. I moved over and took back my seat. In life, I told God who was hiding up in the ceiling with fake clouds, one never knows what's going to happen when you're minding other people's business.

Alice Faye on the screen, as Betsy promised, was gorgeous, dripped diamonds, and the whole world fell at her feet because her character Lillian Russell was so loved, talented and beautiful. The movie, *Lillian Russell*, became my roadmap to what fame and fortune could do for me. Being famous and talented could protect a fat little boy from being abandoned, cursed and not loved. I saw what a beautiful life I could have on a "yellow brick road" lined with Lillian Russell diamonds if I turned into a movie star like Alice Faye. I saw that afternoon what Hatsuko had been telling me for years while I ate her egg salad sandwiches: being a famous movie star, nobody would hit you on your head ever again. Hatsuko and Mother would never leave me, and everybody in the world would love me to death. Even Daddy, Marigold and Grandma would take me sailing in their ships. I yearned to be adored by everyone in the whole world because by being adored, I would not be a cursed boy.

I wanted to be Lillian Russell.

I wanted to be Alice Faye. I wanted to sing "After the Ball" with a hundred dancers waltzing around me. It was the song Alice Faye sang at the end of *Lillian Russell*. I wanted to wear Alice Faye's huge black hat of ostrich feathers and become her.

At Saturday matinees, I would now ask Mr. Sautelle to play on his organ "After the Ball." Bobby Breen songs were thrown in the trashcan. I exiled Bobbie Breen that afternoon out of my life as easily as I scratched other people out of my life because they hurt me, or said a cruel word, or made a fat joke at my expense. My father had been dismissed from my world by a slap of his hand.

As quickly, they - Daddy, friend or actor, were resurrected in my world by a show of kindness. Sometimes, I didn't remember why my friend or actor had been exiled in the first place. Like the stars on the screen, my friends, Hatsuko and Daddy never knew they had been exiled or carved out of my movie-playing mind. Only I, hoarding the heartaches and the list of wounds inside me, knew.

Approaching my eighth birthday, my list of discarded people rivaled Madame LeFarge's long knitted scarf of the doomed aristocrats sentenced for the guillotine in Dickens' *A Tale of Two Cities*. It was a tale I knew by heart because Grandma told me that story over and over again, and I saw the movie with Ronald Coleman in it. I learned by giving an easy smile, a "glad to see you" look, I could hide the real truth of what went on inside my mind. Hatsuko never really did die as one of the stars in my movie.

The Sunday after seeing *Lillian Russell*, Betsy became engaged to Jack. Jack sold his putt-putt and bought Betsy a secondhand two-door Chevy as an engagement present. Checking out the car that Betsy now parked in front of our house, I spotted three big rusted dents on the back right fender of the car. I proudly pointed the dents out to Betsy.

"You have dents. We don't have any dents on our car," I said snottily.

Betsy turned red and sputtered, "Even if my car is dented, Percy, it's better than any old engagement ring. Don't you think so?"

I didn't say anything because I would have preferred a large diamond ring.

Raising her voice because I hadn't said anything, Betsy demanded, "DON'T YOU THINK SO? I love dents on a car, Percy. Dents are precious to me as Jack's heart. Dents give my car character and who would want anything absolutely perfect? I have Jack, and he loves me, and that's as perfect as I want it to get. Who loves you, Percy? Right now I don't find you a bit lovable and I once thought you were my friend." She sounded like one of the girls in her *True Romance* magazine.

Betsy slapped me on the head and ran up the steps to the front door. She turned around, tears in her eyes, and cried, "And Mr. Smarty-pants Percy, now I can go to the movies without getting rained on. Don't you forget that and you can't. You have to go to the movies all by yourself by bus and you'll always get wet. And anyway, who wants you to go with them? I know I don't. Hatsuko doesn't. And as far as I am concerned, right now, I think you are acting like a spoiled, rude, fat little boy. I wanted you to like my car. You're going to end up with nobody liking you." She ran into the house sobbing.

I wished Jack had given her a diamond bracelet.

I knew Betsy was mad at me when she called me fat. She never did that before. She told the truth: I was fat and I did get rained on going to the movies. She had another point; I shouldn't bust other people's bubbles when people are happy and I'm not. It was mean of me to point out the dents, and I should have told her I loved her car. When I heard her slam her bedroom door, I said a little prayer that I hoped that when Betsy walked down her yellow brick road with Jack, she'd be as rich and famous as Lillian Russell so that she wouldn't curse me again. I was going to tell her at dinner that even with the dents on her car, she had started down the yellow brick road, even though the bricks on her road were small.

Flash! Agnes put a thought in my head. Maybe Jack put a diamond bracelet in the glove compartment, waiting for Betsy to discover it. "Wouldn't that be nifty!" I told myself.

Searching through Betsy's car's glove compartment, I couldn't find a diamond bracelet or even piece of jewelry made out of cheap castor beans. I couldn't find one darn thing worth giving to Lillian Russell, just a crumpled pack of cigarettes and a pack of colorless balloons. No wonder Betsy cried.

I missed Jack's putt-putt.

I thought to myself that I was growing up because I could ride the bus alone and I could defend myself from being killed by an amazon. I even claimed back my aisle seat from beer-stinking hoboes and now I had a plan to get rid of the curse that someone laid on me. I was also tired of making other people and myself unhappy by doing and saying stupid things.

Gertrude told me to apologize to Betsy, and that I was out of my mind with my new plan to become Alice Faye. Agnes the happy was ecstatic and sang la, la, la in my mind. Agnes and I had walked down the same yellow brick road ever since we met.

I was determined to dump the ever-present pest - fear in my head. I didn't need anyone to tell me anymore that I couldn't do anything, be anything, just because I was little, wore pink nail polish and was fat. I didn't need Mother, Hatsuko, Marigold, Daddy, or Grandma to tell me what to do anymore. I could take care of myself. It was me who gave his last box of jujubes to Lokilani to keep from being killed, and it was me who was riding a bus by all by himself, and it was me who was acting like a grown-up and telling people they had dents. I walked back into the house trying to puff out my chest further than my fat stomach because I had become a big cheese.

The Advertiser said it was fourteen days till Christmas. *The Advertiser* should have headlined it was twelve months before a war erupts in my backyard, when all the things I feared came true.

My bravery was short lived because fear stuck to me as my third companion. Everyday, it played "Ring around the Rosy" with Agnes and Gertrude in my head.

16

Silent Night

The curse struck me under a Christmas tree. I should have known something was up the day the curse hit because everybody around my house was again being too nice; even Marigold woke up smiling. That morning in the newspaper, I read the following.

The Honolulu Advertiser

MESSAGE FROM THE EMPEROR

His Majesty Emperor Hirohito delivered his message to the War Minister Lieut. Gen. Hedeki Tojo, after the military review, held on the Yoygi parade grounds, Tokyo, to mark the 2600 anniversary of the founding of the Japanese empire.

Advertisement: **CHRISTMAS AT GUMPS**

Square Chinese porcelain low teak stands $2.50 each
Eyeglass and lorgnette cases in Oriental brocade $5.00 each
Crystal swans $3.75 each

NAVY BUILDING IN FULL SWING

At year's end, 1940, Hawaii is probably the busiest microcosm in the complex structure of expanding national defense. And probably the busiest sector on this peace-time defense is Pearl Harbor, where millions of dollars are going into barracks, housing, guns, and ships.

Advertisement: **PAINS AFTER EATING? INDIGESTION? LIVERISHNESS?**
HERE'S THE WAY TO QUICK RELIEF

Take two teaspoons full of PHILLIP'S MILK OF MAGNESIA in a glass of water 30 minutes after eating. Relief comes almost instantly - usually in just a few minutes. Nausea, fullness, and acid indigestion quickly disappear. You feel like a new person.

U.S. NOW SOPRANO LILY PONS' "OWN SWEET HOME."

New Haven, Conn. Singer Lily Pons today renounced her French citizenship and became an American. "Now," she said, "I'll sing Home Sweet Home with new meaning because I am an American."

L. KWAI YOW & CO.

Corner of Waialae & Koko Head   Phone 77502 - 76328
BEST FOODS MAYONNAISE
Per quart...............47c
Per pint.................28c
Per 1/2 pint.............23c
VAN CAMP PORK AND BEANS   16oz tin 3 for 23c

Advertisement: **FOR A NOONDAY FEAST OR A MIDNIGHT SNACK! HEINZ COOKED SPAGHETTI** Made by Our Own Chef and Generously Topped With A Spicy Heinz-Tomato Sauce —-Is A Delicious, Quick-To-Fix Mainstay For Luncheons and Supper!

I learned the passage of time by the holidays celebrated at school. After Labor Day, school began. After Lei Day (May 1st) and before Memorial Day (May 30th), somewhere in between, school ended. In between Labor Day and January first, I had a two-week Christmas vacation. Before that, I had two days off to eat turkey at Thanksgiving. Before Thanksgiving, somewhere in October, I celebrated Christopher Columbus Day. After New Year's Day, I had three months before I hunted colored Easter eggs under coconut trees. In February, I celebrated two presidents' birthdays. Every year, I kissed Lincoln's and Washington's faces in my history books for giving me the two days off.

I told my first grade teacher that if I was the president of the United States, I'd declare a long holiday in April in my honor - at least a week - and make a proclamation: "I hereby make a holiday in honor of Percy, president of the United States, president of the Alice Faye fan club and president of mayonnaise lovers of the whole world."

There were not many holidays in spring. I counted them on one hand. I looked forward to the end of May, because I had three months off in the summer to be free. But from September to May, time passed as slowly as a turtle dragging himself down Kalakaua Ave. From Labor Day on, I wanted to beat up the old turtle to move it along faster. By May, I had lost my patience with slow poke time and turned grumpy. When summer vacation began, the days whizzed by. The turtle turned into a flying fish. Before I knew it, Mother bought me new clothes and colored pencils to start school all over again. I told Gertrude that God had really messed up time. He should have made time pass quickly during the school year and really slowly from June to August. God forgot what it was like to be a little boy and created time only for grownups.

Now the time was for Christmas vacation, Santa Claus and Christmas trees.

I loved Miss Storey, my first grade teacher, even though she never gave me a gold star once. When Miss Storey had her back to the window in the sunlight, she glowed like an angel. I flunked her first grade because I had pneumonia two times. Miss Storey had me from September to May, twice. She was "my first - grade teacher - my *first - grade* teacher." When I said that out loud, she blushed; I was her favorite failure.

By the way Miss Storey touched me on my head, I knew she loved children. After I saw *Lillian Russell*, I knew why I loved her. Miss Storey looked exactly like Alice Faye. Miss Storey was a perfect teacher because she never lost her temper when I made my P's backward or changed my numbers all around the paper. She always said when correcting my letters and numbers that I was improving, but I had to concentrate and to keep on trying. I didn't tell her that my backward P's and D's looked perfectly fine to me, and my numbers stood exactly where they should have been in the first place. I didn't say anything because I didn't want to hurt her feelings because Miss Storey didn't see the world as God created it for me. I didn't want to cause tears in her beautiful blue eyes and make her think she was living in a crazy world because all D's should have been backwards.

Miss Storey giggled when I pleased her. Her giggle sounded like a Japanese glass chime blowing in the wind. I was never bashful in her class and never sat on my hands. I was one of the few students who raised a hand with questions. Miss Storey said she liked when I did that, but when I put my hand up too many times, asking too many questions, hogging the attention, Miss Storey told me to put my hand down and let Wigay have a chance. She never hurt my feelings because she knew that I loved Wigay better than anyone else in my class. I drew pictures when we had to add and subtract numbers. I drew pretty women with large blue eyes, blond hair and big bazooms. Miss Storey had big blue eyes, blonde hair and tiny bazooms.

Christmas vacation was about to begin because Miss Storey pinned a cardboard Santa Claus on the bulletin board. She told us that we were going to have a Christmas party. It was my second Christmas party in Miss Storey's class. At her Christmas party she gave us each a box of crayons and a drawing pad. I gave her a blue bottle of "Evening in Paris" perfume. The blue color of the bottle matched her eyes and I wanted her to smell like Mother. She kissed us each goodbye as we walked out the door and told us she'd miss us and would look forward to seeing us sitting at our desks in two weeks. Christmas vacation had officially begun.

The Friday night after I had said goodbye to Miss Storey in the classroom, the Punahou staff planned their annual Christmas celebration for parents, the principal and the president of Punahou School. Funny skits had been rehearsed for the party since after the Thanksgiving holiday, along with choral singing of Christmas carols and Hawaiian songs. Teachers volunteered to make the refreshments. They put on the refreshment table two massive crystal bowls from the Cooke family filled with sweetened pineapple juice, grenadine, and scoops of vanilla ice cream that floated above the red punch like the Hawaiian Islands. Chocolate cookies and tuna sandwiches surrounded the crystal bowls.

Miss Storey asked me to stand next to the Christmas tree and sing "Silent Night."

The party began at five-thirty and was held in the reception hall of the elementary school building. The room was as large as an airplane hanger and a very scary room for my tiny-sounding singing voice. Rice Hall was a two-story wooden firetrap, waiting for a rat to chew on an electrical wire and turn it into a heap of ashes.

Hatsuko didn't come that night. She was visiting her sister on the other side of the island and still complained of a tummy ache. Agnes and Gertrude dressed in my honor and wore pink organza dresses and purple orchid corsages on their wrists. It was something I would have worn if Daddy hadn't told Mother he was coming.

Mother and Daddy arrived first and stood at opposite ends of the hall. Marigold sat crossed-legged in front of the Christmas tree, plopping herself down where she thought I was going to sing. She chewed on packs of Dentyne gum.

Miss Storey placed me on the program as the grand finale, even after the president spoke his every-year boring, Christmas farewell address. Dressed by Mother in a white shirt, white pants and a red sash around my fat belly, I stood behind a column waiting to be called by Miss Slingerland, the principal, to sing. After what seemed like years - time really went slowly that night - Miss Slingerland made the announcement that I was about to perform "Silent Night."

Only Wigay, Mother and Daddy clapped. Marigold took out her gum and whistled.

I walked over and stood ramrod straight in front of the Christmas tree. I was nervous. My hands shook wildly like the strange boy who lived across the street. He had such bad shaking fits, his father called an ambulance at least once a month to take him to the hospital.

I had that familiar urge in my pants, and if the piano didn't start soon, I knew I was going to do it in front of the audience. To keep from peeing in my pants, I pinched myself on my leg because pee thoughts were starting to make me feel faint. I longed to see Hatsuko's smile in the front row to give me confidence.

I took a deep breath. As I prepared myself, pulling up the sash that had slipped to the floor, Miss Hastings, the piano player, banged the keys on the piano. She started playing "Silent Night" like it was a John Souza march, which caught me by surprise. For a minute, I didn't know where I was, who I was and forgot the words to the song. I was completely lost but started to sing anyway. I sang too fast, then too slow for Miss Hastings' piano playing. We never got together. We were strangers performing to different beats. When I got past the high part of "Silent Night," I wanted to crawl under the Christmas tree because I had croaked out a feeble, weak, high flat note. I sounded like a frog singing underwater. When I finished singing "sleep in heavenly peace," my face had turned red like Daddy's nose when he drank martinis. My shirt had become soaked with my nervousness. My pink nipples showed under the shirt like Christmas lights and the sash was lying like a ribbon of blood on the floor.

No one laughed.

When the applause did begin, it was loud. Everyone started to cheer as if I had won a race. The kids who didn't like me whistled the loudest.

It was the curse.

Afterwards, I sat alone outside on the front steps of Rice Hall. Agnes and Gertrude had their arms around me. Mother and Daddy found me. They said how much they loved my singing. Marigold hid behind my father, with her hands in front of her face, laughing. Mother pulled Marigold out from behind Daddy and made Marigold gush, saying I was just "marrrrrvelous."

As my family went back into the hall to eat Christmas cookies, Agnes whispered, "When your sister said you were 'marrrrvelous,' you know you really hit an iceberg."

Then Miss Storey walked out and sat down next to me on the steps. She gave me a kiss and handed me a box of colored pencils. As Miss Storey talked, Gertrude buzzed in my ear that my teacher was hinting that I should go back to drawing pretty ladies with big bazooms. Gertrude never babied me.

Back home, grabbing food out of the icebox to make a mayonnaise sandwich with everything on it, I moaned to my imaginary girls that I felt lower than the sailors I drew in the bottom of a well calling out for help. I was about to have a mental breakdown like Cousin Bessie did. I wanted to take off all of my clothes and run up and down Rocky Hill even if the moon wasn't full. I sighed to myself, spreading mayonnaise two inches thick on a piece of Love's white bread, that I had just experienced my first big colossal theatrical disaster. I knew just how Bette Davis felt wearing that red taffeta dress to the ball in the movie *Jezebel.*

Gertrude reminded me that something occurred out on the porch. "When your mother, daddy and Marigold told you that you sang good, which they didn't mean because your singing stank like bad poop, they also said they loved you. Even your daddy said that. People who are related do that for each other. They lie to make you feel better so you can try all over again. Daddies and mothers do that all the time for their children." Gertrude never lied to me.

Making another sandwich, bigger than the first, I told the girls I was going to put my plan to become a major star on neutral till after New Year's because I was coming apart. I wanted to shriek and scream, but I couldn't. The mayonnaise sliding down my throat did that for me.

"If you keep on saying you're cursed," Gertrude continued, "something bad will happen to you. You have to watch what you say and do, especially at Christmas time."

After Gertrude said that, I decided that I was going to forget that I was cursed and never mention being cursed again...not to anyone. Not even to God. Then, maybe, the curse would forget all about me and go away and leave me alone.

I took off all my clothes and ran around the dining room table three times, screaming, "Curse, curse, curse."

"KRAFT MUSIC HALL"

TONIGHT -- 7:30-8:30

DUKE ELLINGTON
JAMES HILTON
FRANK McHUGH
BING CROSBY
BOB BURNS
CONNIE BOSWELL

NBC **K G U** NBC

17

Christmas Without Daddy

The night after I murdered "Silent Night," Marigold and I were tucked in our beds, smothered under our pillows, when Mother walked in with an announcement. As she sat down next to me, I took one look at her and I would have bet her a mayonnaise sandwich that she was still thinking about my "Silent Night" performance because she looked so sad.

Before she spoke, she took a deep breath, then said, "Children, I have made plans for Christmas. Your father told me last night that he and Grandma are going to Maui to spend Christmas with Uncle Chadsey and his family. Since Daddy won't be around, wouldn't it be fun for all of us to go to the Big Island to spend our Christmas with Uncle Will and Aunt Ella? They've asked us because they want to get to know you children better. You'll be able to meet your Cousin Kimo. He's their son and my first cousin and you'll like him very much. He's a very special person and has recently seen Hitler in the flesh. Anyway, I've decided that we are going."

Grown-ups never ask children's permission to do anything.

Marigold moaned, "I don't want to go. I want to have Christmas with Daddy."

Mother reached over and touched Marigold's face, saying, "I know, but I'd miss you terribly. You're such a big strength to me right now and I'd hate to have you away from me on Christmas. I'd be lonely without you."

"But, Mother," Marigold protested.

"I know. Your father will miss you terribly too, but Uncle Chadsey and Aunt Barbara have a large family and there is only room for Grandma and Daddy in their house. Maybe next Christmas you can join them," Mother replied.

"Please, Mother, I have to have Christmas with my father." Tears began to well in Marigold's eyes.

"Your father said to call him tomorrow at the office and he'll explain everything to you. When we come back from the Big Island, he's planned something very special for you and Percy. Try to understand this, Marigold. These are very difficult times for all of us," Mother entreated.

Marigold put her face under the pillow and muttered, "I'll try, Mother."

I raised my hand and interrupted, "Mother, I don't want to go to the Big Island either because Santa Claus won't know where to find me. Pleeeeeease let me stay home. You and Marigold go by yourselves and see Aunt Ella and Uncle

Will. I'm going to stay right here."

Mother laughed as Marigold groaned under the pillow. Mother smoothed my forehead and cooed, "And who's going to take care of my baby? You don't have to worry because I've written Santa Claus and told him where to find you. I promise you, Santa will fill your stocking at Aunt Ella's."

I took Mother's hand and squeezed it, "You promise?" I quickly looked at her fingers and toes to see if they were crossed.

"I promise," Mother said, with her hands folded in her lap and her toes curled into the Mickey Mouse rug.

"Okay, but remember, if Santa Claus doesn't come to the Big Island, I won't speak to you for my whole life." I picked something out of my nose to make the point that I was serious.

Settling back on the pillow, frowning because I still wasn't sure that Santa Claus would find his way to the island of real volcanoes, I pleaded, "Tell us about mean old Hunkacha."

"Not tonight, Percy. I'm tired. Tomorrow night," Mother replied.

Whining, I persisted, "You're always saying tomorrow, Mother."

Marigold, taking the pillow away from her face, chimed in, "Please, Mother." Marigold's eyes were now filled with red ink.

"All right. Where did I leave off?" Mother always had to be reminded where she left off because she had a bad case of "the forgets" just like me.

Marigold had a memory like an elephant, so she piped up, "Patty and Little Johnny were about to enter the forest to find the blue pearls that were stolen by Hunkacha. The father gave Patty a gold harmonica that played the sweetest music in the whole world, and Little Johnny had a golden reed that blew the straightest spit balls in the world to help him bring back the pearls."

"That's right, Marigold. You're so smart." Mother leaned back on the bedpost and sighed, "I remember it all now." She collected her thoughts while Marigold and I suddenly forgot that we were going to the Big Island without our father for Christmas and got cozy under the covers, waiting for the story to unfold.

Mother smelled like snow (pine needles) in a forest. She closed her eyes and began the story. "The old father waved farewell to his children and told them that they were about to begin a great adventure and to remember that, whatever happened to them on the path, they must tell the truth. They must also stay on their path and never get off it until they reached the lake where the blue pearls were hidden, miles under cold blue water."

Mother, in the old father's voice, warned, "As long as you stay on your path, you will be protected. Don't, for any reason, leave your path of golden bricks."

Marigold slid out of her bed and got under the covers with me.

"The children entered the dark, scary forest. They were amazed because everything around them was colored bright red. The trees were red, the plants were red, the flowers were red, and even the ground and weeds were colored red, too. Only the path on which they walked was painted bright gold.

"As they walked along the path, the bright red plants stood up and began to frighten Patty and Little Johnny by crying, 'BOOOOOO, we are your fears. You are going to trip and fall off the path and all the poison oak and ivy will cover and sting you. You'll get red welts all over your body in a minute, and you will be so itchy, you'll want to die.'

"Patty yelled at the plants, 'We don't believe you. You are puny, ugly plants and we hate your horrid color of red.' She turned to Little Johnny, 'Little Johnny, touch one of the plants and show them that we aren't scared of them and show them how brave we really are.'

"Little Johnny, holding his reed that blew the best spit balls in the whole world, pointed the reed at Patty, saying, 'You first.'

"Patty walked on ahead as if she hadn't heard Little Johnny because she too was scared of the plants."

Mother took our hands into hers and made her body tremble all over while she growled, "A rumbling noise came out of the forest. It was the voice of Hunkacha, the monster. 'Who has entered my forest?' Hunkacha thundered. Mother roared like a wild beast.

"The children became frightened because no one had ever seen Hunkacha, just his fierce voice was ever heard. Hunkacha cried louder, 'I do not worry about two silly children entering my forest because children are weak and stupid creatures. They are like mosquitoes to me - just a big nuisance. One slap with my fly swatter, I'll smash them like mashed potatoes. I'm going back to bed because I'm tired, but I know one of you children is going to make a big mistake and step off the path, and you'll be my breakfast. Yum, yum! I love to eat small children baked in a tuna casserole.'

"The red plants and trees screamed with laughter, 'Hee hee! See! See! See! One of you will make a mistake. You'll never walk through this forest to the blue lake and bring back the blue pearls to your father. Listen to us because we are your fears.'

"Patty and Little Johnny got so mad at the plants and trees that they took the harmonica and the golden reed and hit the plants - HARD. The plants shrieked in pain and cried out, 'You hit us!' Then in a flash, they all shriveled up and disappeared into a puddle of red ink. One little voice was heard, saying, 'You found out our secret. Fears are nothing when you face them or hit them square in the face.'

"With that, Little Johnny and Patty felt very brave and started to skip and whistle as they continued down the path to find the blue pearls.

"All of a sudden, the forest turned from bright red to bright yellow and was filled with every delicious food that Little Johnny and Patty loved to eat. There were tuna casseroles high on tree branches, and all the leaves had turned into tuna sandwiches. In fact, everywhere they looked, there were the most delicious foods sitting on the forest floor. The biggest surprise of all, mushrooms changed into cream puffs filled with mouthwatering lemon custard, and tree trunks became giant bottles of Best Foods mayonnaise. A rose bush turned into a gigantic hot fudge sundae with nuts and marshmallows that reached for the sky - just for Patty.

"Little Johnny and Patty jumped up and down with joy at the sight of all the food surrounding them. They licked their lips and rubbed their empty tummies because they had never imagined there was such a place in the whole fairy world kingdom. Their stomachs started to rumble like Hunkacha's roar because they hadn't eaten anything since breakfast. The children were so hungry, their tongues began to stick out and they tried to lean over to taste everything in the forest without leaving the golden path.

"This vision of food in the forest was Hunkacha's strongest spell. No one ever stayed on the path after seeing and smelling their favorite foods. Hunkacha liked to catch children gobbling food, put them in his net and then eat them for breakfast, lunch and dinner. One of his favorite dishes other than children in a baked tuna casserole was toasted little children on top of creamed chipped beef and rice."

Hearing that Hunkacha liked to eat little children, Marigold and I got out from under the covers and put our heads on Mother's lap. She continued the tale of Hunkacha while stroking our hair.

"Hunkacha had made his food spell so strong that it was almost impossible for even a brave man like President Roosevelt not to leap off the path and eat everything in sight. President Roosevelt would have sacrificed his life to eat Boston baked beans with catsup.

"Little Johnny pleaded with Patty, 'Let's stop and rest because I am awfully tired and.......sooooooo hungry.'

" 'I am hungry too,' said Patty. 'Father only gave us these stale tuna sandwiches without sweet pickles, and that's not enough food to keep a baby mongoose alive.'

"As the children were saying this to each other, Hunkacha was laughing as he slept in a cave far in the forest. He was dreaming about eating Patty and Little Johnny for supper.

"Little Johnny and Patty heard the voice of their father crying in the wind, warning, 'Don't leave your path; otherwise you'll never be able to find your blue pearls or your happiness.'

"By now, Little Johnny was so hungry he was ready to faint and didn't care if he ever found the blue pearls. He was too hungry to think about anything but a fresh, juicy tuna fish sandwich with lots of mayonnaise. He pleaded with Patty, 'I don't care what Father said about staying on this darn old path. I'm so hungry right now that if I don't eat, I'm going to die anyway. I'm getting off the path and going to make myself the biggest mayonnaise sandwich with tuna, tomatoes, cheese, and pickles and then get back on the path fast as I can. Hunkacha is too old and too mean to catch me.'

"Little Johnny started to step off the path with Patty walking right behind him."

Mother paused and moved Marigold back to her bed and me under the covers, saying, "I'm going to stop here because it's time for all of us to go to sleep."

"We don't want you to stop the story, Mother," I said while putting my feet under the cool bed sheets.

"Please tell us the end of the story," Marigold yawned, rubbing her eyes and snuggling her face into the pillows.

Mother shook her head and turned off the light. We begged for her to stay, but she blew kisses and said, "We have many more nights, all our lives together, to finish the story." She reminded us, "We'll be leaving in a couple of days, so start to think what you want to take to the Big Island. The island of Hawaii has real volcanoes on it and maybe, if we're lucky, we'll see one erupt. Now imagine that in your dreams. Now, go to sleep."

Mother closed the door and went into the living room and phoned Aunt Ella and Uncle Will to tell them that we were definitely arriving on the next boat to spend the Christmas holidays with them.

Hearing Mother talking to Aunt Ella, I turned to Marigold and asked, "What do you think happened to Little Johnny and Patty?"

"What do you think, stupid?" Marigold said, making her pillow into a white ball. "Little Johnny ate the mayonnaise sandwich, and Hunkacha ate him for breakfast."

"And what about Patty?" I asked.

"She ate the chocolate sundae but old Hunkacha never caught her because girls are smarter than boys and run faster," Marigold smugly replied.

"I don't believe you, because nobody has seen Hunkacha and no one knows what he looks like or how fast he runs. Maybe he's fat like me."

"Be quiet, Percy," she sighed. Marigold pulled the covers over her face and pretended to go to sleep. She began to cry into her pillow.

"Hmmm," I thought as I put the pillow over my face and turned to Agnes and Gertrude lying beside me, "Gertrude, I don't think Hunkacha ate Little Johnny. I think Little Johnny is smarter than anyone else in the whole world, and he wouldn't let Hunkacha eat him." Gertrude agreed.

I continued, "We'll have to wait until Mother tells us the rest of the story, but I know it's not the end of Little Johnny and not the end of the story."

Marigold, snuffling like she was coming down with a cold, heard me mumbling and growled like Hunkacha, "Go to sleep, dummy. You're bothering me."

I closed my eyes and went to sleep and dreamt that I ate a mayonnaise sandwich that was as large as a volcano on the Big Island. At midnight, I woke up and went to the bathroom. Running back into bed, I heard Marigold still crying into her pillow.

In a couple of days, Betsy and Jack, the now engaged couple, drove us down to the Honolulu harbor in our V8 Ford because Betsy's car never ran good from the day Jack bought it secondhand. It was sick all the time at the service station with a cracked something or other. I never spoke a bad word to Betsy about her junk car, because she and I had become best pals again, but I still felt she should have held out for a millionaire.

Our interisland steamer was the Waialeale. The Waialeale looked like a bunged-up tramp steamer that leaked its way down the Amazon River in the *Tarzan* movies. Mother had a cabin to herself and Marigold and I slept in a cabin alone and thought we were very grown-up. Our Christmas trip was starting out to be a great adventure.

The ship's cabin was small and furnished with bunk beds. A hardwood desk attached to the wall and a chair were the only furnishings inside the cabin. Our suitcases took up most of the walking space in the cabin. I had a hard time going to the bathroom or in and out the cabin door without tripping over our suitcases or banging into the walls. Two small shuttered windows were across from our bunk beds. The windows let us breathe in the salt air. They were shuttered to keep the Cousin Bessie-types from looking in. Peeping through the slats from inside the cabin, I could see passengers walk by, the liner's shiny mahogany railing, and the murky green harbor water beyond.

Mother, Marigold and I were on deck when the loud steam whistle signaled that the ship was leaving Honolulu. The ship headed out to sea as the sun was setting, spreading its red hues across the horizon. I walked to the stern of the ship and watched the water churn from a pale, milky green to a midnight dark blue as we passed the harbor breakwater and entered the rough seas.

Marigold became seasick as the first wave struck the bow. She ran to the cabin, climbed up to the top bunk bed and never left it till we reached the Big Island. Mother brought her dozens of sick bags and hot chicken broth to settle her stomach, but Marigold only wanted to be left alone, like Greta Garbo in the movies.

Going to sea gave me a seaman's appetite. I went wild at dinner and ordered everything on the menu, including three desserts. Mother wasn't with me at the table because she was seated at the captain's table, so I ate anything I wanted. Men dressed in spanking clean, white uniforms served my dinner. The table was set with silver forks and knives that had the steamship's insignia engraved on them. The dining room was a setting out of a Barbara Stanwyck and Henry Fonda movie. I looked around while eating, waiting for Babs and Hank to fall in love with me.

After dinner, I retired back to the cabin. Marigold was still puking. I ordered room service, "Two turkey sandwiches on white bread slathered in mayonnaise, please." I changed the order to three turkey sandwiches, in case Marigold revived and felt like having something "mushy" in her stomach.

When I plopped into my bed to wait for room service, Marigold moaned she had thrown up everything she had eaten for the past two weeks. Between up-chucks, I'd describe what I had for dinner, then she'd groan and throw up some more. She told me to leave her alone - "goddamit" - and then heaved the Wheaties she had had for breakfast.

Marigold's seasickness was her only weak spot. I took secret delight in her seasickness. Gertrude made me vow to never tell Grandma that Marigold, her favorite old salt, was really a landlubber. "You and your family," Gertrude said, "have to stick together now that your father has dumped you like a sack of potatoes, so no squealing on each other."

When the turkey sandwiches arrived, carried on a tray by a Chinese waiter wearing whites, Marigold asked me, in a weak voice, to please go out on deck and eat them and I could have hers, too. I ate two of the sandwiches on deck as the ship tossed up and down in the waves crashing over the bow. I told Gertrude that salt air made good sailors hungry.

Back in my bunk, Gertrude became as sick as Marigold.

Without a moon, crossing the channel to the Big Island was unusually rough to navigate. Everyone on deck said they had never seen the waves so large. Sleeping was troublesome for everyone because the ship pounded into the waves that were higher than the mountains behind our house. After the ship recovered from hitting a mighty wave, she'd roll back and forth, creaking from side to side, making me think the ship was about to break apart and head at any time for the bottom of the ocean.

Minute by minute, the ship struggled to get over the next wave, forcing itself to the top of a crest. The ship would spill over the wave and plunk down into a trough, trying not to tip over, as the next gigantic wave towered ahead. Passengers on deck who didn't have cabins clutched onto anything to keep belongings and children from falling overboard. Everybody screamed as each mountain-wave covered the ship, "Here comes one big buggah. Hang on, brah." A crate of chickens fell overboard.

Inside the cabins, between screams, I could hear the sounds of muffled laughter, whispered words, and happy songs strummed by a finger on an ukulele. It was the singing by the Hawaiians outside our window that finally put Marigold to sleep. When she closed her eyes, she had used up all the sick bags. Mother checked on her baby every half-hour and used a cool washrag on her forehead while she slept.

I was assigned to take Marigold's sick bags outside to the trash bin. On deck, I saw that the ship had turned into a fairyland of white foam. The snow-capped ocean-mountains had burst salt spray over the ship and turned the Waialeale into a magical ghost fighting for its life.

Back in bed, pushing back the covers, I became part of the rhythmic ups and downs as each wave tried to drown us. I had to hold onto the bunk's railing so I wouldn't fall out on the floor and roll to the wall when the waves hit. When we hit the biggest wave of the night, I called up to Marigold to see if she was still asleep.

"Marigold, are you awake?"

"No, I'm asleep. What do you want?"

"Marigold, do you think we're on the same adventure as Little Johnny and Patty, going through an ocean forest? Do you think Hunkacha's out there? Maybe that's why the waves are so big because Hunkacha doesn't want us to find the blue pearls."

"Shut up, Percy. That's only a story. Go to sleep," she moaned. If Marigold had had the strength, she would have reached down and thumped me on my head.

"Marigold?"

"Now what?"

"I have your turkey sandwich under my pillow, so if you get hungry, I'll pass it up to you."

Marigold gasped for air, "Percy!"

"Yes, Marigold?"

"One more word out of you and you're going to die."

Too bad I had given up on my death plan because Marigold killing me would have been a perfect solution. She could have gone to the electric chair like Jimmy Cagney and she could have played the harp. I called up to her again, "You won't kill me tonight because you can't. Goodnight."

Marigold didn't respond because she was having the dry heaves.

At midnight, while Agnes and Gertrude were sleeping under my pillow and hugging onto Marigold's turkey sandwich, I closed my eyes. I dreamt I was swimming through towering waves with Hunkacha swimming right behind me. He was trying to capture me and was dressed in a shark's costume. He was roaring over the waves, yelling that he was going to eat me up.

Inter-island steamship Waialeale ready to depart from Honolulu pier (1934-37). Courtesy of Farbman, Bishop Museum.

18

Aunt Ella and Uncle Will

I jumped out of my bunk as soon as the sun leapt over the horizon. Mother and Marigold were still asleep. I read an old *Advertiser.*

The Honolulu Advertiser

HONOLULU ADVERTISER EDITORIAL: The next World War probably will be "undeclared!" Many of its battlefields will be of the sabotage order. Poisoned water and food, time-bombs in the front rank, radio that serves a disintegrating purpose, deadly germs that carry destruction, and many other forms of devilishness, will smite the unprepared and unwary during these times of peace.

HENRY JUDD - HAWAIIAN HOSPITALITY

"Sometimes this hospitality has been abused - "wearing out one's welcome." Hookahu la no ka malihini - the stranger has one day. On that first day, he is made much of, entertained and shown every courtesy. On the second day, he is supposed to do his share of the work and cooperate in the idea of this proverb for he would stay on and on and not do a thing toward the work of the household. He would impose on his host and hostess most shamefully.

Many visitors from Kauai, Maui or the Big Island - the Honolulu people would often forget such forms of hospitality - on seeing these Outer Islanders on Fort Street - "When did you come down?" "How long are you going to stay?" "When are you going home?" There was no thought of entertaining these Outer Islanders...so Oahu people, who were entertained lavishly on the Outer Islands, acquired an unenviable reputation of being "pi" or stingy.

Mainlanders were more hospitable.

YOU'LL FIND SANTA'S HELPER AT SCHOFIELD BARRACKS NEAR KEMOO FARM

SHIPPING NOTICE

The SS HUMUULA will LEAVE Honolulu for Kona Ports at 12 o'clock Noon TODAY instead of its regular time of 10:30 a.m.

The SS WAIALEALE will arrive from Lahaina, Maui, and Hilo at 6 a.m.
TODAY instead of its regular time at 7 a.m.
INTER-ISLAND STEAM NAVIGATION CO.

**ACCORDING TO HITLER, THE SECOND WORLD WAR BEGAN AT 5:45, SUNDAY,
SEPTEMBER THIRD, 1939**

VOLCANOES IN HAWAII:

Haleakala - Maui	10,025 ft.
Mauna Kea - Hawaii	13,784 ft.
Mauna Loa - Hawaii	13,630 ft.
Waialeale - Kauai	5,170 ft
Tantalus - Oahu	2,015 ft

Tossing the newspaper back where I found it, I wandered in my pajamas outside the cabin, roaming the corridors, looking for food. On deck, the ship had lost
its ghostly look because the railings were now shined to a mahogany finish. In the
passageways and on the deck, I stepped over Hawaiians curled up in baby posi-
tions, snoring next to roosters in cages. The roosters had collapsed like moldy
feather dusters in their cages. They were even too seasick to crow in the morning.

I awakened Marigold at five by banging the ship's chimes right in her ear. I'd
gotten them from the steward who was walking along the corridor playing on the
chimes and announcing that we were arriving in Hilo. Marigold woke with a start
and banged her head on the ceiling. I quickly sashayed down to Mother's cabin,
chiming away, and banged on her door, yelling that we're docking within the hour.

Marigold, out of her bunk, looked like a dead body that had been buried with
a stake in her heart for over a hundred years. When she came out of the bathroom,
she wandered around the cabin like a zombie, but she now smelled like death who
had brushed her teeth with Colgate toothpaste. Mother rushed into our cabin,
dressed in a white suit, and asked if we wanted breakfast before we landed.
Marigold stuck her finger down her throat and gagged, "Noooooo. Just get me off
this damned ship." When Marigold swore, I knew she was no longer a zombie.

I wanted breakfast, but Marigold's vote won because she looked so awful.
Mother consoled me by saying that we were sure to eat breakfast at Aunt Ella and
Uncle Will's. Thank God, I packed the dried up old turkey sandwich in my suitcase. I had kept it for emergencies. Stewards hustled into our cabin and collected
the luggage. After making a final inspection around the cabin to see if I had left
anything behind, Mother ushered us out on deck.

Leaning over the railing, I glanced down as the ship entered Hilo harbor. The
bay's water was colored "oogie" brown and littered with floating sardine cans,
sticks from trees, and covered all over with fluffy yellow foam that blew in the
wind. Looking ahead, I saw a cone-shaped mountain that blotted out the sky.
Mauna Kea, the volcano, was dressed in pastel purple and fringed at the top with a

layer of white clouds. The mountain looked like a crowned king. Gertrude told me Mauna Kea was the ruling volcano in all the Hawaiian Islands. It was a live mountain that erupted hot lava when it felt like it. Once, long ago, Mauna Kea's lava rivers nearly wiped out the town of Hilo.

The ship limped up to a weathered, wooden dock, jetting black bilge into the bay. The Waialeale was a baby whale nestling comfortably against its mother. It was familiar movement. Brawny Hawaiian stevedores on the dock secured the ship by catching ropes tossed by our unshaven crew. A twist of the ropes around rusted iron posts by powerful brown arms and the whale was hitched to its home.

As the gangway was hoisted into position onto the ship, two white-haired stout people waved a Panama hat and a lace handkerchief at us. The elderly woman had the same colored eyes as my mother. When the gangway was secured, Marigold ran down the ramp and kissed the ground. Mother and I followed, but she turned to me before we stepped onto the pier and whispered, "Percy, don't tell Aunt Ella you wear my dresses."

"What if they ask me?"

Mother squeezed my hand tight, "Don't speak."

Suddenly, I was smothered with leis, embraced and kissed on the cheek by the two elderly people. As soon as the luggage was collected, Aunt Ella and Uncle Will squeezed us into their "banana wagon" and drove us to the outskirts of Hilo. We arrived at their home in a short fifteen minutes. Aunt Ella and Uncle Will's house was a white, one-story rambling home that was perched precariously like a bird's nest, high on a cliff overlooking the dark Pacific Ocean.

It was hard to know what Uncle Will was like because Aunt Ella interrupted him all the time, talking like a machine gun, as we drove to the house. Machine gun talk was a trait from Mother's side of the family and I think Aunt Ella talked that way because she was embarrassed that Mother divorced my father.

I overheard Cousin Bessie tell Cross-Eyed Mama behind a closed door that Mother's divorce was her family's biggest disgrace for that year. A woman held onto her man at all costs. Cousin Bessie breathed into Cross-Eyed Mama's ear, "My dear, every wife in my generation knows that men have that weakness and wives just have to close their eyes and just go along with that tiny, little failing. Divorces, my dear, are only for fast women in Hollywood who drink and smoke, like that Clara Bow."

That was embarrassing for me to overhear because Mother drank and smoked like Clara Bow, the flapper in the movies. Cousin Bessie knew what she was talking about when she talked about men sleeping around. Her husband died on their honeymoon in someone else's bed. Hatsuko told me that. I figured out by myself what Hatsuko meant. Cousin Bessie snored louder than her husband did and that's why he went to sleep with someone else.

I wished Mother had been born Clara Bow and lived in Hollywood.

I was lost in the newness of my surroundings. Aunt Ella's house didn't make any sense. It had been built topsy-turvy and rambled. Wings sprung out of nowhere and at odd angles. Walkways and lanais around the house went nowhere but off the cliff. It was a house that had one long corridor after another in it. I was lost in its maze from the moment I arrived until the day we left. The house was so large that Marigold, Mother and I each had our own bedroom and private bath.

I loved my bathroom. It was three times larger than the one at home and had a gargantuan square porcelain tub held up on metal legs centered in the room. The tub was polished to a Snow White finish, which only a thousand maids and a case of Dutch Cleanser could have kept clean on the Big Island. It glowed like Snow White's tomb.

As soon as I saw the tub, I begged Aunt Ella to let me take a bath right then. She blinked her baby blue eyes in disbelief at my request. I told her that I was a poor, dirty, grimy, neglected kid who hadn't had a bath for a week, and it was all because my mother divorced my father.

I always knew the right words to say.

Handing me the whitest towel I had ever seen, Aunt Ella replied, "Of course, take a bath right now, you sweet, darling boy. Cleanliness is next to Godliness."

Gertrude whispered in my ear, "Oh, brother. Get her."

Aunt Ella sat down on the toilet seat and continued, "You may do anything you want while you're here, Percy. Treat my home as your home. Uncle Will and I are going to make this a very special Christmas for you, your mother, and Marigold, and you can do whatever you want while you're here." Aunt Ella lived to regret those words.

I missed breakfast that morning because I took a bath. Agnes couldn't believe it. My love for bathtubs began when I lived inside my mother's stomach. When I turned the knobs on the tub, brown sludge poured from the taps but cleared to a light tan as I sat my bottom down. I bathed in mud for the first time in my life.

I heard from the maids that the reason for all the muddy water in the tub was because it rained everyday in Hilo. Muddy rivers sometimes overflowed into the Big Island's reservoirs and into Aunt Ella's bathtubs. It was Hilo's best kept secret.

The amazing thing was that no matter how muddy looking I left my bathtub after I bathed, I always returned from a drive to a porcelain tub that gleamed white like a diamond. Still, I never felt squeaky clean on the Big Island. After many baths, my body turned light brown. It was probably why all the people on the Big Island looked tanned, even in rainy weather.

After missing breakfast, I ate my dried-up turkey sandwich. At noon, Aunt Ella called us into lunch. I ran into the dining room screaming for food. I was told by everyone to simmer down. Aunt Ella's meals, I discovered right away, were going to be served formally by maids. The maids carried trays with food on them around the table at breakfast, lunch and dinner. I was going to starve to death on the Big Island because I hated to reach for food on trays. I spilled and never got enough food on my plate. Maids in starched uniforms reminded me to take the food from the left and when I finished, they took my plate away from the right.

For our first lunch, I was served two tiny sardine sandwiches, crusts removed, and a watercress salad smaller than the sandwiches. The salad had only a whisper of oil and vinegar dressing sprayed on it somewhere. Dessert was the smallest small scoop of vanilla ice cream I had ever seen in my life.

There wasn't a bottle of Best Foods mayonnaise in sight. I checked Aunt Ella's icebox before lunch and found a barren desert, but I fooled everyone because I had packed Best Foods mayonnaise in my suitcase, hidden under my Alice Faye paper dolls.

At lunch, being starved to death and no second helpings offered, I got to know Aunt Ella and Uncle Will better because there was nothing to do but listen to the conversation. Aunt Ella was sweet all over. She looked sweet, acted sweet and walked as dainty as a fairy. She spoke her sweet machine-gun words in a tiny, squeaky high voice. She was the baby in her family of eight. My dead grandmother was her oldest sister.

Gertrude told me all last-borns were always sweet and spoiled. I was the baby in my family but I wasn't sweet. I was spoiled...rotten.

Gertrude guffawed into my ear, imitating the black actress Hattie McDaniel in *Alice Adams*, "Youse so bad and spoiled because youse was adopted, honey. Youse was born of gypsies who threw you off a ship passing by Hawaii. A big wave crashed you on the shores of Waikiki Beach. Youse was found by Marigold under a pile of driftwood -like Moses in the bulrushes, and taken home because Marigold wanted someone to beat up. That's who youse is - a spoiled nothing and someone to beat up." Gertrude had a bad habit of interrupting my thoughts.

I never believed Gertrude anyway because I had inherited my mother's nose and her big Eleanor Roosevelt teeth. I also inherited my daddy's fat lower lip, tiny feet and his peepee - only Daddy's peepee was bigger.

Uncle Will was the postmaster in Hilo. He joked that he liked licking stamps because it kept him out of Aunt Ella's clutches. Uncle Will had an abundance of white hair and a fat round stomach like me. He was Santa Claus without a beard and had a Santa Claus jolly, hearty laugh - when he could get it in.

At dinner, I met their only son, Kimo. Kimo is James in Hawaiian. At lunch, Aunt Ella told us Kimo was an artist who lived and painted in a loft above their garage. When I first saw him, I thought he looked like a statue out of a Grecian temple because he was tall, blond and handsome. His face, in profile, looked as if God had chiseled it perfectly. He didn't look like either of his parents.

Gertrude interrupted again, saying that God must have dropped him by mistake from Heaven because he looked like a wild beautiful flower that had blossomed, unexplained, on a black barren lava field. His laughter, she said, came from a wise old soul and once, sitting beside a swimming pool, Kimo told me the people in Hilo thought he was a giggling, naughty, open-mouth Roman mask on a wall.

Kimo loved Marigold and me in seconds.

Aunt Ella told us everything she wanted us to know about her son while he sat at the dining room table, looking down at his plate with embarrassment. Gertrude chimed in that sweet old Aunt Ella liked making her son feel uncomfortable in front of others. Gertrude, poking her bony finger into my head, said that Aunt Ella is punishing him for being different.

Aunt Ella rattled on to us that Kimo hadn't done anything of real substance since he left college and, thank God, he was home at last, doing real work. She went on that Kimo had returned to Hilo a month ago after painting in Europe for two years.

Kimo broke into Aunt Ella's storytelling and told us that he painted with master artists in London, ate raw oysters in Paris and, on one occasion, looked into the blue hypnotic eyes of Hitler in a Munich hotel.

Aunt Ella took back the conversation, rolling her blue eyes to the ceiling, saying in a scolding tone that for months, Kimo wouldn't answer her letters. Worried about a war that was about to erupt with Germany and that her twenty-two-year-old baby was wasting his life away being an artist, in danger, and costing her a fortune to support, she sent her sister, the general, to bring him home.

Wiping her nose with her handkerchief, she continued Kimo's tale as if she smelled something bad. She told us that Aunt Mari found Kimo painting in a dirty garret in Soho and living the life of a wild bohemian. Aunt Mari physically threw out all his friends, poured all his wine down the sink, packed his paintbrushes, and brought him home on the next sailing of the Queen Mary.

Aunt Ella, smiling at me, confided, "Percy, your wonderful Uncle Will got Kimo a job as a bookkeeper at one of the Hamakua sugar plantations run by those smart, thrifty Scots from Edinburgh. Kimo is in his right place now and is going to do right well. He's where he's supposed to be. You can't help but learn about making money from those Scotsmen. They're a stingy lot. Remember that, Percy."

I heard in my mind Uncle Will saying to Kimo, "You've got to be practical, son. Get married and settle down and be like normal people." Gertrude bet me a tuna sandwich that as Uncle Will spoke those words to Kimo, Aunt Ella poked the postmaster's back, adding, "He can't eat canvas, Will. Tell him that, too."

After Aunt Ella finished Kimo's story, I jumped up and ran around the table and shook Kimo's hand. I told him that his life's story was better than any movie I had ever seen. I said to him in front of everyone that I thought he did a stupid thing coming back to Hilo to work for a sugar plantation, which must be very boring after the life he had lead in Paris. I told him I hated arithmetic and when Miss Storey taught me adding and subtracting, I drew ladies with big blue eyes, blond hair and big bazooms. I pointed to Aunt Ella's big bazooms and said, "Like hers."

Kimo laughed and asked if I'd draw one of my ladies with big bazooms for him.

I looked back into Aunt Ella's china blue eyes. They had become clouded. She signaled me to return to my seat. By the way she was acting, she was not pleased with me. By the shape of her mouth, I knew she would have shipped me back on the Waialeale on the ten o'clock sailing if she hadn't loved my mother and if Christmas wasn't coming around the corner.

Kimo was my new best friend.

Uncle Will roared with laughter when I pointed to Aunt Ella's big bazooms.

Mother signaled me to obey Aunt Ella and sit down and to remember what she told me before we stepped onto the pier. She gave me her familiar stern warning look.

Marigold was brooding and didn't hear a word I had said. She sat quietly all during dinner, wishing she was on Maui with Daddy and Grandma. Kimo, who knew about hurt feelings, told Marigold he was going to paint her portrait, as she was the prettiest little girl he had ever seen - even in Europe. Marigold smiled for the first time since we arrived that morning. Rising from the dinner table, Aunt

Ella told Mother that she thought Marigold was a sweet, lovely young lady and so well brought up. She didn't mention my name.

After dinner, I learned from Kimo that he was making goo-goo eyes at his manager's beautiful daughter and painted on his days off in his loft, while playing classical music on his phonograph. I was sent to my room as soon as the adults finished sipping their coffee from German demitasse cups.

"Little boys need their sleep," said Aunt Ella as she put her hands on my shoulders and started to push me out of the living room. I told her that I wanted to stay up like I did at home, but Aunt Ella insisted that it was "grown-up time" and little boys didn't talk back to their elders and went quietly to bed as they were told to do so. Before I left the living room and after I had shaken everyone's hands, I told Uncle Will I hoped they had their address clearly marked on the outside of their house because I didn't want Santa Claus to miss me on Christmas Eve.

Marigold groaned as Kimo and Uncle Will laughed at me. Aunt Ella poked me along with her bony finger, out of the room and all the way back to my bedroom so I wouldn't get lost.

Once the door was shut, alone with Gertrude and Agnes, I ran to the closet for my suitcase. I opened it and brought out a bottle of mayonnaise. I clutched the bottle to my bosom like a long lost friend because I was starved. More starved than I had ever been in my whole life. I knew I couldn't survive two weeks on portions of food that a mynah bird couldn't live on. Here, I couldn't clear the plates and eat leftovers in the kitchen because Aunt Ella had an army of maids running around who took care of everything. Knowing my Aunt Ella now, I knew I couldn't get into the kitchen to eat leftovers nor even make friends with her servants and beg for handouts. The way she talked down to her maids, they weren't chums like I was with my Hatsuko. Aunt Ella had limited her friendships.

Agnes warned me that Aunt Ella was making a deliberate attempt to starve me to death because she thought I was too fat. After I opened the bottle of mayonnaise to eat with my fingers, I remembered a warning from Hatsuko, "Percy, when you open a mayonnaise jar and leave it out in the open air, it becomes poison. Mayonnaise must be kept in the icebox as soon as you open the bottle."

I had to get the mayonnaise bottle into Aunt Ella's icebox without anyone knowing it before I poisoned myself. Agnes, Gertrude and I came up with a great plan: Once everyone was asleep, we'd find the kitchen, which would be like finding a needle in a haystack because the house was so confusing, and put the mayonnaise in Aunt Ella's icebox. I'd hide the mayonnaise behind the milk bottles. Then Agnes said, clapping her hands, having the mayonnaise in the icebox, I could make midnight sandwiches to my heart's content while everyone slept. I'd never starve now and no one would ever know. We all agreed that tonight we would stay up till past midnight and carry out the plan.

Midnight came. A grandfather clock struck twelve somewhere in the house. I opened my bedroom door quietly and looked down a long, dark, black corridor. I couldn't hear anything in the house - not even snoring.

I said to Agnes and Gertrude, "This is it." The three of us tiptoed down the long dark hall carrying the bottle of mayonnaise into nowhere. I bumped into walls as I walked from one corridor to another. I tried doors that were locked. In minutes, I was lost in a maze, like the bushes that puzzled aristocrats in an English garden. After bumping into one wall after another, I arrived in the living room. The grandfather clock in the room struck one. I figured from here, the dining room must be around the corner somewhere and the kitchen nearby.

It was. I entered the kitchen and felt my way in the dark because I didn't want to turn on the light and wake everyone up. I felt pretty spooky as I walked my way like a blind man around the sink, then a table and the icebox.

Bingo.

As I opened the icebox door, the lights in the kitchen flashed on, blinding me. A voice screamed out, "Who's there? I'm going to shoot."

I dropped the bottle of mayonnaise and it shattered into a million pieces of glass and goo on the floor. I looked at the door and there stood Aunt Ella, wearing a terrycloth bathrobe and pointing a gun at me.

"For heaven's sake, Percy, what are you doing in here at this hour? I could have killed you. You scared the wits out of me," she exclaimed.

I should have told her what she just scared out of me.

She demanded, "Answer me, Percy - right now. What are you doing in here?"

My mouth gaped open as I looked at the barrel of a real gun. I finally mustered up a pitiful voice, saying, "I came in here to put my mayonnaise in the icebox."

"What a silly thing to do at this hour. What do you mean, your mayonnaise?"

Wishing I were back in bed with the covers pulled over me, I stuttered, "I brought mayonnaise with me from Honolulu to make sandwiches. I eat sandwiches at night - sometimes I eat them in the afternoons."

"No wonder you're as fat as a pig. Didn't you have enough to eat at dinner?" she demanded.

I lied. I knew I should have told the truth, but I lied when I was frightened down to my toes like Little Johnny did when he heard Hunkacha's roar. "I had plenty to eat tonight, Aunt Ella. Honest. But I'd like some more."

She scolded, "Stop this nonsense right now. No more sandwiches at midnight while you're in my house, young man. Now, let's clean up the mess you made on the floor and go back to bed."

So much for doing whatever I wanted to do in Aunt Ella's house. Grown-ups always broke promises and little boys lied.

Aunt Ella placed her gun on the kitchen table and watched me pick up slivers of glass and my precious glop off the floor. It killed me to throw mayonnaise away into a garbage can and not down my throat. Behind her back, when she was not looking, I licked some of the glop off my fingers as I dropped pieces of glass into the garbage can. Aunt Ella, watchful as a hawk, tried not to miss a trick and hovered over me to see that I was doing the job correctly. Scooping with my hands, I cleaned up most of the mess on the floor.

Agnes told me later in the bedroom that Aunt Ella reminded her of the mean old witch in *Snow White*.

It took me a good hour to finish the final cleaning up because Aunt Ella kept pointing her bony finger here and there, finding tiny bits of glass I had missed. "I want this kitchen left clean as a whistle. What will the maids think if they find you have made a mess of their kitchen?" She kept saying that to me in her machine-gun chatter until she was satisfied that I had rubbed the floor to a shine. "Clean as a whistle. Clean as a whistle. Clean as a whistle." When the floor was clean as a whistle, she escorted me back to my bedroom.

At the door, holding my wrist in a vise-like grip, she cautioned, "This will be our little secret as we don't want to upset your mother. She's having a hard enough time raising you kids, especially after the awful things your father did to her. I hope you don't turn out to be just like your father." After those words, she shut the door and padded down the hallway into some other mysterious corridor where she and Uncle Will slept.

Aunt Ella was a good detective because she probably never slept, kept her good ear attached to the wall, and wore a pistol strapped to her nightgown, cocked and ready to fire at fat little boys. After what Aunt Ella said about my father, I loved my daddy a lot more and wanted to turn out to be exactly like him.

I found Agnes and Gertrude hiding in the closet under my suitcase. They had fled when they saw Aunt Ella pointing a gun at me. I scolded them for not sticking with me, but in the next breath, I admitted I understood because if I had had the chance, I would have run too. Aunt Ella was really Ma Barker, the infamous gun moll of the thirties because Ma Barker, I read, spoke sweet as Shirley Temple did in *The Little Princess* but shot a gun like Billy the Kid. What Aunt Ella didn't realize was that she was up against John Dillinger. I had brought two bottles of mayonnaise in my suitcase. I learned from the movies that a successful gangster always has a backup plan. A second bottle of mayonnaise was resting in my suitcase under Alice Faye cutouts, wrapped in my dirty underwear.

"The next time," I told my girls, "and there will be a next time, we're going to outwit that old gun-toting gun-moll and stake out the house real good before we make our next run for the icebox."

Agnes came up with the idea of putting a sleeping pill in Aunt Ella's coffee after dinner. If I had the pills, I would have dumped a whole bottle in her German demitasse coffee cup. I was not about to give up having mayonnaise sandwiches at midnight for the likes of Ma Barker.

Getting into bed, starved, I told Agnes and Gertrude I was now living in a German concentration camp. Putting my head under the pillow, chewing on the sheets, I told Agnes, "I sure hope Santa piles a ton of chocolates in my stocking this year - forget the toys." As I drifted off to sleep, I heard Gertrude telling me that the reason that Aunt Ella didn't want me to squeal on her was because she didn't want my mother to know that she had pointed a real gun at my head and "she could have killed ya."

During my first night sleeping on the Big Island, I didn't dream of anything because I was too hungry. My brain was down in my stomach, trying to fill it up.

Hilo town in 1948, showing Haili Street from Kamehameha Avenue.
Courtesy of Bishop Museum Archives, Honolulu, HI.

19

Pele's Island

The next morning, after we waved Uncle Will and Kimo off to work, Aunt Ella piled us into her banana wagon. She decided to motor us up the volcano for a picnic. Agnes and Gertrude stayed home. They were afraid of Aunt Ella's gun.

The day was cold and rainy - a perfect day to stay in bed and a terrible day to picnic outdoors. Aunt Ella was determined we were going to see the volcano or bust. "Damn the weather," she said.

Aunt Ella drove her car like a mad woman. Behind the wheel, this little old lady shifted the station wagon into second gear like a race car driver, whizzing through clouds of dense fog. Because Aunt Ella gossiped the entire time with Mother as she drove, she ran off the road three times - once into a shallow ditch. I screamed each time we left the pavement and yelled we were going to die. Nothing daunted Aunt Ella and the journey seemed to go on forever as we passed jungles of tree ferns and rolled onto dirt roads in barren, black lava fields.

Marigold hadn't spoken since breakfast.

We arrived at a picnic park that had large, smelly, sulfur yellow mounds sur-rounding the area. The rain suddenly stopped as we entered, leaving the thick fog behind. Aunt Ella parked the station wagon near a picnic table where we unloaded our lunch things and bundled up in sweaters. I could hardly wait to dig into the wicker lunch basket because at breakfast I had eaten only half a grapefruit and a tiny bowl of corn flakes.

Marigold turned into a jumping bean as she got out of the car, as soon as the cold air hit her face. She ran around the park screaming like a banshee, running up and down the sulfur mounds and yelling, "It stinks like Percy. It stinks like Percy!" Marigold just then blew her cover as the sweet, darling, little girl that Aunt Ella thought she was. She joined me on the bad-kid list. I looked at Aunt Ella and gave her an "I told you so" look.

Marigold was her old self as she screamed "Zoom, zoom, zoom," making her-self into a make-believe dive-bomber and pushing me into the ground. "I killed you," she screamed.

I threw a lava rock at her, bulls-eye, I hit her chest. We started to have fun.

Mother, sitting on the picnic bench across from Aunt Ella, called us to sit down and behave - "Right now. You're upsetting Aunt Ella. Marigold, sit down next to Aunt Ella, and Percy, you sit here." Mother yanked me down next to her. I was panting, out of breath.

Aunt Ella brought out from the picnic basket four boiled eggs, four cucumber sandwiches without mayonnaise, four apples, and four pieces of chocolate cake without frosting.

I was going to faint. It was another no-nothing meal at the "Hilo prison." I ate my share of lunch in seconds. The apple took longer to chew. I tried to steal Marigold's piece of cake when she wasn't looking, but she caught me and slapped my hand, calling me "You Nazi pig!"

I looked down and picked up a dried-up old horse muffin and threw it at my sister. I missed and hit Aunt Ella's left bazoom. Aunt Ella shrieked, fell backwards, crashed to the ground, and screamed that I had killed her. On the ground, with both hands, she wiped away as fast as she could a piece of horse muffin still clinging to her blouse. Getting up off the ground with Mother's help, she whimpered, "I have been defiled. Defiled. This is awful, Deidra."

Sitting on the bench, looking down at the stain on her blouse, she cried at me, "I'm dirty. You threw horse shit at me."

I closed my ears with my hands and pretended I didn't hear the s-word.

Mother ran to the car, grabbed a towel, poured orange soda from a bottle, and wiped away the brown stain from Aunt Ella's blouse. Marigold had her head down on the table, shaking, and biting her tongue to keep from laughing at what a poor shot I was.

I wanted to run away and bury myself in the middle of a sulfur mound.

Aunt Ella recovered after she saw her blouse was clean again, and said to Mother in her sweetest tone, "That's all right, Deidra. Children will be children, and you know I raised a boy, too. I know what dear little dickens they can be."

Then Ma Barker turned to me and with her killer eyes, smiled and said, "Percy, we will have to do something about your manners, won't we?"

Mother interrupted, "Percy, what do you say?" She was ready to hit me with a horse muffin.

"You told me not to speak," I quavered.

"Speak!"

"I'm sorry, Aunt Ella. The horse shit was meant for Marigold. I apologize from the bottom of my heart."

Aunt Ella nodded without saying a word back. In her eyes, I was heading for Jimmy Cagney's electric chair.

Because I didn't want to be shot dead with Aunt Ella's gun and I thought she might be hard of hearing, I repeated, "Aunt Ella, the horse shit wasn't for you, it was for Marigold."

Aunt Ella gritted her teeth and talked through a handkerchief that she had over her face, "Percy, polite little boys don't use dirty words. Let's forget this entire unfortunate incident. After all, it was an accident." Immediately, she took away the handkerchief from her face and bit hard into a cucumber sandwich.

I wanted to tell her that I heard "horse shit" from her own lips, but knew I was already skating on thin ice. In fact, at dinner when I told Kimo he had made a mistake coming home, I had already become a cockroach in Aunt Ella's mind - an insect to squash.

After lunch, the sun burned the fog completely away and the afternoon turned bright, clear and sunny. The lunch basket back in the car, Aunt Ella announced we were going to take a hike. She led us through a forest of tree ferns and down a dirt path till we came to the Thurston lava tube. The tunnel was made during an eruption and had been molded by hot lava into a cave. It was spooky from the outside because it looked like a home for a dragon. At Aunt Ella's insistence, we filed one behind the other to explore the dark innards of the cave. As we walked, I kept thinking the roof was about to crash down on me at any moment and smother me to death.

Water dripping from the ceiling had made the path muddy and slippery. Aunt Ella, leading us like a storm trooper, cautioned me to be careful how and where I stepped. As soon as she said that, I slipped on a rock and fell into a mud puddle. Marigold let loose with a war whoop, then slipped and joined me in the mud. We giggled and immediately began to have a mud fight. Marching orders came from Ma Barker to get up and we exited the cave looking like tar babies. The accident in the mud puddle cut short the hike because we complained about being wet and cold and wanted to go home. Aunt Ella's extolling the wonders of a Hawaiian forest preserve ceased.

Mother could have killed us and had the "I'm going to put you two up for adoption" look in her eyes. She stopped talking to us for a whole hour.

After using a spit bath and towels to get the mud off, we were back in the banana wagon and off to see Halemaumau crater. From the look in Aunt Ella's eyes, we knew Marigold and I were not going to spoil her plans, no matter how uncomfortable we were. She had a lot of "by gum, we're going to do it" spirit in her that her missionary ancestors had when they rounded Cape Horn. It was the old family motto: "We're going to get to the Sandwich Islands even if it kills us, by gum."

Her by-gum spirit aroused, and really furious with us now, Aunt Ella drove at full throttle over the lava roads filled with rocks sharp as knives. We were going to finish this tour even if it killed her tires.

Halemaumau crater was a fire pit where spectacular lava fountains poured out molten rocks that shot up hundreds and hundreds of feet on special occasions. Right now the crater was resting. This was also where the Hawaiian fire goddess, Madame Pele, kept her post office box and where she lived. Her home was an enormous, circular pit in the middle of a black, barren lava field, several miles round.

Pele was a vengeful goddess. I think Aunt Ella had a lot of Pele in her. Teeth grinding, Aunt Ella told us all about the goddess and warned, "Anyone who defiles or defies Madame Pele will feel her raging wrath." She took her eyes off the road again, turned around and looked me straight in my eyes...and ran off the road.

Aunt Ella parked the banana wagon near the crater and ordered Marigold and me to walk the rocky path to the edge and see the view. Aunt Ella crooked a finger at us as we opened the car door and warned, "Dreadful things happen to small boys and small girls who take pieces of lava from Pele's home. They become cursed. The wind picks them up and tosses them down into the crater, and they are left there to die."

Maybe Pele cursed me. I also thought it was wishful thinking on Aunt Ella's part. Ma Barker continued, "Do not under any circumstances take any stone away from Pele's home. I'm warning you." Mother added to Aunt Ella's warning and told us to remember what Aunt Ella said and be careful - and don't get too close to the edge of the crater.

Aunt Ella and Mother, exhausted and needing a nap, told us they were going to sit in the car and have a cigarette. Marigold took one path and I another to the crater rim.

As I walked, I scuffed my feet along the trail. Sulphurous gas and smoke from vents in the volcano cracks began to overwhelm me. The stinky smell and smoke forced into my nose and mouth were so bad, I thought I was going to choke to death. Pele's breath was as bad as Marigold's seasick pukey breath.

I kept losing my balance as I teeter-tottered my way to the crater's rim. The walkway reminded me of Mother's story about Little Johnny and Patty because it looked golden and sparkled with Hawaiian diamonds (olivines). Looking down at the green stones sparkling in the sun, I kept thinking, "Pele won't mind if I steal a bunch of them and take them home with me. I'd hide them with the toys in my window seat. Pele has so many diamonds, she'll never know. And one more curse on my head won't matter anyway." The stones looked magical.

I pinched myself to pay attention because I was only a few feet away from looking down into the fire goddess's home. My palms became sweaty. I hated heights and became afraid. I was certain I was going to fall into the crater and that Pele was going to gobble me up.

A yellow streak rushed up my spine and tingled my mind. I was born a coward. Then, I remembered Ronald Coleman, the actor, who bravely climbed the steps to the guillotine in MGM's *A Tale of Two Cities*. I told myself to act like him even if Pele chopped off my neck. I wanted to be a brave man like Ronald.

I was coming up to the edge of the crater and took each step carefully - one step at a time. I stood at the rim of the crater, not holding on to anything, and looked down.

The crater was huge, as large as a city. Lava cones painted in yellows, blacks, grays, and blues were its buildings. A crimson red light glowed in the center of each cone. Pele's hot blood was boiling underneath the surface. Steam poured out of each cinder cone, making Pele's buildings into huge teakettles whistling on top of a hot stove. The cinder cones were lined up in rows, like battleships anchored at Pearl Harbor.

I looked around and listened. A gust of wind rushed off the barren lava fields, swirled around me, and whispered that I was as tiny as the little pieces of black sand that I was standing on. One mighty blow of Pele's wind would send me flying up into the air like Judy Garland did in *The Wizard of Oz*. I would join the other specks of lava swirling in the distance on a merry-go-round of dust.

Aunt Ella's voice came out of nowhere, "Beware, Percy. Beware. Be afraid because you are a fat, bad, weak, sissy little boy." The yellow streak on my back glowed.

I was dizzy because the steam from the hot teakettles was kissing my face.

Pele's breath, then her kisses began to smother me. Pele was warning me she was going to burst into a thousand explosions, creating a thousand lava fountains that would blow me straight up into God's heaven.

For the first time as a little boy, I was experiencing something that I had only seen in earthquake movies. I wasn't sitting in a darkened movie theater watching a volcano. I was in the movie and I was alone. Hatsuko and Mother weren't around to save me from turning into dust. My heart pounded out of my chest. I couldn't hide under a theater seat to protect myself like I did when I was scared.

I turned crazy and decided to defy Pele. With my two hands, I reached down and grabbed a handful of Hawaiian diamonds and stuffed them in my pocket. I yelled down into the crater, "You can't hurt me, Pele. I'm already cursed. Ha!"

At that moment, a hot gust of wind blew me to the edge. The wind pushed me closer and closer to the rim. With one gust of wind, I could see myself falling hundreds of feet to the bottom of the crater and into one of Pele's teakettles. As I was gobbled up, Aunt Ella cackled in the background like the witch in *The Wizard of Oz*, "See - See -See! See, that's what happens to naughty, bad, fat boys who don't listen to me."

In one of Pele's big black cooking pots, I saw myself swimming around with bunches of carrots, taro, and rhubarb. In my imagination, Pele checked on her lunch. Surprised, seeing she had a haole boy in her stew, she tossed me out because I wasn't the right color to eat. Laughing like a hyena, she screamed, "Hawaiians only like dark meat." Next, I saw myself on top of one of the teakettles - abandoned. I had been called fat; I had been called a sissy; I was named Percy; and now, I was not the right color.

I already knew that I wasn't the right color by the way local people looked at me walking down Fort Street. One thing I did have in my favor, Hawaiians loved fat people who loved to eat.

I reached into my pocket and threw out the Hawaiian diamonds. As soon as the rocks hit the ground, the wind stopped dead. Madame Pele was a powerful goddess.

I looked at my bare feet. My feet were only inches from going over the rim. I stepped back and ran back to the car and found Marigold sitting in the back seat, chewing gum. She looked bored.

I didn't speak all the way back into Hilo. I was thinking, as we were driving down from the volcano, that I had learned new things today. First, you don't fool with a Hawaiian fire goddess. Second, there was something protective in being small, fat, unattractive, and white. In my mind, the good guys may not want you playing kick ball with them, but thank my Sunday school Jesus, neither did those mean witches that wanted to throw little boys in cooking pots. Goddesses and mean witches only liked the pretty boys.

Aunt Ella asked as she turned the station wagon on two tires around a corner, "Did you have a nice time today, Percy?"

Holding onto the door handle, I screeched, "Yes, Aunt Ella, I did. Thank you."

"That's good!" She lit a cigarette and ran a stop sign. I looked to the left and sighed with relief that a car wasn't heading for us. Looking back at me sitting petrified in the back seat, she said, "Percy, when we get home, I have something to show you." Her sweet, tiny little voice sounded threatening.

I stopped feeling protected from witches because a real witch was sitting in the front seat who wanted to do me bodily harm. I figured that it was because I was fat, white, liked mayonnaise, threw horse droppings, fell in mud puddles, was a sissy, and hated her crazy driving.

Aunt Ella sped through another stop sign. I thought I might as well have jumped into Pele's crater and died because Aunt Ella was going to kill me anyway, flying through every stop sign on her broomstick. I was too scared to worry what she was about to show me when we got home.

Once home, Aunt Ella caught me before I took my bath and forced a ruled pad and pencil into my hands. She ordered me to write a hundred times that I would never throw anything bad at an adult again.

Agnes, the naughty, whispered in my ear, "Change 'anything bad' to 'horse shit.'" Gertrude warned me to forget the horse shit business because Aunt Ella was so mad at me right now that if I did one more wrong thing, she was sure to stuff me down the toilet and flush me down with her....

Shit was my new word for the week.

Looking at the pad and pencil in my hand, thinking of all the writing I had to do, I grumbled to Aunt Ella that by the time I finished, I would never see Santa Claus and I'd be as old and wrinkled as she was when I finished, and would probably look like I was about to croak like Uncle Will did.

Aunt Ella huffed and puffed at me to quit being fresh or I wouldn't get dinner and get to work. She didn't scare me because I knew Mother, the good witch, wouldn't let anything really bad happen to me. But maybe with the way I acted today, Mother felt like giving me to Pele for her dinner.

After I wrote out the sentence twenty times, my left hand ached. So, I scribbled tons of words all over the tablet to make it look like I had written the sentence a thousand times.

Aunt Ella forgot to ask to look at the sentences because there weren't enough words or shit in all the world to write away the wrong that I was about to do to her on Christmas day.

20

Santa Claus

Kimo described much of Hilo and its people to me on Christmas Day while we were sitting beside a swimming pool.

Hilo was not a sugar plantation town. It was Lincoln, Nebraska of the Pacific. The town looked middle class. Hilo's architecture was fashioned in the style of the old west and was established to support the cane and cattle industries. It was a town where Sinclair Lewis and the Dodsworths would have happily put down their roots. The only surprise for the Dodsworths: Hilo was on an island and built on the slopes of a volcano, and had a wild river running through its center that spawned a rainbow over a waterfall.

Hilo was exotic only because it was part of the Hawaiian Islands. Gossip ruled in Hilo as it did in all America. Everybody knew everybody else's business and some of the business should have been kept behind closed doors with Cousin Bessie.

On Christmas Eve, Mother and her orphans - that's how I felt we were treated by people in Hilo, were driven by Aunt Ella and Uncle Will to the higher altitudes of Mauna Kea where all the elite lived. The air here was indeed rarefied.

In the evenings, ladies wore long dresses and carried beaded purses. Men wore coats and ties that matched the color of their pants. Everyone - just everyone living on the hill - competed at giving the "swellest" parties on the island. These parties looked like the parties in the MGM melodramas that starred Joan Crawford, Clark Gable and Norma Shearer. They were not the down-home parties like Mickey Rooney's Hardy family had.

The upper reaches of Hilo were considered by people in Honolulu as the Big Island's Beverly Hills, California. The down-to-earth people lived on Banyan Street next to Hilo bay. The folks who had their homes near the volcano, high in the clouds, never considered themselves, for one instant, middle class - which they were. To them, the middle class were "the others" who fished in saltwater ponds, planted taro, and grew orchids in hot houses.

A Christmas Eve invitation came from Hilo's Beverly Hills. It was the cat's pajamas to be invited to this home. The cultural talents of the entire island had been invited to this gathering. The hostess was the grande dame talent of them all, the widow, Mrs. Cornelius Porteous.

Mrs. Porteous's husband, a banker, drowned on a deep sea fishing expedition on the south side of the island three years ago. Rumor had it - at least as Kimo told me - that he got plastered and fell overboard. It was hours before anyone in the fishing party, who used these weekend expeditions to get away from their wives, missed him. Mrs. Porteous kept a candle burning in her window, hoping one day, drunk Mr. Porteous holding onto a life preserver would walk back into her life.

Kimo was assigned to play the piano that evening. He played by ear. Mrs. Porteous modestly told us - she dropped a lot of Hollywood names - that Groucho Marx compared her singing to Jeanette MacDonald's. She told us she had sung at a bar mitzvah that Groucho attended in Bakersfield, California. Groucho was a famous Hollywood jokester.

After we passed around the bowl of colored popcorn for the third time, Mrs. Porteous ended the evening's entertainment by singing "Ah, Sweet Mystery of Life." The mystery was how she got through the song because she was coughing, wheezing and out of breath by the time she finished the last note. Her guests gave her a standing ovation.

I couldn't take my eyes off her gigantic bosom laced with long strands of black onyx beads. The beads and bosom rose and fell with each note she sang. Her rising and falling bosom was like our ship sailing to Hilo in a storm - up and down her bosom heaved through waves. Marigold looked seasick watching her.

After Mrs. Porteous sat down, pleased with herself, Kimo announced that a young talent was sitting in our midst. He said that I had sung "Silent Night" at the Punahou Christmas party to "great artistic acclaim." The "great artistic acclaim" did it. Marigold was behind this embarrassment. I sent a silent prayer to Pele to smear hot lava all over my rotten sister, who was sitting on the couch, smiling to herself and shoving colored popcorn into her mouth.

Mrs. Porteous's guests crowded around me and insisted that I perform. What could I do? Blood was about to be spilt all over this room and that blood was going to be Marigold's. I wanted to join Mr. Porteous floating out in the Pacific. Mrs. Porteous could then burn two candles in her window.

It was too late. Aunt Ella poked me to the front of the room and made me stand next to the piano. Kimo asked me if I was ready. I nodded.

He began playing. My performance turned into a miracle. My singing was perfect, my voice was easy and true.

Mrs. Porteous's guests were dumbstruck when I finished. Mrs. Porteous wanted to kick me in the fanny, and the guests seemed disappointed that I didn't flatten my notes like Mrs. Porteous did or cough or wheeze at the end.

Mother applauded. Not one of the guests gave me a standing ovation except Kimo and Marigold. Kimo winked at me when he sat down. Mother and Marigold had smiled at me with their eyes. I knew I had been really good this time because they didn't have to say anything nice to me about my singing when we got back to Aunt Ella's.

My performance put a damper on the party and Mrs. Porteous fell into a slump.

We left. I learned another a lesson without anyone telling me what the lesson was. A guest should never outshine his hostess who has become very pleased with herself and has a husband floating out in the Pacific Ocean with a drink in his hand.

Before I went to bed, I instructed everyone in the house to keep a watchful eye out for Santa Claus and tell him that I was staying in the guestroom. Uncle Will got the biggest kick out of that. He told me he'd stay up all night to steer Santa into the house and make sure Santa knew where to hang my stocking. Getting into bed, I told Agnes and Gertrude the mayonnaise raid was off tonight because Uncle Will had the watch.

On Christmas Day, I found an old lady's stocking hanging outside my bedroom door. Uncle Will stood his watch well. The stocking was a throwaway from Mrs. Santa Claus because it was riddled with holes and had a run in it. I was disappointed because the stocking was only half-filled. Reaching in, I pulled out pieces of hard candy, a pencil, a box of crayons, and a tiny wooden tugboat. I expected more from Santa Claus. Cousin Bessie must have told Santa I wet my bed or Santa must be going through a financial depression in Santa land. Maybe Santa had to stand in a soup line like the hoboes did in New York City. I couldn't understand why the stocking wasn't filled to the top because I hadn't wet my bed since I left Honolulu and I heard from Wigay that Santa was richer than a hundred Mr. Dillinghams.

Aunt Ella had been padding up and down the hallways in her bedroom slippers since five in the morning. Her voice woke me up as I overheard her giving marching orders to Uncle Will and the maids. She was making final preparations for her annual, stupendous Christmas dinner. Aunt Ella's Christmas dinners were legendary even on Oahu.

After I ate my breakfast, Aunt Ella ordered me to stay out of her way while she ran around the house fixing things up. She told me she wanted to keep her house and especially the living room pristine clean, and she worried that I would mess up her decorations by looking for my presents under the Christmas tree.

She was right. I would have made a disaster under her Christmas tree, looking for presents, if she had let me. Christmas Day excited me to hiccups from the time I woke up until after I unwrapped my last present.

Aunt Ella's Christmas decorations were photographed and featured in the Hilo *Tribune Herald* every year and the guest list was written up on the front page in the society section. Each year, the paper raved that her decorations were more spectacular than the King of England's in Windsor Castle because Aunt Ella gave free tours of her house to the newspaper and post office staffs.

Aunt Ella always started planning her Christmas noonday dinner celebration early in January. By May, she had written to Harrods in England for Christmas crackers and sweet biscuits. This year, she decorated her living room from top to bottom with silver tinsel she ordered from Macy's in New York City and had brought in real Mainland holly from Podesto's flower shop in San Francisco. Uncle Will had everything sent by special delivery.

This year she added a local touch by garnishing the room with Christmas berries grown in Kona. Over each doorway, she tacked large sprigs of real mistletoe that came from the White House department store in San Francisco. Kissing under the mistletoe was the only time our family smooched in public.

Aunt Ella scheduled and planned her Christmas dinner down to the minute. According to the list posted in the kitchen, family and servants were to open presents after lunch. All the outside guests in attendance were to look on as we unwrapped our gifts. Unwrapping gifts was part of the entertainment.

Opening presents in front of strangers was going to be as embarrassing for me as it was for Marie Antoinette when she gave birth to her children while the peasants of Paris looked on. After lunch meant two o'clock in the afternoon, according to the maids. I was beside myself with hiccups as two o'clock seemed a hundred years away.

At home, I opened Christmas presents as soon as breakfast was over. I always cheated. Before anyone was up, I foraged like a weasel under the Christmas tree and in ten minutes, I knew exactly what was inside every present that Daddy and Mother gave me. I never bothered opening Marigold's present to me because she always gave me something she wanted. I gave her lipstick and nail polish and she gave me a baseball. I had cheated since I was five in present opening because I never wanted to look ungrateful at receiving a junky present from Daddy. This way, I'd have breakfast to prepare my surprise act and practice my shriek for joy at getting rubber pants.

Our lunch, according to the maids (we had become best friends), was hard work because Aunt Ella served every known dish ever laid on a Christmas dinner table in merrie old England. Duck, turkey, ham, three kinds of dressing, candied yams, tinned peas, and everything else creamed was on the menu for starts. The oyster soup, served first, was a recipe that Aunt Ella treasured and nowhere else in the Hawaiian Islands was it served but at Aunt Ella's Christmas dinner. The plum pudding, soaked in brandy, arrived in the mail from a specialty shop in New York City that the Rockefellers and Astors shopped at.

Everyone on the Big Island vied for an invitation to Aunt Ella's. This year, the mayor of Hilo and his wife had graciously accepted to attend the luncheon, as did most of Aunt Ella's flossiest friends from the uplands. Every guest's name was written on a place card that was set carefully on the long koa dining room table. We were seated in between the swells. Since her poor relatives were staying with her, she left out some of the regulars because the dining room table held only so many people. The rejected were miffed and secretly hoped that the party would bomb without them. Mother had written out the twenty names on the gilt-edged place cards.

Uncle Will drove into town to get away from the madness. He told me he had to deliver leftover Santa Claus packages personally because Santa forgot to put them in the mail. That worried me because it never occurred to me that Santa left things behind like I did.

Marigold ran outside to be by herself. I wandered aimlessly around the yard, bored with myself, and without anyone looking, made raids into the living room to look for my presents under the Christmas tree. Aunt Ella always caught me rattling a package.

Marigold fished for guppies with a butterfly net in a deep ravine next to the house. I know she was longing for Daddy having Christmas on Maui. Kimo spied her from the window of his loft and went to fetch her. He walked her up from the gully, his arms around her shoulders, buddy-buddy style, and went into his studio. I followed them. Kimo propped Marigold up onto a window ledge. When sunlight streaked in behind her, Kimo started to paint her. The artist said I could watch if I kept quiet.

Marigold sat real still for Kimo as animation drained from her face. The canvas mirrored her thoughts as Kimo's paint brush created a face that brooded dark thoughts. To Gertrude, the painting was of a little girl who had dark, beautiful brown eyes framed in a halo of chestnut hair, flecked with strands of Aunt Mari's golden-red tresses.

At eleven o'clock, Aunt Ella, in her sweet, tinkling Christmas voice, called the troops to get dressed. We all wore white except Kimo. Mother and Aunt Ella dressed in white gowns trimmed with red. Each had on a different style but the effect was the same - fields of white. I wore a white shirt and short white pants buttoned to my tum-tum. Uncle Will wore long white pants snugged tight to his bigger and even fatter tum-tum. In profile, we looked like the Bobsey twins.

Gertrude and Agnes wore red. They said wearing white took the place of snow and wearing red took the place of Jesus's diaper rash. Kimo wore black pants, a blue shirt and a bright red scarf around his neck. He was an artist.

Seeing Uncle Will and I looked twin-like, Aunt Ella brought out her square black "Brownie" camera and made us pose together. Uncle Will held a Santa Claus mask in front of his face and made me pretend a surprised look at seeing him. It was Uncle Will's idea to wear the Santa Claus mask because, as he told me, he had never in his life heard a child create so much fuss over Santa Claus. He wanted a picture of me seeing Santa coming to lunch.

I told Uncle Will that Santa Claus was one of the good things in my life that stayed around. I was thinking about Daddy, Hatsuko and my dog, Uku. *Christmas brings up thoughts like that.*

Aunt Ella ordered that Uncle Will and I stand still and that I hold up my hands as if I was being robbed in a Roy Rogers western. Aunt Ella demonstrated how to put up my hands and how to look surprised. I copied her. Aunt Ella must have held up a lot of banks.

I stretched my eyes and mouth and put my hands up as far as I could make them go.

"Hold still," Aunt Ella coached.

"We are holding still, Ella. It's your hands that's shaking," grumbled Uncle Will.

"They're not. Quiet, Will."

Uncle Will laughed his Santa's ha - ha - ha.

Click.

This photograph was to be my evidence that Santa Claus had come to Hilo in 1940. The photograph would also be a reminder to Aunt Ella that it was to be the last big Christmas party she ever gave in her entire life - a Christmas party that was about to become legendary in Hilo for decades.

Click.

A long shot of a little fat boy and an old man acting out make believe, wearing masks. My mask was pretense: the Santa Claus in front of me.

Click.

Another moment captured. High on a cliff overlooking the blue Pacific, a green grass lawn sloping to its edge, a slight trade wind blowing and a family of relatives standing around dressed in white and red...and blue. It was the last time we would all be gathered together in our lives.

Click.

A moment frozen in time...a happy moment.

Life as presented by God, as told by Gertrude, is only a moment-to-moment process and not all moments turn out happy.

The guests arrived promptly and were herded by Aunt Ella into the living room. The women were dressed for a ball. Some ladies had on every diamond they owned. A goose wore her tiara on the back of her head like a beanie hat while the other women hung pearls like rain drops everywhere on their bodies. The men in tuxedoes were as stuffed as the turkey we were about to eat.

Dinner was late - a bad omen. We entered the dining room fifteen minutes after twelve. I sat between the wife of the mayor - the goose with the tiara, and my mother. There were so many people crowded around the table you couldn't help touching someone somewhere embarrassing on their bodies. The maids, wearing white starched uniforms, served what was probably the most sumptuous Christmas dinner I had ever seen or eaten.

From the start of the dinner, I ate like a prisoner sprung from the Bastille. I piled food upon food upon food on my plate. I ignored the conversation between Mother and the sweet goose on my left. I ate with the gusto of a stevedore, shoveling the food into my mouth with two hands. I ate as fast as I could stuff it in my mouth and took third helpings. Aunt Ella wasn't watching me this afternoon.

I ran a food race with Uncle Will on who could eat the most and I won. It was not even near a draw. By dessert, I was so bloated I had to unbutton all the buttons on my pants. The underwear that Daddy gave me last Christmas showed.

I ate two pieces of mince and pumpkin pies that I layered over with a rich buttery hard sauce. As soon as I swallowed the last bite of mince pie, a sharp gas pain struck; I felt like an oil well that was about to gush. I dropped my napkin and dove under the table to retrieve it. Agnes and Gertrude under the table were shaking their heads at what a pig I had made of myself.

Mother and the mayor's wife, Lydia the goose, with noses leading, curiously watched as I squeezed my fat stomach under the table.

"What's the matter, dear?" Mother asked.

"Nothing," I groaned, holding onto my aching stomach.

The gas was looking for an opening. It found one. I couldn't stop it from coming out. A cannon roared from under the table. I poop-da-pooped...big time. Mother and the mayor's wife must have been blown out of their seats, tiara and all, by the force of the blast. Conversations ceased above me. Gasps were heard as a green cloud rose from under the table. Grandma would have been proud of me.

Hiding under the table, I asked Agnes what I should do. She advised me to crawl out of the dining room as fast as I could and throw myself off the cliff.

Gertrude roared, "Get up, Percy, and face the music." Napkin retrieved, held in my mouth, I emerged from under the table as soon as I heard the conversations resume again. The whale surfaced. A slight odor was hanging in the air.

I sat up straight, took the napkin out of my mouth and pretended that I was a gentleman. Not daring to look at Mother, I stared curiously around the table to see their reactions. One by one, I looked at the pinched faces conversing with one another, all of them pretending that Mount Vesuvius hadn't exploded. My eyes stopped at Marigold. She crossed her eyes while pantomiming gagging and holding her nose. She never let me get away with anything. Everyone else was ignoring the disaster, talking to each other like quacking geese.

Suddenly Uncle Will thundered, "That was a lovely meal, Ella. Let's adjourn to the living room and open presents." Uncle Will signaled, waving his hand to Aunt Ella, the meal had ended. To make it final, he rolled his white linen napkin back into its silver napkin holder. As he did that, I looked at Kimo sitting next to Aunt Ella.

That was a mistake. Kimo looked at me, crossed his eyes like Marigold did and put a naughty smile on his face that spread as wide as the Mississippi River. He quickly stuffed his napkin into his mouth to keep from laughing out loud.

That did it. I burst out laughing. Loud uncontrollable laughter. I couldn't stop myself. Tears streamed down my cheeks. I laughed so hard, I pooped again.

Mauna Kea exploded. Aunt Ella would have forgiven me one explosion, not two. Two explosions were two farts too many at Christmas.

When Marigold heard my second explosion, she shrieked with laughter and the maids started to giggle. Hearing the maids and Marigold made me laugh even louder and explode a third time.

Then Uncle Will farted. Mauna Loa exploded and Aunt Ella swooned in her chair. By Mother's look, she wanted to shoot me. Kimo revived Aunt Ella. She faked the fainting.

The mayor and his wife ran out of the dining room gasping for breath because they were laughing, too. The other guests followed, holding their stomachs.

I ruined Aunt Ella's Christmas dinner and her regal standing in the Hilo community with three poops. Her guests could hardly wait to get home and get on their telephones to spread the news. I had become a celebrity.

As if nothing had happened, we opened presents on schedule beside the Christmas tree as the guests fidgeted and watched the grandfather's clock, longing to get on their telephones. I received from Aunt Ella and Uncle Will a wind-up train that ran around on a track shaped in a figure eight.

After the last guest departed, I was sent into exile. Aunt Ella ordered Kimo to drive me down to the Hilo Yacht Club for a swim. We brought with us a toy submarine that Kimo gave me for Christmas. When he placed the tin boat in the swimming pool, it floated for a minute, then bubbled to the bottom. The sub glued itself to the bottom of the pool and wouldn't surface.

I looked into the bottom of the swimming pool and waited for the submarine to unfix itself and rise victoriously to the surface, as pictured on the box. The submarine didn't hear me. It lay on its side, camouflaged in the blue tile. Kimo dove in, retrieved the derelict and placed the toy submarine between us. We sat silently side by side, dangling our legs in the pool. Water dripped on my head as Kimo affectionately put his arm around my shoulder and talked. "Percy, we'll always be best friends. You and I are kindred spirits."

"I know that, too."

Taking his arm away from my shoulder and looking me straight in the eyes, he said, "Percy, don't let anyone change you. Be who you are! Follow what interests you most. Your passion."

Looking down into the pool, I asked, "Why did you say that? I don't know what passion is."

He kicked the water in the pool, sighing, "Last night, I asked my girl, Sarah, to marry me. She told me no. She said she doesn't want to marry a poor artist and starve for the rest of her life. She said I was too impractical to be a good husband. That was her exact word - impractical. Sarah told me her father wouldn't approve anyway. Her father is going to fire me after the New Year. He told Sarah I'm the worst bookkeeper he's ever hired and he only hired me because of my dad. He's right. All I want to do is paint. I should never have let Aunt Mari talk me into coming back from England. I can't be anyone else but who I am." He sighed and kicked the water again.

I took Kimo's hand and agreed, "I thought you were crazy to leave England, too. Your life sounded as exciting as an Errol Flynn movie."

Kimo squeezed my hand and asked, "Do you keep secrets?"

"I keep lots of secrets right in here." I pointed to my belly.

"What I just told you, let's keep it a secret between you and me - about Sarah and me. I don't want to upset Mother."

Crossing my heart, I told him, "On my honor, Kimo. I already upset your mother tons."

Kimo, looking sadly up at the clouds, said, "You know Percy, I even named the little girl I thought I was going to have with Sarah."

"What's her name?"

"Mary Emily."

I shivered all over. Sitting wet next to my slim, kind, talented, handsome cousin, I wanted to be more like him than anyone else I had ever known. Kimo made me forget in a minute about wanting to be Alice Faye. I wanted to wipe away the tears that were falling down his face.

When Kimo and I returned, the house was in an uproar. Everyone had forgotten I spoiled the Christman lunch because a phone call from Kauai told of another disaster. Aunt Momi's house had burned to the ground on Christmas Eve.

No one had died. Uncle Hans, Aunt Momi's husband, saved his life by jumping out their second story bedroom window. Aunt Momi, Uncle Hans and my first cousins lost all their Christmas toys. The neighbors rescued the icebox while they left the sterling silver tea service melting on the kitchen counter. Saving the icebox, I thought, was a pretty sensible thing to do because at least they'd have mayonnaise sandwiches to eat at midnight.

Talk during the cocktail hour was that Aunt Mari, the really mean old sister of Aunt Ella, hinted over the telephone that a careless cigarette and too many drinks at Aunt Momi's Christmas Eve party had caused the fire.

Sipping an old-fashioned and relaxing for the first time since I messed up her lunch, Aunt Ella breathed a sigh of relief and said, "This old-fashioned hits the spot. It's exceptional, Will. I needed it."

"Thank you, Ella," Uncle Will replied as he chugged down a shot of brandy.

"Deidra, your sister and Hans have the reputation of going around with a fast crowd on Kauai. Mari says there's much too much drinking on that side of the island. Far too many wild and out-of-control parties in Waimea. I want you to talk to Momi about that. She'll end up like you - divorced. We can't stand another divorce in the family," grumbled Aunt Ella.

Mother, staring into her bourbon and water, said, "Yes, Aunt Ella, I'll talk to Momi but she's not about to listen to me."

Mother always stuck up for Aunt Momi since the day their mother died, and she looked Aunt Ella in the face. "Aunt Ella, Aunt Mari doesn't like Momi. She thinks Momi is cheeky because she refused to hand over Mother's inheritance to her like I had to do, and anyway, Aunt Mari exaggerates. She thinks she's a general and runs our family like her own private army and Kauai, if she had her way. Momi has lost everything just now. It's time we stood behind her and not sit around criticizing. The fire must have been awful for her. When I get home, I'm going to send her some of my dresses."

My heart sank.

Aunt Ella put down her drink, looked at Mother, and said, "Percy and Marigold should send their Christmas presents to their cousins. I know Marigold will agree with me on this. Don't you, Marigold?"

I looked over at Marigold, who was watching an ant crossing the carpet. I raised my hand.

Aunt Ella looked at me for the first time since the lunch disaster. "Yes, Percy?"

"All of them?" I asked.

"Every one of them. Don't you think that would be a kind and generous thing to do?" she replied.

"Yes. But I could send them in dribbles. I'll start with the toy submarine and next month, I'll send them the train...something like that. I think my idea is the swellest idea." That idea was shot down and the matter was closed. All my Christmas presents were going to Kauai.

Aunt Ella handed her empty glass to Uncle Will to refill. "Will, I want you to pack all the presents up tomorrow at the post office and ship them off to Kauai on the first boat."

When no one was looking, I hid a Lana Turner coloring book under my shirt.

The phone rang. It was Aunt Mari. The fire chief on Kauai reported that a short in the attic's electrical wiring caused the fire at Aunt Momi's. Mother smiled and made herself another drink.

Back in my room, I told Agnes and Gertrude this was the worst Christmas I had ever had. From now on, I was going to hate Christmas forever.

There was a knock on my door. "May I come in?" a voice said sweetly behind the door. It was Aunt Ella.

I hid the coloring book under my pillow. "Come in, Aunt Ella."

She strode into my bedroom like a prison commandant in a concentration camp. "Percy, sit down on your bed. I have a few things to say before you go to sleep," she ordered.

I quickly sat on the bed like a good soldier. Before she could continue further, I apologized for messing up her lunch.

She told me she had forgotten the entire incident. From the look in her eyes, I knew she hadn't. She paced back and forth in my room, hands behind her back, as she spoke to me in a very General Douglas MacArthur manner. "Percy, there is something I think you should be aware of. It has bothered me since the day you arrived. You act like a baby all the time and you are far too old to keep acting this way. Your constant talking about Santa Claus is very annoying to hear from a boy your age. Uncle Will and I feel responsible to you since you have no father and that is why I am saying this to you. There is no Santa Claus. Santa Claus is a made-up thing, a fairy tale, and it is time for you to forget all about this childish nonsense. You're too old to hang a stocking at Christmas. I knew there wasn't a Santa Claus by the time I was five. Be a man now, Percy. Be a grown-up because you're too much of a weight on your mother's shoulders. I feel sorry for her that she has a child like you to take care of at this time in her life. She needs a boy who will help her. You've got to learn to row your own boat and the sooner, the better. Now it's all been said. Did you hear me? There is no Santa Claus."

I wanted to run screaming from the room but I froze like an icicle on the bed. There was a long cold silence. Finally, in a baby voice, I spoke, "I'm only seven, Aunt Ella. Why did you have to tell me that?"

Aunt Ella stared at the door.

I said thoughtfully, "I guess you wanted to spoil my Christmas like I spoiled yours. I didn't spoil your Christmas on purpose."

All the sweetness faded from her face. She walked to the door and turned, "Didn't you hear me, Percy?"

"I heard you."

"Good!" She continued, "I shouldn't think you'd want to tell your mother about my visit. She might not understand it. You're a big boy now and you can take it. You should be more like your sister. She has spunk."

Getting off the bed, I said, "I can take anything, Aunt Ella. But you shouldn't have told me. I didn't ask you to tell me because I liked believing in Santa Claus. I wanted to be a baby. I liked staying a baby. Santa Claus was the only nice thing I had left in my life. At least babies are kind." Walking to the window and looking out, I said softly, "It's a nicer world with a Santa Claus in it, Aunt Ella. Now, he's gone. I don't ever want to be a grown-up like you."

"Percy, look at me!" Aunt Ella had her hand on the door handle. "I saw you take that coloring book. Please give it to me. When I said everything goes to Aunt Momi's family, I meant everything."

Without a word, I went and reached under the pillow and gave her the Lana Turner coloring book. Aunt Ella started out the door.

I croaked, "Aunt Ella!"

"Yes, Percy?"

Looking at her, my eyes didn't flinch once. "I have two things I want to say to you. Uncle Will didn't apologize for pooping. It's only fair. Fair is fair."

"Your uncle isn't a vulgar man and doesn't break wind in public. You are quite the impossible boy. Have you ever held your tongue? What's the other thing?"

"I wear my mother's dresses."

"Of course, you do. I wouldn't expect anything less of you." She closed the door.

I walked to the window and looked out on a clear, cold, blue night on the Big Island. Agnes and Gertrude joined me at the window.

Gertrude whispered into my ear, "Percy, it is the sweet-acting people you have to watch out for in this world. They are the ones who say nice things to your face and then toss you out of a lifeboat to the sharks. Remember that. Sweet-acting people can be the silent killers in this world."

Frowning, I held my face in my hands, looked out at the sky and started to sing "When You Wish Upon a Star," the Jiminy Cricket song from Walt Disney's *Pinocchio*. A shooting star streaked across the sky. I stopped singing and made quick wishes about a father who disappeared, Christmas presents I didn't have anymore, and a gas attack I wish never happened. Most of all, I wanted to go home and sleep in my bed again.

That night, Agnes, Gertrude and I took my bottle of mayonnaise to the kitchen at one in the morning and I made myself the best cold turkey and mayonnaise sandwich I had ever eaten. I didn't care a tinker's damn if Aunt Ella caught us. I even turned on all the lights. If Aunt Ella wanted me to be grown-up, then she'd have to take me on now - mayonnaise and all.

21

Mr. Hamada

We departed Hilo on a Thursday. Aunt Ella and Uncle Will were all smiles on the day of our sailing. The Japanese maids changed the sheets, cleaned the rooms, and had our luggage in the car before we finished breakfast. Uncle Will couldn't see us off because he went back to work, and Aunt Ella was playing in a bridge tournament. Kimo waved us off.

Our trip home was without incident, except Marigold threw up as soon as she walked up the gangplank. Betsy met us on Oahu. Marigold kissed the ground and vowed to Mother that she'd never sail the seas again. I jumped for joy as I stepped on the dock, thinking that I'd be sleeping in my bed again, bathing in a tub that gushed clear water, eating mayonnaise sandwiches at midnight without Ma Barker's gun in my face, and reading the *Advertiser*.

The Honolulu Advertiser

EDITORIAL: THE NEW YEAR

We enter the year of 1941 with almost the identical ominousness and uncertainty which marked the eve of 1917. No man can pass judgment on the future, yet with the tools which are available to all of us, we cannot fashion any idyllic scenes for the New Year. Peace is the desire of all humble peoples, yet evil forces are still rampant in the world ... For us, as usual, the New Year brings the cherished bounties of sunshine, the beauty of the sea and skies, and the rich products of our lands.

AMERICA'S 1941 ROLE KEY TO WORLD EVENTS

News analysts and important unofficial sources in Honolulu yesterday predict that 1941 may be even more earth-shaking in the march of events than was 1940 - perhaps the most eventful year in modern history.

NAVY BUILDING IN FULL SWING

At year's end, 1940, Hawaii is probably the busiest microcosm in the complex structure of expanding national defense. And probably the busiest sector on this peacetime defense is Pearl Harbor where millions of dollars are going into barracks, housing, guns, and ships.

HAWAII THEATER - MOON OVER BURMA - 10 a.m. Continuous
Starring Dorothy Lamour, Preston Foster, Robert Preston - "Jungle Love
Tease!" "Her Beauty Broke Their Hearts!" Phone 66300

STANFORD INDIANS FAVORED 2 TO 1
Clash today with Nebraska in Rose Bowl Game at Pasadena

LURLINE DUE TOMORROW MORNING FROM COAST WITH 490 PASSENGERS

GOD BLESS AMERICA
Now, in 1941, let us all highly resolve to be better Americans during the coming year—-united in pressing American principle in this land of the free.

Hatsuko was still recuperating in the country with her sister. She was feeling
better but had been in a car accident during the holidays. The car that she drove
crashed into a bridge near Schofield Barracks. Hatsuko now sported a canvas sling
on her left arm. Over the telephone, I wished her lots of Happy New Years and
cooed into the phone that I missed her and gave her lots of kisses into the receiver.
I promised that when she came home I would treat her to a movie and a Hershey
bar with almonds for her Christmas present. I pleaded with her to come home
soon, because I was getting tired of Mother's mysterious creamed dinners. I
longed for her egg salad sandwiches.
     Hatsuko cried. I cried too. After I talked to Hatsuko on the phone, I went into
the kitchen and made a sling out of a dishcloth and told everyone in the house that
I drove my car into a bridge.
     Daddy phoned as soon as we walked in the door. He told Marigold that he'd
pick us up on Saturday to see an air show at the John Rodgers airport. It was his
big Christmas surprise. Marigold was beside herself and started counting the hours
till Saturday.
     Agnes and Gertrude opted to stay home that Saturday. They were only into
seeing matinees and not into Daddy's manly out-of-door events. The real truth:
Agnes freckled. All Hitler's children had that problem.
     On Saturday, Daddy arrived an hour late. He drove madly like Aunt Ella to the
airport. When we arrived, a huge crowd had already gathered. Being late, of course,
Daddy had to drive round and round looking for a place to park and couldn't find
one. He parked the car a good mile away in a grove of kiawe trees. It made for a
long walk in the hot sun to the airfield. Colorful balloons and fluttering banners
guided us to the festivities.
     The air show was a half-hour in progress. I told Daddy I felt like we were
going to a circus without a tent, or a tiger or a bear. The air hung heavy and I was
soaked in perspiration by the time we huffed and puffed to the entrance. As soon
as the man took the tickets out of Daddy's hand, the smell of hot dogs coated with
mustard and sweet pickle relish greeted my nose. My stomach did flip-flops like
the planes were doing above me.

I told Daddy I was hungry. He ignored me and pushed me past the shaved ice and hot dog stands. I longed to rub the shaved ice over my face to give myself a strawberry cool down.

As we entered the field, we saw an army of men, women and children who were stretching their necks, looking up at double-winged planes doing somersaults in the air. Daddy pushed his way into the middle of the crowd so we could get a better look at the action. I felt closed in and couldn't breathe because too many people were mushed into me. People were as tall as the trees in Hunkacha's forest, human trees bending in the wind. They swayed back and forth as they watched planes in the sky make nose dives. I stretched my arms up as far as I could into the forest of people, trying to find a piece of the sky. I could hear the planes but I couldn't see them. I stood frozen, face up and looking for the sky to open up.

"Whirrr - whirrr - zoom - zoom - zoom," went the sounds of the planes.

Suddenly, the forest of people opened up and I saw sky and the playful planes. "I see them, Daddy," I yelled. An airplane went straight up into a cloud and flipped backwards into a complete somersault. I shouted, "Wasn't that's great, Daddy?" I would have jumped up and down, but I couldn't move because I was nosed into everyone's crotch and getting woozy from the different smells.

All of a sudden, Daddy and Marigold were gone. I looked around the human forest. They had disappeared. Poof!

I couldn't believe it. I searched for Marigold's red bandanna and Daddy's blue pants. They were nowhere to be seen. I pushed my way to the outside of the forest and started to run this way, that way. Round and round in circles I scrambled, in and out of the forest of people. I stopped to breathe. I had sucked in air too fast and the human trees were whirling around me. My mind pounded as I spun, singing, "Marigold and Daddy brought me out here to get rid of me."

Panic shifted into third gear. I pushed myself further away from the crowd and ran into the airplane hangar, turned around and ran back to the shaved ice stands. There wasn't a red bandanna or pair of blue pants in sight.

Drenched in sweat, I circled back - darting here, darting there, and cried out, "My daddy and Marigold left me. Hunkacha is going to eat me up. Somebody help me."

My fat legs got me to the parking lot, but I couldn't remember where Daddy parked his car. I ran in more circles and started crying - wailing, actually. The parking lot was empty of people except for a little boy going mad among the kiawe trees as the air show continued in the near distance. No one seemed to have missed a crazy, little fat boy. I scurried from car to car looking for Daddy's Ford, trying to remember what color it was.

I bumped into a Model T vegetable truck. I spied an old Japanese man slouched behind the wheel, asleep. His face looked browned crisp from the sun, wrinkled like a prune, but his cheeks stood out as firm as rocks. From under an old, battered straw hat, his gray hair poked out like the bristles in my hairbrush. The hat slouched over half his face, protecting him from the hot sun and crying little boys.

I shook his leg and said, "Mister." He started to snore.

"Mister!" I cried louder. He snored louder.

I shook both his legs this time and shrieked, "Mister!"

He grunted, "I sleep. Leave me alone."

"How can you sleep when you just said leave me alone?" I demanded.

"I sleep and talk same time. Go away," he grumbled. I wailed louder than the planes flying above.

The Japanese man lifted up his hat and looked down at me. "You sound like girl. I thought you girl. Go way. Why haole boy cry? You one big crybaby, if you ask me. You biggest crybaby I ever heard," he scolded.

Wiping tears from my eyes, I said in one breath, "I'm lost. My daddy left me. He doesn't like me anymore. I wanna go home to my mother. Take me home now." I then wailed like an air raid siren.

The Japanese man sat up, fully alert and said, "I know why Papa no like you. He think you cry like sick dog."

I hollered, "He doesn't like me because I told him I didn't like him. He doesn't like me because I wear my mother's dresses. He just doesn't like me." I wiped away the water running out my nose.

He put on his eyeglasses on the front seat to get a better look at me and said, "If I have son who tell me he no like me and wear girl kimono all time, I t'row him in rubbish pile."

I looked around at the empty cars in the parking lot and realized this Japanese man wearing a funny straw hat was my only hope of getting home. Where were Agnes and Gertrude when I needed them?

"Mister, I wanna go home. Please. I know the way. Please take me home. I'll give you five cents. It's my allowance," I begged. I pulled a buffalo nickel out of my pocket and showed it to him.

He took my nickel from my hand and bit it. "Not enough to take *momona* crybaby in truck." I knew the word momona from Hatsuko. Momona meant "fat" in Hawaiian.

When the Japanese man gave me back my nickel, I started to cry again. He pounded on his horn and yelled, "Enough! You wake up everybody. They come here see me and t'ink I beat up little fat haole boy. Get in. Take you home. Only no more cry like baby."

I stopped crying, ran around to the other side of the truck and hopped in. The man's breath smelled like rotten vegetables. I held my nose. Without another word, the old man started up the Model T and we chugged out of the parking lot toward Honolulu...home.

It was the first time in my life that I had ridden in a truck that didn't have a windshield, a roof or doors. I was riding in the outdoors, so I held fast to the seat. The man drove fifteen miles an hour into the wind. I screamed to him that I lived in Manoa Valley and would show him the way after we reached Punahou Street. As we rode along in the open air, brown dust from the streets blew into my face. I stopped holding my nose and covered my eyes.

We didn't speak at first as we headed into Honolulu but I couldn't stand the silence any longer, so I spoke first. I had to shout because of the loud noises of the truck and the wind. I screamed, "My name is Percy. What's yours?"

The man shouted back to me, "Hamada. Call me Mr. Hamada."

"Mr. Hamada, thank you for taking me home."

"Why you act like girl? Why you dress up in Mama's clothes?"

I thought for a minute. No one had ever asked me that question before. I answered, "I don't know, Mr. Hamada. I guess girls are more interesting than boys. That's one reason. Another reason: girls are prettier and have it much better than boys. Girls slap John Wayne in the face all the time and get away with it. Girls get away with everything and they get FABULOUS presents. I love FABULOUS presents, don't you, Mr. Hamada? I like being taken care of and wearing dresses because dresses are prettier than men's pants. Men's pants are like yours, they look boring. I like to wear bright colors except red. I think my mother is the best person in the whole world and I want to be just like her." I ran out of breath.

Mr. Hamada's question had confused me. I looked at him and yelled again, "I don't know why I like wearing my mother's clothes. I just do it and it gets me lots of attention."

Mr. Hamada scratched his forehead and explained, yelling back, "You born boy. You act like boy. Dress like boy. We born this world one way or that way. You born boy way. Boy not take girl road. Understand?" He poked me on my head with his finger.

I poked him back, protesting, "I like my road, Mr. Hamada. My road goes this way and that way. I like being a boy sometimes and when I get bored, I like wearing dresses. Anyway, I'm cursed but I don't think about the curse anymore because I am making a big plan to see that I will never be left behind like today and never be cursed anymore. My daddy likes my sister Marigold best of all and I know why; it's because she's smart like him. I am like no one I have ever met in my life, Mr. Hamada, and that can be very discouraging."

Mr. Hamada's radiator started to bubble over and in seconds a hot geyser shot up in the air. My new Japanese friend stepped on the brake and turned the truck to the side of the road. "We pull off side road few minutes. Let radiator cool off. Haole boy, hand me water down there." He pointed to my feet where a jug of water stood. "When cool off, I put water in," he explained. "Few minutes, take home then."

He turned off the engine, leaned back in the seat, pulled out a Bull Durham tobacco pouch, rolled a cigarette and lit it. He took off his hat and said, "Haole boy, what make you t'ink you all by yourself?"

I raised my hand and said, "My daddy and sister ran away from me as soon as they saw I wasn't paying attention to them. They wanted to leave me because they don't like having me around because I'm different from them."

"Haole boy, how can be alone? You here, right? Pinch arm."

I pinched my arm hard, "Owww. That hurt."

He said, "If you here, how can be alone? You here all time." He pointed to his heart.

"No can take heart away. Right, haole boy? You here all time. You funny kind haole boy. White skin no think - I t'ink. When I boy-time, Papa he teach me way of bushido - way of samurai warrior. First lesson, be strong here and here." Mr. Hamada pointed to his head and to his heart.

"Warrior - strong body, strong mind, strong heart, but first be strong in here."

He pointed to his heart again. "Then here." He pointed to his head again and then touched my head.

"Body last. No one can take anything away if you no let them take way what inside head. Have strong heart - like fist. If someone leave you - do bad things - they no can if you keep strong heart and head . Haole boy, work on heart and depend on heart all lifetime. Look Roy Rogers - he all time strong because he have big heart, big mind and big body."

"And big horse," I added. "Mr. Hamada, my sister wants to be like John Wayne."

"You funny kind family," he replied.

I looked at him and changed the subject, "I wish you were my daddy."

"No say that about Daddy. Daddy daddy all time for you. He daddy, this lifetime, and give you big lesson. I think lesson he give you is be strong by yourself, like I say. You t'ink you can do that? Now you act like weak girl...you sick kind like Greta Garbo."

"How do you know about Greta Garbo?" I asked.

"I see movie. I no like that kind. My daughter take me. She too much like movies and haoles. Now, you t'ink you can be strong in heart?"

Looking down at Mr. Hamada's front seat, I saw that it was littered with maps, Japanese writing on pads, and a pair of binoculars. I sat up straight and replied, "I can try. I don't think you would run away from me - would you, Mr. Hamada?"

He warned, "You wear my daughter's kimono, I leave you quick like this and catch fish." He snapped his fingers.

"Nah, Mr. Hamada, I don't think you'd do that. May I ask you a question?"

"What question you like ask?"

"Mr. Hamada, are you a Japanese spy?" I queried.

He gasped, spit out his cigarette, coughed, and squashed the cigarette under his foot. "Why ask?"

"Well, Mr. Hamada, from all the movies I have ever seen, spies carry maps, Japanese writing on papers and a good pair of binoculars. You have all three, and your maps, I notice, are of the airport, this island and Pearl Harbor. I think maybe you're a spy for Japan. Are you?" I persisted.

"Percy," he asked, using my name for the first time, "You keep secrets?"
"Yes." I pointed to my fat belly. "I do, Mr. Hamada. I store secrets down here and never let them out. That's why my belly is so big and fat. I could stuff another secret in there," I said, rubbing my stomach. "There's plenty of room inside for more secrets. Are you a spy, Mr. Hamada?"

"I am a spy, Percy, not a very good one." He spoke good English for that one moment and didn't sound like a local man. Then he spoke again like a local Japanese man, "No good spy if crybaby like you find me out."

"Oh, don't feel bad, Mr. Hamada. I'm a pretty good spy myself. One spy always spots another spy. Why are you a spy, Mr. Hamada? Don't you love America? I love America."

He tried to explain, "Percy, you love United States. That's right you. I love Japan. That's right for me. Plenty trouble Japan now. We have to fight. We are all born to walk on funny kind paths. This is my path this lifetime. You and I follow path we born to and walk path best way we know how. You on one path and I on one other path. You do best you can to walk your path. I warrior, you one, too. A warrior man who fight own battles. I see warrior in you."

"You do? Then I'll try, Mr. Hamada. You know, Mr. Hamada, I want to be the best Alice Faye that ever lived. Do you think I could become a warrior that becomes famous and rich and is just like Alice Faye in the movies?" I asked.

"Alice Faye?"

"Alice Faye is big movie star in Hollywood. She's better than Greta Garbo because Alice Faye sings," I explained.

"Greta Garbo no can sing. She only cry."

"I know."

"Percy, only one Alice Faye in Hollywood and only one Percy in Hawaii. You be best Percy in Hawaii and no one else. You write Alice Faye in Hollywood and see what she t'ink. I t'ink she say same," he advised.

"You know, Mr. Hamada, that's the best idea I ever heard. Why didn't I think of that myself? That's what I am going to do, I'm going to write to Alice Faye in Hollywood, California. Mr. Hamada, I get into trouble all the time and I just can't help it. When I am honest, I get hit on the head. So I've decided I'm going to lie all the time," I continued.

He argued, "No lie. Tell truth and be happy you get bumps on head. Bumps on head are better than lies. You troubled-kind boy. Follow warrior path, best path. Boy-san, someday you see what I tell you is truth. Boy-san, better to be troubled person than no person at all. Tell truth. Too many people lie now days. No good. They afraid of what's inside in here and what come out. Lies make weak man. Don't be afraid to find out what inside of you. You t'ink you can do that?"

I picked up the binoculars, looked towards Pearl Harbor and answered, "I can."

I took the binoculars and pounded the seat with them. I was trying to be like Roy Rogers and whooped, "I'm a warrior now."

Mr. Hamada took the binoculars out of my hand and asked again, "You sure I trust you?"

"You can, Mr. Hamada. Tell you what, Mr. Hamada, so that you can really know that you can trust me, let's do what the Indians do in the movies."

"What's that?"

"Let's you and me be blood brothers," I proposed.

"How we do that?"

Picking up a penknife lying on his papers, I opened it and demonstrated, "I cut my palm here and you cut your palm there. We put our hands together, and when our blood comes together, we become blood brothers for life. I never snitch on my sister because we have the same blood. If you're my brother, I can never snitch on you. Let's do it, Mr. Hamada. Let's be blood brothers for life."

"You sure? You sure boy who cry like girl can cut himself?" he asked.

"I can do anything. I got you to bring me home, didn't I? Spies aren't cowards, are they, Mr. Hamada?"

Taking the knife away from me, he lit a match and sterilized the knife. I told him, "You first, Mr. Hamada. I don't want you to chicken out on me."

He made a small cut on his palm and a smaller one on mine. We put our palms together and held them tight for a long time to make sure our blood mingled. I never blinked. When I took my hand away, I said, "Mr. Hamada, we are brothers forever."

"Forever, Percy," he agreed. He looked at his engine. The radiator had cooled down. "Hand me water next to you," he said.

I gave him the gallon of water and he stepped outside and poured it into the radiator. Steam evaporated into the air. After the engine cooled down, he got behind the wheel again, gave me back the empty water bottle, started up the engine, and we headed for home. As we drove down King Street, I asked him, "Do spies tell blood brothers where they came from, if they are married, if they have children - anything like that?"

"No, Percy, a spy is puzzle to brother, in case brother tortured and tells all the big secrets," he answered.

"That's a wise decision, Mr. Hamada. Secrets should be kept down in a stomach for all time. The torture I hate most of all in the world is when Marigold tickles me to death. Even then, Mr. Hamada, I'd never tell on you to Marigold," I promised.

He spoke in good English again and sounded serious, "I count on that, Percy."

As we rounded the corner on Vancouver Street, Mr. Hamada looked over at me and right into my eyes and spoke like a haole, "Percy, you're going to be all right. Remember no one can abandon you, if you stay strong in heart and mind. A warrior is a man who shoots his arrow straight all his life and keeps you inside of you, for you. Tell yourself three times a day that you are strong. Someday you will be strong and no longer be fat boy who cry like girl, but a strong warrior like me."

I jiggled my stomach and replied, "Maybe - I hope so, Mr. Hamada. I hope so."

"Sooner than you think," he said.

I looked down at my stomach hanging over my belt. "I'm so fat, Mr. Hamada, it's going to take years and years for me to become a warrior."

"When you solve problems inside your head, your stomach will be gone and you will become warrior," he reassured me.

Mr. Hamada's truck stopped in front of our house. As I got out, I asked him three more questions. "Mr. Hamada, is Mr. Hamada your real name?"

He spoke again like a local man, "Mr. Hamada name today."

"Will I ever see you again?"

"Maybe."

"Do you like mayonnaise?"

"Yes. Only one kind - Best Foods," he declared.

I clapped my hands and yelled, "I knew it."

Shutting off the engine, he asked, "Knew what?"

"Spies eat mayonnaise."

"So do warriors."

Mother and Betsy ran flying out of the house when they saw me in the truck with Mr. Hamada. They screeched all the way down to the truck, crying, "Percy,

Percy, Percy!" Mother reached me first and shook the daylights out of me as she demanded, "Percy, where have you been? You had us all worried. Your father and Marigold are frantic. They're down at the police station right this very minute looking for you."

"That's a funny place to look for me because I am right here. Look at me, I'm fine, Mother. Really I am. My new friend, Mr. Hamada, brought me home. We are blood brothers."

Betsy gave me a kiss and repeated, "Blood brothers?"

"You wouldn't understand, Betsy," I answered haughtily.

She dropped the subject and continued scolding me, "You're a bad boy today, Percy, because you've given everyone a bad scare."

I took Mother and Betsy's hands. "Mother and Betsy, this is Mr. Hamada. He brought me home. He's a very nice man, Mother. You and Mr. Hamada could be good friends."

Mother shook his hand and said, "Mr. Hamada, how can I ever thank you for bringing this bad boy home? I never know what he's going to do next."

Speaking again in his pidgin English accent, he replied, "No worry baby. He become warrior. He smart boy. He know how to get home. Right, haole boy?"

"Right, Mr. Hamada."

Hearing that, Mother, being her motherish self, kissed me on top of my head. *I liked when she kissed me on top of my head.*

She continued holding onto me when she said to Mr. Hamada, "Please let me give you money for your gas."

"No, boy take care. He say he pay me five cents. Right, haole boy? Boy pay debts like warrior."

I pulled my allowance out of my pocket. "Here, Mr. Hamada, I always pay my debts - from one honorable warrior to another." He took the nickel and put it in his pocket. I felt sad, seeing my new friend was about to leave and said, "Mr. Hamada, you have to come back and meet my best friend, Hatsuko. She's sick right now, but you'd like her."

He looked at me and nodded, "I like meet her sometime." We shook hands, palm to palm, and said goodbye. I waved him off as he chugged his Model T up our Rocky Hill road.

Mother kept hugging me as if I had been lost to her forever and walked me back into the house. Mother phoned Daddy at the police station and told him I was back home.

I didn't want to face my father when he brought Marigold home, so I hid behind the curtains in the living room. I knew he'd explode if he saw me. When I heard his car stop in front of the house, I shook all over.

Mother greeted Daddy at the front door and told him I was resting in my room. She had never let Daddy back into the house since the divorce.

I remembered what Mr. Hamada said, that the way of the warrior is to be strong in heart and head and to be brave inside. I came out from behind the curtains, walked to the front door and stood next to Mother. I said softly, "Hi, Daddy. Hi, Marigold."

Daddy, looking relieved and trying not to explode, said in a measured voice,

"Is that all you have to say to me, son?"

"No. You and Marigold left me and I couldn't find you."

Daddy explained calmly, "We went to get you a hot dog. I thought you heard us say we were leaving and we would be right back. You weren't paying attention. You must have known I'd always come back for you."

"I didn't hear you and I guess I didn't know that you'd come back for me. I really looked all over for you, Daddy. I'm sorry I caused you and Marigold trouble."

Daddy, even calmer, said, "Next time we will both have to be more careful, won't we? It was brave of you to find your way home alone."

When Daddy said that to me, my heart grew strong. I could feel a warrior growing inside of me.

Fidgeting next to Daddy, Marigold snorted, "Percy, you ruined my whole day. I'm going to hate you for the rest of my life. Why can't you stay still once in your life? I'm so mad at you right now I could tickle you to death. And I'm going to do that as soon as I get in the door. You're going to get it. You scared me today, Percy."

"Marigold," Mother scolded, "you should never say you're going to hate your brother for life. Someday, he may be the only friend you have left in the world. "

I interrupted, "Marigold says that to me all the time, Mother. She doesn't mean it. I'm sorry, Marigold, for spoiling your day with Daddy. Next time you and Daddy go by yourselves; I'll stay home with Mother."

"No," Marigold said, stamping her foot, "we want you with us, but next time I'm going to put you on a leash. Treat you like a crazy dog. When I get in there I am still going to tickle you to death."

"You'll have to catch me first," I yelled as I ran to my room.

In my room, Agnes and Gertrude were lying on the floor, reading movie magazines. I was so upset that they weren't paying any attention to me, I went into Mother's room, rustled through her closet, and put on one of her old gingham school dresses. I walked back into my room to play and told Agnes and Gertrude that they had to play cocktail party with me. As we played drinking martinis, I told them about my adventures with Mr. Hamada and even about the spy business. Agnes and Gertrude were part of me so I could tell them everything. Sitting around making idle chit-chat with my imaginary friends like Mother did at her cocktail parties with Aunt Momi, I questioned out loud to no one in particular if there was ever a warrior in all the history books who wore a gingham dress into battle?

Gertrude told me a warrior wouldn't wear a dress because it would get in the way of his using his sword. She said, on the other hand, a great spy would certainly dress up in his mother's clothes, disguised in order to cross borders into foreign countries and steal Nazi top secrets right under Hitler's nose. I decided I would wear a dress when I was a spy and pants when I had to use a sword.

Sniffing the air, I told Agnes and Gertrude I was going to love the smell of rotten vegetables forever. The stench of rotting turnips and tomatoes would always remind me of my blood brother Mr. Hamada's breath.

Agnes and Gertrude wrote a poem for me about my adventures with Mr. Hamada.

Moments in trouble,
A busted radiator,
Life becomes the moment,
A human connection is formed for life.

When everyone in the house had settled in their beds that night, I walked into the living room, turned on the light, and sat at Mother's desk. I took out a piece of her stationery and her Esterbrook pen, opened the jar of red ink and wrote:

Dear Alice Faye of Hollywood, California

22

The Twins

On January 1, 1941, I pored through the pages of *The Honolulu Advertiser*. The newspaper read confusing, interesting, and very scary. A curse was in the air. Betsy sighed that love was in the air. I told her to buy a bottle of Lysol.

The Honolulu Advertiser

Advertisement: **LYSOL - DISINFECTANT FOR FEMININE HYGIENE**
"LOVE MATCH RUINED BY ONE NEGLECT" She didn't know why her husband became indifferent, critical, and nervous. How could he tell her that neglect (or ignorance) of feminine hygiene so often kills romance. Don't be in doubt about intimate cleanliness...use "Lysol" for feminine hygiene. Widely used for more than 50 years. Economical, too...small bottle of "Lysol" makes almost a gallon of antiseptic solution for feminine hygiene. Get a bottle at Benson-Smith Drug Store.

HIDDEN RADIO GIVES 1941 AS HITLER'S LIMIT.
London, Jan.7 -
The German freedom radio station has resumed broadcasts from a hiding place somewhere in Nazi territory. The announcer said Hitler promised to win the war in 1941 because he knew that Germany could not endure it for a much longer period.

WALTER WINCHELL ON BROADWAY
The Duke and Duchess of Windsor may return to Miami mid-January to make personal appearances in four places for the President's British Relief Fund. The Duke, they say, bought $4,000 worth of knick-knacks at Saks on Lincoln Road.

HAWAII THEATER - Phone 66300 - Starts 10 a.m.
Clark Gable, Spencer Tracy, Claudette Colbert, Hedy Lamarr in
MGM'S BOOM TOWN
Tangled Television - Color Cartoon - Feature 10:35 - 1:11 - 3:48 - 6:21 - 8:56
Fox Movietone News

PRINCESS THEATER - Phone 4799 Starts at noon.
THEY KNEW WHAT THEY WANTED
Starring: Carole Lombard and Charles Laughton

TWO ATHLETES WHO DID MUCH TO MAKE 1940 A ROUSING YEAR OF SPORTS ARE ALICE MARBLE AND TOMMY HARMON.

In tennis, Miss Marble was supreme, justly earning the title of No.1 star in America. Harmon dominated the gridiron in equal fashion, concluding his career at Michigan by eclipsing the Big Ten scoring record of the great Red Grange.

JAMES JOYCE DIED. HE WROTE 'ULYSSES.'

After I finished reading *The Advertiser*, I figured out that the European countries were fighting for their lives because Charlie Chaplin (Adolph Hitler) was "tanking" into their homes, killing hundreds of people who looked exactly like me. In *Life* magazine, I looked at photographs of bombed-out cities where Mr. Hitler's airplanes killed thirty-seven-year-old mothers and seven-year-old little boys. Japanese soldiers were doing the same thing, setting up their tents in China and Manchuria. A goose-stepping Mussolini, an Italian fatso who ran trains on time in Rome, was the spitting image of Jack Oakie, the funnyman actor who co-starred with Alice Faye in the movies. Mussolini was too funny looking to be considered much of a threat to President Roosevelt.

A strange new feeling now sat in the pit of my stomach.

Auntie Gladys, Mother's best girlfriend who lived on our hill, advised Mother to buy cases of tuna fish and a pup tent in case the Japanese army landed on Waikiki Beach and forced us to flee to a mountain cave above our house. Hoarding cases of tuna fish was considered a very patriotic thing to do. At Nancy's Hair Salon on Queen Street, Nancy Yoshimoto told Mother of a rumor that was being whispered on Fort Street. The rumor was that a major Japanese invasion was going to happen in June, and that the Japanese army was going to land on the beaches of Santa Monica, California on Memorial Day. Hearing that rumor, Mother stored six more cases of tuna fish in Grandma's shower. By the end of January, Grandma's shower was jammed to the ceiling with cases of canned milk, tuna fish and Vienna sausage. Lucky for Mother, Betsy preferred soaping up in Grandma's bathtub.

The curse was getting closer.

At school, Wigay, Booby the Bully and I were promoted, mid-semester, into the second grade without any explanation. Miss Slingerland, the principal, pronounced the word "experiment" when she told us to clear out our desks. I hated the thought of leaving Miss Storey's blue eyes. I cried as I walked up the steps to the third floor to meet my new teacher, Miss Wood. Her name fit. From the very first day that I sat in her class, I couldn't make heads or tails out of Miss Wood's lessons. They were not only confusing but very boring and she seemingly spoke in Greek. Miraculously, I got A's and B's in her class.

Cynthia and Vinnie were still threatened with a whipping if they so much as spoke a word to me. Whenever Cross-Eyed Mama drove out shopping, Cynthia and I would meet in the middle of a hedge, hiding like spies, and pledge our friendship. Cynthia swore that she was going to convince her mother to arrange a truce with my mother because Cynthia was baking dozens of Cross-Eyed Mama's favorite cookies to sweeten her mama's bad nature. She told me her tragic news. On Christmas Day, after she opened her presents, her mother cut off her tail. Cynthia felt lost without her tail and was sure she was going to end up in the poor house because her mama had taken away her peek-a-boo business. Cynthia was my first friend with a tail on her behind; I knew she would end up a millionaire. She knew how to make a dollar out of nothing. I suggested she glue a fake tail on her behind and continue business.

I turned grumpy. I became so moody that Agnes and Gertrude hid in the window seat. They spat at me that until I became my old self again, we might as well forget we ever met. I slammed the lid on their heads and told them I never wanted to see their faces again.

Best friends fight sometimes.

Don and Roger rolled into my life like German tanks. Don and Roger were Auntie Gladys's twelve-year-old sons. Auntie Gladys was Mother's best girl friend since the day Mother married Daddy.

I called Don and Roger "the Twins." They weren't twins, however. They were the same age but didn't look at all alike. Don was blonde and Roger was brown all over. The reason I called them twins was because Auntie Gladys told me she had brought them home from the orphanage on the same day. She couldn't make up her mind which one to adopt (they came from different storks), so she adopted both of them.

Auntie Gladys and her family lived in the house next to Cousin Bessie's. They had a hundred percent better view of Honolulu than Cousin Bessie did, and they were two hundred percent richer. Auntie Gladys's husband's family was one of the wealthiest landowners in Hawaii and they lived handsomely on their real estate rentals. Everyone in Hawaii knew how rich they were because there were three professional buildings in downtown Honolulu named after Auntie Gladys and the Twins. Uncle Pete, Mr. Moneybags himself, was very shy and named a small liquor store after himself. It was an appropriate gesture because Uncle Pete went through cases of gin every month and routinely passed out into his soup at dinnertime. I told Hatsuko that the Twins drove him to drink.

Don and Roger formed a club, called Skull and Bones, Incorporated. The Twins didn't have much imagination in naming things or anything else, for that matter. Their club met on different afternoons at different times to confuse spies, particularly me. Skull and Bones, Incorporated held their meetings under Don and Roger's house. Only a select few were asked to join. One qualification to be a member was that a member couldn't be seven or fat. That rule was made to keep me out of the club. I found the club's rules in Marigold's desk drawer, so I knew that to be true.

The members kept their meeting times a deep dark secret. As a spy, I became curious to know what they did under the house on those mysterious afternoons. I started to do some real sleuthing. One thing was certain: they didn't bake cookies or eat tuna fish sandwiches.

Don and Roger were the Katzenjammer Kids out of the Sunday funnies. They were the bad, bad, bad boys of Honolulu. Don and Roger were as dangerous, as uncontrollable and as vicious as Hitler's German shepherd, Blonde. They were always in trouble with the Honolulu police because they took pleasure in tearing apart everything they could get their hands on. Their destructive habits started the day Auntie Gladys let them out of their cribs. Uncle Pete was nervous all the time, having the Twins in his house. He lost all his hair the time the Twins dumped three cases of gin down the bathtub drain. He shelled out hundreds of dollars every month to replace something the Twins destroyed in Honolulu. There wasn't a street lamp that hadn't been demolished a thousand times by the aim of their slingshots or BB guns. They took great pride in pretending they were Buffalo Bills shooting holes into plate glass windows. Betsy called them bullies when she caught them carving their initials with a penknife on her car door.

Every afternoon, after school, they'd strut around Rocky Hill, playing tough, sticking out their butts by a mile. They'd come home from Punahou, slam their front door, drop their pants, and throw on something that was dirty, smelly and ripped. They wore men's football helmets that covered most of their faces and shoulder pads that drooped halfway down their bony bodies. They thought it gave them the big bad boy look they wanted. Seeing them in that costume, kids in our neighborhood didn't fool with them, that is, if they didn't want to get killed.

Underneath the football pads were only a bag of bones and not one taut muscle between them. They bragged that what made them strong and tough was that they poured catsup over their scrambled eggs. They told me that Charles Atlas, the body builder, ate catsup every day. They had sent away for his body building program and it was catsup, they said, that made Charles Atlas's body strong and his blood catsup red. After they boasted that, they flexed their tiny little biceps in front of me, trying to look like Charles Atlas. I told them to get their money back, then ran away as they chased me home.

They were so dumb they thought Alice Faye was the name of Gene Autry's mother. Gertrude said there wasn't an ounce of imagination in their heads. If they passed with a D in school, Uncle Pete and Auntie Gladys thought they had raised geniuses. Gertrude warned me, "Watch out, Percy. It's the stupid people you have to look out for. They're the mean ones."

Mother told me Auntie Gladys had wanted to adopt a girl, but Uncle Pete talked her out of it. Uncle Pete made the biggest mistake of his life because they adopted Cain and Abel. God should have sent cases of aspirin to make up for the two troublemakers He sent Auntie Gladys and Uncle Pete.

The Twins' latest devilment was teasing Mr. McLaine's fox terrier, Fluffy. Mr. McLaine lived across the street and had a strange son, Walter, a boy I had never seen. He lived hidden like a mole in the basement of his house. Walter had shaking fits all the time, and an ambulance sirened him to Queen's Hospital at least once a month. Mr. McLaine called Roger and Don to their face "bad-assed" kids and called the police on them all the time. I felt sorry for Mr. McLaine, because he was becoming as high-strung as his fox terrier. Master and dog were barking alike. When Fluffy came home with a tin can tied to his tail, Mr. McLaine yapped from his front door, "You damn kids, I'm calling the police right now. If I catch you touching my Fluffy again, I'm going to see that you both go to jail and your father pays me lots of money."

I thought Mr. McLaine had lots of guts taking on those two bad-assed kids, but he had no choice because the Twins were driving him crazy. Mr. McLaine would rant further, "You better hear what I'm saying because I'm warning you that if it's the last thing I do, I'll see that you're behind bars in Oahu prison." Don and Roger answered by exploding firecrackers in Mr. McLaine's yard and laughing fiendishly. Mr. McLaine and Fluffy would spend the remainder of the afternoon in his bed cuddling each other.

I knew all about their cuddling because I was a terrific spy.

Nothing bad ever happened to our house because Marigold and the Twins were in cahoots. Having a tough-assed sister who associated with bad-assed gangsters was a major plus for our family.

Being bored one afternoon, having no one to play with, my spy nose started twitching; I had the feeling that a Skull and Bones meeting was about to happen. I waddled up the hill. The Twins were outside their house throwing rocks at lizards. Seeing me puff up the hill, they suddenly pretended they were off to China or somewhere farther, like the Chink store where all the Punahou hot stuffs bought soda, candy and gum at lunch. They winked to each other and drawled like cowboys as I walked toward them and said in voices loud enough for the whole neighborhood to hear, "Weah goin' to the Chink store for gum, fatso. Go home."

I kept on walking up the hill.

"Come on, Don, we don't hang around with a fat, fat, fat sissy." They stood, hands on their hips, and gave me their gangster eyes to stop me. I continued walking. As I got closer, they whooped, "See you later, Peeeeeeercy!" They laughed, pulled cigarettes from behind their ears, stuck out their butts, kicked every rock in sight, and swaggered bowlegged past me.

They didn't fool me with that Jimmy Cagney act because I was the greatest spy in Hawaii - other than Mr. Hamada. By the way they tried to get rid of me, I knew a meeting was about to happen. I said to myself, "I'll circle around the neighborhood and make them think I've gone for good. That'll give 'em time to start the meeting."

I yelled after them, "See ya later, guys. Hey, Don, you're dragging your left shoulder pad on the ground. What you need, Don, is a big muscular shoulder to hang it on like Ronald Reagan had in *Knute Rockne*. Ronald Reagan is a real All-American and he doesn't eat catsup. Catsup is for sissies."

Don turned around and gave me the finger.

In a half-hour, I returned to Auntie Gladys's house and found that the Skull and Bones were under the house because I could hear Don's voice. Talking to myself again, I got excited, "Eureka, I am the greatest spy in the world because I found them."

An itsy-bitsy lattice door under Auntie Gladys's bedroom led into the underworld. I opened the door and peered in. It was pitch-black. I couldn't quite make out who was in there, but I saw human silhouettes framed in the little sunlight that filtered through the doorway. Squinting, I saw six or seven kids sitting on benches with the Twins. They faced one another and were holding themselves still as statues.

I crouched down to see if I could see them better. I was determined to have them ask me in. I stood up to think how I was going to make them let me join them.

I put my hands on my hips and stared at the doorway, thinking. Hot sun beat down on my head. It was so hot, a waterfall of sweat poured down my nose. With no specific idea in mind, I squatted down again, cupped my hands over my eyes and looked through the door.

I heard them whispering, "He can't see us!" "Yes, he can!" "I know he can!" "Don't move, Roger!" "Get rid of him!"

I hate people whispering about me.

I stared Superman rays at the gang, trying to make my eyes penetrate into their hiding place. They didn't make a move. They were like rocks. I crouched further into the underworld. Out of the dark came singsong menacing voices, "Percy, go home." "Fat Percy, go home before we beat you up."

I heard Marigold's voice whispering to Don, "Throw a rock at him."

I said, "Marigold, I heard you. I'm gonna tell Mother if you don't let me in."

Marigold's voice boomed out, "That'll be the last thing you'll ever tell her and when I get home, I'm gonna rip your tongue out." *Marigold got so dramatic at times.* I yelled back, "You can't scare me." Getting off my haunches, I stood up, turned around and pretended to go home. Trying to sound like a warrior, I threatened Marigold, "I'm going home and telling Mother you're making doodoo under there."

"You're what?" she screamed.

"I know that's what you're doing. You're making doodoo together." I thought that might get me in.

There was a pause, then I heard Don, the blonde, say, "Let the pest in before he spoils it."

"If he tells, Don, I'll beat him. I promise you. He won't dare tell my mother when I get through with him," said Marigold.

I turned around, put my hands on my hips and said in my warrior voice, "Are you going to let me in, or are you going to let me stand out here and melt in the sun? If I am still standing here when Auntie Gladys comes home, I'll tell her you're all under the house and I'll tell her to make you come out with your doodoo."

That did it. Roger spoke first, "Okay, Percy. Get your fat ass in."

I won. The doodoo and Auntie Gladys talk did it. I clapped my hands, squeezed myself through the lattice door and crawled in on my hands and knees. I said excitedly, "I'm in the club! I'm in the club! I'm in the club!" Clouds of dirt puffed into the air.

I kept saying, "I knew it. I knew it. I found the club. I found the club. Ha! Ha! Ha! I'm not so dumb after all. I'm going to become a member and become a real warrior. I'm gonna talk like Jimmy Cagney and stick out my butt." I practiced my Jimmy Cagney voice, "Ya dirty rat."

I reached the kids sitting on benches. My eyes adjusted to the darkness and I immediately saw who the club members were. They were the neighborhood kids from the top of the hill, my next door cousin, our paperboy Kaina, and Marigold. They sat up stiffly on the wooden benches, acting like soldiers in General MacArthur's army. Their chins jutted out, they faced one another, and there wasn't a stitch of clothing on their bodies.

They were buck-naked.

Their naked bodies, in my humble opinion, cried out for colorful band uniforms from an MGM musical. They looked cold, bony and downright puny, and everyone had an ugly belly button.

They all glared at me as I hoisted myself up next to Kaina. He looked the best naked because he was part Hawaiian and had muscles. Kaina seemed glad to see me because he said "hello" nicely. Everyone else treated me like poison oak. Despite their unhappy expressions at my sudden unwanted appearance, there was a glow of excitement in their faces. Their cheeks were red as apples.

From their faces, I knew I had hit the jackpot. This was going to be a lolla-palooza meeting. Something was about to happen. I lifted my hand and said in friendly Indian fashion, "How."

"SHUT UP, YOU INDIAN FOOL!" It was the voice of General George Custer-Marigold. She was not at all happy seeing her baby brother at the meeting. She was happiest when baby brother was locked up in his room wearing Mother's dresses.

Marigold was seated next to Roger, the brown one. Roger had beads of sweat on his forehead which Marigold was wiping away with her handkerchief. In a first sergeant's voice, she commanded again as she kept wiping the sweat off of Roger's face, "Take 'em off!"

"Take off what?" I piped up.

'TAKE OFF YOUR CLOTHES, FOOL."

"Take off my clothes? It's cold in here, Marigold. I'm delicate."

Now using her four star general voice, she yelled, "T A K E O F F Y O U R C L O T H E S!"

I stood tall, saluted and dropped 'em. Pants first and then I ripped off my shirt. In two seconds, I was naked. I was now a Skull and Bones member and looked like a pink bare-assed cupid ready to shoot love darts.

I sat down as goose bumps started covering my body. Kaina gave me a pat on my knee and told me to feel at home. I replied to the paperboy that no matter how many pats he gave me on my knee, sitting and smelling rat shit (my new word) wasn't what I would call home. I made it clear to him that I didn't make it a habit to sit naked in polite company. I thanked him for his concern and patted his knee back. I didn't know what to do with my nakedness, so I cupped my left hand over my privates to keep them warm, so they wouldn't be covered with goose bumps.

The smell of rotted rats lingered in the air. The ground under my feet stunk, too, because it hadn't had a breath of fresh air in years. The house overhead made every-thing underneath its floor die. The stench of rot seeped into my nostrils, made my nose quiver and I sneezed, Kachooooo.

Once inhaled, the smell of death's perfume is never forgotten.

"Quiet," Roger said, concentrating.

"OOOOGIE. It stinks in here. Let's go outside in the sun."

"Shut up, Percy!" a voice rose next to me.

Kaina put his finger to his lips and warned, "Be quiet, Percy."

I put my right hand over my mouth. I looked around and saw all eyes were cap-tivated by Roger's "weenie." It stood up like a stick.

I thought to myself, "Does Roger have to go to the bathroom? Ooooooo! Don't point your stick at me. Point the stick at Marigold. I don't want shishi all over me. I have enough shishi in my bed."

Roger lifted his hand off his "weenie," flexed his fingers like a pianist about to play, then bang, Roger moved his fingers up and down his stick like he was milking a cow. I imagined I was on a dairy farm as he milked his stick, like Heidi did in Switzerland. We all became cows, sitting on benches, eyes glued on Roger's stick. My eyes were glued on a dead rat lying under his bench, instead.

Roger wasn't looking at anyone, only at his stick. I thought for a boy who lacked imagination and got D's at school, he had great concentration. Minutes passed.

I couldn't imagine what was going to happen next. My stick didn't look as interesting or as pretty as Roger's and mine certainly didn't stand up like a totem pole.

More minutes passed. Sweat streamed down Roger's face. Many more minutes passed.

My mind drifted to a Betty Grable Technicolor movie. In it, Betty danced a South American rumba, beating castanets with her hands while kicking up her long legs. I suddenly stood up and burst into Betty's song, snapping my fingers, "You're romantic, senor, you will surely adore Argentina." I snapped my fingers above my head and danced twirls around the cows, singing "Tsk,Tsk, Tsk."

Everyone screamed, "FAT PERCY, SIT DOWN."

"Percy," Kaina pulled me down next to him and put his hand over my mouth.

Don yelled, "Beat him up, Kaina."

Marigold stood and told everyone she was not my sister and she was going to hate me forever. As she sat down, she looked at me with hot coals burning in her eyes and fumed, "I'm going to kill you - slowly."

"You should have drowned him as soon as he was born." I couldn't see who said that.

Everyone agreed, "YEA."

In the corner, Roger put his hand up in the air and announced, "I've lost it!"

Tears came to Marigold's eyes. She spoke to me again, "See what you've done? You've ruined everything."

"What did I do?"

Don had his arm around his brother's shoulders and said in a sincere voice that I had never heard him use before, "Rog, try it again. For the club."

Everyone pleaded, "For the club. Pleeeeeeeease."

Don told Kaina if I uttered one more word, murder me. Marigold reached over and pinched my arm.

Rubbing my arm, I whined, "That hurt. I thought a little song would help Roger. He looked pretty tired and I wanted to give him a little rhythm. A little beat to milk his stick. Didn't you hear my tsk - tsk - tsk, Roger?" Deep in Roger's eyes was a look that said he was about to put a noose around my neck.

I asked for mercy, "Really, Roger, it could have. I mean it. You were missing some beats."

The cows turned slowly toward me. They were about to make me into a hamburger. They raised their fists and were going to do something to me that seemed pretty awful, so I quickly put my fingers to my lips and whispered, "SHHHHHH-HH!"

That stopped them from killing me.

This club took themselves too seriously. They should take up baking cookies.

Kaina gave me a knuckle punch. My ribs hurt. That shut me up for good.

Now that I had quieted down, everyone turned back to Roger. With a little encouragement (Roger didn't need much because he was a big showoff), the "milk the cow" number began again.

After many long minutes, as Betty Grable still danced in my head, and after a sweaty work-up on Roger's part, a little white seed, a luminous pearl, appeared at the end of his stick. For a moment, the pearl turned blue.

It was the blue pearl Little Johnny and Patty went to find in Hunkacha's lake.

With the sudden appearance of the pearl, Roger screamed and fell backwards. He writhed around like a snake in the powdery gray dirt. After he finished slithering around, he fainted and turned white. Don slapped his face. Roger woke up and turned color again. His face suddenly became beet red and his body a dark, crimson Japanese chrysanthemum. His stick stood out like a weensy Chinese firecracker. Roger was the only bright color in the dark underworld. Everyone else looked blue.

Don sat Roger back down on the bench and crowned him king. The royal courtiers stared at him in awe but the pearl disappeared. It lost its luster and fell off near the dead rat under the bench.

Marigold matched Roger in color. Then everyone else turned from blue to the brilliant red of the apple the bad witch gave Snow White.

I sat watching them, colorless. My left hand still warmed my privates. When it was quiet, I asked, "That's it? That's all there is? Is there anything more? Is this why I had to take off my clothes?"

All heads turned and they yelled, "Get out!" "Get him out, Marigold!" "Get him out of here before I kill him," Roger yelled like he meant it. You'd have thought that I'd interrupted the sacred ceremony of the high priest in *The Mummy* when Boris Karloff boiled tamarack leaves to bring the mummy back to life.

I squeaked out stupidly again, "Roger, a cow gives more milk than you did. Roger, if you poured catsup on your stick first thing in the morning, it might help. Drop your pants at breakfast and pour catsup on your stick."

Roger rose from the bench with his two hands ready to choke the life out of me. He fainted again. He needed to drink a ton of catsup. When they brought him to, he gasped, "Get fatty out of here."

I grabbed my clothes and crawled, bottom up, naked, out of the pit as fast as I could yell, "I'm going, I'm going."

Outside, under Auntie Gladys's bedroom window, I put on my pants and laughed hysterically. I had them in some way. I found a soft spot. I yelled back to them under the house, "MOOOOOO. Any cow does better than that, Roger. You need a new stick. I'm gonna tell your mother to buy you a new stick."

"Over my dead body, Percy," Marigold yelled back, sounding worried.

Calling up to Don and Roger's mother, who had arrived home, I sang, "Auntie Gladys, your baby is under the house milking his stick. Ask him for a quart." I squealed with laughter at my own joke.

Auntie Gladys was cooking in the kitchen and didn't hear me.

Screams came from under the house, "It's a secret, Percy. Don't tell my mother our secrets, you fat, little weasel. You are now about to become a dead rat."

I yelled back, "Marigold, if they touch me or beat me up, I'm going to tell Mother you helped milk a cow." Sounds of clothes being put on were heard under the house. Benches turned over. My alert button went off. A lynching party was being formed. This little outlaw had better run for home - pronto.

I ran.

The Dalton gang came out from under the house in seconds and began the chase. Looking back, I knew from their faces, they were going to string me up on the nearest mango tree. I was fat, but "baby oh baby," this baby boy could run when he had to. I got home safe and free.

I never did tell Mother or Auntie Gladys about the dairy farm under the house. While it lasted, I blackmailed Marigold whenever I could. Whenever she started giving me a bad time, I'd move my hand up and down like I was milking a cow and she'd flee to her room. The "under the house" experience was another secret I stuffed into my belly. Thinking about Roger milking his stick a few days later, while playing with toy boats in the bathtub, I had a warm feeling come over me and I turned the color of a pale, pink rose. Gertrude was shocked. She told me she wasn't going to let me out alone ever again. I was not to be trusted anymore. I told Agnes that I thought Kaina was extra cute.

The Twins put a contract out on me. They told Marigold they were going to drown me in a vat of catsup after they hung me.

My life after school was now confined to the house. Cynthia and Vinnie's Cross-Eyed Mama heard from Cousin Bessie that Cynthia and I were meeting in the bushes, and now, along with the Twins, she was out to get me. Cynthia burned the cookies and the peace offering was off. She tried pasting a tail on her behind but it fell off during recess. I told her to charge the neighbors to come see her mama drinking coffee in her pink panties.

I had run out of friends. I was rubbing people all the wrong way all the time. I blamed it on the curse.

Gertrude told me there was a lesson to be learned, which was to never go under a house until you know who's under there waiting for you. I told Gertrude the lesson was never to sing a Betty Grable song when a good-looking twin was milking his stick. Nobody wants to be upstaged by a fat person with an ugly stick.

To pass the time after school, I'd lie on my bed eating mayonnaise sandwiches and drawing wishing wells. I'd draw fat ladies with big bazooms wedged in wishing wells. They'd have their mouths open calling for help. When Mother came home from school, she'd always find me drawing in my bedroom. She'd tell me to go outside and play. I'd shake my head and continue to draw wishing wells.

Mid-week, Mother announced that the following Saturday I was going to take the bus all by myself to Wahiawa to see Hatsuko. Hatsuko had something important to tell me.

Going to see Hatsuko made life worth living again. I drew Hatsuko in a wishing well waving hello to me.

I still hadn't received a letter from Alice Faye in Hollywood, California.

23

Hatsuko's Surprise

In second grade, I lost my Bobby Breen singing voice. It flew out the window after I had a sore throat. Agnes said my voice flew out the window because Hatsuko wasn't around to coach me. My singing solos at school was out just like Jeanette and Nelson's singing was out at MGM. A Hawaiian classmate now sang the popular songs at the Friday afternoon assemblies. In January 1941, fat was also out. Thin, handsome and Hawaiian were in at school. Jeanette and Nelson were out, Judy Garland was in.

Saturday's visit to Hatsuko arrived at the speed of Superman. Mother drove me down to the YMCA building in downtown Honolulu. At the YMCA, I was to catch the bus to Wahiawa. Mother gave me two dollars wadded up in a white linen handkerchief and a paper sack stuffed with two tuna sandwiches to take on the trip. As I got out of the car, she warned me not to speak to strangers. Mother waited in her car until she saw that I caught the nine o'clock bus.

Agnes and Gertrude stayed home. My girls never felt comfortable around Hatsuko because they were jealous. I forgot all about them when I was with Hatsuko.

The bus was a 1930's touring taxi that had two jump seats and a ride cost fifty cents one way. Since I was the first to arrive, I sat in the back seat next to the window. In the window was a torn blue velvet shade that I pulled down with a golden tassel to keep the sun out of my eyes. All movie stars did that.

The taxi filled up with soldiers from Schofield Barracks going back to duty after a night of drinking gin slings and beers. Most of them were still drunk and smelled of beer, gin, puke, and piss. Each one of them had a grumpy personality. I had yet to meet a happy drunk.

At nine o'clock, every seat in the car was filled with the soldiers and me. There were eight of us including the driver. Two soldiers were squished in the front seat with the driver, two on the jump seat in front of me and three of us took up the space in the back. The private who sat on the jump seat in front of me threw up on the curb three times before we left on our trip.

Our driver was a blown-up, fat, red-faced Portuguese man who took up most of the front seat. He ate sausage sandwiches and drank Coca-Cola during the entire trip. His face looked as full as a moon and was pocked with moon craters oozing pus.

I huddled into my corner because I knew I was on a ride to hell. We left at nine sharp. The sick private made me pull up the shade and roll down the window as fast as I could before the driver shifted into third gear. He threw up again and vomit specks fell on my clean white pants.

The sergeant sitting next to me roared with laughter and said drunkenly, "Sonny, that's the cheapest goddamn meal you're ever gonna get." The next time the private threw up, I ducked, and some of the barf specks flew into my neighbor's face. He screamed at the private, "Keep your fucking shit to yourself. One more time and I'll shove your ass out of this car." He gave the private a slap on the head.

I turned to my neighbor, blinked my eyes at him, and said, "That's the cheapest meal you're ever gonna get." I laughed because I now had the last laugh.

The tough-talking sergeant growled, "Kid, if you want to live, I'd keep my fucking mouth shut."

Everyone in my life was trying to kill me.

The sergeant took the specks off his face and rubbed them hard into my pants.

The rest of the trip, I shut up. So did everyone else. After his remark, everyone pretended to snore. Their breathing smelled like the bathrooms at Ala Moana Park. I pointed my nose out the window like a dog snuffling for fresh air. The trip to hell took two hours.

I watched the sugarcane fields of Aiea, Ewa, and Waipahu pass as we headed west to Wahiawa. At Hickam Airfield, the driver said we were almost there. He stopped at the Schofield Barracks front entrance and dropped off all the drunken soldiers.

Watching them stagger onto the base, I saw they weren't the handsome Robert Taylor types who acted in war movies. Robert Taylor wouldn't have staggered on base drunk, covered head to toe in puke, poop and piss. I made a note to write President Roosevelt that if he wanted to protect America, he should cast the United States Army from MGM Studios.

The driver drove me across the bridge over Wilson Lake into the center of Wahiawa. He dumped me at the Wahiawa Theater located on California Street. He grunted he'd pick me up at four for the ride back home. "Be on time - I no wait for nobody." He drove off as he finished off his last sausage sandwich.

Wahiawa is located in the center of Oahu. It's situated at a higher elevation than any other town on the island, so Wahiawa is cold and windy in January. Once, with record cold, Arctic wind blowing from Russia, heavy hail blanketed the town. I looked at the marquee of the Wahiawa Theater and saw Frank Capra's *Lost Horizon* was playing. The film was set in the Himalayas where people froze to death. It was a very appropriate film to play at Wahiawa because I was freezing to death, waiting for Hatsuko to arrive. I was so cold standing on the street, I was turning into a human popsicle. Alone on California Street, I held my two dollars and sandwiches tight to my breast. Money and sandwiches promised, like Judy Garland's red shoes, to get me back home no matter what happened.

Hatsuko was still nowhere in sight. I wished I had brought a sweater because huge goose bumps were rising all over my body. Maybe Hatsuko wasn't going to show up, I thought. I was pretty certain that if she didn't arrive soon, I'd come down with pneumonia again and die in the middle of the street.

A drop of water fell on my head. I put my hand up to the sky as more drops fell on my head. "It's going to rain," I said to myself.

A car stopped in front of the curb where I was standing. "Percy?" somebody called from inside the car.

I looked into the car and saw a pretty Japanese lady sitting behind the wheel. It wasn't Hatsuko. I remembered what Mother said about not talking to strangers so I looked away and I didn't say anything back to the pretty lady.

She spoke again, "Percy?" If a person calls your name twice, you can speak to her - that's what I think.

"Yes?" I answered.

"I'm Rose, Hatsuko's sister. I'm here to pick you up. Quick, get in. It's going to rain."

I got in the car and rode off with a stranger. I asked, "Where's Hatsuko?"

"She's at my house in Waialua."

"Is she all right?"

Rose concentrated on her driving before she spoke again because she was trying to pass a car on her left. I looked at her while she drove. She was a smaller version of Hatsuko, shorter, and her bones were tinier. She was very pretty like Hatsuko.

Rose's car, an old gray, rusted Plymouth, headed toward the ocean. We passed rows and rows of pineapple fields where Japanese ladies in checkered blouses and elaborate turbans were hoeing the fields. After more moments of silence, Rose responded to my question. "Hatsuko is all right, but since her car accident she hasn't driven much. Hatsuko is not a good driver." Rose looked down at my pants. "It looks like you dirtied yourself."

"One of the soldiers threw up and some of it landed on my pants."

"We'll clean you up when we get home. Can't send you back to your mother looking like that, can we?"

"You talk good, just like Hatsuko!" I exclaimed.

"I better talk good, because I teach English at Waialua High School. My husband Hiroshi is the mill foreman. He talks pidgin, but I'm working on him," she explained.

"Where do you live?"

"Waialua Sugar Plantation. Our house is in Camp A near the sugar mill. I've heard a lot about you, Percy."

"Hatsuko's my best friend and I miss her a lot."

We passed Thompson's corner where the scenery changed abruptly. The land was no longer planted in rows and rows of low growing pineapples, but fields and fields of sugar cane, growing tall and shiny green. We headed into the plantation town; on the left was a park with a bandstand and the sugar mill blowing black smoke out of its stacks. Straight ahead were one-story buildings - the plantation general store, a bank and offices that were doing business even on a Saturday morning.

Daddy said sugar plantation towns in Hawaii were complete communities unto themselves. They had schools, hospitals, and a police force all within a mile radius of its center. Food, rent, electricity, water, and water heaters were free on the sugar plantations. Plantation towns were comfortable cocoons, and once settled in, not many of the old-time workers roamed very far to seek other opportunities or locations. Many of their children, eager to escape the curse of being a plantation worker, eventually left - sometimes bitterly because they felt their parents had been treated shabbily by the plantation system. Daddy said someday the sugar plantations would be unionized.

Rose and Hatsuko were exceptional Japanese women in 1941. They had left plantation life as small girls and completed high school. Rose moved on to middle school and received a teaching degree.

Rose made a sharp left turn and we passed the Waialua Theater. The theater was a huge wooden barn of a building; in the midwest, farmers would have stored hay in it for cattle. This being 1941 Hawaii, in a Hawaiian plantation town, this barn-like building housed movie dramas and musicals that lit up a screen every night at seven. I thought it was the best building in Waialua.

Rose's car headed down a dusty one-lane road where rows of workers' homes stood across from each other. We stopped in front of a house that looked like every other house, but this one had a wire fence around it to protect a small vegetable and flower garden from wandering dogs.

Hatsuko stood on the porch and waved at me as the car stopped in front of the house. The cast was gone from her arm. I jumped out of the car and ran up the steps onto the porch and into her arms. We held each other on the porch for five minutes, crying, jumping up and down. We caused quite a spectacle for the neighbors standing on their porches across the street.

Rose broke us up, saying, "Hatsuko, let the baby alone. We have to get inside and eat lunch because Hiroshi has to get back to the mill. He's waiting inside. We have to clean up the boy and have him back at the bus stop by four. So, stop it, you two."

We stopped crying. Hatsuko took off my shoes, we entered the house and walked into the kitchen.

Hiroshi, a dark Japanese man whose nostrils flared like a mad dog, sat by himself at a small kitchen table. A single light bulb dangled on a cord from the ceiling. Hiroshi's face was black from soot in the mill. His mood matched his face. He pounded his wooden chopsticks on the table and roared like a samurai, "Sit down, boy."

I sat down. Hatsuko sat down. Hiroshi didn't look at us. I had the feeling that he didn't approve of Hatsuko or me wailing on the porch and making him wait for his lunch. He made me feel very uncomfortable as he sucked saliva through his teeth. I don't think he liked the color of my skin.

Rose placed a large bowl of rice, dried fish, daikon, seaweed, and tripe stew on the table. She passed out plates, so we could serve ourselves. Hiroshi dug in. Rose's meal, with no mayonnaise in sight, matched the ride to hell I had.

Out of nowhere, Rose set in front of me two huge egg salad sandwiches. I looked with love at Hatsuko. She smiled back. We still loved each other.

Hiroshi scowled at the sandwiches while stuffing his face with rice and dried aku. We ate in silence, except for the sounds of chopsticks clicking, a ticking alarm clock and my smashing egg salad sandwiches into my mouth.

Hiroshi belched, signaling that he had finished eating, and pushed back his chair and reached for a toothpick on a counter behind him. When he picked his teeth, he made loud sucking sounds like Marigold did when she had a cold. Taking another toothpick, he grunted, "Pau, Rose. What time you take haole boy back?"

"Three o'clock," she answered.

"I back six."

"Okay. I'll be back by five. Do you want me to pick up anything?" Rose asked.

"Beer!" Hiroshi got up and threw the toothpicks into the wastebasket. One missed and landed on the floor. He walked out of the kitchen, through the living room, and out onto the porch, slamming the screen door. I heard him put on his boots and start walking back to the mill, his feet pounding the dirt.

As Rose picked Hiroshi's toothpick off the floor, she said, "Percy, don't mind Hiroshi. It's the first time a haole come our house and eat at our table."

"That's all right. He didn't throw up on me," I reassured her.

Rose and Hatsuko laughed. Rose turned to Hatsuko and said, "We have to clean Percy up. Take off his clothes, Hatsuko. I'll clean and press them while you two talk story. Today is your day with the boy and you have a lot to tell him."

"Tell me what?" I wondered.

"In a minute, Percy." Hatsuko took me by the hand and we went into Rose's bedroom. She took off my clothes and handed me one of Hiroshi's plain blue and white *yukata* (kimono) to wear. I told Hatsuko I didn't like Hiroshi's kimono, it was too ugly. I wanted to wear a pretty one. Hatsuko went into a camphor chest and pulled out a pink kimono decorated in purple flowers. It belonged to Rose.

I threw Hiroshi's kimono down on the floor and wrapped the pink one around me. I showed myself off to Rose, who giggled. She approved by nodding her head and ushered us out of the kitchen so she could get on with her chores and we could be alone.

Seeing a purple umbrella in the corner of the living room, I picked it up and turned to Hatsuko. "Hatsuko, let's go outside and pretend we're walking through the lobby of the Royal Hawaiian Hotel, and you can tell me all your secrets. Let's pretend we are movie stars again."

Hatsuko hesitated, then grabbed my hand and handed me a paper fan. We walked outside on the porch. I slipped Rose's wooden *geta* (clogs) on my feet so I could really look like a perfect Japanese lady. Hatsuko, in a plain brown dress, slid into her slippers. We held hands and started to stroll down the center of the dirt road, in view of all Hiroshi's neighbors. We pretended, once again, that we were Ann Sheridan and Alice Faye from Hollywood. We didn't see the dusty road in front of us as we walked; what we saw was the lobby of the Royal Hawaiian Hotel.

I dragged the hem of Rose's kimono behind me in the dirt road as I twirled the purple umbrella and fanned myself like a geisha girl. I looked adoringly at Hatsuko as we walked. We became unaware of everyone and everything as we lived out the fantasy life we once had in the Royal Hawaiian Hotel.

Hatsuko began speaking seriously, "Percy, I asked your mother to send you to me because I wanted to talk to you in person."

"You're going to leave us," I said sadly.

"How did you know that?" she asked.

"You haven't come back for a long time, so I guessed something must be wrong and that you weren't coming back to me."

"I got married, Percy," she said gently.

"To the sailor?"

"How did you know about the sailor?"

"I saw him come out of your room at midnight," I admitted.

"Well, there isn't much for me to tell you, is there?"

"Do you love him?"

"Yes."

"As much as you love me?"

"It's different."

I stopped in the middle of the street. "Which is better?" I asked.

She paused and answered, "Yours is better. Because you're the first, and my love for you will never leave my heart."

I blurted out, "Is he as handsome as Tyrone Power? I hope he is. When do I meet him?"

"When he comes back. He's not handsome like Tyrone Power, but he's nice to me. He doesn't care that I wear yellow skin. He's on maneuvers in the Philippines and when he comes back, he will be transferred to the Arizona battleship. The Arizona is the best battleship at Pearl Harbor. He's even got permission for me to live on the base."

"Hatsuko, as long as you love me best, you can live anywhere you like, even stay married. What's his name?"

"Charlie Anthony."

"When I meet him, I promise I won't tell Charlie you like me best."

Someone screamed behind us and we turned around. Rose was running down the road towards us, yelling for us to come home. When she caught up with us, she was holding her sides because she was so out of breath. As soon as Rose could talk, she said Hiroshi phoned from the mill to say her neighbors reported that we were walking down the middle of the street. They were embarrassed because a little haole boy wearing a pink kimono was acting like a geisha girl. He told Rose to get me off the street because it was causing him shame at the mill.

We looked around and, sure enough, everyone was out of their houses, at their gates, gawking at us. Old ladies and little girls were hiding their faces behind their hands, giggling. I was amazed because it looked like the biggest audience I had ever played to, and I hadn't even noticed.

Rose turned us around and hustled us back into her house as fast as she could move us. Her head and body were bent down in embarrassment as she pushed us up to her front door. I held my head up because I looked spiffy in Rose's pink kimono. Before I went in, I turned around and waved at the neighbors who were still ogling me. I twirled my umbrella and took a deep bow before Rose dragged me inside. As the screen door closed, I heard a sincere wolf whistle.

Inside the house, Rose scolded Hatsuko for our "flamboyant promenade." She told Hatsuko her Japanese neighbors were not used to such scandalous "theatrics" and Hatsuko should have known better. We had brought "plenty shame" on Hiroshi in the mill.

Hatsuko said when Rose was mad, she used big English words.

Rose went into the kitchen and brought out my clean clothes and handed them to me. She told me to change. I did and left the dirty stained pink kimono lying on the floor. Rose picked up the kimono and threw it into a wastebasket. Hatsuko sat down in a chair and didn't say anything. She was looking far away.

I listened to the windup black clock ticking away on the kitchen windowsill. It was two minutes past two. The clock ticked and ticked and no one said a word.

I sat next to Hatsuko and took her hand when the phone rang. It was Hiroshi from the mill. You could tell he was giving Rose the devil because all she was saying was, "Yes, Hiroshi. No, Hiroshi. Uh-huh, uh-huh. Yes, he's leaving soon."

Rose hung up the phone, looking pale, and saw us looking at her. She walked into the kitchen to wash her hands. Hatsuko followed her and put her arm around her sister's shoulder. "Rose, I'm sorry I got you in trouble with Hiroshi. We're leaving now. Let me drive Percy to the bus. You stay home," comforted Hatsuko.

Rose said, "There are only two phones in the camp. Hiroshi has to have one because of his job at the mill and that nosey Mrs. Kawamoto has the other. She's always getting me into trouble. She's so jealous of me. Her husband used to have Hiroshi's job and they demoted him. I hate this phone." Rose threw the phone on the floor and started to cry.

Pouring a glass of water for Rose, Hatsuko said, "It's my fault and you tell Hiroshi that. He hates that I married a haole. This is too much for you. Tomorrow, I'm going into town and stay with my friend Clarissa till Charlie comes back from the Philippines."

With the glass of water in her hand, Rose brushed a strand of hair from Hatsuko's face, saying, "We were never the Japanese girls we were supposed to be, were we, Hatsuko? You should have been in the movies with Percy," she laughed. "And I wanted to be a big shot and marry the haole plantation manager."

Rose looked at me, sitting quietly in the living room. "You two were quite a sight, parading down the street like you were movie stars. Funny looking movie stars. You're gonna give Hiroshi's friends a lot to talk about for a long time. He hates to be teased and now he'll want to divorce me," Rose worried.

Picking up the phone from the floor, Rose placed it back on the table. She took her purse from the kitchen table and took out her lipstick. As she dabbed color on Hatsuko's lips, she said, "Can't have you going out of here looking ordinary - not with that not-so-ordinary Percy there."

Holding the lipstick, Rose said, "Hatsuko, I never thought I'd marry a Japanese bull and live in a camp again. I never ever wanted that. I hated camp life. But Hiroshi came along and he's a good solid man and loves me in spite of my haole ways. And you know, Hatsuko, I love him in spite of him being such a Japanese pigheaded bull." She paused. "Maybe it's because he's such a bull that I love him so much."

Hatsuko took the lipstick out of Rose's hand and applied Glossy Red to Rose's lips as they must have done a million times to each other when they were little girls. Hatsuko said, "I know he's a good man, Rose. When I get back from taking Percy to the bus, I'm packing up. Tonight, I'll take us to Seaview Inn for dinner. That will make Hiroshi smile...maybe."

Putting the lipstick back into Rose's purse, Hatsuko called, "Percy, we're going. Come in and say goodbye and thank Rose."

I walked into the kitchen with the pink kimono rolled up under my arm. I had fished it out of the wastebasket. I said, "Thank you, Rose." Pointing to the kimono, I went on, "Since you don't want this kimono anymore, maybe you'd let me have it to remind me of this afternoon."

Rose said, patting me on the head, "It's yours." She opened a drawer and pulled out a paper bag and stuffed the kimono in it.

We left Rose's house with Hatsuko behind the wheel. The whole camp was out to watch us drive away. Hatsuko nearly stripped all the gears of Hiroshi's car before we exited the camp. We passed the movie theatre in first gear as we headed for Wahiawa. Hatsuko never had the concentration to be a good driver. Her mind was on Charlie or something else, but never on the highway in front of her. I had to keep reminding her of stop signs that loomed ahead or that we were headed in the wrong direction.

Hatsuko drove a car just like Aunt Ella. Fast!

After three U-turns, we drove in the right direction and passed the pineapple fields again. I turned to Hatsuko and asked, "Hatsuko, I see this all the time in the movies. Why do men marry women that are different from them? Like Rose back there. She's so refined and Hiroshi is the grunting cave man type. I look at the Twins' mother, Auntie Gladys; she's loud and Uncle Pete's so quiet. You'd think Uncle Pete would want to marry a librarian and Rose would want to marry a schoolteacher like her. Why is that, Hatsuko? Daddy and Mother are as different as mayonnaise and mud."

Hatsuko looked off into the distance, not paying attention to the truck ahead filled with pineapples, then answered, "Percy, if I knew that, I'd be a pretty smart person. I'm not smart, Percy. What do you think Charlie is like?"

"I bet he's nice."

"He hates movies!"

Shocked at her reply, I exclaimed, "Hatsuko, how could you marry a man who hates movies?"

"He likes me, that's why, and he'll be a good father. You see, Percy, when I told you that I was a bastard, that meant that I never really had anyone to love me except you and Rose. Now, I have someone who is going to love me forever - just like in the movies, and marrying him is better than the movies, it's real. Now I have someone to take care of me and I'm going to live happily ever after."

As she said that, she watched a rainbow form in the mountains. Then she said softly, "Percy, I'm going to have a baby."

I panicked. "Hatsuko, that's awful! That's really bad. Now, you won't have any room inside you to love me anymore, not with a baby and sailor Charlie around, too."

"I'll always love you just the same - maybe more. You were my first baby, and I told you nothing or no one can ever take the place of a first baby," she assured me.

"Promise?"

"Promise, Percy."

I looked ahead and saw we were coming up too fast on the tail of the pineapple truck. "Hatsuko, watch out!" I yelled.

She braked as we barely missed hitting the truck.

In my seven years, my experience was that promises are made in life only to be broken. Especially when you haven't been paying attention to the one who made the promise, and they are not around you a lot anymore. Broken promises are a "wham" to the heart. It's like smashing your car into the back of a pineapple truck when you're not looking. Even if you paid careful attention to life, driving carefully and thinking your life is going about as swell as it could be, that's when you hear your best friend is married and now going to have a baby. That is, even after she promised you outside Kress Store before Christmas that she'd never leave you.

You can't count on people.

We arrived at the bus station at three. I was an hour early. I didn't tell Hatsuko that we were early because I didn't want her to wait around and get her into more trouble with Hiroshi.

We kissed goodbye.

Hatsuko promised she'd bring Charlie up to the house to meet me as soon as he returned from the Philippines. I told her I'd love to meet him, but inside my black heart, I still wished that Charlie Smarlie had never walked down our driveway at midnight. Why couldn't life remain the same? I felt like Cinderella after the ball, when everything turned back into pumpkins and pineapple fields and not a fairy godmother in sight.

Hatsuko drove away, stripping the gears of Hiroshi's car. I found a store where ice cream cones were sold. I gobbled up two double decker chocolate cones in five minutes and still was hungry. I could have kicked myself because I left the tuna sandwiches on Rose and Hiroshi's bed. I bet myself they were leaking mayonnaise on Hiroshi's bedspread.

The bus arrived on time. This time, I sat in the front seat. The same driver drove me back into town. Driving back, he ate four hot dogs and dripped mustard and relish down the front of his shirt that had hula girls on it. He never offered me a bite, even though I gave him plenty of hints along the way.

Riding back into Honolulu, the soldiers in the taxi now smelled of Bay Rum after-shave lotion and Lifebuoy soap. Not one threw up or swore. They talked about getting laid and guzzling quarts of whiskey on River Street. The trip out of hell wasn't heaven, but it wasn't hell. I slept most of the way and dreamed of Hatsuko's baby looking exactly like me.

Mother met me at the YMCA. She was all gussied up because she was going to a cocktail party at Auntie Gladys's. As we drove up our driveway, Mother told me that we were going to have a new maid. Her name was Helen. She had been highly recommended by Cousin Bessie. If Cousin Bessie recommended Helen, she was going to be "horrible bad."

Mother had a pot of creamed tuna simmering on the stove and warmed white rice in a pan next to it. That was my perfect dinner. Marigold was out with Daddy and Betsy had gone to the movies with Jack. I was left on my own. After Mother walked up to Auntie Gladys's, I sat at the kitchen table and ate mounds of creamed tuna and rice - topped with scoops of mayonnaise. I put the dishes in the sink and turned off the stove. I pooped, peed, pulled down the covers to my bed, and turned out the light. I didn't brush my teeth, take a bath or say my prayers.

I didn't feel civilized.

My house was dark, silent, and empty as the curse hovered over me.

24

Kaina

The next morning, Sunday, my house had turned into a tomb because Mother and Betsy were sleeping late and Marigold was down in Waikiki snuggling with Daddy and Grandma.

Sunday mornings have a quietness all their own. Sunday is different from any other day of the week. It's just a feeling, but Sunday is a day when your engines stop chugging and your boat flounders in a sea without a wind.

I fixed my own breakfast of cornflakes and a mayonnaise sandwich. Our paperboy, Kaina had been at the house, because the Sunday *Advertiser* was lying on the front porch. I brought the paper inside and read it while eating my cornflakes. I started with the gossip and movie sections and worked my way up to the front page.

The Honolulu Advertiser

MARLENE ILL

Film actress Marlene Dietrich was under care of a physician today suffering an attack of influenza. The actress caught cold while working next to the studio wind machines.

PAWAA THEATER Phone 91700 Show times: 6:15 8:30
THE MUMMY'S HAND starring Dick Foran and Peggy Moran

FIVE MEN SEE LEAP TO DEATH FROM PALI RIM.

Kakehaloa gives taxi driver his wallet, jumps from Pali rim. Body recovered. Apparently despondent over a recent family quarrel, a man tentatively identified as Kailama Kakehaloa, 33, of Mailikukahi, walked and leaped to his death from the Nuuanu Pali at 2 p.m. before five horrified witnesses.

ADMIRAL KIMMEL TAKES FLEET COMMAND TODAY.

GENERAL ARRIVES AT DAWN. CEREMONY PREPARED FOR CHANGE IN ARMY CHIEFS.

Final arrangements for the ceremony in which Lt. General Charles D. Herron will turn over command of the Hawaiian Army Department to Major General Walter C. Short at Fort Shafter parade grounds tomorrow morning have been completed by army authorities.

NEW FLEET JAPAN AIM, SOVIET HEARS.

Moscow (UP). Japan is building a secret fleet, understanding that only with a superior fleet can she defeat the United States, the newspaper Red Fleet, publication of the Russian Navy, asserted tonight.

Advertisement: **THE WORLD'S FAVORITE SOUP - CAMPBELL'S TOMATO SOUP.**

REGISTRATION OF HAWAII AUTOMOBILES TOTALS A RECORD OF 46,971.

I set the paper down on the dining room table for Mother and Betsy to read, and with nothing else to do, I walked out on the front porch with Agnes and Gertrude to sit and hear the mynah birds fight with each other in the coconut trees. The morning sun hit my face as we listened, and it felt warm like a mustard plaster. I looked down at the curb and saw Kaina, the paperboy, sitting near our mailbox.

I called out, "Kaina." He didn't call back so I walked down to see what was wrong. His head was in his hands and he was crying.

I sat next to him and questioned, "What's the matter, Kaina?" He wouldn't answer me and kept on crying.

I asked again, "Kaina, what's the matter?" He put his head up. His face was beat up with dark purple moons circling his eyes and red cuts slicing his lips.

"What happened?" I asked, shocked by his injuries.

With his head back down in his lap, he answered, "I got bust up."

"Why?" I persisted. He answered, "My daddy drunk! He do it to me. He beat me up good. I'm not going home this time."

"You want some iodine?" I offered. "No," he shook his head.

"Did you deliver all your newspapers?" He nodded. He patted my knee and asked, "You want to go under the house?"

I pushed his hand off my knee and answered quickly, "No, I'm never going back there again. I hate it under there. It stinks of dead rats. Why did your daddy beat you up?"

Kaina explained, "He no like me. When he hit my madda - I hit him back."

"What are you going to do?" I wondered. He muttered, "I no can think. How about you and me go up Rocky Hill and look at Pearl Harbor."

"I don't know," I said hesitantly.

"Come on. Plenty battleships in now," he urged.

Since I had made no plans for the day, everybody was asleep, I could think of nothing else to do, and I felt sorry for Kaina, I got up and said, "Okay."

Gertrude flew down from the porch and whispered into my ear, "Percy, you're asking for trouble. You stay home. That boy is trouble."

Agnes flew into my other ear and whispered, "Don't listen to her. Kaina is a sweet angel. He's not trouble. Gertrude has never been a good judge of character."

I gazed closely at Kaina. He looked like a fifteen-year-old dark angel with thick black hair, a shock of it falling over one eye like Hitler's. His brown eyes were lashed black and black eyebrows framed them perfectly. His eyes were beautiful but it was the hurt look in them that appealed to me. He looked like a little boy who had lost Christmas. He looked just like me. I made an extra effort to look into Kaina's eyes because he never looked into mine. Gertrude said he was afraid of what I would see inside them.

We walked to the top of the hill. Agnes and Gertrude trailed behind.

The top of Rocky Hill was a point that was as far away as you could get in ten minutes from the houses in the neighborhood. You couldn't be seen there. It was the highest point on the hill and was surrounded by pastureland and lantana bushes. Cousin Bessie's dead husband had built a cement platform for hikers to look out at the view; anyway that's what he told Cousin Bessie. Cross-Eyed Mama said he built the platform to get away from his nosy wife.

Kaina and I sat on the platform and dangled our feet over the edge. He started to talk non-stop about his home life and all the beatings he got from his father from the day he was a baby until today. He told me he was the youngest boy of eight. The only person who was kind to him was his eldest sister, who was married and now lived on the Big Island. He was thinking of running away to live with her. When Kaina ran out of words, we sat in silence and looked out at the view.

Kaina suddenly got up and announced, "Let's take off our clothes."

"What for?" I asked.

Gertrude buzzed back into my ear, "No you don't, Percy. You keep your clothes on."

Kaina took off his pants and shirt and threw them into a lantana bush. "Just for the fun of it," he answered. "Don't you like to have fun, Percy?"

Kaina didn't wear underpants. As he stood on top the hill bare-bottomed, he waved his hands in the air and his thing moved up and down. I noticed he was golden brown all over.

Knowing how fat and white I was, I said, "I like to have fun with my clothes on, thank you."

Kaina took my clothes off. "We'll have more fun without clothes. You'll see," he insisted. I was not a pretty sight naked, but Kaina didn't seem to mind. I wished I looked like him.

"Let's lie down," he suggested.

I did as Kaina told me to do. We laid on the cement platform next to each other. Kaina nestled his face into my chest and put his arms around me. We lay on the cement as the sun warmed us. I looked out at the view.

It was a beautiful, clear Sunday morning and the city of Honolulu spread out like a multi-colored blanket at a Sunday picnic. To the left jutted the razor-cut shape of Diamond Head. A rightward glance brought the fingers of Pearl Harbor in view. I could see the battleships and aircraft carriers sitting in the harbor as if they were toy ships floating in my bathtub. I thought that one of the battleships had to be the one that Hatsuko's Charlie was going to sail on.

I squinted hard to see the airfields and the blue-green mountains of the Waianae Range far in the distance. A spot of pink stood out in front of me on Waikiki Beach: The Royal Hawaiian Hotel took center stage. It was Hawaii's queen of hearts. Waving coconut trees dotted the landscape from one end of the island to as far as I could see on the other side, the largest grove of trees being at the Ward Estate where ghosts roamed.

"Kaina, look down there. See all those coconut trees? Ghosts walk around there at night and *kahuna* (curse) people," I told him.

"Percy, quiet."

"Honest they do, Kaina." My back was getting sunburned. "Kaina, it's time I went home. I'm getting sunburned." My skin blistered easily. Daddy said our skin belonged under the cloudy skies of Norway.

Kaina's arms wrapped tighter around me. I argued, "Kaina, let go! I want to go home."

"Not yet, Percy. We just got here."

I struggled to get loose of his arms, but Kaina was stronger and held me closer to him as I struggled. As I pushed at him, Kaina suddenly stopped holding me. He shrieked in pain, let me go and jumped straight up into the clouds. As he jumped, he held onto his fanny and swore at God. "Goddamit, Goddamit, Goddamit," he screamed with all his might as he rubbed his behind.

Hearing the "Goddamits," Gertrude said it was time to get dressed. I put on my pants, grabbed my shirt and ran for home. As I reached my house, I could still hear Kaina on the hill shouting to God.

Agnes and Gertrude were waiting for me, sitting on the porch and shaking their heads. I told them I meant to keep my clothes on, but they already knew what happened since they followed me. Gertrude then confessed that she had directed a honeybee right onto Kaina's sweet behind. I thanked Gertrude for the bee and I promised that this was the last time I was ever going to be taken in by good looks. Agnes and Gertrude jumped up and ran around the porch, shrieking with hysterical laughter.

When they sat back down, being proper ladies, I told my make-believe friends what I was feeling inside just then. "There was something nice having a warm body cuddling next to me and putting his arm around me, making believe he liked me, even if that person got kinda scary. Nobody ever touches me nice anymore, Gertrude and Agnes, except Mother. Everyone else slaps me on the head or pinches my arm. I liked having someone hold me nice - meaning maybe they liked me."

Being with Kaina reminded me of when I was a baby, when everyone held me nice. When everyone loved me...and I loved them back.

25

Walter

I met Walter, my next door neighbor, the Monday afternoon following my adventure with Kaina. On Sunday night, Mr. McLaine walked across the street to speak to Mother. He told her that he had an important appointment at the bank the next day and he wondered if I would watch Walter, his son. Mother asked him if he thought I was old enough and responsible enough for such a big undertaking. Mr. McLaine said he thought so and asked me, standing next to Mother, what I thought.

I puffed out my chest and told him I could handle watching his son and gave him a definite yes. Anyway, I was bored drawing pretty ladies with big bazooms stuck in wishing wells. Mr. McLaine asked me to report to him as soon as I walked home from school on Monday afternoon.

At one-thirty sharp, I knocked on Mr. McLaine's door, and he answered. In daylight, he was a tall man with dark black holes for eyes and as skinny as a bean-pole. His skin was shiny white like the Greek marble statue without head and arms that I saw at the Academy of Arts. He looked like an undertaker.

I took his bony hand as he led me inside his house. The house was as dark as an undertaker's parlor at high noon because all the curtains were closed. A little light forced its way in through strands of a broken Venetian blind hanging in a kitchen window, light enough to guide me to where I was going.

Leading me into the living room, Mr. McLaine said, "You're not scared of me, are you, Percy?"

I felt like wetting my pants.

"No," I lied.

"Good. Sit down in that chair." Mr. McLaine pointed to a faded red velvet upholstered chair. The chair engulfed me when I sat in it. He sat down on a couch next to me. There was a long silence between us, then he took a pipe off the table and lit it. Sucking on his pipe, talking slowly like an undertaker, he explained, "Since my wife died, I haven't touched this room." He swiped a finger across the table next to him and his finger turned black. "It's pretty dusty in here, isn't it? Pretty gloomy, too, don't you think so?"

"Yes," I tittered, "it's like Frankenstein's home."

"I see you're honest," he agreed.

I raised my hand and asked, "Why am I here? I don't see Walter or any other person around."

A little fox terrier came out of nowhere, jumped up onto his lap and growled at me. I sat way back in my chair. I made it a rule to sit as far away as I could from mean dogs. "He's not very friendly," I offered.

"She'll get used to you. We just don't have many visitors and Fluffy is really a big chicken-heart. She hates Don and Roger and would eat 'em up if she could if she were big enough," he said.

"If I were a dog, I'd eat them up, Mr. McLaine. By the way, I'm the president of the 'I hate the Twins' fan club. I'll make him a member," I said, nodding at Fluffy.

Mr. McLaine laughed. I liked him for that. "Fluffy is a girl, Percy," he corrected. Fluffy showed her teeth at me. He continued, "You asked me why you're here?"

"Yes."

"My son, Walter, asked for you."

I scratched my head. "I don't think I've ever met him, have I?"

"He knows you and likes you," Mr. McLaine answered.

"He does?"

"He'll tell you all about it," he said. "Now here is my proposition. I have to leave the house for business on certain afternoons. While I'm gone, I would like you to be a companion to Walter. I'll pay you a dollar an afternoon."

That was a fortune to me.

He waved his bony finger at me and continued, "But I have to warn you there are certain responsibilities you have to assume. You see, my son cannot take care of himself. When he was your age, I gave him a bicycle. He was quite a daredevil. He went to the top of the hill and rode his bike down as fast as he could. His brakes didn't work and he hit that light pole on the corner. He was unconscious for months, and he hasn't been the same since. Thinking about the boy and the accident all the time - that accident killed my wife. She doted on him.

"Walter has sudden fits now. His fits come out of the blue. He shakes all over, swallows his tongue, and I have to call the ambulance."

"I've seen the ambulance come here lots of times," I confirmed.

"I know you have. When he does have these fits, they're not scary if you keep your head. The first thing you do is put a spoon in his mouth so he won't swallow his tongue, then lie him down and call the ambulance. Do you think that's too much for a little boy to handle? Mrs. Potter used to help me, but she suddenly had to go back to the Mainland to be with her sick sister. This is only a temporary situation until I find the right someone. Presently, I have some very important business to take care of and Walter wants only you to take care of him. Do you think you can handle this? You would be doing me and Walter a great big favor," he entreated.

"Mr. McLaine, I see lots of movies and I can handle any emergency that comes up. I always thought I'd be a great Florence Nightingale. Yes sir, I would be proud to take care of Walter," I assured him.

"That's the boy. Now Fluffy and I are going to take you downstairs to the basement to meet Walter. Can you start this afternoon?"

"I planned to," I answered.

Mr. McLaine led me down to the basement with his bony hand. Fluffy followed, growling behind me. She nipped at my heels as I walked. She was an annoying little dog because she didn't have any manners. I had to keep turning back to her and shushing her. I finally pleaded with Fluffy to quit nipping me and told her that I liked well-behaved dogs. I told her very sincerely that I was very sorry that I called her a boy. I told her I have a bad habit of treating dogs like boys and cats like girls.

Stepping into the basement, I was blinded by bright sunlight. The room ran the length of the house and the walls were made out of bricks. A long bank of windows faced our house across the street. The sunlight burst through these windows into the room. In the center of the room was a long table, three times the size of a ping pong table, with an electric train that ran on tracks running through a landscape of realistic-looking miniature papiermache towns, tunnels, mountains, lakes, cows, and people.

Otherwise, the room looked a typical teenage boy's bedroom, messed up with books, *Popular Mechanics* magazines and clothes scattered all over the floor. In the farthest corner from where I stood was a single bed. A young boy with black hair sat on it. He was bent over like a pretzel. If his face wasn't so distorted, he would be as handsome as Tyrone Power.

Mr. McLaine led me to Walter. My heart pounded because the closer I got, the more Walter looked like Hunkacha. I was afraid he would rise off his bed and eat me up.

"Walter, this is Percy," introduced Mr. McLaine. I put out my hand to shake Walter's hand.

Walter looked at my feet and stammered, "I - I doooona shake hannnnds."

"That's all right, Walter. I just want to be your friend."

He looked up at me, his eyes shining. "Weee allllready friends, Perrrcy." Spit slobbered out of his mouth.

"We are?" I questioned.

Mr. McLaine interrupted, "Boys, get acquainted while I take a quick trip down to the Bank of Hawaii. I'll only be gone a couple of hours. Walter, don't get excited just because you have Percy here."

Mr. McLaine took out a card and gave it to me, as he explained, "Percy, here is a number where I can be reached - and there is the number for the ambulance at Queen's Hospital. If Walter has a fit, call the ambulance and me. Walter wants to teach you himself how to use the spoon so he can't bite his tongue if he has the shakes." Mr. McLaine's undertaker eyes burrowed through me as he said, "I know Walter is in good hands."

Mr. McLaine turned to Walter and asked, "Did you take your medicine? I want you to have a good time with Percy."

Walter nodded his head up and down and with his hands urged his father to go on his errand and to leave us alone. Mr. McLaine patted me on the shoulder and walked back upstairs. Fluffy followed him.

I was scared being left alone with Walter because I didn't know what to say. Walter sat on his bed, body bent over and still looking at my feet in his funny crooked way. I heard Mr. McLaine's car backing out of the garage. I summoned up my courage and spoke, "Walter, do you want to show me how to use the spoon?"

Walter got up and shuffled over to the sink and brought back a spoon. He held it and then put the spoon in his mouth. "Liiiike that!"

"I see. May I try it?" I asked.

Walter held the spoon in his mouth. I went over and took the spoon out of his mouth and replaced it. "Did I do it right?

"Yeeeeasss, riiiight! Youuuu arrrre perrrfect!" he answered. I put the spoon back on the counter next to the telephone.

"Arrrre you hunnngry?" he asked. "Look at me, Walter." I jiggled my stomach. "I can always eat."

He pointed to an icebox next to the sink. "Oppppen it!"

I opened the icebox door and saw two mayonnaise sandwiches piled on a plate. I took out the plate and asked, "Is this for me?"

"Yessss, for you!"

I closed the ice box door and asked Walter, "How did you know I love mayonnaise sandwiches?"

He pushed me to the windows and told me to look out. I saw the side of my house where I ate my mayonnaise sandwiches and played with Agnes and Gertrude.

He explained, "I waaatch you allll the timmme."

I took a bite out of the sandwich. "Walter, you're a better spy than I am. I never knew you were watching me."

"Thasss why we are friennnds. III waaatch yoou alll the timmme. I likkkke you!"

When I had finished eating the first sandwich, I'd forgotten Walter had a bent body, slobbered when he talked, and spoke words funny out of his mouth. We were friends at once.

He told me that he had watched me ever since I was five years old, and he knew I talked to imaginary people. He said he knew me better than I knew myself. Walter was spooky in that department. He told me about his accident and how he can't remember much about anything anymore, especially right after the accident. He cried when he talked about his mother and missing her all the time. His father worried about him too much. He confessed sadly that he thought his father was embarrassed about him and that's why his father never let him go anywhere.

"My faaather thiinks I killlled myy motherr becaussse offf the acciddent," he confided.

I fibbed, "Your father would never think that. He loves you a whole lot - more than my father loves me."

Walter had tears in his eyes when I said that. I continued, "Walter, have you ever seen a movie?"

"Nooo, I caaaaan't leeave my roooom becaaaz I miiight geet sick annnd emmbarraass Daaad."

"Maybe someday your daddy will let me take you to a movie. I promise I won't be embarrassed. Listen, Walter, every movie I see from now on, I'm going to come over here and tell you all about it. I could even act out some of the movies for you. I'm a good actor. Would you like that, Walter?"

"Thhhaaat beee sweelllll, Perrrcy! Peeercy, yooous wan to seee my traiiin work?" Walter asked.

"That'd be swell, Walter."

Walter came alive. He loved his trains as much as I loved dressing up in Mother's clothes and eating mayonnaise sandwiches. He hobbled over to the table and turned on all the switches on the table. The train leaped into action and ran down the tracks with Walter's fingers controlling the speed. I could tell the reason he loved running his train - here he was the master over something. He even forgot I was standing next to him as he concentrated on running his electric train through tunnels, over bridges and past farming villages. By a twist of a dial, he speeded the train to run faster and faster around the track. He pushed his locomotive at a reckless speed - perhaps the same way he rode his bike down our hill into a light pole.

It happened suddenly. The train went too fast and the engine and its cars jumped a bridge and fell off the table onto the brick floor. The train made a terrible crashing sound as it hit the bricks.

Walter took three strides to the other side of the table and saw his engine broken in half. He bent over, picked up the engine pieces and cradled them in his arms. He started to wail as if his favorite child had died.

"Walter, are you all right?" I asked. Fluffy, hearing Walter's moaning, ran downstairs and yapped at me.

Walter started to shake. This was it!

I ran to the counter and picked up the spoon and tried to put it into Walter's mouth. He spat at me at first, but after two tries, Walter let me force the spoon over his tongue. I took the two pieces of the engine out of his hand and he helped me lead him over to his bed. I laid him down like a baby and Fluffy licked his hand. I called for the ambulance and then dialed Mr. McLaine. Everybody on the phone told me to be calm.

Funny thing was, I told them that I was "cool as a cucumber." The ambulance and Mr. McLaine arrived at the same time. When the ambulance men came to get Walter, he was breathing hard and gasping for air. His eyes were spinning like pinwheels. He shook so fiercely, he could have been swimming in an ocean filled with icebergs.

Mr. McLaine went to the hospital with Walter. I walked home, but not before Fluffy wagged her tail and licked my face.

The next day, Mr. McLaine came over with a bottle of Best Foods mayonnaise. It was a present from Walter. He reported that Walter was coming home in a couple of afternoons and hoped that I would still care for his son after he got home. I told him it would be an honor, and when Walter was feeling better, I was going to act out the latest movie I had seen.

In one afternoon, Walter had become my best friend.

I told Agnes and Gertrude I'd made a new friend - no, three friends, Mr. McLaine, Walter and Fluffy. Gertrude was thinking about Hatsuko when she said to me, "When one door closes, three more open."

Two days later, I ran into Kaina delivering newspapers. He told me he was leaving for the Big Island to live with his sister. He blushed and made me promise not to tell anyone what happened on Rocky Hill. He told me he went crazy with me because his dad beat him up. Rubbing his behind, he said he still couldn't figure out why a bee stung him on his okole. I told him that I had it on good authority the bee mistakenly thought his sweet behind was the most beautiful, fragrant flower in all Hawaii. He crossed his eyes at me.

I promised him and crossed my heart that lying together without clothes in each other's arms would be a secret between him and me for all my life. Kaina wrote out his new address on the Big Island and told me to look him up if I came to Hilo. Kaina looked relieved that I had not told Mother anything. He shook my hand. I told him I hoped no one would ever beat him up again because he was a very nice person and if they did, I'd beat them up.

Kaina hugged me.

I was sitting beside my house eating a mayonnaise sandwich the day Walter came home from the hospital. Watching Mr. McLaine carry him into the house, I thought in three days I had sure had lots of adventures. I said goodbye to Hatsuko, lay naked on top of our hill with the paperboy, but best of all, I made new friends who needed me.

I felt wanted now.

I spoke to God in heaven, munching on the sandwich, saying that if God let all those things happen to me in three days, what other doors was He going to open up for me in 1941. Maybe He'd let the curse go away.

That day, I printed a letter to the Twins and put it in their mailbox. I wrote that if they ever again teased Fluffy or Mr. McLaine, my new best friends, the next letter would be to Auntie Gladys, telling her about their club under the house. Marigold was furious that I had turned into a sneaky blackmailer and warned me that the Twins, after receiving my letter, doubled the price on my head - it was now ten cents to anyone who would kidnap me as I walked home from school.

I didn't give a fig because I had the upper hand. I laughed to myself. The Twins wouldn't do anything to me because I'd tell Auntie Gladys that not all the pearls in Hawaii are found around her neck or at the bottom of Pearl Harbor or in Hunkacha's blue lake.

Hiding from the Twins in my bedroom, I was bored reading the latest Batman comic book so I threw it on the floor. I lay back on my pillow and thought about Walter living in the basement across the street. I thought about Mr. Hamada, my spy friend. Mr. Hamada would have been proud that I didn't panic like a girl when Walter had the shaking fit. I wished I could telephone Mr. Hamada but he was probably spying somewhere.

I hadn't heard back from Alice Faye.

Thinking again about Walter, who couldn't talk straight, I now knew someone more cursed than I was and he was my new best friend. Walter was really cursed and I made a vow that I would be his good friend and make all the days of his life happy ones.

26

Kimo

I pretended to be sick so I could stay at home and listen to the radio. I loved Ma Perkins giving out advice in her lumberyard. When everyone left for school, I ran from my bed, pillow in hand and jumped into Mother's made-up bed, pulling back the covers and burrowing in. In a great dramatic flourish, I pulled the covers over my head and pretended I was an Arab under a Moroccan tent in the Gobi desert.

At three, familiar voices floated through the house and interrupted my stolen hours in Mother's bed. Listening to soap operas all day had made me limp as a dish rag. Now I really felt sick.

Coming into her bedroom, Mother skidded to a stop when she saw the mess I had made of the room. "Percy, what have you done to my bedroom? Who do you think is going to clean this mess up?" she demanded. She picked the coverings off the floor and snapped, "Well, it looks like you're well enough to go back to school, young man, even if you're dying."

"But I am dying." I gave her a Greta Garbo tuberculosis cough.

Picking the sheets off the floor, she ordered, "You are not dying and get out of my bed right now and go back to your room so I can clean up in here."

I picked up my pillow and stomped back to my bedroom, muttering, "Nobody believes I'm dying. They'll be sorry when they find me dead in my bed - tongue hanging out, blood oozing out my ears and nose. Then they'll wish they had listened to me. I'll say four final words to them before I die, 'The curse got me.' "

Mother called after me as I jumped into my bed, "Stop this curse business, and well, if you're dying, I guess you can't have dinner with Kimo tonight. He'll be disappointed not to see you because...! Anyway, if you're dying, it doesn't matter and you won't want to know that his world has turned upside down."

"Kimo, my cousin, the artist?" I asked eagerly.

Mother walked into my room, holding the bed sheets in her hands, and replied, "That's the Kimo I'm talking about."

I jumped out of bed and hugged Mother, screaming excitedly, "I'm well. I can feel it." I pinched myself, "Yes, I feel it! Jesus touched me. I'm a miracle, Mother."

Mother looked up at heaven and sighed, "Thank you, Jesus."

I got out of bed and grabbed Mother's hand and pulled on it, saying, "Since

I'm cured, and you won't believe this - I'm well enough to have dinner with Kimo tonight."

"My, we'll really have to thank God for your miracle tonight at prayer time, won't we?" Mother smiled and kissed the top of my head. "You had me worried, Percy. Wash up because God and Kimo don't like smelly little boys at the dinner table. Take a bubble bath and comb your hair and dress nicely."

She added, walking out of the room, holding her nose, "Brush your teeth."

Running into the bathroom and turning on the water in the bathtub, I shouted to Mother, "What are we having for dinner?"

"Cousin Kimo has heard about my cooking, so he's bringing chop suey from Lau Yee Chai."

I yelled back to Mother, who was making up her bed, "Isn't he great? Isn't he great? He's really swell." As I sat down in the tub to wash up for Kimo, I said to myself, "I hope he brings rice. Mayonnaise with rice is my most favorite Chinese dish, and my second favorite is mayonnaise with egg foo yung."

Mother, Marigold and I were decked out in our best clothes when Kimo arrived. As promised, he brought oodles and oodles of Chinese food. The chop suey overflowed the twelve cardboard pint-sized cartons and spilled yellow sauce on our dining room table. It was a banquet fit for a Chinese princess.

Kimo was the only relative I really loved. He was not a person whom I was made to love because we shared the same grandmother or great-grandfather, but I really loved him like I did Hatsuko. In Hilo, he told me I was one of his best friends. I think he told that to Marigold, too.

At dinner, while I was spooning mayonnaise all over my chop suey, Kimo told us he had been fired from the plantation office and had decided to leave Hilo. He had joined the Royal Canadian Air Force and was going away to fight the Germans. He was leaving tomorrow on the Lurline for Canada.

Mother asked, "How did Aunt Ella take it?"

"Not well," Kimo responded. "She stopped speaking to me and didn't see me off on the boat."

Reaching across the table, taking Kimo's hand, Mother said, "Kimo, don't be hard on Aunt Ella. She's feeling that way because you're her only baby and she wants you safe. She doesn't want you killed in a war that we're not fighting in."

"Deidra, there's really nothing for me in Hilo. Never was. I can't do my work there. I mean really my work. I hated being a bookkeeper. That's not a job for me. I'm an artist. I was so unhappy I couldn't even paint anymore. Sarah said I didn't have a future as an artist and stopped seeing me. She's already dating somebody else. It didn't take her long.

"I'm doing the only sensible thing I know how to do. I'm going away. I'm going to fight for something - something bigger than any of us. I know I sound like a corny Army recruit poster but I believe we have to fight Hitler. He's out to destroy my world in Europe. When the war is all over, I'm going back to Paris and paint. When I do, Percy and Marigold, you're going to have to come and visit me. That's what I really want to do and to hell with my family. Come to think of it, it's all I've ever wanted to do - paint pretty girls like Marigold. But now, I'm going to fight the Germans to make it all possible."

He talked just like Errol Flynn acting in a Warner Brothers' war movie.

Kimo looked at Marigold and said, "Marigold, you haven't said one word to me. What's wrong? Don't you like me anymore? Did I hurt your feelings, my darlin'?"

Marigold took her chopsticks and pounded them on the table just like Hiroshi did at Waialua.

Mother commanded, "Marigold, stop pounding those things and don't be rude to Kimo. Tell him you still like him."

Marigold threw the chopsticks on her plate. Holding back the tears welling in her eyes, she looked up at Kimo and burst out, "It has nothing to do with you, Kimo. Even Mother doesn't know."

Concerned, Mother asked, "What don't I know, Marigold?"

Marigold blurted out, "Daddy is getting married!"

"Oh, Marigold," Mother rose and put both her arms around her baby. "Is that why you've been so upset? I thought you were mad at me."

Tearfully, Marigold said, "I am mad at you. You shouldn't have divorced Daddy because then he wouldn't have left us and now he is going to get married again. Even Grandma's upset. She had to move out of his apartment. Daddy is going to put her in the Pleasanton Hotel. She's going to be all alone now. I told Grandma the Pleasanton is an old firetrap and she'll probably burn to death when she moves in there. I told her to move back in with us." Marigold looked back down at her plate. "Grandma feels you don't like her and don't want her here anymore."

Mother didn't say anything. She walked back to her seat and sat down again. Looking out the window, Mother said to no one in particular, "Well, that's that. He's really not coming back, is he? Well, we'll have to take care of ourselves."

Mother turned back to us, a smile back on her face and turned to Kimo, apologizing, "Kimo, I'm sorry this had to happen tonight. This should be a happy night for you."

"I'm glad I'm here." He smiled at us lovingly and talked to all of us, "Deidra, Marigold and Percy - you're my family now. I am glad I'm here tonight. Remember, no matter what happens, you'll always have me. Marigold, remember that. I'll never leave any of you. And if there are problems, you have to promise to write me. Even though I am far away, I know I can help. Promise me you'll write if anything goes wrong."

Now Kimo talked liked Clark Gable.

After Kimo spoke, Mother had tears running down her cheeks. Marigold and I ran around to our cousin and put our arms around him. We held him as tight as we could because we didn't want him to leave us and go fight the Germans.

Marigold ran from Kimo, stood up on her chair and made a toast. Raising up her arm, she cried out, "Here's to Kimo, our best friend, the bravest man we know. Kimo, I've decided to go with you tomorrow and join up with the Royal Canadian Air Force. I'm going to be a pilot just like you."

Marigold talked like John Wayne.

Kimo rose to his feet, glass in hand and toasted Marigold, "Marigold, I'd be proud to have you with me, but you have to be over twenty to join up. In a couple of years, I'll come back and get you and we'll fly together. Here's to Marigold - the bravest girl I know."

Kimo's toast made us all forget that our father was getting married to a stranger.

Marigold jumped up and down and zoomed around the table a couple of times at the thought of becoming a pilot with Kimo. Running around the table, she told Kimo not to forget his promise and that she'll be the best goddamn-ist pilot in the whole world.

Mother let Marigold's swearing pass because she was full of chop suey.

Kimo had turned our evening into a grand celebration and made us laugh from our bellies to our double chins. Then Mother outdid herself. She concocted triple-decker chocolate sundaes for dessert with whipped cream and a red cherry on the top. She knew chocolate sundaes were Kimo's favorite dessert. He called our sundaes by another name - he called them chocolate mousses. I mooed.

After dinner, I walked Kimo down to his car. He put his arm around me and asked, "Percy, you haven't forgotten what I told you by the pool on Christmas Day?"

Looking up at a starry sky, I answered, "I have never forgotten. You are my best friend forever. Someday, Kimo, I know your wish will come true and you'll have a little girl all your own named Mary Emily."

"I forgot I told you about that."

Out of the blue, I mumbled, "Kimo, I want to know everything."

"So do I, Percy," he agreed. We looked up at the stars together. Taking my hand, Kimo said, "Percy, now that your dad is getting married, you're going to have to be the man in the family. You have to take care of your mother and sister. You have to be strong for them like the tallest tree in a forest."

I answered him back, discouraged, "I don't think I'm that strong."

He looked into my eyes, loving me, and said, "You are. You are going to turn into the strongest and tallest tree in your forest. I know you are. I just tried to be someone else in someone else's forest and it made me miserable all the time. And moreover, I found that I wasn't standing very tall in my own forest. Now I am."

"My forest is full of monsters, like mean old Hunkacha and curses," I said fearfully.

Kimo tousled my hair and replied, not hearing me, "Marigold needs a lot of love and understanding and you can help her - even when you think she's being mean to you, love her. Maybe that's hard for a little boy to understand right now, but someday you'll know what I'm saying. Try to see beyond her moods because she's hurting more than she will let you know. She's the best person in our family. Your dad leaving her hurt her a lot. I am saying all this to you because I think you can understand even though you're only seven. I see it in you. I don't think you see it in you, but it's there. Do you understand what I'm saying?"

"I understand everything, Kimo." I didn't.

I wanted Kimo to like me best.

Kimo gave me a bear hug. As he was about to step into his car, he turned to me, "Now friend, you are coming down to the Lurline to see me off tomorrow?"

"You bet. Even if I have to play sick from school again, I'll be there. I won't miss seeing you off. Promise."

As Kimo drove away and I waved goodbye, I vowed that I wanted to be exactly like Kimo...and Alice Faye.

The following day Mother, Marigold and I were at the four o'clock sailing to see Kimo off. The dock and the Lurline were packed with people saying aloha to their friends and relatives. Kimo got us a pass so we could board the ship to see his cabin. It was easy to get lost on the Lurline because there were too many corridors that looked all the same and too many people floating in and out of cabins saying good-byes.

I held fast to Mother's hand so that I wouldn't float away into the masses of people sailing around me. I didn't want to get lost like I did at the John Rodgers airport because if the ship sailed and I got stuck on it, I'd have to jump overboard and swim back to Waikiki Beach.

We found Kimo's cabin in the bowels of the ship. His cabin was overflowing with noisy classmates from Punahou, who were drinking champagne out of a bottle and having a gay old time. Seeing us, they quickly hid the champagne.

Mother and Marigold gave Kimo leis we had brought. I told him we'd better get off because I could hear the ding-dongs of the purser's gong warning all visitors to leave the ship. The ship's whistle blew long and loud and speakers on walls announced, "ALL ASHORE, GOING ASHORE!"

We kissed Kimo goodbye and scurried off the Lurline. I walked fast because I didn't want to become a stowaway and have to sleep in a lifeboat. Walking down the gangplank, I saw Mr. Hamada among the crowds of people milling on the pier. He looked different because he was all dressed up in a coat and tie like a businessman. I yelled and waved, "Mr. Hamada! Mr. Hamada! Over here. It's me Percy! Look over here, Mr. Hamada. It's me, Percy!"

He looked my way, smiled, then disappeared into the crowd in a magician's puff of smoke. I wondered to myself what kind of spying mission he was on. I wanted to ask him that, if he had any pull with Mr. Hitler, to please tell the mean old German pilots not to shoot down my cousin's plane.

Mother asked me who I was yelling at. I told her I was calling to my Japanese friend who brought me home when I lost Daddy and Marigold at the air show.

Down on the pier, we looked back up at the Lurline to see if we could find Kimo at a railing. Marigold found him, and seeing him, we yelled and waved up to him leaning over the railing. He saw us and waved back and threw colored streamers down at us. The ship's whistle blew loudly again, announcing the Lurline was leaving the pier. The Royal Hawaiian Band began to play "Aloha Oe." I looked up at Kimo. He gave a final farewell by blowing kisses to us as the stevedores pulled away the gangplank.

The joy of life and adventure bloomed like a million sunflowers on Kimo's face. He looked truly happy. As he turned towards the horizon, the golden-red rays of the setting sun colored his face. He turned back and threw the leis around his neck into the water, believing in the custom that if they landed back on shore, he would return to us.

Bang! It was if somebody threw a bucket of ice water all over my body. It was as if someone shot a bullet straight through my heart. Watching the ship head out of the harbor, standing on the pier, hearing the Royal Hawaiian Band play Hawaii's farewell song, I knew that this was the last time I was ever going to see my cousin Kimo alive.

I started to cry. Mother asked why I was crying, but I couldn't explain to her what was churning around in my heart.

What I felt, I knew was true - true as true as true as it could be. Kimo's leis were never going to reach the shores of Waikiki. I couldn't tell that to anyone because they wouldn't believe me. They'd think I was crazy like Cousin Bessie. I was drifting further into the doldrums. My ship was cast adrift in a lonely sea.

Kimo caught my curse.

27

A Kiss is Just a Kiss

The next day, Mr. McLaine walked over and he told me that I could visit Walter on Friday. Walter was stronger and wanted me to act out a movie for him. I told Agnes and Gertrude the news and we rehearsed all week the movie that I was going to perform for Walter.

Friday, after school, suitcase in hand, I rushed over to Walter's house. Mr. McLaine and Fluffy let me in. As Mr. McLaine led me to the basement, I turned to him and said, "Mr. McLaine, why did you name a fox terrier Fluffy? There's nothing - and please pardon me for saying this, Fluffy - there's nothing fluffy about Fluffy."

Fluffy growled at me. She just proved my fluffy point.

"Well, Percy, my wife named her Fluffy because when Fluffy was tiny, she was white all over and looked like a snow ball."

"That makes good sense. I had been wondering that forever and it was driving me crazy," I answered. I bent over and said, patting Fluffy on the head, "Fluffy, if I had named you, I'd have named you Bullet because you're as fast and sharp as a bullet shot from John Wayne's gun." She wagged her tail.

As we were walking down the basement steps, Mr. McLaine questioned me, "What do you have in that fancy suitcase of yours, Percy?"

"Costumes, props and everything I need to act out a movie for Walter."

"I'm sure Walter will like your movie."

When we walked into the basement, I could see Walter lying as still as a corpse on his bed. The covers were pulled up to his neck. I looked around the room and saw that Walter's train hadn't been repaired. It lay broken on its side on the table. I walked over to my friend and said, "Hi, Walter. I've missed you this much." I dropped the suitcase and spread my hands out as far as I could stretch them.

Walter reached for my hand and slobbered, "Hiiiii, Peeercy! I'mmm gladdd you've cooome to seee me. IIII misssed yooou toons tooo aaand thannk yoooou foor saaaving mmmy life!"

I wasn't lying when I said to Walter, "I didn't save your life. You saved it yourself. You are the bravest person I have ever met."

"Thannk yoou, Peercy!"

"Well, boys, I'm going upstairs to read the newspaper. If you need me, Percy, call me." Mr. McLaine and Fluffy climbed the stairs back to the living room.

Walter sat up in his bed and asked, "Whhhhat haave yooou gottt inn thaaat suitccasse, Peeercy?"

Opening the suitcase, I showed Walter what I had brought. Inside were Mother's favorite black velvet evening dress, her satin blue high heels, her make-up, perfume, and Marigold's baseball cap. I also brought two champagne glasses, a pack of cigarettes, and Mother's crystal necklace for the props. "I need all of this to help me tell you about the movie," I explained.

"Whaaat's theeee moooviiie?"

"The movie is *Lillian Russell* which stars my favorite actress of all time, Alice Faye. I'm going to play Alice Faye and you're going to play her rich and famous boyfriends."

"Hooow ammm I gooooing to plaaaay her boyfriiiiends?" he wondered.

"That's why I brought the baseball cap." I put the baseball cap on Walter's wobbly head. "We're going to pretend this is a top hat. All the rich men wore top hats in the gay nineties. Take this champagne glass..." I clamped a champagne glass in his claw-formed hand as I explained, "This champagne glass will make you into the richest man in the whole wide world."

Taking out Mother's black velvet dress, I announced, "I'm going to put this on." I slipped the dress over my head, but it fell over my shoulders and cascaded to the floor. I picked it up off the floor and safety-pinned the top of the dress to my shirt. "See," I pointed to the dress, "I am Lillian Russell. Actually, I'm Alice Faye playing Lillian Russell. Now the make-up, and then I'll be perfect."

I took Mother's Deliciously Red lipstick and smeared it over my lips, which made my lips look twice their size. "Big lips are a sign of glamour," I informed Walter. Then I rubbed Rosy Red rouge over my cheeks and powdered my face with Colonial Dames Crystal White vanishing-powder, so I'd look like a perfect Alice Faye.

When I had tried on Mother's high heels, her crystal necklace hanging around my neck, holding a cigarette in my left hand and the champagne glass in the other, Gertrude said I looked like one of Grandma's cheap floozies on Hotel Street. Now in the dress and everything else, I dragged myself around the room and started dramatically to tell the story of Lillian Russell to Walter.

In a low sexy voice, I started, "Lillian Russell was not her real name. Her real name was Helen Louise Leonard. She changed her name to Lillian Russell because she didn't want her mother to know that she had become the biggest musical star in the whole wide world, and she was known by everybody as the most beautiful woman on the moon."

I puckered up my lips, put a cigarette in my mouth, and pretended to inhale to make me look beautiful. Exhaling invisible smoke, I sipped air out of the champagne glass and continued, "Tony Pastor, a big-time producer in New York City, discovered Lillian when he heard her sing in her backyard. He had his own theater and he was the man who made her into a big star. Alice Faye sang this song."

I trilled, "Rosie, you are my posy, you are my heart's bouquet. Come out into the moonlight." My voice cracked, so I stopped singing.

Walter clapped, "Braaaavo. Braaaavo. Morre. Moorre, Liiiilian Russsselll."

Walter was into the act.

I became dramatic and lowered my voice, "Then a boyfriend came along and saved her and her grandma from being killed by a big runaway horse. Now, this boyfriend was the handsome actor, Henry Fonda. He's as good looking as you are."

"I'mmmm nnnot gooodlookkking. Noooo giiirl woooould loook attt me," Walter objected.

"Oh yes, they would, Walter. You are very handsome. Handsome just like any actor in the movies. Better. I think you're handsomer than Tyrone Power," I assured him. I lied. I thought Walter once in his life needed a good lie. "I bet Alice Faye would give a million dollars to kiss you." This time I lied big-time, but I decided to make him feel like he was the handsomest man in the world.

"Now, I'm not going to kiss you but only pretend to kiss you - because that's what Lillian Russell would want to do after you saved her life. Anyway, that's what they do in the movies. They kiss when you save someone's life."

I walked over to Walter's bed and I puckered out my ruby red lips like I was going to kiss him. I bent down, acting out that Lillian was thanking Henry Fonda for saving her life.

"PERCY, WHAT ARE YOU DOING?" Mr. McLaine yelled behind me.

Surprised, I turned around. I hadn't heard Mr. McLaine or Fluffy come down the stairs. I jumped back and in one big breath, I talked as fast as I could get my words out. "Pretending to kiss Walter like Alice Faye would do in *Lillian Russell*. Walter just saved Lillian Russell's life. Walter is pretending to be Henry Fonda. I was pretending to be Alice Faye. I told Walter he was as handsome as Henry Fonda was. Henry Fonda is the big movie star in Hollywood. Don't you think Walter is handsomer than Henry Fonda?"

Mr. McLaine stood before me speechless. His black eyes changed. A door had shut. His undertaker eyes weren't smiling anymore.

"Daaad, I'mmm haaving funnn! Peeercy iiis ooonly preetending. Heee's aaa goood actoor. Peeecy saaays I'mmm haaandsoome," Walter tried to explain.

"That's all right, son. I know Percy is only pretending, but play time is over." Mr. McLaine pushed me toward my suitcase. "Percy, I want you to pack up everything. Take off that dress and go home. Walter is tired now."

I unpinned the dress, and without a word, I folded the dress back into the suitcase.

"I'mmm not tiiired, Daaad," Walter objected.

Mr. McLaine gathered my props into my suitcase and told Walter, "You are tired. I can see it. I made a mistake. It's too soon to have Percy here. Maybe later."

There would never be a "later."

With the suitcase packed, I went over and shook Walter's hand.

We had never touched before.

I said, "Walter, thank you for being Henry Fonda. It was a privilege to act with you today. Next time, we'll do a John Wayne movie. I'll be the horse and you'll be John Wayne."

"Enough, Percy. Let's go." Mr. McLaine grabbed my hand. His hand was freezing cold. I carried the suitcase up the stairs as Mr. McLaine led the way.

Fluffy followed behind. At the front door, I shook Mr. McLaine's hand in full Alice Faye make-up.

"Mr. McLaine, I hope you'll still let me take care of Walter. I can do it - really I can. I don't get scared when Walter has his fits."

"Maybe later when he's stronger. Goodbye, Percy, and thank you," he said. His goodbye was as cold as an ice cube down my back. Fluffy jumped up and kissed me on the mouth, getting lipstick on her face. I patted her and told her, "Goodbye, Bullet."

I crossed the street with my suitcase and went into my house, knowing that Mr. McLaine would never ever let me take care of Walter again because the door in his eyes had shut me out.

"A kiss is just a kiss." That's what Humphrey Bogart sang to Ingrid Bergman. But what is wrong with a kiss when you don't touch lips?

I opened the suitcase and threw Mother's dress and props all over the bedroom. I lay down on my bed, wondering if the wind would ever blow back into my sails. I was more bewildered than ever. Neither Agnes nor Gertrude could help me. They were inside the window seat playing with my old teddy bear stuffed with the stolen box of stars from Mr. Murray's five-and-dime store.

Marigold ran into my room. I turned my face into the pillow so she wouldn't see the make-up smeared all over my face. She commanded, "Percy, look at me, right now. Daddy wants us to go to the beach with him tomorrow. You have to go."

Hiding my face in the pillow, I moaned, "I don't want to go. I'm sick. Leave me alone, I'm cursed."

"Forget the curse. Anyway, I'm tired of hearing about your old curse. I am not going if you're not going with me. Daddy wants us to meet the person he's going to marry. He told me she wants to meet us. You have to go, Percy. Please," she pleaded.

When she said please, I turned to her full face because she hardly used that word with me. I cried out, "You meet her. She won't like me. Nobody likes me. Look at me, I'm a mess. I'll do something bad to her and she'll not want to marry Daddy."

Marigold brightened up and said, "I never thought about that. That's the best reason for you to come. Bring the curse with you. If you don't come, I'll let the Twins in and we'll tickle you to death." She looked at me and around the room. She had been so excited when she ran in, she wasn't thinking about anything but Daddy's new wife. She exclaimed, "What's that goop on your face?"

"Blood, Marigold. Blood. I'm bleeding to death."

"Well, you've got a lot of that blood on your pillow. You better pick up Mother's dress and her make-up before she comes home or she'll give you a spanking so hard, you'll wish you were cursed. Wash your face," she scolded. Seeing her baseball cap on the floor, she demanded, "What are you doing with my baseball cap?"

"I borrowed it to play with Walter. Please don't tell Mother about anything. It's not a good day." I put my face, full of misery, back into the pillow.

Putting on her baseball cap, shoving her hands into her pockets and speaking her best John Wayne imitation, she drawled, "Okay, pardner, I won't tell her anything but you'd better come tomorrow. Daddy is coming by at nine to pick us up."

I warned Marigold, "I'll go, but I'll do something bad and that lady will never want to marry Daddy because she's going to find out that Daddy has a crazy son with a curse on his head."

Satisfied that I was going, Marigold left and shut my door. I heard her say to herself, "I hope you'll pull a doozy tomorrow, Percy. A real doozy. A pipper."

Mother brought our new maid, Helen, home with her. Helen was Japanese, like Hatsuko. She was shaped straight as a stick, without an inch of fat on her. Immediately, I knew that Helen and I were not going to be friends, especially when she announced I was to stay out of her kitchen while she worked for us.

Helen had strict hours. She worked only on Mondays through Fridays from nine to seven, and she wasn't about to live in Hatsuko's tiny little room. She said proudly that she had her own home on Punchbowl Street where she lived with her husband.

Out of earshot of Mother, Helen said, looking me up and down, that she didn't like fat boys. She and Rose's husband, Hiroshi, had to be related. They both were born with sour lemons in their mouths.

After Mother introduced Helen to Marigold and Betsy, she showed Helen around the house and explained her duties. As Mother listed all the things she expected Helen to do for us, Helen walked behind Mother with her hands behind her back, like Grumpy in *Snow White and the Seven Dwarfs*.

Helen's first dinner was pukey. She cooked a pot roast that was as dry as the Sahara desert and she burnt the onions, carrots and potatoes into crispy little pieces of black coal. Helen was Cousin Bessie's revenge. My revenge on her would be to feed Darlene, Cousin Bessie's cat, Helen's pot roast and watch her die. I didn't do it but it was a delicious thought.

After dinner, Mother sorted through her mail and pulled out a large brown envelope from the pile. She looked it over and handed it to me. It was from Alice Faye at 20th Century Fox, Hollywood, California!

I was too excited to open it up in front of Mother. I grabbed the envelope and ran into my bedroom and hid it under my pillow. I was going to wait till everyone was asleep and then open it up when no one was looking. I wanted Alice Faye all to myself.

When the brown envelope arrived from Alice Faye in Hollywood, California, a little wind blew back into my sails - a Hollywood wind.

28

Enter Kathy

Everyone was asleep.

Marigold had moved lock, stock and John Wayne's picture into Hatsuko's room, back of the garage. On threat of death, I was forbidden to enter her new digs. Marigold nailed KEEP OUT PERCY signs all over the windows and doors. I kept out. But now I had my bedroom all to myself.

Putting my ear to their doors and hearing Mother and Betsy snoring, I made sure they were asleep. I returned to my bedroom, turned on the light and pulled out Alice Faye's brown envelope from under the pillow and opened it. Inside, I found a black and white photo of Alice with her golden curls piled on top of her head. It was a photo from the movie *In Old Chicago* with dreamboat Tyrone Power. At the top of the photograph was written in bold black letters, "To Percy" and signed at the bottom was, "Hugs, Alice Faye." I looked further inside the envelope and found a single sheet of pink writing paper. It was a real handwritten letter from Alice. My hand trembled as I picked it up to read. The letter read as follows:

Dear Percy,

It was sweet of you to write me. You sound like a nice little boy.

You asked me how I became a success. Well Percy, I was born very poor in New York City and always dreamed of becoming a movie star. As a little girl I found I had talents - I could sing a little, dance a little, and act a little. But what happened to me was that I had a lot of luck. I am a very lucky person. I was lucky to be at the right place - at the right time - with the right people.

Percy, let me tell you sincerely, you don't want to be exactly like me - you want to be Percy. Always be Percy. Remember that. And pray that you have a lot of luck in your life just like me. When you see a penny with its face up lying on the ground - don't walk by - pick it up. Then, go out and buy a rabbit's foot and carry it in your pocket. They'll bring you luck. But most importantly, pray to God every night and know that whatever happens to you is all for the good. I have

*found it so. Now, if you do all those things, you will be lucky
like me and a great, big success in the movies.
God Bless You.
Hugs,
Alice Faye
P.S. I had a daddy who was a policeman and he loved me
very much and was my best friend all my life. I don't
write personal letters to my fans because I don't have time
to spare while making movies, but your letter sounded
desperate, so I had to write you. I know you must be a
very special little boy. Hugs again.*

Alice Faye wasn't cursed.

I read the letter three times, once out loud to my pals, Agnes and Gertrude. I
told my make-believe friends that everybody keeps telling me to be myself -
Kimo, Mr. Hamada and now Alice Faye. The problem was, I wasn't friendly with
the person living inside my body. I didn't know who that person was. Sometimes I
wanted to be Alice Faye. Sometimes I wanted to be Kimo or Mr. Hamada and
even Mother, a little bit. After I saw the movie *Suez*, I wanted to be Tyrone Power.

Every day, I wanted to be anybody else but me. Life was a big puzzlement.
The only thing I did know was that I hated my name and I hated being fat. Every
morning when I looked into the mirror, a fat lady at the circus stared back. I knew
something was wrong with me and I didn't know what to do about it. I wasn't
even talented anymore.

I learned one thing from Alice Faye's letter. I was going to look for pennies
when walking to school and I was going to ask Mother to buy me a rabbit's foot at
Kress's and I decided to pray to God a lot more. I thought of going back to
Sunday school, which I hated, because maybe sacrificing myself to God on a
Sunday morning instead of dressing up in Mother's clothes might bring Daddy
back and take the curse away.

Gertrude said nothing was going to work because I wasn't born lucky. Not in
any part of my body - not even in my small toe. My success and happiness were
going to be like Little Johnny walking through a forest where Hunkacha lived,
searching for my blue pearl hidden at the bottom of a lake and not finding it. Alice
Faye was born with a blue pearl under her pillow and a lucky star above, and she
had a daddy who loved her bunches.

Daddy was late picking us up that Saturday.

Mother was always on time. She had the habit of arriving an hour or two early
at weddings, funerals and parties. Mother's reputation in Honolulu was she arrived
at a party while the hosts were still in the shower. Daddy timed himself to arrive at
a party when the hosts were seated at the dinner table, sipping soup. His favorite
line on entering a party was, "Hope the ice hasn't melted, sports?" He loved his
ice.

Daddy arrived a half-hour late (which was on time for him) and took us to the
Outrigger Canoe Club. The Outrigger was an exclusive club on Waikiki Beach

where the locals paid dues, ate hamburgers, drank beer, and rode waves in outrigger canoes. Some of the athletic members surfed on long boards made out of native Hawaiian wood. Some of the boards, I was told by Daddy, weighed over a hundred pounds.

Daddy was a charter member of the club. Duke Kahanamoku, the Olympic swimmer, was their star member. Everyone in Hawaii admired the Duke's athletic skills and brown, muscular body. All the women in Hawaii worshipped him from afar because he was so famous and gorgeous. Duke Kahanamoku was Hawaii's movie star and gave out autographs like Tyrone Power did in Hollywood. There was a large photograph of him on the lobby wall of the club showing him taking the Prince of Wales for a canoe ride.

Driving down to the club, Daddy prepared Marigold and me for our first meeting with his fiancee. He referred to his fiancee as his "intended." Daddy asked us to be nice to Kathy because she was going to be very nervous and shy, meeting Daddy's children for the first time. Her full name was Kathleen Mary O'Houlihan. She was Irish and from Boston. (Cousin Bessie said she was lace curtain Irish.)

I asked Daddy if Kathy dressed up as an Indian at the Boston Tea Party. All I knew about Boston was the Tea Party and that Paul Revere rode a horse to warn everyone that the British were coming. Daddy told me Kathy hadn't been born yet and warned me, "Don't ask her stupid questions like that."

Marigold hadn't said a word after she kissed Daddy and slid into the car. I could tell by her silence that she hated every minute that passed by. She had made up her mind long before we left the house, and told me so, that she was going to hate Kathleen Mary O'Houlihan on sight.

Kathy met us in the lobby of the club. She was Mainland white all over and wore her glossy black hair piled high on her head and tied up with a little red ribbon. She wore red lipstick to match the ribbon and had glossy red, sharp fingernails that looked like claws. She rouged her cheeks rosy red and wore a white sun suit trimmed in sky blue stripes. She was very Fourth of July looking.

As we walked into the lobby, she immediately gushed, "Oh Dickie, what adorable children you have. They don't look a bit like their mother."

That was her first dig at our mother.

I thought she was going to cry after she spoke so dramatically.

Kathy lost Marigold immediately because there wasn't an "adorable" bone in our bodies and Kathy had just talked mean about our mother. We stood around fiddling with our hands, sizing each other up. I wanted to suck my thumb. If I had been a dog, I would have sniffed her behind.

Marigold stood apart, glowering and scowling at Kathy like Grandma's gargoyle sitting on top the Notre Dame cathedral. I was waiting for Marigold's time bomb to explode.

Daddy ushered us through the lobby and out onto the beach. He found a place to sit, away from the crowds. He didn't trust Marigold and what she might do to Kathy. I hoped Marigold was going to hit her over the head with a sand shovel.

We plunked ourselves down near the ocean. Daddy sat in the middle. Kathy was on one side of him and Marigold and I sat on the other. Marigold wouldn't let me sit next to Kathy because she didn't want me to make friends with Kathy.

Marigold wanted me sitting next to herself to show Kathy that *we* were the United States of America and *Kathy* was the Nazi enemy.

Daddy pulled a bottle of coconut oil from a small bag and opened it. The oil smelled as exotic as the name on the bottle, Tahiti. Coconut oil was advertised to make you tan like a native from Bora Bora. We oiled ourselves well all over our bodies until we all smelled like fragrant flowers.

Kathy had brought a wicker basket filled with "homemade" goodies that she made with her dainty hands for "my darling new family." She must have been nervous because she really overdid the "darlings" a lot. She hovered over Daddy like a German zeppelin.

Since we'd met, only Kathy talked. She babbled on and on as she unfurled a checkered blue and red tablecloth onto the sand in front of Daddy. Daintily, like a fairy godmother in a Hans Christian Andersen tale, she placed the basket in front of Daddy, cooing sweet nothings into his ears. While fussing over Daddy, she smiled at Marigold and me like she was Jesus' mother.

"Dickie darling, I made everything you love to eat. I just pray that everyone will love it, too." She pulled out of the basket red paper plates and silver forks and knives that she wrapped in red paper napkins. Everything in the basket matched the ribbon in her hair and her claws. Out came fried chicken, coleslaw, potato salad, butterscotch cookies, and chocolate brownies. As she brought out each item, she waved them under Daddy Dick's nose, saying, "OOOOO, Dickie, I made this just for you, my little cootsy, cootsy, coo."

Marigold looked at me and stuck her finger down her throat.

Daddy cooed back and said adoringly to his intended, "Honey, darling, isn't this a little early to eat, my perfect sweetness?"

"Dickie, sweetheart, can't you see your children are just starving? I just wonder, wonder, wonder if they get enough to eat at home," she smirked.

Another dig at Mother.

Daddy turned to us and asked, "Kids, would you like to eat now?"

I piped up, "Pass the chicken."

Marigold elbowed me in the ribs. "Percy was just kidding. He's not hungry."

I piped up louder, "I am too!"

Marigold elbowed me harder, telling me with her elbow that if I said one more word, she'd bury my head in the sand. I got the hint. Wanting to eat everything in sight and feeling faint because everything smelled soooo good, I said weakly to Kathy, "I was just kidding. I couldn't eat a thing right now because I had a huge breakfast at home that my wonderful mother fixed with her own hands. And it was a huge, wonderful, delicious breakfast that only real mothers can make. And my mother is the best cook in the world."

A dig at Kathy.

I should have added, "at making creamed something-or-others." Marigold patted me on the head for being a good team player. "But," I added, "in an hour, I think I might try some of that chicken and coleslaw. Did you make the slaw with Best Foods mayonnaise?" Marigold swatted me.

"No, Percy, darling, I only use Miracle Whip," Kathy cooed.

I could have thrown up on Kathy.

Marigold smiled and told me without words that she wasn't going let me eat anything made by Kathy the Red, even though I could already taste Kathy's fried chicken in my mouth. Knowing I was about to starve to death, I got up and announced I was going swimming. Marigold wasn't swimming. She wasn't about to leave Daddy's side and give Kathy the opportunity to get her red claws further into Daddy. It was too late - her hooks were in tight.

Kathy brushed herself off, got up and dipped her toes in the ocean, squealing, telling Daddy Bostonians never learned to swim and that he'd have to save her if she went into the ocean. She walked back up to Daddy and gave him a big kiss on the lips. I thought Marigold was going to rip the ribbon right out of Kathy's hair and choke her with it.

I walked down to the water and dove in. The water was eighty degrees. I came up from the dive and spat the ocean out of my mouth, making believe I was a fountain in Italy. I loved swimming in warm salt water. It made me feel healthy all over. I jumped up and down and shook the water out of my ears and dove again under the water. I swam with my eyes open, looking at all the fish swimming and circling around me. The fish were all colors, very beautiful and not afraid. I swam around them, through them, and over them. I swam farther and farther out underwater towards the horizon.

All of a sudden, my stomach cramped. I must have been thinking about Kathy's fried chicken. I bent over in pain and hit my head on a piece of coral. The coral hurt and surprised me. I opened my mouth and took in an ocean of water. I started to choke and I couldn't breathe. My lungs started to fill up with seawater. I panicked and went unconscious. I was fat, so I floated to the top.

Marigold, looking out for her baby brother, saw me floating face down in the ocean. She nudged Daddy and cried, "Something's wrong with Percy! He isn't moving."

Daddy jumped up. He and Marigold dove into the water and pulled me out. Daddy laid me down on the sand and punched my stomach. Water came gushing out and I started to breathe again and became conscious.

I heard Daddy say, "Are you all right, Percy?" I shook myself, like a puppy does after having a bath, and told him I was just fine, but my stomach hurt. A crowd had gathered around us and looked at me as if I was dead. Marigold and Daddy helped me up and walked me back to where we were sitting. Daddy said Marigold saved my life because, if she hadn't seen me, I'd still be out there in the ocean unconscious and probably singing with the angels. Instead of singing with the angels, I thought because I was still cursed, I'd probably be humming "I Don't Want to Set the World on Fire" with the devil.

Marigold tried to cheer me up by tickling me. She made her fingers into little crabs and pretended she was talking like a crab, "Pinchy, pinchy, Percy." Her fingers ran all over my body. I shrieked with laughter.

All of a sudden, Kathy became hysterical, too, because Daddy wasn't paying any attention to her. He had to take her to the bathroom to calm her down. One would have thought that she had been out in the ocean drowning. While Daddy took Kathy to the ladies room, I punched Marigold and thanked her for saving my life. I told her I was really hungry and maybe while Kathy and Daddy were gone,

I could eat a chicken leg.

She grudgingly let me plow through Kathy's basket for food. Before Daddy and Kathy returned, I had eaten a chicken leg, two cookies and three brownies. I left the Miracle Whip potato salad for Daddy. Marigold couldn't believe I could be dying one minute and gorging on food the next. I told her it would take a lot more than just dying to keep me away from food, even if the potato salad was made with Miracle Whip.

"I tell you, Marigold, I sure hope heaven has food because it just wouldn't be worth dying if heaven didn't have mayonnaise, tuna fish, rice, and chocolate ice cream in God's cafeteria every day," I continued as I brushed sand off a brownie. "And it certainly wouldn't be worth dying if heaven didn't have a double feature playing everyday in God's theater. If heaven is only a bunch of clouds and playing the harp, keep me down here. What do you think, Marigold?"

"I've heard it before and I think you're silly, and wipe that piece of chicken off your face before Daddy comes back. I don't want Kathy to think you ate any of her oogie food," answered Marigold.

"Don't you like her?" I asked.

"What do you think?" Marigold asked, as she ate one of Kathy's oogie brownies.

"To be frank with you, Marigold, I think Kathy has a lot of Bette Davis in her. I don't know why Daddy wants to marry the Bette Davis type. Bette Davis types shoot their men if they don't do what they want them to do."

Marigold pondered that statement while she ate another brownie.

"Maybe he has to!" I volunteered.

"What does that mean?" she asked.

"I don't know, but that's what Cousin Bessie said to Mother on the phone last night. I was listening in Mother's bedroom. Remember, I'm a spy," I explained.

"What did Mother say?" she inquired.

"Mother defended Daddy and told her she was crazy. Cousin Bessie hung up."

"Then what did Mother do?"

"Mother called Cousin Bessie what Daddy calls her," I said.

"What's that?"

"A bitch. She said that Cousin Bessie likes to make other people unhappy because she's so unhappy herself." I told Mother last night that if Cousin Bessie was my mother, I'd shoot myself.

Daddy came out of the club with Kathy. They were acting lovey-dovey again and biting each other's ears. Kathy seemed to have recovered from her Bette Davis dramatics and was back in love with Daddy. As they sat down, Daddy asked how I was feeling. I told him like a million dollars. I didn't have to ask him how he was feeling because by the way he was looking at Kathy, he looked like a trillion dollars. Daddy didn't ask Marigold how she was feeling because her feelings had gone bankrupt, just like in a Monopoly game.

Kathy settled down and lathered more sweet-smelling coconut oil over her pink body. As she put the cap back on the bottle, she looked at me and screamed like Bette Davis discovering a corpse under her bed. She pointed to my thumb, which was bleeding. I must have cut it on a knife in her lunch basket. It was a small cut and nothing to be Bette Davis about, but the blood wouldn't stop gushing from my finger.

Kathy ran over and took my thumb and started to suck the blood with her mouth. Her sucking away gave me the humongous impression that Daddy was marrying Dracula. When she finished sucking my blood, Kathy told me that she had just taken all the poisons away from my finger and my thumb would soon be well again. She wrapped a red napkin around my finger, telling me that the napkin would keep the sand off. Kathy warned me to keep my thumb clean so it wouldn't become infected and fall off. Looking at my colorful bandage, I wondered if I had any blood left in my hand. Kathy, Daddy's Countess Dracula, looked pinker after drinking my blood.

I whispered to Marigold that maybe now that Kathy has some of my blood in her stomach, she'll think I'm related to her. Marigold whispered, "Don't worry, Percy. If that happens, I'll put you out of your misery and cut your finger off at the same time."

Kathy settled back next to Daddy, looking into his eyes, and played smoochy again. "Dickie darling, did Deidra ever do that for her children?"

Another dig at Mother.

The sun had turned really hot. Heat rays from above steamed the sand all around us, baking us to a crisp. I put a towel over my head to keep out the sunrays. It was two o'clock in the afternoon. Daddy began to get concerned about Kathy because her skin looked red, not pink. Kathy was getting a bad sunburn. He told us it was time to go home. Kathy's image was now complete. The sun and coconut oil had turned her milky Bostonian skin into the color of a crimson firecracker ready to explode on the Fourth of July.

"Kathy!" Marigold told her gleefully, "It looks like you've got a first class sunburn and it's going to hurt like hell tomorrow. You're going to peel bad. Your skin is going to come off in layers and it will turn you into an old, bleeding witch."

"Let me see," Marigold said, pretending to peer with a magnifying glass at Kathy's skin. "Daddy, it's a first degree burn and Kathy is going to die right now. She looks like a piece of burnt toast and has only a few minutes to live. It's too late for the hospital. You're gonna die in one minute, Kathy." Marigold turned to me and ordered, "Percy, while I count the minute, you get a minister."

Kathy swooned into Daddy's arms. He told Kathy that Marigold was only kidding and that Marigold is the greatest kidder in the world, but it was time to get out of the sun. We left.

Burning up inside as well as outside, Kathy, by this time, never wanted to see us again and said a long goodbye to us in the lobby. She told us (I could tell she was lying through her teeth) how darling we were and didn't we all have such a good time today. She was also sorry we weren't hungry enough to eat the lunch that she especially made for us, but she did notice some little mice had eaten some of the food while she was in the ladies' powder room. Adding more guilt, she said, "It cost me a lot of money to make this lunch, and I stayed up past midnight to fix it for my darling new family." Every word she said was meant to kill Marigold and me.

I really took to guilt.

I was thinking that I could have wolfed down the whole lunch if Marigold hadn't been there.

So much for loyalty to Mother.

Kathy gushed on and on about what a joyously happy family we were going to be and how she hoped to see us real soon. What Daddy's "intended" meant was how rude we had been to her, and that her goddamn sunburn hurt so much now that she wanted to jump out of her skin, and that she never wanted to see her darling Dick's brats ever again.

Then Kathy tried to kiss Marigold goodbye. That was a mistake on Kathy's part. Marigold's time bomb went off.

Marigold shrieked at Kathy not to touch her and that she hated her with all her might and that she never wanted to see her again. After Marigold finished her ravings, she yanked me out the door before I could say goodbye and shoved me into the back seat of Daddy's car.

Daddy stayed behind to calm Kathy's nerves because she was beating on the Outrigger's wall, screaming hysterically that she had never been so wounded. Daddy called a taxi for Kathy and sent her home. He should have called the ambulance.

When Daddy got into the car, he was real mad. He looked at Marigold and held his head as if he had one of his headaches. "Why did you do that, Marigold? Kathy is beside herself, crying. I had to give her six aspirins to calm her down. She thinks you hate her," he shouted.

"I do hate her. You always told me to be honest, didn't you, Daddy?" shot back Marigold.

Daddy turned on the ignition, not looking at Marigold, and answered her, "I told you to be honest, but I didn't tell you to be cruel. That was a cruel thing you did just now because Kathy has never hurt you."

"She's taking you away from me. That's hurting me a lot." Marigold paused. She turned from Daddy and said in a slow, deliberate voice, "You've hurt me."

Daddy turned off the engine and said to Marigold, "I didn't mean to hurt you, Marigold, and marrying Kathy isn't hurting you one bit. Marigold, listen to me; nobody is ever going to take you away from me. I love you best in the whole world. I've told you that and you just remember it."

Daddy sounded like Hatsuko when she talked to me about liking me best.

Marigold put her arms around Daddy and sobbed into his chest. It sounded like her heart had broken.

I sat in the back seat, listening to Marigold crying while they forgot all about me. I wanted to tell Marigold not to believe anyone who tells you that they love you best and will never leave you because that person will probably leave you high and dry, like Hatsuko did me.

Daddy told Marigold a secret and told her not to tell Mother. As soon as he told Marigold the secret, Daddy remembered I was sitting in the back seat and made me swear to keep the secret, too. Daddy wanted to tell Mother the secret himself. I thought it was a strange secret and the secret only proved that Daddy never thought about me much.

Daddy's secret made Marigold cry louder. She pulled away from him and jumped into the back seat with me. Daddy also made us promise that we wouldn't tell Mother that I almost drowned. We nodded our heads. I told Daddy I wanted to tell Mother because I wanted Mother to know what a hero Marigold had been and if it hadn't been for Marigold, I would have been as dead as a doornail. Daddy, still mad, told me to be quiet.

When Daddy dropped us off, Marigold didn't kiss him goodbye and ran into the house crying as if her best friend had died. When she got inside the house, Marigold slammed all the doors in the house and then ran to her room outside by the garage.

After I waved goodbye to Daddy, I went into the kitchen to prowl around looking for something to eat. Helen the Terrible had taken the day off so I could make myself a huge mayonnaise and tomato sandwich without her cursing me. After I smashed two pieces of bread over a slice of tomato and mayonnaise, I stuffed the sandwich into my mouth in one continuous, glorious gobble. I realized, wiping the mayonnaise off my face, that I was a lot like Kathy because she and I could pretend good. We were both good actors. I pretended I felt fabulous today even if I had almost drowned, my stomach ached from Daddy's punch and I had a father who forgot all about me. I sighed, lathering mayonnaise on another piece of white bread, that I wished I had had a father like Alice Faye did.

What kind of spell does it take to wipe away a curse? Maybe a rabbit's foot dunked in mayonnaise?

WEEK STARTING TOMORROW
MATINEE DAILY   EACH EVENING
2:15   7:45

LIMITED ENGAGEMENT

FULL LENGTH

NOTHING CUT BUT THE PRICE

GONE WITH THE WIND

IN TECHNICOLOR *starring*

Clark GABLE   Vivien LEIGH

Leslie HOWARD

Olivia DeHAVILLAND

WEEK DAY MATINEE PRICES	Sun., Mat. & Nights
Adults . . . .44 cents	12 Rows . . .55 cents
Children . . .25 cents	Balance . . . .70 cents
(Mat. Not Reserved)	Children . .55 cents
	(Eve. All Reserved)

(All Prices Include Federal Tax)
Reserved Seats for All Night Shows
Now on Sale

29

Gone With the Wind

Mother announced that Helen was going to give our house a thorough cleaning, especially the kitchen floor. Helen told Mother our house was dirtier than a rat's nest in a tree. Helen's terms were that if she was going to clean up our messy house on a Sunday, she wanted us out. Betsy agreed to the terms because she was never home anyway, but Marigold refused to budge out of Hatsuko's room under any circumstances. Mother made Marigold promise that if she stayed home, she would stay out of Helen the Grump's way. I complained to Mother that she had hired Helen the Hun, who was out to conquer our house like Hitler was running his soldiers through Poland.

The Honolulu Advertiser

WAIKIKI THEATER Phone 9967
David O. Selznick's production of Margaret Mitchell's Story of the Old South

GONE WITH THE WIND
In TECHNICOLOR starring CLARK GABLE as Rhett Butler
And presenting VIVIAN LEIGH as Scarlett O'Hara
Reserved seats for all night shows and Sunday matinee entirely sold out the first week.

RESERVED BOX OFFICE OPENS DAILY AT 11 A.M. TO 9 P.M.
NIGHT SHOWS (7:45) All seats Reserved $1.10 incl. Tax
SATURDAY & SUNDAY MATS (All seats Reserved) $1.10 incl. Tax
WEEKDAY MATS. CONTINUOUS - Not Reserved .75 incl. Tax

GONE WITH THE WIND WILL BE SHOWN IN HAWAII IN ITS ENTIRETY EXACTLY AS PRESENTED IN ATLANTA AND BROADWAY PREMIERS

Mother treated me to the 2:15 matinee at the Waikiki Theater, where *Gone With The Wind* was showing. It was one way to get us out of Helen's hair.

David O. Selznick's epic was playing for the second time in the Hawaii movie theaters. Mother and I hadn't seen it, and I heard from Cousin Bessie that the lines at the theater were even longer this time around.

Mother tried to persuade Marigold to join us, but Marigold wanted to be in a foul mood and refused. Mother told her that, if Auntie Gladys invited her for dinner with the Twins, Marigold should accept because we might be late. Marigold har-rumphed, saying she was left out of everything, slammed the door in Mother's face and went back to throwing darts at my picture on the wall.

Furious at Marigold's show of temper, Mother drove us at top speed into Waikiki, flooring the accelerator with her high heels all the way. She ran red lights and rounded curves in the road on two wheels and drove the car as if she was riding a stallion over hurdles at an English foxhunt.

Reaching the theater, we saw that Clark Gable fans had formed a long line down past the Moana Hotel cottages. Looking at the long line, Mother gunned the car and whipped around the nearest corner, looking for a parking place. None in sight, I told Mother, "We're never going to get in to see *Gone With The Wind.*"

"Stop that kind of talk, Percy. You and I are not quitters," she declared. At full throttle, she drove the rocket ship to the Ala Wai canal and saw a car exiting from a parking stall. Mother honked the horn at the driver and bumped him out of the space. After she parked, two wheels on the curb, we ran, hand in hand, for the theater.

Out of breath, gasping for air, holding our sides with our hands, we saw the theater line had stretched and stretched and looked miles long. More discouraging than the long line of people were the football linebackers wearing afternoon dresses and pushing and shoving, to make sure they were going to be the lucky ones to see Rhett Butler kiss Scarlett O'Hara. These women made fifty-yard touchdowns every January, when they smashed through the front doors at the Liberty House girdle and panty sale.

We glumly stood at the end of the line and watched a theater attendant walk up and down the line, counting people. Each time she reached us, she shook her head, signaling that we were two too many for the theater to seat that afternoon. I told Mother that I was not really a quitter, but I knew we were licked and weren't going to get in to see the movie. She tapped me on my head and told me to say three times: think positive thoughts - think positive thoughts - think positive thoughts. I stuck my lower lip out because I couldn't think of one positive thought, only that I was not going to see Atlanta burn or Scarlett kiss Rhett.

The line began to inch slowly towards the box office. The afternoon turned hot because there were no clouds in the sky. Body juices trickled down from my armpits and I began to smell like the lady football linebacker in front of me.

The line halted. Mother stretched her neck to see what was holding up the line. Taking advantage of this momentary standstill, she grabbed my hand and charged down the line. She moseyed us next in line to purchase a ticket. Her move was so outrageous, executed with such daring, that the surly matinee matron football play-ers opened up for Mother as if Moses had parted the seas. Mother whispered to the woman in back of her, who had two anthuriums stuck in her hair, that her boy, that's me, was about to wet his pants and she had to get me into the bathroom. The

woman nodded that she understood because she had children and that Mother must
be having a real problem with such a fat boy in tow.

Since the divorce, Mother had developed a courage that I had never seen
before. After Daddy abandoned us, Mother sat at the dining table like Daddy used
to do and paid the bills all by herself.

Mother was a "dishonored divorcee," in Cousin Bessie's words, in the year
1941, and I overheard lots of people say she had turned into a formidable she-bear
protecting her cubs at all costs. I heard her say to Aunt Momi over the phone that
nobody was going to trifle with her or her children anymore, especially Daddy. Her
independent behavior, like her short hair, shocked her friends and relatives. They
wanted back the fun-loving girl from Kauai who never thought much about any
thing but having a good time. Mother was a girl who grew up on Kauai not knowing how to boil water, wash clothes, make a bed, clean a house, or write a check.
Now, she performed all those tasks extremely well and when Hatsuko left, she
cleaned our toilets and bathtubs to a sparkling shine.

Mother had always worked for a living, as she had no inheritance to fall back
on like her other relatives did. When she and Daddy first married, he earned fifty
dollars a month clerking in a bank and she worked as a teacher, earning far less.
They made do, but, kept their heads above water and partied with the sugar society.

Mother didn't have a savings account when she divorced Daddy. Now she had
one. She never had the opportunity, like her sisters or cousins did, to play bridge in
the mornings, sip gin and tonics at lunch with the girls at the Halekulani Hotel, or
volunteer in the afternoons with the Daughters of Hawaii at Queen Emma's home.
Those society things were never an option nor, I think, as she told me, never an
inclination. For her, that kind of society life during the day was not in her cards this
time around. In my presence, she never mourned not living that life; she only
mourned that she couldn't smoke a cigarette at school.

Mother and I were riveted that afternoon to the screen, watching *Gone With
The Wind*. The four hours seemed like four minutes. We listened to every word and
paid no attention to those sitting next to us while hearing the strains of Tara's
theme, Scarlett's saucy "fiddle dee dee" and Rhett Butler's grumpy, "Frankly, my
dear, I don't give a damn." When the movie ended, I was tightly gripping the seat
and I was forever bound to Margaret Mitchell's South. Movies always played in my
head as if I were having a real-life experience. I believed movies were as real as
eating a tuna sandwich with mayonnaise. I also learned about American history that
afternoon. I learned about a civil war that ripped our country apart, like Daddy and
Mother's divorce had ripped my life apart. In *Gone With The Wind*, people that once
lived happily together like brothers and sisters, side by side in the same country,
killed each other.

I wondered if I could kill Marigold. There had been times since Daddy left
when we had been close.

The movie was also about black people. I loved the actress who played
Mammy, Hattie McDaniel. I loved her because she was the bossy-type lady that I
liked and wore red, rustling taffeta petticoats like Grandma did. I wanted one of

those red taffeta petticoats because I liked the sound of them when Mammy walked. I loved maids in the movies because they always were the nicest people in the story, like Hatsuko was to me. Maids were not stuck up people, and I never saw one maid in the movies who acted as mean as Helen the Grouch did.

Helen the Grouch should go to the movies and learn how to act like a maid.

I never saw a black person in real life. The only black people I saw were on the movie screen. I saw a lot of brown, yellow, pink, chocolate, and sometimes red-all-over people like Kathy, but not once a black person. I had never eaten at a luau with a black person, shaken hands with one, or kissed one on the cheek, or gone to the movies with one. After the movie, I wished I could have met, talked to or touched a black person because they acted as interesting as President Roosevelt did in the newsreels, and every one of them seemed kind and wise. Lots of them had gray curly hair.

My wish to meet a black person was about to come true.

Sometimes black people in the movies made me laugh because they acted really silly just like me. For a week after I had seen *Gone With The Wind*, I pretended to be Prissy, Scarlett O'Hara's maid, who yelled in a high squeaky voice that, "The Yankees are coming! The Yankees are coming!" Every time I saw the Twins come running down the hill, I'd yell in a squeaky Prissy voice, "The Yankees are coming! The Yankees are coming!" and run for home.

When the credits of *Gone With the Wind* rolled up the screen, my allegiance was not to the North, but to the South and the "Aunt Pittypat" way of life. I hated General Sherman and his fiery, Hitler-like Northern army that conquered and burned Atlanta. The Northern types acted like my daddy. The Southern types were like my mother.

Mother cried at the end of the movie when Scarlett, abandoned by old Rhett Butler, sat on a staircase, all alone, thinking about her plantation, Tara. I looked at Mother, wiping the tears away from her eyes, and thought she must be thinking that her own Tara had gone with the wind, too. I wished Scarlett and Rhett had lived happily ever after because I knew about being left alone. Mother knew about being left alone, too. Daddy leaving us, seemingly without giving a damn, changed our lives forever. I don't think he knew it.

Mother's nose was runny and red after seeing the movie. Movies, if they're the Bette Davis dramatic kind, can really do that to a person. Mother wanted a drink before we went home and faced our Tara again. She told me she wanted to think. Looking at her watch, Mother hoped Auntie Gladys checked on Marigold and that Marigold had eaten dinner with the Twins. Lately, Marigold was eating a lot of her meals with the Twins.

We crossed Kalakaua Avenue and walked up to the Waikiki Tavern. We sat at the bar like grownups. Mother ordered a bourbon and water and ordered me a Coke with two extra cherries. We sat together sipping our drinks through straws and didn't say a word for a long time. I was emotionally pooped.

Mother lit a Camel cigarette, turned to me and asked, "Percy, what did you think of the movie?"

"I loved it. I wish Scarlett had kept Rhett though. That was very disappointing. Mother, why do men leave women - like Daddy left you?" I took a sip of my Coke and asked further, "Do women ever leave men?"

Mother inhaled the cigarette, then exhaled smoke through her nose and mouth and answered, "I almost left your father two days after we were married, Percy." She stopped. "I shouldn't be telling you this."

"Tell me anyway," I said, pulling a cherry out of my Coke and eating it.

She thought for a minute, inhaling her cigarette again and continued, "Your daddy and I were on our honeymoon and we went to a party up in the mountains on Kauai. I caught him kissing my best friend in the bushes."

"What happened?"

"Nothing. I didn't say a word to him but he hurt me to the quick. I don't think I ever recovered from seeing him kiss my best friend on my honeymoon. I should have divorced him right then and there. Aunt Mari warned me about him. She said his father was a chaser."

Holding the Coke glass in my hand, I looked at her and said wistfully, "But then Marigold and I would never have been borned."

"You're right, Percy. You and Marigold are my blessings and I wouldn't have had my life any other way," she agreed. Smiling at me, she also looked worried and said, "I'm sorry I'm so busy these days, working like I do, but we need the money. But you and I should spend more time together." Putting out the cigarette and lighting another, she continued, "It's nice having times like this, don't you think so, Percy?"

I nodded.

Mother had acted like Barbara Stanwyck in *Stella Dallas* when she said that. Taking the straw out of her drink, Mother went on, "We'll do this again because I worry about you, Percy. You're alone too much of the time. You don't seem to have any friends."

She didn't know about Agnes and Gertrude or that I never felt alone, ever. I uttered back, "I don't mind being alone. Do you really worry about me?"

Patting me on my head, she said in her Barbara Stanwyck voice, "No, Percy, I don't. I think you can take care of yourself. You don't seem to mind being alone. I never minded being alone until after your father left me." Fingering the ice cubes in her glass, Mother went on, "Now, I hate being alone." I know those words came from her heart because she whispered them in my ear.

Looking at the clock on the wall above the bar, Mother took a last sip from her drink, paid our bill, gathered her purse off the counter, and turned to me, saying, "Percy, we'd better get home. I don't want Marigold to think we've forgotten her." As I started to get off the stool, Mother took my hand and made a request, "Percy, do me a favor, don't tell Marigold what I said about your father. It would hurt her and make her mad at me." Looking in her purse for the car keys, she sighed and added, "She's already so mad at me so much of the time."

I promised Mother that I wouldn't tell Marigold about Daddy's secret honeymoon kiss.

We walked back to the car and found a parking ticket. The ticket was flapping in the wind, under the windshield wiper. Mother had parked next to a fire hydrant. Looking at the ticket, Mother muttered, "My usual luck. I'm not a very lucky person, Percy."

Mother was cursed too and needed some of Alice Faye's lucky pennies.

When we arrived home, Helen was sitting on our front porch. Seeing us drive in, she whooped all around the porch rampaging like Sitting Bull at a war dance. When Mother turned off the engine, Helen ran to the car as if she was going to scalp me, wildly yelling words in Japanese which I couldn't understand as she pointed to the house. I knew from the few words she said in English that her problem had something to do with Marigold.

Mother ran around the car and calmed Helen down by sitting her back on the porch. Helen hugged her mop and blubbered out words that we couldn't understand. After several minutes of watching Helen wailing, Mother calmed her enough to get her to speak in English so we could understand what had happened. In a few words, Helen told Mother that Marigold had scared the hell of her when Helen was cleaning the icebox. Marigold and the Twins had tossed a big string of lit firecrackers through the kitchen window. At the sound of the firecrackers exploding, Helen fainted on the floor. That happened at two in the afternoon, about the time our movie started, and Helen had been waiting for us ever since, sitting on the front porch with her mop and pail. Helen the Miserable told Mother she was going to quit.

I was thrilled that the Hun was leaving and was going to kiss Marigold and the Twins on the lips.

Mother pleaded with Helen to stay and raised her salary five dollars a week. Mother blew it. She should have let Helen, the Nazi storm trooper, take a hike. There had to be a thousand nicer people somewhere in Hawaii wanting to work for us. But oh no, Mother had to keep Helen the Nazi.

Helen, now richer and satisfied she had gotten Marigold into big trouble, went home counting her money. Helen had just now become another Rockefeller.

Mother strode with large steps out to Marigold's room to give her the spanking of the year. I followed right behind her, not wanting to miss any of the action. Mother didn't knock, ignored the "Keep Out Percy" signs and walked into the room. Marigold knew she was in big trouble because she was lying in her bed coughing and sneezing like she had a bad cold, an act she learned from me.

Mother yelled at the top of her lungs, "Marigold, why did you do that to Helen? You almost gave her a heart attack. You could have killed her. She almost quit. Do you know if she had quit, you'd have to clean the house, make the beds and cook the meals. Do you want to do that, young lady?" Mother took a breath before she continued, "You have turned out to be a selfish little brat. You don't think of anyone but yourself. Now, young lady, we're going to march into my room and I'm going to get my hairbrush out and give you a spanking you'll never forget."

Boy, I thought, this was fun.

Mother pulled Marigold out of her bed which Mother could do because she was bigger and stronger than Marigold. Mother had been the captain and the champion basketball player on her high school team. You didn't fool with Mother when she was mad. Daddy found that out.

Marigold screamed, "I'm not well. I have a bad cold. Have mercy on me. Mother, pleeeeeese have mercy on me."

"The only mercy you're going to get is the back of my hairbrush," Mother said as she dragged Marigold out of her room. Marigold screamed all the way into the house.

I followed behind with my arms behind my back, keeping well out of the line of fire. I was sure glad that I wasn't the one who was going to be on the other end of that hairbrush. I hated Mother's silver hairbrush. It was an enemy. I thought of hiding the brush in the potted plant with Daddy's dinner bell, but Gertrude and Agnes talked me out of it.

Mother made Marigold pull down her pajama bottoms and whacked her twice. While the brush was hitting her bottom, Marigold howled as if Mother was murdering her. Marigold, I think, hoped that Mr. McLaine would hear that a mean awful mother lived across the street. Right after the spanking, Marigold had an uncontrollable coughing fit. Mother, still shaking with fury, walked into the bathroom, pulled a bottle of cough medicine out of her medicine cabinet and told me to get a tablespoon from the kitchen. I ran to the kitchen, got the spoon and gave it to Mother. She poured the liquid into the spoon and forced it down Marigold's throat.

Marigold screamed, "My throat's on fire. I'm burning up inside, Mother."

I looked at the bottle in Mother's hand. Mother had given tincture of benzoin, my breathing medicine, to Marigold. I pointed at the blue label on the bottle with the drawing of a skull on it. Under the skull in big letters was written the word POISON.

I yelled, "Mother, you gave Marigold poison. That's not cough medicine. That's my breathing medicine."

Mother screamed. Marigold screamed and collapsed on Mother's bed as if she had died. Mother looked around, confused. "What should I do, Percy?" she pleaded.

Keeping calm, I told Mother that I was going to call Queen's Hospital.

I had memorized the telephone number from the day I took care of Walter. I picked up the phone and called Queen's. I told the operator what had happened and to send an ambulance right away. A doctor asked to speak to Mother so I put her on the line. She told the doctor what had happened. The doctor told Mother to force raw eggs down Marigold's throat and make her throw up. He didn't think an ambulance was necessary right now. The doctor told Mother that if Marigold couldn't throw up, to call him right back.

I ran to the icebox and pulled out a carton of eggs that I brought to Mother. She and I cracked and forced at least four eggs down Marigold's throat before she started to throw up. After she threw up ten times, she didn't burn any more inside her stomach. Marigold started to feel fine again - almost right away, because she kept asking for more raw eggs. She downed the whole dozen and wanted more. From that day on, Marigold was addicted to raw eggs.

Mother put Marigold in her bed that night and treated her like a baby. Mother cooked Marigold's favorite Campbell's alphabet soup and gave her scoops of vanilla ice cream in her favorite blue dish for dessert. Through it all, Marigold grumbled, but I could tell she loved all the attention Mother was giving her. Marigold, I thought, needed lots of attention after our beach day with Daddy and

Kathy. Before Marigold went to sleep, she forgave Mother for poisoning her.

I sat alone with Marigold after Mother had gone into the living room to sleep on the couch. I told Marigold that she wasn't ready to pass through God's pearly gates and, anyway, she wasn't cursed like I was. Most of all, God wasn't ready for her because God didn't think she was good enough to die yet.

I tucked the covers around her neck and said softly, "Marigold, yesterday you saved my life, today I saved yours but I saved you from a real horrible death." I demonstrated by putting my hands around my neck and making choking, gagging sounds. I mused, "I guess what this all means is that we do unto others what we want them to do unto us. Don't you think that's what this is?"

Marigold groaned, "Percy, I hate when you talk like that. Your words make me sick and wish I had really died. Percy?" She put her face up to mine.

"Yes?"

"I like you better when you don't talk. So shut up, turn off the light and leave me alone."

I turned out the light and whispered, "Marigold, I love you."

I closed the door as I heard Marigold grumble, "When I get well, I'm going to tickle him to death and that's a promise."

I found Mother sitting in the living room in Daddy's chair. She had a drink in one hand and a lit cigarette in the other. "Mother?" I asked.

"Yes, Percy."

"Are you all right?"

Taking a drag on her cigarette, she turned to me and said, "Actually, Percy, I'm not."

"Mother, it was an accident," I tried to reassure her.

"I know that, Percy, but I could have killed your sister. Take my hand." I walked over and put her hand in mine. Mother turned to me with tears in her eyes and said, "Thank you, Percy, for calling the hospital. For a moment, I didn't know what to do."

I squeezed her hand and replied, "It was nothing. It's the same thing I did for Walter. It was really an easy thing to do. You just have to know the right number to dial."

"It's not that easy. I'm glad this day is over. I don't think anything more can happen to me tonight, do you? At least, I hope not," she sighed again.

I paused, thinking to myself, should I tell Mother about Daddy's secret? His secret was really bothering me since yesterday when he told it to us in the car.

"Mother, there is something else," I started.

Finishing her drink and snuffing out her cigarette in the ashtray, she said wearily to me, "Can it wait till tomorrow?"

"Yes, it can." I looked really troubled.

Seeing me frowning, Mother lit another cigarette. "All right, Percy, tell me what it is. I can take it," she said.

"Are you sure?" I asked.

"I'm sure. Tell me."

I took a big gulp and said quietly, "Daddy is getting married to Kathy."

"I know that. I told you about that a week ago," she confirmed.

"But he didn't tell you the date. He's getting married to her on my birthday, April eighth," I said sadly.

Mother dropped her glass on the floor and sat up. "What did you say?"

"Daddy's getting married on my birthday."

Having heard it a second time, she said to herself, "That's the oddest thing I've heard in a long time. I knew your father was strange, but I didn't know he was that strange. How very odd to have his wedding on your birthday.

Taking my hand, she said, "Don't take offense, Percy. Daddy meant it as a compliment."

"I don't think that's it at all. I don't think he remembers when I was born," I said morosely.

"Percy?"

"Yes, Mother?" I answered.

"Fix me another drink, please?" I went into the kitchen and made Mother a bourbon and water. When I came back, her eyes were closed. "Mother, wake up. Here's your drink." I handed her the glass.

Mother opened her eyes, looked at me and took the glass. She said, "Percy, everyday try to look forward to something. Make yourself do something - anything - especially if you can do it for somebody else. Try once a day to make another person happy, then you'll be happy, too."

"Yes, Mother."

"We'll do something very special on your birthday," she promised.

"Mother, tomorrow will be a better day for you and thank you for taking me to the movie." Then I walked out of the living room, leaving my mother alone in the dark, drinking a bourbon and water. She lit another cigarette and started to cry. I walked back to my bedroom.

I found Agnes and Gertrude waiting for me on my pillow. Gertrude, seeing the glum look on my face, spoke right into my ear, "Percy, snap out of it."

"I can't," I replied. "I'm feeling sad. My life isn't going well again. My mother's life isn't going well and Marigold's life isn't going well, and Marigold was just poisoned. Everyone in the whole world's life isn't going well except for Daddy and Kathy. Their lives are going well because they're getting married on my birthday."

"Percy, get into bed," said Gertrude. "Crawl under the covers. Agnes and I will sing to you a sweet lullaby, so you'll have sweet dreams tonight."

That night I dreamed that I was one of Kathy's bridesmaids at Daddy's wedding. I walked down the aisle wearing a two-piece maroon bathing suit from Linn's, a famous tailor shop near Honolulu's Aala Park. The shop made to order the best bathing suits in the Territory of Hawaii. My bathing suit, in the dream, was designed to match Kathleen Mary O'Houlihan's fire engine red wedding dress. Mother was the best man and Marigold gave the bride away.

30

The Wedding Plans

Mother reminded Daddy on the phone that his wedding date fell on my birthday. He told Mother it had slipped his mind and that he had chosen April 8th because it was on a Tuesday and he wanted a quiet ceremony.

But Kathy changed Daddy's mind about the quiet ceremony. She screamed at him while taking a bath that she was being snubbed all over town by Mother's highfalutin relatives. She sobbed buckets into the bathtub, saying that she was being treated like a scarlet woman when she walked on the streets of Honolulu.

Scarlet was the right word for Kathy because that color matched her hair ribbon and peeling sunburn.

Mother heard all about Kathy's blubbering from Auntie Gladys daily. Auntie Gladys was not a loyal person, even though she vowed that she was Mother's best friend. (She was the best friend whom Daddy kissed on their honeymoon in the bushes.) Auntie Gladys, so Cousin Bessie reported, sailed where the wind blew best and always to her advantage. When Auntie Gladys heard that the soon-to-be number two Mrs. Dick was from a rich Boston family and had piles of money in a Bunker Hill bank, she became best chums with Kathy right away. It also pleased Auntie Gladys to be able to watch Mother's reactions when she reported back everything that Kathy said about Mrs. Dick number one.

Gertrude warned me about people who told "stink" stories to you about their friends because you could be sure they were talking "stink" stories about you to them.

Loyalty was hard to find in 1941 Honolulu.

Auntie Gladys's latest report was that Kathy wanted her wedding so grand that it would be featured on the cover of *Life* magazine. Kathy wanted to show Mother's stuck-up missionary cousins that she was as good as any of them - even better. Kathy cried for a week in her bubble bath while Daddy sat on the toilet seat listening to her wailing. She cried she wanted her wedding so grand that everyone in Hawaii would take notice of her and see what a sweet person she was. Daddy pleaded, sitting on the pot, that he was as poor as a church mouse. He told her that right now he could barely make ends meet because he had to pay alimony (seventy-five dollars a month) to Mother. He wailed back to her that he didn't have a cent to spare. Daddy's crying and reasoning didn't work with Kathy because she could cry louder than he did and it only made her more determined to have the grandest wedding in all Hawaii. Kathy went to see Daddy's lawyer to see if Mother's alimony could be cut in half. According to Auntie Gladys, black-haired girls from Boston are sharp cookies.

Auntie Gladys, a sharp cookie herself, went on telling Mother that Kathy told Daddy's lawyer that good girls from Boston didn't stoop to work like Mother did and she needed all the money she could get to live like a lady. Ladies were born to keep a clean house, take care of their husband's money, never to wash a window, and to bear thousands of children who would be taken care of by a slew of Black Irish nannies. Kathy boasted that she was a Hail Mary, good-practicing Catholic. What she didn't tell the lawyer was that she had been divorced twice and she ran up huge bills at Liberty House that Daddy didn't know about.

Auntie Gladys said that Daddy was going to end up in the poor house.

After a week of crying in her bathtub, Kathy got her wish. Daddy borrowed money from his brothers and planned a wedding that probably wouldn't make the cover of *Life* magazine, but would at least make the front page of the society section in the *Advertiser*. Kathy's mama also pitched in some of her Boston Tea Party money.

Daddy and Kathy set the date now for Sunday, April 6th, at the home of one of Daddy's wealthiest friends. Daddy's friend lived in a huge eight-bedroom mansion right on the ocean in Waimanalo. Mr. McGregor's home was considered one of the showplaces in the Territory. Some folks considered his home grander than Walter Dillingham's La Pietra mansion.

Waimanalo, where Mr. McGregor's home stood, was near a small sugar plantation town. The house was considered "in the sticks" because it was far away from the slopes of Diamond Head where the Dillinghams and all the other swells lived. Still, the McGregor home was considered chic and everyone who was anyone, including the Dillinghams, accepted the McGregors' invitations - even to Daddy's wedding. When Daddy told me of his wedding plans, I asked if this Mr. McGregor was the same Mr. McGregor in the Peter Rabbit story. Daddy thumped me on my head and told me not to talk baby talk anymore.

According to Auntie Gladys, after hearing that their wedding was to be held at the McGregors', Kathy emerged like Venus out of her bubble bath and bubbled sweet nothings again into Daddy's ear. She insisted that Daddy phone Mother right away to tell her that his darling, darling Kathy soooo wanted Mother to be at their wedding. She would honor Mother as her special guest. Hearing the invitation from Daddy, Mother wanted to vomit into the phone. She told Auntie Gladys that Daddy was marrying a crazy woman. Immediately, Auntie Gladys gleefully reported back to Kathy, who was lounging in a hot tub, that Mother thought her nuts. Kathy screamed for an hour in the suds.

The wedding was the talk of the town. I told Agnes and Gertrude that a lot had happened since the day I almost drowned, Mother poisoned Marigold, and Daddy wanted his wedding on my birthday. Now, with Daddy's wedding around the corner, there was more to come.

Betsy moved out of the house. It wasn't a big shock. I kind of expected it because Betsy and Jack decided to be married on Maui. The date had been set for the last weekend in March. Betsy wanted to go home to her parents, the dairy farmers, and prepare for the wedding. I thought her wedding was really romantic because Betsy told me the reception was going to be held under a tent in one of the pastures. I told her having cows walking down the aisle with the bridesmaids was a very creative thought and I didn't know she had it in her.

She asked if I would be one of her bridesmaids and I was thrilled. I asked her what I would be wearing, Before she could answer, I told her I looked fabulous in yellow chiffon. She said she was joking, but she thought I looked divine in blue satin.

I then asked Betsy point blank if she had to get married. Betsy gasped and told me I was being rude again. I thought that was the usual question everyone asked a bride before she got married. It was the same question Cousin Bessie asked Mother about Daddy when she heard he was getting married to Kathy. Betsy burst into tears and told me she never wanted to see me again and slammed the front door. I watched her from behind the screen door as she dragged her suitcases into her car to get on the steamer for Maui.

Mother overheard me asking Betsy that question and told me I had been a fresh boy and needed to apologize to Betsy. I felt like a lowdown rat after Mother scolded me and told her I would write Betsy a letter that minute if she would mail it. I asked Mother what I had said that was so wrong. Mother shrugged her shoulders and went into the kitchen for a cup of coffee. With the coffee cup in her hand, Mother said I couldn't go to Betsy's wedding because I was still in school, and right now, we couldn't afford that kind of frivolous expense and that after I wrote the letter to Betsy, she would mail it.

I went to Mother's desk and wrote:

> *Dear Betsy,*
>   *I am sorry I made you cry. You are still one of my bestest friends and Jack too.*
>   *I cant come to yor wedding and be yor bridsmade Ha! Ha! but I love you anyways. Mother sass we ar poor. I miss my mvie friend.*
>
> *Love, Percy*
>
> *P. S. I know yor mother and father live on a dary farm. Say hello to the moo cows for me at the weding.*

Marigold abandoned Hatsuko's room and took command of Grandma's room and Grandma's four-poster bed as soon as Betsy walked out the door. She decorated the room just like Grandma had had it. She even had the picture of Grandma's captain, the man who looked like a fox, on top of her bureau. Marigold was all smiles again, sleeping in Grandma's room, that is, when she wasn't thinking about Daddy's wedding. Marigold told me that sleeping high up in Grandma's four-poster bed was like being in hog heaven.

Two minutes after setting up her things in her bedroom, Marigold posted her Keep Out Percy signs all over her door.

Grandma had been cast adrift when Daddy told her he was going to marry Kathy. Grandma was from an old New England family, the Carters, who sailed steerage on the Mayflower. Grandma's very Protestant family never trusted or liked the latecomers that came to Boston, especially lace-curtain Irish. The lace-curtain Irish arrived hundreds of years after the Mayflower had dropped anchor and, according to Grandma, were never up to snuff, especially Kathy's kind of devout lace-curtain Irish Catholic types. From the beginning, Kathy never had a ghost of a chance with Grandma because Grandma wouldn't meet her or have anyone speak her name aloud in her presence.

Grandma was the greatest snubber in the family. Certainly, she was not going to be caught dead at Kathy and Daddy's wedding. As a consolation prize, Daddy and his brothers upped Grandma's monthly allowance and paid for her hotel room at the Pleasanton Hotel.

Mother and I hadn't seen Grandma since the day she walked out our front door. Grandma had visited with Marigold when Marigold had her overnights with Daddy, but Grandma and I had never crossed paths since I waved goodbye as she and Daddy motored away. Mother made overtures for a visit but Grandma always refused.

I told Gertrude the reason Grandma wouldn't see us was because she was embarrassed because Mother had been so kind to her and Grandma had repaid Mother by pooping a lot at dinner. Agnes completely agreed with me.

Grandma went to visit friends on Maui as Daddy and Kathy prepared for their wedding. She wanted to be as far away from Daddy's new bride as she could get. Before she left for the Valley Isle, Grandma wrote Mother a letter.

Dear Deidra,

I apologize, dear, that I haven't conducted myself properly, as I should have done. You were so kind to me after my son died, and though I may not have shown it, I did appreciate your kindness.

When I return from visiting my friends on Maui, I want you, Marigold and Percy to have lunch with me at the Halekulani Hotel. It would be doing a great favor to a very foolish old woman because I have behaved very badly towards you. Please, I would like to see you all again.

I know Dick's wedding must be a very embarrassing time for you, especially marrying that woman. Know that I understand your feelings.

With fond affection,

Grandma.

Mother shared the letter with Marigold and me and told us how much she really loved Grandma. Tears ran down her cheeks. After hearing the letter, I even looked forward to seeing Grandma again. After all, as Mother reminded me, Grandma had taught me how to read, and about France and sailing ships' riggings and because of Grandma, I knew lots of things that my classmates didn't.

I told Mother that I hoped they served huge clubhouse sandwiches at the Halekulani Hotel. I loved big juicy clubhouse sandwiches filled with turkey, tomatoes, crisp bacon and filled with so much mayonnaise that it dribbled on the plate at every bite. I could hardly wait to tell Grandma that she could be real proud of me because I farted just like her...maybe even better.

Mr. McLaine, across the street, hired a fat German lady by the name of Miss Hankins to take care of Walter. The reason I knew he had hired Miss Hankins was that one day after school, I walked over to Mr. McLaine's house to ask about Walter. It had been weeks since the day I dressed up as Alice Faye in Walter's basement and, since that day, I had heard not one word from Mr. McLaine or Walter.

I knocked hesitantly on the door. Mr. McLaine opened the door slowly and Fluffy jumped into my arms. After I inquired after Walter, Mr. McLaine abruptly told me my services were not needed any more because he had hired a cousin of Mrs. Potter to stay with Walter full time.

He introduced me to Miss Hankins. She had a terrible skin disease. Huge, black moles were splattered all over her face and hands like someone threw mud at her. Miss Hankins looked like a Dalmatian puppy dog. By her brisk hello and the sharp sound of her voice, I could tell she didn't have an ounce of humor or dramatics in her. She was not the fun-loving type that Walter needed and probably hated electric trains. Mr. McLaine didn't ask me inside or offer to let me see Walter. I told Mr. McLaine that I was really a very responsible little boy.

Petting Fluffy in my arms, I said, "I loved taking care of Walter, Mr. McLaine. Anytime you might need my services again, I would gladly come back and work without pay. In fact, Mr. McLaine, I miss seeing Walter." With Fluffy kissing me all over my face, I said in all sincerity, "Please tell Walter hello for me. Tell him I miss him."

I put Fluffy back down on the floor and whispered into her ear, "Goodbye, Bullet."

Mr. McLaine closed the door.

31

The Wedding Photographer

Kathy and Daddy's wedding was held on a sunny Sunday afternoon in April. It was a typical Hawaiian day, with warm trade winds blowing that people on the Mainland dream about. It was a perfect day for an outdoor wedding.

Daddy had bought me a small radio from Holster Drugstore so I could listen to the "Lone Ranger" after dinner in my bedroom, and an Eastman Kodak square black Brownie camera as two birthday presents. Daddy said he wanted me to be the photographer of the family. The camera fit in with my plans to be a great spy like Mr. Hamada. I now had the opportunity of not only overhearing conversations that I shouldn't be hearing, but taking photographs of things that I shouldn't be seeing. The Brownie camera made me into a real honest-to-goodness spy. Daddy gave Marigold an Annie Oakley cowgirl outfit to wear to the wedding.

Kathy ordered Daddy to give us something to do at the wedding, anything to keep us busy and out of the way. Daddy did as he was bidden.

Daddy assigned me to be the official wedding photographer and Marigold was to be in charge of passing out the champagne glasses to toast the bride and groom. We were satisfied with our assignments.

Daddy and Kathy's wedding ceremony was set for four o'clock in the afternoon sun. Mother arranged for Auntie Gladys and Uncle Pete to drive Marigold and me to the wedding. Mother invited Cousin Bessie to a late matinee at the Waikiki Theater and dinner afterwards at the Wagon Wheel to keep her thoughts away from the wedding. Cousin Bessie sniffed that it seemed very unloyal of Auntie Gladys and Uncle Pete to attend "that" wedding. Cousin Bessie emphasized that she was a loyal friend to Mother, but then, Cousin Bessie hadn't been invited to the wedding. Daddy hated her guts.

Mother bought at McInerny's an all-white tropical boy's suit with short pants and a bright blue tie for me to wear at the wedding. The blue tie would bring out the blue in my eyes. I told her the white suit was going to bring out my rolls of fat. I wanted to wear her slimming, shimmering, slinky black evening gown. She refused.

Mother wanted Marigold to wear a flouncy girlie dress but Marigold was determined to wear the Annie Oakley outfit that Daddy gave her. Marigold got her way by slamming all the doors in the house.

Auntie Gladys and Uncle Pete picked us up at three o'clock in their brown

Chevrolet coupe. I watched from the living room window as their car jerked to a halt in front of our house. Auntie Gladys, sitting behind the wheel, wore a tight, purple cocktail dress. The purple matched the streaks in her black hair. Uncle Pete, hot and uncomfortable, sat on the passenger side of the front seat. He was stuffed into a scratchy, moth-eaten, blue wool suit, the only suit he owned. He played hard up, trying to look like a bum, because he wanted people to think he was poor so that moochers wouldn't ask him for a handout.

Daddy said the rich are stingy people and that's why they stay rich.

The terrible twosome, Roger and Don, were fighting in the rumble seat and were outfitted in their smelly football uniforms, shoulder pads and helmets included. Between punches, they were throwing a football up in the air and acted like cartoon characters out of the funnies. Auntie Gladys and Uncle Pete were fighting, too, in the front seat. They fought all the time, even when they snored in the same double bed. I could tell by their red faces that they were already three sheets to the wind. They must have been fighting since early morning about who was going to drive to the wedding. Auntie Gladys had won because she was behind the wheel.

Auntie Gladys beat up Uncle Pete all the time. She beat him up so bad once, he had to go to Queen's Emergency to get a hundred stitches sewn in his head. (That was one of Cousin Bessie's don't-tell stories.) On weekends, it was well known in the neighborhood that Auntie Gladys and Uncle Pete drank as soon as they woke up. Today, the Twins were punching each other because I bet Don had used up all the catsup on his French toast, which made Roger mad because he wanted to pour it on his thing.

Not seeing Marigold and me out on the front porch, Auntie Gladys honked the car's horn. She honked so loud, she must have awakened the dead bodies sleeping in the Chinese cemetery. "Deeeeeder," Auntie Gladys screamed out the car window. She always called Mother "Deeder" when she was drunk. "Deeder, we're here. Get those godamned kids out here - right now. We're late. We need to 'hele on.' Did you hear me? We're late."

I ran back to Mother's bedroom. She was sewing a button on Marigold's costume for the tenth time and said they didn't hear Auntie Gladys honking the horn.

Don and Roger were now jumping on our front porch, whooping, "Marigold, we gotta to go. Ma and Pete have got a bug up their nose, and if you don't get out here, they're going to shove one up ours."

We ran out of the house and Mother followed. As I stood beside the car, Roger and Don were back sitting in the rumble seat and Roger looked as if he wanted to eat me up. I wanted to stay home.

Auntie Gladys wagged her finger at me, saying, "Percy, get in the front seat with Petey and me, and Marigold, jump in the back with the brats." That was a big relief. I couldn't understand why Auntie Gladys and Uncle Pete didn't bring their big town car to take us because it had four doors and tons more room. But Auntie Gladys and Uncle Pete never made sense when they drank gallons of gin and tonics.

Marigold yelled a war whoop, carrying her BB gun, and climbed into the rumble seat with the Dead End Kids. She was in a real Annie Oakley mood and was planning to shoot Kathy in the rear end as soon as she said, "I do" to Daddy.

Marigold squashed herself between the Twins and yelled to Auntie Gladys, "Ride'em cowboy!"

Mother cautioned to her best friend, "Drive carefully, Gladys. Take good care of my kids. No drinking till you get there."

Too late!

"Oh, for Christ's sake, Deeder, what do you take me for - of course, I'll take care of your kids - just like I take care of mine. Don't you worry your little finger about that," Auntie Gladys hollered.

Then Mother really got worried.

Auntie Gladys gave Uncle Pete a punch because he was practically on her lap after I had gotten in. She yelled, "Don't crowd me, Petey. I won't be able to drive." She then saw that I was the problem and yelled, "Oh, Percy, for Christ's sake, get back in there." She indicated a small space between the front seat and the back window where Uncle Pete stored his tennis rackets. I hesitated, but Uncle Pete shoved me in and I fit - barely.

As I sat squished, my white linen suit now looked like it had never been pressed. Well, so much for making a good impression on Daddy today.

"Deeder," Auntie Gladys leered at Mother, "I'm going to take in everything and I'll report everything that hussy does. Don't you worry - we're on your side, kiddo. Dick is really the biggest damn prick I know of, other than Petey here."

I screamed from the back, "Stop, I forgot my camera." Everyone groaned. "I've got to have it. Daddy said I am to be the official photographer today. I promised," I pleaded.

Mother ran into the house and found the camera on my bed with the four rolls of film beside it. Mother raced back out to the car and tossed the film and camera to me, smashed in the back seat.

We were off at last. I waved goodbye to Mother, standing alone on our sidewalk, looking as if she had lost Rhett Butler. I sang to the back of Uncle Pete's head, " Hi ho, hi ho - we're off to the wedding to the number two Mrs. Daddy, we go."

On the way to the wedding, I got to know all about Auntie Gladys and Uncle Pete. I knew Uncle Pete was rich, but I didn't know he had been one of the star football players with Daddy and his buddies. He had been a rascal too, but Auntie Gladys, a tub full of gin, a fat stomach, and now a bald head had stopped his naughty shenanigans. That was according to Auntie Gladys. Uncle Pete was now the milquetoast type that hardly spoke. Retreating way back into his mind, he told me of his bygone days without Auntie Gladys.

Listening to their youthful tales while looking at the backs of their heads, I knew why the Twins never had a chance to be good, because both parents had been juvenile delinquents.

Daddy called Auntie Gladys a "pistol packing mama" because she shot off her mouth like one - rat, tat, tat, tat. Some of her shots killed Uncle Pete's youth. Once in awhile, Auntie Gladys aimed potshots at me.

We passed the Diamond Head Lighthouse as Aunt Gladys rat-tatted on what a good looker she had been, and what a handsome guy Uncle Pete once was when he had a thick head of hair, and how goddamn poor she had been, once upon a

time, a long time ago. She rat-tatted, jumping from one subject to another, that she
came from a little mining town in Colorado that went bust and her daddy went
bust along with the mine. He went so bust, he threw himself into the bottom of a
mining shaft. Auntie Gladys took what money she had, shoved it into a small suitcase and left for California and became a professional hoofer. Using her winnings
from a marathon dance contest, she sailed for Hawaii. She landed on Waikiki
Beach dead broke with only her ruby red tap dance shoes on her feet and hooked
Uncle Pete the very week she arrived. I thought Aunt Gladys's life should have
been made into a Judy Garland movie.

There was no question about it - Auntie Gladys wore the pants in her family.
Even the Twins sat up straight when their Ma cracked the whip. It wasn't unusual
on weekends to hear the two football bullies yell out from their house, "Ah, Ma,
have mercy this time. Pleeese, Ma." After the "Pleeese, Ma," I'd hear the whip
crack. The sound of the whip cracking on their behinds was music to my ears.

Being around Auntie Gladys was never boring. Uncle Pete was always boring.
Daddy said he was never going to be boring like Uncle Pete and Daddy wasn't,
because today he was going to have two wives.

I told Gertrude and Agnes that Auntie Gladys had taken all the bullets out of
Uncle Pete's gun. Daddy's gun was still loaded.

Auntie Gladys, weaving over the highway, took the scenic route to the wedding. We drove past the blowhole and Makapuu beach, and I breathed a sigh of
relief when I spotted in the distance the Waimanalo sugar mill stack. We hit upon
the McGregors' mansion straight off. This mansion looked like a movie star's
estate. Acres and acres of lawn were surrounded by tall royal palms that lined the
grounds. Tennis courts and an Olympic-sized swimming pool with an attached
bathhouse were at one end of the estate and a large rambling Spanish hacienda
was built at the other.

A Peruvian architect, Pedro de Ameche, designed the house. He was the most
fashionable architect who was designing houses for the higher social circles in
Hawaii. The architect, as Cousin Bessie cackled over the phone, had washed up
mysteriously on our Hawaiian shores without a dime and just as mysteriously had
become a millionaire. His picture was always featured in *The Advertiser* kissing
Doris Duke, the tobacco heiress. The Peruvian was the first to design courtyards
around the McGregor mansion. Cousin Bessie said, laughingly, it was to protect
the hacienda from an imminent attack by Pancho Villa, the dead, legendary
Mexican bandito.

Ameche named the estate La Casa Grande de McGregor. I would have called
it Versailles because it was the grandest home I had ever visited. It looked much
more impressive than a castle in France because the mansion fronted onto a powdery white sandy beach and the turquoise blue ocean. I once overheard Daddy tell
Mother that Dolores Del Rio, the beauteous, black-haired Mexican actress,
splashed in the McGregors' waves, wearing a black mantilla.

As we pulled into the white coral drive, I saw that Daddy had gone all out for
Kathy the Red because a huge long tent had been erected on the McGregor lawn.
Inside the tent were rows and rows of long wooden tables covered with butcher
paper and rickety wooden benches to sit on. Ti leaves covered the tops of the

tables and cut fresh pineapples were set in the middle of the tables for dessert. Daddy's wedding was going to be a traditional old-fashioned Hawaiian luau. Looking at the elaborate layout, I figured Daddy was going to have to skip months of alimony payments to Mother.

Auntie Gladys parked the Chevrolet next to a whole line of Packards, Cadillacs and Lincoln Town Cars. Marigold and the Twins leaped out of the rumble seat, drunk with excitement, and immediately roamed the grounds like Pancho Villas. Uncle Pete and Auntie Gladys pulled themselves out of the car and headed straight for the bar. I unpretzeled myself out of the back space of the car, legs cramped, and walked bowlegged like Uncle Pete into Daddy's wedding tent.

My white suit looked stepped-on, as if I had been on an Uncle Pete drunken binge for days. I was a fashion disgrace because everyone else wore slinky black dresses. I wanted to hide because I didn't want to embarrass my daddy.

I was determined to make him proud of me as his photographer. With camera in hand and four rolls of film in my pocket, head held high, I walked around the picnic tables, looking for mayonnaise. I pretended to be a successful photographer using my camera.

In the distance, I could see a mound of dirt near the swimming pool. It was the *imu*, the pit where the Hawaiians were cooking a pig for the luau. The pig, wrapped in ti leaves, was being steamed to perfection by red hot stones underground.

My stomach was growling, so I asked one of the workers what we were having for dinner. She told me her family had set up the tent, tables and benches. They were also the cooks and were presently digging out the pig, mullet, butterfish, and sweet potato from the underground pit. They also had prepared steamed Samoan crabs, a tub of *poi* (sticky, gray, cold Hawaiian mashed potatoes), *haupia* (coconut pudding), *lomi lomi salmon* (salmon tartare), *limu* (seaweed), chicken *luau* (chicken stew cooked in sweet coconut milk and taro leaves that looked and tasted like spinach), *wana* (sea urchin), *opihi* (salt water mussels), and coconut cake. Ice cold Nehi orange bottled soda water, and beer, placed on the tables, had been provided by Mr. McGregor, not of Peter Rabbit fame.

The little girl with big brown eyes said in wonderment, "This haole stay get married must be one rich buggah to make all dis."

I told her the buggah wasn't rich enough to suit me. I didn't want to tell her that the rich buggah was my father because then she would think I was rich too and want to borrow the nickel in my pocket. I had brought a nickel along in case Auntie Gladys left me behind. With no mayonnaise in sight on the tables, I left the tent.

A bar was set up near the mansion where a long line had formed. Auntie Gladys and Uncle Pete were already mingling with the people wearing slinky black dresses and tropical suits, drinks in their hands. They must have made a twenty-yard dash to the bar - even old people can run fast when they want to.

Near the bar, a trio of comfortable looking Hawaiian ladies, wearing red and white holokus and green leafed *maile* leis around their necks, sang hapa-haole songs of the Islands. People trying to out-talk other people surrounded the singers. Nobody paid any attention to the ladies singing their melodies.

I stood in the background, listening to the noise of people talking, everyone wanting to be heard at the same time, talking about the weather. I looked for Daddy but I couldn't find him. I wanted his instructions on what exact photographs he wanted me to take of the wedding. I sat down on a bench and loaded a roll of film into my camera.

Nobody paid any attention to me.

Uncle Dutch, the giggler, Daddy's blonde, beefy football buddy whom I hadn't seen since Mother and Daddy divorced, sat down next to me. I knew why he was called Dutch because he looked like he was from Amsterdam. He was white blonde all over - even the hairs on his arms were colored like Jean Harlow's white hair. Dutch cut his hair in bangs across his forehead just like the little boy on Dutch Boy paint cans sold in hardware stores. His eyes were rimmed red like the tulips in Holland and, at any minute, because he expressed himself a lot waving his middle finger, I thought he was about put his finger in a dike to save the Netherlands.

Uncle Dutch looked at me, smiled, put his tree trunk arm around me, and hugged me to death. I could tell he was having a good time because he was laughing at everything I said, even when I said nothing of any importance. He was laughing at laughing and when he stopped, he said, "Well, Percy, me boy, what do you think about Dickie Boy getting married?"

"Oh, it's nice," I answered as Uncle Dutch screamed with laughter.

"I'd say it's nice, boy. She's a real hooker - I mean, looker. She's a corker. She's gonna give your Big Daddy a hot ole time." More laughter roared out of his mouth.

"How's Deidra doing? Your mother is a good sport. Always liked her. Too good for Dickie Boy." As Uncle Dutch said Mother was too good for Daddy, he slapped his knee as if he told me the funniest joke in the whole world.

"I'm going to be Dickie Boy's best man today, Percy. Can you beat that? Your daddy is really some guy and this shindig is gonna cost him a bundle." He laughed again until I thought his sides would break. Then he stopped and said seriously, "Actually, I think old Kathy will be good for him."

"How much will this cost Daddy, Uncle Dutch?" I asked.

"Plenty, Percy. Plennnnty, Perrrcy. Looking around, I'd say this is going to cost your dad a minor fortune. Say, Percy, do you still dress up in your mother's clothes? I never forgot you dressing up like Carmen Miranda. You were something, kid. Never seen anything like it, before or since." Uncle Dutch roared again, thinking of me passing hors d'oeuvres, dressed like the Brazilian Bombshell.

"I sometimes dress up, Uncle Dutch, but not much anymore. I have no one to dress up for. Everyone is too busy, or they don't like me, or like Daddy, they've gone away. Everyone seems to go far away from me - somewhere. Don't they, Uncle Dutch? Uncle Dutch, did you know that I am cursed?"

Uncle Dutch didn't laugh when I said that. Looking at the camera in my hand, he asked, "Say, what's the camera for?"

"Daddy wants me to take pictures of the wedding. I've been looking for him. Have you seen him, Uncle Dutch?"

"He's inside the house getting dressed."

Uncle Dutch was overcome with laughter again, "Say, Percy, I've got a great idea!" Uncle Dutch slapped the table. "It's a real corker. After the wedding, I've got a great set-up for you to take pictures. Your dad's gonna be really proud of you. Don't take any pictures of the wedding ceremony - that's dumb. Don't waste any of your film until you see me. Right, kiddo?"

I nodded.

He looked at his watch. "I gotta go and be your daddy's best man. See you after the ceremony. Remember, don't take any pictures till you see me." He got off the bench and walked towards the house, horse laughing all the way.

Over a microphone, Mr. McGregor announced that the wedding ceremony was about to begin. The Hawaiian music stopped and Daddy's guests gathered in one of the courtyards. I still couldn't see Daddy. I stood alone in the background. Uncle Pete and Auntie Gladys, Marigold and the Twins had ditched me a long time ago. Nobody but Uncle Dutch had paid any attention to me or said hello.

I walked to the courtyard where everyone milled around, waiting for the wedding to begin. An old Hawaiian minister stood in front of the French doors, holding a Bible. Daddy walked out of one of the doors, dressed in a pressed blue suit, and stood next to Uncle Dutch. Musicians began to play a sweet Hawaiian melody as three pretty ladies walked towards Daddy and the minister. Each lady walked behind the other in step as the music played. The tallest and prettiest of the ladies was last and stood next to Uncle Dutch. She kept wiping tears away from her eyes.

A piano inside the house started to play the wedding march. Down the white satin runner marched Kathy, head up, wearing a white wedding dress with a long white veil blowing in the wind and carrying a large bouquet of calla lilies. Kathy was white all over except for the lipstick and red claws. She reminded me of snow fluttering in the wind. She had lost her Fourth of July look. She moved like a blizzard down the white carpet to greet Daddy, who waited for her at the other end. She was like a wind out of the North Pole about to descend and smother my father to death.

Marigold, standing on the wall above the courtyard, watched the blizzard fly to Daddy. As Kathy reached for Daddy's hand, Marigold cried like a banshee and raised her BB gun over her head like a guerrilla fighter. She was ready to shoot her enemy. The sound of the waves crashing on the beach drowned out her cries, so nobody paid the slightest attention to the assassin standing on the wall with tears streaming down her face.

Kathy kissed Daddy. They faced the minister. The minister spoke long and seriously in Hawaiian and English. The ocean waves kept crashing so loudly in the background that I didn't hear a word he said. When Daddy and Kathy kissed hard, everyone clapped so I guessed the wedding ceremony was *pau*. Kathy held on to Daddy and wept a storm of tears and shivered all over.

Marigold, in a crouched position on top of the wall, pointed her BB gun at Kathy's jiggly rear end. She aimed, readied, but didn't fire. She threw herself down on the wall and sobbed while all the guests packed around Daddy and Kathy giving them kisses.

I couldn't walk my way up to them to shake hands because it was so crowded with people. I had been instructed by Mother to congratulate Kathy and Daddy as soon as the wedding ceremony was over and to bite one of Kathy's rosy cheeks.

Mother said she was joking.

I never made it up to Daddy because Uncle Dutch found me first and whisked me away. He said I could congratulate Daddy and Kathy later because we had more important matters to attend to. He hoped I hadn't used up any of my film by taking photos of the wedding. I said I hadn't. He guided me to a spot near the bar, a place where there were lots of thick bushes fronting the beach. Uncle Dutch told me to get inside the bushes, as we were going to photograph some really spectacular sights. When we hid in the bushes, Uncle Dutch ordered me not to make a peep and he promised not to laugh because that would spoil the picture taking.

We didn't have to wait long for Uncle Dutch's amazing sights to appear. The men at the luau who didn't have the patience, notion or desire to pee into the McGregors' toilet preferred the out-of-doors, near the bar, out of sight, and on the beach. It was less troublesome and faster. Sure enough, a parade of peeing men began. There was Mr. Dillingham, Mr. Cooke, Mr. Bishop - all of Honolulu society came before my camera. The tall, the short, the big, the small - all sizes of men unzipped their pants and took a whiz.

Click - click - click; I pressed the shutter of my camera.

Uncle Dutch kept maneuvering me so that my camera could get the best angle. I got some amazing photographs that I had never seen in *Life* magazine - some were more photogenic than others were. I used up three rolls of film in fifteen minutes. Uncle Dutch whispered into my ear, as three of his best friends came into the camera's view, "Percy, point the camera at Uncle Kanaka. You're gonna see the eighth wonder of the world."

Uncle Dutch was right. Uncle Kanaka pulled out a hose that was as long as the one I saw hanging in the Kalihi fire station. I whispered into Uncle Dutch's ear that Uncle Kanaka's snake was longer than a twenty-foot Brazilian boa constrictor that I had seen in Cousin Bessie's *National Geographic* magazine.

Uncle Bip and Uncle Fat, who were with him, couldn't keep their eyes off of Uncle Kanaka's amazing wonder. We overheard their conversation. "Wow, Kanaka, I forgot about that. That's some weapon," Uncle Bip said as he stared goggle-eyed.

Click went the shutter of the camera.

Uncle Fat piped up, "Kanaka, I hear you're taking out Kathy's maid of honor, Babs. She looks hot stuff. I bet she's something in the sack."

"You bet right, Fat," Uncle Kanaka replied, buttoning up his pants.

"Peanut butter legs?" Uncle Fat asked as he finished up and looked out at sea.

"Peanut butter legs, Fat," replied Uncle Kanaka.

"Peanut butter legs?" questioned Uncle Bip.

Uncle Kanaka, smiling like a Buddha, told Uncle Bip that peanut butter legs meant "spreads 'em as smooth as peanut butter." They roared with laughter when Uncle Kanaka said that and slapped each other on their behinds. Uncle Dutch had keeled over in hysterics, stuffing his mouth with his hand, trying not to give us away.

In three-quarters of an hour I used up all the film. Wearily, bones creaking, my white suit spotted with dirt, Uncle Dutch and I emerged from the bushes and walked back into the party. Uncle Dutch went to the bar to order a drink.

While we were gone, couples had started dancing to Hawaiian music. The Hawaiian minister had already said grace and the guests were seated, eating the pig served to them on a big wooden platter. It was five in the afternoon. The sun set at six. The wedding was over when the sun set because Daddy didn't have enough money to pay for strings of naked light bulbs.

Looking for Daddy and Kathy, I saw Marigold serving champagne to Daddy's guests. I also saw that when she thought no one was looking, she picked up used drinking glasses and chugalugged the dregs, mixing gin, bourbon, and champagne together. The Twins were right behind her, hopping from table to table, picking up as many discarded glasses as they could find and guzzling the contents. Marigold and the Twins looked like they were having a contest on who could drink the most and the fastest.

As I saw Daddy and Kathy standing in the tent, shaking hands with latecomers, I realized that I hadn't take a single photo of the bride and groom. Daddy saw me, waved me over, and grimaced disapproval at my rumpled appearance. Sounding annoyed, he asked, "Percy, where have you been?"

Trying to rub dirt stains off my pants, I replied, "Taking pictures with Uncle Dutch, Daddy."

"I hope you took some good ones."

"I did, Daddy. Uncle Dutch really helped me. He said we got some real natural ones."

"Well," said Daddy, putting his arm around his bride, "Kathy and I can hardly wait to see them. Give me the films and I'll get them developed for you. I hope you took good ones of Kathy." Without saying a word, I took the films out of my pocket and gave them to my father. Kathy, melting like an ice cube from the hot rays of the setting sun, smiled wanly at me.

"As a matter of fact, Daddy...."

Uncle Dutch appeared out of nowhere and interrupted my confession. "Dickie Boy," said Uncle Dutch, laughing, "Percy got some outstanding photographs. I'd say they're award winning. They're going to be memorable ones that you and Kathy are never going to forget. Kathy, I promise you you'll want to show them to all your grandchildren."

Uncle Kanaka and Kathy's maid of honor, the tall, beautiful Babs, joined us. She placed herself right next to Uncle Dutch. "What photos?" asked Babs.

Daddy put his hand on my head, explaining, "Percy has been my official photographer, and Dutch says he's done a grand job. I'm really proud of him."

Babs took my hand and shook it. "I'm kind of an amateur photographer myself. You're going to have to reveal some of your photographic secrets to me," she said.

"You bet, peanut butter legs. I'd be glad to. But you see, this is the first day I ever used my camera. Uncle Dutch helped me."

When I said "peanut butter legs," Uncle Dutch fled to get another drink.

Kathy's maid of honor asked, "What did you call me?"

"Peanut butter legs," I repeated.

"That's not my name. My name is Babs. Where in the world did you ever hear that my name was peanut butter legs?"

Daddy and Kanaka left to join Uncle Dutch at the bar. I was alone with Kathy and Babs and confessed, "I heard Uncle Kanaka call you that because he says you spread 'em as easy as peanut butter."

As I was offering that piece of information, Daddy and his sidekicks were ordering doubles and Kathy looked like Miss Fourth of July again. Both Babs and Kathy stood speechless, staring at me. I broke the silence and said, "I like peanut butter with mayonnaise myself. It spreads faster, Babs. You try it."

Kathy was about to swat me across the face, but Babs stopped her. "Leave me alone with Percy," Babs said. She shooed Kathy away and told her to join Daddy and Uncle Kanaka at the bar. Kathy left steaming.

When Babs and I were alone, she took my hand and said, "Percy, it was very embarrassing when you called me peanut butter legs. Did you know that?"

I shook my head no.

"I am going to believe you and think that a little boy like you didn't know what he was talking about. Am I right?"

I nodded my head again, looking into her brown eyes. I liked her a lot and said, "Did I say something wrong? I love peanut butter and mayonnaise."

"You do. Well, so do I. Now, little Percy, we are going to forget all about this peanut butter business, aren't we? You and I are going to let it go and be friends." Babs pulled a Lucky Strike cigarette out from a pack lying on the table and lit it.

She went on, "Percy, I want to tell you something about women. I want you to remember this because, when you become a man, it might help you understand women. Women will never forget a wrong that a man does to them. Their revenge may not be today, tomorrow or next year - but revenge will come as surely as the moon rises. And when it comes, the man that did it to her will probably not remember what he did, but he will damn sure never forget what she will do to him. And that's the truth, kid. And for the record, little man, I do spread 'em as easy as peanut butter, but you'll never tell anyone that, will you, Percy?"

"Actually, Babs, I just did to Daddy and Kathy but I will never say it again and your secret will go inside my stomach, never to come out, I promise you. See this stomach?" I pushed my stomach out. "I store lots of secrets in here."

"I believe you, kid. Now take my hand and let's go to the bar. You can buy me a big drink as I am about to shorten Mr. Kanaka's pride," said Babs, smiling.

I liked Babs better than Kathy because she was more real and knew how to spread peanut butter...and peanut butter, jelly and mayonnaise were one of my favorite sandwiches to eat by the side of the house. If I had the chance, I was going to make Babs one of my good friends and we'd stick together just like bread and jelly and peanut butter.

I took Babs to the bar and acted like her boyfriend as I ordered the bartender to give me a large gin and tonic - with lots of ice. Uncle Kanaka came up and put his arm around Babs. She squeezed Uncle Kanaka's arm as if nothing had happened. As I walked away, Babs and Uncle Kanaka were smooching. I wondered, looking at them kissing, at what date and at what time Auntie Babs' revenge would begin on Uncle Kanaka. Her revenge on Uncle Kanaka was going to be just like my curse because he'd never know when it was going to hit him - big.

Auntie Gladys and Uncle Pete, pie-eyed, spotted me and told me we had to go home because Marigold and the Twins were pie-eyed too. Looking for Marigold, Daddy found her under a coconut tree, passed out with her arms entwined around the Twins. They overdid the sips from the empty party glasses left on the tables. With the help of Uncle Dutch, Daddy tossed the drunks into the rumble seat without anyone seeing them. Daddy ordered Auntie Gladys and Uncle Pete to take Marigold and the Twins home right away. He also warned Auntie Gladys and Uncle Pete not to tell Mother what happened.

As we drove up to the front of my house and the car stopped, I realized I hadn't had anything to eat. I had been too long in the bushes taking pictures with Uncle Dutch. I was so starved I could have eaten the paint off of Auntie Gladys's car.

Uncle Pete carried Marigold into the house and laid her on Grandma's bed. Marigold cried out to Uncle Pete as he left her, "Let me die. Let me die. I want to die." Uncle Pete told Marigold to shut up. He warned Marigold if Mother found out that she got drunk at the wedding, she *was* going to die and so were he and Auntie Gladys. None of them wanted to die by Mother's sword. When Uncle Pete was drunk, he didn't act like a milquetoast.

I waved farewell to the drunks and thanked them for taking me home safely. I stressed "safely."

I went to bed after eating a couple of Helen's dried up chicken wings in the icebox. I smothered the chicken wings with mayonnaise so I couldn't taste her pukey chicken. Helen the Poisoner must have been Attila the Hun's cook in ancient days because only a bad man like Attila could have survived her cooking.

Mother was still out having dinner with Cousin Bessie at the Wagon Wheel. Marigold was living under a good star that night because Mother never found out about Marigold's drinking spree. Each day, my stomach was filling up with secrets.

The next morning, Mother couldn't understand why Marigold was so thirsty and quiet at breakfast. Marigold told Mother she was coming down with the Spanish flu that had killed thousands of people during World War I. I never opened my mouth. Auntie Gladys and Uncle Pete never opened their mouths either because they wanted to remain Mother's friends.

Mother gave Marigold an enema to get the flu out of her. I never had an enema in my life and I vowed never, never to have one after I heard Marigold screaming in the bathroom.

Daddy never told me how my photographs turned out or how proud he was of me for taking them. Every time I mentioned wedding photographs, he'd mumble that they were being developed. One day, tired of my constant badgering, he told me the drug store lost them.

Uncle Kanaka married "peanut butter legs" Auntie Babs on May 1st. I told Agnes and Gertrude maybe getting married was her sweet revenge on Uncle Kanaka.

May Day is Lei Day in Hawaii. I made a report to Miss Wood's class that May 1st is a holiday in Madison, Wisconsin just like our Lei Day holiday in Hawaii. Only in Wisconsin, it is peanut butter day. Banks, schools and cheese factories close on that day so they could spread 'em. I told Miss Wood I knew all that because my Auntie Babs was from Wisconsin.

I made it up.

Daddy and Kathy honeymooned in San Francisco. When Daddy came back, Marigold didn't see him as often because Daddy was too busy doing busy things with Kathy. Marigold threatened Mother that she was going to run away from home and seek her fortune in Timbuktu whenever Daddy cancelled their date. She would have gone, but my sister didn't know how to get to Timbuktu. Even Grandma had flown the coop. She was still on Maui, swapping stories with the famous Valley Isle writer, Armine Von Tempski.

After a phone call to Daddy, Marigold told me that Daddy was angry with me but she wouldn't tell me why. When I heard that, I wet my bed again and felt all over cursed.

32

I Hate Birthdays

I asked Gertrude and Agnes, why do all bad things happen in one month? April started with Daddy getting married to Kathy and then things built up to April 20th, Hitler's birthday. I went for days, weeks, even months without the curse doing anything bad to my life. Then all in one month - bang - everything explodes like a Nazi bomb bursting in the streets of London.

That's what happened to me in April, a bomb burst over my house. I asked God, why?

Gertrude explained, "Percy, as you know there is a big universe up there and there is a mighty force that moves about the universe like a powerful energy, like an electric kite flying in and around the stars. This energy wants to come down into our world and help us, or sometimes it can do us harm. It's how we send for this energy because this powerful energy wants to get into everybody's business. That's why you have to be careful what you pray for.

"Now just imagine there is a big invisible wall that God has built around the earth that keeps this energy from coming down on us all in one month. There is big gate in the center of the wall that God built that doesn't let the energy enter into the world just at any old time, but only at the right time. God attached a hundred locks on the gate so that only He can open up the gate at the right time. These locks look just like stars.

"Lately, God opened up the gate so that Mr. Joe DiMaggio could hit a home run and your Miss Alice Faye could make another hit movie.

"Every bad thought you send up into God's heaven can make the comets go berserk. These comets get out of control especially if God is off having lunch with his Son. God loves his mayonnaise sandwiches too. Can you understand that, Percy?"

I nodded. God loving mayonnaise sandwiches was one of the things I loved about God.

Gertrude continued, "Well, these naughty comets, which are really our bad thoughts that we have sent out into the universe, are like children playing hooky from God. They want to open up the gate and let bad things happen to us here on earth. They, our bad thoughts, hit the locks on the gate until they cause the locks to burst apart like bombs exploding and make the gate open up when it shouldn't have."

Gertrude pantomimed the naughty comets hitting the stars on the gate and continued on with her funny talk in my mind, "When these naughty comets open the gate because of our bad thoughts, that's when the terrible, powerful energy from the universe swoops down on us and unexpectedly causes all sorts of bad things to burst around us like rotten eggs - and all in one month. It happens because someone like you sent bad thoughts out to God and into the universe. Remember, Percy, bad thoughts become bad comets and bad comets change the direction of God's good energy. Good thoughts turn into good comets and that's when the good things happen to you here on earth. Percy, when you think bad thoughts, you're going to create naughty comets that will open up God's gate and have all the bad stardust crash down on you - all in one month."

"Is that my curse, Gertrude?"

"Yes and no, Percy." Gertrude knew I had been thinking bad thoughts all the time lately and that's why she said I had opened up the celestial gate and let some terrible, terrible energy in and made bad things happen to me all in one month. What Gertrude told me made as much sense as any stories I heard from Miss Jones telling me of baby Moses floating down the Nile in Sunday school.

I wasn't prepared for April 20th. Before April 20th, I had acted like a naughty comet-boy and sent three hates flying up into the stars. With my hates, I loosened every lock on heaven's gate and a lot of bad stardust came down on me and poured all over my house all in one month.

Daddy wasn't one of my hates.

I truly hated three things. The first thing I hated was my birthday. I especially hated my birthday parties. Most of all I hated *surprise* birthday parties.

Because Daddy had almost ruined my birthday by having his wedding day on April 8th, Mother did something special to make up for Daddy's booboo after the wedding. She plotted with Marigold to give me a surprise birthday party the Saturday following my real birthday. I knew something was up right away because there were clues all over the house.

Clue 1: there were gallons of ice cream in the icebox. Clue 2: there were cartons of paper plates and forks spread all over the kitchen table. Clue 3: I was outlawed from entering the dining room on Friday night. Clue 4: I found a bag of colored balloons spread all over the living room floor. Clue 5: Being a great spy, I have learned to put two and two together. For that, Mr. Hamada and the Japanese government should have given me a medal. Clue 6: Helen the Awful had been in a foul mood all week because Mother made her work overtime because of my party. As soon as I walked into the kitchen, she'd bang the pots down on the stove, growl to herself, and say in loud voice what a spoiled, fat, ungrateful little boy she worked for. Then she would say louder so that the sailors on the ships in Pearl Harbor could hear her, "You don't deserve a surprise birthday party on Saturday."

Now that's putting two and two together.

Helen the Snitch gave it away. When I heard from her big mouth that a surprise birthday party was about to happen, I wanted to jump off the Nuuanu Pali. The Nuuanu Pali is a windy cliff on Oahu where anyone who wanted to commit suicide jumped. Legend had it the great King Kamehameha pushed his enemies over the pali and after he won his most famous battle there, he unified the

Hawaiian Islands. Daily, I wanted to shove Helen over the pali with Kamehameha's enemies.

I never minded being in front of the class and making a donkey of myself because it was never the real me. I was acting being a silly-billy. But when there was a birthday party planned just for me - *just me* - it made me think of all the things I wasn't, all the things I lacked being a seven-year-old boy going on eight. I made a list.

My shortcomings were:

I was fat.

I was a sissy.

I wet my bed.

I hated my name.

I wasn't Alice Faye or even near it.

I wasn't talented.

I lied when I could get away with it.

For all those reasons, I had to agree with Helen the Skunk and Daddy the Absent that I didn't deserve to celebrate my life. I just wasn't worth it.

When Saturday arrived, Mother made Cousin Bessie take me on an errand. I was to escort her to the Salvation Army. Darlene, her smelly cat, had died. (The neighborhood cheered.) Cousin Bessie was giving the Salvation Army Darlene's leftover worm medicine. Since the Salvation Army was in the wrong part of town, Kaimuki, she needed a protector.

"From what?" I asked Cousin Bessie.

She said, grinding her teeth, "From mashers." She thought all Portuguese men were over-sexed mashers.

"What are mashers?" I asked. Shivering all over, she confided to me that mashers were men who grabbed at ladies' behinds. I said back very sincerely, "Who would want to grab your behind?"

She slapped me on my head and told me that I was bound to be a Portuguese masher because I couldn't keep my mouth shut. I confided to God that even if He forced me, I wouldn't grab Cousin Bessie's behind. She was old, had a flat bottom and there was nothing to grab.

Sentenced to be alone with Cousin Bessie for an hour was enough to make me hate surprise birthday parties for the rest of my life. Hearing her talk non-stop for an hour was like walking over hot coals in bare feet. It was like being stretched out on a rack in a Spanish prison or having a picnic lunch without potato salad or deviled eggs or mayonnaise on anything.

When we got home (the Salvation Army rejected her worm medicine), thirty people jumped out of the bushes, screaming "Happy Birthday." I wanted to tell them to go right back into the bushes and leave me alone. I got out of the car and said "Hi!" I stood in their midst and grinned stupidly.

Someone yelled, "Ain't you surprised?"

I screamed back, jumping up and down and acting surprised, "Oh yes! Oh, boy! Oh boy, what a surprise. You almost gave me a heart attack."

I wanted to kill myself.

After I said "what a surprise" ten times to all thirty of my "very best friends," they went off to play with each other. They left me standing on the curb alone, wanting to drown. I prayed that Cousin Bessie's car would back up and run me over.

I looked up at Mother standing on the porch, watching me, smiling and pleased as a pumpkin. Marigold smirked too, standing next to her. By the look on Marigold's face, I knew she thought she had pulled off the surprise of the century.

I wanted to wipe that silly grin off her face and tell her the truth. I yelled up to them, lying, "Oh boy, isn't this the cat's pajamas. How could you do this to me? I never knew." It was a line out of a Ginger Rogers movie. Pleased that I had been completely taken in by their surprise, Mother and Marigold walked back into the house to help Helen the Snitch with the birthday lunch.

I sat down on the front porch steps and watched "my best friends" tear up our yard, playing tag with each other. I thought, watching them play, that there was not one kid running around whom I would have invited to this party. If I had to have a birthday party, I would have invited:

Hatsuko

Rose - I would have asked her to leave Hiroshi back at Waialua. Actually, he could have played with Helen in the kitchen. They had the exact same personalities.

Alice Faye

Mr. Hamada

Kimo

Kaina

Walter

Fluffy (Bullet)

Vinnie and Cynthia

Grandma - because she wrote a nice letter to Mother

Uku - if he was home

and Daddy - without Kathy. I liked Kathy all right but not with Mother around. That would have been too embarrassing for Mother.

Mother had invited my entire second grade class because she thought they were the ones I played with and liked best. Wigay Wix was my only friend in the class and she was the only exception I would have invited to come with Alice Faye. My teacher, Miss Wood, came late. (I bet she wished she were sunning herself on the beach at Waikiki, playing her ukulele.)

Marigold invited the Twins and some of her chums from school - that rounded out the thirty.

I told Gertrude I was celebrating my birthday with strangers.

Mother called us into lunch. I don't remember what was served, but I do remember I put mayonnaise on everything including the birthday cake and ice cream. Mayonnaise on chocolate ice cream was not a great success, but I was too nervous to really think about what I was eating because I knew what was coming next.

The opening-presents time with everyone watching me, just like at Aunt Ella's, was even more torturous than being with Cousin Bessie for an hour. I would gladly have chosen to be tied and whipped at the mast by Grandma's Captain rather than be made to open presents in front of snarling, bored, greedy little brats who only wanted a second helping of my birthday cake.

Mother piled the presents in front of me. I was sitting in Daddy's seat at the dining room table. I ripped the wrapping paper off the boxes as fast as I could move my fingers. I wanted to get the whole dang thing over with and take the attention away from me. The brats watched me as I pulled each gift out of a box. Their beady eyes told me they were thinking that here in front of them sat a fat sissy who didn't deserve even a dog's bone on his birthday. I hated every minute of it.

After I opened the last present, I thanked everyone. I had learned my correct manners from Mother. I thanked them for:

Two boxes of white linen handkerchiefs, the most useless presents a boy of eight could get.

Pairs of black socks, more worthless than the linen handkerchiefs.

A rubber dog's bone, a joke from Booby the Bully.

A death threat from the Twins written on toilet paper. They were still bound and determined to hang me. They said in front of everyone that the present was a joke. *It was a serious present.*

A box of red and black checkers.

A yo-yo, my best present.

A bag of Hershey Kisses.

A pair of undershorts - used. I could tell they were used because they had a rip in them.

A toy fire truck from Wigay Wix. It was a great toy for a three-year-old.

Lots of books, most of which I had read in the first grade. What I really wanted was a subscription to *Photoplay* magazine.

After the present-opening ceremony, Mother organized games for the rest of the afternoon. I kept saying to Gertrude and Agnes, "When are these brats going home?" The first game was "pin the tail on the donkey." While lining up to play, the rowdies, waiting their turn, chanted:

> Ching Chong Chinaman
> Sitting on a fence
> Trying to make a dollah
> Out of fifteen cents.

There were no Chinese at the party, though we did have one part-Hawaiian, but he didn't count because he acted like a haole. I couldn't understand why kids picked on the Chinese all the time. The chanting got louder as the brats pounded on each other's backs. Mother and Marigold ran around the house, looking for thumbtacks for the game. The house was beginning to tumble down over our heads because a riot was festering. "My best friends" were filled to the brim with cake and ice cream energy and were ready to start the American Revolution all over again.

They yelled at the top of their voices and continued to pick on the Chinese:

Red, white and blue
Stahs ovah you
Mama say, papa say, you *pake* (Chinese).
Let's play a game - NOW!

Thumbtacks were found in Helen the Horrible's kitchen drawer and just in time. The game was about to turn into "pin the tail on the birthday boy." The game began. Kids screamed and rolled on the floor when someone pinned a tail on the donkey's nose or some part of the donkey body where it wasn't supposed to be. The afternoon turned into a success because everyone forgot about me.

Mother's genius at keeping the kids under control came after that game and she made sure everyone went home with a present. I would have given them all my presents. Since Marigold was the only one in the family who knew how to use a hammer, Mother told her to build a makeshift screen to play "fish in the pond." It was a game where everyone at the party received a gift without doing anything. It was the last game in the afternoon.

Bamboo fishing poles with strings and hooks attached were placed outside the screen. Mother and Marigold, hunched over on the other side of the screen, attached a surprise gift to the hook at the end of the fishing line. Sometimes the fishing game became hilarious because Mother and Marigold didn't know who cast a line over the screen.

The bully of the class, Booby, hooked a kewpie doll. We howled and teased him mercilessly when the doll came into view. Booby ran crying into the bathroom and wouldn't come out until he got another present. Sweet Wigay Wix knocked on the bathroom door and exchanged her pencil flashlight for his kewpie doll. Bullies are all crybabies.

The party ended at three and proved a real success because everyone went home full of hot dogs, cake, ice cream, and a present to boot. Each brat said goodbye to Mother and they asked to be invited back next year because, clutching their presents to their chests, they said they had had the most woooonderful time.

I never wanted to see them again. As far as I was concerned, I hated my birthday party. After the last little brat was driven away by his mother, I gathered up all my presents, took them to my room and shoved them down into my window seat. I vowed I was going to send them all to Kauai to my cousins whose house had burned down and now played with my Christmas presents. I grumbled to Agnes and Gertrude that the presents would only remind me that I didn't deserve all the attention I got because everyone knew I was the big sissy of my class.

Daddy told me that a million times over just by the way he looked at me.

My classmates didn't like me either. They only came to my house because of the hot dogs and ice cream and cake.

I stuck out my lower lip. By the side of the house, Agnes and Gertrude told me to shape up and quit feeling sorry for myself. They said together, "You're eight years old today and it's time you grew up." They repeated that I had turned into a spoiled brat and yammered into my ear how spoiled and thoughtless I had become. I hadn't given a single thought to all the work and expense my mother had gone to just to make me feel special.

"And don't forget Marigold," Agnes said, which surprised me because she was usually very critical of Marigold. "She went all out, too. But she must have taken some nice pills today."

"You'd better thank them - so your mother and sister will think you reeeeally mean it!" sniffed Gertrude. "They are the only ones who don't care if you're fat," Gertrude said snottily, looking down at her stick figure.

I told them that I knew all that. I went to bed that night feeling confused and guilty. I told Gertrude I wouldn't know how my family felt about anything, including me, because we all faked that everything was all right, all of the time, when it wasn't.

I just couldn't help it. I hated my birthdays. Agnes and Gertrude warned that if I put hate thoughts out in the universe, something terrible was bound to come back and smack me in the kisser.

I unlocked one of the star locks on the celestial gate.

33

Two More Locks on the Celestial Gate Opened

My second hate was the Honolulu Zoo.

On Sunday, the day after my birthday party, Mother took Marigold and me to the zoo. It was my first visit. We drove down in Mother's rocket to Kapiolani Park where the zoo is located. Kapiolani Park lies at the base of Diamond Head on the Waikiki side. Most of the year, the park wears a layer of brown grass on its open fields because the rain clouds hanging on the mountains seldom drift overhead.

This Sunday afternoon was a scorcher and I could smell the zoo even before Mother parked the car. I felt like I was under the Twins' house, breathing the stench of decaying rats. It was same rotted smell. Gertrude said the heat of the day was burning the animals to a crisp inside their cages. Agnes added that the animals were in Hatsuko's oven, baking like a turkey for Thanksgiving.

After Mother paid for our tickets, we walked through the zoo's turnstile gate and down the path into the zoo. As soon as we entered, thousands and thousands of birds perched in the trees screeched, "Let me out, let me out." That's how it sounded to me. As we walked from cage to cage, the animals were crying, wanting to get out, and staring from their cages with dead, desperate eyes. I stared back at them and saw that they had given up on living - every animal one of them.

The lions that I read about in *National Geographic* magazines and saw in movies, especially Tarzan movies, were the kings of the jungle. Here in the zoo, they wandered around in circles, going nowhere, with their skin hanging over their ribs like brown duffel bags. They weren't anything like the lions I had expected to see. I expected to see lions run, attack, and fight each other, to watch ferocious beasts roar and eat bones, just like they did at the movie matinees when lions ate Christians in the Coliseum.

Even the monkeys were goofy - jumping here, jumping there, and always hitting smack into a wire fence. These little "Chitas" were acting stupid as if they were in a Three Stooges movie. In Tarzan movies, monkeys swung on real vines high in the trees, teasing lions and tigers that roamed on the jungle floor. In the zoo, monkeys swung on dirty ropes, spit, and screamed "yeeeeeeeee," showing me their red gums.

I wanted to be a naughty comet and unlock all the gates in the zoo and let all the animals out to wander with the tourists on Waikiki Beach.

After fifteen minutes of being dragged from one cage to another, I told

Mother and Marigold I'd wait for them in the car. I complained that I didn't feel well. Mother said I ate too much birthday cake yesterday and it had made me sick in the stomach. I pouted that it wasn't the cake, it was the bag of stale peanuts in my hand. Everything in the zoo was stale because they caged *life* in here.

I feared that someday a policeman would haul me into a cage like the one the lion was in. With the same dead eyes of the lion, I would look out at the world from inside a cage as the people walked by with stale peanuts in their hands. I'd be buried alive.

The pride of Africa, the lions, and all the animals just happened to be at the wrong place at the wrong time and got caught. None of them had Alice Faye's luck. That afternoon, curled up in the back seat of the car, I vowed I would never have dead eyes like the lions. I hated zoos.

I broke a lock on the celestial gate.

That afternoon, I read in the newspaper about the Bishop Musuem.

The Honolulu Advertiser

BISHOP MUSEUM - 30,000 VISITORS EACH YEAR ATTEND EXHIBITS
Article by E.H. Dryan, Jr., Curator of Collections. Bernice P. Bishop Museum is famed throughout the scientific world for its researches on the ethnology and natural history of Pacific Islands. Yet, like the oft-mentioned prophet, it is scarcely known to the residents of Hawaii.

My third hate was the Bishop Museum.

Learning Hawaiian history in the second grade meant the promise of an excursion by school bus to the Bishop Museum. We second-graders fainted with excitement anytime we got out of school for anything. Going to the museum was especially appealing because it was as adventurous as going to see the Great Wall in China. It was one glorious day free from learning math, spelling and sitting on hard, wooden seats. As the chorus girls sang in a Warner Brothers' musical, we were going to be "footloose and fancy-free."

Wheeee!

I imagined all sorts of exciting things that I was going to do at the Bishop Museum. To say that I was about to be disillusioned would be like me discovering that Best Foods mayonnaise had been Miracle Whip all the time.

The Bishop Museum was located on the outskirts of Honolulu and housed the only collection of Hawaiian artifacts in the Territory.

We played "jan ken po," Hawaii's version of the paper, scissors and rock game, to decide who got to sit shotgun next to the bus driver. I lost. Miss Wood walked me to the back of the bus, under protest, to sit down on a broken, springy seat. My whole day went badly after I sat down because the curse had followed me to school that morning and showered me with bad luck all day. I had looked for an Alice Faye penny and only found a lot of dried-up dog doodoo. I should have known that was an omen that I was going to be exiled to the back of the hot, stuffy bus for most of the day. The museum visit became one disaster after another for me.

We arrived at the museum at nine o'clock. Miss Wood said that was when the museum opened to visitors. The Bishop Museum was a large, gray, two-story stone building and it struck me at first glance that it was a castle somewhere in Germany, near the Black Forest, near where cuckoo clocks were made for Dr. Frankenstein. It looked scary.

We shoved and pushed each other off the bus almost before the bus came to a stop. Miss Wood shushed us to be quiet as we lined up in order outside the front door. When men and women who looked like Dr. Frankenstein's servants opened the creaky door, Miss Wood ushered us into a large reception hall. I told Wigay, by making oooing sounds, that this was where Hunkacha lived.

Three employees in long white coats, looking like weird keepers in a mental hospital, shushed me. They scolded me to speak in whispers and quit my oooing. From the looks in their eyes, I knew they pegged me as the class troublemaker. As their eyes bored through me, I pretended not to notice their looks. Fat people always stand out in a crowd and I could see in their eyes that they thought me a termite.

One attendant instructed the other attendant, who had a long black hair sticking out his nose, to follow me. He whispered to a lady with a pencil in her hair that if I made one false move, he was going to lock me in a padded cell. He was the only man I ever observed who whispered so I could hear him, and he made a Dracula laugh every time he ended a sentence. HAAAAAAH! His mouth didn't know how to whisper or laugh normally.

I tiptoed into the first gallery mincing like an Egyptian princess. The room had a high ceiling and I felt a cold, shivering sensation as if I had entered a sacred tomb in Egypt. I was not wrong. The museum, I found out, was dedicated to dead people and things. I wandered from room to room, looking for anything alive, anywhere. Even the ants had died because there weren't any crawling through the cracks in the wood floor.

A dried out carcass of a huge sperm whale hung from the ceiling in the center gallery. It was dead, too. One side of the whale showed its skin and a poppy eye and on the opposite side, the whale's skeleton was visible, as intricate as the inner makings of a sailing ship. I had wanted to see a real whale swimming in the sea and spouting, not hanging on a clothesline out to dry.

Down below in the center gallery was a grass hut covered with *pili* (native) grass. I waited for a Hawaiian native to walk out the front door, pound poi, cook a pig, and play with me. The grass house, however, was empty inside and out. Only the stone articles used by a family of the past was left on display. I told Agnes, playing inside my head, that I imagined that the daddy and mommy living inside the grass house had to flee with their kids because Pele had hot lava roaring down the mountain ready to *kaukau* (eat) them up.

In another room, wood spears hung lifeless on the walls. I was disappointed that warriors weren't holding them, ready to battle on lava fields on the Big Island.

Near the spears were royal crowns, glittering with rubies and diamonds, displayed in a glass case. There wasn't a king or queen sitting on a throne to wear them. I kept on looking at dead things - dead - dead - dead - things. Even the small round stones weren't in the hands of children playing checkers (*konane*). There wasn't a human being on display except for the man in the white coat with a long hair sticking out his nose who kept following me.

Then I remembered a portrait of a lady hanging on the wall where we first entered. She looked nice and almost real. I tiptoed back to the entrance and looked up at the lady in the painting who stood regally like a queen. The brass label on the frame read that she was Princess Pauahi Bishop, whose husband built the museum in her memory. She had beautiful eyes. I stared and stared at her painted eyes. They were kind eyes and the only live thing I could find in the entire museum. I reached up to touch her face.

The caretaker with the hairy nose yanked my hand away and howled, loud enough for all the dead in the museum to arise, "Don't touch that painting! You're going to ruin it. You've got oil on your dirty fingers."

I pulled back my hand and whispered to him, "Shhhhh."

The watchdog yelled back at me, "Don't you shush me, you stupid little fat boy. Didn't your teacher teach you manners?"

Miss Wood and all my classmates heard the commotion and ran into the room to listen to everything the guard was yelling at me. In fact, everybody in the museum heard the guard yelling at me. The pig with a hair sticking out his nose didn't follow the rules because he was yelling. I was so mad, I wanted to yank the black hair out of his nose. Instead, I hid my head in embarrassment as Miss Wood and my classmates kept watching the guard, who had steam pouring out his nose. The black hair now stood at attention and his face was crimson like Kathy's red ribbon. He finally clasped his chest as if he was going to have a heart attack and die.

I wished he had.

My classmates yelled at me, "*Bakatare* you!" meaning in Japanese that I had done something embarrassingly stupid.

I defended myself to Miss Wood, saying, "I didn't do anything. I was only going to touch the lady in the painting. I didn't, Miss Wood. Promise."

No one believed me because I was known to exaggerate a little and lie...sometimes. My classmates turned into a chorus of witches, shaking their fingers at me, singing, "Ahana koko lele, ahana koko lele. Percy is a bad boy. Percy is a bad boy." Their eyes danced as they chanted and now everyone was breaking all the rules.

Life wasn't fair. I wanted to take a snake to my breast as Claudette Colbert did in *Cleopatra* and kill myself. There are no snakes in Hawaii but if there were, I would have grabbed one. "Honest, Gertrude, I would have," I said to her.

Miss Wood smoothed it over with Mr. Big Stuff In-Charge and made me apologize to him. I did so grudgingly and meant not one word of it. I still wanted to yank the black hair out of his nose.

The incident was quickly forgotten and the museum became dead again, but I was now the leper of the class and nobody wanted to walk with me. I sauntered listlessly into another gallery, pretending nothing had happened, and hummed under my breath, "Who's afraid of the big bad wolf, the big bad wolf." I bent over to look into a case that displayed lava stones with Hawaiian diamonds, olivines, the same semi-precious stones I had seen on Pele's island.

Suddenly, Booby the Bully kicked me in the rear. I shoved him into a glass case. I was not in a good mood.

He shoved me back into a round koa table on which stood a Chinese vase with Hawaiian red ginger flowers arranged in it. Vase and flowers crashed to the floor and the sound of the crash echoed in all the galleries. Crash - crash - crash - crash - crash...CRASH!

I was blamed for the accident because Booby cried in Miss Wood's arms, saying that I had shoved him and he had hurt his arm. Booby received a kiss from Miss Wood and was sent off with Wigay to soothe away his hurts.

I was banished from the museum just as Napoleon had been sent to Elba. My personal attendant with the hair in his nose was at my side in a flash, glowering. He made a twenty-yard dash, knocking over a chair, to where I was standing in the midst of the broken vase. I was guilty as charged. He grabbed my arm so hard I thought he was about to squeeze all my blood out through my fingers.

He obviously was related to Hunkacha. The monster pulled me out of the museum and told me he was going to lock me up in a padded cell. He didn't, but he did shove me into the back of the hot bus and ordered me to stay put, not to move from my seat, until the bus left for school.

After touring the museum, my classmates got to picnic under a cool, shady monkeypod tree while I baked in the boiling bus. Booby the Bully and Wigay and all the kids who came to my birthday party played tag and ate sandwiches and were having lots of fun. No one paid any attention to me.

I watched from the bus window, like the caged lion in the zoo who wanted to get out and be free like everyone else. I watched them having fun with dead eyes. I just happened to be at the wrong place at the wrong time.

Wigay brought me a peanut butter and jelly sandwich from Miss Wood which was so dry that parts of it stuck to the roof of my mouth. Getting peanut butter off the roof of my mouth with my tongue was my occupation all afternoon. Wigay was the kindest girl in our class because she didn't play favorites. Looking at Wigay take roll for Miss Wood after lunch, I thought she'd make a great diplomat for President Roosevelt. When she sat next me on the bus ride back to school, I promised her that I was going to write President Roosevelt to send her to Berlin to keep us out of the war.

Miss Wood snitched to Daddy as soon as we got back from the museum. Daddy promised her he'd send a check to the museum to pay for the broken vase.

After work, Daddy drove up to the house, stood outside the front door and yelled at me, shaking his head, and saying that I was a careless boob. He moaned that he hadn't paid for his wedding and now this. Because of me, he would really be in the poor house. Daddy then asked for the camera back and told me I was a menace to society.

After my father left, I told God I hated the Bishop Museum.

As soon I said that, the last lock of the celestial gate snapped open and a flood of bad angel dust dumped all over our house.

34

Aunt Momi

One of the worst things that ever happened to me was on Hitler's birthday, April 20th.

In the morning, Mother walked into my bedroom and announced that we were all going to stay home from school. Aunt Momi and her three daughters, my first cousins, were arriving by plane from Kauai. Mother was going to have an important meeting with Aunt Momi and wanted us home to entertain our cousins.

Gertrude said it must be important because Aunt Momi was spending a lot of money to fly from Kauai to see us. Nobody flew from Kauai just to see us on Kapaka Street - only movie stars traveled in planes. We had to travel in a slow, leaky boat if we wanted to visit Kauai.

Agnes, Gertrude and I racked our brains, trying to think what Aunt Momi had up her sleeve. I hoped she was going to give me a million dollars. Gertrude guessed that Aunt Momi was going to become a Catholic nun. Agnes said Aunt Momi didn't have a saintly bone in her body and was announcing she was leaving for Hollywood to become a movie star. None of us were even close. We were a million dollars off.

Aunt Momi arrived with her brood. She never walked into a room - she swept in. She was a glamour puss from the day she was born and had always been her father's favorite. Grandpa, Mother's father, told his poker-playing friends that his Momi had the pizzazz in his family.

Mother said Aunt Momi had *IT* because Aunt Momi was sexy. She was the aunt who sent me her discarded *Photoplay* movie magazines. She attracted men like flies were attracted to a fresh cow pie. She couldn't walk into a room without every man in the room sniffing around her like a dog in heat. That's what Daddy said.

Uncle Hans, her husband, was a German through and through. He had a bald head to match his Germanic posture and wore shiny black boots to match his bald head. He looked like a Nazi. He shaved and shined his head twice a day and servants polished his black boots every night. He had two matching German shepherds at his side when he roamed the sugar plantation. Mother called him the Kraut behind his back.

I thought Aunt Momi and Uncle Hans were the usual, typical, happily married couple because they fought a lot. Aunt Momi and Uncle Hans had four children, three daughters and a son. I knew them only slightly because they lived on Kauai. They were the cousins to whom I sent all my Christmas presents from Aunt Ella's house after their house burned down.

At ten in the morning, a Cadillac limousine with a chauffeur behind the wheel stopped in front of our house. Out swept Aunt Momi with her girls trailing behind. Nancy was the oldest. She was a dark beauty and knew it the day she was born.

Betty, the middle child, was chubby, blonde and full of personality. Marsha, the youngest and littlest, wore glasses as thick as the bottom of a green Coke bottle, and she and Marigold were considered by everyone in the family who counted as the brains in the family. Marsha carried a red leather classic book under her arm all the time because she said it made her feel like an intellectual.

Little Hans was always left at home. He and I were the same age. I wet my bed; he pooped in his. We were kindred spirits. Little Hans was the spitting image of his father - Germanic looking at eight and already getting bald. Aunt Momi's children were a year and a half apart from each other.

Aunt Momi and her girls stampeded into our house like wild horses. In two seconds, they took over our living room, sitting in every chair in the room. Even Marigold was cowed by their enthusiasm. They used up so much energy, they sucked all the air in our house into their bodies. It was hard for me to breathe when they were around. I found myself having to excuse myself every so often, saying I had to go to the bathroom, in order to run into my bedroom and breathe in air.

Aunt Momi herded her troops out of the living room into our outside lanai. My cousins brought a Parker Brothers Monopoly set with them, so Mother and Aunt Momi ordered us to play Monopoly and not to bother them in the living room because they had a serious matter to discuss.

While we played, Mother and Aunt Momi sat in the living room and conducted their powwow. They really had something serious to discuss because once in awhile, their voices rose, loud and angry. I can't remember them ever being angry with each other. I do remember when they came out of the living room because I had landed on Park Place. Betty had a hotel on it and I was flat broke, all out of Monopoly money. Betty screamed at me to hand over the rent money or lose the game. For a fun-loving cousin, she was a Hunkacha at the Monopoly board. She was a very serious player and she always elected herself as the banker.

Aunt Momi told us to stop playing. I could have kissed her for that because I hated to lose. I was the poorest loser in the family at anything. I whined for days if I lost and cried that nobody loved me, I was cursed and everyone cheated.

Aunt Momi and Mother sat on the *punee* (couch) on the lanai facing us. Aunt Momi crossed her legs and lit a cigarette just like Marlene Dietrich did in Ciro's Hollywood nightclub. Mother sat next to her sister, wearing an unhappy expression on her face and looking like an actress who had just lost the Oscar as the best supporting player.

"Well, kids," Aunt Momi directed her words to her three girls, "I have an announcement to make and there's no other way to get around it. I'm divorcing your father."

Nancy burst into tears. She was her father's favorite.

Not paying any attention to Nancy, Aunt Momi continued, "I am sorry about it but your father and I are just not suited to each other any more. Your father wants a divorce and so do I. I came up here to get advice from your Aunt Deidra on what to do." Aunt Momi patted Mother's knee. "Aunt Deidra told me to wait before I did anything about a divorce, and that's probably good advice, but I'm not taking it. You see, girls, I have fallen in love with Lono."

Aunt Momi turned to me, "Percy, you'll like Lono because he is a real, live Hawaiian prince and I'm about to turn into a princess."

With that statement, all the girls wailed and held on to each other. Marigold and I watched them, not knowing what to do because we didn't belong in the room.

Aunt Momi clapped her hands and continued, "Stop that crying, girls. Right now. I mean it. Crying won't help. I've made up my mind and I am not going to change it. Aunt Deidra disagrees with me, but I've set my star on Lono and I am going to follow it. You girls are just going to have to like it - like Lono and live with me. Your father wants custody of Hans, but you three are mine. Until I'm married, I'm going to put you girls in the boarding department at Punahou School and that way you'll be near your Aunt Deidra, jolljamit."

Brushing her hands back and forth like she just finished making an apple pie, Aunt Momi turned to me and said, "Percy, how'd you feel about having a princess in the family?"

"Oh Aunt Momi, I love it. Can I wear your tiara sometime? I've always known deep down inside that we were royalty and now we really are. Aunt Momi, are royalty cursed?" I asked.

Aunt Momi swept around the room, speaking like a princess, "I don't believe in such things, Percy. Ask your mother, she thinks we are. Hah! It's all bunk." With that, she gathered up her brood like a princess, Monopoly board and all, and ushered them back into the limo. Aunt Momi's Hawaiian prince paid for the limousine and air trip.

She was now leaving to enroll her girls at Punahou. My cousins looked wounded, as if Aunt Momi had shot an arrow into their hearts. Nancy, Betty and Marsha sat in the limo, clinging to each other and crying with all their might, because in a minute Aunt Momi had turned their world upside down.

If Hawaii hadn't become an American territory and remained a monarchy, Uncle Lono would have been king and Aunt Momi would have been his queen - and I would have been Cinderella at the ball.

After royalty left, the air around our house was still topsy-turvy. I had to take in deep breaths because Aunt Momi and my cousins' energy still lingered on the ceiling. Mother sat down exhausted, trying to make sense of Aunt Momi's visit. She brooded, but not because Aunt Momi was divorcing Uncle Hans. Mother was upset because Uncle Lono, Aunt Momi's fairy tale prince, had killed his second wife by breaking her neck with a tossed plate. This marriage was not to be made in heaven and dark days loomed ahead for all of us because royalty was cursed.

The celestial door had opened wide and I was about to suffocate in bad stardust.

April 20ᵗʰ was not over.

Charlie Chaplin as Hitler in "The Little Dictator." (United Artists)

35

April 20ᵗʰ - Hitler's Birthday

The Honolulu Advertiser

THE QUEEN'S HOSPITAL BEGAN AS A 40 BED UNIT IN 1859

The growth of Queen's Hospital since its beginning in 1859 - 82 years ago - well represents the growth of Honolulu as well. When founded, the hospital cost $16,000. Today the plant is valued at $1,500,000.

SUNDAY, APRIL 13, 1941 - THOUSANDS ATTENDED THE SUNRISE RITES AT PUNCHBOWL. PUNCHBOWL HAS THE LARGEST SERVICE IN HISTORY THIS EASTER 1941.

APRIL 20 - HEART OF LONDON IN RUINS AFTER NAZI BLITZ

Germans drop 100,000 bombs on East End. (UP) Cheering, waving men, women and children in London's East End scrambled around King George and Queen Elizabeth today, attempting to shake hands with their majesties when they toured the East End areas devastated in Saturday's night raid which the Germans claimed was a reprisal for the British raid on Berlin Tuesday night.

It was still early afternoon on the 20ᵗʰ. Mother went shopping. Marigold roamed the neighborhood looking for the Twins. I sat on the front porch reading the newspaper, thinking about nothing, which was very unusual for me. My mind never took a nap.

All of a sudden, out of Walter's house ran a screaming Dalmatian. It was the wart-faced Miss Hankins, the lady taking care of Walter. She raced up and down our street like a madwoman, calling for help. I ran to her and asked what happened.

"It's Walter!" she cried.

I knew immediately what was wrong. I streaked into Walter's house, ran downstairs into the basement and found Walter twisting on the floor and turning blue. I grabbed the spoon off the counter and tried to shove it in his mouth. Holding the spoon next to his mouth, I yelled, "Walter, it's me, Percy. You're going to be all right. Open your mouth. Come on, Walter, open your mouth. Just for me." I cried into his ear, "Please, Walter - just for me, Percy."

Walter opened his mouth and I shoved the spoon in. His tongue was bleeding.

I ripped the bed covers off the bed and covered him - then I called Queen's Hospital for an ambulance. While I was on the phone, Walter turned a pale gray but was breathing. He was shivering all over.

Miss Hankins stood on the steps of the basement, watching me and sobbing uncontrollably. I lay down next to Walter and put my arms around him. I held him tight to keep him warm. I whispered into his ear that help was coming and to please hold on and please don't die.

I wanted to push my life into his body.

Marigold must have heard Miss Hankins screaming because she too flew down the stairs, careened the Dalmatian lady to the floor, and kneeled next to me. "What happened, Percy?" she said excitedly.

"Walter had a fit. He needs our help. Lie down on the other side of him and hold him like I'm doing. We have to warm him up," I urged. I whispered into Walter's ear that Marigold was my sister and that we loved him. Marigold lay down next to Walter. We both held our arms around him, helping him take our life into his body and loving him as much as we could until the ambulance arrived.

That's how the ambulance men found Walter - two little children holding on for dear life to a boy who had turned dark purple. As they lifted Walter onto a stretcher, the men in white told us that we had done the right thing. We were heroes as far as they were concerned.

Marigold stoutly said, "No, my brother is the hero and I am proud of him. He acted like John Wayne today."

I followed the ambulance driver and said seriously, "My sister, Marigold, is my pal. We did it together."

As the ambulance drove Walter away, Miss Hankins told us that Mr. McLaine had taken Fluffy to the vet, Dr. Pinkerton on School Street. I phoned him at Dr. Pinkerton's as Miss Hankins watched. She had become so pale that the spots on her face disappeared. After I spoke with Mr. McLaine, Miss Hankins thanked us for all our help, walked into her bedroom and closed the door quietly. As we left Walter's house, I heard her taking a bath.

Marigold telegraphed the news like Paul Revere, running from door to door, telling everyone her brother was a hero like John Wayne. Within minutes every-one, and I mean everyone including Cousin Bessie, came to our house to congratu-late me. Even Cross-Eyed Mama came to our door with Cynthia and Vinnie. They shook my hand. Cross-Eyed Mama said she would let me play with Cynthia and Vinnie again and they beamed like an Edison electric light. Life must have been pretty dull for them since I had been banished. I hoped Cynthia's tail had grown out. I longed to see it again.

I told Agnes and Gertrude later that when you turn into a celebrity, even your enemies love you - at least to your face.

The Twins were the last to arrive. They carried a little white flag and called a truce. They told me they were not going to hang me anymore. I was free to roam our streets again because they only hang pests, not heroes. They had their fingers crossed.

All this happened before Mother arrived home from shopping. She was flab-bergasted when Marigold gave her the news. With her arms around me, then smoothing down my cowlick, she said proudly that when she left to shop at Matsuda's, her son was her Clark Kent, and now when she came home, I was her Superman. When she told me that, the color of her eyes turned an extra blue. She kissed me not once, but twice on each cheek.

Mother phoned Daddy at work. She told him about my heroism. He curtly replied he was very busy in a meeting and for her to congratulate me. He added, ready to hang up, that if he had time he'd buy me an ice cream soda at Dairymen's.

I basked, being the star of the neighborhood, for one whole day. I told Agnes and Gertrude that when you're living life to the fullest, you really don't have time to sit around and plan it. My planning for the future had taken a detour again because I was basking in my glory.

I found a bottle of Best Foods mayonnaise propped against my front door before the sun went down. Wrapped around it was a note written in Japanese, and underneath the Japanese, was written in English, "To Percy the Samurai." Beside the bottle, rolled into a ball, was a long band of blue and white cloth. The note said Japanese warriors wore this around their heads after they had become heroes. I wrapped the cloth around my head. The present was from Mr. Hamada. He always knew everything. On certain days, coming home from school recently, I felt he was watching me, protecting me from the Twins.

The day was not over.

That night, after dinner, we heard a slight tap on our front door. I went to the door. There stood Mr. McLaine whom I hadn't seen since the day I had inquired about Walter. He was crying.

"What happened, Mr. McLaine?" I asked.

"Walter died!" Tears tumbled down his cheeks.

"That can't be," I cried. "I saved his life. He's got to be alive!" I opened the screen door and joined Mr. McLaine outside. I thought to myself that I had to shut that celestial gate because I couldn't take any more of the bad stardust.

After a few minutes without saying anything, Mr. McLaine uttered softly, "You did save his life, Percy. It was his heart. His heart just couldn't take it any-more."

I shouldn't have said it, but it just came out. Without looking into Mr. McLaine's eyes, I mumbled, "Mr. McLaine, if you had let me take care of Walter, I know he would still be alive." I thought he might hit me. I waited for it.

He didn't. He looked towards his house, down to Walter's basement windows, and murmured, "I know that, Percy. I'm sorry." He took me into his arms and cried and cried and cried. I could hear his bones cracking up all inside himself. He had broken into pieces.

After he controlled himself, he pulled away and took something out of his coat pocket. It was Walter's train engine, the same little engine that jumped the track and fell on the floor when I first met Walter - Walter's broken train. "I want you to have this to remember Walter by. I know he would want you to have it," he said sadly. Caressing the engine as if it was Walter, he said, "He loved this engine more than anything in the world - perhaps even more than me." He paused. "I want you to have this, Percy."

He put the train in my hand and walked off our porch, and started to cry again. Mr. McLaine stopped, turned back and hoarsely uttered from deep down in his throat, "Percy, please come and visit Fluffy and me." He looked at his house and then back at me. "We're going to be very lonely." The tall stooped figure, looking like death itself, shuffled back to his empty house. He was wearing his bedroom slippers. After he was in the house, the lights in Walter's basement went out.

I stumbled back into the house, wailing as if a truck had hit me. Between sobs, I told Mother and Marigold the terrible news. I wailed to them that I was no longer a hero and that I had lost my best friend. I ripped the white and blue cloth off my head.

Mother and Marigold surrounded me like covered wagon trains protecting settlers from savage Indians, trying to breathe life into me as I tried to do Walter. They told me that, as far as they were concerned, I was their hero.

That night, clutching Walter's toy train to my heart, I told God I had had it. It was enough of His bad angel dust. God heard me. That night, He closed and locked the celestial gate. The bad stardust force evaporated out of our house and floated back up into the stars - until the next time.

36

Nothing Lasts Forever

"Nothing lasts forever." That's what Gertrude said on the night Walter died. It's not something a person of eight wants to hear.

I hated the word "goodbye." After Walter died, I spent sleepless nights thinking about him. All the "what ifs" flooded my mind like tidal waves:

what if I had reached him sooner; might he have lived?

what if I hadn't played Alice Faye with him,

what if I had made more attempts to see him.

The "what ifs" tortured me, awake and asleep. The worst dream was Walter lying on the floor, trying to breathe and calling to me for help. I lost the key to his room and couldn't get in.

Walter's funeral was set for Thursday afternoon.

The night before the funeral, Mother came into the bathroom as I was finishing brushing my teeth, and she watched me spit the toothpaste out of my mouth and gargle with Listerine mouthwash like movie actress Rita Hayworth did in *Life* magazine advertisements. Mother took me by the hand and led me into her bedroom without saying a word. I thought to myself, "Oh, oh, I've done something wrong again."

She didn't head for the silver hairbrush on her dressing table; instead, Mother took her favorite photograph off the wall. The photograph was of her mother wearing a white wedding dress. Mother sat on her bed and, without a word, gazed at the photograph resting on her lap.

I sat next to her and immediately asked if I had done something wrong. I could think of a list of things a mile long, but I was going to make her say them, in case she missed a few.

Mother shook her head and took my hand in hers. Tears welled in her eyes. She turned to me and said quietly, "Percy, we are not going to Walter's funeral."

I took my hand away and blurted out, "I want to go! I really want to, Mother. Please let me go. Walter was my best friend and I haven't been able to sleep, thinking about all the things I didn't do for him." Mother kept looking at the photograph of her mother. I spoke more determinedly, "Things I *should* have done for him, Mother. Please, please, please, please let me go."

"Percy, listen to me," Mother said, caressing my hair gently with her fingers. "When I was just a little older than you, my mother died. It was a terrible shock because I didn't expect it and I loved her very much. We all did. All my sisters did. What made it worse - I believed she was cursed to death by the Hawaiians." She paused.

I thought to myself, I knew it. I always knew it. I am cursed.

Shaking her head, warding off bad thoughts filling her head, Mother continued before I could ask her what the curse was, "I will tell you about that another day, when you're older."

"But I want to hear about it now," I pleaded.

Mother stood up, photograph in hand, looked out the bedroom window, pretending not to have heard me and thinking thoughts that didn't include me. She stared at the shadowy forms in her rose garden.

Then she spoke about a time before I was born. "Though we lived on Oahu, my mother was buried on Kauai. The funeral was held at Aunt Mari's house. They placed Mother's casket in Aunt Mari's living room, dead center, right next to Aunt Mari's grand piano. It was an open casket and Aunt Mari covered Mother's body with cheesecloth to keep the flies away. The air was blue and filled with a sickening sweet odor - jasmine perfume to cover the smell of death. I refused to see my mother lying in the coffin. The thought of seeing her dead scared me. I wanted to remember Mother alive, not dead. I told Aunt Mari to please leave me alone because I didn't want to see my mother dead. Aunt Mari forced me to look at her, pushing me up to the casket, saying I had to be brave. I closed my eyes but Aunt Mari made me open them and look down. Mother was lying in a bed of blue satin. She wasn't there. She had gone away. Mother had turned into a wax doll.

"To this day, my strongest memory of my beautiful mother is a lifeless wax doll lying in a coffin. I collapsed on the floor and lay next to the coffin. I wouldn't leave. Aunt Mari couldn't pry me away. Every time someone tried to lift me away, I held fast to the casket. My uncles came and one of them held me while they took her away to bury her in the family plot. She rests in a cemetery under a marble stone. They left me behind, lying on the floor, weeping for someone who would never come back to me. To this day, I hate looking at painted dolls propped up in a store window."

I sat on the bed, filled with thoughts of curses, looking at Mother's darkened figure standing at the window, her eyes fixed on nothing alive. I didn't know what to say.

Mother broke the silence, "Percy, come here." I rose from the bed and moved towards her. Her arms reached out and smothered me into her. I couldn't breathe. With her arms around me, as if protecting me from evil demons out in the rose garden, she swore an oath, "Percy, I promised that no child of mine would ever go through such a horrible experience."

Now, her eyes focused on me, she said, "Mr. McLaine told me he is having an open casket for Walter. I advised him that you, Marigold and I would not attend the funeral. I told him why. He understood. Tomorrow, during the funeral, we are going to a movie in honor of Walter. Do you understand what I've been saying, Percy?"

People always asked me if I understood what they were saying. It gave me the impression that people thought I was deaf.

I wanted to hear about the curse.

I nodded, still scrunched into her bosom. Hearing her heartbeats, all of me wanted to go to Walter's funeral. I didn't say anything because my mother was emotional. Her heart was beating like a tom tom.

Mother and I saw a Lana Turner movie the day of Walter's funeral. The movie was called *Zeigfeld Girl*. It wasn't a happy movie because at the end, sexy, red-headed Lana Turner fell down a long staircase because she was sad and drank too much champagne. At the end of the movie, she died because she had become too stuck-up, too rich, too famous, and worst of all, she hadn't been nice to her old boyfriend, pimply-faced Jimmy Stewart who had loved her since the day they drank chocolate sodas in a drugstore. I told Agnes, a person had to die if you did terrible things to Jimmy Stewart.

In bed, I told Agnes and Gertrude to tell me something funny because people around me were dying, and I might be the next victim lying in a coffin with cheesecloth over me.

Marigold talked her way out of going with us to the movies with the excuse that she had a ton of homework to do. What she really did was to sneak to the funeral with the Twins because they wanted to see a dead body. Marigold reported back that Walter looked better dead than alive. I believed Marigold because my last memory of Walter was him lying on the floor, blue in the face, shaking all over, and a spoon sticking out of his mouth. I didn't tell Mother what Marigold said, that Walter looked better dead than alive, because I didn't want Mother to think about painted dolls lying in a coffin.

Mother wouldn't tell me about the curse.

37

My Last Visit With Grandma

Grandma returned from her hike (I called it her hike) on Maui. She was berthed in her room at the Pleasanton Hotel. Mother and Marigold religiously talked to Grandma every night on the telephone because Grandma told Mother she was blue. Daddy didn't call her every night because he was playing house with Kathy.

Grandma was cast adrift so, at the invitation of friends, she made up her mind to leave for Oakland, California. Her friends insisted that she live with them. They were rich ex-ladies of the night who retired and had become the pillars of San Francisco society. Each year, Tessie and Hilda were counted on to donate wads of money to the opera house and art museums. The "girls" had fond memories of Grandma and her Captain and they, too, were lonely for good company to sit at the kitchen table and talk about the good old days.

Grandma requested a visit with us before she departed for California. She even asked that I be included. Our audience was set for the following Saturday at one in the afternoon. At two bells, Grandma always took her nap.

The Pleasanton was an old shipwreck of a hotel. In its heyday, it had been one of the grandest hotels in Hawaii. It now reeked and sagged with old age. The lobby of the hotel smelled like Grandma, especially on the days when she forgot to splash her face with lavender perfume.

We arrived exactly on time to the second. Promptness was considered next to godliness by Grandma, a trait Daddy never inherited. We elevatored slowly up to the second floor. Marigold, Mother and I creaked our way down the hall, stepping on a faded rose-patterned carpet that hadn't been cleaned since Moses broke the Ten Commandments. Purple mildew hung like icicles from the ceiling and brought color to the hallway. The heat of the afternoon intensified the smells of age.

Walking to Grandma's door, I understood why she wanted to set sail for Oakland; she was living on a sinking ship. I imagined the rats in the attic were packing their bags along with Grandma and moving to the Royal Hawaiian Hotel - that is, if they had any rat sense. Daddy told me rats and eight-year-olds had no brains to speak of.

When we arrived at Grandma's door, Room 205, Marigold knocked. We heard a faint "come in." Mother opened the door.

Grandma was sitting in a fan-shaped wicker chair next to the window. She had shrunk and the chair had swallowed her. A towering force of hurricane winds that I once feared, Grandma had magically wizened into a little old lady. Her chair looked five times bigger than she was. It could have been her coffin. Grandma and the hotel were dying together.

Marigold ran into the open arms of her ninety-year-old great-grandmother and burst into tears. Mother and I remained at the door, embarrassed because we didn't want to interrupt them.

The room looked as if an army had fought a battle. It was chaotic. Grandma's nightgown and underwear were strewn on the floor, the bed was unmade, and the bed sheets, worn and yellowed from years of use, were partially on the floor. The only thing that was orderly in the entire room was the round table next to Grandma, where black and white photographs of the people she loved were displayed. Photographs of her Captain and grandsons set in old-fashion ornate frames were placed in a neat semi-circle. An eight-by-ten photo of Mother, Marigold and myself, taken in Mother's rose garden, was placed in front of her grandsons. I was pleased to see that Grandma included me as some of the people she loved. It warmed my heart.

Marigold was on the floor, holding onto Grandma's legs and crying, anchoring Grandma so she wouldn't leave her. Since Daddy left us, Marigold cried every day. Marigold always slammed doors when Daddy lived with us - that wasn't new, but crying was. One day, I caught her sobbing as she looked at a picture of Daddy. I told her John Wayne didn't cry. She got up and punched me and started slamming doors again. I felt better.

I walked over and stood next to Grandma, not knowing what to say to her because Grandma hadn't noticed me when I came in; she only looked at Marigold. With no words to say, I glanced out the window next to Grandma's chair and watched a mynah bird chirping sassily in a shower tree. I named the mynah bird Michael. (I had a habit of giving animals names.) The mynah yacked to me that he wanted to eat a worm. I liked Michael because he reminded me of myself, always hungry.

At the door, Mother coughed to get Grandma's attention and said, "Grandma, I've got a lot of errands to do. I'm going to leave the children with you so you can have a good visit with them. I'll be back in a half-hour or so." Mother always used the "or so" to give herself lots of leeway in time. Sometimes her "or so's" turned into hours and hours and hours.

Because she knew I upset people by asking too many questions, Mother warned, "Percy, remember to be a good boy and don't talk too much to Grandma and be a help to Grandma if she needs it. Marigold, you too."

I faintly heard what Mother said because I wasn't paying attention. I was watching Michael, the mynah bird, eat a worm. I turned around to answer Mother but she had gone.

When Marigold was upset, she never spoke because she kept all her deep feelings down in her toes. When I got upset, I had to jibber-jabber as fast as I could to keep from getting nervous. My mouth couldn't stop talking. I hated silences and always had to fill in the blanks. I, too, had locked places inside myself but they were not down in my toes. Marigold and I were born with locked closets, but hers was in the basement and mine was in the kitchen.

Silences - empty moments - empty spaces in time were a part of Grandma's legacy. She could sit for hours as people sat around her paying their respects, watching her every move, and waiting for her to speak, while she fidgeted with a handkerchief, looked out into space and never uttered a word. She made people so uncomfortable that they spilled out every secret they were not going to tell her.

Grandma's ancestors learned silences when they sailed on the Mayflower, huddled down in their cabins. Grandma said her ancestors ran out of talk even before they left the shores of England and sailed the Atlantic without uttering one word until they stepped out on Plymouth Rock. Their first words upon stepping on the Rock were, "Watch out, it's slippery." Our ancestor, Ishmael Turner, fell face forward into the bay. (That's the story I made up in Miss Wood's class.)

I took after Mother's side - I filled in all the empty spaces and would have talked non-stop while coming over on the Mayflower.

When Mother closed the door, Grandma began one of her long silences as Marigold sat on the floor, hugging her leg. Grandma's hand rested softly on Marigold's head and they were content to be in each other's hush time. The room became so quiet, I'd swear on a pack of law books that I could hear the room creaking like a ship at sea. The hotel was sinking like the Lusitania.

Michael, the mynah bird, flew away.

Grandma's silence was driving me to madness so I said, louder than I meant it to sound, "GRANDMA." Marigold and Grandma jumped. I even scared myself.

Grandma, recovering her composure, laid down her twisted handkerchief on the table next to the photograph of us in the rose garden and said sternly like the Grandma I used to know, "Yes, Percy?"

I looked right into her eyes and stated, "Grandma, I want you to know that I am a chip off of your own block."

"How's that, Percy?"

"I'm a good sailor. I never get seasick. I love rough water and big waves. The rougher the sea the better for me." I took a sailor's stance. "I think the Captain would have hired me on as a mate. I really think he would have."

"Really," said Grandma, surprised.

I sang to Grandma to prove that I was a real sailor, "Ship ahoy, Sailor Boy, don't you get too springy. The Admiral's daughter waits down by the water, she's out to grab your dinghy."

"Percy! Where in heaven's name did you learn that terrible song," Grandma scolded.

"Marigold," I answered.

"You did not. Grandma, Percy is lying," Marigold retorted.

Speaking to Grandma about the sea had gotten Marigold's attention. She started giving me her Captain Marvel shazam rays because she thought I was about to squeal on her upchucks at sea. I wanted to tell Grandma that Jack London and Marigold were two peas in a pod, upchuck sailors.

Grandma beamed, "That's good, Percy. Now, Percy, you forget about that song. It's not a nice song. You mustn't lie. Marigold would never teach you such a song. Now, what about Marigold, Percy? Is she a good sailor?"

I spoke up quickly so Marigold wouldn't have to lie, "Marigold is a great sailor. You would be proud of her. She's got your fat sea legs too." They didn't know what to make of that compliment.

Grandma thought about it for a bit and finally looked pleased. I could tell she was pleased because her mouth stretched really far apart like a rubber band. Her smile made her look like a jack-o-lantern. Using her Charles Laughton as Captain Bligh in *Mutiny on the Bounty* voice, Grandma barked, "I knew that. Marigold could be the captain of any ship I ever sailed. Isn't Marigold a darling, Percy?"

If I lied about Marigold being a darling, I would for sure go to hell. Saying Marigold was a darling would take a real stretch of my imagination. So I changed the subject. "Grandma," I said softly, "I'm like you in other ways too."

Grandma, annoyed that I hadn't answered her question, roared, "What? Speak up! I can't hear you."

I said as loudly as I could in her deaf ear, "I fart just like you. Maybe louder. Anyway, people say I fart so loud that sometimes the general at Schofield Barracks thinks a cannon has shot off."

Grandma gasped, sucked in air, and made a little poop. The little poop was not like the old big ones I was used to. Taking her handkerchief off the table, she coughed into it. It was her way to hide the sound of the poop. Old ladies did that. The air in the room was filled with the scent of lavender. She took my hand and spoke to me like a grandma, "Percy, the word fart is not a word to be used in polite company. I should have corrected that long ago - but you were a little boy then, but now you're eight."

I thought to myself, eight must be a magical age when a boy is supposed to change into King Arthur. But being eight years old, I didn't feel different inside from when I was seven or six.

Grandma continued, "I thought you would grow out of using that word. But since I am leaving and we may not see each other again, I want you to stop using that vulgar word right now."

"If you say so, Grandma. I used to say whoosh whoosh poop, but Marigold told me only sissies used those words. She said, he-men said fart! Marigold told me that you liked he-men and told me to say fart. Fart was a word you liked and that every time you made your noise, I should say fart. So I've always said fart to you but I always liked whoosh whoosh pooooop much better. I think that sounds like a real fart. Don't you, Grandma?"

Marigold stood up, shook her fists and yelled in my face, "I did not tell you to say that to Grandma. You're such a liar. You're always lying, Percy. Grandma, Percy always lies."

I yelled back, "You did, too."

"Stop it, children. Sit down, both of you and be quiet!" The admiral spoke and the swabbies sat down on the floor. The hotel was afloat again because Grandma was no longer decaying. Yippee!

Her eyes blazing hot, Grandma continued her lecture, "Percy, when in polite company, a gentleman does not say anything when a lady makes an indiscretion of any kind. If you must refer to it at all in your own privacy, you say 'breaking wind.'"

"Like a hurricane?" I ran around the room making loud hurricane sounds.

"Settle down, Percy. Come back here and stand next to me. Now let's change the subject," Grandma ordered. She put her handkerchief on the table with her photographs, took in a deep breath and spoke seriously, "Children, your great-grandmother wants to leave you something to remember her by before she sails for Oakland. Percy, go to that drawer." She pointed to her bureau. "Pull out the gold watch you find in the drawer."

I did as she told me and brought back a gold watch with a gold chain attached to it. I held the watch up by its gold chain and swung it back and forth, trying to hypnotize Grandma like Count Dracula did in the movies.

Grandma started to sway, watching me swing the watch, but she caught herself and commanded, "Percy, give me that damn watch."

I handed Grandma the watch and she held it tightly in her fist. She said, "This watch is for you, Percy. It belonged to the Captain. This gold watch is very valuable and my Captain considered it his prized possession." She opened the back of the watch with her fingernail and told me to look at the inscription. Inscribed inside the watch were her captain's name and the date 1865. Grandma handed the watch back to me and asked, "Percy, do you think you can take care of it?"

"Yes, Grandma," I replied.

"Will you think of me?" she asked.

"You're in my prayers every night," I promised.

"I like that, Percy. Always keep me in your prayers."

Marigold watched our "goings on" with jealous green eyes. Grandma turned to Marigold and said, "Now my darling, go into the closet and bring out the Captain's sword."

Marigold ran to the closet and brought out an elaborate sword that any officer would have proudly carried into battle. Grandma explained, "That sword is for you, Marigold. My Captain wore it when he was in the Civil War. He was a brave officer and was very good to his men. They were very loyal to him. My Captain saved many lives on both sides of the war. My Captain was a man of integrity. He helped free the slaves because he volunteered to go into the army and left the sea he loved to fight for the country on land."

"Which side was he on, Grandma?" I asked.

Marigold pulled the sword out of its scabbard and waved it in the air and shouted, "Percy, that's a stupid question to ask Grandma. He was on the winning side, of course."

Grandma said proudly, puffing out her chest, "That he was, Marigold. Look at the blade. There's blood on it."

I ran to Marigold to look at the blade. I saw faded dark brown spots splattered on the steel. I turned to Grandma and said, "It's rust, Grandma."

Marigold gave me a boot in the rear and using her General Ulysses S. Grant voice, menaced, "Twerp, one more word out of you, and I'm going to run you through with my grandpa's sword. If Grandma says that's blood, that's real blood. Right, Grandma? It's going to be your blood next on this sword if you don't shut up."

Marigold had the point of the blade at my throat. Retreating behind Grandma's chair, I thought to myself that Grandma made a big mistake giving

Captain Grandpa's sword to Marigold because I saw myself - because I never kept my mouth shut - dangling at the end of it.

Grandma brought order back by thumping her hand on the table. "Now, calm down, both of you. Marigold, that sword is not meant to hurt your brother or anyone else for that matter. That sword is to symbolize bravery and honor. My husband had both those traits and both those traits I see in you, my darling. Sit down next to me." Marigold sat down and put her arm around Grandma's fat leg.

Michael the mynah returned to the tree branch. He hopped from branch to branch, pecking at lice on his body and watching me with one eye. The room was no longer boring.

Grandma picked up a round jewelry box studded with diamonds and pearls from the table. A scene of Madame Du Barry being pushed on a swing by cherubs was handpainted on the box cover. I loved that jewelry box and remembered it in Grandma's room, on her bureau, placed next to the Captain's picture.

Putting the jewelry box in Marigold's hand, Grandma murmured like Diamond Jim Brady giving Lillian Russell diamonds in a flower basket, "Marigold, this is for you, too!"

Marigold took the box and opened it to find Grandma's treasures, diamond, sapphire and amethyst jewelry. Marigold ooohed and ahhhed as she pulled out necklaces, brooches and rings, but from her eyes, I could tell she liked her sword best. She was just ooohing for Grandma. I would have traded my gold watch in a minute for just one diamond bracelet and Marigold would have traded the whole kit and caboodle for the gold watch.

Marigold batted her brown eyes at Grandma and said in her sweetest voice, "Grandma, can I have the whip too?" I almost fainted. Hearing Marigold's request, I got on my knees, crocodile tears flowing, and pleaded with Grandma not to give Marigold the whip. I told Grandma I would be at the other end of the straps.

Grandma calmed me. She had given the whip to the Hawaii Humane Society. I wished she had given it to the Daughters of Hawaii. Anywhere, but not where Uku might be living.

Calmed now and resting my hand on her shoulder, I asked a question, "Grandma, you love Marigold best of all, don't you?"

"I do love Marigold, Percy. I love her a lot because she was my first grandchild and she was a girl. All my married days, I lived my life with men. I had the Captain, my husband, an only son and four grandsons. I never had a little girl to spoil until Marigold came along. All my life, men surrounded me. When I sailed with the Captain I was the only woman aboard ship, so I had to be strong. I could never be a lady because I didn't want the crew to see me as a weak, helpless female. Dealing with those lazy loafers made me tough and I carried a whip to protect myself and make them carry out my orders. When I said jump, I'd crack the whip and those sailors jumped. You bet they did."

Grandma laughed like an old salt, thinking about it. "Me, a tiny little thing beating up on those six foot bruisers." Patting Marigold on the head, she continued, "That's why I loved you like a boy. I never knew how to treat you any other way. You're just like me, darling."

I interrupted Grandma's train of thought. "Grandma, do you love me?" I didn't know why that came out of my mouth.

"I do, Percy," she answered.

I persisted, "Why do you love me, Grandma?" Marigold groaned, trying to shut me up.

Taking my hand, Grandma said, "Percy, I love you because you amuse me. I never know what's coming out of that mouth and that amuses me."

"Me too, Grandma. I never know what comes out, too. Words just come and I surprise myself all the time by saying things that surprise me."

Grandma squeezed my hand. "Don't lose that, Percy. Amuse people. We don't laugh enough in this world."

I sat down next to Marigold with her sword lying between us. We both thanked our great-grandmother for being like our grandmother because we never had a grandmother. Both our grandmothers died before we were born. We thanked her for loving us, each in her own special different way.

"Grandma," I piped up, "tell us your stories again till Mother comes back."

Marigold took over, "Tell us about that big storm at sea with waves a hundred feet tall that crashed over the bow of the ship and how you almost drowned. Tell us about the Captain in the Civil War...."

I interrupted, "And about the French revolution and how they chopped everyone's heads off. Tell us stories, Grandma," Marigold and I said together, "just like you used to do."

Grandma instantly grew taller and became bigger than the chair. She was no longer a dying pigmy in a wicker coffin. She spent the rest of the afternoon telling us stories we had heard a thousand times, and in those few hours, we were once again back on the Kapaka Street lanai, sitting at Grandma's feet, hearing her tales. They were tales she told us before the divorce happened, and when Marigold and I thought our lives were going to be always sweet and secure.

Mother came for us at four. Her "or so" had run into a couple of hours. I was glad she was late and Grandma said she was glad she missed her nap. Mother looked harried, her hair tossed every which way as if she had been running around doing a ton of errands. Mother told Grandma she'd take Grandma to lunch the next day, and then they could have their own private visit. Grandma smiled and took Mother's hand and said she'd love it.

Mother also suggested she'd bring us back before she left on the ship for Oakland. Grandma paused, then said, "Deidra, don't bring the children back. This has been a perfect day for all three of us and it would break my heart to see them again. We've had such a lovely afternoon, and it's hard enough for me to leave them now. Let's keep it as it is. We've said our good-byes."

I hated good-byes.

We kissed our great-grandma farewell forever. For the first time I saw on her road-mapped face that once looked as fierce as a figurehead on her Captain's ship, a tear running down her cheek. I watched the tear as it meandered its way down her roadmap of earned wrinkles. A smudge of pink face powder stopped the tear from continuing its voyage to her chin. Watching Grandma's tear disappear in her pink face powder, I never loved her as much as I did that afternoon. That tear is my most cherished memory of the Captain's mate.

Riding down in the creaky elevator, we learned where Mother had been that afternoon. Seeing the terrible state of Grandma's room, Mother was so furious with the hotel management that she immediately went into the manager's office and told him off. She told the manager (I imagined him cowering behind his desk) what a disgrace Grandma's room was and they, the hotel, had better - before the sun set - have it cleaned and put in perfect order. Mother made it very clear to the manager she would check daily on Grandma till Grandma left for the Mainland, and if she ever again found Grandma's room in the same deplorable state, Mother would see to it that her cousin, Chief Justice Judd, closed the hotel down immediately.

Mother was also furious with Daddy and his brothers for ignoring Grandma and letting her live in that "uncalled-for state of squalor." Before we stepped out of the elevator, in a voice filled with emotion, Mother told us she was most of all ashamed of herself because she had let Grandma down. She shouldn't have let a divorce from Daddy stand in the way of taking care of an old lady who was her children's great-grandmother.

Mother took Grandma to lunch the next day and they renewed their friendship. The hotel manager kept to his word and Grandma's room was spick and span until she left for Oakland. Mother checked on Grandma every day. Her grandsons, my father included, filled her room with her favorite flowers, yellow day lilies and white roses.

Grandma left on the next sailing of the Lurline. We would miss Grandma's stories forever, and much of what she told us on those days when we sat at her feet has been forgotten in time.

I told Agnes and Gertrude, if Daddy so easily abandoned Grandma, who loved him more than all the riches in the world, to the Pleasanton Hotel and Oakland, California, I worried that he'd abandon anybody, even his precious Marigold. I never considered myself in the running for his affection.

I did have Mother and I pledged to take care of her even when she became an old lady of forty and to make certain that she didn't rot away in a room at the Pleasanton Hotel.

38

Charlie

Mother had good news. Hatsuko was coming to visit and going to introduce her Charlie Anthony to the family. Charlie returned from active duty in the Philippines and was now stationed on the battleship Arizona, anchored in Pearl Harbor. Hatsuko and Charlie, the newlyweds, had finished moving into their new quarters on the Pearl Harbor Navy base. Hatsuko was the only full-blooded Japanese that I knew who was living on an American base.

Hatsuko and Charlie set their visit for Sunday afternoon at teatime. That after-noon, Mother and I caught the early matinee of *Tin Pan Alley* at the Princess Theater. It starred Alice Faye and a 20th Century Fox upstart, Betty Grable. Betty Grable was trying to take over Alice Faye's stardom at Fox. Betty didn't have a fat chance, as far as I was concerned, because she had dumpy legs. Gertrude and Agnes said that I looked at Betty Grable and people I didn't like with a warped eye.

Hatsuko and Charlie drove up to our house in a beat-up 1938 Dodge sedan. When Hatsuko got out of the car, I saw she had painted her lips like Maria Montez did, the sultry movie actress in the movie *South of Tahiti*. She had lost her Ann Sheridan look. Her lips were smeared grape juice purple and she tied a Shirley Temple purple bow in her hair. The bow matched the Maria Montez purple blouse and slacks outfit and she looked a thousand times prettier than Dorothy Lamour ever did.

Charlie got out of the car, ran around it, and stood beside Hatsuko like he owned her. He put his arm around her waist and beamed a hundred sunbeams into her eyes. A hundred thoughts raced through my head as I looked at Charlie with Hatsuko. I saw right away that he had crooked teeth and was much too skinny to be a manly sailor. I couldn't imagine him fighting on a battleship and defending my country because he looked so puny. A small gust of wind could blow him overboard into the propeller. Giving him another once-over, I saw that his uniform hung on his body like an old rice sack and beneath the middy blouse, only bones showed. Shaking hands with Mother, Charlie had to pull up his pants to keep them from falling to his ankles, and I told Agnes that he must have a huge tapeworm in his stomach eating up all his food because he was so skinny. He wasn't fat like me.

When Charlie shook my hand, I looked up at a face that had ugly fuzz on it. I don't think he ever shaved in his whole life because a fine layer of orange fluff grew almost invisibly where a dark manly beard should have bloomed. Charlie was a total mess and I could see that he was not the right man for my goddess, Hatsuko. I felt sorry for my best friend having to hitch herself up to such a goofy looking person, when she could have married Tyrone Power. As I walked behind Hatsuko and Charlie into the house, I thought that it must have been a real dark night when they met because Charlie was no dreamboat. Hatsuko probably married Charlie out of the goodness of her heart because Hatsuko's heart was as kind and pure as the Virgin Mary's, and she couldn't hurt anyone's feelings, so she just couldn't say no when he asked her to marry him.

Hatsuko needed eyeglasses.

Mother escorted Hatsuko and Charlie into the living room as if they were the king and queen of England. She sat them down and passed teacups, after pouring tea from her precious sterling silver tea set. Mother never did that for Cousin Bessie. Helen the Vomit-Head had made two dozen tiny tea sandwiches the day before, which were on a silver platter in front of them.

Marigold ran into the living room in her bare feet, late like Daddy and stinking in her ripped blue jeans. My sister had a bad case of impetigo, an infectious skin disease that had turned round, purple and pussy on her left ankle. She showed off her pussy, purple sore to everyone like it was a Purple Heart medal.

Right off the bat, even before Hatsuko took her first sip of tea, I tried to make her jealous. Ignoring Charlie, turning my back on him, I said in a sassy voice, "Guess what I did today?"

"What, Percy? What did you do today? Charlie and I would like to know," Hatsuko replied.

"I saw a movie."

"What did you see?" she asked.

"Alice Faye in *Tin Pan Alley*! It's the best movie I have ever seen. Too bad you couldn't have seen it with me. But then I didn't miss you," I gloated.

"Oh, I liked it too. Charlie and I saw it last week," Hatsuko answered.

I yelped, "You saw it last week without me?"

"Yes, aren't I the lucky one? Charlie takes me to the movies now that you seem to be so busy going to movies with other people - and Charlie hates going to movies," she added.

I pouted, "I'm not that busy and I only go with Mother or by myself."

Hatsuko didn't look at all concerned that I had seen an Alice Faye movie without her and she wasn't acting jealous at all. All Hatsuko seemed interested in was Charlie because they kept holding hands and looking at each other.

I stopped talking because I was so mad at her. Mother and Marigold were chatting like magpies to them as if they were very best friends and as if they had known Charlie forever. I kept thinking to myself, "Hey, wait a minute, Hatsuko is *my* best friend. Boy, oh boy, where did my best friend go to?"

Marigold and Charlie had become buddies in seconds because he told her he once had impetigo on his rear end. After he told her that, he laughed like a hyena and showed every one of his crooked teeth. Charlie sucked in a lot of air when he talked.

He bragged on to Marigold that he was a gunner's mate. (Marigold loved any-thing to do with guns, so that made her adore Charlie even more.) Not to be out-done, Marigold ran into her room and brought out the Captain's sword - blood and all - to show off to Charlie. He had Marigold in the palm of his hands and she snuggled up to him like he was Daddy, and they told tall stories to each other like they were seasoned old salts.

I bet he got seasick too.

I overheard Charlie inviting Marigold to his next open house onboard the Arizona. He promised to show her his gun emplacement and where he planned to shoot down enemy planes if they attacked Pearl Harbor. Marigold giggled like a Girl Scout as he lied about his heroic deeds as a sailor. I could have strangled them both.

The afternoon was a disaster. A San Francisco earthquake would have seemed a fairy dance to all the shaking that was going on inside of my belly. Nobody was paying any attention to me so I started counting how many finger sandwiches everyone was eating. Hatsuko had four. Charlie had twelve. Mother held back. I forgot how much Marigold took because I watched Charlie eat most of them and I crowned him the biggest pig of the afternoon. Charlie told Mother at least five times that they were the best sandwiches he had ever "et" in his whole life. After he'd say that to Mother, he'd grab two more sandwiches off the platter, one in each hand, and stuff them through his crooked teeth into his mouth.

Hatsuko turned to me, looking at her watch, and questioned, "Percy, why are you so quiet this afternoon? We have to go pretty soon. Isn't there anything you'd like to tell me?"

"No," I said as I grabbed the last cheese sandwich away from Charlie. I was tired of his gobbling up all *my* sandwiches.

Hatsuko persisted, "Percy, would you like to feel my baby?"

I had forgotten about the baby. Swallowing down the cheese sandwich in one bite, I said, surprised, "Your baby? How do I feel a baby when it's not here?"

"Come over and sit next to me," she said. I moved next to Hatsuko and put my hand on her belly. I hadn't noticed until then how big her belly had grown. Hatsuko wasn't skinny any more but I knew she was too nice to have tapeworms like her Charlie had. I was going to suggest to Hatsuko to take him to Dr. Pinkerton's and get him dewormed.

I placed my hand on Hatsuko's belly and felt boomp ta, boomp ta, boomp ta sounds. Then something moved under my hand. Startled, I asked, "Is that your baby?"

"It's my baby, Percy. Come, Marigold, feel my baby, too."

Marigold slid over and we both placed our hands, then our heads on Hatsuko's stomach. For several minutes, we listened to the baby's heartbeat and I forgot about being jealous. I sat up, turned to Mother and asked, "Did I sound like that when I was in your belly?"

"Both you and Marigold did," Mother answered.

"Was I in a swimming pool in your stomach? I mean did I swim around inside of you?" I asked.

Lighting the first cigarette for the evening, Mother crossed her legs and answered, "Yes, you might say that but I never thought about it in that way."

I turned to everyone and exclaimed, "I knew. I knew it. I just knew it. I knew I swam around in my mother's stomach."

With her ear on Hatsuko's belly, counting the baby's beats by drumming her fingers on Hatsuko's belly, Marigold looked up at me and said, "Percy, I'm going to haul you off to the loony bin if you keep talking like that. You never knew anything like that." Putting her head up, Marigold turned to Charlie and said solemnly, "Charlie, my brother can be very embarrassing at times. Most of the time, he just doesn't make any sense. No sense at all and I apologize for him."

"Marigold, stop talking about your brother like that. Percy is just being creative," Mother defended me as she squished her cigarette in the ashtray.

"I just wish he'd be creative by himself. When he's in company why can't he just act normal." Marigold sighed, meaning I was hopeless, and put her head back down on Hatsuko's stomach. Hatsuko squeezed my hand. She and Mother understood me like no one else ever did.

Listening to the baby's heartbeat again, I watched Charlie eat the last egg salad sandwich. He sure was a fast grabber. Mother had lectured me before the guests arrived for "family to hold back." What she meant was "Percy, hold back" because she didn't want me to eat up all the food before the guests arrived. I always cheated. After the movie, I had sneaked into the kitchen before Hatsuko and Charlie arrived and, without anyone looking, ate two tuna sandwiches in two swallows. Egg salad sandwiches were not touched because they were Hatsuko's favorite sandwiches.

Hatsuko rose from the couch after looking at her watch again and announced that she and Charlie had to leave because they were going to meet Rose and have *saimin* (Japanese soup) at a new Japanese restaurant on the corner of Kalakaua and Beretania Street. Charlie groaned as he got off the couch, rubbing his belly, and said that his stomach was now as big as Hatsuko's. He shook Mother's hand hard and gushed, "Thank you, ma'am. Best sandwiches I ever 'et.' You were real sweet to ask us into your home."

I swore to Gertrude and Agnes that those were the only sensible words I overheard him speak all afternoon. Otherwise as far as I was concerned, he was as dumb as a hillbilly from Arkansas.

Standing by the car, I kissed Hatsuko goodbye and whispered in her ear, "Please, Hatsuko, take me to a movie soon. Helen doesn't make egg salad sandwiches like you do and she's not like you at all. She hates me."

Hatsuko whispered back, "The first Saturday Charlie has day duty, we'll go to the movies. Promise."

I put my lips right next to Hatsuko's ear and said as softly as I could, "Don't name your baby Percy. Percy is an awful name." Hatsuko whispered back, "I like the name Percy."

Putting my lips closer to her ear, I pleaded, "Hatsuko, please don't do that. Please. Percy is a cursed name."

She said, "Give me a kiss on the cheek and I'll do anything you ask, Percy." I kissed her hard on the cheek and another one right on her Maria Montez lips.

Looking to see if Charlie was listening, I whispered softer, "Thank you,

Hatsuko, for not naming your baby Percy. I'll love you always. And please don't say goodbye to me." Hatsuko kissed me on the cheek as Charlie, standing next to Mother, watched us. I swear his crooked teeth almost fell out of his mouth when she kissed me.

After Hatsuko and Charlie chugged off in his beat-up Dodge, Mother and Marigold walked back into the living room to straighten up. I couldn't believe my ears at what they said about Charlie. They were praising him to the heavens as if he was a Greek god. Mother, speaking like an elementary school teacher who was talking about an A-student in her class, said to Marigold, "Marigold, I think Hatsuko has done really well for herself. Charlie is such a fine, bright, outstanding, handsome young man. I'm really glad for her and he's sooooo good looking."

Mother handed the empty sandwich dish to Marigold, who replied, her eyes showing adoration, "Mother, he asked me to come aboard the Arizona on family day. Isn't that keen, Mother? He's woooooonderful. Please let me go?"

Mother agreed, "I'll let you go with him any day. There's a man you can trust. That's a man who will really protect our country. I feel safe just having him around and serving Uncle Sam."

I gagged and wanted to throw up all over them.

Marigold swooned around the room like a star-struck movie fan, mooning to me, "He's the handsomest sailor I have ever seen in my life. He's better looking than your old beat-up Tyrone Power. Mother, what a wow he was in that sailor suit. I can see why Hatsuko married him. Can't you, Percy?"

I wanted to punch her in the face.

Mother and Marigold made more swooning sounds around me as they giggled their way out into the kitchen. I wanted to take Grandpa's sword off the couch and run them through, and then beat them to a pulp until they talked sense to me again. I stood flabbergasted hearing what they were saying about dorky old Charlie, and my mouth hung open like a whale ready to swallow a squadron of Japanese flying fish. What Mother and Marigold saw through their eyes sure didn't match what I saw through mine.

One of us was crazy, and it wasn't me because Charlie the sailor was as skinny and as ugly as a monkey in the zoo. He was even uglier than Hitler. While I was counting all the ugly facts about Charlie, if I had looked into the mirror, I would have noticed that my face had turned a repulsive shade of green, the color of the snake in the Garden of Eden.

While Mother and Marigold were in the kitchen, giggling like schoolgirls and washing dishes, I pounded my fists in a jealous rage on the couch where Charlie sat. I turned into a madman.

and Bad Breath is to Blame!

39

More Goodbyes

Two nights after Charlie and Hatsuko's visit, while listening to the "Lone Ranger" on my radio (the radio Daddy gave me for my birthday that I expected him to take back), Mother asked if she could come into my bedroom. She asked me quietly to turn off the Lone Ranger because she had something very important to tell me. I knew it must be important because she knew how much I loooooved the Lone Ranger and Tonto. I told everyone in the house that I was not to be interrupted when I was listening to the Lone Ranger, even if the house was burning to the ground.

Mother sat down on my bed and folded her hands. I thought she was going to pray when she said, "Percy, I want you to pay attention to me. I have something very important to say to you and I want you to hear me clearly. Are you listening?"

I nodded. Actually, one part of my mind was still roaming on a prairie with the Lone Ranger, who was about to rescue Tonto who was hanging from a tree. Another part of my mind said I wished she'd hurry up and get to the point and wondered why she kept asking me to pay attention.

"Are you sure you're listening to me?" she repeated. I nodded a fast yes, yes, yes, trying to please her, but I wanted to turn on the radio again. Fidgeting with her wedding ring, Mother started to speak slowly. It was as if she wanted everything she was about to tell me to sink in my brain. "Before Grandma left, she gave me some money to do something nice for myself. Grandma said I needed it. And I do, Percy, I do need it. It's been a hard year for me. Now I hope you'll understand this - and this is not permanent - but I'm going away."

Mother now had my full attention. The Lone Ranger galloped out of my mind and my alert buttons were beeping. I gasped, "Going away? You're leaving me too? You can't." I started to gulp for air because all of a sudden, I was dying.

The phone rang. Mother got off the bed and went to answer it. She instructed me as she was going out the door, "Percy, I'll be right back. It's not as bad as it sounds. You stay put and calm down until I get back. Please, don't act so dramatic."

I began pacing the room as she talked on the phone. I walked round and round in circles. Faster, faster, faster, I walked. I was little Black Sambo turning into butter. My alarms were ringing so loudly in my head that I couldn't think straight about anything. All I could hear was my mother's voice saying that she was leaving me and I was drowning in her words. Agnes and Gertrude were trying to reach me and telling me to calm down, but my line rang busy.

Mother stayed on the phone for a long time. It seemed like a hundred birthdays had gone by before she returned. Her face looked as if Dracula had sucked out all her blood. The only color in her face was her bright, blue eyes ringed in red. Without a word, she grabbed me and held me tight into her body. Tears were rolling down her face.

She moaned and then began to talk to me, like the minister does when he gives a sermon, way down in his throat. "That was Aunt Ella. She and Uncle Will are at The Young Hotel. Kimo is missing in action. They just heard by wireless that his plane went down in the English Channel. There doesn't seen to be any reason for it as there weren't any German planes in the skies. His plane just crashed. God has taken Kimo away from us."

Mother's tears fell on my head so hard that they plastered down my cowlick. Her tears were like Kimo's swimming pool water dripping on my head at Christmas time, when Kimo and I were sitting by the side of the pool and he had just rescued my toy submarine. Mother kept holding onto me, not saying a word, as I was remembering that time. We were both crying.

I remembered Kimo's water dripping on my head - plunk, plunk, plunk, as he dried me off. He had become serious, looking at the toy submarine lying beside us. He told me that no one should die of neglect, not even a toy submarine. He said the submarine met a disgraceful end for a valiant little toy. He called it an ignominious ending.

I had asked him what "ignominious" meant because that was a new word to me. He said it meant that this toy submarine had died with dishonor because someone had been careless at the factory, or worse, someone had been lazy and knowingly sent the submarine out from the factory with a missing part. He spat out the word lazy as if he had drunk in dirty sewer water.

Kimo, drying off my hair, warned me, "Don't be a lazy person, Percy. Make every moment count and pay attention to life. Be alive. You know, Percy, I dreamed recently that one day I was going to end up like this submarine, dead at the bottom of a big swimming pool."

"You mean dead like dead?" I asked him.

"Dead like dead, Percy. Laziness kills and is the biggest sin in the world."

I pried myself from Mother's arms, walked over to my window seat, sat down, and said to no one in particular, "I knew it. I just knew it. I just knew I'd never see him again when he left us on the Lurline." I looked up at my mother and said, "Everybody is saying goodbye, Mother. And now you're leaving me, too. Where are you going?"

She replied, "Percy, it's not as bad as it sounds. I'll tell you all about it when I come home. Right now Aunt Ella and Uncle Will need me terribly. I have to go to them."

In my little boy voice, I called to her, "But I need you, too."

"Percy, you're eight. You're a big boy. I'll tell you all about it when I get back. Don't pout. Go into the kitchen and have a dish of ice cream. I'll be home before you know it. Aunt Ella has just lost her baby and I know how I would feel if I lost you. Have some ice cream. It will make you feel better. I just bought your favorite Dairymen's chocolate ice cream."

"Mother?" I asked. "What?" she answered as she walked away.

I added, "Tell Aunt Ella I miss him too. Tell her that he wanted to have a little baby girl named Mary Emily." Mother nodded and left for The Young Hotel.

I walked into her bedroom, down in the dumps, and jumped on her bed to wait for her to come back. I lay on top of the covers so she'd be forced to wake me and talk to me when she came home from visiting Aunt Ella.

Mother didn't drive into our garage until past midnight. I was not asleep. I could hear her tiptoeing through the house, trying not to wake anyone, and she was surprised to find me awake on top of her bed. She sighed wearily, "Percy, I hoped that you'd be asleep by now."

I sat up and said loudly, "I'm not. How could you expect me to sleep when you're leaving me? Tell me where you're going?"

Mother sat next to me. "Please, Percy, not now. I'm bone weary. It's been very hard on me being with Aunt Ella and Uncle Will. Be my sweetheart and go to bed. I promise you, I'll tell you all about it tomorrow. There is nothing for you to worry about. Please believe me."

"Did you tell Marigold?" I demanded.

"Yes," she answered.

"What did she say?"

"She thinks it's going to be a great big adventure. In the morning, I'll tell you all about it," Mother promised.

"Marigold thinks everything is a great big adventure. I don't trust her great big adventures. She thinks digging for worms is a great big adventure," I grumbled.

Lifting me off her bed, Mother said crossly, "Get in your own bed, Percy. Please, I have to teach tomorrow."

I thumped the floor going back to my bedroom, thundering that no one loved me, and got under the covers. I knew for certain that I wasn't going to sleep and was going to stay wide awake, like on those nights when I watched Charlie walk out of Hatsuko's room. Looking out the window, I saw that the moon was new, a silver crescent shape hanging in the sky, going in and out behind dark clouds.

I slept. I dreamt that Kimo was trapped in his airplane at the bottom of a swimming pool, trying to get out. He couldn't open the cockpit window because I had locked it by mistake. Kimo waved to me, under the water from inside the cockpit, yelling at me to find the key. I burst into tears because I didn't know where I put the key. He kept telling me to look inside the icebox next to the mayonnaise jar. I looked, but it wasn't there. He was dying. I failed him because I had been careless.

I woke up sweating. Agnes and Gertrude were lying next to me. I cried to them that if Mother left me like Daddy did, I wanted to join Kimo at the bottom of the English Channel, drowned in his cockpit.

My head throbbed for the rest of the night, tapping out Morse code signals; "Why is Mother leaving me? Why is Mother leaving me? Why is Mother leaving me?"

The next door neighbor's toilet flushed. It was morning.

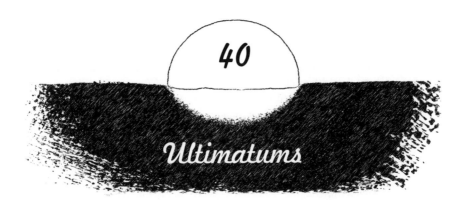

40

Ultimatums

The Honolulu Advertiser wrote that Alice Faye had eloped in Mexico. She married Phil Harris, the loudmouth jokester on the Jack Benny radio show. I wrote her a letter of congratulations.

1941

Dear Alice Faye - my favorite movie star
I red in the newspapers that you maried
Mr. Fil Harris.
Congratulatons.

I red in my anut momi's fotoplay magazine that yoo said kising Tyrone Power was like going to henven. Whot does kising fil harries feel like?
I gues it's bettre to have some one to laugh with than going to heaven. Fil Harries makes me laugh. I hope he makes you laugh becuz he is not as handsome as Tyrone Power.
Sincerely yor friend,
Percy
P.S. I stil wold like to be just like you!
P.S. S. My mother is going to Tahiti - that's where Dorothy Lamour was borned and raised! (Sme peole say Dorothy was borned in Texas and run an elevator in Chicao. I nevr believed that because she wore a saroong.)

"What you think about strongly, all the time, every waking moment of your life, is what you will get someday." That's what Gertrude said on the day Mother announced at breakfast that she was taking a cruise to Tahiti.

Since the day Daddy left, I feared that Mother would abandon me, too.

Gertrude said the fear that I kept down inside my stomach had now come true. I moaned to Gertrude, "I'm like Kimo. He believed he would drown at the bottom of a swimming pool - and look, Gertrude, he did. I believe, in my heart of hearts,

that one day everyone in my world will leave me. Even you and Agnes will leave
me. I know it."

"Stop it," Gertrude snapped.

"I can't help it. I know I'm going to end up dead like Kimo at the bottom of
something. I'll be dead like that baby in China - that *LIFE* magazine photograph I
hate." Gertrude and Agnes yelled back, "No, you're not."

The morning after I heard Kimo's plane was missing over the English
Channel, Mother broke the news. At breakfast, she told me she was spending
Grandma's money to board the Matson liner, Mariposa, for a three-week cruise to
the South Seas. She had booked to leave for Tahiti the week after school let out for
summer vacation. She was traveling in a party with her cousins and a few school
chums from Mills College.

After Mother gave me the news of her trip, I finished my bacon and eggs, and
I decided to throw a major, major tantrum to keep her from leaving me. I started
by putting a napkin over my face and crying, "Mother, I am dying of a terrible disease and I have only a few weeks to live. Have pity on me." I got up and choked
myself, fell down and wiggled all over the dining room floor as if I was dying of
the Spanish flu.

Mother crossed her legs and lit a cigarette.

Next, I acted like I was taking a painful dump on the toilet. "Ohhhhh, Mother,
my doodoo smells awful. I know I have worms as big as dinosaur eggs. They're
ooogy green and make me smell like a rotten egg." Holding onto my stomach, jiggling my fat, I continued, "They are moving around in my stomach and eating me
up. They're making a sandwich of my liver right now. I can feel them. You have to
stay home and see I do number two good again."

Mother picked up the *Advertiser* and held it in front of her face.

I hit the newspaper. "I'm going to read in the newspaper that you were torpedoed by a Japanese submarine and eaten up by sharks." I ran around the dining
room table, making like a torpedo heading for a ship and shouted a huge explosion
in her ear.

Mother put down the newspaper, rolled her eyes to the ceiling, picked up the
newspaper, and went back to reading the society page.

I got on my knees and begged, "Mother, please stay with me because
Marigold will behead me with Grandpa's sword if you're not around to protect
me." I put my head down on the table, made my arm into an ax and pretended to
chop my head off. I rolled my head on the table, making gagging sounds and finally sticking out my tongue.

Mother yawned and kept sipping her coffee. I ripped *The Honolulu Advertiser*
out of her hands, sat down and pretended to read the front page, "A passenger ship
has just been hit by a Japanese mine floating off Bora Bora and the ship sunk to
the bottom of the sea. All women drowned first." I pretended I was Alice Faye
drowning. A giant squid was strangling me. I screamed "help, help" and sang
"Alexander's Ragtime Band" at the same time. I picked up Mother's glass of
water, drank, and spit water up into the air as if I was drowning.

Mother picked up a napkin and wiped off her face. I had sprayed my pretend
ocean water on her unintentionally. She still wasn't reacting to my acts. Mother

grabbed the newspaper away from me without saying a word and started to read again.

I took her napkin and pretended to cry. "Mother, we have never been parted before. Why do you prefer a trip to the South Seas over me?" I watched her face for a trace of guilt, but there wasn't a flicker showing, not even in her eyelashes. She just wasn't biting.

Next, I wailed, "Mother, you're never coming back to me because you're going to marry the king of Tahiti and have a thousand children and forget me." I made my arms into a cradle and cooed to an imaginary baby, "You're much cuter than fat little Percy I left back in Hawaii."

Finally, a smile whispered across her lips.

In the grand finale that I hoped would plunge a dagger into her heart, I performed a scene, playing it like screen actress, Bette Davis, in her role as the tyrant Queen Elizabeth the Great of England. I drawled slowly like Bette, "If you go away from me, I'll never speak to you again and I will never 'evah, evah, evah, evah love you - evaaaaah again.' " I said this loudly straight into her face, drawing up all the hurt feelings stuffed down inside my stomach. After I finished saying the "evahs," I plopped myself down in a chair, exhausted.

Across the table, Mother stared at me without any change in expression. She folded her napkin, placed it in its silver napkin ring, set it next to her plate, looked me straight in the eye, and said without a speck of feeling in her voice, "Percy, you're acting silly again." She rose from her seat as calmly as a sea at low tide and started to walk out. Then she stopped, turned back, and spoke so softly I could barely make out what she was saying to me. She whispered, "Percy, don't you want me to be a little happy? I'll be away only for a couple weeks."

She lied. The cruise was scheduled for a three-week voyage, that is, if you took the ship onto New Zealand and Australia. Mother turned, walked out of the room and drove to Punahou to teach her class of twenty-three third graders who treated her a thousand times better than I just did. Mother left me with a dagger sticking in my heart and bleeding because of her parting words. She engulfed me in a cocoon of guilt.

Mother was like President Roosevelt to me. President Roosevelt and Mother were gods who were centers of my universe. I could not think of living in a world without either one of them.

In a week, Kimo was officially reported dead by the Royal Canadian Air Force. His body was never recovered. If anyone thought to ask me, I knew where he was. Kimo was trapped in his plane's cockpit at the bottom of the English Channel because I had lost the key to get him out. I dreamed that dream every night for a month.

Aunt Ella and Uncle Will received a cable that a plaque in his memory had been placed in a little English cemetery near Windsor Castle. They received letters of sympathy from the King of England, Prime Minister Winston Churchill and even a telegram from President Roosevelt. Agnes sighed that those letters and telegram were worth dying for. I was shocked at Agnes saying such a thing because I wanted Kimo back alive.

Gertrude, on the other hand, wept. She told me there was nothing worth dying for when you were young, handsome as a Greek god and living in the best part of your life. Good men shouldn't die because of a mean old nasty Hitler, who was killing harmless women and children in Poland and France. Hitler should be dead at the bottom of the English Channel.

Daddy was right. War, like a divorce, does terrible things to people.

Gertrude beat Agnes over her head with my pillow, yelling, "GOD IS UNFAIR. I DON'T UNDERSTAND WHY WARS ARE SO POPULAR? SOME PEOPLE LIKE WARS BETTER THAN EATING A BEST FOODS MAYON-NAISE SANDWICH." Gertrude, sounding a lot like Hitler, hit Agnes every time she opened her mouth that afternoon.

Daddy phoned the night after I heard that Kimo died, on the day when Mother told me she was going to Tahiti, and at dinner, I ate three huge helpings of creamed tuna and rice. Mother had mailed my report card to him. My grades were not up to snuff - not an A, B, or C in sight. My D in math lay down at the bottom of my wishing well, making nodding acquaintance with my other D's. Comments from Miss Wood written at the bottom of the report card read, "If Percy wasn't so dreamy in class and applied himself more, he could be an excellent student again and should be getting A's." The last sentence was underlined in red ink - "Percy is not reaching his potential."

When Mother told me that Daddy was on the line and wanted to talk to me, I knew I was in big doodoo. I picked up the telephone like a hot potato and heard, before I said hello, Billy Goat Gruff's voice boom, "Percy?"

"Yes, Daddy! It's me."

"I received your report card," he said.

"That's good, Daddy."

"What do you have to say for yourself?" he asked.

"It's a pretty card if you like D's," I lamely answered.

"What are you going to do about it?" he demanded.

"I am going to try harder, Daddy."

Daddy paused and drank his "oats." After a long sip, Daddy Goat Gruff snorted and pawed the dirt in frustration, as he thought about his next sentence. "Percy, why can't you be more like Marigold?"

I replied quickly, "Marigold was born smart. I was born different. That's the reason, Daddy."

"You were born smart, too. You just don't apply yourself. Are you listening to me?" he asked.

There was that "listening" word again. If my parents talked to me about interesting things like Alice Faye, mayonnaise and movies, I would listen more. Returning from dreamland, I replied, "I'm listening, Daddy. I promise I will try harder. (Pause.) Daddy, can I say something?"

"I'm listening, Percy.

"Don't forget about Marigold," I told him.

Daddy died on the spot because he stopped snorting. I heard him take another sip. He suddenly became so quiet, I thought maybe I'd better hang up and call for an ambulance. Then Daddy breathed again. "Percy, that's none of your business.

You may be sure I haven't forgotten about your sister. Her report card is a joy to read," he said.

"Daddy, that's because she's smarter than God. (Pause.) Daddy, please see her more often. Please. She misses you. All she talks about is wanting to run away from us to see you," I explained.

"You tell her we can all go to a ball game next Saturday."

"I hope so, Daddy, otherwise I'm going have to give you a D on your report card. Then I'll really be a chip off the old block," I retorted.

Daddy Goat Gruff's voice roared, "Goodbye, Percy." He hung up.

"Goodbye, Daddy!" I hung up the phone, too.

That night, I gave Billy Goat Gruff a big D on his report card.

I was determined to buckle down at school because I didn't want any more grumpy phone calls from Billy Goat Gruff and I wanted more than anything to keep my mind busy because my anchor, my mother, was leaving for Tahiti. The first thing I did, thinking it would raise my grades was to tryout to be a star at the May Day celebration. In Aunt Momi's *Photoplay* magazine, Hollywood gossip columnist Louella Parsons wrote that when you become a star, fans forget that you had the D's on your report card. Joan Crawford had D's in everything from the fifth grade on.

While Mother busied herself writing for a passport and buying a new set of luggage at Liberty House, I sat in my bedroom, pondering my curse. I shuddered to think what was going to happen to me in the months to come without my protectors, Mother and Hatsuko, to save me from myself.

41

The Pageants

The Honolulu Advertiser

MAY 1ST IS LEI DAY IN HAWAII

Lei Day is distinctively a Hawaiian holiday devoted to perpetuating what the world knows as the island's most charming custom, the wearing of gay flower garlands. Wear a lei today, for this day is set apart to honor the spirit of friendliness.

The mayor asks everyone to wear a lei today and announces the Lei Day Program below:

Noon to 12:20 - Concert by the Royal Hawaiian Band at City Hall.

12:30 p.m. - Lei exhibit open in the City Hall. May Queen and court appear. Chants by Malia Kau.

12:30 to 1 p.m. - Royal Hawaiian Band Glee club.

1 to 1:30 p.m. - Music by Al Kealoha Perry's Surfriders.

1:30 p.m. Music by Josephine Ikuwa and singers and Police Glee Club, with Joe Ikeole Jr. leading.

2:30 p.m. to 3:30 p.m. - Music by John Almeida's singers from the recreation and playground commission.

3 p.m. -Mayor Petrie awards lei prizes.

5 p.m. - Lei Day pageant and coronation of Lei Day queen, University of Hawaii amphitheater.

STORY OF PUNAHOU SCHOOL'S CENTURY

A pageant is going to turn Honolulu upside down - figuratively and literally. Picture, if you can, a cast of more than 1,000 - special costumes for 640 of them - the largest revolving stage ever to be used in a Hawaii production - an actual railway operating in the course of the presentation - an expenditure of more than $8,000 - cooperation of every leading firm in the city and county of Honolulu - if you can, then you have some idea of the magnitude of the Punahou Centennial Pageant.

It's a vast undertaking that writers, directors and the cast of this production are participating in. For not only will this pageant picture 100 years in the life of Punahou, but also 100 years in the life of Honolulu, with all the pomp and ceremony attendant to the hey-day of royalty, the excitement of the annexation when the Islands became a territory of the United States, and the public examination before King Kalakaua, among a few of the scenes which will require hundreds of players and hours of technical background.

Elroy Fulmer, Honolulu Community Theater director and a member of the Punahou faculty, is general director for the entire pageant.

I loved May Day. It was an all day festival honoring the arrival of spring. The Lei Day celebration was unique to the Hawaiian Islands. It was a day when a court of pretty women reigned over special kingdoms. A queen and several princesses made up the courts, each princess representing the seven major islands in the Hawaiian chains. The queen and her court rules for one whole day. Their kingdoms varied; some were elementary schools like mine, others were the city hall and parks on various islands.

On May 1st, I was crushed because no one asked me to wear a crown.

Another school event that caught my attention, which I hoped would make me a star, was the centennial celebration of Punahou School. Punahou was founded in 1841, the first private school west of the Rockies. The trustees of the school asked Hawaii's most notable, prominent and richest citizen to be in charge of the centennial celebration. Mr. Walter Dillingham, sitting at the head of the volunteer table and at the urging of the school's drama teacher, Elroy Fulmer, was convinced that this was a time for Punahou to pull out all the stops.

Therefore, this centennial celebration was heralded around Hawaii to be the pageant of all pageants - *kilohana*, not to be compared. All the trustees wanted a theatrical spectacle to bring Punahou and Hawaii to world and national recognition. The school, therefore, spent a minor fortune on the event that included constructing a gigantic outdoor theatre on the track field that advertised a revolving stage, a first in the islands. Railroad tracks were laid in front of the stage so that a steam locomotive with cane cars could puff by the audience watching from the bleachers. The locomotive was there to dramatically depict the overwhelming influence of the sugar industry in Hawaii. Mr. Fulmer cast thousands of local people to enact not only the history of Punahou but of the Hawaiian Islands. The pageant was titled "Punahou, One Hundred Years - the Story of an Era." The script was written by a group of the finest writers in Hawaii and it narrated the 100 years when Hawaii turned from being a royal kingdom, to the revolution, annexation, and becoming a United States territory.

Through Mr. Dillingham's influence, letters of congratulations and money poured in from all over the world. A letter from the Duke of Windsor, who was the Governor of the Bahama Islands and a visitor to the Hawaiian Islands a decade before, was printed boldly on the front page of *The Honolulu Advertiser*. The Duke didn't send a farthing.

Punahou's centennial celebration was very important for the people in Hawaii because it was an opportunity to be taken seriously by people living across our ocean. Some of those were the farmers baling hay in South Dakota and, of course, those goose-stepping Germans in Berlin thought we lived in grass houses, laid in hammocks all day, drank gin slings, wore no clothes, and married Dorothy Lamours who wore red cellophane grass skirts to bed. People in Iowa heard we cooked people in iron pots for breakfast. The average Americans had no idea that the largest natural harbor in the world, Pearl Harbor, anchored the biggest battleships and aircraft carriers in the American fleet.

Mr. Dillingham hired the best artistic talent he could find in Hawaii to support this outdoor production of Hawaiian history and formed a twenty-piece orchestra to heighten the acting that was to be performed on stage. I dreamed of being the STAR of this production and saw, in my dreams, my name blazing in lights above the stage. I asked my principal, Miss Slingerland, to let me open up the colossal production by singing the "Star Spangled Banner" with the twenty piece orchestra. I knew I could do it with my dynamic personality. I planned to sing our national anthem in a Carmen Miranda chika-chika-boom-ba-boom-ba rendition.

In my enthusiasm, I gave Miss Slingerland my impersonation of Carmen Miranda singing the "Star-Spangled Banner." After I finished, I put my hands on my hips and asked her, "Wouldn't I knock 'em dead?" Miss Slingerland, with her hands on her hips, said I'd kill them for sure.

The good gods were with me after all because I got a role. I was given the part of a missionary boy who stands next to an overturned rowboat holding a paddle upright in his hand. The part was small and without lines, but I knew I could make something out of it - after all, Charlie Chaplin didn't speak in the movies.

Being a star, I was very fussy about my costume. I wanted it to be authentic. The costume committee found an original, little missionary boy's blue dress suit in a rusty old trunk in the dungeon of the Mission House Museum. Now I knew I was really authentic because I smelled of mothballs. I swooned.

I was on time for all rehearsals. I told Miss Wood that homework would take second fiddle to my art. A star had responsibilities to be a star and I couldn't be bothered with her little interruptions like reading, writing, and arithmetic. Miss Wood threatened to call Daddy Goat Gruff. She furthered her threats and told me that if I didn't get my homework in on time, she would take the role, the paddle and the costume away, and I would immediately be replaced by Booby the Bully. Miraculously, my homework was on her desk at eight the very next morning. I got to keep the role.

In class and at rehearsals, I daydreamed about Alice Faye, eating mayonnaise sandwiches, and becoming a star in the Punahou production, and I pushed away the curse that my mother was leaving me to marry the king of Tahiti.

The night of the production arrived. The smell of grease paint filled the fragrant Hawaiian air. The stage became a circus of people in colorful costumes. Hawaiian chiefs strutted around naked in red, orange and yellow feather capes - well, almost naked. Women in sapphire blue, hoop-skirt gowns waltzed around backstage, practicing "The Blue Danube." All around me was show biz as I imagined it.

Chinese coolies in colorful orange pajamas scurried between the dancers, carrying bags of rice, smoking long, black cigarettes and spitting out black crackseed. Hawaiian kings and queens, crowns on their heads, walked behind the flats as if they once again ruled the Islands. On cue, the kings and queens made grand entrances on the stage and sat on gold thrones in front of a Republican, missionary-descended sugar plantation audience. The royalty part slowed the production down a lot because the stagehands couldn't talk the kings and queens off their thrones even after the lights went on again for the next scene. Royalty growled imperiously that they were remembering the good old days.

Waiting to go on, I peeped through all the holes in the canvas flats, looking for anyone I knew among those sitting on the concrete bleachers, eating hot dogs and popcorn. I got the reputation real fast as being "that fat little missionary boy who wore a blue suit, to avoid." I stopped everyone, even those running to make their entrance on stage, because I wanted to ask them a thousand questions on how I could get into show business. The actors always held their noses when I talked to them; my mothball smell was pretty strong. A Chinese coolie asked if I had been embalmed.

On opening night, everyone who was anyone, from all the islands and the Mainland, came in by ship for the extravaganza. My powerful and rich relatives from Kauai sat in the reserved seats on the bleachers. Opening night, my mother was there. Hatsuko and bad-teeth Charlie were there. Every loud-mouthed politician in Hawaii was there. All the people living on the slopes of Diamond Head were there. Governor Poindexter was there. Doris Duke was there. Duke Kahanamoku was there. Marigold and the Twins were there. I bet even Mr. Hamada disguised as a spy was there.

Daddy wasn't there. He and Kathy were on Maui, attending a sugar meeting.

My scene came just before the choo-choo train smoked down the railroad track, tooting its whistle, and closed Act I. The train always got a standing ovation. I went green with envy every time the audience stood up for the train. I hated to be upstaged.

The missionary act, of which I was a part, had actors marching around the stage, pretending they had just gotten off a sailing ship. They were all costumed in black suits and dresses and looked fierce as Hunkacha. The missionary ladies sang hymns off key as they marched up and down stage as if they were off to a witch burning. I thought they put a damper on the show. They should have at least costumed the ladies in gold hoop skirts with red tassels on the gowns. The missionary scene needed lots of color.

Some of the missionary actors, trying to be real, acted seasick and pretended to throw up. A skeleton-thin lady overstuffed herself to look as if she was about to born a baby. She overdid the stuffing because she looked as if she was about to burst out twenty of the famous Dionne quintuplets from Canada. She got the biggest laugh opening night, which killed me, when her pillows fell out from under her dress. She looked as if she had hatched feather pillows. The audience screamed for more pillows. The stick lady ran off stage in hysterics. I could have done real wonders with that role.

At the stage manager's signal, after the missionaries walked off stage pretending to preach, five of us children were placed next to the overturned rowboat. I held an oar and stood stiff as the oar next to Wigay, who was dressed as a peasant girl from the Madeira Islands. I never knew what our scene represented or where it fit in the scheme of the pageant, but I didn't care - I was thrilled to be on stage.

After we were set in place by two stagehands, the blinding stage lights illumi-nated us like a thousand lit candles. The brightness of the lights began to fry my brain and eyes. I never knew that being in show business was going to be that painful. The audience's eyes were on me as the scene plodded on and on. The nar-rator droned on about the different kinds of people who had arrived in Hawaii to work in the sugar plantations. I felt like I was standing in the middle of a desert at high noon without a hat.

The heat of the lights began to bake the tiny particles of the mothballs flaked on my costume. Stinking fumes entered my nostrils. My hands began to sweat. I felt a warm sensation rise from my toes, to my ankles, into my stomach, into my heart, and finally fountains of hot blood burst into my brain. I fainted.

I fell over the rowboat. Everyone, especially Miss Wood, thought that I had pulled a Percy and decided to become creative. Thinking I was acting, Miss Wood left me unconscious on the stage. Seeing my lifeless body on the rowboat, the nar-rator went with the action and adlibbed about how many of the missionary chil-dren died of consumption - just as "that little boy died" over the rowboat. The audience applauded that I had died so well. If they had given me a standing ova-tion as they did the train, I would have risen, flapped my fat arms like wings and pretended I was going to heaven.

When the lights went out and I didn't walk off stage, Miss Wood finally real-ized something was wrong. She sent the stagehands to retrieve me before the choo-choo train started to chug down the tracks to end the act.

Mr. Fulmer, the director, liked my dying (fainting) on stage so much that he told me I could die every night. Each night I took a little longer to die. Mr. Fulmer, the spoilsport, on the third night, told me to quit "milking the act." That was actor talk for overdoing it. I nodded and purposely forgot his words. I stuffed them down into my stomach with all the other things I didn't like to hear.

On the last night, I performed a sensational Greta Garbo (Camille) dying with lots of coughs. I slowed Mr. Fulmer's production down by a good five minutes, the stage manager said, especially when I spit up a lot of fake blood-catsup all over the stage. That night, I got more laughs than the stick lady did.

Exhausted and lying in bed, I confided to Gertrude and Agnes the night the pageant was over, "You just never know what opportunities come your way when you're not thinking about what's coming ahead. I would never have imagined to die onstage if I hadn't fainted." I sighed to them as I drifted off to dreamland, "Isn't life wonderful when you let it just happen?"

For the whole week of the centennial production, I was at peace because I was doing what I loved best. Acting. While acting, I forgot that I was fat and that my mother was sailing on a ship for Tahiti without me.

A few days after the centennial celebration drew down its curtain, our school year 1940 - 41 ended. Miss Wood kindly put on my report card that I was the most creative child in her class, but the laziest.

Kimo would have died another death if he read that.

Mother didn't send Daddy Goat Gruff my report card because he didn't call and I pleaded that I would do better the next year. After all, I was going on nine and at nine, I promised her, I would become the Einstein of the family. I would outshine Marigold's brilliance by a hundred sunrises and be an A-plus student in math. To further make sure she'd keep my report card away from my father, I swore an oath that I would stop wearing her dresses and quit eating quarts of mayonnaise to save her money.

Boy, did I love lying. When I said I would quit eating mayonnaise, Agnes and Gertrude, inside my head, told me that I was living with the devil and that I deserved to be cursed. Liars are cursed people.

The day I feared arrived.

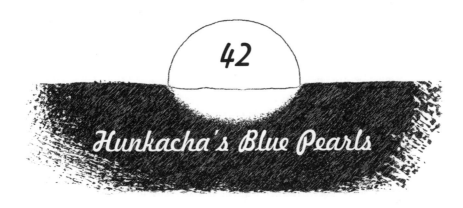

42

Hunkacha's Blue Pearls

As Mother was leaving for Tahiti, I read in *The Honolulu Advertiser* that the curse lurked outside my house. It was out on the horizon, waiting to strike me down with my mother.

The Honolulu Advertiser

Up The Gangplank by LaSalle Gillman. Cruise Ship. When the Mariposa sails, a number of Honoluluans will be aboard for the second round-Pacific cruise via Tahiti in a year. The very fact that people can go on long Pacific pleasure cruises in these perilous times speaks for the confidence of Americans in their own ships and safety in the open sea lanes. There will be a lot of Mainlanders, mostly Californians, aboard the ship making the same trip.

In short, while there are always alarmist and timid souls in our midst, most people have as yet failed to get the wind up about reports of mines in the Pacific to the extent of abandoning plans to go traveling. The tourists (on this cruise) should see something interesting...and we're sure the natives of Tahiti will find the tourists interesting!

RESIDENT'S ATTENTION

Tonight there will be a territorial-wide blackout sometime between the hours of 9 and 9:30. When the "enemy planes" are sighted, alarm signals will be sounded. Immediately turn off all lights, inside and out, as well as all illuminated signs. Automobiles will stop and extinguish head and taillights. Don't use flashlights or matches. Make the blackout complete.

While this is only a rehearsal for an event we hope will never come, nevertheless we should all cooperate, just as if the aerial raid was real and not imaginary. As citizens of Hawaii, it gives us the opportunity of demonstrating to our military services how we can cooperate in the defenses of our Territory.

"Out black the Last Blackout." Territorial Blackout Committee.

HAWAII THEATER - Phone 66300 - Air Conditioned for your comfort.
Three Days Starting Today at 12:30 p.m. Alice Faye - Betty Grable in *TIN*

PAN ALLEY. The Musical of our Exciting Times. With a Merrie Melodie Cartoon, "Elmer's Pet Rabbit."

Two nights before her ship was to sail, Mother gathered Marigold and me into my bedroom. I assumed she was planning to say her last farewells and give her final instructions on how we were to behave ourselves when she left for Dorothy Lamour land.

I was wrong.

Marigold climbed into bed with me. I hadn't seen much of her since Daddy's wedding. At night, she usually stayed alone in her bedroom, pounding pillows, and in the afternoons, she played "king of the mountain" with the Twins on top of Rocky Hill until Mother called her home.

We hadn't snuggled as a family for a long time. When Mother asked if we wanted to hear a bedtime story, we screamed yes, and pleaded with her to continue the Hunkacha story.

"You really want me to?" she teased. We screamed louder, "Yes."

Amazingly, Mother remembered where she left off in the story. We didn't have to prompt her once. Since the divorce, Mother hadn't had time for story-telling, so we thought she had forgotten all about Hunkacha, Little Johnny and Patty. We hadn't.

Arms around each other, Marigold and I sat on my bed just like we did the last time Mother told the story of Hunkacha, the night before we took the ship to the Big Island to spend Christmas with Uncle Will and Aunt Ella.

Mother took our hands and said, "Now, Percy and Marigold, the Hunkacha story is a good one to tell because we are all entering on new adventures."

Marigold clapped her hands and said, "Adventures. Samentures. Hurry up. Just tell the story." Marigold was anxious to hear what happened next because she thought she was just like Patty.

"All right," Mother said squeezing Marigold's hand. Mother began, "As you remember, Patty and Little Johnny were sent out by their old father into the forest to bring back the blue pearls, a gift from the angel Husskelson that the evil, evil, evil monster Hunkacha stole and hid at the bottom of a magical blue lake. Now these children had been warned by their father to never stray from their path and to tell the truth, or they would be eaten up by Hunkacha and never find the pearls.

"The evil old Hunkacha had turned his forest to a fairy delight of foods to tempt the children. Tree trunks were made out of mayonnaise jars and branches held hot fudge sundaes dripping with hot chocolate. Everywhere Patty and Little Johnny looked, they saw every kind of food that they loved. The children were so hungry and so tempted, they started to step off their path into the forest of delights. That's where we left off, remember? And remember Hunkacha is still fast asleep in his cave."

I jumped up and down on the bed and said, "I remember that. Now what happened? This is just as exciting as the serials in the movies when Don Winslow of the Navy was about to be crushed by an avalanche."

"Calm down, Percy," Mother shushed me. She continued, "As they were about to step into the forest, they heard their old father's voice coming to them on a strong wind, commanding them to stop what they were doing and not to forget what he had told them. And guess what happened?"

Marigold raised her hand. "Yes, Marigold?" Mother asked.

Marigold, puffing out her chest, said knowingly, "They stopped. I know they stopped because Patty is a smart girl."

"They did and then they continued on their path," Mother exclaimed. "And you know what happened next?"

"Tell us," I screamed.

"Suddenly, the forest turned green again like all forests are in the whole wide world. Hunkacha's spell was broken. The forest now looked like a real forest filled with beautiful trees. The magical food disappeared. Then, right in front of Patty was a huge hot fudge sundae and in front of Little Johnny was the largest egg salad sandwich in any fairyland, loaded with mayonnaise. The treats were from their father who was very pleased that they had minded him - like good children should do. They ate their treats in three gulps and found new strength to continue on their journey. They were very grateful to their father and thanked God for such a wonderful father who guided them. Hand in hand, tummies full, they continued their quest to recover the blue pearls.

"All of a sudden, in a miraculous instant, they arrived at the magical lake. This was the magical lake where the blue pearls rested on its muddy bottom, waiting to be rescued by the children. Patty and Little Johnny devised a plan. Patty would play beautiful songs on her gold harmonica to keep the monster Hunkacha asleep in his cave. This was the same beautiful harmonica her father gave her. Little Johnny would take his gold reed into the lake, and use the reed to breathe in air while he was underwater. With the reed, he could dive to the bottom and bring up the treasures.

"And that's what they did. Patty played sweet music on her harmonica as Hunkacha slept peacefully in his cave, and Little Johnny dove into the lake, using his golden reed to breathe while he went underwater and search for the blue pearls. Little Johnny found a big surprise at the bottom of the lake, a treasure chest filled with the most beautiful jewels anyone has ever seen. Among the jewels, at the top of the open chest, lay the blue pearls side by side. Being an honest boy, Johnny took only the two blue pearls that belonged to him and Patty and nothing else. Little Johnny swam to shore with the pearls and showed them to Patty. He gave the prettiest one to Patty. She was so surprised at seeing the pearl in her hand that she stopped playing music on her harmonica.

"When the music stopped, Hunkacha woke up with a start and smelled that something was terribly wrong in his kingdom. Hunkacha had a very keen, magical sense of smell, so he knew immediately what had happened and roared like a den of lions. He rushed out of his cave like Joe Louis ready to fight Max Snelling and, sounding like a herd of elephants, he ran towards the lake saying he was going to eat the little children for lunch because they stole the pearls. Hunkacha was really mad.

"Patty and Little Johnny heard him coming because the ground shook like an earthquake. All of a sudden, two paths appeared before them in the forest. They had to make a quick decision. Should Patty take one path? Should Little Johnny take the other? Or should they take the same path together? They had to make up their minds that very instant because they could hear Hunkacha coming around the corner."

Mother paused and asked, "Percy and Marigold, what do you think Patty and Little Johnny did?"

We both piped up, "We don't know. Please tell us."

Smiling like the calico cat next door, Mother patted our hands, pursed her lips and answered, "Think what you would do if you were Patty and Little Johnny. Think about it while I am gone. I'll tell you the ending when I get back from Tahiti."

We yelled, "That's not fair. Tell us now." Marigold scolded Mother like she would a naughty child, sounding a lot like Grandma when she ordered sailors to swab the decks, "Mother, right now! Now. Tell us now. If you don't, I'll give you twenty lashes."

"No, you won't because I am bigger than you and I am your mother. You have to wait. Patience, Marigold," Mother resisted.

"Mother," I said, pouting like Shirley Temple, "I don't want to wait. Anyways, I don't care because whoever is going to take care of us when you are gone can finish the story, and I'm not going to tell you the ending. So there." I stuck out my tongue.

"Don't be fresh, Percy. Nobody is going to take care of you here," Mother replied.

"What do you mean?" I asked, surprised.

"You and Marigold are going away too," she revealed.

I cried out, "Going away? Nobody told me I was going away. Where to?" I looked at Marigold and said crossly, "Did you know we are going away?"

Marigold looked down at Mother's lap and mumbled, "Yes."

I shouted, "YES! MARIGOLD, YOU KNEW? YOU KNEW?" I looked at her with my killer eyes. "YOU ARE A BIG PIG. YOU ARE A BIGGER TRAITOR THAN BENEDICT ARNOLD. WHY DIDN'T YOU TELL ME? WHY DOESN'T ANYBODY TELL ME ANYTHING? AFTER ALL, I'M EIGHT YEARS OLD."

I jumped off the bed and started pacing around the room. "I'M NOT GOING ANYWHERE AND YOU CAN'T MAKE ME!" I screamed, "I MEAN IT!" At that moment, I sounded like Grandma, too. I'm sure the neighbors heard me screaming but I didn't care because I wanted everyone to know that I lived with a mean mother and a Benedict Arnold.

With eyes flashing, Mother spoke with a firmness I wasn't used to hearing from her. Her voice became deadly, like a cobra spitting poison. "Percy, you sit back down on the bed, right now. Be quiet. I MEAN IT!" Now she sounded like Grandma, too, and from the tone in her voice, she meant business.

I sat down but as far away from Benedict Arnold Marigold as I could sit. I collected my thoughts and finally spoke up. Shaking with anger, I asked, "Where am I goooooing?"

Mother answered, "You and Marigold are going to Kauai. Marigold is going to stay with Aunt Mari and you are going to stay with cousins of mine. They have a little boy the same age as you are. You are going to live with Cousin Rose and Nigel Powderhurst."

I moaned, "They sound awful. I don't like them already. Pooooowderhurst! What an awful name."

"You've never met them," Mother replied. "How can you say you don't like them?"

"I just don't. Let me stay home by myself. Let Marigold go. I'll even sacrifice myself and stay with Daddy and Kathy, if I have to," I wailed.

"Your father doesn't have room," Mother said. "His apartment is too small."

I looked at both Mother and Marigold as tears came into my eyes. "I want to be adopted. I don't like my family anymore," I cried.

Mother took me in her arms and cooed, "Percy, you're being perfectly silly. You'll love being on Kauai and when I come back, I'm going to take you both on a great big adventure, just the three of us. Please, Percy, try to act a little grown up for me."

"I can't. I'm still a little boy and everybody forgets that," I said pitifully. I looked at Mother and Marigold. Mother had tears in her eyes and Marigold looked more miserable than I had ever seen her.

Marigold reached for my hand. "Percy, I'm sorry I didn't tell you, but I knew how you'd react. I wanted to stay with Daddy, but Kathy doesn't want me to stay with them. She says they'd be too cramped. I'll be nearby at Aunt Mari's and if you really hate it at the cousins', I'll come get you. We can hide in a mountain cave till Mother comes back. I promise you," she said.

Like I was George Washington's father, I looked at her, searching to see if she was telling the truth. I said, "Promise, Marigold, and don't you cross your fingers."

"I promise, Percy." Marigold held up her hands. "See, my fingers aren't crossed. I promise, you'll be all right. I'll see to it. We'll be Little Patty and Johnny fighting Hunkacha."

Mother grabbed both of us into her arms and whispered into Marigold's ear, "Thank you." We clung to each other because we were, at that moment, bobbing up and down in a stormy sea of emotions, each wearing a life preserver of hope and love. The life preservers were there to protect us as we sailed off in a leaky ship of life.

My stomach growled like a mating panther, breaking the spell. The three of us looked at one another, got up, and without a word, walked into the kitchen and gobbled down big bowls of Dairymen's chocolate fudge ripple ice cream.

In three days, Mother left for Tahiti. In four days, Marigold and I boarded the Waialeale, an inter-island liner, for Kauai. Daddy drove us to the ship. He kissed Marigold goodbye.

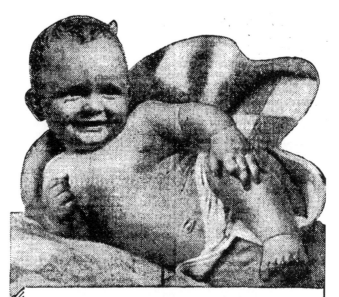

43

Odds and Ends

Before I sailed for Kauai, a few odds and ends occurred to the people in my life.

Aunt Momi married Uncle Lono, but Mother wouldn't attend the wedding. She warned Aunt Momi that her marriage to Uncle Lono was destined to be fatal. Mother further prophesied that after three weeks of marriage, in a drunken brawl, Uncle Lono would push Aunt Momi over the Nuuanu Pali and she'd end up dead at the bottom of the cliff with a broken neck. Aunt Momi, being in passionate love, was not amused.

Gertrude advised me to tell Mother that if you have the guts to tell your sister truths, laugh at the end of each sentence, signaling that maybe what was just said was a joke. Mother's refusal to attend the wedding was no joke to Aunt Momi, therefore, when the royal wedding bells rang, Mother and Aunt Momi were not speaking.

On a hot afternoon in a judge's office downtown, without her beloved sister at her side, Aunt Momi became a Hawaiian princess in fifteen minutes with her neck still intact. The gossip was that after the ceremony, Uncle Lono and Aunt Momi had a monumental honeymoon night drinking schnapps in one bar after another down Kalakaua Avenue, and ended up in the wee hours of the morning in their honeymoon suite at the Royal Hawaiian Hotel, where they passed out.

The day after Aunt Momi married Uncle Lono, Mother rented our house to Betsy and Jack, now happily married, for the two months while we were gone. The couple had been looking for an apartment to rent, and not finding one, were grateful to Mother for a temporary place to light and make babies. Marigold told me about the making babies part. Helen the Horrible was kept on to take care of household chores and do their cooking. I told Mother that Helen's cooking and disposition were going to ruin Betsy's marriage.

Another odd thing happened before Betsy and Jack moved in. Mr. Hamada, the greatest spy in the world because he knew what I was going to do even before I knew it, left a bottle of Best Foods mayonnaise on my front doorstep. He wrote instructions that I was to take the mayonnaise bottle with me to Kauai. The word *sayonara* (farewell) was written under his instructions in black ink.

The night before I left, I talked to Hatsuko by phone and told her I had the perfect name for her baby if it was a girl. I teased her that I wouldn't tell her the name until I came back from my summer vacation on Kauai. I added, pleading, "Please don't see any new movies without me, and if you do, I won't tell you the baby's name." Hatsuko promised by crossing her heart over the telephone that she wouldn't see a movie, even if Charlie begged. Inside my head, I knew Hatsuko broke promises, but Gertrude said I must be grown up and quit making people swear to things they can't keep.

Acting odd and out-of-sorts on the night before Mother left, I begged on my knees for Mother to bring back a koala bear from Australia. "After all, Mother," I reasoned, "Australia is next door to Tahiti and I love the koala bears' flat noses. They remind me of yours and they can sleep in my bed like Uku did." More promises that couldn't be kept. I just couldn't help testing the people I loved.

The odd-acting Twins were sent away to a detention summer camp on the other side of Oahu two days before my ship sailed. They were to study what they hadn't learned that year at Punahou and if they didn't bring their grades up, they were going to be banished to a rival public school, Roosevelt, forever. I loved the idea.

"Only the classless and poor white trash went to Roosevelt," according to snotty, old, class-conscious Cousin Bessie. Aunt Gladys and Uncle Pete, big keepers-up with the Joneses and Dillinghams, and living next door to Cousin Bessie, were horrified at the prospect of being demoted to common folk if their wayward children went to a public school. Snobs are snobs are snobs and will always be snobs, according to Gertrude. Snobs didn't know how to be anything else. Agnes told me that if I looked into one of the Twins' ears, I'd see daylight at the other end.

When I was certain that the Twins were a thousand miles from home and from me, I advised Auntie Gladys that the only way to make them study was to lock 'em up in cages. Then, I told her to have Uncle Pete beat them daily with sticks until they pleaded for mercy and became saints and, therefore, he would protect me and the world from two potential, hard-hearted, upcoming Hitlers. Auntie Gladys kicked me out of her house and threatened that she was going to lock me up in a cage with the Twins and have them beat me up. I learned another lesson: to never criticize other people's children to their mothers, even if the mother had Hitlers sitting at her breakfast table, eating scrambled eggs with catsup.

The last afternoon before I left, I made a secret rendezvous with Cynthia and Vinnie. They told me Cross-Eyed Mama promised them that I could play with her darlings when I returned from Kauai. Flashing a quarter at Cynthia, she and I went into the bushes. She pulled down her panties and I found her birthmark tail had grown back in all its glory. In fact, it was more magnificent than when I last saw it flying from her upstairs window. It was longer and blonder, but her bottom was fatter. I told her that her tail now had a modern sleek Art Deco look. Her tail looked like Loretta Young's house in *Photoplay* magazine. Sometimes, I never made sense, even to myself, but looking at the tail, it was worth at least twenty-five cents.

I told Cynthia that we'd make a lot of money with her magnificence because her birthmark was far more impressive than any lady's black beard at the E.K. Fernandez circus sideshow. I visualized us in business when I returned. We would set up a booth in front of her house with a sign, written in pink, featuring Cynthia's bare bottom and her tail hanging out to dry. I told her I'd provide the ice-cold lemonade and cookies. I estimated that thirty-five cents was a fair price because I added in my refreshments.

Agnes and Gertrude opted to stay behind in my window seat with my crayons and coloring books for the summer. They were upset with Mother because she just flung the Kauai trip on us without giving us notice. They moaned they didn't have time to shop for something new to wear. Gertrude told me that if I really needed them, knock three times on my heart and, in a flash, they'd be right there beside me. I told Agnes and Gertrude that I was going to hold my breath until I came back from Kauai because only then could I return to a normal life again. I hated going away because my plans to make something of myself and to make my father like me were all discombobulated, and I was certain that in going to Kauai, I'd never find out what the curse was.

Wrong again. The curse was waiting for me on Kauai.

Mother's last two instructions as she walked up the gangplank were: "Remember what Dr. Mansfield told you; only one helping at meal time. We're going to try to lose weight this summer, aren't we? And please, Percy, don't ask to wear Cousin Rose's dresses."

The night before Marigold and I left, I found a book on Kauai in our living room bookshelf that was written by a famous Hawaiian author, Ned Harlow. Gertrude and Agnes had advised me to read up on this strange island before I landed on its shores.

The chapter on Kauai read as follows: "Kauai is known as the Garden Island by visitor and resident alike. It is a 555-mile round island. In its center is a large dormant volcano, Mount Waialeale, which is the tallest mountain on the island. The peak is known in *Ripley's Believe It or Not* as the wettest spot on earth. It rains an average of 450 inches a year at the top. Thus, Kauai has many deep rivers, some of them navigable, and lots and lots of trees and flowers; therefore, it was named the Garden Island.

"Because Mt. Waialeale is centered on Kauai, everyone lives on the island's perimeter. On the northern end of the island, there is a large section of impassable, razor-sharp cliffs that plunge into the ocean. They are known as the Napali. These cliffs prevent any residents from driving completely around the island in a circle, making the north and west ends of the island isolated communities. All Kauai communities, isolated or not, think their fiefdoms are the only places worth living on the planet earth. Some of the residents have never even ventured a mile from their townships. Like the people in Christopher Columbus's day, they have never glimpsed or wanted to glimpse their island beyond the bend in their road - maybe they think ferocious monsters are waiting for them around the corner to eat them up. Some of the natives never learned to swim, even though the ocean all around them threatens possible tidal waves.

"Everyone on Kauai considers themselves a king or a queen. They live in a variety of grand dwellings: mansions in valleys with glass-covered swimming pools, or sugar plantation houses, batten and board wooden structures roofed with tin, to mention just two. Every plantation worker's home has a boiling hot *furo* (outdoor bath) in their backyard to soak in after a tiring day of cutting cane. Somewhere in the hinterlands of the island, grass houses still stand nestled in coconut groves, near lagoons, and are holdouts from days when only the Hawaiians roamed the island. Each home, big or small, is considered a castle by its dwellers.

"The men and women living in these castles rule their homes and their communities as if they live in a mythical kingdom. Filipinos speak to each other as if a Spanish grandee lurks in their blood, even if that grandness jumped the fence. Portuguese conduct themselves, in church affairs, as direct Catholic descendents of Queen Isabella and King Ferdinand of Spain. Chinese walk into stores like a prince and princess - mandarins who have arrived from the court of the Empress Dowager in Peking. The Hawaiians on Kauai sniff the rarified air around them, acting more royal, bluer of blood, than all the Kamehamehas put together. The Japanese consider themselves from the samurai class, every one of them. They each proudly show off a family crest and, without a word spoken or sword raised, lord it over all the other races. One of the haole families at a Kauai Historical Society meeting proved last year to other members, by holding up an old piece of parchment, that they were related to Old King Cole, that merry old soul that once ruled in England before the days of King Arthur.

"Royalty rules everywhere on Kauai and everyone, because they are royalty, looks down on somebody. The Japanese snub the Okinawans. The Filipinos from the northern end of Luzon don't speak the dialect of those immigrants from Manila. The Chinese, the first to arrive on Kauai after the whalers, turn up their noses at all unworthy souls who can't save a nickel. Stout Germans from Bremen, being German, look down on everyone. If you find yourself at the bottom of the social totem pole on Kauai, there is always a dog, cat or fighting cock you can reign over. Though royalty rules in every crook and cranny on Kauai, royal blood doesn't mix with the royalty of different race, color or creed.

"A Hawaiian *kahuna* (priest) was known to chant that it is the strong magical, potent waters from Mount Waialeale, the wettest spot on earth, that makes Kauai people act peculiar."

Ned Harlow was right. At age eight, I never met a peasant on Kauai.

On Kauai, my end got stuck with my first enema.

44

Buckingham Palace

The morning Marigold and I arrived on the Garden Island, the air was so muggy that buckets of water poured from my body. Sailing into Nawiliwili, Kauai's deep-water harbor, I smelled like a rotten mango as I stood on the boat's deck.

Marigold and I had traveled alone. She, true to form, had been sick all night and her breath smelled like rat poopoo. I, also true to form, ate sandwiches all night, and after I finished munching the last turkey sandwich, rivers of mayonnaise and mustard were running down the front of my shirt and pants. Without a wash, or putting a toothbrush near our teeth or a comb to our hair, or a change of underwear, Marigold and I walked barefooted down the gangplank. We held onto the railing as we walked to keep our balance, wearing the clothes we slept in.

At the end of the gangplank, the ugliest, scariest apparition waited to greet us. The monster looked as if she arrived out of the sky in an orange soap bubble and burst in front of us like a bomb. Her head and arms were matted with orange hair, and she glowered like a dragon, breathing orange smoke out of her nostrils. It was the infamous Aunt Mari, the wickedest queen on Kauai. Looking at her made me want to shishi. She stood like an orange praying mantis, studying us with her pince-nez glasses. I knew that in her presence, God rode in the rumble seat. We were not halfway down the gangplank when the witch of Kauai boomed out to us, "I have never seen such a raggle-taggle, filthy, dirty pack of children in all my life."

At the sound of her voice, which sounded like a cannon volleying across the harbor, everyone jumped a mile, including the four-hundred-pound stevedores unloading the cargo. I froze as if an arctic wind had struck me.

Aunt Mari screamed at the onlookers, who were gawking at us, in a voice that sounded like it could shatter cities, "WHAT ARE YOU FOOLS LOOKING AT? MIND YOUR OWN BUSINESS. THESE CHILDREN ARE NO CONCERN OF YOURS. GET BACK TO WORK, TURN AROUND OR I'LL HAVE YOU FIRED."

The workers jumped, hustled, bumped into each other in confusion, and went back to unloading the ship. It was as if President Roosevelt had just ordered them into war to fight the Germans.

Aunt Mari turned back to us and continued her assault. Marigold and I had stopped walking, frozen in motion as if icebound, and stood looking at Aunt Mari like two dirty strawberry popsicles.

She roared, "Come down here. You two are a disgrace. From where I stand, you look and smell like pigs. I have a half a mind to send you packing back to Honolulu." She put her orange hands on her large General Douglas MacArthur hips, looking ten feet tall, and ordered, "Come down here, right now! Both of you! Step lively!" When I heard that command and saw her menacing look, I wanted to blow a bugle, retreat, run back into the cabin, and hide under the blankets for eternity. I had never been so scared in my life.

Marigold took my hand and said under her breath, "Sewer stink, let's go." We inched our way down the gangplank to the hell that awaited us. When we got within arms' length of the queen of the uglies, Aunt Mari grabbed Marigold by the hair and pushed her into a beat-up old station wagon.

She swooped back to me, as I stood galvanized with fear at the end of the gangway, and snarled, "What a complete mess you turned out to be. I knew it the day you were born. At least, you didn't disappoint me. I have never seen such a fat, filthy child in my life. You wait here for Rose."

My mouth had dropped open and collected flies as Aunt Mari kept on talking. She snorted to herself, "Humph. Powderhursts seem to think that it's their royal prerogative to be late. I'm getting out of here before the royal highnesses arrive on their high horses. Do you have anything to say for yourself?"

I shook my head, indicating no.

Aunt Mari, giving me a final look, snarled, "For your information, I don't cotton to Rose's high-handed ways and you can tell her so. Ha! You're going to be a good joke on them. It's almost worth staying to see the look on their faces when they get a load of you."

I tried to look past the monster spewing orange acid for Marigold, sitting in the station wagon, but she had her head down and wouldn't look at me. I mouthed to her, "Marigold, let's go hide in a cave."

The wicked witch of the East saw me signaling and demanded, "What are you doing?" I put my head down like Marigold and didn't answer.

"Sassy too!" She slapped me on my head and then in a fizz of orange, hoisted herself into her station wagon and drove away from the pier with my sister. The wicked witch disappeared on her broom with my Dorothy as fast as she had appeared, leaving Toto behind - alone, unwashed and feeling like an orphan.

One of the pursers on the ship, an Australian, came up to me, put his hand on my shoulder and said, "You're well rid of her, mate. I've seen the likes of her before. She's like those tough rich birds in Sydney who think they're next to God and drive old beat-up cars to prove they are like one of us. The Rockefeller types and we, the bloody middle class, need to buy a new V8 Ford every year to prove that we're as good as one of them." I looked up into kind, deep blue eyes as he gave me a pat on the back.

Then a sleek, black Bentley zoomed around the corner and screeched to a halt in front of me. Out of the car stepped a tall man with a brown moustache and thick, bushy eyebrows. Dressed as if he were about to attend an afternoon tea party with the King and Queen of England, he wore a fitted tweed jacket and pressed dark brown slacks and held a lit pipe in one hand. The gentleman marched up to me like an officer in the King's guards, snapped to attention, straight as a rifle, and saluted me. I saluted him back. The man looked me up and down as if he was inspecting one of his soldiers before leading them into the King's birthday parade. As he gave me the once-over, he gasped at the raggedy sight in front of him and blinked three times to make sure that what he saw was real. The stranger then smiled at me, as if he had just discovered one of the oddest creatures in the world, and blurted out, "I daresay, you can't be Percy?"

I nodded.

He kept on staring at me as he spoke in a very clipped English accent, saying, "Oh dear, dear, dear. My, this will never do. I think a ragamuffin has just landed upon our shores today. My boy, a chimney sweep in England covered with black soot would be a far cleaner looking lad than you are right now." After a further inspection, he murmured, "Hmmm. It looks as if you have landed most of your dinner on your shirt, dear boy. Well, never mind that, we'll turn that right, again."

I stuck my hand out and said, "I'm Percy."

"Well, my lad," he said, taking my hand, "I'm your Cousin Nigel." Calling back into the car, he announced, "Rose, come on out, I think we've found our muffin."

A large woman wearing a flowing lavender chiffon dress appeared out of the car. She dripped in pearls and wore the sweetest queenly expression. She looked just like a rose blooming in an English garden because her complexion was pink and white and her lips were cherry red. She was the color of the loveliest single rose in a Cornish flower garden. Her figure was in full bloom and she wore it well.

She made tiny graceful movements as she floated over to me on two tiny little feet. Because her two tiny hands wafted the air as she walked, she had a dancing grace that took away from the fact that she was fat. Cousin Rose whistled when she walked and because of her round shape, she made herself into a lovely, walking, porcelain English teapot. Her delicate, well-shaped ankles were her finest features. I learned later from Cousin Rose that her petite ankles were what drew Cousin Nigel to their marriage bed.

She touched me lightly on the head, knighting me with her finger, and spoke in a high shrill voice, "Ah, this is dear, sweet Cousin Percy." She looked over at Cousin Nigel and said, "It looks as if our dear cousin has had a rough voyage. We must get him home to be washed and scrubbed. Have you had breakfast, dear Percy?"

I didn't answer because I was embarrassed. I smelled like a garbage pail and was surrounded by sweet-smelling English gentry. I was so nervous meeting real royalty that I wouldn't dream of eating, not even a mayonnaise sandwich.

Looking at my feet, Cousin Rose said, "Dear cousin, where are your shoes?"

I stammered, "Somewhere. I can't remember. I think they're in my suitcase."

"And pray tell, where is your suitcase?" Cousin Rose countered.

"I don't know, Cousin Rose. Maybe Aunt Mari took it."

Her eyes widened, and she said in a surprised voice, "Was dear Aunt Mari here before us?"

I replied quickly, "Yes and she took Marigold away. She said she wasn't going to wait for you." Turning thoughtful, I asked my cousin a very important question, "Cousin Rose, is Aunt Mari related to God?"

Without hesitation, she answered, "She thinks she is, but we know better, don't we, Percy?"

"Yes ma'am." At that moment, I knew that I had found best friends, the Powderhursts. I wanted to add "your majesty" and curtsy to everything I said to them, but I knew better because you only curtsied and said "your majesty" in a throne room. Hearing Cousin Rose and Cousin Nigel speak, I immediately felt an English accent growing inside of me, ready to blossom, ready to converse as an equal with my newfound "favorite" cousins.

"Well, Cousin Percy, there is someone we want you to meet. Our dear son, Tom." Cousin Rose turned back to the car and motioned to someone sitting in the back seat. Walking towards the car, Cousin Rose called, "Tom dear, get out of the car and come meet your dear Cousin Percy."

Tom pushed himself out of the Bentley and at first sight, I thought he looked like a little old man. Mother told me we were born in the same month, in the same year, and only two days apart. Tom was a half-inch taller than I was and as skinny as a beanpole. He was scrubbed clean, dressed in a blue blazer and fitted short white pants. His hair was slicked down and parted in the middle. Cousin Tom wore thick eyeglasses. He appeared sickly frail, like a real flesh-and-blood little Lord Fauntleroy that I had seen in the movies. Cousin Tom marched up to me like his father, held out his hand, and said in an English accent, "Hello, old chappie."

I put my hand out and, with an English accent that blossomed out of my mouth, replied, "Hello, old chappie yourself. I am so glad to meet my dear, dear, dear cousin at last." I sounded more like Cousin Rose than I did Cousin Nigel because I overused the "dears."

With all the introductions made, they hustled me into the Bentley, telling me that they'd check on my suitcase with Aunt Mari. On the drive to their home, to make me feel comfortable, they told me all about themselves, and especially, how much they loved the King of England.

Cousin Nigel, I learned, had been a hero in World War I. He had been gassed twice, wounded once, captured by the German Huns once, and shuffled around into five prison camps with French, Russian and American soldiers. He escaped three times and three times, he was captured, punished and tortured. After the war, he was sent to Shanghai by the Bank of England and traveled all over the Far East as far as Tibet. He met Cousin Rose on the American ocean liner, USS Wilson, when she was returning from taking a holiday in Hong Kong. Walking his morning constitutional on the liner's deck, he saw Cousin Rose lying on a deck chair. It was at that moment that he noticed her ankles.

Cousin Rose continued their story, fiddling with a strand of pearls around her neck, "Percy, I was as thin as a bud vase then and when this handsome banker from Shanghai, a war hero to boot, courted me, how could I resist? I fell in love with his English accent, his moustache and his delightful courtly manners. Manners, dear Percy, are very important to have in our uncivilized world."

She giggled now like a schoolgirl. "Your Cousin Nigel fell in love with my ankles and worked his way up to my face. American boys are so crude in their courtship of women and Englishmen are the gentlemen of the world. When you court a girl, Percy, send her roses every day. Cousin Nigel sent me a dozen yellow roses every day while he was courting me. We were engaged after five days on shipboard and married when Nigel came back from his leave in England. We were married on Kauai, lived in Shanghai, and had Tom in Peking. We were forced to come home by my father because of the present terrible Japanese peril. So your dear Cousin Nigel now runs Father's newspaper on Kauai. It's now a newspaper to be read. For once, sentences are strung together in a paragraph that makes sense. Tom, tell your Cousin Percy about you."

In the back seat, sitting next to me, Tom kept eyeing me as if I was an orang-utan that had just escaped from the Honolulu zoo. Sitting straight as an ironing board, he turned to me, took off his glasses to wipe them and spoke as if he was talking to a scullery maid. "Cousin Percy," Tom said in all seriousness, "Mama schools me at home and I am so glad you have come to visit me." He talked like the English gentry did in the movies. He continued, "I don't have anyone with whom I can play. Do you know about English history? I adore it, especially Lord Nelson and his bloody naval battles with the French. I have formed a club I call the Royal English Navy Club of Kauai. I do hope you will join it and then there will be two of us in the club."

I bowed to Tom, sweeping my head toward the car's floor, and said that I'd be honored to be a member of his club.

Putting on his glasses, continuing to be ever so polite, Tom asked me, "Cousin Percy, what interests you?"

I wanted to reply that it was Cousin Rose's chiffon dress but quickly remembered what Mother told me not to say. I answered safely, "Alice Faye."

An imperial "Whooooooo?" rose out of Cousin Rose from the front seat. I repeated again for all of them to hear, "Miss Alice Faye."

Cousin Rose coughed a little cough and asked, "Isn't she one of the cousins I haven't met yet? She must be from Joshua's side of the family, the ones that left for the mainland to make their fortunes before I was born. That side, dear Percy, is considered the black sheep of our family. They own gas stations and movie houses."

I liked my newfound relatives immediately but knew I had just landed in never-never land - never heard of Alice Faye and never spoke of lowly Hollywood movie stars and never mentioned relatives who are the black sheep of the family. I decided to tell a big lie and said, "No, Alice Faye is one of the royalty back in London, somewhere on my father's side. She discovered lipstick and girdles."

"How fascinating, Percy," said Cousin Rose, looking astonished. "You must tell me all about her girdles at lunch," she purred. I knew that by mentioning girdles, I hit one of Cousin Rose's soft spots. I could tell by the way they were treating me that my cousins were putting their best foot forward and had dressed to the nines to make the right impression on their dear cousin from Honolulu.

Cousin Nigel, steering his Bentley as if he was riding a horse on a foxhunt, spoke to me in the back seat like an officer talking to his new recruit. "Rose, I believe we have a fine fellow visiting us. I think it's up to us to show him how we live. Percy, if you don't mind, I'd like, with son Tom, to show you the ways of how a proper English gentleman comports himself. Would you like that, Cousin Percy?"

I gushed, "I'd love it, Cousin Nigel."

Very pleased with my answer, Cousin Nigel continued, "And let's call him Muffin, Rose - like the ragamuffin we have just found on our doorstep. Righto, Muffin."

"Righto, Cousin Nigel," I responded. "I like the name Muffin ever so much better than Percy. I have never, ever, liked my name."

"Righto, Papa," Tom spoke up, beaming at the thought of making me his project.

Pigmalion had arrived at the home of Pygmalion. I was going to be the statue from the Greek myth that Miss Wood read about just before school ended. I was going to become something wonderful. Though dreadfully homesick for my mother, at that instant, I fell in love with Cousin Nigel. Here was the hero father I always dreamed about. Maybe the curse had flown away.

We drove to their mansion located in the heart of the county seat of Kauai called Lihue. Their mansion was a long, rambling, white structure nestled among gigantic monkeypod trees. I thought I had arrived at Buckingham Palace because the manor was so enormous that I couldn't see the end of it. The palace opened up to the outside through tall French doors without screens, and inside, it was filled with antiques from England and China. Chinese incense burned all day in brass kettles to keep mosquitoes from raising itchy welts on Cousin Rose's delicate royal limbs. The house smelled oriental. There were grand Hawaiian calabashes filled with rare shell leis from the nearby island of Niihau in every room. These calabashes were a reminder that the Powderhurst castle was in Hawaii, not next to Hyde Park.

As she showed me around her stately mansion, I told Cousin Rose that she had two advantages over Buckingham Place that I was sure Princess Margaret Rose and Princess Elizabeth would have given up their royal titles for. One, the Powderhurst house was directly across the street from Kress store. The store was built squat on Cousin Rose's grandfather's dairy farm. The second reason I believed the princesses would have been jealous was that the Royal movie theatre stood next to Kress Store and boasted a neon sign that blinked all night: R - O - Y - A - L, then flashed the whole name ROYAL all at once. I knew the theater had been named after the Powderhursts, but they were too humble to say so. The movie house proudly featured John Wayne in the western movies on weekends. I swooned at the thought of what stood across the street from the Powderhurst Buckingham Palace. I declared on bended knee to Cousin Rose that living in a royal palace across the street from a movie theater and Kress store was better than being in heaven.

Cousin Rose, always the lady, said grandly, "Muffin, I try to forget what's across the street, but I can understand why a little boy like you would say that. I hoped you wouldn't have noticed because it's so plebian. I had our Japanese gardener plant that thick, pink oleander hedge so I can't see Kress Store and the Royal Theater. But one day, you, Tom and I will make an excursion across the street and you can buy something you would love to have, and pray tell, Muffin dear, what would that be?"

"A movie magazine. I adore movies, dear Cousin Rose," I answered.

Thinking I might have delved into something more substantial in literature, like Charles Dickens's *David Copperfield*, Cousin Rose spoke crisply, stretching out her vowels, "Well, my little Muffin, I see we're going to have to start your education immediately."

And so they did. As soon as I arrived at the palace, I was taken to their bathhouse. I was scrubbed and polished to a shine by their maids. Within the hour, wearing new clothes that Cousin Rose bought at Lihue Store, I now looked related - at least on Cousin Rose's side. Cousin Rose and I were the fat side of the family and Cousin Nigel and Tom were the sticks of it.

Cousin Nigel took the day off as editor of the local newspaper and started on my enlightenment. He instructed me how to walk like a soldier, shoulders back, and stomach in. As far as pulling my stomach in, we found that was kind of hopeless.

At lunch, he informed me that gentlemen did not eat with their left hand because that bumped rudely into their neighbor eating with his right. He made me eat using my fork in my right hand. It was difficult at first, being naturally born a lefty, but I was determined to master it for him. I wanted Cousin Nigel to love me right away. I told them my doctor said I couldn't have second helpings, but would they mind piling on the food on my first helping. That wasn't cheating too much.

In the afternoon, Cousin Nigel taught me how to make a bed by squaring the corners, to part my hair in the middle, to memorize the poem "If" by Rudyard Kipling, and to spit shine my shoes. He told me that when he was captured by the Germans in World War I, it was the British who kept themselves in perfect order, uniforms pressed, shoes shined and moustache trimmed. The French, American and Russian prisoners were a slovenly, unshaven bunch of beggars until the armistice was signed.

"A mark of a civilized gentleman, Muffin, is how he keeps himself. A gentlemen always shaves before breakfast." He lived his words and I wished I could have shaved.

I was determined to emulate the gentleman that Cousin Nigel wanted me to be. I was a fast learner. After two days of marching around the Powderhurst palace, I began to look like a soldier in Cousin Nigel's British brigade. I overheard the cooks in the kitchen remark that I was the spitting image of Field Marshall Hermann Goring, Hitler's Luftwaffe air force general. When the cooks peered out the kitchen window, watching me march, I'd do a goose step for them. I never took what they said as a great compliment.

My suitcase arrived from Aunt Mari's. I opened it and found a note from Marigold and a present of three whoopee cushions. She signed it "Happy Farting!" In her note, she wrote that she'd keep her promise and to call her if I hated the Powderhursts, and she'd come get me by hook or crook. She then added a P.S. to the note. She had discovered a cave we could hide in.

I didn't want to leave Cousin Rose and Cousin Nigel's castle, though at night, lying in their guest bed, I cried myself to sleep while thinking about my mother in Tahiti and Agnes and Gertrude stuffed in my window seat. I had no one in bed to comfort me. I was bound and determined not to let Cousin Nigel or Tom see me cry because I learned right off the bat that an English gentleman never shows his feelings.

Cousin Nigel and Cousin Rose, by their kind actions, were determined to see that I was going to be a happy little boy in their home. They knew by looking at me that food was a very important part of my life. At lunch, our first meal together, when Cousin Nigel made me eat with my right hand, they asked what my favorite foods were. They told me I could ask for anything I wanted and they'd have Masa, the head cook, make it.

Cousin Nigel, puffing on his pipe, queried me, "Muffin, would you like rare roast beef with Yorkshire pudding, beef Wellington, chicken Diane, or Indian curry with your Cousin Rose's delicious homemade mango chutney on the side? Which is it to be, Muffin?"

I gave it serious thought and replied, "If it wouldn't be too much trouble, I'd like to have creamed tuna." Cousin Nigel stamped his hand on the table and said, "That's jolly good, Muffin, and that, my boy, is what you'll get."

Creamed tuna at the Powderhursts' was not like any creamed tuna I had eaten in my life. When I saw it served on a platter, I called it a volcano. Set before Cousin Nigel on a china turkey platter was a massive mound of rice that was covered with creamed tuna and surrounded by a spinach souffle ring. Like everything else at Buckingham Palace, the ordinary became royal.

During that meal, I presented the family with a gift. I had packed Mr. Hamada's quart of Best Foods mayonnaise in my suitcase. When I placed the jar in Cousin Rose's hand, she made such a fuss over it, you would have thought I presented her with the king's crown jewels. Her reaction pleased me so much that I curtsied. After dinner, Cousin Nigel taught me how to make a royal bow like Sir Walter Raleigh.

The second day at the Powderhursts' palace, I was knighted in Tom's Royal English Navy Club. I exhibited curiosity in everything Tom was interested in, though most of what he said went completely over my head.

I was trying with all my might to become the English gentleman Cousin Nigel wanted me to be. My shoes now gleamed with a mirror shine. I wore them inside and outside of the palace. Everyday, my face, hands and feet were scrubbed raw as soon as I woke up and definitely when I retired at night. Living with royalty had a price because, as a member of the royal family, I couldn't do or think what I naturally had done and thought at home all my life. I couldn't act like a pig.

I was now acting the role of a crowned prince in a British J. Arthur Rank film production titled by me, "Living with the Royal Family on Kauai." My English accent had developed so fast and was so broad that there were times I couldn't even understand myself, much less Cousin Rose.

On the third day at the Powderhursts', a package arrived for Tom from Liberty House. When Tom opened his package, it was a present to him from my mother, a wind-up toy train. Tom was thrilled. He told me it was the first present he had ever received from anyone other than his parents. My cousin told me my mother must be a very kind and thoughtful person.

I thought my mother was a big slurp. Where was my present? I asked Cousin

Rose to phone the post office to check if there wasn't a present for me from my mother that was left in the post office. Cousin Rose phoned twice and even drove to the post office three times to inquire about a missing package. Each time she came back, she told me that there had to have been a mix-up in the mails and for me to remain patient. Being very kind like royalty always is, especially to the unfortunate, Cousin Rose walked me across the street to Kress's and bought me a box of crayons. I remained heartsick, sulky, and felt entirely abandoned. I also was consumed and overwhelmed with jealousy over Tom's present, especially since he played with the train all day. I crayoned guns, arrows, blood spurting out of fat ladies' hearts, and beheaded people in wishing wells on a lined tablet.

In the afternoon, as I looked on, Tom continued to run Mother's present around the track. I tried to divert my jealous thoughts by reading the adventures of the Rover Boys, another consolation prize from Cousin Rose. It wasn't enough.

Nothing could change the feeling that my mother had forgotten me and I wanted to get even. I still had no present from my mother. Tom, tired of playing with his train, asked me if I'd like to play with his present. I said yes with a vengeance. I took his train and ran it around the track until I deliberately broke it. I showed Tom, with a smile hidden inside my face, that his train was now beyond repair. He burst into tears and ran into his room. My heart jumped for joy.

I told Cousin Rose it was an accident. I lied, but Cousin Rose and Tom believed that I told the truth.

I told Cousin Nigel at dinner that I accidentally broke Tom's train. Looking into my eyes, he knew I lied. After all, Cousin Nigel was a real hero and lived years in a prison camp. He was wise about traitors and liars. That night, being ever so polite, Cousin Nigel stopped calling me Muffin. He referred to me as Cousin Percy when asking me to pass the salt. Cousin Rose and Tom continued to call me Muffin.

The following day, true to Cousin Rose's prediction, a package arrived from Liberty House. It was from my mother. The box contained a stuffed koala bear that I hated on sight. I wanted Tom to have it. Tom, raised as a gentlemen's gentleman and brought up by royalists, wouldn't consider the offer, even if he had wanted the koala bear more than anything else in his life.

Alone in bed that night, with the koala bear packed away in my suitcase, I knew what a terrible person I was because I had deliberately hurt someone who had only been kind to me. I was being punished, without words, by the man I so wanted to love me. Cousin Nigel punished me by doing something far worse than taking a hairbrush to my bare fanny; he withdrew his friendship.

I lost another father because I had failed to meet Cousin Nigel's code of honor. "God," I asked, "Is there a father out there - somewhere - who would want to have a little fat boy for a son? Tonight, let me die before I wake and, please, if I don't die, please, please, please, send me back home to my mother."

I told God that Mother is the only person in the whole wide world who loves me fat and sassy and even loved me when I ripped her favorite black velvet dress. All mothers do that and some fathers don't.

I cried myself to sleep, promising God that one day I would make up my error to Tom. I also beseeched Him to please let Cousin Nigel call me Muffin again.

Rice and Kress Streets, circa 1940, Lihue, Kauai. Courtesy of Kauai Museum Archives, Lihue, HI.

45

Making Whoopee

Inside the Powderhurst castle, my days were scheduled as if the King of England was in residence. Cousin Nigel, the prince, was noticeably absent. My commanding officer went back to publishing the local newspaper. He left my training to Cousin Rose and continued to call me Cousin Percy.

After breakfast, Cousin Rose's first order of the day was that Tom and I sit on the throne. We were decreed to sit there until roses bloomed on our cheeks. After our cheeks looked like Cousin Rose's, she motored us in the Bentley around the island on morning excursions. We'd swim at a beach, inspect a Hawaiian temple, and sometimes before lunch, visit dour German relatives, who shelled out dollars on each visit.

In the afternoons, while Cousin Rose attended volunteer committee and board meetings, Tom and I were left to play in the backyard. Alone with Tom, I learned English history and Tom listened to historical French sagas that Grandma taught me. Tom was fascinated when I acted out Madame DuBarry's execution. I tore my hair, then played the Madame being guillotined by hanging my head over the railing of the garden pavilion, screaming.

Late in the afternoon, when Cousin Rose returned from a meeting, she would stretch out on her chaise lounge in the sunroom, eat Whitman's chocolates and read us children's classics. We would lie on the floor next to her and listen to tales of heroic deeds, while we looked up at a large oil portrait of Cousin Rose painted by my deceased cousin Kimo.

The book I liked the best was *Swiss Family Robinson*, the story of a family shipwrecked on an island where they had to live by their wits in a tree house. The reason she read that novel was because a film version of the book was to be featured at the Lihue Theatre on Saturday. Cousin Rose promised we could attend the matinee. It was to be the second movie Tom had been allowed to see in his whole life. *Snow White and the Seven Dwarfs* was his first and last and the only movie that Cousin Rose allowed him to attend. She considered the story of a cruel witch giving Snow White a poisoned apple a masterpiece. Tom was a total ignoramus about movies and my movie stars, Alice Faye, Tyrone Power and Carmen Miranda. I thought, in that department of his learning, he was deprived.

Feeling comfortable with Tom, I decided to share a secret. I took him into my bedroom, opened my suitcase and pulled out the three whoopee cushions that

Marigold sent me from Aunt Mari's. Tom read Marigold's note and asked what the word "fart" meant. I described it - by farting. Tom shrieked with laughter until tears rolled down his cheeks. It was the first time I heard my cousin laugh.

To show how the whoopee cushions worked, we went into the living room and blew them up. We then placed them under the sofa and chair cushions and made funny sounds all afternoon. Tom couldn't have been more pleased and laughed harder each time he sat on a chair and made a rude sound. Tom said this was the best day of his whole life.

"Cousin Muffin, let's put one of these under Daddy's chair to surprise him when he comes home from work," Tom said gleefully while clapping his hands and thinking about his father's startled look.

"Oh no, Tom," I warned. "Your daddy will get mad and spank us."

"Muffin, you don't know Father. Father loves a joke. I'll take the blame for it, Muffin. Just don't put one under Mummy's chair. I promise you, dear Cousin, Daddy will think it great fun."

Persuaded by Tom, I blew up one of the whoopee cushions and placed it under the pillow on Cousin Nigel's chair. After we tired of the whoopee cushions, we went outside to play "English Navy battles French ships." We forgot all about the inflated whoopee cushion that lay in wait for Cousin Nigel's homecoming. We also forgot that this was the afternoon of the annual meeting of the Lihue Public Cemetery Association of which Cousin Rose was president. At 4:30, its members were to convene in Cousin Rose's living room. High tea and sandwiches without crusts were to be served as the group elected next year's officers. Cousin Rose prayed and lobbied for another term as president.

While we were shooting broadsides at one another in our imaginary ships, we heard the ladies arrive. We remembered at the same time Cousin Rose telling us about the meeting, and then Tom remembered the whoopee cushion under the pillow of Cousin Nigel's chair. We ran to retrieve the joke, but we were too late. The matrons of the committee were walking into the living room like tombstones - heavy, white, and "holier than thou" inscriptions chiseled across their foreheads. Each lady had on a hat and a pair of gloves and they were girdled to their ample chests, which made them look as if their maids had stuffed shovels of wet cornbread dressing inside their blouses. One of the tombstone-ladies was colored orange.

Tom and I watched in horror as Cousin Rose assigned each of the ladies to a chair. The chair of honor, Cousin Nigel's, went to the orange tombstone, Aunt Mari.

Hands over our mouths, wide-eyed in fear, we peered through the window and watched Aunt Mari duck-walk to sit in Cousin Nigel's chair. She turned around before she sat, raised her hand holding up an Irish linen hankie, looked everyone in the eyes, fluttered the hankie, nodded like a regent, and all the ladies sat down in unison.

Pooooooooooooop!

The horrified look on Aunt Mari's face was worth standing in front of a firing squad. Before the ladies reacted, Tom and I ducked under the window and slithered back to the pavilion. We couldn't stop laughing as we ran. Reaching the pavilion, we stuffed pillows over our faces so the tombstone-ladies couldn't hear our hysterics.

It didn't take long before we heard the shrill voice of Cousin Rose calling,

"Tom, Percy, come in here this instant!"

Not looking at one another for fear of bursting into further gales of laughter, we marched into the house, thinking we were about to face our own funeral. We halted dead center in a cemetery of grim looking tombstones. The ladies sat bolt upright in their chairs looking gray. The orange tombstone had turned blue. Standing in the center of the room, her dainty feet wide apart, all the sweetness gone from her face, Cousin Rose demanded, "Well, which one of you did this?"

Before Tom could answer, I saluted and said, "I cannot tell a lie; it was me, Cousin Rose."

"It was I, Percy," she corrected. "Well, what do you have to say for yourself?" Cousin Rose demanded.

A laugh was working its way up from my toes. I said, gagging, "I am very sorry, Cousin Rose, it was meant for Aunt Mari."

Gasps went around the room as each lady reached for their smelling salts.

Tom hit me and I realized immediately that I had made a big mistake. I corrected myself, "I meant, it *wasn't* meant for Aunt Mari."

"Who was it meant for?" the Orange Witch said, spitting fire out of her mouth.

"Cousin Nigel," I said, looking above her orange hair because the laugh was now up to my belly button. I wondered, looking at the witch fuming, if a pail of water would melt her away like the Wicked Witch of the West did in *The Wizard of Oz*?

Tom raised his hand, "Mummy, we wanted to play a joke on Daddy. We thought he'd like the joke."

"That's enough, Tom," Cousin Rose interrupted. She saw her re-election flying out the window.

Aunt Mari, not to be put off, held up the deflated, ripped rubber sack and demanded, "Where did this dreadful thing come from?"

Not wanting to get Marigold into trouble, I said, "From my mother. She sent it from Liberty House. They were on sale." All the ladies tittered and nodded to each other, saying hmmmmm and expressing with a look, that's what you expect from a divorced woman.

Knowing I lied, Cousin Rose dismissed us by saying to her committee, "I know the boys are very sorry for what they have done. Aren't you, boys?"

We nodded. She motioned us to leave and not a moment too soon, because the laugh bubble had reached my throat. I sneaked a look at Aunt Mari as I left. From her stare, I knew someday, in some way, the orange witch was going to wreak sweet revenge on me, especially when she hissed as I passed her chair, "I'll be seeing you soon, Perrrrrcy."

Outside the room, the laugh bubble burst and I screamed with laughter. All the tombstones heard me.

At supper that night, Cousin Nigel discussed the incident and chastised us firmly. I put my elbows on the table, placed my face in my hands, and spoke with such fervor that everyone stopped eating. I said abruptly, "Cousin Nigel, why is it that God, of all the chairs to sit in, let Aunt Mari sit in that one?"

Cousin Nigel, knowing from Tom that the joke was supposed to have been on him, answered in the same serious manner, "As far as I am concerned, Cousin Percy,

God couldn't have chosen better seat for Mari."

He winked. Cousin Rose started it. We all burst into gales of laughter from thinking about Aunt Mari. We laughed so hard that I got the hiccups. As I looked around the table at my cousins laughing, I loved living in a palace where a king and a queen and their little prince laughed at silliness. Cousin Nigel still wouldn't call me Muffin.

Leaving the dining room table, Tom said to his father, "Daddy, I learned a new word today. I think I have to whisper it into your ear." Cousin Nigel leaned down as Tom whispered the word into his father's ear. It was the word he had seen written on Marigold's note.

Cousin Nigel rubbed his chin and explained, "Tom, I haven't heard that word since I was in that blasted German prison camp. It's a very American word. I don't think we should share that word with your mother. Where did you learn it from, son?"

Tom, who never told a lie, said, "Percy." Turning to me, Cousin Nigel sniffed as if he was smelling something bad and asked, "Percy, from where did you learn that word?"

"From my sister, Marigold, sir." I was learning to tell the truth.

Cousin Nigel took me by the shoulders and said, "Well, boys, let's drop that word from our vocabulary, shall we? What say, everyone?"

Sounding like an English Boy Scout, I agreed, "I think that would be a jolly good idea and my great-grandmother would think so, too." We shook hands like English gentlemen and sealed our bargain. I immediately dropped that word from my vocabulary - that is, until I saw Marigold again.

Marigold was always enriching my word power. I wanted to share the new word Marigold taught me when she was seasick on the ship coming to Kauai. Every time she threw up, she said it. I was saving that word for Aunt Mari because Marigold told me it was a perfect word to use on Aunt Mari if she did something bad to me. It was a strong word to stop a person doing something mean to you. Lying on her bunk and puking, Marigold told me that she and the Twins read that every American general in the United States used the word when they went into battle. She warned me to use the word only as a last resort. I was saving "fuck you" for that time when Aunt Mari dished out her revenge on me.

Tom and I wrote long, flowery letters of apology to Aunt Mari. The wicked witch of the oranges never replied. I imagined Aunt Mari, like the witches in the fairy tales, was too busy putting toads, lizards and sheep guts into a boiling pot of water and making incantations to turn me into an orange orangutan. There was a happy ending; Cousin Rose was re-elected as president of the Lihue Cemetery Association.

That night, I was asked to move out of the guestroom into Tom's room to sleep. I was being exiled, not because I had lied or caused the whoopee cushion incident, but because someone was visiting the castle for a night. After the visit, Cousin Rose assured me, I would be back sleeping in the guestroom.

Now knowing my nature, Cousin Rose took away the whoopee cushions because the lady arriving was someone very famous.

46

The Opera Star

The famous lady in question was an opera star. She had been engaged by Cousin Rose's cultural club to sing on Kauai. The recital was to be performed in one of the local movie houses located in the town of Kapaa.

The Roxy Theater was a drafty barn of a theater that had a balcony held up by termites. It had rotten acoustics because a strong wind blew off the ocean through the large cracks in the walls. Kapaa looked like a Kansas town out in the middle of the wild West. It was a town where Jesse James, if he had roamed on Kauai, would have robbed banks. It was widely known to have the wildest drinking bars in Hawaii, the Blue Lei being the most notorious. Drunks made their first appearance on the streets of Kapaa by ten in the morning.

The opera star, unfortunately, thought she was to perform her arias in the cultural mecca of the Pacific. The tickets were very expensive, set at an unheard-of price of five dollars per person. Her performance was a sellout.

Cousin Rose, being the chairman of the event, claimed the honor of housing the famous singer. Hotels on Kauai in 1941 were mainly for businessmen (drummers) or adventurous tourists who had left the civilized beaches of Waikiki for the wild jungles of the Garden Island. People of substance never stayed in hotels.

Two days before the concert, the Powderhurst castle was polished to a gleaming shine. On the day of the star's arrival by plane, Tom and I were scrubbed and dressed as if we were about to meet the Queen of Sheba. And we did.

When the Bentley drove into the porte-cochere, the servants, Tom and I lined up at the door to welcome the famous lady to Kauai by presenting flower leis. When Cousin Nigel opened the car door and the guest stepped out, I was struck with wonder.

The opera star was the first black lady I had ever seen in my life. I had seen black ladies in movies but never in the flesh. God had answered one of my prayers.

The lady looked like a gorgeous chocolate cake and acted like the Queen of Sheba getting out of the car. The first thing I noticed on her face were her lips, which were large, soft and luscious and the most kissable lips I had ever seen in my life. Wearing a short purple dress, a purple velvet hat, purple gloves, and a mammoth, shiny black patent leather purse under her arm, she strode past me into the castle. Inside the living room, the light warmed her skin as if someone had wrapped her all over in a dark piece of brown velvet.

After I gave her my lei, she shook my hand. She crunched it hard, like she was squeezing an orange. I was very disappointed that I didn't get a kiss from her big juicy lips. After she shook my hand, I bowed low and said, "Your highness." She paused for a moment, arched her eyebrows in surprise at the sound of the royal title and moved on without saying a word. Cousin Rose took her arm and led her into the guest bedroom.

When Cousin Rose came out of the bedroom, she pulled Tom and me aside and cautioned us that we must be very quiet, as opera stars need their rest before giving a concert. The opera star wasn't speaking because she was saving her voice for tonight's performance. She had confided to Cousin Rose that she caught a slight cold singing in a drafty hall on Maui. Cousin Rose said to us, "Wait till she sings in the Roxy Theater; she'll have pneumonia." Aunt Mari had booked the Roxy Theater.

Cousin Rose whispered further that if we were very good that afternoon, we could have supper with the opera star after the concert. Cousin Rose, trying to explain how special our guest was, said, "Tom and Percy, staying with us is one of the most famous contralto singers in the world. We are very fortunate to have her sleeping in our house."

"Mother, what is a contralto and what's her name?" Tom asked, impatiently.

"Her name is Marian Anderson and a contralto is a singer who sings lower than a high-sounding soprano. Listen to her low, rich tones tonight. She is truly one of the great wonders in the singing world. And Percy dear, tonight at dinner, please don't ask any embarrassing questions about her color."

"Why, Cousin Rose?" I asked. "I like her color."

"Because, boys, a couple of years ago, Miss Anderson was barred from singing in Constitution Hall in Washington, D.C. because her color is different from ours. It was a shameful incident but she rose above it and sang her concert in front of the Lincoln monument. We must make her feel at home tonight and give her the impression that she is one of us."

I offered, "As a matter of fact, Cousin Rose, her color is far more interesting than mine. I've always preferred chocolate to vanilla. How about you, Tom?"

Looking at his mother, he smiled, "I like Mummy's color ever so much better because it's just like mine." Cousin Rose gave Tom a kiss on his forehead and said, "Thank you, dearest, but we must enjoy everyone's color. It'd be a pretty boring world if all of us were pink and white. Now, you boys, go play quietly in the garden and be dressed by six."

That afternoon we were as good as gold just like Cousin Rose wanted us to be and spoke only in whispers. Needing no one to remind us, Tom and I were dressed at six sharp. Miss Anderson left the house early for the theater to warm up her voice. We soon followed by car. We took our seats in the third row, and promptly at seven, after Miss Anderson's accompanist sat down on the piano bench, from the wings walked "our" black goddess.

The audience stood and cheered. Miss Anderson wore a long dark maroon gown made of velvet and had a white carnation lei around her neck. She carried a long purple handkerchief in her right hand which she trailed on the floor. She looked just like an opera star should look. For two hours, I sat fascinated, listening to her singing, though I couldn't understand one word of it. Even so, I understood her greatness. Just before the recital ended, she sang "Swing Low, Sweet Chariot" in English and "Ave Maria" in Latin.

"Ave Maria" I knew because I had heard Deanna Durbin, the Judy Garland of Universal Studios, sing it in a movie that I saw with Hatsuko at the Hawaii Theatre called *It's A Date*. Deanna sang it dressed like a nun. "Swing Low, Sweet Chariot" I had heard at a church picnic. Knowing all that, I felt like an intellectual.

After a standing ovation and five curtain calls and a half-hour reception in the lobby, Miss Anderson and we drove back home for Cousin Rose's late supper. I was exhausted, because I was only used to hearing the Andrew Sisters sing "Beer Barrel Polka."

There were only five of us sitting around the dining room table. Tom and I sat together. Miss Anderson was across from us and seated on Cousin Nigel's right. I started the conversation while we were eating the first course, a chilled alligator pear cocktail, because I wanted Miss Anderson to know right away that she had a professional in show business seated across from her. I mooned, "Miss Anderson, you really sing good. You're a better singer than Jeanette MacDonald in my book, but I do have to tell you that Alice Faye is a big threat to anyone that sings. Don't you think so? Do you know them?"

"I have met Miss Faye in Hollywood!" she replied. I was dumbstruck. I had never met anyone in my whole life who had touched Alice Faye. Mute in wonderment, I kept staring at Miss Anderson because here, in front of me, was a real goddess and only a real goddess could meet another real goddess like Alice Faye.

Cousin Rose picked up the conversation, "Miss Anderson, I want you to know how ashamed I am of what happened to you in Washington, D.C."

Miss Anderson smiled, spooning her avocado cocktail, and replied, "Thank you for the thought but it's been awhile now. I've put that out of my mind." Miss Anderson put down her spoon and spoke more forcibly, "That's not true, but I do like to forget the bad things in life as much as I can because hate can poison a person. Hate has poisoned me many times and I see it happening all around me. My people have much to hate and much hate inside them. I've seen what it has done to them and to me. But, I have a wonderful family and my love for God has kept me strong to get through these troubled times. It's God first. God and my family are the reasons I am here tonight and the reason I sing. I have much to be grateful for."

"That's a perfectly lovely sentiment, Miss Anderson," replied Cousin Rose, feeling uncomfortable that she brought up the subject in the first place. Making Cousin Rose feel more uncomfortable, Miss Anderson replied, "I think it's more than a sentiment, Miss Rose - at least I hope so."

Cousin Nigel rose up from his seat and tapped his fork on a glass and spoke in a princely manner, changing the subject, "A toast, gentlemen, to Miss Anderson. Gentlemen, stand." Tom and I stood with Cousin Nigel and toasted the great opera star. I liked toasting because it was right out of a Cary Grant movie. After we sat down, Cousin Nigel cleared his throat, trying to take away the frown from Cousin Rose's forehead, said, "Miss Anderson, I understood what you said about the bad times. When I was captured and put in a German prisoner of war camp, wounded, gassed, head full of lice, thinking I was about to be killed, what kept me alive was the thought that someday a beautiful rose would grow in my garden." He looked across the table, smiled at his wife, blew her a kiss and said, "And so she has."

Speaking in her warm, velvety low voice, Miss Anderson replied while look-ing at Cousin Rose, "I can understand that just by looking at your wife's gentle face. Miss Rose, you have the face of a perfect rose and that's the loveliest strand of pearls I have ever seen in my life. You wear them well. They suit you."

Cousin Rose paused, looked with love at Cousin Nigel, then back to Miss Anderson, reached behind her neck, unclasped the pearls, placed them in front of Miss Anderson, and said, "They're yours."

Miss Anderson gasped, "Mrs. Powderhurst, I wouldn't dream of accepting such a priceless gift."

Cousin Rose wouldn't be put off, insisting, "In Hawaii, whenever someone genuinely admires something we have, it gives us pleasure to share it with them. Please take the pearls. It would be insulting your hostess if you didn't."

Miss Anderson was truly flabbergasted and said, "I don't know what to say."

Cousin Rose said, smiling again, "Don't say anything more about it. Now, tell us about your life. I would be fascinated to hear all about it. It would be something the boys will always remember and treasure for all their lives." I added to Cousin Rose's request, "Please, Miss Anderson, tell us all about your life. I bet you had a real nice daddy, too. I can tell the people who have nice daddies, like Tom here. Everyone who has a nice daddy has to be a nice person."

For the rest of the evening at the table, Miss Anderson told stories about growing up black in America. There were funny moments when I laughed till I almost cracked my head on the table, and some very sad ones when it was hard for me to swallow my food. What most impressed me of what Miss Anderson told us that evening was that she could never hide being colored black. Her color stuck out all over her like a flashing light - all the time. Black skin was not something she could wash off her body with soap and water whenever she wanted to. And people attacked her for just being painted different at birth. She said that by being whitewashed, I had the privilege to hide lots of things.

I told her if I were black, I'd take off all my clothes and stand naked outside on a night without a moon so people couldn't find me. She laughed and said that even on a night without a moon, someone would find me stark naked and send me to jail.

One of the things I could hide from Cousin Nigel, being colored white outside and privileged, was that at home, I wore Mother's dresses. I knew that if my cousin found out my secret, he'd kick me out of the house because he said real men wore army uniforms. Being white, I realized after hearing Miss Anderson's tales I could continue to keep all my secrets stuffed in my belly without being attacked as long as I didn't open my mouth. Looking around at my cousins, proper and pink, seated at the dinner table, I felt I was as colored as Miss Anderson was, only I was colored different inside.

After dinner, I walked into the living room with Cousin Nigel. Tom, Miss Anderson and Cousin Rose were already in the living room, eating mints. Cousin

Nigel leaned down to my ear, patted my head, and whispered with relief, "I'm glad your Cousin Rose wasn't wearing her good pearls."

Wearing her new strand of pearls, Miss Anderson left us the next morning. Again, we stood at the front door and waved goodbye. This time when I gave her a lei, she kissed me on my lips. It was the best kiss I ever had in my life. After the kiss, I said swooning, "Miss Anderson, you're the best kisser in the whole world and you have the softest and most beautiful lips I have ever seen." She kissed me again.

As she was getting into the Bentley, I called to her, "Miss Anderson." "Yes, Percy?" she said, smiling. Making my lips as big as I could, I called, "Say hello to Alice Faye for me, and please don't tell her this, but you're a much better singer and kisser than she is. I bet you sing 'After the Ball' real good, too."

She winked, "Honey, I sing a helluva 'After the Ball.'" The opera singer left for the airport.

I had one regret as I heard her plane fly overhead. I wished she had sung my favorite Alice Faye song. It would have been a song that everyone at the Roxy Theater would have understood the words.

Mother had returned from Tahiti. She was about to land back on Kauai, and over the phone she said she had a big surprise waiting for me.

47

A Hero

I only had one more day to live in exile at the Powderhurst castle. Being my last day, Cousin Rose wanted to make it a special one. After breakfast, Cousin Rose, Tom and I walked over to Kress's. She told me I could spend two dollars on anything I wanted. Without hesitation, I bought three movie magazines, a Carmen Miranda coloring book and a paper doll cutout book of Linda Darnell, the dark-haired movie beauty at Fox. From her disappointed look, I could see that she thought our afternoon reading sessions had been a dismal failure.

Later that morning, we packed a picnic lunch and drove down to Kalapaki Beach. Uncle George, her father and Mother's lawyer, had his home nestled among coconut trees and fishponds. While Cousin Rose was visiting with her father in his house, Tom and I, wearing blue wool swimsuits, ran into the surf for a swim.

Since we had seen the movie *Swiss Family Robinson*, we decided to jump up and down into the waves and pretend we were members of that family, fighting the surf because our ship had crashed on the rocks. We made believe we had just been shipwrecked and faced the oncoming waves, standing tall and letting them hit our tummies. When the waves hit our stomachs, salt water spewed high in the air and we'd laugh, spitting seawater out of our mouths.

When we turned our backs to the horizon to let the waves hit our bottoms, we didn't see the largest wave of the day coming towards us. It hit us by surprise. The wave smashed into our backs, tossed us up in the air and then pummeled us nose down into the sandy bottom. Ocean foam was all around me as I was flung up and down, twisting and turning underwater in Neptune's washing machine. For a moment, I didn't know where I was. I couldn't tell the sandy bottom from the air above. I held my breath, hoping I'd surface because my lungs were ready to burst apart. Suddenly, I hit the sandy floor with my toes and shoved with all my might to let my body reach up into the sunlight.

Reaching the surface, I gasped for air, spitting saltwater out of my mouth, and swam for shore. Standing on the shallow sandy bottom, shaking my head to get the saltwater out of my ears, I searched for Tom. I couldn't find him anywhere. He wasn't swimming out in the waves and he wasn't standing on the shore. He wasn't anywhere to be seen.

Cousin Rose had told me Tom wasn't a very good swimmer and to watch out for him. My heart burst and I began to panic. I started to swim out to where we had been playing. I dove underwater as three big waves crashed over me. I couldn't find him.

On the beach, two Hawaiian boys were throwing a football to each other. I screamed to them for help. They thought I was crying wolf and ignored me. I dove under the water again. This time, I saw the green of Tom's bathing suit. I swam towards the bathing suit and saw Tom floating unconscious underwater. I grabbed him under his arms and, lucky for me, he was built like a matchstick and light enough to pull to the surface.

When I got his head above the water, I screamed for help again. This time, the Hawaiian boys knew I wasn't playing wolf. They ran into the water and we pulled Tom out of the waves and onto the shore. They lay Tom down on the sand and pressed on his chest. I ran for Cousin Rose.

My screaming brought her out of the house, and with her "two-ton Tony" father puffing behind us, I led them to Tom, who was lying on the sand. The boys had Tom breathing again but he looked blue as death and couldn't speak. He could only stare wide-eyed at us, throwing up seawater. The Hawaiian boys told Cousin Rose that it was me who saved Tom's life.

The ambulance arrived and sirened Tom all the way to the G.N. Wilcox Memorial Hospital in Lihue town. I got to ride in the front seat with the driver. Cousin Rose rode in the back, holding Tom's hand. After Tom was admitted to the hospital, I told both Cousin Rose and Cousin Nigel what had happened. Cousin Nigel said he hoped we had learned a good lesson that every Hawaiian knew - never turn your back on the ocean.

Doctor Wallis told us Tom had had a close call, but he would be fine in a couple of days. The doctor wanted to keep Tom in the hospital under observation because having so much water in his lungs might lead to pneumonia. Cousin Rose and Cousin Nigel went to visit Tom in his room. I stayed in the waiting room as only adults were allowed to visit patients. When they returned, they told me that Tom said he was ever so grateful to me for saving his life.

After the hospital visit, Cousin Nigel drove down to Kalapaki beach and gave the Hawaiian boys fifty dollars each as a reward.

My last night with my cousins was subdued. No one was a bit hungry. I said out loud that I couldn't think about eating a mayonnaise sandwich. For dinner, we were served a bowl of cottage cheese with two Ritz crackers spread thinly with peanut butter. Cousin Rose was emotionally undone and couldn't eat, so she went to bed early. I ate her Ritz crackers. Cousin Nigel excused himself to write an editorial for the next day's newspaper and I walked back to my room to pack.

Suddenly, Cousin Nigel appeared at my door and asked me quietly to please join him in his study. I left my packing and followed him. The library was his sanctuary and was shelved from floor to ceiling with peeling, red-leather bound books. "Close the door, Cousin Percy, we don't want to disturb dear Rose," he instructed.

I closed the door. Cousin Nigel sat in his chair, took out his pipe and lit it. He pointed to a chair across from him and said, "Sit over there and make yourself comfortable." I sat down and began to inspect my hands. Looking at my fingernails, I saw the change that had occurred since the royals had met me at the dock. My nails were cut and as clean as a whistle.

Smoking on his pipe, seeing me fiddling with my hands, he coughed to get my attention. "I wanted you to come in here so I could thank you for saving Tom's life. I don't know what I would have done if my Tom had drowned. You see, Cousin Percy, Tom is the most precious thing that I have in my life."

"I know that, sir," I said, looking down at his shined shoes. I continued, "Tom is a very lucky boy to have you as a father." I paused, looked back down at my fingernails, then said the same thing I had said to Mr. Hamada. "I wish you were my father."

"You have a father," he replied.

"That I do, sir."

Now was the time to say what I had wanted to say to him for a long time, but I had never had the courage before. I stumbled, saying, "Cousin Nigel, there is something I have been meaning to tell you."

"What is it, Percy?"

I sputtered it all out in one breath, "I broke Tom's train on purpose. I wasn't mad at Tom. I wasn't. I was mad because I thought my mother had forgotten me."

"I knew that, Percy, and I am glad you told me. I was a little disappointed in you when you did that. Now that you have told me, it makes you a man in my book. Telling the truth is an important thing in a man's life. It's a sign of honor," he assured me.

"I am really sorry that I did it and I will make it up to Tom. I promise."

"You just did." Cousin Nigel rose from his chair, took a book from his bookshelf and handed it to me, saying, "I want you to have this book as a present from me, Percy. It was my favorite book when I was a lad your age. It's all about a boy who learns to become a man."

I looked at the book and saw it was *David Copperfield* by Charles Dickens. Thumbing through the book, I said, "Thank you, sir, it will be one of my great treasures for all my life. I will never lose it."

"I hoped you'd like it. I hear your mother has a surprise for you when she comes in tomorrow," he continued.

"A surprise? Will I like it?" I asked.

"I think you will," Cousin Nigel said with a smile.

"Do you know what it is?"

"I do, but I can't tell you because then it wouldn't be a surprise, now would it?" Cousin Nigel sat down again and stoked his pipe.

"No, it wouldn't." I hated surprises but couldn't tell Cousin Nigel that.

Speaking like a daddy, Cousin Nigel said, "Now, it's time you went to bed. We've all had a big day and tomorrow will be a bigger one for you. You must be happy, thinking about seeing your mother."

"I am, sir." I rose from my seat and walked to Cousin Nigel. He stood and we shook hands. Looking into his eyes, I mumbled, "Thank you, Cousin Nigel, for making me into a gentleman."

He looked down at me and placed his hand lightly on my shoulder as he said, "I should have done more for you. I'm sorry I didn't. I want you to know that it was as much my fault as yours because I forgot you were a little boy."

"I'm eight, Cousin Nigel, and you did nice things for me and I really learned lots. Really." I walked to the door and opened it. I turned to him and spoke like an Englishman, "I still wish I had had a father just like you."

Cousin Nigel, standing ramrod-straight, spoke to me as an officer does to his first lieutenant, "Close the door quietly as you go down the hall so you won't disturb your Cousin Rose. Pick up your feet when you walk. You don't want to sound like a herd of elephants, do you? I'll see you in the morning at breakfast."

I nodded and whispered, "Thank you again for everything, Cousin Nigel. I'm going to miss you."

Cousin Nigel looked at his pipe, paused and whispered back, "I'm going to miss you too, Muffin."

I closed the door quietly and walked down the hall, picking up my feet as high as I could so I wouldn't disturb Cousin Rose. I could hear her snoring in bed.

I crawled under the covers without turning on any of the lights and thanked God for making my wish come true. Cousin Nigel called me Muffin again. On my last night at the Powderhurst castle, for the first time since I arrived there, I went to bed without washing my feet because the Cinderella ball was over. The prince was turning back into a ragamuffin and was going to live again among the common folk.

Before I drifted off to winken, blinken, and nod land, I felt anxious all over. I wondered when the sun rose in the morning what my mother had in store for me. I hated surprises.

48

The Surprise

My exile ended when Mother, driving Aunt Mari's station wagon, gunned into the Powderhurst porte-cochere, careening the car into a potted plant. Seeing what she had done, Mother reversed quickly, and destroyed more of Cousin Rose's rare plants. When she turned the engine off, feeling safe, I ran to the car.

Gingerly stepping over the broken pieces of the clay pots, I immediately asked, "What did you bring me?" Cousin Nigel and Cousin Rose, watching on the steps, looked embarrassed.

Getting out of the car, hugging me, Mother said, out of breath, "Is that all you have to say? Didn't you miss me at all?"

"I did lots, Mother." Pointing to my cousins, I said, "Cousin Rose and Cousin Nigel have been swell." Getting quickly into the back seat of the car with my suitcase, I ordered, "Let's go home."

"Before we do anything, young man, you get out of that car and say your thank you's politely," Mother scolded.

From inside the car, I told her that at breakfast, I had already said all my thank you's. Cousin Nigel and Cousin Rose walked over and embraced her and told her that last night Tom caught pneumonia and they were about to leave for the hospital. Mother thanked them for taking care of me and was sorry about Tom, my poor manners and their plants. They said not to worry and hurriedly headed for the Bentley. I waved a final goodbye to my cousins as Mother started the engine, backed out of the drive, and steered the station wagon away from the direction of the harbor. I asked her why we weren't headed for the ship to take us home.

Running over a tin can, Mother lit a cigarette and said, not answering my question, "Percy, I have that surprise I promised."

I blurted out, "You married the king of Tahiti and we are going to be very rich and we're going to have a castle all our very own like Cousin Rose and Cousin Nigel. That's the surprise, isn't it? I have a list of the things we can buy."

Mother stopped the car in the middle of an intersection and spoke to me in the back seat, "What am I going to do with you? I have something much better than being rich. We are going to Kapake."

"What's Kapake?"

"It's Shangri-La, a magical valley my family owns, hidden way over that mountain there." She pointed to a mountain far in the distance that was shaped like the back of an elephant. "It's a secret place that very few people even know about because the only way we can get there is by riding a horse over a very steep and dangerous trail."

I yelped, "Mother, that's no surprise. That's death! Mother, stop joking and let's get on the ship and go home. You know I hate heights and I hate horses."

Because cars were honking behind us, Mother put the car back into first gear and continued, "Don't you want to make me happy? Not many people ever get to see this valley. It's a privilege to be invited there and it's my very favorite spot in the whole world and, once you've seen it, it will be yours, too."

I grumbled, pressing my face into the back seat, "I don't care if Lana Turner, Clark Gable, Alice Faye, everyone I know in the world hasn't seen it. I want to go home. Pleeeeeese."

Mother concentrated on her driving, biting her tongue and keeping her thoughts to herself, while I continued talking like a sulky brat, "Mother, I think I've been making you happy all summer. Now it's my turn to be happy. If that's the big surprise you have for me, shoot me - kill me. I want to go home. I wanted you to come back queen of Tahiti and rich. You don't know how disappointed you have made me."

Mother's voice rose as she said, "Now stop that. We're going to Kapake and that's all there is to it. Not another word out of you, young man. Be a good sport and don't spoil it for the rest of us."

The words "good sport" were right behind the word "stupid" as the most hateful words Mother used from her personal dictionary.

"Mother?" I said.

"Yes?"

"I want to go home! Pleeeeeese!"

Mother pressed the accelerator and whipped down a long palm-tree lined drive to Aunt Mari's two-story mausoleum. The orange witch's house looked as mean and dark as she did. My darling mother, whom I hadn't seen for almost a month, told me that we were going to spend the night at Aunt Mari's and quickly emphasized that it was only for the night. In the morning, we would ride horses over the elephant-shaped mountain to Kapake.

I screamed to her that I was being shanghaied to hell and complained since Daddy left us I was either living in heaven or hell, and couldn't I start living somewhere in between. I shrieked on, "Compared to spending a night in the witch's house, then a horseback ride over a mountain, Mother," I paused so she would get the point, then went on, "facing a firing squad would be a picnic to me. Being dead and singing with the angels, at least I wouldn't have to get on a horse. Mother, you don't know what's it like to be a cursed person."

"I should have stayed in Tahiti," Mother said, handing me a spoonful of guilt.

I continued having Bette Davis hysterics.

Aunt Mari, the witch of terror, stood spread-eagle on the steps of her plantation mansion, clasping my sister's hand. Marigold was hunched over like a flying monkey in *The Wizard of Oz* and looked like she had become Aunt Mari's evil second lieutenant. They were nestled next to each other as if they had been glued together with peanut butter. Mussolini and Hitler waved at us as Mother lifted her high heel off the pedal and braked the car to a stop. She hit a potted bougainvillea plant.

As I walked up the steps, anticipating a beheading, Aunt Mari spoke thunderously, sounding like a thousand Queen Elizabeths, "Marigold, take your brother upstairs. Keep him in your room until lunchtime. See that he washes his hands and is seated promptly in the dining room at twelve sharp." Inspecting me up and down with her pince-nez glasses, she gave me the same look she had given me when she met the ship, and snarled, "Hmm - staying with Rose might have done you some good. You smell better and at least look presentable. Hair combed and shoes shined. Young man, need I say, that I haven't forgotten what happened at Rose's." Peering down into my face, she hissed, "You just remember that."

I was a cooked goose because no one had forgotten about the whoopee cushion incident. The whole island knew about it five minutes after it happened. The Japanese maids had a communication system that was faster than the telephone. Everyone who had ever felt the sting from the Orange Witch and those who had been fired from her employ knew the witch always got her pound of flesh and the whole island was waiting to see what was going to happen to me.

A Portuguese-Hawaiian man delivering groceries from Lihue Store had just been fired the week before because he wouldn't yield to the witch on her driveway, as she drove home after tending a sick Hawaiian family. As he forced her to pass around him in her car and drive on her manicured lawn, she rolled down her window and yelled, "Who in the hell do you think you are?" He found out who he is, because now, without a job, he was one of the poor, sick Hawaiians. Cousin Rose told the story at breakfast, warning me about Aunt Mari's clutches.

Without a word, Marigold grabbed my arm, doing a Brunhilda the Mighty act for Aunt Mari, and marched me upstairs, suitcase in hand, to the guest bedroom. Once inside the room, Marigold drilled into me that this was where we were to sleep, to be quiet, to not stomp my feet on the floor, and over there was my bed, the lumpy one with a blue and white checkered bedspread.

As I unpacked, I tried to impress Marigold with my new Powderhurst English accent and intoned, "Dear, dear, dear sister, how delightful. This room has such charm and it's so good to see you, dear sister, looking so absolutely handsome. I shall try to keep absolutely quiet for you."

Hearing my accent, Marigold collapsed on the bed, cackling like a chicken laying an egg. After she controlled herself, she got off the bed, put her arms on her hips just like Aunt Mari did downstairs, looked me straight in the eye, and ordered, "Cut the crap, Percy. Talk American or I'll tickle you to death. Take off your goddamn shoes."

I immediately dropped my English accent, ripped off my shoes and threw them at her stomach. I would have thrown the suitcase because she was sounding as mean as Aunt Mari, but it was too heavy.

We started to sniff each other's behind - that's dog language for getting to know one another again, and sat down on the floor and caught up. For better or worse, my sister was back into my life again and we'd have to make do. I told her about my adventures at Buckingham Palace and showed her the *David Copperfield* book that Cousin Nigel had given me. I offered to let her read the book first.

Marigold, gnashing her teeth, told me that the first week at Aunt Mari's, she caught trench mouth. She opened her mouth to let me inspect her bloody gums and the three teeth she could wiggle. She was forced by Aunt Mari's doctor to spend a week in Wilcox Hospital because she was so infectious. I told her Aunt Mari gave her trench mouth because Aunt Mari caught it fighting the Americans in the German trenches. Trench mouth was Aunt Mari's punishment for fighting on the wrong side in World War I and now she passed it on to Marigold to make her as mean as she was. After I finished telling Marigold that Aunt Mari was a dirty-mouth old Hun, she gave me the familiar "ouchy" Indian punch because she said she loved Aunt Mari. I answered that was because they were two chips off the same block of rotten wood and if she didn't watch out, she'd turn into a Hunkacha beast.

Marigold got up and pulled something out from her bureau drawer. It was a present that Aunt Mari had given her after she got well. She threw a pair of brass knuckles on the floor. She told me they once belonged to Aunt Mari's brother Uncle George, who is the sheriff on Kauai, Mother's lawyer and Cousin Rose's father. He used them on prisoners who tried to escape from jail. The reason Aunt Mari had them was because, after her husband died, she was robbed in the middle of the night. She told her brother that she needed something to protect herself. He gave them because he knew she could pack a mean wallop. Aunt Mari beat him up a lot when they were little children. Aunt Mari now stuffed a .22 pistol under her pillow like her sister Aunt Ella did. Not having any use for the brass knuckles and knowing Marigold could also pack a mean wallop, the orange witch gave them to my sister to use on me.

I told Marigold I couldn't understand why Aunt Mari was so worried about robbers when her ugly old face was protection enough. I received a slap on my head. Fifteen minutes after being back with my sister, I was my same old slap-happy person again.

Marigold put on the brass knuckles and lunged at me, making me into her punching bag. Trying to keep her fists from flying into my face, I jumped around and told her the brass knuckles were just great, hoping that would make her stop. I went on giving her lots of sugary words, saying she could knock out Joe Louis and become the next world champion, but leave me alone. I warned her that if she punched any closer to my nose, she'd knock me out.

I retreated back up on the bed and yelled, "Stop it. You've turned into a mean old orange witch or worse, a gangster like Dillinger. And you know what happens to orange witches, don't you? They melt and die when a pail of water is thrown over them. And you know what happened to Dillinger? He got shot dead after seeing a John Wayne movie."

Marigold laughed out loud like an orange witch "HA - HA - HA" and made an ugly face, pretending to be Aunt Mari cackling, and rode around the room on an invisible broom. She yelled that she didn't give a fig what she became. Watching her, I knew Marigold had stayed too long at Aunt Mari's because her mind had turned squishy. Aunt Mari must have cast an evil spell over her. I read witches can do that. They can turn people into witches just like them if the people lived with them long enough.

I slapped my head in wonderment, watching her battle-ax performance, and yelled, "Why is it that you always get swords and brass knuckles and I don't?" I jumped up and down on the bed and yelled above Marigold's cackling, "But I'm not going to let you become Aunt Mari. You're too nice to be a bad witch and, anyway, you're my sister. You're a Patty, not Hunkacha. And anyway, if you end up in prison at thirteen, you're gonna wish you hadn't because I can't bake a cake with a file in it. I just won't let you go to jail. You're just going have to stay plain old Marigold. Anyway, I don't want you to punch me in the face for the rest of my life. You're gonna make me permanently ugly."

I stopped jumping and said to Marigold, "I just thought of something - if you go to prison, you can't punch me anymore. Let's call up Uncle George and send you to jail right now." I fell down on the bed and sighed, "I'm exhausted! You tire me out, Marigold. I'm going to sleep." I pretended to sleep and made fake snoring sounds.

Marigold stopped riding around on her invisible broom and in a normal voice, said, "Percy, wake up." With one eye, I watched as she put the brass knuckles back into the sock drawer.

Feeling safe again, I sat up. "What do you want?" "Shut up," she said as she slammed the bureau drawer. "Oh." I lay back down on the bed and made snoring sounds again.

Sitting on the floor, Marigold started to pick at a scab on her foot. She snuffled, "Percy, come down here."

I got off the bed and sat beside her. Trying to get her out of her witchy mood, I handed my book to her and offered, "You can still read my *David Copperfield* book first if you want to."

Marigold took the book out of my hand and flipped through the pages, saying, "Percy, even if I had trench mouth, I would have rescued you and hid you in a cave if you had called me. I would have escaped from the hospital just to save you." She handed me back the David Copperfield book as I replied, "I know that, Marigold."

At Aunt Mari's house, the rule was that children were not to be seen except at meals, and certainly not heard from, except when asked a question by an adult - at least while I was in residence. Thankfully, because of those rules, I kept out of Aunt Mari's aim.

After dinner, Marigold and I sat quietly on the stairs, out of sight, while we overheard Mother and Aunt Mari gossip. Mother got first prize because she had traveled with a prissy bachelor cousin to Tahiti. When they arrived at the dock in Papeete, three lovely Tahitian maidens with children in their arms waved at Cousin Bertie, leaning over the railing, waving back. The children were yelling up to him, "Papa." It wasn't April Fool's Day.

Mother and Aunt Mari giggled like teenagers over the improbability of Cousin Bertie having a hidden brood of native children. Good gossip even made a witch giggle like a kid. Marigold and I giggled, too, because they were giggling.

Back in our room, I jumped up and down on the bed, excited because Aunt Mari was downstairs and I was upstairs, and tomorrow I would be leaving her house and her. I sang bravely, "La, la, la, la. Who's afraid of the big bad wolf, the big bad wolf." I flung my arms up in the air and made a big jump on the bed. The bed broke and crashed to the floor with a loud thump.

The next thing I heard was Aunt Mari, puffing up the stairway, two steps at a time, seeking revenge.

49

Shangri-La

The next day after Aunt Mari spanked me, I sat on a blistered bottom and my bones ached from sleeping on the floor. I was in a bad mood. To make matters terrible, the orange witch and her companion decided to come with us to Kapake.

She woke us at five by ringing a bell, and after breakfast drove us to the family ranch. At the stables, we were to mount the horses for an early ride over the mountain. Aunt Mari wanted to reach Kapake before the sun heated up the trail.

As we drove to the stables, Mother told us the story of her father and mother's wedding day. My grandparents had married in Lihue and jumped out a bedroom window during the reception because they were so eager to start their honeymoon. By moonlight and the light of torches held by Hawaiian cowboys, they rode over the mountain to Kapake. My grandfather not only hated horses, but he was allergic to them, and he sneezed and wheezed his way over to Kapake. Being madly in love with my grandmother, Grandpa was a good sport but broke out with a severe case of hives on their first night. He spent the rest of his honeymoon in bed, scratching. When Mother finished her story, Aunt Mari commented that my grandfather was a weak man.

Mother replied defensively, "Aunt Mari, you are talking about my father."

"I know that, dear," she said, patting Mother's knee. Ignoring Mother's comment, she continued on, "nevertheless, a weak man, Deidra." Aunt Mari looked at me in the rearview mirror and declared that all men were weak and the only way to control the beasts was to treat them like wayward boys, with the exception of her brother, Uncle George.

Waiting for us at the stables was a party of travelers. The person gathering the supplies and lining up the horses to ride was Uncle George. I could tell he wasn't a weak man because he bellowed out orders and everyone jumped.

Horses scared me silly. Of course, they didn't scare Marigold. She mounted her horse, Sweet Pea, as soon as we arrived. She rode him as if they had been best friends since the first grade. In minutes, she had Sweet Pea prancing in and out of the stables, showing off for Aunt Mari. As Marigold led her horse away from the stables, she tenderly patted Sweet Pea's neck and fed the horse sugar cubes like Gene Autry did in the movies. She trotted off to where the line of travelers was waiting to start the journey. Sweet Pea and Marigold were in love at first sight.

Uncle George had to ride the biggest and strongest horse because he weighed over three hundred pounds. A cowboy told me Uncle George's favorite horse, Peewee, died under Uncle George after a Thanksgiving dinner. He had too many helpings of mashed potatoes. A huge horse was being led out of the stalls for him to ride. Its name was Zeus.

Mother was given a gaunt-looking nag that looked ready for the glue factory. Of course, Aunt Mari jumped on the grandest looking horse of all. She called the horse Athena. Astride the horse, Aunt Mari looked like General George Custer getting ready to fight Sitting Bull because she wore jodhpurs, black boots, a pith helmet, and a khaki Army commander's blouse decorated with epaulets and brass stars. She looked as fierce as Kaiser Wilhelm II, the Emperor of Germany, and there wasn't any doubt in my mind that Attila the Hun, after seeing Aunt Mari on her horse, would have run screaming for his mother.

I hid from everyone and stayed far away from the four-footed monsters that were prancing around the stable yard. I was scared to death that someone was going to find me and attach me on top of one of the hoof-pawing Frankensteins.

Uncle George found me hiding behind a feed barrel. He picked me up, stuffed me under his arm, and tossed me up on a riderless horse. Seeing me sitting wide-eyed in terror, legs barely hanging over the horse's back, he burst out in a loud guffaw. As I gripped the horse's mane, terrified, he thundered, "Hang onto the pommel, fat boy, or you'll be spattered down here like scrambled eggs. And I'll be damned if I'm going to clean up your mess."

"Uncle George?" I asked timidly.

"What, fat boy?" he roared. Uncle George liked playing the bully.

Then I screamed at him as loud as I could, "Get me off this horse! Now! I want to go home." Taken aback, he turned around, and walked away. I watched him lumber down the road, shirttails flapping in the wind, as three cowboys helped him mount Zeus.

Looking at my hands, I saw that my fat fingers were shaking while holding onto the pommel. I leaned over and peered down to my right and saw immediately that the ground was a thousand miles away. As I adjusted myself back on the saddle, I pretended I was at home playing dress-up with Agnes the Awful and Gertrude the Good. As I tried to keep my mind elsewhere and think other thoughts, the horse turned around and looked me in the eye. We stared at each other eyeball to eyeball.

Trying to make friends, I introduced myself, saying, "Hi, horsey. My name is Percy." The horse blinked his eyes twice, telling me that he didn't like me on sight. I blinked my eyes back at him, telling him I hated him instantly and that we were never going to be friends. I snarled to his face, "I hate you, Stinkweed."

That was a mistake. After he heard me call him Stinkweed, he swished his tail back and forth, and tried to unseat me. Not succeeding with his tail, he shook his entire body in a forceful rippling motion, trying to toss me off the saddle. Doing his jitterbug, his tail swished faster and faster, twirling around like a revved up airplane propeller. I jiggled all around and danced on top of Stinkweed, holding onto the pommel. Slap, slap, slap, up and down, went my sore bottom hitting the saddle. I yelped, "Mother, help me. Rescue me. Your son is being killed by a horse."

Mother, far away, wore a red bandanna tied over her ears. Forgetting about me, she had fallen in love with her horse, too, and was patting its mane. I wanted to feed

Stinkweed arsenic and make him die.

Horses, Agnes said, like girls better than they do boys. I could vouch for that now and should have worn a dress to fool Stinkweed. Slap, slap, slap, my bottom continued to hit the saddle as riders ahead circled, frustrated because a locked gate kept them from entering the pasture where the trail began. I watched the riders pull on the reins of their horses, trying to make them behave. They couldn't move forward, backwards, sideways, any which way, because the gate was locked.

Missionary descendents were not in the habit of being kept waiting, especially by a locked gate. Grandsons and granddaughters of the first preachers to Hawaii were used to having all gates "open sesame" for them, just as they did for Ali Baba in *Arabian Nights*. Aunt Mari, especially annoyed, yelled to her brother, "Who are we waiting for, George? Which numbskull has the key? Someone, get the key and bring it to me so we can get going."

I hid my head down on the saddle. I didn't want her to think that I was the numbskull that had the key.

"This is it," I said under my breath to Stinkweed. "I'm getting off. I've had enough of you. I don't care if all my brains get splattered and Uncle George has to clean them up. I'm not going to Kapake. I'm jumping off and no one is going to stop me. Even that orange witch out there can't stop me now. I'm going home even if I have to swim."

As I shifted my body, moving my right leg over the saddle to leap off, a Hawaiian cowboy, large as the mountain, grunted and plopped into the saddle behind me. A large, muscled brown arm clasped around me and pulled me into his stomach. He charged, "Hold on, baby." The cowboy, Solomon, smelled of horse manure, worn leather and human sweat, odors of the earth on which he worked. His musk seeped into every pore of my body, a smell he wore with pride.

Solomon had on a dirty blue denim shirt, worn Levis, and a battered lauhala hat that covered his black curly hair. I could feel his strength pulsing in his arm as he held me fast. I could tell here was a man who railed at the winds, at the stars, at the seas, and would squash a skull with his bare hands and then, in an instant, turn into my protector. Solomon was a champion, a guardian, a killer, and saint.

In the distance, I heard, "Yippee, coyote. *Imua* (forward)." The gate had opened, which brought cheers from all the riders. Solomon dug his spurs into the horse and we jerked forward and trotted to the back of the line of riders filing through the gate.

The riders were dressed to make a movie about David Livingston and Henry Stanley, the men in Africa who discovered each other and the source of the Nile. Some of the riders were costumed in formal tropical whites, others in khaki World War I uniforms, and those in current 1941 fashion wore off-the-rack grayish Abercromie and Fitch riding britches. Most riders had on squashed felt hats to protect them from the sun and some carried fans to swat the flies away that fed on horse dung. Red, white and blue feathered leis encircled the men's hats. All the cowboys wore lauhala hats. Only Aunt Mari wore a pith helmet. The riders who were dressed in Vanity Fair fashion had on long, polished black leather boots. Marigold, Mother and I were the only ones barefooted. All the men and Aunt Mari slung hunting rifles over their shoulders to shoot a goat if he stupidly crossed our path. Also in the lineup were Japanese servants wearing muted kimonos that flapped over the backs of their horses. The servants held ropes and led the mules. They brought up the rear. On the backs of the mules were tied our food supplies and toilet paper. Ranch cowboys of all nationalities rode the outside fringe of the line to scold the horses to behave if they became too frisky.

Marigold was in the lead with Uncle George. Solomon and I rode in back with the servants and mules. Our riding party had the combined looks of a Tarzan safari, an outdoor picnic with the king of England, a samurai raid, and a Gary Cooper movie filmed in lower Borneo without "lions, tigers, or bears" to kill.

All my fears of heaven and hell surfaced during the entire trip because Uncle George laughed liked Hunkacha did in his cave. Uncle George's laughter scared me because it echoed in all the valleys. Because of his laugh, I was sure that we were going to travel into a forest of monsters and demons.

At the beginning of the journey, we wound through a maze of green pastures, unlocking and locking gates. Then, abruptly, the horses nosed straight up a mountain trail like in the Grimm's fairy tale I read in Miss Storey's class, and we began to climb a mountain of glass. The trail, in reality, was a wet, steep, slippery, winding, cobblestone trail built by Hawaiians to take my early ancestors over into the valley. A glass hill would have been easier to travel than the green, mossy rocks under us. One false, careless slip by a horse, and a rider would plunge down a two-hundred-foot ravine onto the rocks.

This trip was one of the worst days of my life and, to make matters worse, Solomon didn't talk. I was stuck in his stillness that made the fear gurgling in my stomach rumble like thunder.

Clop - clop - clop, the horses inched slowly up the stone trail. Every time the trail became slippery and dangerous, Uncle George roared with laughter. I observed after a horse and rider almost slipped into a ravine, he attached a rope to Marigold's horse and led her. When we heaved our horses up to the gap in the mountain, there were gasps of relief. In celebration, the horses streamed out long strands of cellophane from their noses. Uncle George couldn't stop laughing.

At the top, I saw on one side Lihue, from where we came, and on the other side, the valley of Kapake, the Shangri-La that awaited us below. We steered the horses down into the valley as color returned to our faces. The personalities of each rider changed, too. It was if a wizard waved a magic wand and turned witches and gnomes into nice human beings. Politicians became fishermen and witches became maids who cleaned scales off fish and peeled potatoes, and even thought that making a bed was a lark. It was as if, as we rode down the trail into the valley, a magical window shade had been drawn to the outside world, and all the powerful roles played in Lihue were left behind.

Aunt Mari took off her pith helmet.

The Kapake house greeted us like a great lady. High on a knoll that overlooked the ocean, the house was built of lumber that was floated in by ships in 1893. Ocean salt preserved the wood, so the original house still stood, even after tropical storms and decades of warm, raucous family gatherings threatened its very survival. However, at our arrival in 1941, the house had decayed badly from years of neglect and needed a proper paint job.

As we rode our horses up the knoll and tethered them to the ironwood trees surrounding the house, I could see from the top of the hill a small swimming bay, protected by a reef that was shaped like a turtle. Next to the bay, a land formation bellied out into the ocean, forming a fortress that protected the house from southern Kona hurricane waves and wind. The rock formation was in the exact shape of a crocodile. The beach house, built to last decades, was architecturally unpretentious and simple. It was designed to embrace and keep the residents safe from the wild, natural elements that roared outside.

As soon as we were off our horses, everyone ran into the house, unfastened the shuttered windows and pushed them out with wooden battens. Immediately, the salt winds blew into the house. With a gust of wind, all the smelly, trapped stale air was ejected in one mighty blast and the salt air sweetened every corner in the house.

A whirlwind of activity began. Aunt Mari, without her pith helmet, gave out instructions, saying sweetly, "Deidra dear, air out the bedrooms. You and your children can have Mother's room. Kimiko, unload the mules. Bring in the ice first, then the vegetables. Don't forget to put the meat on ice."

Pushing black droppings on the floor with her boot, Aunt Mari exclaimed, "Oh, my God, look at this, George. Rats. Rats have made their home in here again. Get the broom. George, don't look at me like that; the servants can't do everything." Uncle George laughed and pinched Aunt Mari's bottom as he went to get the broom.

Aunt Mari, with a twinkle in her eye, called after him, "George, you stop your foolishness. We have children here and you know where the broom is. If you don't know, it's in the pantry. Hurry up and don't let the others see this mess. You know how Dora hates rats. If she sees this, she'll make us all to go back to Lihue."

Dora was a distant cousin and a spinster who had recently come to live with Aunt Mari as a companion. You never saw her much, as Aunt Mari kept her in the shadows.

Aunt Mari found my sister outside, feeding her horse more sugar cubes, and instructed, "Marigold, go down with the boys and help them unsaddle the horses. Tell Solomon to keep my horse saddled. I want to ride her down to Long Beach to look for glass balls this afternoon." Mother told me that hundreds of Japanese glass balls (fishing floats) were found on the beaches of Kapake. Some glass balls, she said, were as big as basketballs and others, not round, looked like long hot dogs.

Marigold, happy as the Lone Ranger riding out on a Texas range, led her horse down to the stables to play cowboy. For the first time in her life, she was about to become a real flesh-and-blood cowboy like her hero, John Wayne.

Aunt Mari found me lying on the hikiee. I loved the *hikiee*, a king-sized bed to relax on in a living area, which was especially wonderful to lay on after filling up on a ten-course meal. The hikiee always has tons of colorful pillows on it to smother yourself with, especially when you're relaxing on a full stomach. I was exhausted from the ride of terror, and my fanny ached and so did every bone in my body. I had gone through hell and I didn't care who knew it. I placed tons of pillows over my face, thinking no one would find me.

Aunt Mari, born with the nose of a bloodhound, peeled the pillows one by one away from my face, and ordered, "Percy, get up. Go into the kitchen and get a sandwich and a glass of juice for lunch. Go outside and play on the beach. Stay out of my way. We have lots to do around here and you're better off out on the beach."

Her words were music to my ears. I skirted around her, looking to see if she had the paddle in her hand, and thought, "Dear God, let Aunt Mari stay out of my way for the rest of my life." I skipped into the kitchen and the maids made me a ham sandwich without mayonnaise. A ham sandwich without mayonnaise was created by the devil to torture me. I placed a ham sandwich without mayonnaise in the same category as sticking a toothpick under my fingernail and lighting it. After gagging down the torture sandwich and gulping a glass of lemonade, I put on my bathing suit and walked down the hill to the beach to look for shells and glass balls.

Kapake was Shangri-La because, without walking two steps, I found hundreds of perfectly formed seashells, more than I had ever seen in my life. They glistened in the sun, wet from an ocean wash, and were waiting for me to pick them up. After a half-hour making piles of seashells, Mother appeared on a sand dune behind me. She was wearing her bathing suit, holding a bathing cap in her hand and a towel around her neck. She motioned me to follow her. Holding hands, we disappeared behind a sand dune and walked far away from the prying eyes up at the house.

Once hidden behind a dune, Mother smiled and said breathlessly, "We've made our escape." Giggling like a naughty little girl, she spoke in a low voice, "I don't think Aunt Mari will miss us, do you? Everyone has gone into their rooms to take naps. Follow me, Percy." Hand in hand, we walked over the white dunes until we came to the top of one that overlooked one of the longest beaches I had ever seen in my life. It encircled a green-blue sparkling bay. We sat down at the very top of the dune.

Mother said sadly, "I always come here as soon as I can get away from the house without anyone seeing me. It was here on this spot that my mother was cursed by the Hawaiians. Remember, I told you I'd tell you about the curse one day?"

I jumped up and looked around and shrieked, "I knew we were cursed, Mother. I just knew it. It's spooky up here." I sat down and pleaded, "Tell me about the curse."

"Dig," Mother said. We both used our hands and shoveled deep into the sand. In seconds, we dug a deep hole. I hit something hard with my fingers at the bottom of the hole. I dug around it and brought out a broken human skull. I looked at it in wonderment. A wind rose and whipped grains of sand into my face, stinging me like little bees.

Wiping the sand away from her face, Mother looked out to sea and started her story. "It was here that brave Kauai warriors fought terrible battles to save their island from being conquered by King Kamehameha. The battles are legendary and are said to have been bloody and fierce. King Kamehameha's warriors were defeated and were left on these dunes to rot away, without a burial. The Kauai warriors cursed their dead enemies for eternity. It was for the wind and the drifting sands to bury them. These dunes are filled with thousands and thousands of bones, and anyone who disturbs them or takes the bones away from here takes the Kauai curse with them. The curse will follow wherever the bones go. My mother took...."

I dug around a little more and pulled out a leg bone. It looked like a big, long, oversized turkey drumstick. I interrupted Mother and said, "Look at this!" Mother paused and looked at me as if I hadn't been paying attention to what she was saying, and asked, "Are you listening, Percy?"

"Of course I am. What happened to Grandma, Mother?"

Playing with her hands, sifting sand through her fingers, then looking down at the beach where waves were crashing on the shore, she whispered the story of Grandma's curse, "I told you many times that when I was a little girl, we lived in Berkeley, California. Next door to us in the Uplands lived a dentist. Once at a dinner party, Mother told the dentist about this valley, the sand dunes and the Hawaiian bones. He asked her if she should ever find a skull with a beautiful set of teeth, to bring it back to him. He needed one for research.

"Our last summer here as a family, Mother was riding her horse on this very dune and found a perfectly formed skull with the most perfect set of white teeth. She did as she promised and brought the skull back to the dentist in Berkeley. The Hawaiians heard what she was doing and pleaded with her that the skull must remain where she found it, but Mother wasn't a very superstitious person and didn't listen.

"She died an accidental death four months after we got home and left us orphans. Aunt Momi and I remember, to this day, the skull rolling back and forth on the bureau in Mother's cabin as we sailed for California. It is a memory that has never left my mind. Someday, I want to find that skull and bring it back here and bury it where it belongs.

"You see, I think the skull cursed my mother and maybe cursed all of us. The dentist still lives in the San Francisco area. Momi and I have made it a project to bring the skull back here and bury it where it belongs. If we don't, you must promise me that when you grow up, you will do it for us. But in the meantime, every time I come back here, I come to this very spot and say a little prayer, hoping that my prayer will make the curse go away. Sometimes, I feel the curse is very strong around me. But then, maybe it's all silly superstition. Percy, let's not tell them back at the house what I just said." Mother pointed towards the house. "They'll think we're crazy, so let's keep this our secret."

Putting my hand on my stomach, I said, "Mother, I know it's true because since I was little, I knew I was cursed. I keep lots of secrets and this will be one of the most secret of secrets, and, I promise you, I'm going to make the curse go away. I thought Aunt Mari had cursed me, but I knew inside she was just a mean old lady who likes to beat up little boys." Placing my hands in a praying position, I said to Mother, "Let's ask God to protect us until we bring the skull back here because I don't want anything to happen to you, or to me, or to Marigold and...to forgive Grandma in heaven for taking the skull."

Mother asked, "Would you like to say the prayer for us, Percy?"

"Yes, I would," I said, stroking the skull in my hands. I paused and looked all around me before I started the prayer. The wind had risen now and blew small cyclones of sand up into the air. Because the sun had gone behind a dark cloud, running shadows from the clouds were dancing across the dunes like maidens holding hands. I thought they were fleeing Hunkacha. The wind suddenly stopped. God was listening now.

I began, "Dear God, please don't let anything happen to my family any more. Please, let the curse go away, and make everything all right again. My grandmother didn't know what she was doing, and, if she did, she wouldn't have done it if she had known the curse would hurt us." Scratching my head at my last words, I added, "That might not make sense to you, God, but you understand what I am saying, especially if you were me, and anyway you know all things. Please make the curse go away right now, like poof. Thank you, God, and say hello to Jesus for us. Amen. P.S. Tell Daddy we are not cursed anymore."

Mother kissed me on the cheek. "That was a nice prayer, Percy. You can be such a good boy at times and even if I don't say it very much, I love you and Marigold very much."

I answered, "We love you, too, Mother. Isn't it fun that you and me are here all alone and able to play together like we're best friends? Come to think of it, we don't have much time together any more, do we? Just like you said after we saw *Gone With the Wind*, we need to play together more. And Mother, don't let Aunt Mari spank me again. She hurt me."

Mother gave me another kiss and said, "I didn't know what happened last night because I was taking a bath when she heard the bed break. I made it clear to her to never touch you again. You are my child, not hers. Percy, what we have is today, and that's all that counts, so let's have fun."

We blessed and buried the skull and leg bone again and felt free from the curse.

"Let's go swimming," I said, jumping up and running as fast as I could towards the ocean. I called back to Mother when I was almost at the water's edge, "Last one in is a rotten egg."

Mother screamed, using her Hunkacha voice, telling me I wasn't playing fair, and chased me into the ocean. Together, holding hands, we dove into an incoming wave. As we emerged from the other side of the wave, the sun appeared from behind a dark cloud.

"Mother," I said excitedly, jumping up and down in the ocean foam and splashing the water with my hands, "the curse is gone! I know it is! I can feel it."

Mother, wiping away the saltwater from her eyes, sputtered, "I hope so, Percy. I do hope so."

"Mother, you're the rotten egg because I got in the ocean first." After I said that I dove underwater looking for fish. Mother swam for shore and yelled as I surfaced, "The last one out of the water is a double rotten egg." I was the double rotten egg because Mother was already walking on the beach as I ran out of the water.

A laughing seagull screeched as it dove to where we were picking up our towels. The bird swooped right above our heads, close enough to peck something out of my hair. The bird frightened me. In the distance, Uncle George was laughing again. His laughter echoed in all the valleys of Kapake.

I looked at my mother, toweling the saltwater off her body, calling to the bird above, and I felt a shiver run up my spine.

50

Uncle George's Last Laugh!

The valley became magical because Aunt Mari was no longer colored orange. She turned into a wrinkly, white-haired old lady who sat outside in a bathing suit, eating mangoes with her fingers.

The beach house was a fairy-tale castle and had the biggest kitchen I had ever seen. There were three stoves in the square room, two kerosene and a large wood burning one near the back door, a stone's throw from the turkey pens. Every day, the servants prepared meals suited for knights sitting at King Arthur's round table. The menu varied from roast duck to baked chicken to rare rib roasts of beef, goat that had been shot on a mountain cliff that morning, and fresh reef fish plucked from a throw net. Every day, I ate as if I was going to fight King Kamehameha's warriors on the sand dunes.

The house was not magical for the Japanese cooks. They had to slave over the hot stoves from sunlight to sunset. Every morning, the Japanese ladies burned incense and prayed to Buddha for a quick return to Lihue because at high noon, the kitchen with all the stoves burning felt as hot as a thousand rising suns.

Separate from the magical castle was a seven-holer outhouse. Seven holes, seven doors, seven cubicles. The outhouse looked like portable dressing rooms nailed together for Hollywood movie stars and every morning I expected to see Alice Faye walk out of one them, dressed in a Gay Nineties costume, ready to face the camera.

The holes in each cubicle were shaped to fit different sized bottoms. Once, I made the mistake of taking door one, which belonged to Uncle George. I almost fell through his hole and if I hadn't hung on for dear life to the sides, I would have joined Uncle George's breakfast in the pit. I never made that mistake again. Door seven was mine. Like in the story of *Goldilocks and The Three Bears*, that hole fit my bottom just right.

The most amazing thing about the outhouse was that in the mornings, after breakfast, it became the gathering place for the family. When the cubicles filled to capacity, the occupants sitting inside the cubicles would chat merrily with their neighbors, chirping away as if they were eating crumpets with the King of England. Nothing disturbed their conversations, except if someone ran out of toilet paper; then there was hell to pay, especially if that cubicle housed Aunt Mari. But some royal person would wave a magical wand, and in seconds, the kind-acting princess would pass down a page torn from an old Sears and Roebuck catalogue to the screamer.

The only person who didn't chat on these social occasions was Cousin Dora, the spinster and the companion of Aunt Mari, who stayed in the shadows. I never saw her go, not once, not ever, and that made her a very special person to me. I thought she must be an angel in disguise because angels didn't go either, like movie stars. Anyway, anyone who lived with Aunt Mari had to be an angel. Cousin Dora was so skinny, she ate like a minnow and was worrisome about everything that Aunt Mari did, so I figured there wasn't much to come out of Cousin Dora. She looked like a ghost.

Real ghosts did roam the castle at night, so said Uncle George. He called them night marchers. They were dead Hawaiians who tramped through our rooms at midnight looking for fresh water and my blood. Uncle George, showing his teeth, said that he heard that the night marchers this year were out looking for a fat, little boy to eat up. After hearing that, I never once walked down to the out-house after dinner. I wasn't going to be stupid enough to have a hungry ghost make me an ala mode for his apple pie. The cooks added to my fears of going to the bathroom in the dark because they told grim tales of poisonous centipedes crawling in cubicle seven, waiting to sting my white, fat bottom. I never once wet my bed sleeping in Kapake, which made the castle truly magical.

I slept with Mother and Marigold in the front bedroom which faced the ocean. The bed frames were made of metal and the bedsteads had rusted brown from the blowing salt wind. Mosquito netting hung from the ceiling, protecting me from squadrons of mosquitoes flying around that hungered for an evening meal. Sardine cans filled with water were placed under each bedpost to discourage centipedes from crawling up into my bed and from stinging my peepee.

The days at Kapake were ordinary - yet not so ordinary. In an enchanted valley, the days could not be ordinary. After breakfast and our chats at the outhouse, we were on our own until lunchtime.

Marigold, now smelling like a real cowboy, hitched up her pants and walked bowlegged down to the stables to ride Sweet Pea, or brand a calf or learn a hundred different ways to tie a rope. On the first day, Solomon taught Marigold to saddle her own horse. She still adored Sweet Pea and now began to look and act like her horse. Marigold's legs even quivered like a horse, and when I walked by her, she kicked me whenever I came within kicking reach. Sleeping next to Marigold was hell. It was like sleeping next to a dead horse because she smelled like a hundred Black Beauties who hadn't taken baths. I itched all over like my Grandpa did on his honeymoon and complained to Mother that I was breaking out in hives. Mother turned a deaf ear because she wanted to keep Marigold happy.

I decided to take the situation in hand, especially because the smell was getting stronger and the wind wasn't blowing, so I called from my bed, "Marigold, would you please take a shower? You're making me itch. I'll do something that I don't for anyone. I'll share my Loretta Young Palmolive soap with you."

Marigold neighed like Sweet Pea and hollered her two favorite words, "Shaaaad up." Then she added, "Runt, if you don't shaaaad up, I'll brand your fat ass with a big M or put a fat centipede in your bed."

Given the choice between a centipede bite and a red hot M branded on my bottom, I chose the centipede bite and shaaaad up, of course, scratching my tummy and holding my nose for the rest of the night.

Every morning, when Uncle George was on his own, he and his favorite cowboys hiked the mountains behind the house to shoot goats. I was amazed at how nimble he was climbing over rocks, carrying three hundred pounds of his fat. With a gun slung over his shoulder, he skipped up the cliffs like a young boy, always champing on his big, fat black cigar. Everyday, Uncle George and his cowboys shot dozens of goats for our dinner. We had more goat meat than there were jars of mayonnaise at the Piggly Wiggly grocery store. Uncle George could have fed the entire American army with his goat meat.

I hated eating goat meat. Roasted goat tasted like its own poo poo, seasoned with Marigold's bad breath after she was seasick. I poured gallons of Twins catsup over the goat meat to take away the taste. At dinner, most of the goat meat went into my napkin. I coughed a lot. Goat meat was tougher to chew than shoe leather, but everyone at the table oohed and ahhed that gnawing the goat was as tender as a baby's bottom. Aunt Mari, fluttering her eyes and making loud smacks with her mouth, said the taste was ambrosia. Cousin Dora, sitting next to me, came out of the shadows and told me that ambrosia meant food for the gods. I whispered to her that the only god who would say that would be the god of the big poops. Cousin Dora choked on a piece of goat meat.

Cousin Dora liked me because I said things she would have said if she weren't so scared of her own shadow. Skinny as a pencil, she was scared of everything, especially when Uncle George was around. The spinster hid in the darkest corners of the house, reading poetry, until summoned by Aunt Mari to do the witch's bidding. Cousin Dora did everything for Aunt Mari, from cutting her toenails to fixing her hair. I whispered to Cousin Dora at the dinner table that Abraham Lincoln had freed the slaves, if she hadn't heard. She spat a string bean out of her mouth and patted my hand, whispering, "Dear boy, never be poor. Never have to depend on the kindness of relatives. Your mother understands that."

Of all the relatives staying at Kapake, Mother was the kindest to Cousin Dora. Mother made notice of people who weren't noticeable.

I promised Cousin Dora that someday President Roosevelt would free her and bring her out of the shadows because our president was more powerful than Aunt Mari. She placed a finger on my lips and shushed me, reminding me that President Roosevelt was a Democrat and Aunt Mari hated Democrats, and she slithered back to a corner of the lanai to read her poems.

Aunt Mari spent her days on horseback roaming the beaches, collecting driftwood and odd relics from shipwrecks and, of course, Japanese glass balls. She wore old clothes and, like Mother, wound a red bandana around her white hair. Nature calmed her here and she became one of us. She made beds, peeled potatoes, chopped onions, and read romantic novels on the hikiee in the afternoons. The romantic novels were about lovers kissing on the moors of Scotland, and the books had happy endings with the romantic couples sailing off into the sunset, arm and arm. While reading her sappy novels, Aunt Mari flushed like a pimply teenager. Gertrude the wise told me witches can turn into anything that they want to become, and that's why witches are dangerous. Aunt Mari also planned picnics, played charades and took Marigold on horseback rides up to waterfalls in the mountains. Aunt Mari and Marigold were like two peas in a pod. Once in awhile, I saw the orange look come back into Aunt Mari's eyes. I told Mother that Aunt Mari was still a mean witch and not to be trusted.

Once when Aunt Mari and Marigold nuzzled their noses together like Eskimos and rode off to find more treasures on the beach, Mother took my hand and walked me down to my shelling beach. After she spread a towel on the sand, she sat me down on the beach and explained about Aunt Mari. "Percy, you must try to understand Aunt Mari. She has had a very tragic life. A sad life, really. How you see her at Kapake is what she must have been when she and my mother were little girls. Notice how full of fun she is here. Aunt Mari always loved the outdoors. She was like Marigold, a tomboy. But God wasn't as kind to her as He was to my mother. My mother was beautiful and Aunt Mari was a big boned child and grew to almost six feet tall by the time she was sixteen, and she wasn't pretty - that's a terrible curse for a woman."

I asked, "How come she has white funny hair here and orange hair in Lihue?"

"She wears a wig, Percy. We never question the wig but I think it makes her feel more attractive or more noticeable in the outside world," Mother answered.

"Having orange hair all over your body where you don't want it growing and wearing a funny wig like Queen Elizabeth isn't going to make you into a Miss America, Mother." I shook my head in disbelief, thinking that Aunt Mari's hair change wasn't magic at all.

"Percy, you exaggerate too much. Aunt Mari doesn't have orange hair all over her body," Mother retorted.

"Yes, she does. You look at her at dinner; there's a lot of hair coming out of her nose. I can't help thinking of all the hair in her brain that wants to come out. That's a lot of orange hair in my book." I inspected Mother's nose as I said that.

"Percy, what is it you see through your eyes? Never mind, don't tell me. Now let me continue. Do you want to hear the rest of the story?" she asked.

"I love your stories. Of course, I do, and for your information, there's nothing wrong with my eyes. You look at Aunt Mari's nose tonight at dinner," I insisted.

Mother ignored that last remark and continued, "Well, after my mother married my father, Aunt Mari thought she was going to end up like Cousin Dora, that is, until Uncle Edward came along. She and Uncle Edward had known each other all their lives and suddenly, they fell in love. He was Aunt Dilly and Aunt Margaret's brother."

Aunt Dilly and Aunt Margaret were on the trip with us at Kapake. I never saw them much except at meals. They were from another missionary family that owned two or three large sugar plantations. They were the retiring types and kept to themselves. Mother told me that Aunt Mari always included them on these trips because they were her sisters-in-law and they were never invited anywhere else because they were so shy. I overheard Aunt Mari telling Cousin Dora that these sisters had more money than Uncle George did. The sisters looked similar and had big teeth like Mother. They were known to have driven ambulances in France during World War I and they never spent a penny on themselves. Aunt Dilly and Aunt Margaret wore the same dresses they had bought back East when they attended college. The dresses were now faded cotton prints that were hemmed up a thousand times.

Aunt Dilly and Aunt Margaret were like the shy fairies in a fairy tale, who didn't want to be seen and would have disappeared just after "Once upon a time." Mother told me to watch these two ladies because they were the kind of people we should all aspire to. She said that they may be stingy with themselves, wearing old dresses, but they gave away money to hospitals, museums and to Japanese boys and girls for their college tuition. They did other generous things, but they would have died if Cousin Nigel wrote about them in his newspaper. I said to Mother that I would have died if I had to wear one of their dresses.

Smelling a beach flower, Mother continued her story about Aunt Mari, "Uncle Edward was short, thin and dark, and quiet like his sisters. Aunt Mari - well, we all know what Aunt Mari is like. Everyone was surprised they married because Uncle Edward was so shy. But after they married, Aunt Mari changed. She became docile and sweet and he blossomed, too. She became the perfect wife and he ruled the roost. Everyone in the family was amazed at the change in each of them.

"Then the accident happened. Three years after they were married, Uncle Edward went swimming out on Long Beach, got caught in a current and drowned. He had a weak heart. Mother, home for the summer, swam out to save him but she was too late. Aunt Mari was inconsolable. She wept night and day and threatened to kill herself. The family made Mother give up her baby, my youngest sister, to Aunt Mari to keep Aunt Mari's mind off the tragedy."

I exclaimed, "That was a terrible thing to make your mother do. If you left me with Aunt Mari I would have killed myself, even if I was a baby."

Mother explained, "It's a very kind, Hawaiian thing to do to give up a child to someone who needs one. The Hawaiians call it *hanai*. Now this is a family secret, Percy, along with Aunt Mari's wig. You mustn't tell anyone this." Mother made me "cross my heart and hope to die," promising that I would never speak of this.

My family was loaded with secrets that everybody in Hawaii knew anyway, even to the tiniest details. Hawaii was too small a place to keep secrets. Secrets were the delicious fodder to chew on at all bridge tables and, of course, behind closed doors.

Mother broke into my thoughts and more of the story unfolded. "Mother and Papa were very indebted to my mother's parents, your great-grandparents, because they supported us financially in Berkeley. My father was not a very good businessman because he always chose partners who cheated him out of everything he owned."

"I'm going to be just like Grandpa. I can feel it," I said as Mother took a breath. "What happened to your baby sister?" I asked.

"She died too! She suffocated in her crib at Aunt Mari's. Those deaths turned Aunt Mari..."

I finished Mother's sentence, "Into a mean old, sour, orange witch that wears a wig."

Ignoring my comment, Mother said, "Perhaps I am to blame."

"Why?" I asked.

Quickly, Mother explained, "Aunt Mari wanted to adopt me first, but I wouldn't leave my mother."

"I'm glad you didn't. You're much too nice to grow up in a witch's cave." I changed the subject and said to Mother, "It's the curse, Mother, and we've got to get the skull back. It's the only way that Aunt Mari will be nice again."

By Mother's look, I could see she was afraid that I might forget to keep my promise and blab the stories she had just told me at someone's dinner table. I reminded Mother when I saw that familiar look in her eye that when I made a promise, I kept it. That's what good spies do in the movies.

Mother always kept her promises to me and she was much too nice for this world and for those who lived in it with her. She was always doing something nice for someone else. Once, she sacrificed shaking hands with President Roosevelt when he visited the Territory of Hawaii. Grandma was so sulky when she heard that she, an old kamaaina sea captain's wife, hadn't been invited to stand in the receiving line with the governor that Mother let Grandma stand in her place and shake hands with the president.

Mother spent her days at Kapake making everyone else's days happy. She'd walk with me in the early morning, telling me about sea turtles that crawled up on our beaches in the dark of night to lay their eggs. She would ride horses with Aunt Mari when Marigold was too occupied branding calves down at the stables. She made sure Aunt Mari was never alone because Aunt Mari always had to have someone around her - especially to beat up.

Mother cozied up with Cousin Dora in the shadows in the afternoons, while Cousin Dora read some of her own handwritten love poems to Mother. Even the reluctant, standoffish sisters-in-laws would entice Mother to meet them behind a sand dune and smoke a half a pack of their Lucky Strikes. The ladies were chain smokers and died a thousand deaths until they could inhale a cigarette down to their toenails in secret.

Aunt Mari made it known to her subjects that she did not approve of smoking cigarettes or drinking spirits. She ordained that, being a true daughter of missionaries, alcohol was strictly forbidden in her presence except for a few exceptional exceptions. Uncle George was an exception.

Mother, Uncle George and the sisters-in-law would wait until Aunt Mari took her bath before hauling out the bourbon bottle from under Uncle George's bed and pouring stiff drinks on the rocks. Cousin Dora was the lookout person. As soon as she signaled that Aunt Mari had finished dressing, splashed 4711 perfume on her bust and was about to make her entrance - zip, the bourbon bottle would disappear under the bed and, poof, all the glasses were now filled with iced tea.

Only Uncle George, all 300 pounds of him, kept his bourbon glass held high in hand, filled to the brim with Kentucky bourbon, and he toasted his sister as she walked out of her bedroom smelling like a Parisian streetwalker. In everything, Uncle George was her exceptional exception.

Uncle George could get away with anything because he was Aunt Mari's older brother and had a powerhouse personality. She called him her naughty, naughty lit-

tle boy and he pinched her bottom, called her an old hag, made fun of her wig, and
told her to shut up when she talked like a witch. She loved every minute of his
teasing because she adored him. Uncle George was the only person in the family
who could take on Aunt Mari and get away with it.

Uncle George hunted in the mornings and fished in the afternoons. With a
throw of his net over a hole in the reef, he caught dozens of Hawaiian reef fish
called *moi*. Hawaiian and Japanese fishermen could never compete with his form
or the skill of his throw. An old photograph on the wall of the beach house showed
Uncle George, looking like a bronzed Adonis, casting a net over a reef. It was a
black-and-white moment of long ago, a fish net caught midair, flaring out in a hor-
izontal position into the horizon, and thrown by a man who looked like a god.
Uncle George, who laughed all the time, didn't have one handsome feature left on
his fleshy face that gave any hint of his long-ago movie star handsomeness.

Uncle George told a thousand off-colored stories, especially stories about his
old girlfriends. He was the most powerful Republican politician in Hawaii and was
used to having his way and saying anything that came to mind, and never mind
how the other person felt.

Uncle George lost his wife, Aunt Elsie, two years before to a cancer that he
never spoke of. His daughter, Rose, was a puzzlement to him because she was
much too, too refined "for her own good." He blamed her refinement on her marriage to "the Brit," as he called Cousin Nigel from Shanghai. He told me his
grandson was a bookworm, so he left him alone. I told Uncle George out loud that
Tom was a gentleman. I picked up my fork, looked Uncle George in the eye, and
stuck a piece of goat meat in my mouth as an exclamation mark. He never talked
as if Aunt Elsie had ever lived. Mother said when they were courting, everyone on
Kauai who saw them dance thought that they were the most romantic couple in the
world and a perfect match.

One of the best times at Kapake was in the afternoon, around four o'clock,
when everyone took a swim together. The ladies wore white rubber bathing caps to
protect their marcelled permanents from the Tip Top Beauty Shop in Lihue. Tip
Top permanents were then the rage on Kauai. All the ladies, including Cousin
Dora, bobbed up and down in the waves, chattering like magpies. From the
seashore, they looked like a flock of ducks floating on the waves. I searched
around to see if a duck hunter was hiding in the bushes because surely they'd get
shot.

Uncle George was the only man in the ocean. A ladies' man, he reveled in
being surrounded with females. He'd tease them by trying to rip off their bathing
caps and they'd splash water in his face. Every time he tried to say something to
Aunt Mari or the sisters or my mother, he'd have to yell above the waves that
pounded on the beach, and they couldn't hear him anyway with their bathing caps
on.

The ducks would call, "What?" or "George, speak louder," and get annoyed
with him because he wouldn't speak loud enough as he was telling a juicy story.
Uncle George knew every scandal that happened in Hawaii and he loved telling
about them. As he said many times at the dinner table, "I know where all the dead

bodies are buried in Hawaii."

Every afternoon like clockwork, three big waves loomed out on the horizon. One wave always dunked Uncle George and his smoking cigar. We'd laugh at him as he sputtered to the surface with the cigar still in his mouth. The other waves crashed on our heads and we'd get sand everywhere on our bodies. Getting out of the water, shaking the sand out of our bathing suits, some of the ladies' bathing caps always floated out to sea and their hair hung down like wet spaghetti. Watching as Uncle George and the ladies ran for their towels to dry off, I thought that life is like swimming in the ocean, feeling fine one minute, but the next minute a big wave looms up and crushes you with a ton of water. You can take the pounding as long as you don't keep your back to the incoming waves. I was never good at being surprised.

The other best time of the day was that special moment between lingering twilight and dark nightfall, when a blue-black blanket covered the sky and shut out the sun. The blanket had lots of holes in it, so a thousand stars appeared in the sky. It was when God told the mynahs and all the other birds to put their feathered wings over their eyes and go night night. The birds sitting in the trees would protest and scream to God, just like I did when Mother forced me to go to bed early after dinner. The birds, like me, wanted to stay up with the grownups because we feared that going to sleep meant dying. It was at that time the evening star appeared. I called the evening star God's engagement ring because the star sparkled like a white diamond hanging on God's sapphire blanket for everyone to admire. The North Star gave me something to wish on.

Every evening at this time, Aunt Mari and Uncle George walked out the kitchen door, sat on the steps, one above the other, and played brother and sister. Uncle George would scale the fish he caught and Aunt Mari would hold a bowl in her lap and a knife in her hand and peel vegetables for dinner. It was their special time alone when they put aside playing king of the mountain. Amusing myself by the corner of the house by making castles in the sand, I overheard everything they said, and they acted as if I was not there.

On our last night, whittling away at a carrot, Aunt Mari complained angrily about their brother, Pip, and his politics. Finally, Uncle George's voice came down like a meat clever and snapped. "Mari, stop it. I don't want to discuss Pip anymore. Trust me - it's all taken care of. Go in and take your bath. There's lots of hot water now."

Another star appeared in the sky. God's sky was turning into a very holy night.

Picking up another carrot to scrape, then looking up at the star, Aunt Mari put her hand on her brother's shoulder and asked, "George, is everything all right?"

"Everything is fine. Why?" he asked.

"I was just wondering," Aunt Mari sighed and put the carrot back in the basket.

Uncle George looked over, squinted his eyes and called, "Percy?"

"Yes, Uncle George?" I answered.

"Maybe tonight, you'll see the night marchers. They come out on nights like this," he said, trying to scare me.

My eyes widened and replied, "Really?"

"Don't scare the boy. He's much too impressionable, George," Aunt Mari scolded her brother.

Ignoring her, he continued on, "Percy, they have faces like this." He took both his hands and pressed his eyes and mouth together and squished his face into rolls of fat.

I laughed, "You don't have to make a face like that, Uncle George. You have a funny face all by itself."

Aunt Mari shook her paring knife at me and warned, "Don't be fresh, Percy."

"Leave him be, Mari. I like seeing him show a little spunk. He acts like a *mahu* (sissy) most of the time," replied Uncle George.

With her left hand, Aunt Mari scraped the leftover peels into the bowl with the carrots, wiped off her lap and rose to go back into the house. "I'm going in for my bath. Come inside, Percy. It's getting cold and you'll be getting your death, staying out here. Before you come to the dinner table, young man, be sure to wash your hands and face. I can see from here that you still have lunch on that face. Wipe that mouth now."

I wiped my mouth.

Aunt Mari turned to Uncle George and asked, "Coming?"

"In a minute, Mari." Uncle George sighed, wishing Aunt Mari would leave so he could have a drink of his whiskey.

She remarked, "You know, this was Papa's favorite time of day. You're so like Papa, George. Why don't you steam the fish tonight like Papa did for us every summer?"

"Good idea, Mari."

"Don't be out here long." She turned and walked back into the kitchen.

Uncle George put his head down and, for a long time, stared at the scaled fish neatly placed in the galvanized bucket by his leg. He lifted his head, shook it as if he wanted to get saltwater out of his ears, looked at me, and said, "Don't forget this place, Percy. Come back here often. This valley is really what life is all about. My wife loved this place."

Herds of peacocks down by the chicken pens shrieked as if they were in pain. They blasted the silence like an air raid siren except that their cries sounded more like maidens being ravished. The sky blackened. Uncle George walked over, reached for my hand, took it and with bucket in one hand, my hand in his other, he and I started to walk into the kitchen. Going through the kitchen door, I said, "Uncle George, I will come back here again."

"You will, Percy?"

"Yes, I have something to finish here. It will help you, too."

Uncle George stopped to look at me and questioned, "Help me?"

"Yes," I answered.

"What is it, Percy? I don't think anything can help me right now," he said, while he turned and looked down where the peacocks were strutting.

"I can't tell you that because I promised, but I can give you a hint. Do you believe in curses, Uncle George?" I replied.

He paused, put down his bucket of fish and hugged me. He hugged me for a long time. Then he said, "Yes, Percy, I do believe in curses." There were tears in his eyes. I liked Uncle George when he acted like a fisherman.

After eating Uncle George's steamed fish for dinner, everyone went out on the lanai and lay down on the hikiee. We talked of ghosts by candlelight. "I remember Mama telling me of the time she saw Alika coming in here and touching Papa on the forehead while he slept," Aunt Mari said, holding a pillow on her tummy. "Mama knew it was Alika back from the dead to bless him."

Aunt Mari told the story of Alika, a wise Hawaiian kahuna who lived in a grass house on my great-grandfather's property. The grass house was built next to the main house. Alika raised my great-grandfather after he lost his father to tuberculosis. Alika taught him to speak and learn Hawaiian ways. My great-grandfather became more Hawaiian than many of the Hawaiians who had readily adopted the ways of America and England. Even after he married, my great-grandfather spent nights with the old man in the grass house. Alika taught him the secret language and the secret ways of the ancients who lived in Hawaii long before Captain Cook landed on Kauai.

My great-grandfather, who was governor of Kauai during the reign of the last Hawaiian queen, Liliuokalani, never revealed to anyone the secrets Alika taught him. The ancient secrets are buried with him in the family cemetery. Aunt Mari ended her story saying, "Alika appeared here on this lanai just before Papa died."

Lighting a cigar, Uncle George said in the dark, "Papa never talked to me about Alika. Mari, you were much closer to him than I was. I always wondered if Papa told you anything about what Alika said. I always wanted to learn Alika's ways, but Papa always put me off, saying 'later.' He loved you best, Mari."

Aunt Mari, shifting herself on the hikiee and putting a pillow behind her neck, answered, "Papa never told me anything, George. He loved Mary best. Deidra, your mother was always the apple of his eye. The fact is everyone in our family loved your mother best."

Uncle George blew his cigar smoke into the air and interrupted, "If I believed in ghosts, I'd think Alika was here with us tonight."

Aunt Mari coughed and said, "Quit teasing, George, and I wish you'd quit that filthy habit." Blowing the smoke away from her, she continued, "Anyway, George, girls are always much closer to their fathers, but I was thinking tonight, looking at you, you're so like Papa was."

"I'm not. Wish I were, Mari." Taking a long puff on his cigar, he changed the subject. "Marigold, you and Keoki did a good job penning up the calves today."

"Thank you, Uncle George," Marigold answered.

Cousin Dora piped up, "Deidra, sing us a song before we go to bed." A wave crashed on the reef.

Aunt Mari interrupted, "George, what makes you live so well?"

Smoke curled up from the corner where Uncle George lay, and he chuckled to himself, saying, "Good food, good cigars and lots of women, Mari."

"Oh, George." Aunt Mari blushed, putting a pillow over her face. Uncle George burst into laughter at his joke played on Aunt Mari.

The two sisters from the other missionary family, who lay next to each other, ached for a cigarette. Another wave hit the reef.

Cousin Dora raised her voice tentatively again, "Deidra, please sing us a song."

"I'm too full, Cousin Dora," Mother answered. "Please," Cousin Dora gently insisted.

Mother grabbed the ukulele off the table and started to tune it while Uncle George sang out, "My dog has fleas."

I yelled out, "So does Marigold." Marigold jumped on me and punched my arm, yelling, "I do not."

"Yes, you do and I can prove it!" I proceeded to look through her hair while Marigold punched me.

"Stop it, children! Simmer down right now! Let your mother sing us a song for Uncle George," the lady general ordered. Marigold and I separated. I noticed the two sisters had left quietly while we were fighting and I could see them walking on the beach, smoking cigarettes.

Mother played and sang her mother's favorite Hawaiian song, "Nani Wale Lihue." Uncle George and Aunt Mari joined in singing.

A soft wind blew across the lanai. A candle went out. Another wave crashed on the beach. The song was over. Mother put the ukulele back on the table as a wind howled through the ironwood trees outside and then rushed into the lanai, extinguishing the last candle. The lanai turned to total darkness.

Uncle George boomed out, "Percy, it's the night marchers." I put my head under a pillow.

Aunt Mari relit a candle as we all said our goodnights and felt our way to our bedrooms. I crawled into bed, pulled the mosquito netting down over me and fell fast asleep. I forgot to say my prayers.

Around midnight, I heard a loud BANG! I woke and sat straight up. My heart pounded as I listened for a second bang. Nothing was heard. The house went back to being as quiet as an empty icebox. I looked over at Marigold's bed and she too was sitting straight up. Her eyes were opened wide as saucers.

I whispered, "Marigold, did you hear that?" She whispered back, "Yes." I looked over at Mother's bed. She was still fast asleep. Old people can sleep through anything, I thought. Pushing back the mosquito netting, I got into Marigold's bed and whispered, "What do you think it was?"

Marigold cocked her ear, turned to me with an evil grin and said with absolute pleasure, "Percy, it's the night marchers."

"Do you really think so?"

"Yeeeeeessssss! And let's go find them."

'Nooooooo, I'm staying right here." I hid under Marigold's covers.

"Oh, no, you're not. We're going to see them together," she said, pulling the blankets away from me.

"You just want me to go with you so they'll eat me up and leave you alone."

Marigold said, eyes glittering, "Yeeeeeeees."

"Well, I'm not going." I was adamant. Marigold got out of bed and pulled me with her, saying, "Yes, you are, and don't worry. I'll protect you."

"Promise?" I begged, hoping she'd say no.

"Promise."

"And promise me if they want to eat me up, you volunteer to take my place."

She didn't answer me, but dragged me by one hand out of the bedroom onto the lanai. It was so dark, I couldn't even see my hand in front of my face. There wasn't a star left sparkling in the sky. God had covered his sky with a blanket without holes. A wave crashed on the reef.

"Let's go back, Marigold," I said, pulling her back into the bedroom.

"No, I want to see the night marchers," she said, yanking me back onto the lanai. The wind whistled through the ironwood trees, its sound making us shiver.

I whispered, "It's too dark to see anything. I have to go to the bathroom, Marigold."

"Hold it," she ordered. I did. I always questioned myself what it was about Marigold's voice that made all my bodily functions dry up like a desert.

A flickering light shone under Uncle George's bedroom door. "I smell something burning, Marigold," I said, pointing to Uncle George's bedroom. "It's coming from there." Marigold also pointed to Uncle George's room.

"Maybe Uncle George is burning up the night marchers. Or maybe the night marchers are burning up Uncle George," I guessed.

"Let's go see," Marigold said as she headed us towards Uncle George's door. Holding my hand in a vise-like grip, she pulled me next to the door. She opened it slowly and we looked in. A kerosene lantern sat on a table lighting the room. The first thing we saw was Uncle George's cigar on the floor, which was burning a hole in the lauhala mat. We rushed over and beat out the fire with a Bible that lay next to it. The room was beginning to fill with smoke.

I looked at the bed where Uncle George slept. His head lay quietly on the pillow, but his eyes were wide open - ready to pop out. I pointed to Uncle George, saying, "Marigold, look at Uncle George. His eyes look funny."

Marigold finished smothering the fire with the Bible and looked up as I called softly, "Uncle George, wake up. You almost burned the house down." When Uncle George didn't respond, I took his foot that was outside the covers and shook it, and said louder, "Uncle George, time to wake up. The house is on fire."

His eyes didn't blink. We inspected him further. In his right hand, next to his head, lay a pistol. On the right side of his face, there was a round, crimson spot on his temple. On his stomach lay a magazine featuring a Zane Grey western about a bank robbery. Marigold inspected Uncle George's face as I kept wiggling his feet.

"Percy, Uncle George is dead!" she exclaimed.

"His feet don't work either. Move over. Let me see him. I've never seen a dead body in my whole life." I pushed Marigold out of the way.

Marigold said, "Well, I have and he's dead as a mackerel."

I gave Uncle George's face a real once-over. "Yep," I said, "he looks as dead as they do in the movies." I thought for a moment. "Marigold, we're supposed to close his eyes. That's what they do in the movies and I know it's the right thing to do. And then we're to put pennies on his eyes. You close his eyes and I'll look around for some pennies."

"No, I'll look for the pennies and you close his eyes," she offered.

"Marigold, are you a sissy?" I said, with my hands on my hips.

That did it! Without looking, she reached for Uncle George's eyes and closed them. I found two pennies on his bureau and placed them carefully on his eyelids. "Do you think we should take away the pistol? I asked.

"It might go off again," replied Marigold, "and the detectives have got to see the evidence." She sounded like Sherlock Holmes.

"What do you think happened, Marigold?"

She paused and rubbed her chin. "Percy, it looks to me as if the night marchers were here and killed him."

I gasped, "The night marchers? Really?"

"THE NIGHT MARCHERS!" Marigold said, with terror in her eyes.

"Marigold," I said breathlessly, "if the night marchers killed Uncle George, they must still be around here somewhere." I got heated up. "And if they're around here somewhere, they're going to kill us too."

With that sudden realization, our hair stood on end and we screamed in unison, "MOTHER!" We immediately ran from the room, yelling, "MOTHER! MOTHER! MOTHER! UNCLE GEORGE IS DEAD AND THE NIGHT MARCHERS DID IT. THEY'RE COMING TO KILL US!"

I yelled louder than Marigold and screamed, "THE CURSE IS BACK!"

In the darkness of the night, a black wave broke across the reef.

51

A Suicide Ruins a Vacation

A suicide takes all the fun out of a summer vacation. From the moment Marigold and I woke everyone up, yelling that the night marchers were going to kill us and that the curse was back, and the very instant that Mother found Uncle George with a bullet smack through his head, our life at Kapake turned upside down.

Because there were no telephones in the valley, we couldn't call the police to come get the body. On top of that, there was neither electricity nor an icebox large enough to keep Uncle George from decaying in front of our eyes, so we had to pack up quickly to climb the mountain and get to Lihue and the icehouse.

As soon as the sun rose, a flurry of activity began. The beds were stripped, all the floors were swept, our clothes packed, and leftover food tossed to the pigs. In an hour, the cowboys sewed a canvas bag to carry Uncle George's body on his horse over the mountain. It took four big cowboys to lift the body from the bed and cram him into the canvas bag. To preserve the body for the trip, Solomon packed Uncle George with all the ice that he could find in the kitchen icebox and put rock salt into all his open parts.

Solomon was a great cook because he took as much care stuffing Uncle George with salt as Hatsuko did when she stuffed our Thanksgiving turkey. I know, because both Solomon and Hatsuko let me watch. After he finished his stuffing chores, I told Solomon proudly that it was I who put the pennies on Uncle George's eyes.

Everyone else around the castle acted emotionally. Aunt Mari collapsed on her bed, wailing and calling out to Uncle George to come back to her. Cousin Dora, trying to console the orange witch, ran back and forth from the kitchen to her bedroom and laid cold compresses on Aunt Mari's forehead.

The burden of closing up the house was left to Mother and the cigarette-smoking sisters. One of the sisters, a known saver who kept a hundred balls of old string stuffed in her kitchen drawer, said to Mother that she had packed up all the leftover toilet paper in the outhouse. Being a former ambulance driver in World War I, she also warned that we ought to get out of the valley before high noon because the heat would soon make Uncle George "smell to high heaven. And", she added, "there is a lot to smell there."

Without any assigned job, I wandered around the house following everybody, asking them a thousand questions. My main question was, "Why did Uncle George shoot himself?"

Mother caught me and made me stand still. She ordered me to walk down to the beach until it was time for us to leave because now wasn't the time to ask any more questions. I looked around for Marigold to ask her my questions. She ignored me, too, because she was busy down at the stables, helping the cowboys saddle up the horses.

The Japanese maids also ignored me. They were cleaning up the kitchen and were speaking to no one. I could tell by their glances at one another while washing down the walls, that they were ecstatic at the abrupt leaving. I imagined that at any minute, they'd break into a chorus of "hallelujah" with hands waving to the ceiling. When the Japanese servants first heard the news about Uncle George, they got down on their knees in their hellish kitchen, snuffed out the incense and thanked Buddha, not for Uncle George dying, but for being able to leave the hot kitchen.

Aunt Mari burst into tears at the sight of the maids on their knees, calling Buddha's name. She thought they were praying for Uncle George's departed soul.

After awhile, understanding that no one was going to answer any of my questions, I followed Mother's instructions and walked down to the beach. I sat in the sand, looked out at the sea, and pondered the big question all by myself. Why did Uncle George shoot himself?

Breathing in the salt air, I cleared my head and smelled the fragrant morning glory vines on the sand. Turtles had buried their eggs at midnight. I beat on my heart five times as Gertrude instructed, and suddenly, my imaginary friend was sitting at my side. Looking around, I asked, "Where's Agnes the bad?"

"This is our vacation too, Percy - remember? She's having her toenails cut and polished this morning. What's up?" Gertrude demanded.

I explained to Gertrude what had happened to Uncle George. "Why did he do it, Gertrude?" I asked.

Gertrude thought for a minute, making her voice low and sounding like a wise baldheaded monk, and said, "I don't know, Percy. The only person who will ever know is your Uncle George and he's dead. There are some mysteries in life that will always remain mysteries. We will never know about what went on in Uncle George's mind and what made him do it. Remember when you read about Amelia Earhart, the lady pilot who disappeared while flying over the Pacific Ocean? Poof - she disappeared just like your daddy did when he divorced your mama, but your daddy's not a mystery because we know where he lives. Amelia Earhart, that's another story. We will probably never know what happened to her, and that's okay, Percy. You don't have to know everything in this life just as long as God does. That's all that counts - that God knows, and that's just the way things are here on earth, and you should stop asking questions because no one up at the house can give you the answers. It's a mystery to them, too. You'll just have to be content knowing that we'll never know the answers to some things and you just go on living, knowing that."

"That's hard to take, Gertrude," I said, picking up a shell and showing it to her. "I want to know everything, even how shells are made."

Gertrude sighed and spoke slowly to me like I was a halfwit, "And so does everybody else, but that's the way it is. So forget it. You don't need to know everything and get on with your life, here and now. Stop living other people's lives. Anything else?"

Sounding like a baby, I said, "I miss you and Agnes."

"We're around if you need us, but I think now is a good time for you to be by yourself and to give us a little rest. You're not the easiest person to be around all the time, you know," Gertrude confessed.

"I know that, Gertrude. It's even hard for me to be around me all the time," I said, dejectedly. I lay down on the beach, looked up at the sky, and said, "Sometimes, I get really exhausted being me."

"Well, Percy, if that's all you want, my nail appointment is right after Agnes', so I've got to get back. I'm a mess. Look at my toenails. Oh, one more thing for you to remember, Percy: anyone who laughs too much, too loud, may be the saddest person in the whole wide world. See you in August, Percy. I have a feeling this is going to be a very busy year for all of us. Get some rest."

I nodded. Gertrude kissed me on the forehead and disappeared in the wind as a green wave with a frothy, snow-white crest crashed over the reef, slid to the shore and touched my toes.

Mother called from the house that it was time to go. I ran up to the house and everyone, including Aunt Mari looking like death's companion, was standing on the lanai, waiting for me. I thought Uncle George, dead and packed in ice, looked a thousand times better than Aunt Mari did alive. She was wearing her wig again.

"Percy," Mother said, "come here and stand by me. We want to say something to you. Now, this is important to Aunt Mari. We want you to listen. I want you to hear this."

I nodded.

Mother said, "We don't want you to say anything to anybody about how Uncle George died. We're telling everyone that Uncle George died peacefully in his sleep. We don't want you to say that he...."

I made my hand into a gun and said, "Bang, bang, shot himself in the head."

Mother nodded and continued, "Do you think you can do that for us?"

"But that's a lie. Mother, didn't you tell me never to tell a lie?"

Aunt Mari interrupted me, placing her pith helmet squarely back on her head, and shouted above the sound of the waves, "Percy, that is not a lie. Your Uncle George did die in his sleep and it's better for everyone to think he left us peacefully. You don't want to upset your Cousin Rose, do you? Think of all the nice things Cousin Rose did for you. We don't want anyone asking our family nonsensical questions."

"Yea," nodding my head up and down, I agreed, "you're right, Aunt Mari. We don't want anyone asking us questions we can't answer. When somebody puts a bullet, bang, bang, bang, into his head, that's a real big mystery. And no one can answer that except God."

She thundered, "Stop your constant palavering with me. Can we trust you?"

"Yes," I said determinedly, "I can tell as big a lie as you can, Aunt Mari."

Cousin Dora swooned into my mother's arms. As she held Cousin Dora, Mother quickly put her hand over my mouth before I could speak again.

Aunt Mari took off her pith helmet and was going to beat me over my head with it to make me shut up, but Mother stood in her way, saying, "Aunt Mari, you can trust Percy, I promise you that."

I nodded but I crossed my fingers behind my back. Cousin Dora saw my crossed fingers and swooned again into my mother's arms.

Aunt Mari turned heel and commanded me to sign the guest book before we left. She flew off the lanai on her broom to the horses waiting at the stables. The others followed the witch's wake.

I opened a page of the guest book and found that Jeanette MacDonald, my favorite MGM singing star, had spent her honeymoon at Kapake. Her husband, Gene Raymond, must have been the happiest man in the world here, that is, if he wasn't allergic to horses. I signed my name right under Jeanette's and wrote, "Had a great time in the outhouse. Your next future MGM singing movie star, Percy! Ha! Ha! I was just joking."

I walked down to where the cowboys were standing, waiting for me to get on Stinkweed again. There was a great commotion among the cowboys. I thought they were mad at me for being a pokey boy but they weren't. Solomon told me that last night, the cowboys killed an old horse and put his guts and blood in the water to attract sharks. They threw the dead horse's head into the ocean where I swam every day. A rope and hook were attached to the head. In a minute, a twenty-foot shark swam in and bit part of the horse's head off, and on his second bite, the shark was gaffed and it took three men and two mules to haul the monster onto the beach.

As Solomon finished telling the story and was lifting me on the saddle, I yelped, "Solomon, I swam in that water everyday. I could have been that shark's afternoon snack. Lucky for me, that shark liked a dead horse's head better than fat old me to eat. Just think, the shark and Uncle George died on the same day."

Squaring me on the saddle, Solomon spoke more words than I had ever heard him speak, "Fat boy, da buggah was watching you all da time. I know for sure because da buggah shark told me. Da shark no like you because you haole. But he know all haoles all time get stink taste - so he no eat." He roared with laughter at his joke on me. Solomon laughed just like Uncle George now.

Holding onto the pommel, I chortled, "Funny joke, Solomon, but I think he was waiting for you, because you look more like a dead horse's rear end than me."

Solomon jumped on the saddle behind me and slapped my head like everybody else did. I was tired of people slapping me on my head, and someday, I was going to do something about it, but so far it never made me keep my mouth shut. I said to myself, smelling Solomon's overpowering musk, "When I get home, I'm going to borrow one of the Twins' football helmets and play lots of jokes on people."

Solomon and I took the lead on the ride back to Lihue. Marigold and her Sweet Pea were in back with Aunt Mari and Mother. Uncle George's body in the canvas bag, slung over his horse, brought up the rear. Uncle George's favorite cowboy, Pinky, had tears streaming down his face. He led Zeus with a rope.

Riding back to Lihue was slow going. We plodded up the mountain like a funeral procession. The riders in back of us rode their horses slowly, with their heads bowed in reverence to the body that brought up the rear. I heard the horses' hoofs beating like drums, going boom, boom, boom - bang, bang, bang. Everyone wore a solemn face and no one dared to squeak a word. I actually missed Uncle George's laugh.

Riding back over the mountain seemed quicker and far more pleasant than the first time because this time, I wasn't scared. As we reached the mountain pass, the trip down was a breeze because we slid down the mountain of glass. When Solomon and I got to the bottom of the mountain, he asked me if I wanted him to gallop to the stables.

Feeling very brave now and thinking I had been saved from a shark bite, I said, "Giddy-up, Solomon. Let's go." Old Stinkweed gave his best effort and we arrived at the stables a good fifteen minutes before anyone else. I loved beating Marigold.

While standing around with Solomon, waiting for the rest of the party to come in, I asked Solomon a question that had been going through my mind while we were riding over the mountain, and I needed a man to talk to. "Solomon," I asked, as he was taking the saddle off Stinkweed, "you know what my grandmother did, don't you?"

He didn't answer. He lifted the saddle onto a sawhorse.

"I mean, about the skull."

He took a cloth and cooled Stinkweed down. I followed right behind him, talking, "Do you think that Uncle George's death had anything to do with my grandmother taking the skull away from Kapake?"

Without a word, he kept rubbing his horse. I kept on talking. "I don't know what to think. I know one thing, I am going to bring that skull back to Kapake, bury it in a sand dune, and break the curse. I have to find a way to go to San Francisco and get the skull. When I bring it back, will you take me back to Kapake and help me bury it?"

Solomon stopped rubbing his horse. He looked at me, thought for a minute and came over and slapped my head again. He turned and finished rubbing down his horse.

Marigold rode in and gave me a look like a dark thundercloud because I had beaten her back to the stables. I teased her with my biggest smile, showing her all my front teeth. She stuck her tongue out at me. I knew she hated being stuck with Mother and Aunt Mari because she had to ride like a lady.

Everyone dismounted their horses and gathered up all their belongings and headed for the cars. The cowboys unfastened Uncle George's body from his horse and dragged him into the icehouse. I noticed that Aunt Mari's wig glowed bright orange in the sun as she got into the car.

Back at Aunt Mari's house, the family gathered in her living room to make plans for the funeral. It was going to be a big funeral because Uncle George was so famous. Cousin Rose wanted to have the funeral in Honolulu and then to have the body brought back to Kauai for final burial. There was a lot of talk over Cousin Rose's idea because that meant lots of planning. It meant putting the body on a ship, holding the funeral services in Honolulu, and then bringing the body back again by ship to Kauai. There were further discussions on lining up the right church, who was to sit where, the hymns to be sung, and asking the governor to give the eulogy.

Aunt Mari wanted the funeral held on Kauai. She wanted it performed simply, missionary style, which meant sitting on hard benches and listening for hours to a minister who preached fire and brimstone. Aunt Mari "grrrd" like a tiger, pounding on the table and determined to have her way, blasting the family and saying that the funeral will be in her daddy's church. Cousin Rose, standing tall and being Uncle George's daughter, won the moment.

Aunt Mari, a poor sport, threw up her hands, and like Bette Davis, dramatically screamed that she wasn't going to have anything to do with Cousin Rose or the funeral and that Cousin Rose could go straight to hell. Aunt Mari added, looking around as the family ran for cover, "Tell me where and when the funeral is going to happen and I'll be there - under protest, of course." Of course.

Outside the window, I jumped for joy after hearing that Cousin Rose beat Aunt Mari without having to dump a bucket of water over her. She was the first person I knew that had triumphed over the orange witch but in Aunt Mari's eyes, I saw a look for revenge.

Cousin Rose was made to believe that her father, Uncle George, died peacefully in his sleep after smoking a black cigar and reading a western. Someday, I knew Aunt Mari was going to take great delight in telling her the truth.

Aunt Mari, grieving over everything, especially losing to Cousin Rose, packed Cousin Dora and all of us up to her mountain cabin because the funeral, by Cousin Rose's decree, wouldn't take place for at least ten days. The delay was to give time for the dignitaries and relatives on the Mainland to arrive by ship. Aunt Mari wanted to hide in the mountains until Uncle George's body journeyed to Honolulu and lay in state at the altar of Central Union Church. Then, and only then, would she make an appearance.

Before she left Aunt Mari's house, I asked Cousin Rose where she was going to keep Uncle George's body till the funeral. She told me Aunt Mari was keeping his body frozen in the ranch's icehouse. The maids told me that the body was wrapped in burlap and propped up, next to the hanging sides of slaughtered beef. The beef was waiting to be shipped to my favorite market, Piggly Wiggly. When I heard that, I warned Cousin Rose that, because Aunt Mari was so mad at her, she should make sure Uncle George wasn't shipped to Piggly Wiggly with the dead shark.

I told Cousin Rose I could see Mrs. Dillingham buying a leg of Uncle George at Piggly Wiggly on sale for twenty-nine cents a pound. Cousin Rose sniffed into her handkerchief, looking as if she was about to faint as Cousin Nigel held her, saying to me, "Thanks for the advice, Muffin. I'll see to it that Aunt Mari doesn't do anything mean to my Rose."

She didn't. In three days, Aunt Mari took her revenge out on me.

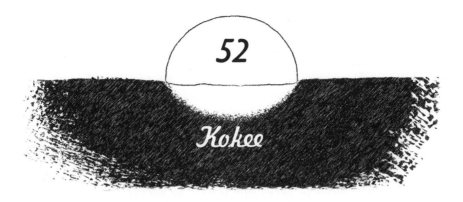

52

Kokee

I had two weapons to protect me from the curse. I used both of them on Aunt Mari at Kokee and neither of them worked.

Aunt Mari drove us up to Kokee to await Uncle George's funeral. Kokee is a mountainous retreat on Kauai. To get away from the summer heat, haole families built cabins in its valleys. While married, Aunt Mari built herself a four-bedroom wooden cabin with a stone fireplace in the living room for the wet, cold days. Kokee has many wet, cold days.

The trip up the mountain was a long three-hour journey by car. Motoring up the steep, twisting, two-lane dirt road was slippery and dangerous. Once, a cousin in a Model T died because he slid down into the Waimea Canyon. Traveling anywhere on Kauai was dangerous.

The mountains in Kokee go up to four thousand feet and surround a canyon that rivals the beauty of the Grand Canyon in Arizona. The purple and red colors of the canyon's pinnacles were extolled in Ned Harlow's book to be more vivid than the Grand Canyon, and during Kauai's wet season, a hundred waterfalls plummet dramatically into a river below. Kokee's valleys are filled with dark magenta roses, purple plum trees, blue hydrangeas, blackberries, and orange nasturtiums imported by the early German, Norwegian, and English settlers. The plants mixed and grew and sometimes snuffed out the fragrant green native plants that are not found growing anywhere else on earth, including on any other Hawaiian island.

Odd-looking native Hawaiian birds with hooked beaks, wearing bright red and yellow feathers, once flew about the trees, and have also disappeared because new cousins, brought in from China by my German nature-loving relatives, copped their food.

Driving into Aunt Mari's yard, and seeing the Kokee house covered in mist, I knew that this had to be the home of the leprechauns. Actually, a mythical, teeny-weeny race of people still played games in the valleys of Kokee. These creatures were as strong as a brick house and at night, they constructed amazing stone walls for fishponds. They were known to be very shy and were embarrassed if seen, because they were much shorter than their Hawaiian brothers. Because of their shyness, they hid in the forests like the leprechauns did in Ireland, and especially, hid from little fat, white people like me. These little folk were called *menehune*. I was told that they could be seen on moonlight nights, wandering in the Kokee cabins looking for a tuna sandwich.

As soon as we entered Aunt Mari's cabin, lit a fire, and settled in, rain began to fall - hard. Aunt Mari said it looked like we were going to be housebound. The terror had brought only her cook Kimura with us because Aunt Mari's maid, Kimura's wife, was pregnant, so she stayed behind. I wished I were pregnant. Thus, Aunt Mari assigned us jobs to make up for Kimi's absence. Aunt Mari first instructed Marigold and me to make the beds and clean the house everyday, implying that we were to be the grown-ups' slaves. So, side by side with Cousin Dora, who never left the slave list, we toiled away doing a hundred things. I hated putting my hands in a pan of dirty dishwater most of all.

The first day, as the rain sheeted down outside like waterfalls, we sat near the fireplace to keep the wet and chill out of our bones. The orange witch was unusually quiet as she rocked by the fire, humming a tune I didn't recognize, all the while knitting a long, red scarf. I knew she was planning mischief. I asked Aunt Mari if she had seen the movie *A Tale of Two Cities* in which Madame Lafarge had knitted the names of her enemies that she was about to send to the guillotine on a long red scarf. Aunt Mari kept on knitting as I persevered with my questions, asking if she was knitting the names of her enemies. I was sure I had seen her knit in bold stitches Cousin Rose's name at the top of the scarf. She ignored my questions and kept humming to herself, rocking back and forth, and acting as if she was deaf. I had a strong sense that she was plotting some dastardly deed on me. As her needles clicked away, I was sure that the curse was going to help her carry out her plan, especially because I was certain that she had knitted my name just below Cousin Rose's.

As the rain continued to fall, Mother and Marigold read books about horses and Cousin Dora wrote poems on yellow lined paper. I spread myself all over the floor and crayoned Carmen Miranda's hats. I used up all of my orange crayons first on Carmen Miranda's platform shoes because I hated that color. I thought the rain was never going to stop.

The second day, the hard rain did stop before breakfast. The day began as a cold, drizzly, misty morning. I woke up freezing. My sheets felt like slabs of ice. I had never been so cold in all my life. My teeth chattered - clack, clack, clack, when I brushed my teeth. I prayed as my teeth clacked uncontrollably that I'd lose one of my double chins.

Aunt Mari had trucked horses up from the ranch for our excursions into the wilderness. She insisted at breakfast that, no matter how bad the weather turned out, a picnic and horseback ride to a waterfall was the order of the day. Keoni, a cowboy from the Kokee ranger's station, on pre-arrangement, would saddle the horses for our outings. Aunt Mari announced, as I stepped out of the house for the ride, that I was old enough to ride a horse by myself. Aunt Mari's orange eyes glittered with devilment; this had been one of her Madame Lafarge plans as she knitted by the fire. It was payback time. Aunt Mari was sending me like Marie Antoinette, to the guillotine.

I was not about to give her the satisfaction of knowing that she had scared the fingernails off my fingers, so I walked past her to Keoni and said loudly, "Which horse is mine, amigo?" (a line I remembered from a Gene Autry movie).

Keoni pointed. My heart sank. The horse he pointed to was big, gangling, chewing on the grass, and the ugliest, boniest horse I had ever seen. This horse, if you could call it a horse, was covered in white mange and I could have played "chopsticks" on its ribs. I named him George because he looked dead.

Keoni helped me up on Dead George. Dead George had a sweeping hollow in his back so that, when I sat in the saddle, I could barely see over his head. As I readjusted myself on him, the horse neighed like Greta Garbo dying of tuberculosis and offered me a world-weary, snuffling hello. He put his head down, pooped a road muffin, turned around, and clopped back into the stable. In the middle of the stable, we stood like a stone statue in the middle of a town square. Dead George's eyelids dropped to half-mast, and with his stance, he defied me to move him back out into the cold. Aunt Mari rode her horse over to where we were standing and screamed into the horse's ear, "Get out of there, you big, useless old nag. Right now."

Dead George, no longer dead, perked up his ears, wiggled them, and trotted out to join the picnickers. No living creature in his right mind defied Aunt Mari to her face - except Cousin Rose and me, but then, neither one of us had any horse sense.

Aunt Mari, riding alongside of Dead George, scolded me, "It's all your fault, Percy. You have to show a horse who's boss and, for God's sake, stop hanging onto the pommel. Pick up the reins! Hold them in. Now, give your horse a swift kick and show him you're a man. Don't you know anything?" She kicked my horse in the ribs and rode off as her horse slung mud in my face.

Of course, I didn't know anything. My daddy wasn't around long enough to teach me how to ride a horse and, like the piano lessons, I never wanted to know how to ride a horse. What I yearned for was to sit by the fire and color Carmen Miranda's face blue, but on we trekked single file to the waterfall. Dead George never once cooperated. If I wanted to go right, Dead George went left. If I wanted to stop, he kept on going. All during the ride, the horse's eyes kept turning back with longing to stare towards the stables that was left behind. In a half-hour, Dead George and I were as cold and miserable as a beggar in New York City and we lagged behind last.

When I finally looked up, I saw that we were riding through a beautiful tropical forest where Hunkacha and menehunes would have lived. Jesus sunrays slanting through the trees lit the way to the falls. Birds sang "Happy Days Are Here Again" as Dead George and I stumbled over fallen tree trunks. Like Patty and Little Johnny in Mother's story, we clopped our way down a forest path surrounded by trees that bloomed with beautiful red flowers. I kept looking for tree trunks made out of mayonnaise jars.

When we arrived at the top of a waterfall, our destination, I saw gallons of rainwater spilling over a cliff and plunging thousands of feet down into a canyon. After we got off our horses, I observed that one of the black pools right above the falls had a swift current; one slip into the current, and over the waterfall I would fall.

Kauai was a dangerous island.

Aunt Mari immediately spread a blanket out on the large rocks as Cousin Dora unloaded the food in the picnic basket. Before lunch, the orange witch made us take a dunk in one of the pools seemingly filled with ice cubes, while she sat and watched us. She covered herself with a blanket. I jumped in and jumped right out, toweled off and sat on a rock as far away as I could from the witch, and ate a ham sandwich without mayonnaise. The sandwich was the second torture Aunt Mari planned for me. The foul weather was the third. A misty rain fell on us all afternoon, like iced confetti continuously falling down my back. I watched Aunt Mari, cozy under a blanket, sharing a bottle of sherry with Mother and Cousin Dora and saying that she was warm as toast. Under the blanket, she challenged us by saying that only sissies got cold. She challenged us further, asking if there were any sissies in the party. I put up my hand and then put a wet towel over my face so Aunt Mari wouldn't have to watch a sissy freezing to death.

Marigold and Keoni jumped in and out of pools, not being sissies. They rode the swift current of the black pool until they reached the edge of the waterfall and stopped themselves from going over by holding their feet against a rock. They screamed for me to come join them. Plan four by Aunt Mari wanted me to join them and go over the waterfall. Not answering, I pulled the towel further over my face and hid from everyone for the rest of the afternoon.

All during lunch, Marigold and Keoni scooped pork and beans out of cans with their fingers and spread the gunk on saloon pilot crackers. In an hour, they polished off two cans of pork and beans and three ham sandwiches. Trying to make goody goody with Aunt Mari, they stuck out their stomachs as far as they could and said that pork and beans and ham sandwiches "were real man's food, pardner." Marigold, sassy as can be, yelled at me hiding under a towel, "A sandwich without mayonnaise is a John Wayne sandwich, Percy." She was acting so obnoxious, showing off for Keoni and Aunt Mari, that I wanted to run and shove her over the waterfall. *That was my plan.*

After lunch, just as we were mounting our horses to go back, clouds gave way with one whooosh and down came the hard rain again. As soon as Dead George felt the rain pouring on his back and knew that he was headed for home, the horse that I thought was ready for the glue factory turned into Sea Biscuit, the famous horse that won the Kentucky Derby. He reared back on his legs, took in a deep breath, and galloped for home at top speed with me on top of him, holding on for dear life. Dead George became Alive George.

"Yeeeeeeooooooooooeeeee," I screamed. That was the only intelligent line I could remember from a John Wayne movie. I glued myself onto the pommel as we sped through the forest. There was never a doubt anywhere in my mind that before we reached the stables, a low-hanging branch was going to sweep me off my saddle, and the "coup de grace" would be to get trampled by Aunt Mari's horse. Plan five. Surprisingly, the curse was asleep, and I arrived safely back at the stables twenty minutes before the rest of the party galloped in. Once back in his stall, Alive George threw me to the ground and heaved up his oats all over me.

Standing up, wiping the oats from my face, I felt a burning sensation on my behind. I pulled down my pants and turned around, and saw two round, red cherries painted on my bottom. At that moment, Aunt Mari strode in like General

Custer, shouting, "Percy, where in the hell were you?" In her second breath, she yelled louder, "Pull up your pants, you dirty boy."

I neighed, pulled up my pants and shut my mouth. I had enough horse sense to know that a private doesn't talk back to a general when she's mad. After the rest of the party arrived, Keoni unsaddled the horses, Cousin Dora gathered up the picnic things and Aunt Mari patted her horse on the nose. She told Athena that she had just experienced the best picnic in the world. The horse was the only one in the stables that looked at her with love in her eyes.

As I tried to sneak back into the house to warm up, Aunt Mari called out, "Percy?"

I turned around, annoyed at being caught and snapped back, "What is it, Aunt Mari?"

"You look peaked to me. You need roses on your cheeks."

I told her I looked peaked because I just finished a ride of terror to a waterfall of death. I told her because of the ride, I had all the roses I needed on my cheeks, and pulled down my pants again and showed her the red flowers plastered on my behind.

She screamed, "You're absolutely disgusting." Marigold and Keoni fell on the stable floor, hooting at me, as Mother ordered, "Pull up your pants right now, Percy."

I pulled up my pants, angry to the point of bursting, and faced Aunt Mari squarely, declaring with stupid courage, "Aunt Mari, I am not going riding with you tomorrow or ever."

"Why not?" she demanded.

"Because I have to finish coloring my Carmen Miranda coloring book and then I'm going to cut out my Linda Darnell paper dolls." Linda Darnell, Alice Faye wrote in the May *Photoplay* magazine, was a 20th Century Fox dark beauty who was about to make it big into the stardom category. They were about to co-star in a movie.

"What did you say, Percy?" Aunt Mari asked, hoping her voice sounded so menacing that I would be too scared to answer her back.

Mother cut in, "Aunt Mari, Percy has some reading to do before school begins in September."

"I heard what he said, Deidra," Aunt Mari snarled.

I spoke up, "If you didn't hear me, what I said was that I am going in to color Carmen Miranda's face orange, a color I hate with all my heart."

Marigold butted in, snuggling up against the orange witch like a horse and said, "I can hardly wait to go riding with you tomorrow, Aunt Mari."

Resting her hand on Marigold's shoulder, man to man, Aunt Mari smiled and said, "I know that, dear. You're such a treasure to me."

Cousin Dora, carrying the picnic basket, passed Aunt Mari and whispered, "Leave him alone, Mari."

Aunt Mari blinked like a cobra ready to strike and hissed back at Cousin Dora, "I hope I didn't hear you correctly... dear."

Cousin Dora kept on walking. Cousin Dora and I, with my pants back on, entered the cabin, arm in arm. She walked straight to the kitchen and deposited the picnic basket on top of the sink and then stood by the fire to thaw out. Warming her hands next to me, she kissed the top of my head. For the rest of day, lying on the floor, pants up, I snuggled next to Cousin Dora as she wrote a poem about love and I colored Carmen Miranda's face blue.

On the third day, it rained so hard that Noah would have blown a conch shell to tell all the animals in the world to hurry aboard the ark. God may not have heard Noah's prayers, but God heard mine because there was no horseback riding that day. After breakfast, nestled around the fireplace, Aunt Mari kept nattering about the lack of roses on my cheeks. I was tempted to pull down my pants and give her another look at my flowers, but I was too content cutting out clothes for my Linda Darnell paper doll. I also felt safe from Aunt Mari because, no matter what she said, as long as I had Cousin Dora and Mother around, they'd protect me. When Aunt Mari wasn't looking, I'd pinch my cheeks like Scarlett O'Hara did in *Gone With The Wind* to make roses bloom on my face and just to keep her off my back.

Suddenly, we were jolted out of our quiet time when a car horn blared. We looked out the cabin window and saw through the rain, a 1940 green Hudson with Aunt Momi at the wheel and her three girls beside her, driving on the lawn.

Hearing it was Aunt Momi, Aunt Mari gathered up her knitting and fled for her bedroom, beckoning Cousin Dora to follow her. Aunt Mari told Mother, before she locked the door, that Aunt Momi gave her a migraine.

In a bomb burst, Aunt Momi and her girls, with newspapers protecting their hairdos, crashed into the room. Dripping puddles on the floor and carrying paper sacks, Aunt Momi looked around and immediately asked, "Jollyjamit, Deidra, where's the old girl gone to?"

Mother pointed to the bedroom. Aunt Momi strode to Aunt Mari's bedroom door, pounded on it and called, "Aunt Mari, I know you're in there and you can stay in there for all I care. I just wanted to say hello. Anyway, I really came to see my sister. I brought lunch and a bottle of bourbon and if you want some, come on out and join us. I'd love to see you, old girl. Brought mangoes with me. What say, old girl?"

A voice roared from inside the bedroom, "Go away. You're making me sick."

Aunt Momi shouted through the door, "Keep your headache, Aunt Mari. Cousin Dora, leave the old spoilsport and come out and join us. Big kisses from me and the kids."

Aunt Momi turned around, looked at Mother, and said, "Deidra, our not talking to each other is just plain stupid. Let's kiss and make up right now and forget anything ever happened between us. How's about it, kiddo?"

One look was all they needed and they ran to each other, hugged, and cried like little girls. The fact that Mother didn't come to Aunt Momi's and Uncle Lono's wedding was forgotten and forgiven in a split second. Mother and Aunt Momi broke apart, sat on the floor, and talked lickety-split, gossiping and making up for lost time. Catching her breath, Aunt Momi pointed to her girls, "Nancy, Betty, and Marsha, take the food into the kitchen, put it on plates and fix it nice. Serve the food like I've taught you to. Go on, now. I've got to talk to your Auntie Deidra."

Turning back to Mother, she continued without skipping another beat, "I'm so damn hungry I could eat a cow right now. Jesus, Mary, and Joseph, I have a roaring hangover." Pulling a bottle of bourbon out of a paper sack, she toasted, "Let's have a little bit of the old dog, Deidra."

Mother laughed, "I've missed you, Momi."

Aunt Momi yanked paper cups out of the bag and poured whiskey as her girls danced into the kitchen, frolicking and jabbering away like little puppy dogs. Marigold followed them like a hound dog. I could hear them dumping the contents of their paper bags into Aunt Mari's kitchen sink and starting to make a colossal mess. I could hear Marigold joining in the mess making. I hoped they cleaned up after themselves because I knew which slave would have to fix the mess if they didn't.

After Aunt Momi finished pouring a second cup of bourbon, and there was a lull in the conversation, I asked, "Aunt Momi, what's it like to be a real princess?"

She held out her left hand and on her third finger sparkled the biggest diamond I had ever seen outside of the movies. "That's some rock, Aunt Momi. Anything else?" I said, holding her finger.

She reached up and swung around her neck three long strands of the largest matching pearls in the Hawaiian kingdom. My princess aunt told me they were once part of the royal Hawaiian jewel collection and now were hers to keep forever and ever. She intoned like a princess, "These pearls, my boy, were a gift from Uncle Lono's mother. Percy, the Princess is considered the highest muck-a-muck roaming the islands today. Hawaiians still bow to her on Fort Street."

Aunt Momi continued that the Princess Mama was so royal, she shopped at Day and Company, the fanciest grocery store in Honolulu, and never once had to get out of her car. She just sat in the back seat of her big, black Rolls Royce and passed her shopping list out the car window for the owner, Mr. Day, to fill. Mr. Day bowed and scraped to her exactly the way the English gentry did in front of royalty.

Aunt Momi continued telling me that Doris Duke, the millionaire cigarette heiress, did the Princess Mama one better. She motored in her speedboat all the way from her home on Black Point to the downtown harbor, then walked up from the pier and shopped at Day's to buy caviar and toilet paper. Day's was so expensive, the dowager Hawaiian princess could only afford to shop on Tuesdays and Thursdays. Doris Duke, who had twice as much money as the Hawaiian princess, shopped at Day's from Monday through Friday. Now that was what I called being really rich.

I sighed, looking at Aunt Momi downing her third bourbon, and thought she would be really rich if she and the prince didn't spend so much of their money on bourbon and waters. I sighed again to myself, thinking about Mother, who had to shop at Chun Hoon Market on Nuuanu Street on Wednesdays because that's when they had sales. I understood that the rest of us were cursed because we didn't have a boat like Doris Duke used when she shopped for a tube of toothpaste or Princess Mama who sat in the back seat of a Rolls, wearing a tiara, when she bought a can of tuna fish.

Aunt Momi intoned in a voice starting down in her toes, waving her diamond ring in front of my face, that now her prince gave her charge accounts at Day's and Liberty House and she was in her glory. My princess-aunt could buy all the whiskey, cigarettes and dresses she wanted and the Princess Mama picked up the bill. Trying to speak like a duchess, she roared, "Son of a bitch, Percy, these are the good old days. Ha! Ha! Ha!" Aunt Momi always laughed at her own jokes.

I seriously warned my aunt, "Aunt Momi, I'm sure glad you made it big. But I hope Uncle Lono won't cut off your head, because, otherwise, you won't be able to keep your pearls, charge accounts or diamond ring. By the way, before you get your head chopped off, could I wear your pearls sometime?"

Without blinking an eye, she answered, "May I, Percy!"

"May I, Aunt Momi," I chirped.

"Yes, you may, my man." I loved it when Aunt Momi spoke to me like a royal. Her future with Uncle Lono looked ominous because I had just overheard Mother and Aunt Momi talk about the prince's bad temper. He had the reputation of throwing plates of tripe stew at anyone he didn't like. Aunt Momi confessed to Mother that last week, after drinking whiskeys in the kitchen for most of the day, Uncle Lono threw her down a flight of stairs.

Then I came up with my idea. "Aunt Momi, I think we should practice," I suggested.

Lighting a cigarette and blowing smoke rings in the air, she asked, "Practice what, Percy?"

I explained, "Daddy says that practice makes perfect. Let's throw dinner plates at each other after lunch. I'll pretend to throw a plate at your neck and you pretend to duck. I bet that will keep your neck in one piece."

I had a gift for making a room go silent. In a drumbeat, Aunt Momi swerved the conversation away from breaking necks to the subject of Daddy. Aunt Momi told Mother that Kathy and Daddy were fighting in public and the honeymoon was over. Mother and Aunt Momi giggled gleefully as they drank another cup of bourbon at the thought of Kathy beating Daddy up. Their fights were over how much money Kathy was spending on making herself beautiful in red and on decorating their new house on the Ala Wai canal. The inside of the house was painted pinker than the Royal Hawaiian Hotel.

My first cousins, who always acted like puppies, and Marigold served lunch. It was hard for them to concentrate because they could not stop chatterboxing about anything that came into their minds. They ran around the room singing hit parade songs while holding trays high in their hands like carhops at a drive-in, and served the food as if we were doughboys in the army. They were as energetic and lively as a gaggle of geese and sucked every ounce of oxygen out of the room. After they finished serving us lunch, the fire in the fireplace fizzled to a tiny wisp of smoke. Everything in the cabin was exhausted, pooped out. During lunch, they made me get up and show them how to do the conga ten times. Royal princesses' daughters aren't cursed because they are very exhausting and they'd tire a curse out. Marigold was so bushed, her tongue hung out like a dog's as she spread-eagled out on the floor.

"Time out" wasn't in Aunt Momi's vocabulary but "son of a bitch" was - and they made us play son of a bitch games with them all afternoon. Aunt Momi was definitely hilarious to be around, even if she pooped me out. No wonder the prince of Hawaii loved her because he'd be too tired out not to love her. Just as we thought royalty was leaving, they brought out an ukulele and sang and danced hulas for us. They couldn't keep still.

The song I loved the best was called the monkey song. Aunt Momi told me she learned it from a man who had been at the Scopes trial where the people in Missouri attempted to prove that we were related to monkeys.

Aunt Mari's headache, I imagined, had blistered into a fire by now, hearing us sing, and I was sure I saw smoke coming out from under her door like Uncle George's bedroom door at Kapake.

We blasted:
"You can't make a monkey out of me,
I don't look like one that's plain to see.
I refuse to think that I'm the missing link,
And when I meet my baby bradda,
We don't scratch each odda.
My old mammy was no chimpanzee,
Pappy didn't swing from tree to tree,
I ain't never had no fleas,
On my them or those or these,
You can't make a monkey out of me."

We finished the song, hooting and hollering, and then sang it again, this time louder. On the second chorus, Cousin Dora burst out of Aunt Mari's bedroom and streaked for the kitchen. With a wet cloth in her hand, she sprinted back into Aunt Mari's room, holding the wash cloth up like a marathon runner carrying the Olympic torch. In a few minutes, out minced Cousin Dora from Aunt Mari's room, and she said quietly that Aunt Mari had a blinding headache and wouldn't we "please keep it down." After she said that, she gave us a big wink and walked back into the bedroom. I would have bet a dollar that Aunt Momi's name was now needled at the top of the knitted red scarf, right above mine.

As the royals finally packed up to leave, I asked Aunt Momi about my cousin, her son, little Hans. I had never met him. Sadness filled Aunt Momi's face as she mumbled to me, holding back tears, "Big Hans, that son of a bitch, won't let me see him anymore. Since I asked for the divorce and married a Hawaiian, he thinks it wouldn't be good for my boy to be near me. I'm fighting that son of a bitch in court. At least, he lets me keep my girls but I want my baby. That son of a bitch!" When she said the last "son of a bitch," she hugged her girls.

"Well," I said and frowned, "I wish my daddy...." I stopped mid-sentence, thought better of what I was going to say, and continued down another path as I put Aunt Momi's bottle of bourbon back in the paper sack. "No," I said, "I like it just the way it is."

"You do?" Aunt Momi asked, taking the paper sack out of my hands.

I whispered into Aunt Momi's ear, "Yes, Mother lets me wear her dresses and I'd look swell wearing your pearls and diamond ring. Daddy doesn't like me doing things like that. Don't you think wearing Daddy's coat and tie with your pearls and diamond ring, I'd look pretty stupid?"

Aunt Momi gave me a big kiss and whispered, "Percy, you're a godamndest character. You're either gonna be a famous bijeezus actor or the biggest damn criminal in America." I voted for being a famous actor. Gertrude, the grump, always said that someday I'd end up in Sing Sing.

Aunt Momi kissed Mother and offered, "Deidra, as soon as you get home, bring the kids over to the country and come see my new bijeezus house that my broken-down old prince bought for me. Percy, if you come see me, I'll let you wear my pearls."

"OH, BOY!" I said, jumping up and down.

The country Aunt Momi referred to was on Oahu, on the opposite side of the island from the city of Honolulu, where she now lived in splendor with Uncle Lono. Aunt Momi shoved her girls into the green Hudson as the rain still came down in waterfall sheets. She turned on the engine and skidded out of the yard.

I yelled after her, "Don't fall down the canyon and break your neck. Uncle Lono wouldn't like that and I wouldn't be able to wear your goddamned pearls. Don't forget to keep your son-of-a bitch neck attached to your son-of-a-bitch head."

Mother, waving to Aunt Momi, said firmly, "Percy."

"That's what Aunt Momi says," I answered, innocently.

"That's your Aunt Momi."

Marigold, standing at the door, wiped her brow and uttered two words, "Good God." She, too, had been dazzled by her cousins' and aunt's performances. She added, "Give me air."

It had been an exhausting afternoon, a five-hour talking marathon, and we walked back slowly into the cabin, letting the rain pour down our heads. As we entered, the fire in the fireplace exploded back into roaring flames as Aunt Mari burst like a genie out of the bedroom. Her face glowered fiercely like the flames, and there was an orange tinge of revenge in her eyes.

On the fourth day, the rain stopped. By now, everybody was frothing at the mouth to get out into the sunshine, so Aunt Mari planned another horseback ride to the world famous Kalalau valley, which had been immortalized in a story by Jack London.

I declined the ride for two reasons. One, I didn't want to ride Dead George and two, I desperately needed to finish cutting out my Linda Darnell paper doll dresses. Underlining it all was a third reason - I wanted to get away from Aunt Mari's constant reminder that roses weren't blooming on my cheeks.

There was the usual scurrying around to ready the picnickers for the ride, the lunch had to be made, the horses saddled, and just as everyone was going out the door to mount the horses, Aunt Mari switched. She decided to stay behind. She told Cousin Dora that her splitting headache had returned and she decided to spend the day in bed.

Mother, Marigold and Cousin Dora said how sorry they were and left under protest. I was alone with the orange witch resting in her bed, but I could smell the curse filling the cabin. Nervously, nevertheless, I settled down by the fireplace and attached paper dresses to the cardboard cutout of Linda Darnell, content to be left alone. I didn't hear Aunt Mari open her door behind me. From the bedroom door, her voice boomed as loudly as if God was speaking to me from heaven.

"Boys shouldn't be playing with paper dolls - that's for girls. What's the matter with you, Percy, anyway?" hissed Aunt Mari.

Jolted out of my fantasy world, I turned around and there stood the orange witch glowing from the reflection of the fire in the fireplace. She didn't look sick. I was so startled by her booming voice, her glowing appearance, and seeing her looming above me like Dracula dripping blood from her mouth, that my mind scrambled. I couldn't think of anything to respond with.

She walked towards me like a panther and said, "Put those things away right now" I kept looking at her, frozen, dumbfounded by her actions. I had been caught by surprise because I had imagined her in bed, holding her head with one hand, pulling tissues out of a Kleenex box and wiping snot from her nose with the other. I was amazed at how tall she had become.

"Stop staring at me like a dumb bunny - ANSWER ME AND PUT THOSE SISSY THINGS AWAY," she demanded.

I picked up the Linda Darnell paper doll and the cutout dresses and slid them back in the paper doll book, all the time watching Aunt Mari with one eye. She roamed around the room, like a tiger waiting for a kill. There was something devious up her sleeve. Seeing I was finished, she walked over and yanked me off the floor and announced, "Percy, you're going to have an enema."

"A what?" I screamed.

"An enema," she repeated. "It will put bright red roses back on your cheeks."

I pulled away from her and cried out, "I don't want red roses back on my cheeks or anywhere else. I hate roses." Furious that I was captured, I yelled, "I HATE YOU!"

Grabbing my hand again and pulling me towards the bathroom, she grew angrier and said, "That's the last straw, young man, you're not going to sass me again. You're going to have an enema and that's all there is to it. You've needed a good cleaning out since the day I met you."

Breaking away from her, I ran into the kitchen, yelling, "I want my mother."

Aunt Mari ran behind me, yelling, "That's your problem, young man. You're too tied to your mother's apron strings. Your mother isn't here now to save you and what you need more than your mother's coddling is a little starch put in you."

I stopped at the kitchen sink, turned around to her and said to her blankly, "What is an enema, anyway?" I was stalling for time.

Like the wolf in *Little Red Riding Hood*, she gave me an evil smile and cooed, "Come to the bathroom and I'll show you."

"No, you tell me first, " I demanded.

"It's a flushing out," she replied.

"What do you mean, a flushing out?"

"I put water up you and clean you out. It's good for bad, little boys," she smirked.

"Where do you put the water up?"

"Up your behind," she said as she started to come closer.

"With what?" I said, backing away as she came closer and closer.

"A pink nozzle!"

"How long?" I asked.

She measured out with her hands a distance that looked too long for anything that I wanted up my behind. I gasped, "That long!"

Aunt Mari was now within arms' reach just about to grab me, when I turned around to the sink, picked up the pan of dirty dishwater and threw it all over her wig. We looked at each other - surprised.

I screamed at her, "Melt! You're supposed to melt! You didn't melt. Why aren't you melting? Melt. Melt. Melt. All bad witches melt when they have water poured over them." I started to cry because I was so disappointed that she was still standing in front of me and not melting through the floor. I wailed, "You're supposed to melt. Son of a bitch, all bad witches melt into the ground when water is thrown over them. Why aren't you melting?"

Wiping the dirty dishwater off her face, she screamed, "What are you talking about? Look, what you've done to me, you've ruined my good kimono."

I added gleefully, "And your wig."

"This time, young man, you've gone too far." She made a lunge for me. I ducked under her arm. She made a grab for me and missed. I ran back into the living room and stood defiantly next to the fireplace, ready to take on the orange witch. Aunt Mari charged out of the kitchen without her wig, looking like a gray German tank ready to roll over me in a final assault.

I had saved this one thing for my last ditch defense against the invading German Nazis and the curse and Aunt Mari. Marigold promised me it would work and promised me it would stop Aunt Mari from doing horrible things to me. I picked up the fireplace poker and held it high in my hand, like a sword Errol Flynn used in the *Adventures of Robin Hood*. I yelled loud enough for all the birds in the forest to hear me, 'FUCK YOU, AUNT MARI. FUCK YOU! FUCK YOU! FUCK YOU!"

My words stopped her all right. She gasped, clutched her chichis as if I had shot an arrow into her heart, and hollered, "NOOOOOOW, YOU'VE REALLY GONE TOO FAR, PERCY! WHERE DID YOU HEAR SUCH FILTH?"

I thought I had her because she was frozen still. The words worked. But she moved again. She was angrier than ever, and took a huge lunge at me, arms outstretched and strong as a stevedore's. She grabbed me by my hair and pulled me into the bathroom.

I dropped the poker and screamed all the way, yelling, "Marigold told me. Marigold told me that word. Marigold told me. Stooooop it, Aunt Mari. You're hurting me."

I was furious, thinking to myself as Aunt Mari hauled me into the bathroom that Marigold never gets anything right. Aunt Mari pushed me into the bathroom wall. I froze in fear. Aunt Mari then ordered me to take down my pants and underpants. I did. In a rage, she filled up a rubber bag with water, attached a syringe with a pink nozzle on it, and told me to bend over. Like a good prisoner, I bent over and she thrust the nozzle up into me until it hurt. She filled me with water till I screamed that I was going to burst, pulled it out, and told me to sit on the pot.

I think that's what happened, as I don't remember much of the details. Sitting on the pot, I thought my insides were burning up. When I finished evacuating, nothing left inside to come out, I pleaded, "I want to get off the toilet now."

Standing by the door, inhaling hard and breathing fire, Aunt Mari kept on watching me and didn't answer. I wouldn't look at her face. She scared me because now she looked like the devil. I kept my head down, looking at the wood floor and counting the cracks.

She finally hissed, "You sure you're finished?"

I nodded.

"We're going to do it one more time," she threatened.

I looked up at her with murder in my eyes. "Don't you touch me with that thing again. I'm bleeding." I didn't know if that was true but I felt like I was. My words slowed Aunt Mari.

In a controlled voice, she said, "Let me see."

I flushed the toilet and got off the pot, picked up my clothes and walked past her as she stood motionless in the doorway. I stopped just before I walked into my bedroom, looked at her and said in a deliberate voice seething with hate, "Aunt Mari, I'm going to tell my mother what a bad person you really are."

She leaned against the door and laughed, "She won't believe you. I'll tell her you are imagining things again and we all know," she said sarcastically, "what a sissy child you are."

I closed the bedroom door. After I wiped myself off and dressed, I walked out of the bedroom. Aunt Mari was on her knees, cleaning up the evidence off the bathroom floor and I said in a quiet, determined voice, "Aunt Mari?"

She replied curtly, and kept on scrubbing, "What do you want?"

Coming into the bathroom as she crouched below me, trying to remove one of my spots off the floor, I said, "Aunt Mari, look at me. My mother will believe me because she knows I always tell her the truth on important things and I can show her the blood on my underwear."

I stopped speaking to let my words sink in. I learned about blackmail from the Boston Blackie and Charlie Chan movies. I continued, looking at Aunt Mari's frightened eyes, "But I thought about it while putting on my pants and decided I'm not going to tell Mother because she has enough troubles right now. But if you ever touch me again or do anything to Marigold or Mother, I'll tell the whole world what you did to me, and the whole world will be mad at you for treating a little boy like you just did. I'll even put on the front page of the *Advertiser* that Uncle George shot himself because I saw the hole in his head."

Seeing I had finished talking, Aunt Mari got up slowly, leaned on the bathtub to brace herself and breathing hard, said, "I want to see the underwear."

I snapped, "I've hidden it where you can't find it."

Aunt Mari looked ancient without her wig and every bit as worn as the rag in her hand. Her white hair was scraggly and thin and hung down like an old mop on her face. Maybe witches did melt after all. Lifting herself up slowly, towering over me, she said sadly, "Percy, I've had troubles in my life, too."

I cut in, "I know all about them. Mother told me all about them. But you don't have to act like a mean old witch just because your husband died. I think he was lucky." I spun out of the room, furious that she hadn't melted and the "fuck you" didn't work. I was so foot-stomping mad I could have spit thumbtacks into the fire.

My mind raced and I said to myself, "If I can't believe in the movies anymore, what can I believe in? I'll never see *Wizard of Oz* again and I'll never, NEVER, believe anything Marigold tells me ever, ever, ever again in my whole life. And worst of all, I've nothing left to protect me from the curse."

For the rest of the afternoon, and without a word, Aunt Mari scrubbed the bathroom, dried off her wig, and polished the kitchen floor to a sheen, while I played, as little boys shouldn't do, with my Linda Darnell paper dolls.

When Mother, Marigold, and Aunt Dora arrived back from their ride, I pulled Mother aside and whispered, "Don't ever again leave me alone with Aunt Mari."

Mother looked concerned and asked, "Did anything happen while we were gone?"

"No, nothing. But don't ever leave me alone with her ever again. Promise me that," I said with a vengeance.

Aunt Mari never touched or spoke a harsh word to me for the rest of that visit. We conducted a polite truce, but I kept a watchful eye to insure that she was never within reaching distance to stick a pink nozzle up my behind again. I learned from that incident to never turn your back on an enemy.

I also gave up using the words "fuck you" forever because they were words that were as dirty and useless as the dishwater I threw at Aunt Mari. There was never hidden anywhere in the Kokee cabin the bloody underwear. The bloody piece of clothing line was just a line from an old Bette Davis movie.

The night after that incident, I prayed to God that one day Cousin Dora would give Aunt Mari the biggest enema in the world with a nozzle that was as long as the Empire State Building. I also knew that I was going to have to become rich, famous and royal as Aunt Momi because people like Doris Duke and the Princess Mama just weren't cursed and never got a pink needle stuck up their behinds.

Or, at least, I had to figure a way to get the skull back to Kapake because I knew for certain that, without anything to protect me now, bad things were still going to happen to me.

53

Maui

Cousin Rose pushed Uncle George's funeral up three days. Aunt Mari, in a snit, packed us up and headed back to Lihue. On our way down the mountain, Aunt Mari steered the station wagon like a beefy truck driver, swerving all over the muddy road, skidding us into grassy embankments. While honking her horn, Aunt Mari kept muttering to herself that she was mad as hell that Cousin Rose had changed the date.

Clinging onto the door handle for dear life, Mother revealed that she was sending Marigold and me to Maui. She wanted us out from underfoot during Uncle George's funeral. She was afraid that I would blab during the eulogy that Uncle George did himself in. Mother announced that we would be staying with Betsy's parents, the Richards, until the funeral was pau (over). I would have agreed to stay anywhere, even with Frankenstein, because at that moment, Aunt Mari was driving like a crazy woman.

Everybody in Hawaii is a bad driver. I told Agnes and Gertrude that it was the fresh drinking water in Hawaii that made people go mad behind a steering wheel.

Marigold pouted until she remembered Betsy's parents had the largest dairy farm on Maui. She perked up and said that she could hardly wait to get her hands on a cow's teat to milk it, and then she yanked on my nose with her fingers. As she was milking my nose, visions of milkshakes burst into my mind. I began to describe the milkshakes to Marigold as Aunt Mari whipped the car around a hair-pin curve. The dizzy turn made Marigold throw up but thankfully, it made her stop milking my nose. Cousin Dora, on the other side of me, followed next, throwing up out the back window. Sitting between the "sickies," I kept on imagining thick chocolate milkshakes with peanut butter and bananas mixed in, washing them down with a gooey mayonnaise sandwich. The more my seatmates upchucked, the hungrier I got. I leaned forward and tapped Mother on the shoulder and asked if there was anything to eat on the front seat. Cousin Dora and Marigold pulled me back next to them and choked my neck and threatened that if I ate in front of them, they'd throw me out of the car with their throw-up. Cousin Dora must have been really sick because she had never said a bad word to me before. Marigold was her same old "poopy" self and punched me. One thing I knew for certain, in the food department, I wasn't cursed.

The night before we sailed for Maui, I searched for a book by Ned Harlow on

Maui. I found it next to Aunt Mari's Bible. I took it off the shelf and opened it to the chapter on the Valley Island. It read as follows:

"Maui is a *haole* island. Everyone on Kauai told me that though the people of Maui may look Hawaiian, Japanese, Chinese, Portuguese, or Puerto Rican, they act like a haole. The term haole was defined by a man I met guzzling a beer as he fished off the wharf at Lahaina on Maui. He said a haole is a person wanting to have a good time - all the time. The missionaries, the guzzler slurred, were never true haoles because their good time was telling everybody else how not to have a good time. The whalers on the other hand, harpoon held in one hand and a mug of grog in the other, were the best damnedest haoles in the world. After the whalers arrived on Maui, the fisherman said, 'Living on Maui was one good time after another.' After imparting that information, my source passed out.

"Throughout my travels in the Hawaiian Islands, I heard many a definition of haole but this definition was the most unique. When I traveled on Maui from Lahaina to Hana, I found the Mauians beat their own drum with a different stick. I never felt the Maui people considered themselves a part of the other Hawaiian Islands - they lived in their own universe and to hell with the people on Kauai and Oahu. They weren't stuck-up necessarily, but you felt Mauians knew a secret and they weren't about to reveal that secret to anyone, no matter how famous you are.

"I think their secret is Haleakala, a dormant volcano that dominates most of the island. The volcano is shaped like a strawberry sundae. Hawaiians consider her a rainbow goddess and chant about her in hushed, reverential songs. The mountain is one of the most magnificent, temperamental and powerful dormant volcanoes I have ever seen in my travels. Everyday when I was on Maui, I prayed for clear weather to see her in all her glory. I never did. She was very shy when I was visiting on Maui.

"One thing I did do – and you must consider it a must while on Maui, was to hire a car and see the sun rise from the mountaintop. Bring a sweater.

"Maui is two islands put together - one side Haleakala, the volcano, and a saint; the other side, Lahaina, the sinner. In between, where the saint and sinner meet, the isthmus is a swamp, a no man's land, where no man in his right mind should ever want to live. They should build a prison there." So ended the chapter on Maui in Ned Harlow's book.

If haole meant people who had a good time all the time, when Marigold and I were on Maui, we met gobs of haoles. I never met a haole on Maui who didn't have a drink in his hand.

Mother booked passage for us on the Humuula, a rusty cow ship that took cattle from one island to another. We creaked over monstrous waves going from Kauai to Maui. In the bow of the ship, cows mooed all the time, getting seasick as dogs. Marigold barfed, too, and so, hoping to make her feel better, I told her that the cows got seasick. She screamed for me to get out of the cabin and stay out until I had something nice to say to her. As I retreated backwards out the door, I told her that the reason I told her that cows got seasick was that Cousin Dora told me that misery loves company, and then I mooood at her. She threw a barf bag at me and missed.

Out on deck, looking down at the bow of the ship going up and down in the waves, I looked to see if Uncle George in his canvas bag was with the cattle. He wasn't.

I wasn't sleepy that night, so as I lay back on my bunk and tried to remember everything Mother told me not to do when I was with the Richards. She told me to always be a gentleman and to say, "yes, thank you" and "please" and "excuse me." "Don't tell any stories about me and remember don't tell Auntie Louise that Uncle George shot himself. And, please keep out of Auntie Louise's closets." I thought that was a lot to remember.

Arriving by ship at Lahaina was real scary because there was no wharf for the ship to dock at. The ship had to anchor off port, as passengers were bodily lifted off and transported to shore in small boats. I was the first person to be transferred off the ship while the morning was still dark as midnight. Without warning, a Hawaiian picked me off the deck, tossed me out into the air, screaming, to some-one waiting on a little boat with open arms. After he caught me, I thought I was going to lose the turkey sandwiches I ate at midnight. The sailor rowed me into shore as little waves slapped against the boat. In minutes, we arrived at the dock. I scrambled up a rope ladder and onto the wharf.

The sun was beginning to rise so I could see Lahaina outlined ahead. It was a town of quaint two-story white buildings that were laid out in a semicircle around a park. I had to wait for Marigold because she was three boats behind. Marigold staunchly believed, like Grandma did, women and children went first.

When Marigold joined me, she looked her miserable seasick self. We stood together, holding hands, our bags next to us, and waited for someone to pick us up. As the morning sun was lighting the dock and buildings in a blinding yellow, everyone headed for the bars. When the men appeared again, they were drinking beer, and walking on the dock with fishing poles in their hands. Marigold held her nose as they passed her because they smelled of fish guts, stale rum and their morning beers.

Out on the horizon, the Humuula blasted her horn three times. The cows mooed, black smoke jetted from her funnel and the old freighter jerked forward to the Big Island. At that same moment, chugging down the main street of Lahaina, an old Model B headed straight for us. The truck was without a roof or doors but had a sturdy wooden bed attached to the cab, filled with empty, silver-colored milk cans clanking all over the truck bed. The pug-a-junk looked as if a thief, in the middle of the night, had ripped everything from the truck's body but the front seats, the hood and the wooden back. The culprit was the thieving salt air that had rusted everything away before the truck was five years old.

Seeing the truck, I thought that my friend, Mr. Hamada, was coming to get me to spy with him on Maui. With a further look, I saw a big lady behind the wheel who stopped the truck right in front of us. The lady was the biggest woman I had ever seen in my life. She was two times bigger and stronger than Aunt Mari and was much larger than Charles Atlas. She wasn't fat because she had tennis balls for calves, biceps like cantaloupes and bosoms bigger than watermelons. She was way over six feet tall and acted like a real, living, breathing Hawaiian goddess. This lady was a human skyscraper.

"Hi!" she greeted, getting out of the truck. She wore a big flowered printed muumuu and a lauhala *papale* (hat) that barely covered a mass of salt and pepper hair. The lady had painted her toenails different colors, like a rainbow. She had the most beautiful bare feet in the world. The lady grabbed Marigold and me with her arms and crushed us into her watermelons and said, "I'm your Auntie Lulu." I liked her right away.

I stood tall trying to reach her face, and said back, "I'm Percy. This here's Marigold, and she's been seasick all night. You have to excuse her right now because she isn't talking or breathing." I jabbed my finger down into my throat, demonstrating what Marigold had been doing all night.

Auntie Lulu immediately adopted Marigold. She picked Marigold up like a sack of rice, and placed her gently on her right shoulder and laid her down like a baby on the front seat, next to her. Then the big lady picked up our bags and tossed them back with the empty milk cans and told to me to get in. I hitched myself up on the other side of the truck. I looked around for something to hold onto to keep from falling out, but couldn't find anything to hold onto but air and luck.

"Eh, kids," she said, starting the engine. "Good you come visit your Auntie Lulu because I show you good time." After Auntie Lulu said that, Marigold nestled into her side and fell asleep. As we drove out of Lahaina, Auntie Lulu waved and shouted at everybody on the street. It seemed like she was running for president of the United States because everybody in the town knew her and waved back madly. I would have voted for her for president of anything, anywhere, because I loved her painted toenails.

People screamed as we drove by, "Lulu." "Eh nea, Lulu. Auntie Lulu, howz'it? What kind *opala* (rubbish) you pick up?"

She laughed, "You like?"

Her truck engine "kachook kachooked" leaving the town. I loved the sound of her rattletrap kachooking down the road. We headed west.

Auntie Lulu never looked where she was going and didn't care. She loved watching the passing parade on the side of the road. She gave a final call to no one in particular, yelling above the sound of the engine, "Everybody come my house tonight. We party. Look what I picked up. Ain't they cute? Real cute, yea?" We kept on kachooking and kachooking down the road. After Auntie Lulu yelled we were cute, I waved at everybody, too. I was running for vice-president with Auntie Lulu and gave my cutest smile to the people on the street.

When we arrived at Auntie Lulu's, I saw the Richards' dairy farm went as far as I could see from the sea to the mountains, and there were more cows in pastures than Bartholomew Cubbins (in a favorite Doctor Seuss story) had hats.

The main house was built next to the beach. It was built low to the ground so as not to block the view of the ocean from the cows across the street. All the rooms in the house faced the islands of Molokai and Lanai that were etched on the horizon. The house had been designed so those islands would never be out of sight from the people living in it.

As soon as we settled into our room, Marigold recovered. She became her perky old self again and asked Auntie Lulu if she could run cross the street to see the cows and visit the dairy. Auntie Lulu gave Marigold another big hug and nodded. Marigold went off with her fingers making crab-crawling movements in front of her, itching to milk her first cow. My red nose had been saved.

Auntie Lulu's kitchen was her fortress. It was the biggest room in the house and there was a huge pot of beef stew simmering on the stove. I never sat anywhere else in the house but around her oak table in the kitchen. The table sat ten or more people at one sitting. Empty dog and cat bowls were all over the floor and newspapers tied with a string were stashed in every corner for the dog doodoo pickup. I never saw the top of the counters because empty cans were piled high next to bowls of leftovers waiting to be thrown into the garbage can. Dirty dishes sticking out of a soapy pan sat in the sink, ready to be scoured before the next party began. An open bottle of bourbon, with the label partially eaten off by a cockroach, was always on the kitchen table in wait for a sudden drop-in. Two iceboxes against the far wall stood like treasure chests waiting to be discovered. Opening the door of these stuffed treasure chests was a real challenge to see how much food I could keep from falling on the floor. Auntie Lulu called me Joe DiMaggio when I caught a bowl of potato salad in mid-air as it catapulted out of the icebox. The rest of Auntie Lulu's house was picture perfect because no one ever sat in the living room except for funerals or weddings. Auntie Lulu's kitchen was the messiest, dirtiest kitchen I ever ate in.

When I first entered the kitchen, I made a beeline for the nearest icebox. I opened it and made my first catch, a dish of leftover rice spilling off a shelf. Shoving the bowl back inside, I felt the icebox coolness on my face. It was Alaska in July. The westside of Maui is blistering hot in August. I quivered with excitement as I looked further into the icebox because in front of my face on the second shelf, staring at me, were three unopened bottles of Best Foods mayonnaise. I had come to heaven. Browsing further, moving this here and that there, I found a vat of poi, two bowls of lomi lomi salmon and every kind of milk in the world - chocolate milk, vanilla milk, strawberry milk, and even green pistachio milk. These glass milk bottles were neatly lined up on the bottom shelf.

I sprawled on a chair at the kitchen table as Auntie Lulu prepared lunch. I made my fingers into little people grabbing any tidbit Auntie Lulu threw my way. In an hour, I watched her cut up vegetables, whip up a lemon cream pudding, and put fresh ingredients into her stew, all the time sipping on a glass of bourbon. Being in a warm, loving surrounding, without Aunt Mari breathing down my back threatening to put a pink nozzle up my bottom, I relaxed and became very full of myself and completely forgot about the curse. I started to do everything Mother didn't want me to do; I began to blab.

As she kneaded with both hands boiled taro into poi, I told a wide-eyed Auntie Lulu great, whopping lies. As I wove every lie into a spider's web, she'd say, "Oh, no" and take a sip of her drink. As I spooned globs of mayonnaise on bread, I told her that I had saved three people from drowning on Kauai all by myself. Next, I told her I was almost eaten up by a thirty-foot shark, but I saved everyone by throwing a dead horse's head with a silver hook into the ocean and I had brought the beast in single-handedly. I added that I had sung a duet of "Don't Sit Under the Apple Tree" with Marian Anderson, the famous opera star, at the fabulous Roxy Theater and that Alice Faye, the movie star living in Beverly Hills, California, was my best friend. And topping all those fibs, I bragged that all the cowboys on Kauai named me the best horseback rider on the island.

Munching my sandwich and dripping mayonnaise on the tablecloth, wound up, eyes ablaze because of the lies I was spinning, I whispered, "And you know, Auntie Lulu, Marigold and I were the ones that found Uncle George dead. He was dead as a doornail. His eyes popped out of his head like fish eggs." I paused, wondering how far I should go on with Uncle George's story. Hearing Aunt Mari's voice cackling in my head, warning another enema, I added, "from choking on his cigar."

Because of the grand time I was having in Auntie Lulu's kitchen, gorging on food, making myself out to be grandest person in all the Hawaiian Islands, I disregarded everything Mother told me not to do and had thrown caution to the wind. Adding to my performance, Auntie Lulu believed everything I told her. Auntie Lulu was a very intoxicating person. When I finished telling her all the tales I could think of, I plunked down my head on the table, closed my eyes and took a shut-eye. Lying had been very exhausting.

Lunch was ready. While listening to my stories, Auntie Lulu fixed a pile of tuna sandwiches just for me and a potato salad with hardboiled eggs and sweet pickles for Marigold. Noticing right away that I adored mayonnaise, she added gobs of mayo onto everything she made for me. She placed the potato salad in a green glass bowl in the center of the table with the platter of tuna sandwiches next to it. With a rusty can opener, Auntie Lulu opened up tins of vienna sausage, corned beef and chopped olives for "my man." She sighed when she uttered "my man," sounding like a lovesick turtledove. She spooned his food onto a plate and placed it next to the potato salad. For her final preparations, she took Tabasco sauce, homemade hot chili pepper water, Heinz tomato catsup and Lea & Perrins Worcestershire sauce from the cupboard, and set them dead center on the table. She said they were the frosting for our lunch. Out of the icebox then came bowls of poi and lomi lomi salmon, more food for her Tony.

On cue, Marigold, Uncle Tony, and his five dogs walked in for lunch. Uncle Tony, Auntie Lulu's husband, was a big surprise because he was a skinny man, all muscle like Auntie Lulu, but barely five feet tall. He was as wiry as his black hair and a Frenchman.

Antone Pierre Richard was from Alsace-Lorraine. He was proud of his name and where he came from. He once had been a sailor on a freighter that docked outside of Lahaina. After a drunken brawl at the Pioneer Inn, he woke up and found himself married to Auntie Lulu. Not having a choice of leaving her, he jumped ship and they soon had Betsy, and he became the best dairyman in Hawaii. In five minutes, I knew who the boss was around the house; it was Uncle Tony. Looking at Auntie Lulu and Uncle Tony holding hands while eating my fifth tuna sandwich, I never would have imagined Betsy was their daughter. Betsy looked like a starlet - slim, pretty and blonde, and very shy. Betsy didn't in any department resemble her tall, outgoing mother or her short, Napoleonic father.

Uncle Tony wore a cowboy hat, high-heeled boots and grew a tiny moustache like a pencil-line above his lips. Upon meeting me, he gave me a smack on my back, poured a drink and sat down. He lit a cigarette and ate immediately, gulping down food like he was a dozen stevedores. I never saw a little man eat as much as Uncle Tony did, and he never showed a poochy belly like my daddy did. Uncle Tony was a wonder to watch when he ate because he was a bottomless pit.

Right away, I saw Marigold and Uncle Tony had become a team. They were well-suited to each other because they acted like toughies and looked at you square in the eyes when they talked.

Wiping the food off his face, pushing back his chair, Uncle Tony belched and called to Auntie Lulu, "Louise, I'm taking Marigold back wiz me to the dairy. Sheez already a beeeg help. I hire her. You like come work for me, Marigold?"

Marigold beamed, meaning she liked to very much.

"Percee, you like come wiz us, too?"

"I'll come later, Uncle Tony. I'm gonna stay here and help Auntie Lulu. She's gonna bake a chocolate cake this afternoon."

"Maybe I stay too. Louise, who come tonight?"

"The regulars."

"Good." With that, he downed his drink, motioned to Marigold to follow him, and they and the dogs crossed the street to milk more cows. As soon as they left, I ate three more tuna sandwiches.

That night the regulars arrived at seven. Some of them were the same people Auntie Lulu waved at as we drove from the ship. They were a chop suey bunch of people but all loved a good time. I met a bank manager, a seamstress, a school-teacher, a ditch digger, a beachcomber, a member of a singing Hawaiian family, and others that I never did hear what they did or who they were in the hubbub. Everyone brought something to Auntie Lulu: booze, vegetables, fruits from their gardens, and lots of cut tropical flowers to smell up Auntie Lulu's kitchen.

Marigold and I squeezed in at the table with the regulars. As soon as they arrived, we were treated as part of the gang. Auntie Lulu gave Marigold and me a jelly glass of beer to sip on. One sip of beer and I knew I had hit the big time. I was big stuff.

Everything went swimmingly until, in the middle of the dinner, Auntie Lulu stood up. She clinked with a spoon on her whiskey glass to get everyone's atten-tion. When Auntie Lulu stood, she loomed like the Empire State Building, and with a couple of drinks under her belt, she got your attention - or else. With two glassy eyes, she told everyone to look straight into my two glassy eyes. Everyone turned and looked - at me.

Slurring her voice and pointing a finger at me, she said, "You know, today I hear fantastic stories. Dis boy here, he something, I gotta tell ya. I never met one boy like him."

Marigold immediately perked up her ears, twitched her nose like a curious rabbit, and gave me a funny, "what have you been up to" look. She turned to Auntie Lulu and asked, "What stories did he tell you, Auntie Lulu?"

I quickly spoke up, "Nothing, Marigold. Anyway, nothing you'd be interested in hearing." I got out of my chair and stood by Auntie Lulu. I beckoned her down to my level and whispered into her ear, "Those stories were between you and me, Auntie Lulu. Please, don't tell them." While speaking to Auntie Lulu, I kept looking at Marigold to see what she was going to do next.

Marigold's eyes turning into slits, she kept on questioning, "Please, Auntie Lulu, tell me what my little brother told you this afternoon."

I squeezed Auntie Lulu's hand hard and pleaded, "Please, Auntie Lulu, I'll give you five cents if you don't tell anything in front of Marigold."

Auntie Lulu wasn't to be bribed at any price. As if she hadn't heard me, Auntie Lulu started with, "Percy told me he pulled in a thirty-foot shark all by himself."

I interrupted Auntie Lulu and looked at Marigold, pleading with my eyes for mercy and said, "Marigold helped too - in fact, Marigold was the biggest help in pulling in the shark." Marigold and I stared at each other for a long time in a real John Wayne standoff.

Then my sister took in a deep breath, and having two little glasses of beer under her belt, looked at everyone around the table and announced, "Yea, I did that, whatever Percy said I did."

I looked at her gratefully and sat down. Then we both started telling stories, each one trying to outdo the other and each building more fantastic stories on the ones the other told. Our stories, together, were far better than the ones that I told to Auntie Lulu before lunch. We dazzled the regulars, playing like Patty and Little Johnny walking hand in hand through Hunkacha's forest. But no matter how far we expanded on the stories, or how much we got carried away, we never told the regulars that Uncle George shot himself, bang bang, in the head.

I think what saved me from exposure as being the biggest liar in the world were the glasses of beer Marigold drank because, instead of being her usual growling self, she purred like a cat all night. I made a mental note to buy Marigold a case of beer when we got home because Marigold was the first happy drunk I ever met.

The evening was over when Uncle Tony passed out. Auntie Lulu picked him up, tossed him over her shoulder and took him to bed. With the hosts gone, everyone got up and staggered home to their own beds. I could tell Auntie Lulu enjoyed when Uncle Tony got drunk because then she became the boss of the house.

I went to bed feeling that I was a balloon floating in the sky and that nothing could touch me, not even the curse. Lying through my teeth, making up all those grandiose stories, made me a big shot in Auntie Lulu's eyes. But I wish someone had warned me that people who think they are big stuff, floating in the air like a balloon, made themselves into a target for a curse to bring them crashing to the ground. And that's what happened next.

54

Back to Zero

CLANG! CLANG! CLANG! Somewhere in the middle of the house, an alarm clock rang. Auntie Lulu rushed into our bedroom, stripped off our blankets and commanded, "Get up."

Marigold turned over on her stomach and yawned back, "It's still night, Auntie Lulu. Go back to bed. I need to sleep." By the smell of Marigold's breath, she had a hangover.

"Get up," Auntie Lulu insisted, "we go see sunrise at Haleakala."

"NO - NOT ME!" Marigold moaned and shoved her head under the pillow.

"Uncle Tony he make suggestion. He want his little Marigold to come."

Hearing Uncle Tony's name, Marigold jumped out of bed, brushed her teeth, and we were both sitting in the back seat of Uncle Tony's Packard before I could say, "Where's my breakfast?"

Wearing a gray cowboy hat cocked on one side of his head, a Camel cigarette dangling from his mouth, and a beer in one hand, Uncle Tony turned on the ignition with his other hand and started the car. Auntie Lulu, from the front seat, handed back to us two mugs of hot chocolate as we headed for the top of Haleakala to see the legendary sunrise. It was three o'clock in the morning. Auntie Lulu next passed back old sweaters to put on and instructed, "Gonna be freezing like ice water up there. Take these and put them on. Keep you from turning into one snowball."

Sitting in the back seat, basking in the glory from the night before, I talked like a big shot. Sipping my hot cocoa, preening at my reflection in the car window and hoping for more brownie points from Auntie Lulu, I said affectedly, "Auntie Lulu, I just read Ned Harlow's guide book on Maui. He said seeing the sunrise at Haleakala is one of the great wonders of the world."

She growled, "Percy, no mention that son a ka bitch's name in front of me. Next time he come Maui, I kill him with my two bare hands, that no good son a ka bitch! You know what he calls us?"

I peeped, "Haoles?"

Uncle Tony looked back and warned, "Percy, no get Auntie Lulu mad at youze. She seez dat man she say she gonna break, with one hand, zat man's two kumquats."

"Keep your eyes on the road, Antone. No talk like that and you know somet'ing, Antone, if you don't look at the road, you're gonna make me mad. Drive, Antone. And I no break no man's kumquats in two, except yours, Antone."

Uncle Tony snapped his eyes back to the road. I got the picture. Auntie Lulu's dander was up. Swiveling her body back around to me, she asked me in a biting tone, "Percy, do I look like one haole to you?"

Wide-eyed, I peeped back, "No, Auntie Lulu. It would never occur to me that you look like one haole."

"Good! Now no mention that son a ka bitch's name to me ever again and read something good next time - like *Popular Mechanics*." She turned back fuming to watch Uncle Tony drive up the mountain and grumbled, "Antone, you one lousy driver."

Uncle Tony's driving proved again that there wasn't one good driver left in Hawaii. They all took lessons from Aunt Mari and drank Hawaiian water. Uncle Tony didn't say a word until we reached the top of the mountain. Watching the road, scrunched in the back seat, I tried to hide from Auntie Lulu's angry mouth. Marigold, looking over at me, whispered, "Can't you keep your mouth shut? You and Ned Harlow are the two most stupidest son a ka bitches to ever set foot on Maui."

It took us three hours to reach the top of Haleakala. Each mile we climbed, I froze more. By the time Uncle Tony drove into the ranger's station at the top, I thought I was living inside an igloo with three polar bears. Before we got out of the car, Auntie Lulu made sure we had on our sweaters and wrapped blankets around us. It was six o'clock in the morning.

We ran, freezing, and snuggled against the stone wall of the ranger's station like frozen cattle in a snowstorm to watch the sun rise. Huddling close to each other as a freezing wind blew into our faces, we waited for the first ray of sun to streak into the volcano.

"Anyone like more chocolate?" asked Auntie Lulu with her teeth chattering. The cold air had calmed her down.

"I would, Auntie Lulu," I answered sweetly, trying to make up for bringing up Ned Harlow's name. Hoping to get on her good side again, I offered, "I'll get it from the car, Auntie Lulu. Anything else you want?"

Uncle Tony slurred, "Get me ze beer, Percy, and bring your Auntie Lulu's thermos. We want to keep her in ze good mood."

Pinching Uncle Tony's fanny, Auntie Lulu growled, "There's nothing wrong with my mood, Antone. Percy, they stay inside the trunk of the car. Here're the keys." Grabbing the keys from her hand, I smiled, playing my best little boy act, and said, "I'll get it for you, Auntie Lulu."

Turning to my sister hiding under the blanket, I cooed into her face, "Anything for you, my sweet little Marigold? She peeped out from her blanket, glowering, showing her fangs and her pukey face. As far as she was concerned, I was still a son a ka bitch.

I ran to the car with breath coming out of my mouth like steam, and opened up the trunk of the car with the key. I took out Uncle Tony's beer, the thermos of bourbon for Auntie Lulu (I unscrewed it and smelled it to make sure I had the right thermos), and then picked up the thermos of hot chocolate for "sweet"

Marigold and me.

I discovered *it* then. I couldn't keep my eyes from it. The temptation was just too great. The IT was the picnic basket that Auntie Lulu fixed for our lunch. I couldn't resist it. I put everything back down in the trunk and opened the basket. I first spied egg salad sandwiches wrapped in wax paper and a package of graham crackers at the top of the basket. My tummy told me I needed a "fill'er up." I ripped open two egg sandwiches and shoved them in my mouth fast as I rearranged the food in the basket. I wanted to cover my tracks so that Auntie Lulu wouldn't suspect a thief had been at her lunch. As I was about to grab for two graham crackers, Auntie Lulu's voice rang out, "PERCY, WHAT'S KEEPING YOU SO LONG?"

I smoothed out the dishcloth that covered the lunch, closed the picnic basket, picked up the beer and thermos bottles, slammed down the car trunk, and ran back to Auntie Lulu with a great big smile on my face. I gave them their beer and bourbon, and even Marigold showed her front teeth when I handed her the hot chocolate. I was a hero again, even as I wiped off a trace of egg salad on my mouth.

At 6:20, God's show began. He started to play on His light switches. From out on the horizon, a sunray appeared. Then another streak of light burst through the clouds and then another and another and another, until before us spread a volcano large enough to house the city of Manhattan. God designed this volcanic city in magnificent colors of red and gold. I clapped my hands when the curtain came down because seeing the crater glowing before me made me want to run down into the crater and play within God's city. I turned and told everyone that I just saw Apollo riding in his chariot, whipping his golden steeds, and lighting up the sky. Didn't they see him?

Marigold said to Uncle Tony that I was a cuckoo person.

After the show ended, Uncle Tony and Auntie Lulu were back in a good mood. Even Marigold smiled sweetly under the blanket and said to Uncle Tony that it was the best damn sunrise she had ever seen. She hugged Auntie Lulu and thanked her for waking her up at three o'clock in the morning.

Uncle Tony, downing the last of his beer, spoke to Auntie Lulu, "Louise."

"Yes, Antone."

"I'm hungry. Let's feed ze kids. Give me ze keys. Marigold and I go get ze food." He had his hand out to take the car keys.

"We go with you," said Auntie Lulu. We turned and walked to the car.

As we reached the car, Uncle Tony put his hand out again and said, "Louise, the keys." Auntie Lulu rifled through the pockets of her dress looking for the keys, and then turned to me and asked, "Percy, didn't I give you the keys?"

"Yes, but I gave them back to you," I replied quickly.

"You sure?" she asked.

"Yes, I'm sure, Auntie Lulu," I said, nodding that I was telling her the truth.

Uncle Tony stepped in, "Louise, I bet you dropped zem on the ground."

"I did not, Antone," Auntie Lulu said back, curtly.

"You always lose things. I look around." Uncle Tony huffed as we all looked on the ground for the keys.

Auntie Lulu came back to me and said, "Percy, do you think you might have left the keys in the trunk of the car?"

I thought a minute and then it dawned on me. I had put the keys down in the trunk of the car and I could now see where they were still laying. I put them down while I was thieving the egg salad sandwiches from the picnic basket and forgot to pick them up. The keys were locked in the trunk.

Auntie Lulu saw immediately what was floating around in my mind, and she asked again, "Percy?"

I looked right in her eyes and lied, saying, "I don't think so, Auntie Lulu." My nose started to grow.

"Are you sure?" she said, giving me another chance to tell the truth.

"Yes, I gave you back the keys," I answered more firmly than before. This time I couldn't look her in the eyes because my nose felt longer than Pinocchio's.

"Percy, you lie to me?" Auntie Lulu growled, getting mad.

"Auntie Lulu, I wouldn't lie to you!" That lie was as big as the volcano below me. I was turning into Pinocchio.

"Percy?" Auntie Lulu not letting up, said, "Tell me the truth."

More determined not to be caught, I said, "I gave them back to you. You were the one that lost them, Auntie Lulu." My nose was now as long as a tree branch and housed a nest of birds.

Auntie Lulu turned her back on me and shouted at Uncle Tony to come back. Uncle Tony didn't hear her as he was lifting stones to see if the keys were under them. She yelled again, "Tony, come back here. Percy locked the keys in the trunk."

I could have died.

Uncle Tony and Marigold ran back as I heard a hissing sound behind me. Air was coming out of the left tire as it went flat. I could have killed myself.

Looking at the locked trunk and the tire going flat, I thought Auntie Lulu was going to pick me up and toss me over the rim into the volcano. The look on her face was: "good riddance to bad rubbish - toss'em over."

Auntie Lulu said very slowly, "You have one more chance, Percy. Where are the keys?"

I stuck out my lower lip: I felt that I had to stay with my lie or else Auntie Lulu would know that I was really a fake since the moment she met me. So I determinedly said again, "I don't know. I gave them back to you. Honest, injun."

Auntie Lulu shrugged her shoulders and looked as if I had just slapped her in the face. While Auntie Lulu was talking to me, Uncle Tony and Marigold tried to pry open the trunk with their hands but it wouldn't budge. Uncle Tony picked up a stone and started pounding the lock. Each pound dented and scraped the paint off his beautiful Packard.

A park ranger arriving at work ordered Uncle Tony to stop what he was doing. He thought Uncle Tony was a robber. After Uncle Tony told him what had happened, he suggested we take the back seat out of the car and have Marigold crawl through the small open space and unlock the trunk from the inside. That's what happened.

Marigold, Uncle Tony and Auntie Lulu's big hero, found the keys in the trunk where I left them. Uncle Tony snarled at me as he opened the trunk and changed the tire. His precious Packard, which he had kept in mint shape, was ruined. Everybody was now in a black mood, especially Auntie Lulu. After opening the picnic basket and finding two of her egg salad sandwiches stolen, she put two and two together. She made the egg salad sandwiches especially for Uncle Tony.

As the sun rose high in the sky and warmed the day, I became yesterday's hero. I was now an icky worm that everyone wanted to stomp on. The curse took aim, shot his arrow and burst my balloon, and I was now a fallen angel. Riding back home, no one talked to me. I didn't peep a word because I feared that Auntie Lulu would jump over the front seat and break my kumquats. I had to go to the bathroom.

Driving home in the fog, Marigold now sat between Auntie Lulu and Uncle Tony, and she chatted away, telling them that she was an only child. If I had had Uncle George's gun in the back seat, I would have shot myself.

After we got home, Auntie Lulu and Uncle Tony tossed down three drinks and relaxed. The more they relaxed, the more I became the butt of their jokes. My hauling in a thirty-foot shark turned into a hilarious comedy and the loss of the keys became a Charlie Chan caper, a whodunit. The story they were telling their friends was about a fat little boy who misplaced the car keys, who lied, and who stole Uncle Tony's egg salad sandwiches.

I couldn't face the regulars coming that night because I knew I would be teased mercilessly and as much as I tried, I couldn't wangle the disappointed look out of Auntie Lulu's eyes. Her hero had tossed himself off his pedestal - all by himself. I asked her if I could go to the movies in Lahaina. She gave me permission but I was to be escorted by one of the hired hands working at the dairy. They paid him overtime to be my babysitter.

In the car with Moki, driving into Lahaina, I hung my head down to the floor, thinking about the swiftness of life. One minute I was a hero, the next minute an untouchable. I had become a leper, the people that Auntie Lulu told me about whom nobody wanted to be around because everyone was afraid they'd become lepers, too, if they touched them. Lepers lived on Molokai, the island across the channel from Auntie Lulu's house, and farmed in a valley surrounded by tall mountains that kept them prisoners. Nobody liked lepers because they had pussy sores all over their bodies and their fingers dropped off.

I guessed that people touching me would catch my lying disease and turn into crooks or murderers or even worse, be cursed. I now had developed invisible sores all over my body that everybody knew about, and I was sure from now on, nobody wanted to be around me anymore. Life had changed a big notch that morning. All of a sudden, I was living in a world that I couldn't trust because I couldn't trust me: I couldn't trust what I said or what I did.

Moki dropped me at the movie house. He paid me fifty cents not to squeal that he was going off to see his girlfriend. Fifty cents was big money and a boy who lies is easily bribed.

The Lahaina movie theater was another big barn of a movie palace. The seats sloped down, listing on their hinges as if I was sinking on the Titanic. There were blobs of gum wadded under each seat, enough rubber to make tires for Mr. Ford's cars. The tin roof above me was like the Waikiki Theatre in that it showed a starry sky through holes in the ceiling - but looking up at the Lahaina theater, the holes and sky were real. The large rusty holes in the ceiling let rain, dust, mill soot, and moonlight fall on our heads. The biggest attraction before the movie started was watching rats as big as cats dance back and forth on the rotten beams above. The theater stunk like the toilets in a public park. Little boys in back of me let go, whenever they felt like it. All through the movie, yellow rivers would stream past my bare feet, especially when the movie got exciting. I was in such a foul mood, I pretended I was the devil, God's fallen angel, sitting in his house in hell.

The movie playing that night was perfect. It was *A Woman's Face* starring Joan Crawford. It was about a woman whose face had been scarred badly, but only on the right side. The other half of her face appeared sweet as an angel's. I felt like Joan Crawford's character that night because sometimes I was good, and sometimes I acted rotten bad. Right now, I was acting rotten bad as Aunt Momi predicted. I was a lying son a ka bitch criminal that should be sent to Sing Sing and be electrocuted. I never saw how the Joan Crawford movie turned out, whether she became all good or all bad, because halfway through the movie, the projectionist burnt a hole in the film with his cigarette lighter. A lot of "goddamns" and "shits" were heard up in the projection booth and then the lights went on. We were told by an old man to go home. Everyone walking out of the theatre grumbled, "All time happen. That buggah should be fired." I had company that night; the man in the projection booth had also become a leper.

Standing under a banyan tree, waiting for Moki to finish loving up his girlfriend, I knew I was just like Maui - half-good and half-bad.

When I got back to the house, Mother had phoned. She told Auntie Lulu to put us on the next ship. The funeral was over, but I was planning mine again - this time without the MGM spectacle. This time, I wanted to be sewed in a bag like Uncle George and dumped at sea.

Auntie Lulu booked us on Humuula and we were ticketed to leave in two days. I was glad to go because Auntie Lulu kept looking through me as if I had worn out my welcome. The day before we left, Auntie Lulu drove us into the county seat of Maui, Wailuku. It was the town where Daddy had been raised. My grandfather's house had been torn down years before and in its place stood a building that housed The Salvation Army. Auntie Lulu told us the river that ran through Wailuku once ran red with Hawaiian blood. The blood was that of defeated warriors whom the great King Kamehameha killed in a major battle. There was nothing in the town that reminded me of my daddy. I looked and looked but I couldn't find my daddy anywhere. Everywhere Marigold looked, she saw Daddy. I just saw a river that ran red. I wanted to go home to be with my mother again.

Auntie Lulu saw that we boarded the Humuula safely. She wrapped two egg salad sandwiches in wax paper for me to eat on the ship. The disappointed look never left her eyes. As soon as we sailed and were out at sea, I threw the sandwiches overboard. Marigold told me that she was happy to leave, too, because she was tired of milking cows and drinking beer and she wanted to see Daddy. Our summer was over.

Mother met us at the ship and the first thing she told me was Hatsuko had a surprise for me. When we were alone, I confessed to Mother everything bad I had done. I told her about breaking the train she had given to Tom, about lying to Auntie Lulu and about acting like a big conceited fathead. I didn't tell her about the enema. Mother gave me a stern look and said she would send Tom another train and that I must write everyone thank you letters, including one to Aunt Mari. I must especially apologize to Auntie Lulu and Uncle Tony for being a liar. She told me liars were not permitted to live in her house. I nodded I would never lie again.

Lepers are really good and kind people and what they have isn't their fault. Liars are not good and kind people and everything is their fault and all liars should be sent to a concentration camp. From the look in Mother's eyes and the touch of her hand, I knew my mother would always love me even if I continued to be the worst liar in the world, and that's why I would love my mother till the day I died in the electric chair.

After I confessed to Mother, I ran into my bedroom and pulled Agnes and Gertrude out of the window seat. "Well," said Gertrude, sitting on my lap, "what did you learn this summer?" Pulling Agnes up beside us, I answered her grumpily, "Nothing. Absolutely nothing, Gertrude, just nothing. I'm back to zero!"

Kissing them both on the cheeks, I added, "Actually girls, I'm minus zero and the curse is still out to get me." This time, I wasn't lying.

55

Making the Rounds

After I unpacked, the first thing I did was to look for the old *Advertisers* and catch up with the news. I found piles of newspapers under the sink in Helen's kitchen.

🦋

The Honolulu Advertiser

SLEEPWALKING FARMER BOY IN WRONG JOB

There may be a place for farmers in the navy, but apparently it isn't shipboard if they walk in their sleep. A young bluejacket, fairly recently off the farm in Kansas, was sleeping on deck one night aboard the lead ship of a cruiser division operating in Hawaiian waters. Presently, he got up, walked to the rail, climbed it and plummeted into the sea. After a bit of confusion, the third cruiser in the line picked him up, a little startled but uninjured.

He had, he said, been dreaming he was back on the farm and, in the course of his dream, found it necessary to climb a fence.

July 1941 (UP) GERMAN ARMY DRIVES SWIFTLY TOWARD MOSCOW AND LENINGRAD.

UNITED PRESS'S GRAPHIC SURVEY COVERS PACIFIC DEFENSES

July 1941 by Julius O. Edelstein. Key to Defense: Hence, in American military judgment, the key to the defense of the west coast remains in Hawaii, in its huge naval operations base, and in the great army establishment which is charged with the defense of the Islands against seizure or attack.

The entire defense system in the Pacific...Guam, Samoa, Wake and Midway-are specialized links in a chain of fortifications whose central stronghold is in Hawaii. While Oahu stands inviolate, the entire system will remain functional, even though individual bases might be seized by an attacking enemy.

Greatest Naval Base: In Pearl Harbor is the greatest assemblage of dry-docks in any naval base in the world. More are under construction. The navy yard has its own power station, now being proofed against air attack, its own railway system, machine shops, cold storage facilities and shelters for personnel. This retreat has served as the home base for the entire U.S. fleet since April 1940, when it was suddenly ordered from its station at San Diego base in Southern California. The fleet has remained in Hawaii ever since, exerting a powerful influence on the politics of the Pacific.

Aug 6, 1941. ISLANDERS MAROONED IN JAPAN.

(UP) 1700 Territory of Hawaii Residents, Mostly Alien Japanese, Stranded as Result of Suspension of Sailing. Japanese hotelmen of Honolulu estimated yesterday that mostly alien Japanese but including a number of Americans of Japanese ancestry, are stranded in Japan as a result of the suspension of sailing of Japanese ships to Hawaii and the Mainland.

HOWARD HUGHES GROOMS STAR.

Howard Hughes, wealthy sportsman, flyer and movie producer who discovered Jean Harlow, is grooming a 19-year old beauty, Jane Russell, for stardom.

AUG 12. TOKYO PRESS WARNS U.S. TO 'STOP SHOVING' JAPAN!

Returning home after two months, I felt like Buck Rogers coming back to earth after a long spaceship journey around Mars. Everything seemed strange, even our house looked smaller. Betsy and Jack left a note next to the telephone saying they had found a "darling" apartment and thanked Mother for the use of our house and would take us all out to dinner soon.

The day after I came back, I scribbled thank you notes to Cousin Rose, Cousin Nigel and Tom, thanking them for teaching me to wash my feet before I said my prayers at night and feeding me tons of volcano, my now all-time favorite creamed tuna dish. I printed a short note to Aunt Mari and wrote a big THANK YOU in orange letters that took up most of the card. Before I signed my name, I inquired in small letters if she had roses on her cheeks. I made a PS at the end of the note asking the orange witch to send back my Linda Darnell paper dolls I left up at Kokee, and would she please send them by special delivery. I found old yellowed lined paper in Mother's desk drawer and wrote Cousin Dora separately. I drew big kisses all over the yellow page and signed my name "with love." I found an old Christmas card lying under a stack of letters and sent it to Auntie Lulu and Uncle Tony. I put a thank you under the season's greetings and signed it "Love, Percy." I hoped that after receiving a Christmas message in August, they'd forget that I was the biggest liar in the whole wide world. I also thought the card would remind them that at Christmas time, everybody forgave one another.

Mother called Marigold and me into the living room. She had a letter from Grandma who was still living in California. She sat us down and read us Grandma's letter.

"Oakland, California. August 1941 - Sunday afternoon

Dear Deidra and Children:
  I miss you all so dreadfully.
  It's not the same here as it is in Hawaii especially being with you all. The weather now is most foul, and most of the time I look out the window and see the rain and fog.
  I have made new friends. Some are real characters. One of the most interesting new acquaintances is Sally Stanford. She had the biggest "house" in Northern California. We have become quite close though I don't approve of her old profession. But she knew the Captain and I like her because she's a square shooter.
  Deidra, I want to request something from you and my great-grandchildren. I want to come back home to my family. I want to come back to Hawaii to die. I would like, with your permission, to move back into my old bedroom and sleep once again in my four poster bed. Those days, with all of you on Kapaka Street, were some of the happiest memories of my life.
  Deidra, you were always so kind to me...and you, too, are a square shooter.
  Will you let me come home? If you all say yes - I will return on the Lurline after the New Year - towards the middle of January 1942. I've given my word to spend the Christmas holidays in Santa Barbara with my friends.
  Looking forward to hearing from you. I do miss you all.
Love, Grandma"

Mother put the letter down on the table and asked, "Well, children?" We answered joyously that we both wanted our grandma back. Mother, tears in her eyes, blessed us and said, "I'll write to Grandma tomorrow and tell her to come home."

After reading the letter, Mother headed for the telephone with her cup of coffee and began her morning ritual - telephoning. She was addicted to talking on the telephone, day and night. In three hours on the telephone, Mother knew more news going on in the Islands than *The Honolulu Advertiser*, God or even Cousin Bessie. When Mother wasn't teaching, she knew everything about everybody by noon. Auntie Gladys was her first dial in the morning.

Wearing new Levi's, Marigold put on her cowboy hat, jingled coins in her pocket, and walked out the front door as she told Mother she was taking the bus downtown to see Daddy at his office. She was as happy as a bumblebee, because she was having lunch at the Young Hotel with Daddy to herself.

Knowing Mother would hog the phone all morning so I couldn't call Hatsuko, I decided to make the rounds. I had been away for so long, and being my mother's son, I wanted to find out what had happened around the neighborhood since the day I sailed for Kauai.

I first checked Mother's closet. She hadn't bought a new dress since I looked last. At this moment, pushing the dresses back and forth on the rod, I wasn't as interested in playing Mother or dressing up. I had found a new interest at Kokee that I hadn't even shared with Agnes or Gertrude. I now adored playing with matches. It started when I lit the logs in Aunt Mari's fireplace. I got the biggest kick watching things burn to ashes. I now carried a box of Lancer matches in my pocket.

My first peek-a-boo hello was to see Helen the Horrible. I stuck my head into the kitchen and waved, "I'm back!" She lifted up her wooden spoon and waved back at me, snarling, "Get out!" I sighed as I went on my way, thinking, "Helen has remained horrible. Some things never change - thank God."

I walked up the hill to Auntie Gladys and Uncle Pete's house and rang their electric buzzer. Buzzzzzzzzzz! Auntie Gladys opened the door. She was wearing purple curlers in her hair and had a smidgen of cold cream left up in her right nostril that looked like snot.

I grinned, "Guess who?"

"Let me see. Greta Garbo?" She answered, scratching her fanny.

"Guess again," I persisted.

"The biggest goddamn pest is back," she answered, and then pretended to close the door.

"That's me. Got anything to eat?" I insisted, putting my foot in the door.

"Come on in," she sighed. "We're having breakfast."

Fully inside the door, I smiled. "I'm starved because I haven't eaten all summer." I gave her a kiss on the cheek.

"Follow me," she said, sounding like she had a doozy of a hangover. She turned and padded down the hall to the dining room, wrapping her terrycloth bathrobe around her as she walked. I followed behind, mimicking her unsteady walk. As we headed towards the dining room, she kept on blabbering, "Was out late with your father and Kathy last night. That dame, Kathy, is a pistol, if you ask me. Damn good for your father. She doesn't let your father get away with anything."

I advised, "I wouldn't tell Mother that and by the way did you make any blueberry muffins, Auntie Gladys?"

Turning back to me, she chortled, "Tell your mother anything good about Kathy? What, do you think I'm crazy? Your mother is my best friend. And by the way, you're in luck, blueberry muffins are just out of the oven."

Fearing the death contract was still out on my head, I asked quickly, "Are the Twins back from summer camp?"

"Yea. They're having breakfast with Petey and me!"

I stepped backwards, making a retreat and howled, "I'll come back later."

She grabbed my arm and forced me into the dining room, laughing, "You come with me, Percy. My angels ain't going to harm you. They love you, Percy." Auntie Gladys lived in la la land when it came to her Twins.

When we entered the dining room, Don was hitting Roger, the good-looking one, on his head with a catsup bottle. Pushing me into the dining room, Auntie Gladys announced, "Look who the cat dragged in." Then, she picked up a glass of vodka and orange juice off the dining room table and chug-a-lugged it.

Seeing me in the doorway, the Twins stopped beating up on each other and looked me over, licking their chops, because dessert had just arrived.

I finger-waved at the boys, "Hi, Don. Hi, Roger. How was camp?"

Auntie Gladys interrupted, "They passed."

"Yea," said Roger, "we're real Einsteins. I got an A in wood shop." He laughed a fiendish, "Ha! Ha! Ha!" He then poured half a bottle of catsup over his scrambled eggs. Grabbing the catsup bottle out of Roger's hand, Don mumbled, "Yea and I got an A in finger painting." Don poured the other half of the bottle onto his eggs.

Uncle Pete spoke up from the other end of the table, "Hi, Percy." He was sitting up like a mummy in his chair, nursing a tall Bloody Mary with a piece of celery sticking out of the glass and he slurred, "Wanna have some breakfast?"

I said quickly, "No, Uncle Pete, I just came over to say a quick hello and to tell you we're back, and I've gotta go."

Auntie Gladys interrupted and said sarcastically, "We all know you're back because your mother called me up at six-thirty this morning."

I smiled, "That was nice of Mother to wake you up. Well," still trying to make a quick getaway from the Twins, I uttered, "I got things to do." Whispering to each other as if they were deciding my fate, the Twins looked at me with evil grins and said, "What things, Perrrrrrcy?"

I answered, "I gotta go." I just couldn't resist asking, "Auntie Gladys, can I have one of your blueberry muffins to take with me?"

"Sure, Percy, I'll wrap one up for you." I could always count on her.

Don grabbed the basket of muffins off the table, set them on his lap and said, "Come get them, Percy. We want to show you something."

Dumb I'm not. I said, "That's all right, Don. Show Marigold. She's having lunch with Daddy and I know she'll want to see your little tiny peepee when she gets back. She can tell me all about it."

I certainly knew how to make a room go silent.

Before Don could get up and sock me, Auntie Gladys walked over, slapped him on the head, grabbed the basket of muffins out of his lap, picked out two, wrapped them in a paper napkin, and gave them to me. I held onto the muffins for dear life because I saw from the mean looks on Don's face that I was still on his most wanted hate list. Some things just never change.

I backed out of their house, a maneuver I learned from Aunt Mari and her enema nozzle. From now on, I was never going to turn my back on an enemy. As Auntie Gladys would say, I got the hell out of there.

Muffins in hand, I walked next door to Cousin Bessie's house. I rang her chimes. Ding, Ding, Ding, Dong! Cousin Bessie, dressed to the nines, opened the door. "Why, Percy, you sweet thing, how I've missed you. You are my most darling boy and you look just wonderful. Handsomest boy in the neighborhood." I knew by her insincere greeting that I was going to be invited into the spider's web.

I asked, "Cousin Bessie, are you going somewhere? You're all dressed up."

She flounced her dress and replied, "All dressed up and nowhere to go. My daddy said when you wake up and you have nowhere to go, dress up like you're going somewhere and then something is bound to happen to you. And sure enough, look what's happened."

"What's happened?" I asked, looking startled.

Blinking her eyes like Mary Pickford did when she looked into the camera, she chirped, "Sure enough, Percy, you're here."

"Well, ain't that real nice of me," I answered, imitating Auntie Gladys.

"Isn't, Percy. I can tell you've been next door with that 'ain't we awful' Gladys. Ain't is a common word spoken by common people. And that Gladys is as common as they come."

I spoke in my proper Powderhurst English accent and tilted up my nose in the air and said, "May I come in, dear Cousin Bessie? I have in my hand two delicious blueberry muffins and I'll share them with you and tell you everything that happened to me this summer."

Her eyes lit up like diamonds as she pushed me inside, saying, "Come in, sweetness. You've just got to see Darlene's replacement. You know, Darlene died. This new one is mama's new sweetie. She's a dear cat. I've named her Martha." Martha crawled out from under the couch, arched her back, and spat at me. She looked as mangy as George the horse and appeared as loaded with worms as dead old Darlene. I could tell she was wormy by the way she "fannied" her way across the rug trying to get away from me.

As Cousin Bessie fixed a cup of Ovaltine, I unwrapped Auntie Gladys's blueberry muffins and shared one with Miss Nosy Parker. Cousin Bessie sat me at the kitchen table for what looked like a serious hour of interrogation because she straddled one leg over a chair, the way Marlene Dietrich did in the movies, and gave me a once-over look before I began. Miss Nosy Parker would have made an excellent Gestapo agent because without torture, I gave her every bit of news that I had overheard and made up some more. I told Cousin Bessie on my second cup of Ovaltine, confidentially, of course, that Aunt Mari had syphilis.

Syphilis was a word Marigold used when she referred to Kathy, Daddy's wife, and a word that I read in *The Honolulu Advertiser* about people who worked down on Hotel Street. Cousin Bessie ran for the bathroom, she was so thrilled with my news. When she returned, she asked, "Percy, did you make that up?"

"Kinda. But I read in *The Advertiser* that there is a huge rise in syphilis cases at Schofield Barracks and on Hotel Street. I thought since Aunt Mari acts like a general, she must have it, too, and believe me, I know she has it."

"I wouldn't spread that around, Percy, because syphilis is a bad disease and it makes you go blind. It's not like the chicken pox, you know."

I leaned toward her and confided, "Okay, Cousin Bessie, I understand that. But don't forget when you hear that Aunt Mari has gone cuckoo in the head, you heard it from me first. Trust me, she has a bad case of it. Now it's your turn to spill the beans."

From then on, I couldn't get a word in edgewise. When her gossip faucet turned on, it gushed out poison on everyone. She told me that Mr. Murray crashed his car into his neighbor's garage once again and this time, Mr. Murray broke his arm and a leg.

"And your friends down the hill, Cross-Eyed Mama - well, she's now got a big drinking problem. She's turned into a complete mess and stays in bed all day, nursing a bottle of gin. Remember, Percy, birds of a feather flock together. So you stay away from that family. And your other friend, Mr. McLaine - now there's a real oddity. He keeps to himself all the time. Never speaks to me. When he sees me coming, he hobbles back into his house. It wouldn't surprise me, Percy, if we'd find out that he was a Jack the Ripper-type. Watch out for anyone who has yellow eyes. Mark my words, Percy, yellow eyes are the sign of a rapist."

Finishing my cocoa, I said time was up and got off the chair, wiped my face with a napkin, and sniffed, "Thanks for the Ovaltine."

She pushed me back down in the chair and speaking like a Nazi, ordered, "Percy, I know you haven't told me everything. Have you? You're keeping a secret from me, aren't you?"

"I have told you everything. Honest, Cousin Bessie, I have." I crossed my fingers.

Smacking her lips, smiling like Martha, she pounced and announced, "You haven't told me about your mother's new boyfriend."

"What new boyfriend?" I demanded.

"Percy, don't fool with me. Everyone in Honolulu knows about him. Did your mother tell you not to say anything to me about him?" she said as she drummed her fingers on the table.

"There is no boyfriend. You're making that up just to upset me." I threw the napkin in her face.

"You just ask her, sweetums! He's in the Army and maybe he's the one that has the syphilis around here."

I jumped up for good this time because she made me hopping mad by saying things like that about my mother. I went face to face with Cousin Bessie and blasted her, "I know what you said isn't true. I also know something really big, that is the biggest scandal anywhere in the world and you don't know what it is, but you'll wish you did, and I'm not going to tell you." I was thinking about Uncle George with a bullet hole in his head.

I stomped out of the kitchen and slammed the front door. Cousin Bessie always got me into a bad mood when I stayed around her too long. I ran down the hill to Cross-Eyed Mama's house fuming, wanting to see if Vinnie and Cynthia could play with me. I hit the brass knocker on their door three times - hard. Clank, clank, clank! Cross-Eyed Mama opened the door.

"Hi!" I sang, "I just got back."

"I heard," she said, looking at me as if Hitler had just returned from his summer home in Berchtesgaden. She put her hands on her hips and uttered to herself, "We've certainly had a peaceful summer without you around."

"Can I play with Cynthia and Vinnie?" I asked, hopefully.

"No."

"No?" I couldn't believe my ears at what she just said. "You promised before I left that I could play with them when I got back."

She yelled, "I said when the summer was over. Summer is not over. Do you understand that? SUMMER IS NOT OVER!" As if yelling would make me understand her better.

"When is summer over?" I asked.

"Next week," she screamed and slammed the door in my face.

I yelled at the door, "I'll be back in the fall."

Walking home, I picked up some stones and threw them at anything, muttering to myself, "I'm sure glad I was missed around here." I walked up the front steps of my house and beside the door sat a bottle of mayonnaise. I knew from the Japanese writing on the label that it was from Mr. Hamada. It seemed he was the only friend I had left in the world who was glad to see me back. I took the bottle into the kitchen and made myself a huge mayonnaise sandwich and then I lay down on my bed with Agnes and Gertrude and thought, "My life is falling apart." The curse was out to get me good for sure.

As I was about to doze off, I heard Marigold storm through the house, heading for her bedroom. She slammed every door on her way, shouting, "I'm gonna run away from this dump. I hate this world. I hate everybody." After she banged her bedroom door shut, the house turned quiet again. I told Gertrude and Agnes that lunch with Daddy must not have gone very well. Maybe she ate a bad tuna sandwich but I knew Marigold had planned to ask Daddy to dump Kathy.

Next, I heard Mother drive in. I had the *big* question to ask her. I struggled out of bed and met her at the front door. She carried two bags of groceries in her hands and asked, "Please help me with these." I took the bags from her arms and we walked into the kitchen.

As I put the bags on the kitchen counter, I asked, "Do you have a boyfriend?"

She paused and then said, "Who'd you hear that from?"

Pulling the cans of tuna out of the paper sack, I answered, "Cousin Bessie."

Turning me around so I had to face her, she questioned, "Do you always believe everything she tells you?"

"Sometimes. Is it true? Do you have a boyfriend?" I looked her squarely in the eyes.

"I met someone on the ship going to Tahiti."

"Is he gonna take Daddy's place?"

"Of course not."

I turned around and pulled three cans of peas out of the paper bag, and mumbled, "Are you gonna love him more than you love me?"

She put her arms around me and kissed the top of my head, and murmured, "Do you think that would be possible?"

I dropped my head and threw a can of tuna into the sink, sighing, "I think the way things are going, and the way I've been acting lately, I think anything is possible."

Turning me around, Mother looked me in the eyes and said, "Well, you put that out of your mind. Anyway, you have something much more important to think about. I just saw Hatsuko in the hospital. She's had a baby girl."

I jumped and exclaimed, "Hatsuko has a baby girl! I've got to see her right away. I hope she hasn't named the baby yet."

Mother calmed me down by saying, "She's waiting for you to name the baby and that's why she wanted you to call her."

"I couldn't call her because you hogged the phone all morning. Then I forgot about it. When can I see her?" I demanded.

"Tomorrow. Tomorrow we're all going to the hospital to see her and the baby."

"Mother, now this is serious. This is important. Now, please pay attention to me. Does the baby have Charlie's teeth? Please, tell me no." I waited breathlessly for the answer.

"The baby is as beautiful as a movie star."

I yelled, "I knew it. I just knew Hatsuko's baby had to be as beautiful as a movie star."

I helped Mother take the rest of the groceries out of the paper bag and after we had finished, I said, after thinking about the baby's beautiful teeth, "Then Charlie can't be the father."

"That's an awful thing to say. Go right into the bathroom this very minute and wash your mouth out with soap! That's not a nice thing to say about anyone. Charlie is a nice boy and has nice teeth." Mother sounded really angry.

I walked to the bathroom, soaked a washrag in soapy water and gave the inside of my mouth a good cleaning. After washing my mouth out with soap, I walked out on the lanai. I felt the matches jiggling in my pocket. I pulled them out and jiggled them again in the box and wondered, looking up and down the street, which house in the neighborhood I wanted to burn down.

56
And Baby Makes Three

I was so excited about seeing Hatsuko's baby that I couldn't sleep. In the middle of the night, I read old *Advertisers* to keep my mind from jumping out of my head.

The Honolulu Advertiser

Advertisement. Headachy PEPLESS from sluggish bowels? Take FEEN-A-MINT The Chewing Gum Laxative

FILIPINOS OF HAWAII UNITE!
For National Defense - For 100% cooperation with the United States -
BUY NATIONAL DEFENSE BONDS

MISS AMERICA.
Atlantic City. (UP) Rosemary LaPlance, of Los Angeles, was named Miss America of 1941. She is five and one half feet tall and weighs 120 pounds. Miss LaPlance said she hasn't a boyfriend and plans to enter the movies.

HIROHITO TAKES CONTROL OF ARMY HEADQUARTERS. AIM BELIEVED TO KEEP JAPAN OUT OF WAR.

THOUSANDS OF ISLAND CATHOLICS GREET NEW BISHOP OF HONOLULU.
The Most Reverend James Joseph Sweeny, new Bishop of Honolulu, arrived yesterday to assume leadership of Catholic work in the Islands.

JACKIE ROBINSON SAILS THURSDAY TO JOIN BEARS.
Jackie Robinson, fleet-footed former University of California at Los Angeles football star, said tonight he would leave Thursday for Hawaii to play in the Islands. Robinson will play for the Honolulu Bears at $100 a game for expenses and a job.

JOE LOUIS READY IF ARMY CALLS.
Received news he might be drafted in October. He said "I hope I will be able

to carry out the Lou Nova fight Sept 29. But I'm not going to ask deferment or any other favors. I think I'll like the Army!"

HARRIET'S POI SHOP - POI EATERS!
Poi arrives fresh from Kauai every Wednesday and Saturday. Best Quality Kauai RED POI. 5pds @.50cts 10pds@$1.00
207 Namokueha Street Phone 68062

Mother, in a rage, stormed into my bedroom and demanded, "Did you tell Cousin Bessie that Aunt Mari has syphilis?" I put the newspaper down on the floor, sat up in bed, calmly fluffed up the pillows, and said nonchalantly, "Yes, I did."

"Why did you say such a thing? Where do you learn such terrible words? You certainly don't hear them from me." Mother was so angry she was ready to shake the daylights out of me.

"Mother, if you will calm down and sit on my bed, I'll tell you all about it." As I said that, I smashed a stick of gum into my mouth. Mother sat down, ready to reach over and strangle me.

"First of all," I continued, "nobody ever believes anything Cousin Bessie ever says. She's known as the biggest liar in the world. And second, Mother, I read about syphilis in *The Advertiser*. Everybody has it now. All the movie stars have it. The new general at Schofield Barracks said that all his men have it and the governor should close down Hotel Street. Well, Aunt Mari acts like a soldier so I thought she's got to have it too, and I bet she buys her dresses on Hotel Street when she shops in Honolulu."

"That was a terrible thing to say about Aunt Mari and you know it," Mother scolded.

"Well, she might have it. Remember when I complained that I had the chicken pox and you said I was making it up, and the next day I broke out with red spots all over my face. Aunt Mari might have that disease and she doesn't know it. You ought to call her up and tell her to go to the doctor right away."

Mother squinted at me and said, "You have a naughty mind and that was really a naughty thing to say about Aunt Mari. Don't you think so?"

I closed my eyes and didn't answer her. She pressed on further, "You do, don't you?"

I opened my eyes and smiled, saying, "Yes, I think I have a very naughty mind. It's part of the curse."

Folding her hands on her lap, she asked, "What do you think syphilis is?"

"It's a disease that Kathy has. It will make her go blind and go goofy in the head in a year." After I said that, I nodded my head up and down like a wise monk sitting in a Buddhist temple.

"Your father's wife doesn't have that disease and what makes you think Kathy has it?" Mother kept pressing on.

"Marigold told me. She says that only awful people get it so I thought Aunt

Mari must have it too. Marigold was going to tell Daddy to leave Kathy because he might catch it and go crazy."

"Kathy doesn't have it and neither does Aunt Mari. It's a terrible disease that no decent person mentions in polite company. Aunt Mari would die if she heard such a thing was said about her. It would just about kill her."

"Really, Mother?" I said, perking up.

"Yes, Percy," Mother said solemnly.

I got out of bed and started for the door, saying, "Let's call her up right now and tell her she has it and reverse the charges."

"Percy!" Mother had to laugh in spite of herself. "Come back here and sit down. You're impossible. You know what you have to do?"

"Soap out my mouth?" I offered, sitting back on the bed.

"Make it a good job this time. Percy, you must stop saying these things about people. People will think what you say comes from me. What am I going to do with you? You're just getting out of hand." After saying that, Mother looked down at her hands, shaking her head.

"I think we should sew up my mouth," I offered, pantomiming pulling a needle and thread through my lips.

Mother looked at me, thought a moment and said, "That's a very good idea. Bring me the sewing kit."

I looked dead serious and said, "Mother, I'm going crazy and becoming real goofy. I must have syphilis too. I need a good dose of milk of magnesia."

"What makes you say that?" Mother asked.

"Because I still believe everything Marigold tells me and I know she's a bigger liar than Cousin Bessie. She's even a bigger liar than I am and it makes me so mad because she never gets caught."

"Marigold is going through a hard time now, so be nice to her," Mother said kindly.

I picked up my comic book, got out of bed, shook the loose marbles in my head, and said, "When am I going to learn anything?"

We heard a door slam. Marigold was out of her bedroom and running for the front door. Mother quickly got up and said, "I'd better go see what's wrong with Marigold." Mother rushed to intercept my sister as she ran out of the house on her way to nowhere.

After soaping my mouth out with Palmolive, I turned to Gertrude and Agnes and showed them my teeth, "Look, my teeth are turning green." They ignored me and kept on playing jacks on the floor, mumbling to themselves, "He never learns. He never learns. He never learns. And he never listens to us anymore. We might as well not even exist." They now referred to me as "he." They picked up their jacks, hiked back into the window seat, pointed at me, and said, "He is in big trouble and he doesn't know it." They jumped in and shut the window seat over them.

After Mother calmed Marigold down, I heard from Mother that Marigold's lunch with Daddy had been a disaster. It started out hunky-dory because Daddy ordered Marigold's favorite meal - a hot roast beef sandwich piled with mashed potatoes on the side and tons of hot gravy poured over everything. During lunch, Daddy just talked about Kathy and how sick she was these days and how worried he was about her. After fifteen minutes of that dribble, according to Marigold, she smashed her fist into the mashed potatoes. She told Daddy that she was sick and tired of hearing about his drippy old Kathy. She screamed at Daddy in her loudest voice, so loud that everyone at the counter looked at them, and told Daddy that Kathy had syphilis and he better watch out because he was going to get it, too. Daddy got really mad and yelled at Marigold and said she had better get used to having Kathy around because he wasn't coming back to our house ever. Marigold ran out of the coffee shop and cried all the way home on the bus.

After hearing the story from Marigold, Mother phoned Daddy and gave him a piece of her mind. I overheard her say that Marigold adored him, as her sun rose and set over him, and he should be careful what he says to her.

"She's still a child, Dick, you must remember that. She's a hurt baby and she's going to say things that we might not like to hear, but listen to where her heart is coming from, Dick. Her heart is broken. You've broken her heart. We've broken her heart. Our divorce has broken her heart." They both agreed that having Grandma home would make all the difference in the world for Marigold. They hoped Grandma would mend the broken heart. In the meantime, Mother said that they had to act together as parents and be patient with Marigold and that Daddy needed to see more of her and me. At his end of the phone, Daddy must have complained that I was acting impossible because I heard Mother say that I was just going through another phase.

After telling Mother about the hot roast beef sandwich lunch with Daddy, Marigold ran around the house, slamming doors and yelling lots of "goddamns" that the relatives on Diamond Head must have heard five miles away. She screamed that she hated Daddy for marrying Kathy, she hated Mother worse for divorcing Daddy, and she hated me most of all because I was stupid, pretending not to see what was going on around me. Frustrated that nobody was listening to her, she ran into her room, packed her suitcase, came out, and announced that she was going to join the Navy. She marched out the front door whistling "Anchors Aweigh." Mother told me not to worry because she was certain that Marigold would be back before lunchtime. Lunchtime came and went and Marigold hadn't returned. Mother got worried.

She ordered me to get into the car with her and made me her copilot. We drove around the neighborhood ten times looking for the runaway. Mother made me call out the car window for Marigold to come home and yelling that we loved her. It felt like calling Uku to come home. I became a little sad, after rounding the block for the tenth time, calling and thinking that Uku never came home and that Marigold might not either. I imagined Marigold was now on a Navy destroyer, manning a gun, heading out to sea with Uku at her side. Mother finally drove home and into our garage.

Mother was really scared now that Marigold might be lost to her forever and was just about to call the police when I heard a tiny noise under the house. I took a flashlight and went under the house and found Marigold sitting on her suitcase, looking miserable. She had been under our living room floor all the time.

I yelled at her, "Marigold, Olli, Olli Oxen Free! I see you." That's what I said when I raced to touch a tree when we played "hide and go seek." I pleaded with her, "Please come out. I'm hungry and I can't eat till you come out. Please. Join the Navy tomorrow." It didn't take much persuasion to make her crawl out from under the house. In ten minutes, after we washed our faces and hands, once again we were sitting around the dining room table eating lunch without our father.

As promised, Mother took us after lunch to see Hatsuko and the new baby at Queen's Hospital. On our way to Hatsuko's room, we passed Rose and Hiroshi sitting in the waiting room and looking glum. Rose looked more and more like Hatsuko. She waved at me. Hiroshi scowled, put his head down, and nudged Rose and said, "Da haoles come, we go home." Rose looked angrily at Hiroshi as we passed them.

I squealed at Hatsuko when I entered the room. Hatsuko looked as pretty as Snow White, lying in her bed and holding her baby. I never saw Hatsuko look so beautiful - not ever, and she smiled at her baby like she never smiled at me. I didn't know what to say, watching her play with her baby. I wondered to myself, should I be happy or act angry like Hiroshi? I just stared at Hatsuko and the baby without saying a word. In back of me, Charlie stood in the corner, beaming at Hatsuko and his child.

Mother and Marigold ran over and kissed Hatsuko. They made all sorts of cooing sounds at the baby. Hatsuko, smoothing out the baby's "blankey," called to me to come over. "Percy, we've been waiting for you all morning. We want you to name our baby. Actually, Charlie wants you to name our little girl. You did say you had a name for her, didn't you?"

I hesitated because my mind was a jumble of jealous thoughts. Somehow, Gertrude's voice punctured my brain and told me to snap out of it. I collected myself and answered, "I do, Hatsuko." I took a deep breath and continued, "I had a cousin who died in a plane crash fighting the Germans. He always wanted to have a little girl named Mary Emily. If you and Charlie would please do it - would you name the baby Mary Emily? I know that my cousin Kimo in heaven would really like that."

Charlie came out of the corner, took the baby out of Hatsuko's arms, held her to himself and said, "Welcome, Mary Emily." He kissed his daughter's forehead. Charlie turned to me with tears in his eyes. "You have been named the sweetest name for the sweetest little girl in the world, by the swellest guy in Hawaii." He looked at me as if I was his best friend and continued, "Thank you, Percy. It's a wonderful name. It's funny, isn't it, Hatsuko, you must have told Percy that my mother's name is Emily." Charlie took the baby's hand out of the blanket and waved it at me. He looked very handsome with the baby in his arms.

Hatsuko took the baby back into her arms and suddenly looked very serious and spoke carefully, "Percy and Marigold, Charlie and I want you to be Mary Emily's godparents."

Marigold, holding Mother's hand, asked, "What does that mean? What is a godparent, Mother? What do we do?"

Mother replied, "Marigold, being a godparent is a very big honor. You and Percy are going to have to be responsible in all sorts of ways for Mary Emily for the rest of your lives. It means that you two will have to watch over her and see that nothing bad ever happens to her. Do you think you two can do that?"

"I know I can and so can Percy. Can't you, Percy?" Marigold said, nudging me.

I stood straight like a sailor, saluted and replied, "If you can do it - I can, too. Mother, does that mean that sometimes we can take Mary Emily home with us? She can sleep in my bed just like Uku did. I bet Mary Emily doesn't have any fleas." Everyone laughed. I liked it when I made people laugh.

"No, Percy, Mary Emily stays with Hatsuko and Charlie forever. But you and Marigold can watch over her. Maybe when Hatsuko and Charlie want to go see a movie, you both can babysit her."

I puffed out my chest and agreed, "That would be swell - then Marigold and I can take her to see an Alice Faye movie." Marigold pinched my arm and argued, "Mary Emily ain't gonna see no Alice Faye movie. She and I are gonna see John Wayne movies. She's gonna grow up to be just like me."

Mother intervened, "Children, no fighting over Mary Emily. Hatsuko is tired and she has to feed the baby, and we have to leave."

Mother passed Charlie an envelope, adding, "Here's something for the baby. You buy Mary Emily something she will need when you take her home. Hatsuko, are you sure you want my children to be Mary Emily's godparents?"

"Yes. Hiroshi won't let Rose do it. He never approved that I married a haole. You and Marigold and Percy are my only family now. Please."

"Of course, Hatsuko. You are like a daughter to me and my children will be proud to be Mary Emily's godparents," Mother said, with tears in her eyes.

I walked over to Hatsuko and looked down at Mary Emily snuggled in Hatsuko's arms. I pursed my lips and crossed my heart and said, touching the top of Mary Emily's head, "I promise you, Mary Emily, you will never be cursed." A cool breeze blew into the room.

I kissed both Mary Emily and Hatsuko before we left and made a point of shaking Charlie's hand. As I was leaving the room, I took another look at Hatsuko's Charlie and thought he was the handsomest sailor in the navy. When we walked back through the waiting room, Rose and Hiroshi had gone.

Two nights later Mother introduced us to her boyfriend, who was a colonel in the army. He was coming to our house to pick her up and take her to a formal dinner and dance at Fort Shafter. He was in Army Intelligence and met Mother when they took the same cruise to Tahiti.

Mother "spit and polished" us to meet her colonel. She told us her date's name was Colonel Seibert and we were to show him our best manners. When Marigold and I acted as a team, trouble brewed. Without saying a word to each other, we were determined to lower this army man's flag to half-mast.

Mother instructed us to sit properly on her newly slip-covered couch in the living room and to be good. She bought the expensive fabric again at Grossman and Moody's. The couch now matched the plants that grew by the side of our house. She chose the fabric to ensure protection from spilled red ink and me.

Marigold and I sat on the couch next to each other, dressed as if we were going to a birthday party. Our hands were placed sedately on our laps and we looked absolutely angelic. Mother looked like Lana Turner coming down the stairs in the movie *Ziegfeld Girl*, when she walked into the living room. Her hair was now longer, golden blond, and swept up into round rings around her head - very Irene Dunne, the classy movie actress who acted in sophisticated movies with Cary Grant. Mother had on my favorite black velvet gown that sparkled with rhinestones circling the neck. Wrapped around her wrist sparkled a bracelet of diamonds and sapphires she had inherited from her mother. Mother sat in a chair across from us, crossed her legs, and smoked nervously while we waited for the colonel. She kept looking at us, flicking cigarette ashes into a blue porcelain dish, giving us a look that implied she wasn't sure how her children were going to act when meeting her new beau. This was going to be a first.

Mother's date was late. A bad omen. Finally, we heard the colonel's brown army car screech to a halt in front of our house. He got out, slammed the car door, ran up on our porch, and knocked on the front door. Mother put out her cigarette and went to greet him. After she opened the front door, we could hear them kiss. She brought him in to meet us. We watched him like vultures as he walked into the living room. We looked at him with wide-eyed innocence as devilish thoughts ran through our heads. We stood up like the polite children that Mother hoped she had raised to shake his hand.

Mother said, tentatively, "Warren, these are my children, Marigold and Percy."

Before we shook his hand, we wiped our hands on the couch.

The colonel was dressed in formal army whites and had lots of brown hair. The sides of his head were shaved army style and he looked more like the drill sergeant I had seen in Abbot and Costello's movie, *You're In the Army*. He acted very military, stiff, and seemed the type of army man who, if I stepped out of line, would send me to the brig, rationed on bread and water. He wore lots of blue ribbons and colorful bars pinned on his white coat. Mother and the colonel looked handsome together, he in white, Mother in black. They looked too perfect together.

Marigold and I stood at attention and gave him the once over, and then the once over again, and again, and again.

"Well, children," the colonel snapped, "you both look like healthy specimens. Maybe a little toughing up would do with this young man." I could see by the look in his eyes that he meant six months of boot camp with a hundred laps around the base and a thousand push-ups before breakfast. He continued on at his peril, "And what do you think about your Mummy? Doesn't Mummy look beautiful tonight?" The word "mummy" was all we needed for his destruction.

We shrieked and laughed because he had just turned our "Mummy" into a dead Egyptian princess. We dropped to the floor and rolled over the living room carpet belly laughing, tears streaming down our faces. We couldn't make ourselves stop. We visualized Mother as Boris Karloff swathed in Red Cross bandages, meeting Frankenstein. Between laughing hiccups, we sang from the floor, "Da Da - Da Da - Da Da Da Da Da DA! Mummy. Mummy. Mummy. Our Mummy is a mummy."

Mother was aghast at our performance. She quickly demanded that we get off the floor and comport ourselves like ladies and gentlemen - "AT ONCE!"

We picked ourselves up off the floor, not looking very army-like, and sat down once again on the couch, chewing on our cheeks to keep from bursting into further fits of laughter. We pretended to act very serious because we knew it would be all over if we even glanced at the other. I knew if I did, I'd lose it and I'd be back on the floor, rolling around and screaming with laughter. To keep me from further hysterics, Marigold whispered into my ear to pretend that we were buck privates in the army and that we had a mean commanding general in front of us.

Mother knew she had to get the colonel out of our house as fast as she could if she ever wanted to see him again and immediately excused herself by saying, "Warren, I'm dreadfully embarrassed. I don't know what to say. I really don't know whatever took hold of my children." She touched the colonel's arm and started to leave the living room. "I'll be right back, Warren. I'm going to get my purse before anything more happens."

She turned to us and gave us a withering look that told us, "You just wait till I come home." A second look signaled that one more incident like the one we had just pulled, and she was going to give us back to the Indians.

Standing on the landing of the living room, Mother said firmly, "Marigold and Percy, I want you to apologize to Colonel Seibert right now and say how sorry you both are for acting in such a childish way. Warren, I'm going to the bedroom to get my purse. I'll be gone only a minute." To us again, she instructed, "Show the colonel what nice children you are."

We nodded our heads up and down as she left. Marigold and I knew we had more than a minute before Mother came back because she'd have to "freshen up" and that meant more lipstick on her lips and more powder on her nose. We had time for one more thing so I put my elbow into Marigold's ribs and said, "Marigold, you go first."

Marigold turned to me and nodded, looked back at the colonel and said, "We are very sorry we acted like brats. We apologize very much, don't we, Percy?"

"Yes," I agreed, "and we are very sorry because our mother has a hard time taking care of me since I came down with leprosy last night. I have a bad case of it, too. It's affected my head. Not many people want to touch me anymore. Some people call it impetigo, but I know what it really is. I caught it from Marigold. Don't tell Mother we told you because if she knew we told you, she'd put us in a basket and send us out to sea to drown. She threatens us with that all the time."

Marigold piped up, "And I am double jointed in my teeth which is very catching. I'm on my second batch of teeth and the dentist tells me I have only three more sets to go. I hope you didn't catch my mouth disease when we shook hands."

The colonel pulled a Lucky Strike out of his pocket and lit it. I had the feeling he wasn't taking us seriously.

I punched Marigold and said, "I think you should ask him the big question because our father wants to know. By the way, Colonel Seibert, you know our father is still living and has a bad temper. He shot three men dead just last year."

Marigold faked a shock look and said, "Percy, don't tell everything."

"You mean I can't tell him what Kathy has?" I asked her.

"I don't know what you're talking about," Marigold said, wondering what I meant.

I jabbed her again in the ribs. "Yes, you do. The big S disease."

Marigold caught on and said, "Yesssssssss! You ask the question, Percy. You're more an expert on that disease than anyone in Hawaii. Most of our relatives have it, Colonel Seibert."

The colonel took a long drag on his cigarette, opened his mouth and exhaled a long stream of smoke that touched my nose. "Ask me, Percy. Ask me anything."

"Well, Colonel Seibert, Marigold and I hear everyone in the Army has it. Do you have syphilis? We're dying to know because we hear it's very catching and we wouldn't want Mother to bring it home to us. Daddy told us to ask you that question because he's got it too. He caught it from our stepmother."

The room went silent. It never ceased to amaze me how I could stop a conversation in a room. Mother broke the silence when she walked in looking more beautiful than Alice Faye and said, "Did you both apologize?" We nodded.

"Have they been good, Warren?" Mother asked.

The colonel snuffed his cigarette out in an ashtray as Mother put her hand through his arm and he said, "I'm ready, Deidra." Without another word, the colonel escorted Mother to his car. We waved them off from the front porch, yelling, "Don't do anything we wouldn't do." As they drove off, I had an uncomfortable feeling that we might have gone too far. Mother never brought the colonel to our house again.

I visited Hatsuko and my godchild everyday while they were at Queen's Hospital. One day coming home on the bus after a visit, I heard a familiar voice ask, "May I sit here?" I looked up. It was Mr. Hamada.

"MR. HAMADA!" I screamed.

"Not so loud, Percy," Mr. Hamada said, trying to hush me as he sat down. He was dressed in a black business suit.

I quickly said in a whisper, "Mr. Hamada, I want to thank you for all my presents. I think you're the only friend I have left in the whole world." Whispering even lower, "How's the spy business?"

He ignored the question. Then in a very soft voice, talking like a real spy, he spoke into my ear, "Percy, I want you to do something for me."

I sat closer to him. Barely moving my lips, I whispered, wanting Mr. Hamada to know that I could be a spy, too, "Whom do you want me to spy on? Cousin Bessie? Don't tell your spies, but she's a real Nazi!"

He hushed me and quickly said, "No! No! I want you to tell your mother to buy food - cases of food. I want her to store them in your house in case there is an emergency."

"What kind of emergency?" I asked.

He paused for a moment then spoke, "Like an earthquake - something like that. But you must tell her it is very important that she does that. Can you do that for me?"

Thinking ahead, I said, "Yes, I'll tell Mother to buy five cases of mayonnaise. That should do it."

"I am serious, Percy. Tell her to buy soups, tuna fish and tell her to get a first aid kit." When he finished, he watched my eyes to make sure that I understood what he had just said.

I looked at my friend as he put on a pair of dark glasses, and I said in a perplexed voice, "Mr. Hamada, you sure don't look like a vegetable farmer anymore or talk like one. You talk like President Roosevelt. Are you running for something?"

He got up to get off the bus but first leaned down to me one more time and gave me his final words, "Percy, I have to get off at the next stop. Remember what I told you...and I watch you all the time, so I'll know if you did as I told you to." The bus stopped on King Street and without another word, Mr. Hamada got off. I waved to him from the bus window as he stood on the corner looking up at me, waving back. The bus driver closed the door and I headed for home.

I looked down where Mr. Hamada had sat. There on the seat was a small package lying next to me. I unwrapped it. Inside the package were a pink baby rattle and a twenty-dollar bill with a small note attached. The note read: "This is for Hatsuko's baby." I knew then for certain that Mr. Hamada was the smartest spy in America.

As I walked home, I thought of the important message I had to give Mother from Mr. Hamada while reflecting on the responsibility of being a godfather to Mary Emily. It weighed on me heavily. I was feeling that I was over a hundred years old. I guess taking on responsibility meant getting old and turning into a grown-up.

I gave the message to Mother from Mr. Hamada. The next day Mother bought and stored cases of food in Grandma's empty shower. Auntie Gladys, always ahead of Mother by a day, had already stored cases of Campbell's alphabet soup in her broom closet. She told Mother to buy a pup tent in case we had to flee up into the mountains.

I asked Mother, "We're not expecting an earthquake, are we, Mother?"

"No, Percy. People say a war with Japan is coming. Colonel Seibert says it's around the corner and someday we may have to run for it and hide in a cave." I saw myself being thrust in the air at the end of an enemy bayonet and wanted to throw up.

The next day, I gave the twenty dollars, the note and the pink baby rattle to Hatsuko. She cried when I placed them on her bed.

That same afternoon, I took all the discarded letters out of Mother's wastebasket, made a pile of paper by the side of the house and lit it with my Lancer matches. I watched the flames lick the walls of our house. After awhile, the letters crumpled down into a mass of gray ashes and fizzled out. I took a hose and washed the mess away. Putting the Lancer matches back into my pocket, I went inside the house and made myself a mayonnaise sandwich.

Reading the newspaper, I felt the curse was breathing down my neck. To keep the curse away, I started to burn up parts of the newspaper by the side of the house.

The Honolulu Advertiser

RIGGS CAPTURES NATIONAL CROWN

Forest Hills, N.Y. Sept 7. (UP) Bobbie Riggs and Mrs. Sarah Palfrey Cooke won the men and women's national amateur single tennis crown.

R.A.F. PLANE CRASHES INTO BUSY STREET, STRATFORD ON AVON.

A Royal Air Force plane crashed and burst into flames 300 yards from William Shakespeare's birthplace tonight. The plane narrowly missed a woman pushing a pram.

JIMMY FIDLER IN HOLLYWOOD.

"Lowdown." I hear test of actress for the Maria role in "For Whom the Bell Tolls" is pure publicity. Ingrid Bergman is set for the part. "Unhappy" baseball fans and writers are protesting Gary Cooper as Lou Gehrig on the screen because Lou was left-handed and Gary isn't.

CAPTURED CONVICTS ADMIT 4 BURGLARIES.

Henry Estrella and George Raymond, Oahu prison escapees who were recaptured at 11.a.m. yesterday by prison guards, have admitted to four car thefts and four burglaries, police said last night. Questioning of the men is continuing. The convicts, who escaped July 28, were captured in a grass shack hideout two miles back of the Oahu Country Club golf course by Guards Isaac Harbottle, Moses Kapoi, and Augustine Dias. Unarmed, they surrendered quietly.

Editorial. ADMIRAL KIMMEL'S ADVICE.

Officers and men of the fleet know that their commander in chief is intolerant of half measures and won't take the will for the deed. Admiral Kimmel, whose chief business is America's sea defenses in case of war, places a large measure of his trust in Hawaii's impregnability, but he knows that no matter how hard his navy men work, these Islands cannot be impregnable until the inhabitants themselves, the citizens of Hawaii help carry the load.

Admiral Kimmel spoke sharply of inadequate emergency legislation, traffic bottlenecks, rent gougers ("Get rid of them!" he urged), and lack of provision against a sudden shipping shortage. "The more we collectively prepare in peace, the less collectively we suffer in war," he said.

The navy's commander in chief knows what he is talking about. We believe Hawaii will take heed, profiting by the advice given and understandingly accepting the spirit in which it is offered.

I thought I had met the scariest people in the world, Daddy and Aunt Mari, but I hadn't. Uncle Lono was the scariest of them all.

On Labor Day weekend, Mother drove us over the Pali to Punaluu to spend four days with Aunt Momi and Uncle Lono. Punaluu is located on the wet side of Oahu. It reminds me of Kauai because it rains buckets all the time. Amateur photographers swooned, looking at the lush slippery green mountains that had a trillion waterfalls falling down their sides into freshwater swimming pools. One waterfall is so sacred, so dark and so mysterious, the Hawaiians named it sacred. Punaluu was also known for a celebrity, a Hawaiian man who lived in a grass house and cultivated taro. He was the genuine thing, not the Hollywood make-believe type like Harry Owens, the bandleader at the Royal Hawaiian Hotel. People all the way from Iowa came to have their picture taken with this Hawaiian. David Kaapu of Punaluu in his malo is what people around the world hoped to find living in the Islands.

I felt a little anxious driving over the Pali to meet my dangerous Hawaiian uncle, whom Cousin Bessie reported had killed his first wife by tossing a plate of tripe stew at her neck. I vowed to myself to do everything I could to keep Uncle Lono from tossing a plate of tuna sandwiches my way.

We arrived mid-afternoon at Uncle Lono's palace on the beach. His palace was a modest, single-story whitewashed house that spread out between lines of coconut trees. The house had been modified at the whims of Aunt Momi, so bedroom wings thrust out at right angles and a screened porch protruded from the middle of the living room. Actually, Aunt Momi's creativity had made the house topsy-turvy. You never knew where you were or what door opened to where because it wasn't a house built on logic. A kitchen door wandered into a bedroom that wandered into a pantry that wandered into a bathroom - you needed a seeing-eye dog to get you around that house.

A long, winding, sand drive led to the front door of the house, which was screened from the curious by large, overgrown red croton bushes that grew around the house. Our Ford was chockablock full of food, changes of clothes, Mother's silverware, a pup tent, jugs of whiskey, and her and Daddy's monogrammed, pressed, white linen sheets. Mother said she didn't want to be caught with her pants down and not having the basic essentials with her. *The Honolulu*

Advertiser's editorials screamed everyday to be prepared because a war with Japan could be imminent, and I predicted to Mother before we left that the Japanese army was about to land on Waikiki Beach to dance the hula with Hilo Hattie.

When our car stopped at Aunt Momi's front door, Mother kicked herself because she forgot my rubber sheet. She turned to me, lounging in the back seat, and warned me sternly, "Percy, be sure to go to the bathroom before you go to bed and don't drink any water after dinner. I don't want you to wet Uncle Lono's bed. Uncle Lono can be very fussy." Fussy was the wrong, wrong, WRONG word for Mother to describe Uncle Lono. I would have used Cousin Bessie's word to describe him - killer.

Aunt Momi whooped out the screen door like a mad Indian and opened up all the car doors. She sported a black eye and new diamond earrings. In one breath, she said, "Jolljamit, Deidra, where have you all been? I fixed lunch an hour ago. That broken down prince of mine is out in Kahuku playing golf, so we got the whole house to ourselves. I've made a ton of sandwiches, Percy, and Marigold, you look great and getting prettier all the time." Marigold groaned.

Out of the house romped my cousins, Nancy, Betty, and Marsha. In five seconds, they unloaded the car, took our bags to our bedrooms, unpacked them, and in another five seconds, we were around their round koa table eating tuna sandwiches.

Wiping mayonnaise off my mouth, I asked, "Aunt Momi, where'd you get that black eye?"

"Made the wrong turn in the dark, Percy. Rammed right into that jolljamit wall," she lied as she pointed to a wall in back of her. Reaching for another sandwich, making believe I believed her, I told the truth, "You sure got a fat shiner."

Aunt Momi changed the subject. "Kids, clear the table and wash the dishes. I wanna talk to your Auntie Deidra. After that, go outside and play. Betty, show them your new toy." We hopped to it and cleared the dishes, but before I went outside with Marigold and my cousins, I walked back into the dining room and found that Mother and Aunt Momi had fixed themselves a couple of stiff drinks and were huddled in deep conversation. As soon as I appeared, they stopped talking. Giving me the eye and sounding annoyed, Mother said, "Now what, Percy?"

I ignored Mother and cuddled up next to Aunt Momi and chirped, "Aunt Momi, I brought you a present." I pulled a bottle of Best Foods mayonnaise out from a paper bag and showed it to her, saying, "It's better than a bottle of bourbon. Every house should have an extra bottle of mayonnaise so you can't run out while I'm around."

"That's very sweet of you, Percy, and just what this house needs," Aunt Momi answered. She smiled as she took the mayonnaise out of my hand and kissed me on the cheek. I felt very pleased with myself and added one more thing before they dismissed me, "Aunt Momi, don't forget you said that I could wear your pearls when we were up at Kokee. You didn't forget that promise, did you?"

Aunt Momi faked being hurt, replying, "Percy, do you think I would forget a thing like that? Jolljamit, what kind of auntie do you think I am? Tomorrow, Percy. Tomorrow. Your mother and I have a lot to discuss now. Go out and play with the girls." I kissed Aunt Momi's hand and sauntered outside, thinking how grand I was going to look wearing Aunt Momi's pearls tomorrow.

Betty stood in the middle of the driveway, beaming, holding up a brand spanking new green putt-putt scooter. It was an exact copy of the one Jack took us on for thrill rides around our neighborhood. While I was talking with Aunt Momi, Marigold had already had a turn and run the putt-putt into a coconut tree. Nobody seemed to mind. The more spills we took, the "funner" things were for Betty and her sisters. We each had a turn, but because no one trusted me, I had to ride with Betty, who was even a bigger daredevil than Marigold. We fell off twice and once we ran into the wall of the kitchen, screaming, "We're going to die." Everyone clapped.

After we played daredevil on the motor scooter for an hour, Uncle Lono appeared. Without honking, he whipped down the sand driveway in his convertible with its top down and golf bag and clubs sticking out the back seat. He drove so fast and recklessly that he almost hit Marsha, who was wheeling the putt-putt in circles in the middle of the driveway. Without her glasses on, she didn't see him until he was about two feet away from her, which made her crash into the bushes. Marsha squealed from inside the bushes as if she had been killed. Uncle Lono slammed on the brakes and stopped the car on a dime. He leaped out to see how badly Marsha had been hurt, looking scared as hell - an Auntie Gladys expression. After he helped her out of the bushes and found that she didn't have a scratch anywhere on her, he hollered, "For Christsake, I could have killed ya! Didn't you see the car coming?" Marsha, Miss Smarty-Pants of the family, was so shook up that for the first time since I met her, she stood speechless. I pinched Marigold and whispered, "That's a first."

From behind as he scolded Marsha, Uncle Lono looked very scary, and when he turned around and looked at me, I wanted to faint. Betty and Nancy jumped quickly in front of Marsha to protect her and trying to divert his attention from Marsha, they said, "Uncle Lono, this is Marigold and Percy, our cousins, Auntie Deidra's children." Marigold, throwing caution to the wind, swaggered up to the giant like a brave cowboy, held out her hand and drawled, scratching her armpit, "Jesus, Uncle Lono, you're bigger than John Wayne." Uncle Lono roared like a lion and shook Marigold's hand and in eight words, she cemented their friendship.

I stood back and gaped at Uncle Lono because he loomed higher than Aloha Tower and was bigger than three King Kamehamehas. Aunt Momi's Hawaiian prince stood over six feet tall in bare feet, had shoulders broad enough to carry two worlds and biceps shaped like hundred-pound Armour hams. His eyes were dark pools of midnight, but it was the yellow that surrounded the dark pools that were the scariest part of him. They made him look like the wolf that ate up Little Red Riding Hood.

Uncle Lono stared at me, looking as if he was about to *kaukau* (eat) me up or was about to throw a poison-tipped spear into my heart. He was the real flesh and blood Gulliver from *Gulliver's Travels* and I was just a little, little Lilliputian. It was David and Goliath time.

He roared, "Speak." I couldn't think of a thing to say, but inside my head, a voice was screaming, "Heeeeeeeelp!" Finally, I pulled the first doohickey out of my mind, trying to sound as brave as Marigold. I spread out my legs, put my hands on my hips like Mae West, and challenged him, "Do you like Alice Faye?"

"Who in the damned hell is Alice Faye?" he thundered.

Marigold gave me a kidney punch, meaning for me to shut up. She then spoke quickly to block a punch that she was sure was coming my way from Uncle Lono's fist, and said, "Uncle Lono, she's just an old movie star that can't sing worth a damn that Percy wants to be like. You mustn't mind my brother; he's been off his head since the day he was born. You wouldn't like Alice Faye, Uncle Lono, and that's why you don't know her."

I gave Marigold a pinch on her arm and defended myself, sputtering, "I am not off my head and Alice Faye can too sing. And maybe she wouldn't like Uncle Lono, Marigold." I turned to Uncle Lono because Marigold made me mad and spit words at him, "You can't know very much, Uncle Lono, if you don't know who Alice Faye is."

Marigold was right. I was off my rocker. I was sassing a wolf-eating prince who threw plates at people he didn't like. But darn it, I had to stick up for my darling Alice Faye. We stood and stared at each other. Nancy, the pretty one, shoved Marsha and Betty out of Uncle Lono's aim and retreated like little mice behind a coconut tree to watch the killing. Marigold, the brave, stood beside me without saying another word and I could feel her legs quivering next to mine. Swords had been drawn. The smell of blood was in the air and it was my blood that was about to be spilled all over the sandy ground.

Uncle Lono's yellow wolf eyes darted back and forth, deciding what to do with me. I knew what I wanted to do - I wanted to run into the house and hide behind Mother. Uncle Lono stepped slowly towards me. I wanted to run but my bare feet were glued to the sand. His yellow eyes fixed on me spoke a thousand words of doom as he kept walking towards me step by step. My doom was that he was going to throw me into a big boiling pot of stew. He had to be Pele's brother.

Trying to make friends and call a truce, I quickly stuck my hand out. When he was inches away from my belly, he rasped, "If she's your sister, you can't be all that bad." He smacked Marigold on the back and walked past me without shaking my hand. I turned around and behind his back mouthed silently, "I'm all bad, Uncle Lono. I'm as bad as they come. You'll find out." And he did! When he entered the house, I stuck my tongue out and lucky for me, he didn't see it.

In the kitchen, he pounded on the counter and yelled, "Momi." The rasp of his voice told me that he had drunk gallons of whiskey and smoked hundreds of cigarettes since he was eight years old. Once he was in the house, my cousins came out from their hiding place and acted as if they had been as brave as Marigold. We looked at each other and, pretending it never happened, went on playing as if Uncle Lono had never appeared, like all good children do when bad things happen to them. We continued to take turns on the putt-putt, but this time we rode the motor scooter only around in circles without hitting the house, falling down or laughing. Uncle Lono was home.

After that first meeting with Uncle Lono, I was more determined than ever to keep a china plate out of his hand and make sure he wasn't going to use me for target practice. While waiting my turn to ride the putt-putt, I peered again through the kitchen window and watched the dark uncle make himself a drink. He filled up the entire glass with bourbon and no ice. The color of the drink matched his skin. Then I watched him walk like Frankenstein out of the kitchen, drink in one hand and a china plate of cheese and crackers in the other. I made a mental note to plead with Aunt Momi to throw away all her china and stock her house with paper plates. As I watched Uncle Lono sit down at the dining room table and join Mother and Aunt Momi, they, too, stopped laughing.

Aunt Momi and my cousins had changed since their Kokee visit. They no longer grabbed everyone's energy out of the air and, I, for the first time, breathed freely around them. It was Uncle Lono who now sucked the energy out of us, and it was because he had to fill up his big body with our air so he could be a giant.

A little later, a royal summons was decreed from down the street. Uncle Lono's mother, the real princess, and his stepfather were holding a command performance dinner that night at their beach mansion. I had nicknamed her the Princess-Queen because I felt she was the most royal of them all. Their castle was appropriately named Valhalla; Mother translated Valhalla as meaning the home of the gods. Valhalla was only a five-minute walk from Uncle Lono's house. Uncle Lono and Aunt Momi, so Cousin Bessie told me, lived on the largess of his mother's fortune, and whenever the Princess-Queen commanded, they jumped.

Nancy, Betty and Marsha begged to stay home because the night before, they had been called into action by the Princess-Queen to play "fish" with her weekend friends-in-waiting. Aunt Momi and Mother ordered Marigold and me to walk down to have an audience with the Princess-Queen for appearance's sake. Mother spiffed us up before she left and in bare feet, we walked by ourselves down to Valhalla.

Valhalla was a majestic two-story mansion built on five acres of land that Ned Harlow, in his book on the great Hawaiian estates, had erroneously compared to Marjorie Merriweather Post's estate, Mar-A-Largo on Palm Beach. Mar-A-Largo has a big, white sandy beach fronting it. Valhalla sported a small, dirty, brown sand beach with lots of sticks on it because a small river flowed nearby and deposited all sorts of rubbish on the sand.

When we arrived at Valhalla, the Princess-Queen's guests were already seated at tables eating dinner. Marigold and I were ushered by two Japanese servants wearing formal kimonos to the Princess-Queen's table. Following the maids, we wended our way through a maze of tables outside the main dining room that were set for the common folk, the hoi polloi. In the main dining room, where the hoity-toity sat, a long table seated twenty of the royal-royals. This table was located on the lanai where the trade winds blew, but the tables of eight set inside the living room didn't get the trade winds, and the non-family guests suffocated from the heat.

Hoi polloi, a word Grandma taught me, were hard to distinguish one from another because they were equally tanned from the sun. Some of them acted like scared ferrets, furtively looking around, searching for someone to put them on the cover of *Photoplay* magazine. As we passed the common folk, they didn't pay us the slightest attention, but kept leaning into each other, head to head, smoking cigarettes, drinking martinis, and conversing about polo and breeding - animal and the other kind. With a quick look, they dismissed us as we passed as small, poor, uninteresting children who weren't worth a second glance.

The Princess-Queen came into sight. She was a stout Hawaiian woman in her sixties and was seated at the head of the dining room table where she was ruling her guests like a queen. The Royal of all the royals wore an off-the-shoulder black lace *holoku*, a formal Hawaiian dress with a long train that sweeps the floor whenever the queen marched to her throne. Salt and pepper hair was piled up high on her head and held in place by a large tortoiseshell comb. A diamond necklace sparkled around her neck, making her look very handsome and appearing every inch the queen I imagined. In one hand, she held a dozen white ginger flowers and sniffed them on occasions when her subjects spoke to her. The other hand held up her double chins, which made her look more royal. Mother and Aunt Momi were seated as guests of honor near her and Uncle Lono, acting like a nervous little boy of eight, was on her right.

Seeing us heading towards her, the Princess-Queen held out her hand that held the flowers and motioned us to stand next to her. As we came nearer, she said in an upper-class Hawaiian-English dialect, resembling the King's English, "Children, stand on either side of me." We obeyed.

As I walked next to the Princess-Queen, I furtively looked down the mile-long table. The royalty at the table were nibbling on celery sticks, sipping their drinks while making sidelong, furtive glances while they talked to their partners at the tables in the living room. It looked as if some of the royals wanted to sit with the common folk. When we stood on either side of the Princess-Queen, all eyes at the table lifted out of their boredom and curiously fixed on us. Marigold and I had turned, momentarily, into the evening's entertainment - a slight amusement.

"Auwe, Deidra, are these your *keiki* (children)?" the Princess-Queen asked Mother.

"Yes, Princess," Mother said, putting a finger to her mouth, warning us not to embarrass her.

"Well, they look veddy substantial, Deidra. Well fed. Ha, they look more Hawaiian than Sissy's children. Don't you think so, Lono?" Uncle Lono sat bolt upright when his mother spoke and answered her like a dutiful son, "Yes, Mother." I could see by the look in Uncle Lono's eyes now fixed on me that he still wanted to cook me in a stew or steam me up in his imu with Uku. Ancient Hawaiians, I heard, ate puppy dogs.

The Princess-Queen tapped her crystal goblet, signaling her guests to stop what they were doing and to listen to her. Speaking like Cousin Rose, she intoned, "Look, everyone. Say hello to Deidra's darling keiki. Speak your names, deahs."

"I'm Marigold," my sister said, looking out at sea and wishing she was having dinner with John Wayne.

"I'm Percy," said I, copying Marigold while sniffing the flowers in the Princess-Queen's hand.

Fiddling with her diamond necklace, not glancing at us because royalty never want to look you in the eyes, the Princess commanded, "Don't they look well fed? They just must *ono* (love) their poi. Deidra, deah, they are really very sweet looking."

Everyone craned for a better look at us, stretching their necks out like swans, twitching their upper lips as if they were smelling something bad, and observed not one ounce of sweetness or grace standing before them. But dutifully, they agreed with the Princess-Queen, nodding their heads up and down like jack-in-the-boxes.

Marigold and I stood dumbfounded. We never, ever had been called sweet in our entire lives, and hearing those things said about me made me want to stick my finger down my throat or pick a goober out of my nose to show them the real me. As Princess-Queen rambled on about us, I couldn't help but stare at the Princess-Queen's diamond necklace. I longed to wear it and yearned to say to her, "That's a nifty holoku you're wearing, Princess-Queen. Could I come over tomorrow and try it on with your spectacular diamond necklace?"

Mother always read my thoughts, so she interrupted the Princess-Queen when there was a pause and coached us quickly, "Marigold and Percy, what do you say to the Princess for saying all those nice things about you? Don't we say thank you?" Hearing Mother, Marigold and I came out of our daydreams and said together, making a little bow, "Thank you, Princess." The Princess-Queen then handed us each a ginger flower as a blessing. I held the flower high in front of my face and pretended it was a sliver from the cross of Jesus.

We were about to be dismissed when in walked a hulking man to the other end of the table. He had bright red hair smashed down with brilliantine, parted in the middle. He plunked himself down in a chair directly opposite the Princess-Queen. He had a huge politician potbelly, wore dirty khaki work clothes and sported a scraggly red beard. He looked like a plumber.

"Kiki," he shouted, "sorry I'm late! The meeting ran on late because that goddamned Price was trying to cheat me out of my deal in Ewa. I set him goddamned straight. Where were you, Lono? You were supposed to be at that goddamned meeting with me."

I was about to raise my hand and squeal on Uncle Lono that he was out playing golf and scaring a little fat person. Marigold, also reading my mind, pinched my fanny, warning me not to speak. Uncle Lono mumbled something unintelligible, put his head down on his chest and uttered loudly enough for the red-haired man to hear that he had forgotten about it.

"You're always forgetting," the big man shook his head in disgust. Noticing us standing next to the Princess-Queen, he bellowed out, "Kiki, what you got down there?"

"Deidra's children, deah," the Princess-Queen answered. She continued on so he couldn't interrupt her, "Scottie, why didn't you change? It would have only taken you a minute and you know, my darling, that would have pleased me very much."

"Ah, Kiki," he groaned, "I just couldn't stay away from you another minute. You're the best damn looking woman in this whole damned room and you know I can never keep my damn eyes off of you."

Shaking a finger at him, she said, annoyed, "Scottie, you're not getting around me like that. None of that Scottish nonsense! You're in the doghouse."

The big man pointed at us and ordered, "You kids, come down here and protect me from that mean old Princess. Come see your old Uncle Scottie." Marigold and I never knew what to do when we were in the middle of a grown up fight.

He waved at us. "Come on, I'm not going to bite you. Come here."

Mother whispered, "Go see your Uncle Scottie. It's all right."

"Don't scare the children, Scottie. You're such a big bully," the Princess-Queen said, waving her flowers at him while she signaled with her other hand for us to join the redheaded man.

With heads down, we single-filed the length of the dining table to the big man with the flaming red hair waiting for us. My heart beat so hard in my chest that I could hardly breathe as I walked. Here was another big man who had also scared me on sight. All the people at the table watched as we headed for what seemed a certain hanging. As we reached the old man, he pushed back his chair and bellowed, "You, lassie, up on this knee and you, laddie, up on the other. Come on, get up here." We did as we were told and sat on his knees. Without asking, we introduced ourselves.

After we finished our introductions, he asked, "Do ya know who I am?" We shook our heads, no. He guffawed, "Ha! That's a good one. I'm your Uncle Scottie. I'm the richest damn man in Hawaii and sitting way down there is the richest damn woman in Hawaii. Together we make the Rockefellers look like the poor people in Ireland."

The Princess threw her flowers down on the table and yelled, "Scottie, that's just not true and stop your bragging, right now." Everyone at the dinner table hushed as husband and wife began sparring with one another.

"Oh yes, we are, Kiki," he countered.

Shaking her head, she scolded, "Deah, you've been drinking. And you're quite impossible when you drink. You say things you shouldn't."

"A few pints, my dear," he answered. "Listen, Marigold and Percy, do you want to hear a story?" We nodded, yes.

"That beautiful woman down there," he said as he pointed at the Princess-Queen, smiling like a man in love, "that's my wife and don't you think she is the most beautiful woman in this room? That lassie first married a Hawaiian prince. He died. He was lord over all the crown lands in Hawaii. They had Lono there and that beautiful darlin' over there." He pointed to a beautiful Hawaiian woman seated at the middle of the table. "That's Kaiki and she's almost as beautiful as her mother, but she'll end up marrying some good-for-nothing French royal ass something or other. They're my children now and I treat them like my own." He blew a kiss to the woman.

Pointing to Uncle Lono, he continued, "Lono should have been king, but we don't have kings anymore in Hawaii and anyway, Lono, you drink too much and you have no sense of responsibility. You wouldn't have been a good king."

"That's enough," the Princess commanded.

Uncle Scottie ignored her and looked at Aunt Momi. "Momi, what's that you're wearing in your eye?"

"A black eye, Papa," Aunt Momi responded.

"Did my son give it to you?" he asked.

"No, Papa, I walked into a wall last night," Aunt Momi said, lying again.

"If I ever hear that wall is Lono, he'll hear from me, and I'll tell you, lass, not one red cent will go to Lono from me or his mother if he harms you. The next time it will be prison, no matter what your mother says, Lono. Did you hear me, Lono?"

The room went silent as Uncle Lono sat up straighter in his chair. He answered like a bad boy who had been caught doing something naughty and said as meekly as a lamb, "Yes, Sir." I observed that around his parents, Uncle Lono acted not like a big shot, but like Darlene, Cousin Bessie's dead pussycat.

"Percy and Marigold," Uncle Scottie continued his story, "after I married that beautiful woman, we had that girl over there and that one there and this handsome young lad here." He patted a tall teenage boy who sat to his left.

"My oldest girl is Sissy." Looking at blonde Sissy, he pounded on the table and asked, "Sissy, where's that no-good-for-nothing husband of yours?"

"Racing his boat at the Pearl Harbor Yacht Club, Papa," she answered, taking an olive out of her martini glass and eating it.

"Sissy, you tell that good-for-nothing husband that when he's invited to have dinner with me, he'd better be here. You understand? You tell him that the next time he doesn't come to dinner, he's going to lose all his fancy-assed privileges that I bought him at that worthless Pearl Harbor Yacht Club. I think, my darlin', he loves his goddamned racing boat more than you, darlin'."

"Yes, Papa," she said, looking as if she had heard him say that a thousand times.

He pointed at a redheaded lady and continued, "That other girl of mine, Horsy, is mighty unhappy with her Papa. She hates it when I start talkin' like this. She isn't married. But kids, see all those men over there at those tables in the living room, looking at us? They're all, every one of them, New York City pansies. They just waiting to get in my little girl's pants so they can get my money. Right, boys?" He waved at the men sitting at the tables, yelling, "Boys, no touch. Touch and I'll de-ball you faster than you all can say King Kamehameha." Horsy blushed with embarrassment.

He reached out and tousled the hair of his boy sitting next to him. "This is my youngest, Little Red. He's got a big, kind heart. Too kind for a boy who's gonna be as rich as he's going to be. He'll never be the thrifty sort. He's like his mama, spend, spend, spend. Gonna have to toughen him up if he's gonna take over my money. Are you a mama's boy, Percy?"

"Yes sir, I am. Sir, may I say something, sir?" I asked tentatively.

"Speak ahead, young lad," he said, pinching me on the cheek.

I looked into his face and said, "My mother is the prettiest woman in this room."

Marigold, wiggling around on Uncle Scottie's other knee, spoke up, "I think so, too, Uncle Scottie."

"Well, if you two hadn't said that about your mother, I wouldn't have thought much of ya two. Ya got spunk. Listen to these innocents. Hear what they're saying about their mother."

I piped up, feeling brave because my smart mouth started working again, and said, "I know how the Princess got so rich!"

Looking a little uncomfortable, he queried me, "Well, my lad, just how did she get so rich?"

I said out loud so everyone could hear me, "Princess-Queens are just born rich. Have you ever met a poor princess, Uncle Scottie?" When Uncle Scottie heard that he roared with laughter.

"That's a good one, Percy. I like that - Princess-Queen. Ya know, laddie, I've never met a poor princess either." He gave me a funny look and said, "You look like your daddy."

"No, I don't. Marigold does. I'm the spitting image of my mother," I said, defending myself.

"Uncle Scottie, I look like my daddy." Marigold grimaced, making a Daddy-look.

Looking at Marigold, he asked as if he really meant it, "Little Marigold, what do you want to be when you grow up?"

"A cowboy like John Wayne," she answered truthfully.

He kissed her cheek and said, "Marigold, a pretty little girl like you, I bet, is going to change her mind when she grows up and probably marry a cowboy that won't be worth a damn. Be careful whom you marry, Marigold. Marry rich. It's just as easy to love a rich man as a poor man."

He turned to me to ask the same question, "Percy?"

"A movie star. I..."

Uncle Scottie interrupted me, swearing bad words before I could continue to answer - "like Alice Faye!" He howled, "That's the worst goddamnest, most worthless profession God ever invented. And the most dangerous. See that pretty blonde sitting over there? Dorothy, stand up so this boy can see what a damned fool looks like."

A blonde lady at a table in the living room stood up. She looked as fragile as a Dresden teacup, but when she opened her mouth, she spoke like a salty sailor. "Chief, who in the hell are you calling a damned fool, you fat slob? You goddamned, rich snobby bastard who has made too much goddamned money for his own good and now keeps measuring people by their bank accounts. Marry for love, Marigold, and be a movie star, Percy."

"Where'd it get you, Dorothy?" Uncle Scottie grimaced like Daddy as he spoke back to the lady.

"A kick in the ass, Chief. But I'll take a kick in the ass any day than have to end up to be a stingy slob like you."

"Sit down, you made my point. I wish you'd quit opening your mouth like a drunken seadog in heat and start acting like a lady, and quit calling me Chief. You're mixing me up with your friend, Mr. William Randolph Hearst. He's the Chief - I'm Scottie."

Looking back at me, he smiled with affection as he talked about the lady, saying, "That so-called movie star there is Miss Dorothy McKail. She was once a big time Ziegfeld Follies star and is now making it big in the talking movies. She's damned lucky because she has a damned smart mother, Percy. She made Dorothy invest in blocks of land on Wilshire Boulevard. Buying land, boy, will make you rich every time. Unless you have a smart mother who knows real estate and knows how to make a buck, you stay out of the movie business. Just pansies and crazy people go into the movie business. You ain't never going to be rich being an actor, and she's only worth a damn because she now has money of her own - outside the movie business."

Dorothy stood up again, "Don't listen to him, Percy. He's so full of shit and himself. Percy, because I'm a movie star, I've never had to make a bed in my life. So there." With that she sat down and tossed a gin and tonic down her beautiful throat.

Uncle Scottie yelled at a servant to bring him a beer as he drew us closer to him, lowering his voice, "Percy and Marigold, here's a little advice for free that I give to all my children. Here it is: be each other's best friends. You can trust your brothers and sisters but never your husbands or wives, especially if you're rich and they're poor. Except my darling wife, sitting there, but of course, she's rich. Make your brothers and sisters your best friends. You may not agree with each other or have much in common - but they're your blood, young'uns. Blood is blood and that means a lot. But if they mess you up, there is only one thing to do - kill 'em. Hear what I'm saying?

I squiggled on Uncle Scottie's knee and wouldn't look at Marigold after he finished speaking. I was thinking of all the pinches, the punches and the blood I had lost in our battles.

He repeated again, "Did you hear me, bairns? I want to see you shake each other's hands in front of me and pledge your undying loyalty." We remained silent and unmoving. Uncle Scottie roared, "Did you hear what I said?" We continued to sit on his knees, not looking at each other, just breathing in the salt air.

He took our hands and ordered, "Take Percy's hand, Marigold. You're the oldest. Percy, take Marigold's hand." We continued to hesitate.

"Percy and Marigold," repeated Uncle Scottie. He began to sound mean, so we reached over and grudgingly shook hands with each other. When we did, I felt invisible blood passing through our fingers.

Sachiko, the maid, rushed up to Uncle Scottie and gave him a note. She looked as if the Japanese army was knocking at the front door. He flipped open the note and read it. Without looking up, he ordered the maid, "Sachiko, send him in." She left and brought back a Hawaiian policeman with her. The room sobered up.

Looking at the note, then at the policeman, and then at Uncle Lono, Uncle

Scottie announced, "Well, Lono, I think you might be in some danger tonight. Your friend, Harold the Butcher, escaped from Oahu prison. Officer Kealoha came to warn us."

Uncle Lono took ice out of his drink and rubbed it on his face and snorted, "I'm not afraid of him, Papa."

"Mr. Kealoha thinks you should be because Harold has told everyone he's coming to Punaluu to collect on his debt by putting a knife into your throat. He's threatened to kill you in front of a lot of people because you turned evidence against him last year. Don't you forget that because I don't think he's forgotten it. Any advice, officer?" Uncle Scottie asked.

The officer looked at everyone and said, "I'd be careful tonight. Everyone, lock the doors because you'll never know who he'll take his revenge out on." The pansies from New York started to get up to flee for Honolulu.

Uncle Scottie saw them and shouted, "EVERYONE SIT DOWN. I'LL TELL YOU WHEN THIS PARTY IS OVER!" The pansies wilted back down into their chairs. Giving the policeman a ten-dollar bill out of his pocket, Uncle Scottie said, "Thank you, officer, I'll see we're taken care of."

Putting his hands on our shoulders, Uncle Scottie spoke softer and said, "Kiki, have someone take these kids home now and let's eat. I could eat a horse." He winked at us, saying, "Maybe even a killer." Looking up at people sitting at the inside tables, he growled, "I don't go for pansies in my salad, but Harold the Butcher does." He roared with laughter at his joke on the people in the next room.

As I was getting off his knee, Uncle Scottie asked, "Tomorrow, will you come play with my grandchildren?"

"Where are they?" I asked. "They live in a house across the street. They're just your age and I think they need a new friend," he answered.

"Who do they belong to?" I said curiously. "Sissy over there and that good-for-nothing sailing husband of hers that never shows up," he smirked.

The Princess-Queen rose from her chair and walked down to us and took our hands, "That's enough, Scottie. Follow me, children. I'll have Sachiko walk you home. We don't want the boogie man to get you."

Our hands in hers, Marigold asked, "Does the butcherman carry a big knife?"

She sighed, "Probably. But we won't worry about that, will we, deah? I don't think he likes little children - only big children."

We left and walked home in the dark with Sachiko, who screamed at every sound she imagined in the bushes. Any moment she expected a madman to rush out and thrust a knife into her back. When Sachiko got us home, she was too scared to walk back by herself, so all my cousins, Marigold and I escorted her back to Valhalla. Sachiko pleaded with us not to tell the grown-ups that we walked her back to the mansion. We promised.

As we ran back to Uncle Lono's, we scared ourselves to death, running in and out of bushes, playing the mad killer. Back at the mansion, Nancy heated up the stew and we played Monopoly till we were sick of it and each other. They wouldn't let me play the last game because I was caught stealing five hundred dollars from the bank. I actually stole two five-hundred-dollar bills. I did it because everyone cheated, but I was the only one that got caught. Before we went to bed, we explored every dark corner in the house looking for Harold, the mad killer. I wondered, stalking from room to room, if Harold knew Hunkacha. Not finding the mad killer, we jumped into our beds and pulled the covers over our heads for protection.

When Uncle Lono came home, I overheard him tell Aunt Momi to hide a .22 pistol under her pillow. I went to sleep dreaming about Harold the Butcher, Hunkacha and Uncle Lono. I, with my own little .22, wet Uncle Lono's guest bed. I soaked the best mattress in the house, a mattress that had been imported from England, the same type of mattress that the king of England slept on. The mattress was a wedding present from the Princess-Queen. When Uncle Lono and my Princess-Aunt awoke the next morning, every nook and cranny of the palace reeked of my stale piss.

58

Harold the Butcher

"This place stinks! Where's that little bastard?" Uncle Lono roared, turning every room upside down and looking for me. He had awakened at ten with a "helluva" hangover and was greeted by the smell of the offending mattress, drying out on the lawn. At dawn, I had hosed it down and now it was thoroughly ruined.

Before Uncle Lono dragged himself out of bed to fix a Bloody Mary, Mother, wanting to crawl into that mythical hole to China, wrote Aunt Momi a check to replace the pee-soaked mattress. Aunt Momi advised all of us to make ourselves scarce while she handled the prince. Mother, Marigold, and my cousins took towels, books and the Monopoly board and fled to the beach. I, wearing Aunt Momi's pearls, hid in the croton bushes by the side of the house and played with matches. I hid right under Uncle Lono and Aunt Momi's bathroom window.

Soon, I heard Aunt Momi dragging Uncle Lono into the bathroom, ordering, "Get in here, Lono, and close the door." Uncle Lono joined Aunt Momi and slammed the bathroom door shut. Immediately, he started a fight with Aunt Momi, yelling, "I could kill that little turd. He's ruined my best mattress and the house smells like a toilet. I want him out of this house today."

"Not so loud, Lono; do you want them to hear us? Sit on the toilet and listen to me," Aunt Momi said, taking charge of the fight.

"I don't give a damn who hears me and don't order me around," he said, slamming his fist into the wall.

"Sit down, Lono!" yelled Aunt Momi, sounding like she meant business. Uncle Lono sat on the toilet. Her voice now quivering because she was mad, she continued, "Now, listen to me, Lono. Deidra is my favorite sister, and she and her family stay here as long as they want - as long as I want them to. Don't interrupt me. Percy is damned scared of you."

"How do you know that?" he asked, sounding like a little boy.

"Watch him. He looks at everything you do, especially when you get near the dishes. He's waiting for you to toss a plate at me," she answered, running water in the sink.

"Jesus Christ, Momi, where do you get off saying that? He's a kid. How does he know about that?" he mumbled.

"Come out of your stupid bubble, Lono. Everyone in Hawaii knows about that. And why the hell are you making such a fuss about a jolljamit mattress?

Jolljamit, there are more important things to get upset about than a mattress. I'll
see it doesn't happen again. It was my mistake, I shouldn't have put him in that
bed."

"You better do something," he roared.

"Don't worry your handsome head about it. Leave it to me." Aunt Momi finished washing her hands as Uncle Lono got off the toilet.

"Momi, sometimes I could just kill you," he said quietly, as if he meant it.

"Try it, Buster. Just try it. Touch me and you say bye-bye to your money for
good. Remember, Lono, I give as good as I get. Your mother won't come through
this time, believe me, Toots. Scottie will see to that," Aunt Momi retorted.

"You're not scared of me, are you?" he questioned.

"If I was scared of you, Lono, I wouldn't have married you. Get the hell out
of here and go cool off. Go play golf with the boys. When you come back, I want
you to be nice to Deidra and her family. You're scaring the hell out of my girls,
too."

"You know I like Deidra and that little girl of hers, and your kids, too, but
keep that fat turd out of my sight," he warned.

"That little turd's name is Percy, and you be nice to him. He couldn't help
what happened any more than you can help being a bastard. I bet right now he
wishes that he was back home in his own bed. They're only here for one more
night, so start acting like a prince for once, and make things pleasant for me. And
quit roaring around here like a jolljamit lion in heat. If you can't behave yourself,
go and stay in a hotel in Waikiki. Now, Buster, take your broken-down old golf
clubs and get out of here and go play with the boys. Cool off, Buster." There was
long pause and I could hear only a lot of heavy breathing.

Uncle Lono spoke first, "Momi, some day you'll go too far."

"When that day comes, Lono, let me know. Till then I'm going to shoot
straight from the hip. You're not going to change me, little princey, just to suit
your whims. I've whims of my own - look at this house, jolljamit, and thank you,
darling, for teaching me how to shoot a gun. Don't forget you're the one who
named me Dead-Eyed Dick.

"That was the biggest goddamned mistake of my life," he growled.

Talking lovey-dovey now, she said, "I don't know why I love you, you big
stinker, but I do, in spite of your jolljamit ways and you know, baby, you love me,
too."

"Don't count on it!" he warned.

"I don't." I heard them kiss.

Uncle Lono started to open the door as he said to Aunt Momi, "Did I see that
fat boy running outside wearing Mama's pearls?"

"I promised Percy he could wear them." There was a sound of menace in his
voice when he said, "Have him take'em off."

"I will. I'm going to send him down to play with Sissy's kids this morning. I
feel sorry for those kids. Nobody seems to be paying much attention to them but
Mina," Aunt Momi said, brushing her hair.

"I don't care how you do it, just get rid of that little turd. And Momi, remember, don't go too far with me. Remember your place around here."

"How could I forget it? You keep reminding me of it everyday. But remember, princey charming, you knew who you married and I'm not about to change. And don't forget, I shoot straight as a goddamned arrow."

"Remember, my darling, you married a killer." With that, Uncle Lono slammed the bathroom door, walked into the kitchen and made breakfast, a Bloody Mary.

Aunt Momi washed her face, put on fresh lipstick, combed her hair again, and breathed a sigh of relief. She joined Uncle Lono in the kitchen and made herself a gin and tonic; as an afterthought, she cooked him a cheese omelet.

After Uncle Lono drove away from his castle with his golf clubs sticking out the back of his convertible, I crawled out from under the bushes and handed Aunt Momi her pearls. Putting the pearls back around her neck, she told me that I had been invited to spend the day with Aunt Sissy's children. Aunt Sissy, she reminded me, was the sun-bleached blonde whose husband sailed and who was sitting at the middle of the table. Aunt Sissy was the exact opposite in looks from her dark half-brother, Lono.

Children of Valhalla were raised as if they were the offspring of English gentry, children hardly seen and who never spoke a word unless spoken to. Sissy's children, Daisy and Neal, had impeccable manners and were like the perfect looking sister and brother photographed standing next to wolfhounds in *Town and Country* magazine. They were close enough in age for us to become friends. Actually, Daisy was exactly my age and Neal was a year-and-a-half younger. They lived in a two-bedroom, little white cottage across the street from the big house, with a maid all to themselves. Except for their Japanese maid, Mina, there would be days when they didn't speak to or see another adult. They lived as privileged prisoners surrounded by a high wire fence and a locked gate that protected them from Harold-the-Butcher types. Their parents said they feared a Lindbergh-like kidnapping. The fence not only separated them from their mother and father who lived across the street in the big house, but also the Princess-Queen.

Daisy and Neal were blonde, generous, open faced, slim, and shy as two fawns. They had been raised since birth in a fairytale forest, a forest Hunkacha never inhabited.

When I reached the gate, I called out for Daisy and Neal. Mina, a thin, stern Japanese lady wearing a black kimono and holding a ring of keys, clumped briskly down the stairs of the cottage to open the gate. Fumbling for the right key, she unlocked the gate and I stepped inside. Mina never looked at me as she locked up the gate behind us. Without a word, still not looking at me, Mina pointed to the house and indicated by crooking her finger that I was to follow her. For a minute, I thought I had the wrong address and entered Sing Sing.

What impressed me most about Mina was her black hair. It was dyed coal-jet black except at the roots, where white hair was starting to streak up like the Japanese rising sun. What made her hair really interesting was that it burst out of her head at different angles because she cut it at different lengths. She looked like a Japanese porcupine. When I knew Daisy better, I asked if Mina combed her hair before breakfast by sticking a wet finger into an electric toaster.

Daisy and Neal met me inside as I entered, and we immediately connected because they were beautiful children and I was a curiosity. I don't think they had ever met a fat child before. My timing was perfect because it was lunchtime.

Daisy and Neal had table manners that even Cousin Rose and Cousin Nigel would have envied. They used their knife and fork as if the Duchess of Windsor had given them etiquette lessons. I watched fascinated as they cut their liver into teeny-teeny little cubes, took insy-insy bites and chewed each bite for several minutes. No wonder they were thin; they hardly had time to eat anything before lunch was over. It took them so long to eat a piece of liver that I was sure by the time they'd finished that piece, it would be dinnertime.

I, on the other hand, traumatized by overhearing Aunt Momi and Uncle Lono fight about me, ate like a pig at the trough. I couldn't push enough food into my mouth fast enough. Daisy and Neal sat wide-mouthed in amazement, watching me swill in the food. They couldn't believe their eyes, seeing the amount of food I smashed into my mouth before they had even taken their first swallow.

Feeling sorry for me, Daisy started passing food from her plate to me, and before it had hardly settled on my plate, I gobbled it up. Mina was beside herself at what Daisy was doing and ran around the table trying to intercept the food. My hands were faster than greased lightning when it came to food and I outmaneuvered Mina in every instance. Soon Daisy and I turned the food-passing into a baseball game, with Mina running around the bases trying to catch the ball. It all just happened spontaneously and Neal got into the act by blocking Mina with his foot. Daisy, shrieking with laughter, pitched the food like a curved ball over the table to me. A roll arrived by a smooth overhand toss and a pat of butter smacked into my palm.

The biggest disaster of all was when I knocked over the gravy bowl while throwing rice at Daisy and spilled gravy all over the Princess-Queen's white lace tablecloth. The Princess-Queen now had two scores to settle with me - a ruined mattress and a Belgian lace tablecloth. Ned Harlow wrote that in the old days, Hawaiian royalty buried people alive for a lesser offense, and the look in Mina's eyes, the Princess-Queen's high priestess, indicated that I was living on borrowed time.

Neal, Daisy and I didn't care about Mina or anything else because we had turned crazy-silly. We split our sides with laughter, now running around the dining room table, throwing food at each other. I belly laughed when I made direct hits of food on Daisy's face. Some of the food splattered on the wall. A fat pig had turned Mina's precious darlings into raving maniacs before dessert.

Mina gave up. Out of breath, she sat in a chair, spread her legs wide apart, pulled out a cigarette, lit it, and watched us turn crazy. We finally ran out of steam because most of our lunch was now on the ceiling, on the walls, on the floor - stuck everywhere but on our plates. Having nothing left to throw, we flattened ourselves out on the floor, exhausted.

Mina, whose face had turned glossy red like Linda Darnell's nail polish, rose from her chair like a tsunami wave and uttered one word - "Baka" (stupid). Then she pointed to the table and yelled, "SIT!"

We hustled back into our chairs and pretended we were angels as we looked around at the once clean, pristine dining room, now in shambles. Sitting straight in her chair like a lady, and in her most proper voice while delicately picking pieces of rice off her face, Daisy asked Mina to bring in the dessert.

Mina snarled, "No dessert. Bad children!"

Smiling sweetly, Daisy pleaded, "Please, Mina, we promise to be good." Daisy had such a gentle halo about her and Mina loved her more than a precious diamond necklace and could never refuse her anything. We ate Mina's Royal chocolate pudding without further incident. From the way Mina looked as she placed the pudding in front of me, I had the feeling she had sweetened my chocolate pudding with rat poison, so I asked Neal to change desserts with me. As he did, I thought Mina was going to faint.

Daisy asked, "Would you like anything more, Percy?" Mina, hovering in back of me like the wicked witch in Snow White, signaled to Daisy, shaking her head back and forth, that I had had enough - more than enough. Feeling Mina's signal prickling at the back of my neck, I responded in a gentleman's voice, like a butler in a Fred Astaire and Ginger Rogers movie, sniffing like a snob, "My gracious no, Daisy, I am sufficiently sufficient. Thank you so much, Neal and Daisy, for asking me over for this wonderful lunch. It has been a magnificent repast. I don't know when I have been more amused. Ha! Ha! Ha!" As I said that, Mina yanked a string bean out of my hair.

Daisy blotted her napkin daintily on her mouth, rolled her napkin into a silver monogrammed napkin ring and indicated that the meal was over. Neal, following Daisy, took his napkin off his lap. I picked up my napkin, wrung it out like a washrag, squeezing the gravy drippings onto the already ruined tablecloth, and pushed it through the napkin ring.

Mina grabbed the napkin out of my hand, hit me on my head with it, and ordered us, "Go play outside. I clean up mess before Grandma come over." We didn't need another encouraging word from her and ran out the front door. Outside on the lawn, we rolled and rolled on the grass like tumbleweeds blowing in the wind. I love everything about grass. I love the smell and the fresh taste of green leaves.

Daisy called us to order. We sat in a circle, chewing on grass when Neal whispered to Daisy, "Let's tell Percy our secret. Tell him what happened to us two days ago."

Daisy put a finger to her mouth and said, "Percy, you can't tell on us or we'll get into big trouble with Mummy. Mummy doesn't like us to leave here without her permission. Come in closer, Percy." We three huddled in so close that our foreheads conked together.

Daisy whispered, "Two days ago, Mummy played polo in Kapiolani Park. Percy, Mummy is the best polo player in Hawaii - lady polo player, that is. Daddy went sailing like he always does, and Grandma went into town and went shopping at Day's like she does every week. So with everyone away, Mina took us away from here, in secret, to Uncle Takeo's house in Kahuku."

"She drove us in her old pugajunk," Neal interrupted, spitting out a chewed blade of grass.

Daisy continued, "Mina's brother, Uncle Takeo, was dying. Mina told us we had to go with her to help keep him alive. It was a real scary thing to do, Percy."

Neal took up the story from Daisy. "When we arrived at the house, Mina made us go into the bedroom. Uncle Takeo was lying in his bed, not saying anything, just looking up at the ceiling and moaning. Everybody around him was eating, smoking, talking loud...like a party at Grandma's. I didn't want to go in."

Daisy made a face and said, "But Mina made us go in. We had to do it."

"Do what?" I asked.

Daisy, with her piercing blue eyes, looked straight at me. "Pull on his big toe."

"Pull his what?" I gasped.

"On his big toe," Daisy said again.

"Did you do it?" I gasped in wonderment.

"Yes - twice," Daisy explained.

"Me, too. I did it too," Neil said excitedly. Daisy, breathing hard and really getting into the story, said, "And Mina did it, too. Everyone took turns pulling on his big toe."

Daisy paused and let me sit and think a minute, imagining Uncle Takeo's room with people pulling on a dying man's big toe. I looked at them with great expectation and asked excitedly, "What happened?"

They screamed, "He died!" We burst into hysterical laughter and began pulling on each other's big toes. We screamed and laughed so hard, we couldn't make ourselves stop.

Slamming the screen door, Mina rushed out on the lanai with a broom in her hand and screamed, "What you doing? You make humbug for Mina, I think. You want Grandma come over here and spank you? She think crazy people live here now and Mina no good." No matter how sternly Mina talked and looked at us, we couldn't stop laughing. When we didn't stop laughing, she ran down the steps and hit us with the broom, yelling louder, "Stop! Bad! Bakatare!"

We stopped laughing when she threatened to hit us with the broomstick. Coughing in a haze of dust from the broom pounding, we promised to be good, but Mina kept beating us on the head until we said that we were really sorry. After we said three times, "We're sorry, Mina," she quit and stomped back into the house.

With our hair full of broom bristles, we lay back down on the grass and held hands. Daisy and Neal told me that at five, Mina scrubbed them up and walked them over to the big house to say hello, curtsy and bow, and kiss their parents and their guests as a goodnight ritual. It didn't happen every night, only when word came over from the big house that "the children were to make an appearance." I silently thanked my lucky stars that I had been born a commoner.

We got off the grass and walked over to the fence next to the road, the fence that separated us from Valhalla. Daisy, Neal and I hung ourselves down from the fence rungs as we listened to familiar voices talking in the big house. We also could hear people playing tennis, and once I was sure I heard Mother's voice calling to someone to serve. We were prisoners locked in a stockade, kept far away from the "others" who were taller and bigger. After our arms hurt from hanging so long on the fence, we put our noses through the rungs and tried sniffing the air of freedom across the street. Daisy and Neal had been sentenced since birth to be kept separated from grown-ups because they were - children. I said a silent prayer that one day I would spring my new friends from the gates of Sing Sing and take them to see an Alice Faye movie.

The time drew near for the evening's walk over to see their parents. Mina called Daisy and Neal into the house to take their baths. While they were in the bathroom polishing their halos and putting on clean underwear, Mina told me to wait in the living room, and then we'd all go out the gate together and I could walk back to Aunt Momi's.

I sat in a chair in the living room and glanced through Daisy's books. She obviously liked horses because all her books were about horses. After checking on her wards, Mina sat down across from me. She rapped her knuckles on the chair to get my attention. "You want something, Mina?" I asked.

"How come you so fat?" she snuffled as if she was coming down with a cold.

"I don't know," I answered.

"You too fat. Make you look ugly. You eat too much." She snorted. Mina had adenoid problems.

"I know that, Mina." I answered, not being at all upset by her questioning.

"You big troublemaker, too," she said, blowing her nose into a handkerchief.

"Yes, Mina," I agreed.

A pause, then out of nowhere, she said, "I like you."

"You do?" I said, taken by surprise. She smiled and answered, "You make my babies laugh. They no laugh too much. They have good time today but you no more t'row food when you come next."

"Yes, Mina," I said, pleased to learn that she liked me.

"You come back see my babies?" she asked.

"Yes, Mina. I would like to very much."

"Good," she said, slamming her hands on the arms of the chair. Mina retied her kimono and startled me again, saying, "Percy-san?"

"Yes, Mina?" She burst out laughing and said, "You funny kine."

I blushed and said, "Thank you, Mina." The little old Japanese porcupine reached over and put a cookie in my hand, then went to get her babies.

When Mina unlocked the gate, I was free again. Before Daisy, Neal and Mina crossed the street to Valhalla, Daisy promised me that we would be friends for the rest of our lives. I promised Daisy that if I couldn't visit her all the time, at least we could become telephone friends. As I watched them, starched, clean, and aristocratically beautiful, cross the street with their little old Japanese gnome, I felt their loneliness. Retracing my steps back down the street to Aunt Momi's, I thought that tonight I was even going to be glad to see Uncle Lono again.

When I returned, I found Aunt Momi cooking in the kitchen. Everyone else was in the dining room whooping it up, and from the sounds of it, having a good time without me. Tasting her stew, Aunt Momi said, "Well, Percy, did you have a good day with Daisy and Neal?"

"I had the best day, Aunt Momi, but I'm glad to be home," I said, looking longingly at the stew cooking on the stove.

"Here, taste it!" Aunt Momi filled a wooden spoon with her meat and vegetable concoction, blew on it and placed the spoon carefully in my mouth. Feeling the stew slide down my throat, I closed my eyes and purred, "Aunt Momi, you are a magician. That stew is better than anything I ever ate."

"Percy, you always say the right things to me." Her eyes filled with tears.

"Aunt Momi, do you miss your little boy?" I asked.

Stirring the stew, she replied, "I miss him all the time, Percy. Go on in and see your mother, she's missed you." Aunt Momi put salt and pepper into the stew.

"It sounds like everyone is having such a good time that if I go in there now - well, they'll just remember there was a stinking mattress out on the lawn this morning. If you don't mind, I think I'll fix myself a mayonnaise sandwich and sneak into my room. I've had a very emotional day, Aunt Momi," I sighed.

Aunt Momi walked over and held me tight to her bosom. Kissing me on the head, she said, "I understand that, Percy, I really do. I've had an emotional day, too."

I brightened up, "Thank you, Aunt Momi, for understanding, and Aunt Momi, I don't think I want to wear your pearls anymore. Could I have a little bowl of your stew with my sandwich?"

Pulling me way from her, she said, "Are you sure you don't want to wear my pearls anymore?" I nodded. I lied.

Looking serious, Aunt Momi said, "Percy, because I think you are an adventurer, I've made a special little nest for you under the bed. Your little nest reminds me of back when I was a little girl and we were in the San Francisco earthquake. A chimney fell between my bed and my older sister's. I think a brick hit my sister's head. From that day on, Mama made us sleep under the bed. I have loved sleeping under a bed since I was a little girl and you will love it, too." Aunt Momi was a real good storyteller like my mother. She could make the unbelievable believable. I had heard the real story in the bathroom that morning.

"Thank you, Aunt Momi, for my little nest, and tonight, before I go to sleep, I'll pretend that I was just in an earthquake and that my Aunt Momi came to my rescue and put me under the bed. As they say in the movies, she was trying to save my bacon." I took the mayonnaise sandwich and a bowl of stew and ate them under the bed.

Around three o'clock in the morning, while dreaming of falling through cracks on the streets of San Francisco in an earthquake, I heard the icebox door open. Marigold and I were sleeping in the maid's room located off the kitchen - nearest to the icebox. Thinking Mother and Aunt Momi were having a three o'clock snack, I walked towards the kitchen door. I opened it a crack and saw a local man with a flashlight taking my mayonnaise bottle out of the icebox. I knew immediately it was Harold the Butcher. I tiptoed to Marigold's bed and shook her. She groaned, "Percy, damnit, what now?"

"Shhhhhhhhhhh!" I whispered, "Harold the Butcher is in the kitchen and he's stealing my mayonnaise. He's come to kill Uncle Lono. I think he wants to eat something before he shoots Uncle Lono. He doesn't want to kill Uncle Lono on an empty stomach."

Marigold, now wide awake, said, "Are you sure?"

"Yesssssssssss!" I whispered.

Marigold slid like an eel out of bed and ordered, "You go wake Uncle Lono and I'll see that the killer doesn't get away."

I panicked, "No, you go get Uncle Lono. He'll forget about Harold and kill me first."

She slapped my fanny and said, "Don't be a coward. I'm braver than you are and I can keep Harold the Butcher from leaving the kitchen."

"How?" I asked.

"I don't know. Go." She shoved me towards Uncle Lono's bedroom.

Having no choice, I crept into Uncle Lono and Aunt Momi's bedroom while Marigold crawled on all fours towards the kitchen door. When I walked stealthily into the bedroom, Uncle Lono was snoring louder than an army of bullfrogs and Aunt Momi was snoring croaks beside him. I quickly chose to leave Uncle Lono alone and wake up Aunt Momi first. I crept to her side of the bed and shook her. Quiet as I could be, I whispered, "Aunt Momi, wake up. Wake up. Harold the Butcher is in the kitchen. He's going to kill Uncle Lono."

Aunt Momi jolted awake, "Whaaaaaat?"

I whispered louder, "Aunt Momi, Harold the Butcher is in the kitchen and he is stealing my mayonnaise."

Aunt Momi reached over and shook Uncle Lono. "Lono, wake up. We have a burglar in the kitchen."

"Whaaaat? Whaaaat? Leave me alone, Momi. Go back to sleep," he mumbled. Uncle Lono put his head under the pillow and started serenading the frogs again.

Aunt Momi punched him angrily and grumbled, "You useless kanaka." She got out of bed, took the .22 from under her pillow, put on her robe, dabbed lipstick on her mouth and combed her hair. She uttered under her breath, going out of the room, that she didn't want to be found dead without a little make-up on.

We tiptoed to the kitchen door and found Marigold on all fours, watching the killer eat Aunt Momi's stew and rice and spooning my mayonnaise all over it. I thought, watching him enjoy my mayonnaise on his stew, that he couldn't be all that bad. I saw a gun on the table next to his food.

Aunt Momi told us to get behind her and to be quiet. She looked at her gun and then at the killer, took a deep breath and yelled from behind the door, "Stick'em up, ya bastard."

Peeping from behind Aunt Momi, I saw the killer spit out his food and grab for his gun. Before he could pick up the gun, Aunt Momi shot three shots. Bang! Bang! Bang! The killer yelped and grabbed his gun, and fired wildly at us, and then ran for the outside door, cursing Aunt Momi. Aunt Momi turned into a vigilante and ran after him, shooting in the air. The killer dropped his gun as he ran down the beach, yelping, and then disappeared into the night, trailing blood.

All the lights in the house, except in Uncle Lono's bedroom, were turned on. Aunt Momi, gasping for air from the chase, called the police. Mother and my cousins joined us in the kitchen. After Aunt Momi told everyone what had happened, Mother made coffee. Marigold and I, showing off, walked the trail of blood from the kitchen, to the lawn and onto the beach.

When the policemen arrived, they asked us questions and we showed them the killer's footpath of blood and told them what a fabulous sharpshooter our Aunt Momi was. The policeman told us to lock all the doors just in case the killer decided to finish the job, but they doubted it, because he had dropped his gun and was wounded. Before the police left, they said they would be back in the morning to finish their investigation. They dropped a bombshell before they left, however, telling us that Harold the Butcher had been captured and was safely behind bars again.

Mother decided after that bit of news that Aunt Momi deserved a stiff drink and fixed her four fingers' worth of bourbon on the rocks. Mother joined her. We couldn't sleep because we were so excited, so we sat on the kitchen floor and played Monopoly till the cows woke up. Under his pillow, Uncle Lono continued to serenade the frogs.

59

"I Don't Want to Set the World on Fire. I Just Want to Start a Flame in Your Heart."

While everyone was taking a shower, I read the newspaper.

The Honolulu Advertiser

ITALY DARES BRITAIN TO BOMB ROME

Rome. 1941 (UP) Italian reaction to Prime Minister Winston Churchill's statement that the British will not hesitate to bomb Rome if necessary today was —- "Come and try it!"

UNIVERSITY OF HAWAII VS WILLAMETTE UNIV. (OREGON)

Coming on December 6th. For the benefit of the Shrine Hospital for Crippled Children "Honolulu Unit". PRICES - Sections 4-5-6-7-8 (makai) $2.00, Sections 41-42-43-44-45 (Waikiki) $1.00

THERE ARE NO EXCHANGE TICKETS THIS YEAR

LAWYERS BLAST RESOLUTION TO IMPEACH PRESIDENT ROOSEVELT.

Indianapolis, (UP) - The American Bar Association convention today almost unanimously rejected a resolution asking for impeachment of President Roosevelt on charges that he deliberately is leading the United States into war.

JAPANESE CABINET SET UP 3 MONTHS AGO QUITS EN BLOC.

Tokyo, (UP) - The cabinet of Premier Prince Fumimaro Konoye resigned en bloc today. The cabinet left office three months to the day after the previous Konoye cabinet's resignation, thereby becoming the shortest-lived cabinet in Japanese history.

CLARE BOOTH LUCE, writer, who came in from the Philippines, was the guest of the Dillinghams' at La Pietra Wednesday night. She is now visiting with Mrs. James H.R. Cromwell (Doris Duke) until she takes the Clipper back to the Mainland.

HIGHLIGHTS OF PRESIDENT ROOSEVELT'S RADIO SPEECH FROM WASHINGTON LAST NIGHT:

We will not hesitate to use our armed forces to repel an attack. Defense means more than merely fighting - it means civilian as well as military morale. We must be realistic on the subject of attack - the Bunker Hill of tomorrow may be thousands of miles away from Boston, Massachusetts.

TOKYO, (UP) TOJO MADE FULL GENERAL; WILL REMAIN ON ACTIVE DUTY.

At six in the morning, after everyone had showered, the policeman arrived for the second time. He asked more questions and made a great production of looking for fingerprints. The policeman told Aunt Momi that, as far as he was concerned, the robbery was an "open and shut case" and that Turkey Brown was the culprit. The first clue was, according to the policeman, that Turkey Brown escaped over the prison wall with Harold the Butcher and must have learned where Uncle Lono lived. The second clue was that he loved to eat. The last time he was caught, he was gorging on a turkey sandwich slathered with mayonnaise in the midst of robbing the police chief's beach house at Waialua. The third clue that "he stay more stupider than a turkey" was that he left a hundred other clues around. Blood was everywhere and gobs of it trailed to the beach. The most damaging evidence, he felt, was that there were small greasy fingerprints all over the mayonnaise jar.

After he said that, I confessed in a flash that those fingerprints were mine. I had eaten a mayonnaise sandwich while everyone was taking a shower and unintentionally erased Turkey's fingerprints. I imagined, looking at the policeman's handcuffs hanging on his belt, that before sunset, my photo would be tacked on the wall of the Honolulu post office next to Turkey's.

After I came clean, I blurted out to the policeman that I "kinda" felt sorry for Turkey Brown because we had a lot in common. We ate Best Foods mayonnaise at any cost and were by reputation, stupid gobblers.

All morning, Aunt Momi kept calling Marigold and me her jolljamit heroes and told the policeman that, without us, everyone would have been shot dead in their beds. Aunt Momi jolljamed that hero stuff up, especially after the policeman left and Uncle Lono finally came out of the bedroom. She kept repeating the hero stuff while he rummaged around the kitchen, opening and slamming the cupboard doors shut, looking for something. He found the vodka bottle under the sink where Aunt Momi hid it before the policeman arrived the second time. Not looking at us or saying a word, his breath stinking like rotten fish, he poured ten fingers of vodka into a Walt Disney jelly glass jar with ice and a splash of tomato juice. It was my very favorite water glass in the house because on it was painted Goofy, "yuck yuck yucking" as he grabbed for a screaming Minnie Mouse. Uncle Lono, acting a little goofy himself this morning, speaking to no one, walked down to the beach with his drink.

Mother decided it was time for us to go home. We packed quickly, said our good-byes to Aunt Momi and our cousins and left for Honolulu. As we were

departing, the policeman phoned and said they had captured Turkey Brown a couple houses down, hiding in a boathouse, and that Aunt Momi had wounded him in
his right leg. The policeman told her to tell me that Turkey was sitting in the
police station whining for a turkey sandwich with eggs, bacon and lots of mayo.

"Aunt Momi," I said, after hearing about Turkey's capture, "I thought you
were Dead-Eyed Dick. You missed hitting him where it counts."

"Where'd you hear that expression, Percy? Percy, jolljamit, I am just the best
crack shot around here because that's exactly where I aimed to shoot that jolljamit
crook. Right in the thigh, toots. Do you think I wanted to kill the poor bastard? I
wouldn't kill a fly, Percy."

"That's not what you said to Uncle Lono in the bathroom yesterday," I
replied

My cousins, my mother and Marigold converged on me like a tidal wave
and shoved me into the back seat of the car. As we drove off, Aunt Momi, standing in the driveway, looked dumbfounded. I thought to myself, I must get over
the habit of dropping bombshells on people's heads. Before we reached the end
of the driveway, the Princess-Queen and Uncle Scottie drove into Aunt Momi's
yard. They waved and yelled that the word was out and all the houseguests were
coming over to congratulate Uncle Lono, the hero. I wanted to tell them the real
heroes were inside our car and their hero wasn't speaking because he was
ashamed. Uncle Lono was standing on the beach, holding my Goofy glass, facing the wind, and thinking how he was going to cook me up in his stew.

September 1941. The new school term began. I had been promoted into the
third grade by the grace of God and a miraculous C average. My third grade
teacher was Mrs. Mott-Smith, a tall, lovely-looking lady whose distinguishing feature was a long, aristocratic nose. When she first spoke to our class, her voice
warned that she wouldn't suffer fools or any of my nonsense this coming year. We
would no longer be treated as second grade crybabies.

Mrs. Mott-Smith was a drinking buddy of my mother's, therefore, I was
doomed because they attended the same cocktail parties and exchanged confidences. This year, I wasn't going to get away with anything because she sat me in
the front row, dead center in front of her. She could gaze right into my daydreams.
Mother and Mrs. Mott-Smith made me pledge that I was going to buckle down
this year and concentrate on making myself into an A student. They kept repeating
that this year, I was going to live up to my potential. I told them I already had
because I remained the fattest child in our class. Some things never change.

Actually, some things do change. This school year I had more homework to
do and that meant less time to spend with Agnes and Gertrude gossiping by the
side of the house and eating a mayonnaise sandwich. When I found time to play
with my make-believe friends, I missed Walter looking at me from across the
street.

Everyone else who inhabited my world changed, too. They seemed to be running on different courses. Marigold was more active in after-school activities and
had joined the swim team. Mr. McLaine volunteered every day at the downtown
Red Cross, and Auntie Gladys and Uncle Pete were considering a divorce - that

was the rumor floating around. The Twins walked around the neighborhood in a
blue funk and sat in front of Cousin Bessie's house every afternoon smoking cigarettes. Marigold told me they contemplated quitting school and joining the Marine
Corps. Cousin Bessie had joined with her granddaughter, Pamey, in visiting a
crazy doctor that treated crazy people and that was God's crazy truth. I heard
Mother tell Mrs. Mott-Smith that piece of gossip over the telephone, when they
were discussing my habit of farting before the lunch bell. I told them I couldn't
help it because it was my signal that I was hungry.

Mother continued dating but never brought the dates home, especially after
the disaster with Colonel Seibert. She was still dating the colonel because his
name came up whenever she brought home something to protect us if a war
arrived on our doorstep. Her latest protection was a .22 pistol. She bought it on
River Street in a pawnshop and hid the gun under her mattress. She forgot to buy
the ammunition, which was a blessing. Mother was not Aunt Momi and couldn't
shoot straight if my life depended on it. But Mother had something better than a
.22 pistol to protect us. She could talk anybody out of anything, so I was certain
she'd talk the Japanese soldiers out of shooting us - so I wasn't worried about a
Japanese invasion. I was worried that she'd buy ammunition and shoot me by mistake.

A letter came from Kaina, my Rocky Hill companion. He wrote that he still
lived with his sister in Hilo and from his address, I realized that his home was near
Uncle Will and Aunt Ella's. In a scrawl that was worse than mine, he invited me to
come visit him and asked about Marigold.

Mr. Hamada disappeared from sight. Since our meeting on the bus, we had
not met nor did I find a bottle of mayonnaise on my doorstep.

I talked on the phone with Daisy every other day. She and Neal were going to
a private school that was much more exclusive than Punahou. They had moved
back to their Honolulu estate and she asked me to her birthday party two days
after Christmas, when she promised me a gigantic food fight after we sang "Happy
Birthday." Screaming with laughter, Daisy told me that their mother, Sissy, had
treated Mina to a permanent in the Liberty House beauty salon. According to
Daisy, after the permanent, the Japanese porcupine had corkscrew curls sprouting
all over her head. Mina, as soon as she got home, shaved her head. Now, she
looked liked a Japanese cue ball.

War news was everywhere. It was discussed by the grocery clerks, on the
radio and found on every page in *The Honolulu Advertiser*. Scanning the pages in
the morning, looking for an Alice Faye movie playing, I read that the Japanese
Empire was about to go to war with the United States.

The Honolulu Advertiser

NEW JAPANESE PREMIER IS CONSIDERED 'CONSERVATIVE.'
Washington, Friday, Oct 17. (UP) First reaction to the selection of General
Hideki Tojo as new Japanese premier was a "relief," but diplomats cautioned

against jumping to conclusions before the structure of the cabinet is known. Tojo is regarded as the more conservative of aggressive nationalists.

Daddy now took Marigold and me out every Saturday. Kathy didn't come with us. We hadn't seen her since their wedding. Daddy said Kathy wasn't feeling well, she had an upset tummy. Marigold told me Kathy had an upset tummy because she heard that we were telling everyone in Honolulu that she was riddled with syphilis. Daddy and Marigold were friends again and there was nary a mention of the disastrous luncheon at The Young Hotel.

On our first Saturday outing, we went to a circus at the Civic Auditorium. The main show started at three o'clock. I was impressed because Daddy paid sixty cents a piece to get us the best seats. We sat in the front row and watched the Naito Troupe, a daring aerialist family, fly through the air without a safety net. A baldheaded man, acting fake-drunk, almost fell off his tightrope, and Marigold and I screamed him back to safety. I saw real lions outside their cages for the first time. Mean lion tamers cracked whips to make them behave like pussycats.

The best part of the circus was the "Ripley Oddities" featuring Mona, a large black-haired lady with a red beard. What was even better than the bearded Mona, or the sea lions, bears or chimpanzees, was "Polar" the iceman. Every afternoon, he was buried in a coffin made of ice. Without any air, and for what seemed like hours, we watched him turn blue in his coffin. We counted the minutes out loud, until he was lifted out of the ice prison. Polar, shivering all over, was colored blue-green. When he took his bow, wearing his underpants, ice fell off his body. I thought he was thrilling.

The next Saturday, Daddy took us to Al Karasick's wrestling matches. It cost him fifty cents a piece for ringside seats. I was dazzled at how much Daddy was spending on us. I figured he must be up to something because he was forking out a fortune.

Every week, Al Karasick had a full line-up of beefy wrestlers. Killer Morelli, Hillbilly Hefner and Gust Johnson were his main stars. They each looked different and were very colorful. I became a screaming fan of Gust Johnson because he had the biggest belly, the longest blonde hair and wore the tiniest, red, white, and blue bathing trunks I had ever seen, outlining his peepee. We never went to a movie.

Before Daddy drove us home, he'd take us to his favorite Japanese restaurant on Kalakaua and Beretania Street. He'd order us saimin soup, rice and teriyaki meat sticks. He let me order a side dish of mayonnaise for my rice. He called my mayonnaise, served in a large Japanese dish painted with blue koi fish, Percy's soup. I spooned it into my mouth like I was eating Campbell's soup. At dinner, Marigold and Daddy would snuggle up next to each other like good ole buddies, and talk about football, baseball and her swimming exploits. I could have been living on the moon for all they cared, but I didn't mind because there weren't many days since Daddy left that Marigold showed her teeth and smiled. Alice Faye's name never came up in conversation.

Each week, Daddy told us that he had bought us the best seats at the stadium to see the Shrine football game - University of Hawaii vs Willamette, Oregon on Saturday, December 6th. Marigold yelled with excitement when he told us that. I had the vapors. I hated football games because they were boring. Maybe if the players wore feathers in their helmets or livened up their uniforms with glittering sequins, I might have had some interest in the game. Football games were as colorless as eating a gray dinner on a gray day.

I told Gertrude and Agnes that my father was a big disappointment. Why couldn't God have given me a father who liked movies - even corny ones that starred Kay Francis, the movie actress who lisped when she talked. I was not only cursed but I was born cursed. It was the skull's fault and it was all Aunt Mari's fault, too, because she waved an evil wand over me at birth. I planned to be sick with syphilis on December 6th!

The curse was getting closer because everyday I read in the newspaper that Japan was moving towards war.

The Honolulu Advertiser

OCT 17 (UP) JAPAN MOVES TOWARD WAR.

Japan is moving swiftly toward war with first, the Russians and second, the United States and Great Britain. The rises and falls of Japanese cabinets, the question of war or peace in the Pacific every two to three months is not children at play. They are leading to a conclusion, a serious reckoning which Japan is evidencing no desire to avoid. It now seems reasonably certain that war will be difficult to escape. The Pacific is not to remain static. The hope for improvement is gone.

Our household routine had broken down. Mother and Marigold were out for dinners more often than not because Mother was dating and Marigold was up at Auntie Gladys's, consoling the Twins because Uncle Pete lived at the YMCA like Daddy did. I had Helen the Horrible to myself. At dinnertime, I ate her creamed tuna without peas, alone in my bedroom, listening to the radio. My favorite program was Owen Cunningham's Amateur Hour. I thought it was the "bestest" program on the radio. Fritzi Macwiggen, the singing hostess, would start the show by belting out -

> "It's everybody's hour, so everybody sing,
> Join the throng and sing along
> And make the laughter ring.
> It's brought to you by Listerine and
> Prophylactic too...."

In heaven, I'd lay on the floor with the radio next to me and sing and sing and sing. I'd sing louder, louder and LOUDER as each contestant performed. My dream then was to become a contestant and win first prize and go to Hollywood. I knew my voice sounded just as good as Ronnie Tanaka's from Waipahu, and he won first place singing "America the Beautiful." The Eloise Chun types were always voted the grand winners because they could belt out a song like Ethel Merman or Kate Smith. When one of them sang "You're In the Army Now," she made me want to join the army. I noticed girls won the grand prize, mostly.

After I'd turned off the radio, I'd take my bath, soap up, and sing at the top of my lungs, hoping that Owen Cunninghan was driving by our house. On hearing my voice, he'd stop his car, rush through the front door into the bathroom and sign me up, nude, to a five-year contract at 20th Century Fox. During these months of war talk and eating by myself, Agnes and Gertrude were forgotten in the window seat. They were now as alone as I was.

Once in awhile, I saw Aunt Momi when she drove in from the country. She had placed her girls in the boarding department at Punahou and used our house to freshen up her make-up and take a shishi on her way to visit them.

More war bulletins were in the newspaper.

The Honolulu Advertiser

TALK PEACE OR ELSE JAPAN SAYS
Nov 1 - Tokyo - Saturday. Patience is wearing out, Tokyo newspaper warns United States to finish negotiations.

Hyde Park, New York Nov 4 (UP) PRESIDENT ROOSEVELT ISSUES BLUNT WARNING TO AMERICAN PEOPLE THAT THEY MUST FACE HEAVY HARDSHIPS TO PRESERVE FREEDOMS.

SEEKING QUICK UNITED STATES SHOWDOWN
Tokyo, Wednesday Nov 5. (UP) Former ambassador to Berlin Saburo Kurusu is en route to Hong Kong to board a clipper for the United States, where he will assist Ambassador Kichisaburo Nomura in conversations with officials, it was learned today.

KURUSU ABOARD THE CHINA CLIPPER
San Francisco, Nov 9. (UP) Pan American Airways revealed tonight that the China Clipper carrying Saburo Kurusu, Japan's special envoy to the United States arrived at Midway Island from Wake at 5:27 p.m.

Thanksgiving holiday arrived and my grades had improved. Hallelujah. On my report card, I passed everything but math. I told Mrs. Mott-Smith that if math had feathers and sequins on their numbers, I'd be more interested. Helen went home for the holiday so Hatsuko, Charlie and Mary Emily joined us for Thanksgiving dinner with Hatsuko roasting the turkey. Betsy and her dreamboat

were last minute drops-ins and Mr. McLaine came at Mother's insistence, but
without Fluffy and her fleas. So did the Twins. They brought their own catsup bottle. Auntie Gladys and Uncle Pete were dining at the Royal Hawaiian Hotel, making up. We didn't invite Cousin Bessie or Martha, her cat.

We ate lots of food and I had a nice time, even without Daddy carving the
turkey. Once or twice Marigold forgot about Daddy and she showed her teeth.
Standing up at the table, I recited a joke before dessert arrived to make everyone
happy.

"Old Mother Hubbard went to the cupboard to get her dog a banana.
When she got there, the cupboard was bare so her poor dog ate sponge cake."

Nobody laughed. Marigold told me to sit down and not embarrass her. We had
phone calls from Uncle Will, Aunt Ella, Aunt Mari, and Cousin Dora. Five minutes later Cousin Nigel and Cousin Rose phoned from Kauai and told us that Tom
was back in the hospital with pneumonia. Even Auntie Lulu and Uncle Tony called
from Maui. After Betsy talked to her parents, Auntie Lulu asked to speak to me.
She thanked me for my Christmas greetings and said, "let bygones be bygones." I
told her I would never lie again. I always made promises that I couldn't keep.
Grandma sent a Thanksgiving telegram from Oakland - with love. Our cousins
from Baltimore, the two old maids, Nelda and Louisa, wrote Mother a Happy
Thanksgiving note and added that we should get out of Hawaii and come stay with
them because of the Japanese threat. I remembered them fondly because they
taught me to eat liver to make my blood red. Mother planned to answer them
when she wrote her Christmas cards in December.

I had a happy Thanksgiving because everyone I loved was at home and eating
turkey with me. That day, I even loved the Twins. Daddy called while we were
clearing the dishes and that made Thanksgiving perfect. After dinner, we strolled
out on the lanai, lounged on the couch and listened to more war news on our
radio:

> Saburo Kurusu, special Japanese envoy to the United States, it was
> learned is carrying a personal message from Premier General Hideki Tojo to
> President Roosevelt. The note declares that if a Japanese-American rap-
> prochement is not readily achieved Japan will be forced to "use other means"
> to protect her existence against economic and military encirclement.

> Representative Martin Dies, a Democrat from Texas, said that the United
> States 'will be at war with Japan within two or three weeks for the entire matter
> will be settled.'

> From Warm Springs, Georgia. President Roosevelt talked to Secretary of
> State Cordell Hull by telephone tonight. It is thought that the president may cut
> short his visit here and leave for Washington on Sunday. It is understood that
> the president has received several reports on the Pacific situation since his
> departure from Washington yesterday.

Tyler Dennett, former advisor to the state department, said tonight that the United States and Japan always have been and always will be natural allies, but Japan's "political madness" now has reached a point "where we are ready to meet the Japanese challenge to fight it out."

Hearing all that news, the pumpkin pie digesting in our stomachs soured.

The Monday after our Thanksgiving dinner, back at school, Peggy Potz, the class brain, said she found a new word in her father's large Webster's dictionary during the holiday. After we pledged allegiance to the flag, Mrs. Mott-Smith asked, "What did you learn during Thanksgiving vacation?" So that's when Peggy shared her new word with us. She said she discovered the word while writing her book report on *Little Women*. The word was "PURSY!" Peggy primly stood up, pulled out a little card from her purse and read in a squeaky voice, "PURSY is defined (she blasted out so everyone in the school could hear her) as asthmatic, baggy, fat, obese, plump, puckered, pudgy, puffy, pursed, stout, swollen, and wealthy." She slurred the word "wealthy." After she finished reading, the class snickered behind their hands, looking at me.

Peggy, now very pleased with herself, smiled sweetly, and said, "That's a darling word, just for you, Perrrrrcy." After she sat down, she gave Mrs. Mott-Smith her "see how smart I am look." Crinkling her nose and smoothing out the ruffles in her skirt, she grinned an evil grin and folded the card back into her Shirley Temple patent leather purse that her mother bought her at Liberty House. I could have socked her in the eye because she ruined my day. Someone wrote on the boy's bathroom wall at recess time, "Percy is a Pursy."

I told Wigay about it. Before lunch, she whispered, "I put a lizard in Peggy's lunchbox."

Gertrude said in life, the only person you can really count on is you, but she was wrong - I could always count on Wigay Wix. At noon, Peggy turned hysterical. She was taken yowling and foaming in the mouth to the nurses' office. While eating her watercress sandwich, she bit the lizard in half. After school, I walked home in a stinking mood and wanted to kill everyone in sight but Wigay.

Seething with horrible thoughts over the embarrassment Peggy had caused me, I decided to bite the bullet and I walked over to Cross-Eyed Mama's house. I rapped her brass knocker loudly. BANG! BANG! BANG! Ten times I rapped it.

Cross-Eyed Mama whipped open the front door and yelled, "WHAT DO YOU WANT?"

I yelled back, "SUMMER IS OVER AND A PROMISE IS A PROMISE."

"Well," she said, startled.

"IT'S ALMOST CHRISTMAS, FOR GOODNESS SAKE," I continued yelling.

"I..." Cross-Eyed Mama started stuttering because she didn't know what to say. She was dressed to go out because she had on her hat and gloves. Nothing matched.

I calmed down and said, "May I play with Vinnie and Cynthia?"

Recovering from her stuttering, she replied like a lady, "I have a meeting right now at the Outdoor Circle."

I informed her, "I didn't come to play with you."

Mollified that I might have grown up and become a more responsible boy, she instructed, "Percy, if you want to play with my children, you must learn to mind your manners and not yell at adults."

"I can't help it," I said, close to tears. "I've had a very bad day."

She looked at me and could see the sadness all over my face, and she sighed, "I know I'll regret this, but, all right - come on in." I walked into the vestibule.

Jumping all over me again, she cried, "Wipe your feet on the mat there. Your feet are filthy dirty. Percy, do you ever take a bath?" I ignored that stupid question.

It had been a long time since I had been in her house and I didn't recognize the surroundings any more. She had redecorated her house. It was now furnished for Madame Pompadour, not her children. Cross-Eyed Mama had turned everything in her house igloo white and the living room was filled with fragile French chairs made out of ivory matchsticks.

Standing in front of me, she commanded, "I have new rules around here. First rule: don't touch anything. Keep your dirty paws off my walls. I spent a lot of money to make this house look nice. Another rule is that my children are not to play over at your house. You all go wild over there. You are all to stay here and upstairs. I'll instruct my maid to watch you. Is that clear?"

Looking past her, I asked, "Where are Vinnie and Cynthia?"

"Upstairs doing their homework," she answered.

"Upstairs?" I asked again. Giving me final instructions, she said, "Upstairs. And lastly, do not go outside for anything. I'll be back in a couple of hours." She said to herself, "I know I'm going to regret this."

Not waiting to hear another word, I ran up the staircase, taking two steps at a time, to see my friends. From behind, I heard her call out, "PERCY, REMEMBER WHAT I JUST SAID!"

I yelled back, "Yea, yea, yea," forgetting everything she had said immediately.

I burst into Cynthia's bedroom and yelled, "I'M HERE!" Cynthia screamed and Vinnie, hearing Cynthia scream, ran into her bedroom. Seeing each other, we jumped up and down, holding onto each other, yelling at the top of our lungs. While we were screaming, Cross-Eyed Mama backed her car down the drive and after five minutes, we caught up on everything that we had done.

Resting from all the excitement, I asked Cynthia if her mother had a drinking problem. I told her what Cousin Bessie had said and as usual, Cousin Bessie was off her rocker and got things botched up. Their mother had splitting migraine headaches, not hangovers, and sometimes she had to stay in bed for weeks. I told them Cousin Bessie should be put in a concentration camp with Nazis and have her tongue cut out.

After the initial excitement had passed, we became completely bored with each other because there was nothing to do in a house decorated with matchstick furniture, and we didn't dare touch the white walls. Nothing, nothing, nothing. We couldn't dress up in Cross-Eyed Mama's clothes, nor have Cynthia stick her fanny out the window and play Rapunzel or any game that might turn Cross-Eyed Mama's white house a smudgy brown.

I asked to see Cynthia's tail so she dropped her underpants. Her birthmark looked more beautiful than ever and I told her so. I reminded her that if she ever ran out of money, she could make a fortune in a circus sideshow. I told her her tail was a much better attraction than the bearded lady that I had just seen, but was on a par with the iceman who had buried himself in ice in his underpants. I bet her a hundred dollars that she could get a whole dollar for one peek at her hairy wonderment. I told her I would have given her a dollar right then, but I was broke.

We just sat on Cynthia's bed doing nothing but looking at each other. I became exhausted doing nothing. The anticipation of our meeting had been far more exciting than the real meeting. Sitting around, out of conversation and bored, I sensed they wanted me to go home so they could finish their homework. When friends are away too long from each other, you lose interest in their company because you've changed,

I had to think of something to do. I reached into my pocket and pulled out the box of matches and said, "Vinnie and Cynthia, here's something really exciting to do. Too bad we can't go outside because I'd show you what I've been doing lately."

"What do you do with those matches?" Cynthia asked, taking the matches out of my hand. Her fascination in me suddenly revived. Cynthia told me a long time ago she liked me because I did things that were really crazy.

My voice getting inflamed, I said, "I burn things. I take a wad of paper, smash it up and burn it. I don't know why, but it's really exciting. I'd burn my house down, but I'd be sent to jail and be out of mayonnaise."

Vinnie grabbed the matches and urged, "Let's do it up here."

I got a little nervous and said, "I think that could be dangerous. What would your mother say?"

Vinnie stamped his foot and spoke like Teddy Roosevelt, "Naw, she won't know anything about it because Mother has a wastebasket in her bedroom that's fireproof. She told me so." Spoken with the determination of his favorite American president, Vinnie ran to get the wastebasket.

Cynthia clapped her hands and giggled, "We haven't had this much fun since you were last here and I stuck my fanny out the window. If it gets too dangerous, I'll put the fire out in the bathtub." Vinnie brought me the wastebasket and we stuffed it with school paper torn out of Cynthia's notebook.

"I want to light it!" Vinnie said, holding the matches. He struck a match and put the match to the corner of a piece of paper. The fire took hold immediately and went from paper to paper. Soon, long flames began to curl to the ceiling. We stood mesmerized as if we were in a movie watching Atlanta burn. All of a sudden, the flames became real to us because they were licking the curtains beside Cynthia's bed. Cynthia ran to grab the wastebasket but it was too hot to carry to the bathtub, and her curtains were beginning to smolder. She ran to the bathroom for water as Vinnie ran downstairs yelling, "Fire!" The maid phoned the fire station.

I grabbed for Cynthia's bathrobe, wrapped it around the wastebasket, picked it up and ran downstairs, flew out the front door holding it high in my hands, and threw the wastebasket on the front lawn. Upstairs, Cynthia splashed a wastebasket of water over the curtains and put the fire out in her room.

The fire engines, hooting their horns, arrived at Cross-Eyed Mama's house in seconds. The firemen pulled out their hoses, rushed through the house, and ran upstairs, breaking one of the matchstick pieces of furniture and dirtying the white walls as they climbed. After the firemen were completely satisfied that the fire was under control, they came downstairs and told us we were heroes. We had saved the house from burning to the ground, but in the next breath, they scolded us. They said that if we ever played with matches again, they'd throw us in jail. They asked whom the matches belonged to. I raised my hand. They nodded at each other and said that I looked the type - Percy the Turkey-Head.

When the fire engines hooted back to the station, Cross-Eyed Mama's house had smoke still coming out the upstairs windows. The house inside now looked as if children played in it. The maid had called Cross-Eyed Mama at the Outdoor Circle meeting, so I ran home before she came home and beat me to a pulp.

That night, Mother had a meeting with Cross-Eyed Mama and her lawyer-husband. Cynthia had saved my neck from being completely chopped off because she told her parents who lit the fire, who saved the house, and that all three of us were equally to blame. Cross-Eyed Mama, who took the upper hand at the meeting, screamed at Mother and her own husband that until I came over to play with her darling children, there wasn't a thought in their dear sweet, innocent heads about lighting a match or burning down her house. She continued, jabbing her fingers into her husband's chest and gulping in air, that her once beautiful house, decorated pristine white, was now completely ruined. She ended her spewing of hate that Cousin Bessie heard while leaning out her window, that I was a disciple of the devil, and heaven help her now because she felt a migraine from hell coming on.

When the meeting ended, Cross-Eyed Mama decided that I was to be banished from her house forever, and I was to write a thousand times that I would never light a match again. She instructed Mother that after I had finished writing the thousand sentences, I was to go over, paper in hand, kneel before her and make a personal apology. Cross-Eyed Mama also insisted that Mother fork over two hundred dollars to pay for the broken furniture and smudged walls. Cross-Eyed Mama's husband, being a lawyer and a fair-minded fellow, felt that Mother should only pay half. Furious at her husband's interference, Cross-Eyed Mama ran home, bolted upstairs, locked herself in her bedroom, shut the blinds, threw herself on her bed, and waited to suffer the worst migraine headache of her life.

After hearing about the fire, Marigold came into my room, punched me on the arm and told me she was real proud of what I had done. Burning down a house was just the niftiest thing she had ever heard of in a long time and that even the Twins couldn't have thought up a good one like that. Leaving my room, she announced that I was beginning to act like a real brother.

Mother cancelled her date that night, pulled me into her room and said that I should be ashamed of myself because I could have burned down a house and I had cost her a lot of money that she didn't have. While holding a pillow tight to her chest, she sighed that she didn't know what to do with me any more. She sighed that I was getting out of control and began to cry.

I hated it when she cried because I always felt helpless. I took her hand, squeezed it and apologized, "I'm sorry, Mother. I promise from now on that I will be the best little boy in Hawaii. You'll be proud of me someday, I promise you."

She dropped her pillow, held me to herself and rocked me back and forth like she used to do when I was a baby. After she wiped the tears away from her face, she told me it was probably all her fault. Shaking her head, sniffling, she confessed she probably shouldn't have divorced Daddy, and she had been kicking herself of late for not sticking it out with him. She pulled me away, looked at me square in my eyes, and stared a long stare, full of love for me for a whole minute.

That is my favorite memory of her.

Mother collected herself and said, nodding her head ever so slightly, that she just hadn't been paying enough attention to me or Marigold. She then spoke with determination, "I love you, Percy, and from tonight on, you and I are going to turn over a new leaf. We're going to make ourselves proud of each other. I'll tell you what - you, Marigold and I are going to spend all next Sunday together. We'll make a picnic like we used to do when Daddy lived with us. Where shall we go?" she asked.

"Kailua Beach, Mother," I answered. She kissed me hard on the cheek. Mother didn't kiss me like that very often.

That night with Agnes and Gertrude prodding me, I started to write a thousand times that I wouldn't play with fire. While scrawling out my fiftieth sentence, I realized again that Mr. Hamada had disappeared from my life, but I knew the curse hadn't.

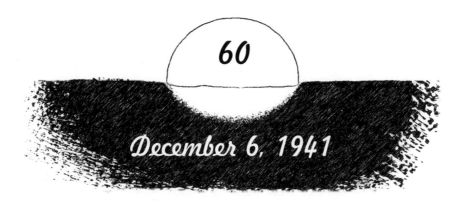

60

December 6, 1941

After reading Saturday morning's *Advertiser* on December 6, 1941, I should have known the sting of the curse was around the corner.

The Honolulu Advertiser

Jimmie Fidler In Hollywood: Idol Chatter: Isn't Joan Crawford mighty quiet these days. No smile more completely wins your confidence than Lana Turner's....Too bad good singers aren't as much at ease on the screen as Bing Crosby...Marlene Dietrich is unmatchable at expressing utter nonchalance.

Washington, Tuesday, Dec 2 (UP) Rep. Andrew J. May, D., Ky. Chairman of the House military affairs committee, in a statement to the press today, urged President Roosevelt to tell the Japanese that unless they renounced their ambition for an empire in South Asia, the United States "will blast them off the land and blow them out of the water."

DEC 2 (UP) JAPAN WARNED THE UNITED STATES THAT THEY (JAPAN) CAN SHOOT STRAIGHT AND HAVE A MIGHTY ARMY AND NAVY.

NEW YORK, DEC 2 - JAPAN FACING CATASTROPHE, JOURNAL SAYS
(UP) The Wall Street Journal carried on its front page today a survey, which concluded that "economically" Japan is living on borrowed time. If ever there was an empire on the brink of conflict which was 99 per cent certain to result in catastrophic liquidation of that empire, it is the Nipponese," the survey said. It pointed out that Japan gets 80 per cent of its materials from Britain, the United States and The Netherlands.

RECORD MAIL GOES OUT WHEN LURLINE DEPARTS
A record load of passengers and a record load of mail left Honolulu aboard the Matson flagship Lurline Friday noon for the Mainland.

DEC 6 - THE BIGGEST GAME OF THE SEASON: WILLAMETTE VS UNIVERSITY OF HAWAII - SHRINERS' ANNUAL HOSPITAL BENEFIT GAME

So that less fortunate children – afflicted with bodily ailment may have an equal chance in life, is the major purpose of the Shriner's Hospital. Toward the maintenance of this Hospital goes every cent of the proceeds from this great annual sports football classic.

The big sporting event arrived in Honolulu, the Willamette Bearcats vs University of Hawaii Shrine football game. Daddy spent a fortune on tickets, which were double the price of one admission to see *Gone with the Wind.*

I didn't want to go and sulked around the house all morning. I wanted to go to the Hawaii Theatre to see *She Knew All the Answers* starring Joan Bennett and Franchot Tone. It had just opened and I loved the ad in the morning's *Advertiser -* "Heaven will protect this working girl...but who will help the man she works on." I phoned 66300, the Hawaii Theatre, to check on show times, but Mother wouldn't listen to my moans and insisted that I go with Daddy and Marigold.

She scolded me, "You'll hurt your father's feelings if you don't go. This football game isn't cheap and he spent a lot of money to give you and Marigold this treat. It's going to be an exciting game."

She said that because she had other plans. She was meeting Aunt Momi and they were going to do "girl things." Girl things didn't include me anymore. I overheard Mother telling Aunt Momi that they were going to have lunch at the Kewalo Inn and then going on a shopping spree. Aunt Momi wanted to replace a broken table lamp and a silver cigarette case. The cigarette case she threw in the ocean after a big fight with Uncle Lono and the lamp had to be replaced because she cracked it over Uncle Lono's head.

Mother and Aunt Momi had been looking forward to this lunch date for weeks because, for the first time in a long time, they were going to spend time alone without children or Uncle Lono. I was not included beyond having lunch with them at the Kewalo Inn. Gertrude kept telling me that nobody wanted me around any more because I repeated everything I heard. I had the reputation for being as big a gossip as Cousin Bessie. Gertrude scolded me further, saying that my ears were too big for my own good and that my mouth was as loose as a cannon shooting at the German army. Mother told me that Daddy was picking Marigold and me up after lunch.

The Kewalo Inn was a restaurant next to the waterfront where Japanese fishing sampans moored. A tuna cannery hummed nearby. Everyone asked for a table by the window because you could see fishing boats entering and leaving the harbor. The restaurant excelled in fresh fish and coleslaw soaked in mayonnaise.

The four of us arrived at the restaurant at eleven-thirty. The room was empty except for a table where three Japanese men in black suits talked in loud voices. They were eating sashimi and drinking bottles of sake. A fourth person, a blonde woman, joined them as we arrived and she ordered champagne immediately. They were acting as if they were celebrating someone's birthday. The waitress marched us as far away from the noisy table as she could get us. As we walked by their table, I recognized Mr. Hamada. I started to speak to him, but he looked away, and I got the message immediately that he was spying. I had seen enough spy movies to know that when a spy worked, he never recognizes friends or even best friends. I chose a seat at the table so I could watch Mr. Hamada spy, hoping to pick up a few pointers. Watching him drink sake, I thought to myself, "Boy, spies have a lot of fun because they eat at restaurants." From what I observed, a spy drank sake, laughed loudly, told jokes, and pretended someone was turning twenty-one. Being a spy meant going to a birthday party every day with people you liked.

I ordered a mahimahi sandwich and a double order of slaw right away. Marigold ordered a hamburger with a pickle, french fries and lots of catsup. Mother and Aunt Momi ordered martinis with olives.

After they got their drinks, Aunt Momi said to Mother, swirling an olive around a frosted martini glass, "Did you sell your stock to Aunt Mari?"

"I need the money, Momi," Mother said, looking troubled.

Looking into her martini glass, Aunt Momi said, "Watch out for that witch. She's a shrewd operator and has kept every dime she's ever got. She's got a heart like an iron fist. I bet you sold your stock to her for peanuts. Never trust a woman who wears a red wig." After Aunt Momi spoke, I noticed her hair had turned California orange since I last saw her.

Spearing an olive, Mother sighed, "I owe it to her for educating me. Really, looking back, she did a lot for me after Mother died." The olive disappeared from Mother's toothpick into her mouth. Aunt Momi, downing her drink, said loudly, "Jolljamit, Deidra, you don't owe her a damn thing. Believe me, you don't. Is there anyone in this world you don't like?"

"I could name a few," Mother responded, sipping her drink.

Aunt Momi raised her glass and toasted, "Here's to our goddamned relatives. God bless them one and all. They certainly do take care of themselves. I told that old battleaxe when she called me that if she wanted my stock, she'd have to talk to Lono. She hung up." Aunt Momi laughed a throaty chuckle.

A loud burst of shouts exploded from the table where the spies were drinking. Aunt Momi, looking at their table, said to Mother, "Damn it, what's going on over there? That's looks like a party I'd like to have been invited to."

Marigold, fidgeting with her napkin, wasn't paying any attention to anything around her because her mind was focused on the football game and Daddy. She had finished her hamburger in three bites and kept watching the door for Daddy.

Another explosion came from the spy table because Mr. Hamada stood up and cheered, "Banzai! Banzai! Banzai!" He sat down and everyone at his table screamed as if he had told the best joke in the world. The blonde lady laughed the loudest. When they saw us looking at them, Mr. Hamada shushed them to be quiet.

Ordering another martini from the waitress, Mother looked at Mr. Hamada's table and said, "Isn't it wonderful to see people happy?" Looking down into her empty martini glass, she continued wistfully, "I wish I had something to celebrate, for once." I thought she was thinking about me and my matches and all the trouble I was causing her.

Trying to keep the guilty thoughts from flooding in my head, I turned and watched out the window as a sampan left for the open sea. Two Japanese men heaved ropes onto the pier as the engine started up. The boat, chugging like a putt-putt, backed up and pulled away from the dock as two fishermen scrambled around the deck searching for their fishing poles. Finding them, they set them in place on the back of the boat as the sampan motored out beyond the breakwater.

I interrupted Mother and Aunt Momi's conversation, pointing to my plate, and whined, "I want some more coleslaw."

Mother corrected, saying, "May I have some more?" She answered herself, "No, you may not have more because you haven't finished your fish. Fish is good for you." I argued, "I want more coleslaw, Mother. If I have to go to a football game, I need more coleslaw for my strength."

"Eat your fish," Mother commanded. "You eat my fish," I pouted.

"Don't be rude to your mother, Percy," Aunt Momi said sternly, finishing up her second martini. Jabbing her finger into my ribs, she continued to scold, "You're turning into a spoiled little brat." Marigold stopped looking at the front door and nodded in agreement.

Aunt Momi wouldn't let up and ordered, "Eat your fish. Don't make your favorite old auntie angry. Fish is brain food. EAT YOUR FISH." Those last words were said loudly enough for Mr. Hamada to hear at his table and spoken to me in the same tone of voice she had used on Uncle Lono in the bathroom.

After I finished eating my fish, Daddy walked into the restaurant. He stood in the doorway as Marigold ran to him and kissed him all over. Holding onto Daddy, Marigold yelled louder than Mr. Hamada's banzais, "Can we go now, Mother?"

Mother, wiping a piece of slaw from my mouth, yelled back at Marigold, "You can go." Mother waved her purse at Daddy and called out, "It's already the sixth of December, Dick. The check, remember?"

"In the mail," Daddy replied, smiling sheepishly. Aunt Momi lifted her third martini and gave Daddy a salute, saying, "We've heard that one before."

Under my breath, I leaned over and whispered to Mother, "Please let me go with you and Aunt Momi." She whispered back, "No, Percy. You go with your father and Marigold - now." Putting my napkin on the table, I got up and whined, "You're no fun any more." Aunt Momi gave me a slap on my fanny.

As I walked to Daddy, two of the Japanese stood up and banzied me. I gave them the Churchill V for victory sign. They laughed, sat down and slapped Mr. Hamada on his back. Mr. Hamada looked embarrassed. The haole lady still laughed the loudest and looked drunk. We left for the stadium.

The Honolulu Stadium was located in the heart of town, a couple of blocks from the Varsity movie theater. It looked like the Roman coliseum but was made out of wood. It was so creaky and old that it shook like an earthquake when we walked up to our reserved seats. Each step up, I thought I was going to fall through the spaces in the bleachers to the cement floor below and die. It was a spooky walk to our seats.

In our seats, Marigold and I sat on either side of Daddy. Holding onto Daddy's shirt, I looked over the crowd as they were filling up the stadium. There was old, young, fat, slim, all nationalities, sitting and fanning themselves because it was turning into a hot afternoon. All the adults smoked cigarettes and all the children, sitting next to them, breathing in their smoke, were stuffing their mouths with hot dogs.

I felt sick in the stomach because of all the coleslaw I ate at lunch and I was having a hard time breathing because my nose was stuffed up with snot. I was just plain unhappy sitting next to Daddy at the football game and I was nervous sitting so high off the ground in that rickety stadium. I wanted to leap down the steps and flee to a matinee at the Varsity Theater. To top it off, the day was not only hot, but the trade winds stopped blowing on December 6th.

Daddy bought us each a hot dog and a bag of popcorn. Marigold ate her hot dog in three big bites. Without anyone noticing, I shoved pieces of my hot dog and bun through the spaces in the floor and watched them fall on people's heads as they walked below me. Nobody paid any attention to me.

Daddy bought me a Nehi orange soda while he and Marigold jumped up and down on the wood planks, waving and yelling at their friends coming in. I didn't know anyone at the football game because all my friends were sitting in a movie. Every time Marigold jumped up and down, I held on for dear life waiting for the stadium to collapse. Daddy saw that I was scared and said gently to my sister, "Sit down, Marigold, you're scaring Percy." I could tell she was scaring Daddy, too. Marigold glared at me as if I had ruined her whole afternoon and growled, "Percy is a sissy."

She quickly changed the subject and said, "Daddy, we're going to lick those bastards, aren't we?" Daddy corrected her, laughing as he did, "Marigold, don't say bastard." "That's what you say," she said back, looking at him with adoring eyes.

"That's not a word nice girls use," he scolded her, giving her a little love tap on the arm. Punching Daddy hard on his arm, Marigold screamed, "I don't want to be a girl. Girls are just silly, silly, silly, silly."

Putting his arm around her, he said, "Don't let me hear you use that word again."

Pulling a nickel out of his pocket, Daddy asked, "Honey, will you buy us a program?"

When Marigold left, I told my father he had it all wrong because bastard was a good word. "What do you think it means, Percy?" he asked. I looked him square in the eye and said, "Bastard means that you are loved and the reason you don't say it out loud is because bastard is a special kind of love."

"Who taught you that?" Daddy said, taking a drag on his cigarette.

"Hatsuko," I said smugly.

Daddy lifted his eyes to the sky, and shook his head and replied, "Percy, let's sleep on that word for now. When you get older, I'll tell you another meaning."

"Thank you, Daddy," I said, pleased because I knew something that Daddy didn't know.

I looked at Daddy's face while he smoked his cigarette and asked another question, "Daddy?"

"Yes, Percy," he said, looking at his cigarette.

"You're a bastard, aren't you, but we'll keep that to ourselves." Taking a last drag from the cigarette, he threw it on the floor, stamped on it with his shoe, closed his eyes, and said, "I wish you would, son."

Marigold returned and handed the program to Daddy and purred, "Daddy, this is the best day of my life." It wasn't mine.

Daddy turned to me and pointed, "Percy, you're going to like this. Look over there." At the far end of the stadium, I saw a line up of bands at the stadium's entrance. A voice came out of a loudspeaker and announced, "LADIES AND GENTLEMEN, WE PROUDLY PRESENT THE HIGH SCHOOL BANDS OF HAWAII." Horns trumpeted, drums rolled and in marched a hundred teenage boys and girls playing "God Bless America." Everyone stood and cheered. The band goose-stepped up and down the field like the Nazi soldiers in Berlin. After the bands left the field, a tenor sang "the Star Spangled Banner" and a whistle blew and the game began. I immediately fell asleep next to Daddy and dreamt about the midgets in *The Wizard of Oz.* They were playing football with Dorothy and Toto on the yellow brick road.

Daddy woke me at halftime. I tried eating a hot dog as I watched floats with pretty girls standing on them motor slowly around the field followed by funny-looking clowns doing somersaults. At the end of the parade, hundreds of colorful balloons were released into the sky and floated out to the ocean. Looking at the balloons in the sky, I wished I could have been the yellow one that floated out to sea.

When the second half of the game began, I amused myself by secretly dropping anything I could find on the heads of people walking below me. I bulls-eyed a small pebble on a bald-headed man. He looked up to see if the sky was falling. I laughed to myself and felt very pleased because I was as accurate with my dropping as Aunt Momi was shooting her gun. I looked for other pebbles but I couldn't find any. Nobody paid any attention to me.

When the last quarter of the game began, the sun hid behind the stadium wall and it started to get cold. I leaned against my father, felt his warmth and fell asleep. When the game was over, Daddy woke me. I opened my eyes and saw Daddy and Marigold slapping each other's backs, cheering, whistling, and screaming, "Yea, Team." It had been a great day for our little University of Hawaii football team because they won. They beat the growling Mainland Bearcats. Everyone on our side of the stadium was jumping up and down like Marigold and Daddy were. The bleachers groaned as I held onto my seat and prayed for a parachute. As my body kept undulating up and down from the towering waves of stamping feet, it reminded me of a rough ocean and I got hungry. I wanted to eat a hamburger with everything on it. I looked over to see if Marigold was seasick.

She wasn't but her voice was kaput. Gone. Now, she croaked like a frog. Croak, croak, croak, she croaked, "I knew we'd win, Daddy. Those Mainland guys can't beat us...the bastards." Daddy put his arm around Marigold and beamed, "You're right, honeybunny. I guess they are bastards but they fought well." Reaching down, he put his other arm around me and said, "Well, Mr. Sleepyhead, did you like it?"

"You bet I did, Daddy," I lied.

Clapping his hands, Daddy asked, "Okay, kids, where do you want to go for dinner?" I thought he'd never ask. We both piped up, "Kau Kau Korner."

"That's it. Kau Kau Korner for my favorite kids." Those moments when Daddy talked about food, I really loved him and most especially when he was in a good mood. Thank God, Mother didn't tell him that I had almost burned down Cross-Eyed Mama's house.

Kau Kau Korner was a drive-in restaurant on Kalakaua Avenue. Kau kau means food in Hawaiian. Meals were served on trays attached to your car by eager beaver young girls who wore white boots, tiny red skirts and tall helmets fringed with red tassels. They marched around the parking lot like an army of high school drum majorettes. Their helmets were not practical because when the girls leaned down and took an order, they thumped on the roof of the car. Thump, thump, thump.

Daddy drove his yellow Dodge into a front stall. In a flash, Pua, one of the majorettes, was at his window, thumping. She passed us a menu through the window. Pencil poised and pad in hand, she spoke local, "Eh, watcha like? Good hambuggah special tonight."

Marigold and Daddy nodded to Pua from the front seat, nestled next to each other as they looked over the menu together. I sprawled out on the back seat, waiting patiently, because I had decided what I wanted to eat by halftime. Daddy and Marigold took ages in deciding what to order, so from the back seat, I rattled off to the waitress, mimicking her, "I like one hambuggah with tomatoes, onions, cheese, pickle, and lots of mayonnaise, please."

Daddy looked back at me and cautioned, "Don't be a smarty-pants, Mr. Percy."

Pencil still poised in the air, Pua looked at me in the back seat, "Eh, not so fast, speedy gonsalves. Watcha tink, I one track stah? Go like one turtle."

I stretched out my words as slowly as a turtle crossing a desert and said, "I want a hamburger with tomatoes, onion, cheese, and lots and lots of mayonnaise! Got it?"

Shaking her pencil at me, she said, "No make smart, kid. You like one drink?"

I leaned out the back window and said as slowly as I could, "Give me a thick, thick, thick, thick, thick, large, large chocolate shake with plenty of chocolate and chocolate ice cream." She wrote as she said to herself, "One shake!" My eyes rose to the ceiling, thinking she was hopeless. I flopped back down on the back seat, prayed to God that she heard me and belched out loud.

Marigold and Daddy, after going over the menu a thousand times, finally made up their minds. Daddy ordered two toasted tuna sandwiches and two vanilla shakes. Some things never change; Marigold and Daddy were two peas in a pod.

After Pua wrote our orders, she took back the menus and went off mumbling that she wished haoles would make up their minds. I yelled after her, "Don't forget, thick." Marigold leaned against Daddy and cooed, "This has been the best Saturday of all, Daddy. Best Saturday of my life. What are we going to do next Saturday?"

Daddy coughed and mumbled, "Sorry, honey, next week Kathy and I have been invited to a party at Kanaka's."

Marigold asked, "The Saturday after that?"

"Maybe, honey." Daddy sounded funny when he said that.

Adding my two cents from the back seat, I asked, "Maybe next time we can go to a movie? Maybe, Daddy?" Nobody was paying any attention to me because they were talking to each other about the game. So I talked out loud to myself in the back seat because certainly no one in the front seat was listening to me. I rambled on, "I liked the circus best, Daddy. Pooooolar the ice man. I like Tyrone Power movies, if anyone is interested."

Daddy changed his voice from fun to serious and said, bringing me into the conversation, "Kids, I have something important to say to you." He turned around to me to be sure I was listening and said, "I've been meaning to tell you kids this every weekend, but it never seemed the right time."

Sensing that something terrible was about to happen, Marigold slid away from Daddy and moved next to the window. She asked cautiously, "What is it, Daddy?"

Daddy blurted out his news, "Kathy is going to have a baby." I could see Marigold's body slump next to the car door. I sat up, leaned forward and rested my face on the front seat, next to Daddy, and said, trying to be cheerful for Marigold, "That's good, Daddy. If it's a boy, give him my name."

Daddy acted surprised and asked, "Why? Don't you like your name?"

"No, Daddy, I don't. I hate my name." I didn't lie that time.

"What name would you like to have had?" Daddy asked. Alice Faye's name came to mind. "Tyrone Power," I said.

"Why Tyrone Power?"

"It's not a fat name!" I exclaimed.

"I'm afraid you're stuck with Percy," Daddy said gently.

Leaning back into the seat, I said, discouraged at my fate, "I think so, too." I continued, sighing, "I wished you and Mother asked my permission before you named me Percy."

"Your mother named you." I groaned, "She made a big mistake."

He laughed and then turned to Marigold, who was looking out the car window, and asked, "You're quiet, honey. What do you think of the baby?"

"It's fine, Daddy. It's really fine." It wasn't and Marigold was lying tons.

"Daddy," I leaned forward again, having a brilliant thought, and said, "don't have any more girl babies, only boy babies. We have Marigold and she is just right. She's all the girl we need. Have a boy baby who likes football." Marigold reached over and smacked my head and told me to "shut up."

Dinner arrived. The milk shake was really thick, so thick I couldn't suck it up with the straw. I was so happy with my milk shake that I tapped Daddy on the shoulder and said, "Daddy, I really love Kau Kau Korner." Marigold was sad and wasn't eating her tuna sandwich, just kept staring out the window at nothing. I tried to get up the courage to ask her for her tuna sandwich if she wasn't going to eat it, but I turned chicken because I could see she wasn't in a good mood.

Daddy, looking concerned, asked, "Aren't you hungry, Marigold? Eat your sandwich, honey. It's good for you." Sounding like she was about to cry, she answered, "I'm not hungry, Daddy. When is the baby coming, Daddy?"

"Soon. In two or three weeks."

Sounding angry, she said, "You took a long time telling us."

"I just never found the right opportunity, honey. I'm sorry," Daddy said, knowing how upset Marigold was. Looking out the window, she mumbled, "Daddy, I'd like to go home now. I'm feeling sick. Anyway, I promised Mother to have Percy in bed by nine." That was the biggest lie of the night.

Daddy honked the horn and Pua came and took away the tray. I looked longingly after Marigold's untouched tuna sandwich as Pua took it away. We drove home without speaking. The air in the car was full of electricity. I sat back in the car and sang quietly:

"Somewhere over the rainbow.
Way up high,
There's a land that you've heard of,
Once in a lullaby,
Somewhere over the rainbow,
Skies are blue....."

"Shut up, Percy," Marigold snarled from the front seat. Her words held a thousand meanings and I shut up. After we arrived at home, I thanked Daddy for taking us to the football game and dinner at Kau Kau Korner. Marigold, still not speaking, ran into the house. Daddy called after her, promising he'd call on Wednesday. I waved goodbye as he drove off and walked into the house. I turned on the lights on the lanai. Marigold had gone into her bedroom and, for the first time, closed her door quietly. I stayed up until ten listening on the radio to Al Perry and his singing Surfriders. Mother was still out on a date. After shopping with Aunt Momi, she had gone to a dinner/dance at the Pacific Club to honor a Navy submarine commander. Before bed, I read in *The Advertiser* our horoscopes for December 7th.

HOROSCOPE BY STELLA - DECEMBER 7TH

ARIES - (Percy) Be cautious in all morning activities. Don't be hasty in the face of irritating complications.

VIRGO - (Mother) Don't let haste make waste for you this morning. Think before you act; avoid impulses. A social evening ahead.

TAURUS - (Marigold) You will need to keep a calm head on your shoulders all day. Use your head and don't be stubborn. Be adaptable.

I awoke early and wrote 400 sentences of "I will not play with matches."
Flipping through the handwritten pages, I hoped it looked like a thousand sentences. After breakfast, pages in hand, I intended to walk over to Cross-Eyed
Mama's house and make the annoying apology. I was pretty sure that at seven in
the morning, Cross-Eyed Mama wasn't about to count every sentence. Aunt Ella
hadn't.

When I walked into the dining room, Marigold was already seated at the
breakfast table eating her cornflakes. Mother was sleeping because she got in late
last night after attending the submarine party, and Helen the Horrible had the day
off. On Sundays, Marigold and I were on our own, so I went into the kitchen and
made myself breakfast, a mayonnaise sandwich. Coming back into the dining
room with my plate, I was remembering Mother's promise that today we were
going on a picnic. As I sat down to eat my sandwich, a big boom burst outside the
house. The house shuddered on its foundations. It was as if an earthquake had
struck Oahu. Then another boom, and then another. The house was quaking as if it
was falling apart.

"What's that, Marigold?" I asked.

"Diamond Head is erupting. Shut up and eat," she snarled. I could tell
Marigold was still in a bad mood.

"Where's *The Advertiser*?" I persisted.

"Didn't come," she said, finishing the last of her cereal.

Boom. Boom. Boom. Boom. The house wobbled on its foundations. I was
surprised Mother hadn't awakened but then again, she was a sound sleeper.
Marigold, concentrating on the booms, started to get excited thinking that
Diamond Head had really erupted. She jumped off her seat and announced, "I'm
going to see what's going on. Be quiet this morning, Percy, and don't wake up
Mother."

"I won't. Anyway, I make less noise than what's going on outside. Don't forget to come back because Mother is taking us to Kailua beach today. Oh, by the
way, I'm going next door to hand in my 'I won't play with matches' sentences," I
said, while wiping a dab of mayonnaise off my face.

"How many did you write?" Marigold asked.

"Enough," I said, evading the question. Another boom shook the house.

"I bet you cheated. Anyway, I'm out of here. If Mother wakes up, tell her I'm up on Rocky Hill." After she said that, she slammed the front door, sounding louder than all the booms.

I picked up my papers off the table, mushed them together in my hand and walked next door. I rapped Cross-Eyed Mama's brass knocker. Cross-Eyed Mama's husband answered, wearing his BVD's. Looking him straight in the eye, I said, "Here," and shoved the papers into his hand.

"What are these?" he asked, perplexed, examining the papers I handed him.

"My apologies," I answered, looking down at his bare feet.

"Thank you, Percy. You're a man of your word." I looked back into his face; he was smiling at me. I answered back, "I'm kind of a man of my word." I should have told him the truth that I was a hundred or more sentences short, but he acted so nice, I didn't want to tell him the truth.

Still looking me in the eye, he lowered his voice and said, "Percy, if you and Vinnie are very quiet, why don't you go out in the backyard and play."

"Really?" I asked. I thought to myself, boy, Mr. Cross-Eyed Mama is a thousand times nicer than his wife. Boom! The ground shook underneath my feet but the explosion didn't seem to bother Mr. Cross-Eyed Mama because without a word, he pointed me to the backyard and closed the door. I thought Cross-Eyed Mama's husband had to be a saint.

In the backyard, Vinnie was waiting for me. We decided right away to play war. Playing war meant we'd shoot each other with our fingers and fall down like we were dead. I shot Vinnie first and he rolled down his driveway, dying without making a noise.

I heard our telephone ring.

Next, it was Vinnie's turn to shoot me. As he shot me, I heard Mother scream, "Marigold and Percy, come home - right now! Right this very minute." Her voice sounded like she meant business, so I waved goodbye to Vinnie and ran home, holding my chest as if I had been shot in the heart and wondering what kind of scolding I was about to get.

As I ran around the corner, Mother was standing on our front porch, wearing her bathrobe, looking around for us. I ran up the steps of the lanai as Marigold came running down the hill, screaming something I couldn't understand. We arrived home at the same time.

Looking like a ghost, Mother said, before either of us could speak, "Auntie Gladys just phoned. The Japanese are bombing Pearl Harbor."

Marigold burst out breathlessly, "I know, I know. I saw it all. Japanese planes are all over the place. Pearl Harbor is burning up. Flames are this high." Marigold stretched her arms as high as she could make them go.

Boom. Another explosion occurred in the far distance. At the sound of that boom, I threw up on Marigold's bare feet. "Ahhhhhhhhhh," she screamed. Looking down at the mess I made, I threw up again. Mother grabbed my hand, started to tug me into the house, and ordered, "Marigold, clean it up and then come inside. Percy, why do you always have to make a mess." I kept throwing up as Mother was pushing me into the house.

Marigold was shrieking, "Whaaaaat? Tell Mr. Throw-Up to clean up his own mess." She was running around the lawn, wiping her feet on the grass, trying to get rid of my throw-up.

Standing at the door, Mother pleaded, "Please, Marigold, I'm at my wit's end. I need time to think. I'm going inside and as soon as you finish cleaning up, come help me. Gladys told me to turn on the radio. Percy, get inside and go to the bathroom and wash yourself." Turning back to Marigold, she added, "Please, do this one favor for me."

"I'm always doing you favors and cleaning up Percy's messes," she barked, then stomped away to get the water hose. After she washed her feet, Marigold hosed down the front steps, yelling at the top of her voice for a Japanese pilot to drop a bomb on my head.

Mother turned on the radio on the lanai, and we immediately heard Webley Edwards, KGMB's commentator, instructing the people of Hawaii that "this is the real McCoy." Pearl Harbor was being bombed and everyone should fill up the bathtubs and stay off the streets. He instructed everyone to immediately get cars off the road and stay inside.

After Mother filled up the bathtubs, and I had changed clothes and Marigold's feet were clean, we gathered around the kitchen table as loud booms continued exploding in the distance. Marigold, itching to see the action, pleaded, "Mother, please let's go up on Rocky Hill and watch the bombing. Please. Everyone is up there. Please, Mother."

"Marigold, that's a dangerous suggestion and I don't want anything to happen to you and Percy. We're in a war now and it is very dangerous outside," Mother answered firmly.

Marigold continued pleading, "Nothing will happen to us up there, Mother. The planes are too far away, and Mr. Murray is up there telling everyone how we can protect ourselves from a Japanese invasion. He has some really good ideas."

The phone rang. It was a second call from Auntie Gladys. Hysterically, she told Mother her babies were visiting relatives who had a home next to Pearl Harbor. She and Uncle Pete were getting in their car and going to rescue them because the relatives weren't answering their telephone. She was sure her babies were dead. Uncle Pete and Auntie Gladys were back together again after their Thanksgiving dinner. Without another word, Auntie Gladys hung up, and in minutes, we heard their car screech up their drive and out to rescue their babies. I told Mother that the Japanese had better watch out because the Twins had to be our best secret weapons.

At the sound of Aunt Gladys and Uncle Pete's car leaving, Mother felt alone and abandoned. Having no one around to advise her what to do, alone, and with two children on her hands, Mother was persuaded by Marigold to join our neighbors up on Rocky Hill, who were watching the bombing. Mother said she wanted to hear Mr. Murray's plans because Daddy wasn't answering his telephone.

Mother wearing her bathrobe, Marigold leading, and I trailing behind, wanting to throw up, hiked up Rocky Hill. Arriving at the very spot where Kaina was stung by the bee, we saw Marigold was right; our entire neighborhood was standing on the cement platform and watching the action. Even Cousin Bessie was there, holding Martha in her arms.

From the top of the hill, I could see the battleships in Pearl Harbor burning. From where we stood, all the ships in the harbor looked on fire because black smoke was all around, belching into the air. In the midst of the black smoke puffing into the air, shooting red flames were licking the sky. Out of the clouds, Japanese planes were taking turns zooming into the harbor, dropping bombs and torpedoing our fleet. The surprise raid looked under Japanese control because no one was shooting Zeros out of the sky. Once, I saw a big splash in the harbor when a Japanese bomb missed a ship.

Right above us, a Japanese Zero and an American fighter were duking it out, shooting at each other. Everyone on the hill cheered the American pilot by shouting encouragement at him, waving and clapping our hands. Marigold yelled, "Get the bastard!" Just when the American pilot was about to get the upper hand in the fight, another Japanese Zero joined in and the American plane headed for the mountains. The Japanese pilot had seen us cheering the American plane and booing him and suddenly turned his plane around and dove down straight for us.

"Oh my God," Mr. Murray yelled, "the Japanese plane is coming for us! Everybody run for cover." We ran for home.

Mother, running in back of us, yelled, "Go, kids! Keep in front of me. Run." We were running faster than Flash Gordon when I heard the rat-tat-tat of bullets in back of us. The pilot was strafing us as Mother kept shouting, "Run, run, run. Faster, kids. Faster. Get in the house." Rat-tat-tat-tat, the bullets whizzed over our heads. The sound of a flat tire exploded in back of me as the plane flew right over our heads.

Behind me, Mother gasped, "Ahhh, I've been hit! Kids, run. Go. Go faster. Get into the house." I looked back and Mother was holding her chest. Spurts of blood were soiling her bathrobe. I yelled to Marigold to stop. I screamed, "Mother's been hit!" I turned and grabbed Mother to keep her from falling down on the street as Marigold ran to her other side to help me hold her up. Mother was too heavy for us and fell to the ground. She was gasping for air, pleading, "Get me off the street."

Marigold and I dragged her to the curb in front of our house as Mother kept repeating, "Get inside the house. Get inside. Protect yourselves. Listen to me, now."

My eyes began darting back and forth, thinking what to do, when an idea came into my head. I said, "Marigold, you stay with Mother. I'm going to call an ambulance." I ran into the house and because I had memorized the Queen's Hospital number when I took care of Walter, I dialed 2381. A busy signal rang. I dialed again. Another busy signal beeped. I ran into my bedroom and pulled a blanket off my bed and ran outside to Mother, who was now lying flat on the sidewalk. Marigold had stopped the bleeding by pressing her hands and body on Mother's chest. They were talking quietly.

I yelled, "Queen's Hospital line's busy, Marigold. Here, put this blanket around Mother like we did for Walter. I'm going to get Mr. McLaine. He'll take us to the hospital."

I ran over to Mr. McLaine's and pounded on his door, screaming, "Mr. McLaine, wake up. The Japanese shot Mother. Pleeeeese, Mr. McLaine, unlock the door. Now." The door opened. Mr. McLaine stood in the doorway in his pajamas, Fluffy at his side. I pointed to Mother and Marigold across the street and explained everything in a sentence.

"I'll get the car," he said. Without a word, he closed the door, looking like a man who knew how to take charge in a crisis.

I ran back to Mother and Marigold and said, breathlessly, "Mr. McLaine is going to take us to the hospital. You're going to be fine, Mother." She reached her hand out for me and said weakly, "Thank you, Percy."

Marigold was acting as brave as Joan of Arc, with her body next to Mother, trying to stem the flow of blood with her hands, and her eyes brimming with tears. I said, "You're lucky to have Marigold, Mother, because she's better than any old doctor at Queen's Hospital."

"I know that, Percy," she said. Looking at both of us, Mother took our hands and confessed, "I haven't said it for a long time but I love my children more than anything else in the world. You must always remember that."

Marigold, wiping tears away from her eyes, pressed her hands on Mother's chest, and started sobbing, "And we love you, too."

Before we knew it, Mr. McLaine had his car parked next to the curb. He helped us put Mother in the back seat and brought a pillow so she could rest her head comfortably. We sat in the back with Mother, as Marigold caressed her forehead and I rubbed her feet.

"Children," Mr. McLaine instructed as he started up his car, "keep your mother talking. Don't let her sleep."

"We will, Mr. McLaine," Marigold answered. She kissed Mother on her forehead and said, "Mother, tell us the story about Hunkacha."

"I can't, Marigold. I'm feeling funny right now," Mother answered softly.

"Please don't feel funny, Mother. Please tell us the story," Marigold pleaded. Rubbing Mother's feet, I begged, "Please, Mother, please don't go to sleep."

In a quiet voice, she whispered, coughing up blood, "Once upon a time there were two little children named Johnny and Little Patty. Their mother loved them very much...." She stopped the story and whispered, "Let me tell that story another time. Talk to me, Marigold. Keep me awake."

Marigold talked and talked and talked, making Mother answer questions she made up. Mr. McLaine drove like an American fighter pilot, ran red lights and honked his horn as he drove down Beretania Street to the hospital.

Marigold kept on saying, "Mother, I love you. Don't die. I'm sorry we went up to Rocky Hill. It's all my fault." Her tears fell on Mother's face.

"It's not your fault, Marigold. Please, don't think that. Please," Mother mumbled, trying to keep awake and trying to make Marigold feel better.

Marigold asked, gulping in air, "Mother, did you know Daddy and Kathy are going to have a baby?"

"No, I didn't. Oh, Marigold, that must hurt you very much. But it's all right, just remember there'll never be another Marigold in the whole wide world in your Daddy's eyes. You remember that, Marigold, because your Daddy has told me that a thousand times how much he loves you." She paused, coughing and asked, "Percy, are you there?"

"Yes, Mother," I answered. "Mother, I'm rubbing your feet. Your feet are getting cold!"

"Percy?" she asked again. "Yes, Mother, I'm here."

"You mind Marigold," she said weakly. The crimson spot on her bathrobe was getting larger.

"Why should I mind her? I'm only going to mind you for the rest of my life," I told her, rubbing her feet harder.

Mr. McLaine tried to maneuver the car into the porte-cochere of the emergency room but he couldn't because there was a terrible traffic jam. The army and navy ambulances were lined up at the entrance, bringing in oil-soaked, wounded servicemen from Pearl Harbor. He finally had to stop his car in the middle of the street. Looking around and seeing there was no one to help us, he sprinted out of the car to get help. I could hear him shouting at everyone, yelling, "I have a woman in my car that's been shot by the Japanese."

Waiting for him to come back with help, we tucked the blanket under Mother's chin. Marigold caressed her hair, saying, "Hold on, Mother. Hold on. Mr. McLaine is getting a doctor. You're going to be okay now."

It seemed hours before Mr. McLaine returned with a dark-haired woman. They wheeled a gurney to the car. Mother moaned as they lifted her onto the gurney. Once she was settled on it, we followed behind them quietly as they pushed Mother into the emergency room. The emergency room was jammed with sailors soaked in black oil. I looked around at the men lying on cots. They were men without faces. Each had on black masks that showed only two red eyes and a red mouth. Some of them were screaming for their mothers. The room smelled just like I knew a war would smell. It was the rotting smell of decaying rats under a house.

The dark-haired woman without a nurse's uniform told us we couldn't go any further because children were not allowed in the emergency room. She pointed to another room where we could wait. She gave us her name and told us not to forget it. Her name was Heather. She patted our heads kindly, pushed us into the waiting room and told us our mother would be just fine, and she'd come back later and get us as soon as Mother was settled in her room. Mother was taken over by an orderly, who had blood all over his whites and they disappeared into the crowd of dying sailors. Heather told Mr. McLaine to go home because he looked like he was about to have a heart attack and they didn't need any more casualties. He nodded sheepishly.

Starting to leave, Mr. McLaine asked, "Are you kids all right?"

"Yes, Mr. McLaine," Marigold said, "and thank you. Mother would have died without you."

"I am the one who owe you both everything for what you did for Walter," he said. When he said that he looked far away, as if he was thinking sad thoughts about his son.

"Mr. McLaine," Marigold interrupted. Reading her thoughts, he asked, "Anyone you want me to call, Marigold?"

"Yes, Mother told me to call Aunt Momi."

"Do you have her number?" he queried.

"No," Marigold said, looking at me, not knowing what to say next.

Trying to be helpful, I offered, "Her name is in the phone book under Prince and Princess."

"I'll find her. Don't you worry, kids." Mr. McLaine hugged us tightly like we were Walter. When he left the hospital, he was limping on his right foot. I always knew that Mr. McLaine was a kind old man.

Marigold and I sat in the waiting room all morning without saying a word to anybody. We were too scared to speak because everyone was running around in a panic. Heather never came back to get us. Holding hands, we watched the minute hand go around on the big clock on the wall. We had Mother's dried blood spattered on our clothes and smudges of it on my face. All morning, as every half-hour passed, the waiting room filled up with more people. Because there was no room, some of them sat on the floor with their backs to the wall. Everyone was crying.

Marigold asked the lady next to us what time it was, checking to see if the clock on the wall was correct. She looked at her watch and said it was around noon. Confirming we had been there for over three hours, Marigold grabbed my arm and said that we were going to find Mother's room. We went back into the emergency room and saw a Japanese lady sitting behind a counter. She acted like she was in charge. The lady had a sweaty face and big dark bags under her eyes.

Marigold asked, "Do you know the room where they put the lady that came in here about three hours ago? Her name is Deidra. She was shot by a Japanese pilot."

Rustling through a thousand papers and trying to answer the phones at the same time, the lady, not looking at us, said an off-hand manner, "Oh, yes, I remember her distinctly. She died a few minutes after they brought her in." Not looking up, she asked, "Who are you?"

"Just her children," Marigold mumbled.

The lady sat up and saw us for the first time, and reached out for Marigold's hand, saying, "Oh, I'm sorry. I am really sorry. Do you have a daddy I can call?"

Marigold's eyes welled with tears and she started to moan, crying out, "We have no one. Not any more. He's having another baby."

I put my hand on my face to make sure Mother's blood was still there. It was. I vowed to never wash my face again. I couldn't cry like Marigold.

The curse had finally struck.

U.S. Navy ships sunk in attack on Pearl Harbor, December 7, 1941.
Courtesy of Bishop Museum Archives, Honolulu, HI.

62

They Didn't Live Happily Ever After

"Where are they?" Aunt Momi shouted, pushing the emergency room doors open. She immediately spotted us next to the counter with the Japanese lady. Seeing Aunt Momi, we screamed and rushed into her arms. She rocked us back and forth, soothing us, saying, "That's all right. That's all right. It's all right." Marigold cried and cried.

I pulled away and asked, "Where's Mother, Aunt Momi? Where's my mother? I want to see my mother. I want my mother." I kept on insisting that Aunt Momi take me to my mother.

"Percy, you can't see her. You don't want to see her," Aunt Momi tried to explain.

"But I do want to see her," I demanded.

"Well, you can't," Aunt Momi said, wiping tears from her eyes.

"Have you seen her?" I asked.

"Yes." With that, she grabbed our hands and pulled us to the entrance doors, saying, "Let's get out of here. The radio says the Japanese planes are coming back."

I held my ground next to the counter and demanded, "I want to see my mother, Aunt Momi. I'm not leaving here until I see her." Aunt Momi took hold of me, shook me and yelled, "Percy, you listen to me. Your mother is dead and you cannot see her anymore."

I yelled back, "Dead like Walter? Dead like Uncle George? Dead like how?"

She yelled louder than I did, "Dead! Just dead."

Under my breath, I said angrily, "People disappear when they die, don't they, Aunt Momi."

"Yes," she answered softly, calm once more.

I looked up at Aunt Momi and said, "I don't want my mother to disappear. I want her here with me. Where do people go when they die? Why can't I disappear with them? I don't like it when people disappear."

Taking my hand again and leading me to the door, she sighed, "Me, too, Percy. Me too. Now, let's go to the car. I want to get back to Punaluu before dark and before the Japanese planes return. Now mind me."

I was so confused at that moment, I didn't know which way to turn, so I followed Aunt Momi and Marigold to the car. I sat in the front seat next to Aunt

Momi as Marigold curled herself up into a ball in the back. Marigold hadn't said one "shut up" since we had heard Mother died.

Aunt Momi headed the car towards Punaluu and flew faster than a Japanese pilot flying his plane. She kept telling me to look out the window to see if a Zero was following us. Nobody was following us. We met few cars on the road and nearly flew over the Nuuanu Pali. Aunt Momi smashed the accelerator to the floor and took the famous hairpin turn on two wheels. Soon, we whizzed past the Kaneohe airfield where soldiers were standing around dazed, looking at their bullet-riddled burning planes lying cockeyed on the airfield. Fire trucks were whirling around the field trying to put out the fires. I stuck my hand out the window when I saw a soldier on the road and made the V for victory sign.

Aunt Momi told me that this was her second trip into Honolulu. As soon as she had heard the news of the bombing on the radio, that this was the real McCoy, she raced into town and plucked her girls from the Punahou dorm. When she got home the first time, she tried calling Mother. After ten tries, she called Cousin Bessie, who tearfully told Aunt Momi that Mr. McLaine had taken Mother to the hospital. Aunt Momi tried to phone the hospital but all the lines were busy. Then, when Mr. McLaine didn't answer his telephone, she decided to make another dash for Honolulu. She told me "no Japanese planes were going to stop her." But when she drove back for the second time, the police blocked the highway into Honolulu. They wouldn't let her drive any further until it was fairly certain the Japanese Zeros had left - at least for the moment. The official word from military sources was that the fighter pilots had probably gone back to their aircraft carriers to refuel. Everyone in Honolulu, including the governor, was certain that an out-and-out invasion was to occur at any moment.

After Aunt Momi finished telling us about her morning, we screeched to a halt in front of her palace. She silently marched us through the house into the guest bedroom where Aunt Momi told us to take off our clothes and clean up. Marigold took the first shower. Betty gave her a pair of her jeans and a clean cowboy shirt to wear. After I showered, Aunt Momi brought me one of Uncle Lono's shirts. It was so big, it hung on me like one of Mother's nightgowns. By the time we finished showering and dressing, Aunt Momi had burned our bloody clothes in the backyard. I didn't wash Mother's blood off my face.

Marigold and I walked into the living room, sat down on the floor, and watched Nancy, Betty and Marsha play Monopoly. After awhile, Marigold crawled into a corner and curled herself up into the wall. No one said Mother's name aloud. My mind, by this time, had turned to mush and I couldn't think or feel anything. I was living in a big, blue bubble. I pretended I was a Portuguese man of war.

While Marsha was winning at Monopoly again - she owned everything including Park Place and Boardwalk - I overheard Uncle Lono giving orders in the kitchen, sounding like he was in charge. I tiptoed to the kitchen door and peeked inside to see the Princess-Queen, Uncle Scottie, Aunt Momi, Aunt Sissy, and her yacht-sailing husband sitting around the kitchen table, taking instructions from the prince. There wasn't a vodka bottle in sight.

The war had turned the prince into the king of the family. Uncle Lono's eyes were feverishly alive as he instructed his warlords, "If it looks like the Japanese are going to land on this beach, I want Momi to take the children up to Sacred Falls. There is a large cave above the falls where they can hide in. Momi, pack enough food to last you and the kids for at least two weeks. Take the first aid kit in the medicine cabinet and your gun. Scottie, you and me and Derek (Sissy's husband) will take rifles and protect the cave from the ridge above the falls. Sissy, you'll be the courier between the cave and us. Mama, you and Scottie go with Momi." That was one plan - there were other plans - but it was clear to everyone in the kitchen that no matter what plan was being discussed, Uncle Lono made the final decisions and he was their leader. A golden light shone in Uncle Lono's mama's eyes as she watched her baby take charge. It was a light of recognition that I would never see in my mother's eyes, a light that her son had suddenly become all that she had dreamt him to be.

Governor Poindexter declared martial law over the radio. He decreed that no one was to be out of their homes after dark. He further ordered that anyone who was caught wandering outside after curfew would be arrested or shot on the spot. We were also ordered to blackout our houses completely and, if any speck of light escaped from any home that could lead enemy planes back to Hawaii, the occupants would be sent to jail without a trial. The governor implied that because we were now in a war, the people of Hawaii had lost all their rights as democratic citizens. The governor meant business and was going to do everything possible to protect the people of Hawaii from the Japanese Imperial Navy that lurked somewhere out on the horizon.

That night we ate dinner at five and Aunt Momi tucked us in bed at six. Uncle Lono sent his family home, and he and Aunt Momi had a quiet dinner by themselves, drinking soda water. In the dark, under the bed, I heard the radio playing in the kitchen with the same bulletins broadcast over and over. I kept waiting for The Shadow to break in with his sinister cackle, saying, "Who knows what evil lurks in the hearts of men" and declare that the evil Japanese army had landed on the beach at Waikiki. I longed to hear Jack Benny's funny voice again.

Just after dark, two men from the National Guard had set up a machine gun post out on Uncle Lono's beach. They told Aunt Momi how sorry they were to hear about my mother. By six in the evening, everybody knew everything because as soon as the raids were over, rumors, true or not, flew fast and furious around the island. By nine, everyone was asleep except me. From under the bed, I could hear Uncle Lono serenading his frogs in his bedroom. At ten, when the stars were out, a plane flew right over the roof of the house and shook it, but afterwards there were no gun shots or bombs bursting.

Hearing the plane, I sat straight up and conked my head on the bedsprings. I had just fallen asleep but the plane brought me out of a bad dream. In my dream, Mother was in our kitchen cooking me a creamed tuna dinner, but she was on fire.

I got out from under the bed and looked around the room. Marigold was curled up in a corner, crying without making a sound. I couldn't go back to sleep because the top of my head hurt and I wanted to get out of the room and walk outside. I didn't care if the soldiers on the beach shot me dead on sight; I just wanted to get out of the house. I waved to the soldiers as I walked out on the lawn. They recognized me on sight as the fat boy whose mother had died, and waved back. I lay down on the grass and looked up at the sky that was filled with a thousand, twinkling stars. God had spread a very hole-y blanket that night.

A voice loomed out of the darkness and whispered, "What are you doing?" It was Uncle Lono towering above me. His voice scared me speechless. He said he was checking up on me and when he couldn't find me, went looking and saw me lying on the grass. With a blanket in his hand, he leaned down and whispered again, "What are you doing out here?"

"I'm looking at the stars, Uncle Lono," I whispered back.

"May I lie down with you?" he asked. I nodded.

Shaking the blanket out, he said, "Here, get up and let me lay this blanket down so we both don't catch cold." I got up as Uncle Lono spread out the blanket on the grass and when he finished, we lay down next to each other.

Uncle Lono asked, "You all right?"

"Yes, Uncle Lono, I am not all right. Uncle Lono?" I asked.

"Yes, Percy." Looking up at the stars, not wanting to look at him, I confessed, "I haven't cried. Does that make me a bad person?"

Uncle Lono took a little time to answer, then in a soft voice, he said, "Sometimes it's hard for a man to cry."

"Do you cry?" I said, still looking up at the stars. "Not for anyone to see me," he admitted.

"Uncle Lono?" "Yes, Percy."

I turned to him and stated, "You sounded like a king today in the kitchen. King Kamehameha would have been proud of you today."

Uncle Lono rolled over onto his side, away from me, and didn't speak.

"Uncle Lono?" I asked again. Heaving a long sigh, he muttered, "Now what, Percy?"

"Did you kill your wife with a plate?" A long silence ensued. I listened to the waves crash on the beach, waiting for his answer.

Uncle Lono rolled back to me. "Who told you that?"

I said, truthfully, "Cousin Bessie, but she lies about everything."

Uncle Lono smoothed my forehead with his finger and answered me, barely moving his lips, "I did, Percy. I killed a person, but it was an accident. I'm sorry it happened. I didn't mean to do it. I don't even remember doing it. Nothing. But I think about it a lot."

Looking into his troubled face, I wanted to smooth the deep furrows on his forehead and try to make it all right for him again, so I said, "I think you didn't mean it, too. Thank you for telling me, Uncle Lono. I like you, Uncle Lono." More waves crashed on the beach as the army men moved their machine gun to another location.

Still looking at me, Uncle Lono asked, "Percy, did you find your mother in the stars?"

"I did, Uncle Lono. Look up there." I pointed to a star. "See that star there and that one over there? I think she's living right between them. Don't you think so? Do you believe in God, Uncle Lono?"

Shaking his head, he said, "I don't know, Percy. Do you?"

I agreed with him, "I don't know either, but if there is one, I hope He's taking good care of Mother." I kept looking at the stars, trying to remember Mother's face, especially the time she had looked at me in her bedroom - loving me for a whole minute. I looked at Uncle Lono and confessed, "I'm going to really miss my mother a lot. Don't tell Aunt Momi, because that will make her sad."

"I'm going to miss her too, Percy," he said, pressing one of his fingers on my forehead. "Thank you, Uncle Lono." I wiggled my forehead up and down, thanking him for his touch.

"Now, let's go to sleep," he mouthed, "and try not to disturb the soldiers on the beach. They have a big job to do tomorrow."

"Okay," I whispered, "but after I say my prayers. I'll say them silently so I won't disturb you or them." Uncle Lono turned back onto his right side.

"Uncle Lono?" I said, tapping his back.

He started to sound annoyed and mumbled, "Yes, Percy."

"I just want you to know that I'm going to mention you in my prayers," I said, pressing my finger on his back like he had rubbed my forehead. He grunted something back that I couldn't understand.

After I had said my prayers to where I thought Mother was living up in the stars, I put my nose into the crook of Uncle Lono's back and smelled him. I mumbled into his back, "You should have been king of Hawaii, Uncle Lono, because today you acted like one." The prince didn't hear a word I had said because he was serenading his frogs. As I heard him snore, I said into his back, "My mother was cursed. I am cursed and someday I am going to break that curse. I promise you that, Mother."

I woke the next morning as the sun was lighting up the sky in crimson. It meant rain. I looked around and saw the two men at the machine gun station were fast asleep, folded in half over their gun. They looked dead, as if the Japanese had shot them in the night. Uncle Lono was gone. Then I remembered yesterday's nightmare and panicked. I ran into the house expecting to find everyone dead like Mother, but was relieved because I found Aunt Momi, Uncle Lono, and my cousins eating oatmeal at the kitchen table. I didn't see Marigold anywhere.

"Where's Marigold, Aunt Momi?" I asked.

"She's in the car waiting to go back to Honolulu." As she handed me a bowl of mush, she announced, "Eat your oatmeal because we're leaving after breakfast."

Wiping the sleep from my eyes, I took the bowl and informed Aunt Momi as I sat down, "I'm not going back to Honolulu. I don't want to go home. I want to stay with you and Uncle Lono. Nobody's going to make me go back. There's nobody living at my house anymore."

Aunt Momi, using a stern motherly voice, cautioned, "You are going back to your house because that's where you belong. That's where your mother wants you to be and furthermore, young man, I need your help. Uncle Scottie phoned early this morning and told us that the Army Corps of Engineers took over Punahou School last night, and they want all teachers' personal things out now. I want to get in there before any of your mother's belongings get destroyed, and I want to collect my babies' clothes from the dorm. You and Marigold can help me. Now eat your oatmeal."

I stood up and spoke like a mighty midget, "I'm not going. Nobody is going to make me. I'm going to stay right here. I don't want to go home. I mean it. Nobody's going to make me. Didn't you hear, there's nobody at my house any more." Looking straight into Aunt Momi's eyes, I continued, "You're going to have to catch me and make me. You're going to have to toss me into your car, but Aunt Momi, you can't because you're too old and too fat. I'm not going and that's that." I put my hands on my hips as I finished.

Uncle Lono banged his spoon on the table and said to me, "Don't you speak to your aunt like that, Percy. Make up your mind right now, you're going back. Do you hear me, Percy?" Like a boogey man, he rumbled, "I can catch you, fat boy, but don't make me do it. If you make me run after you, you'll wish you hadn't." He pounded his fists on the table and my cousins jumped out of their seats.

Uncle Lono then roared, getting up from his chair like an erupting volcano, "Are you going to be a good boy or am I going to have to turn you over my knee and wallop you?"

I took his challenge and snapped, "You'll have to catch me first, you big fat pig."

"Who did you call a big fat pig?" He looked at me and started to reach for a paper plate.

I yelled, " YOU! YOU BIG FAT PIG! And I'm not scared of you." I ran out the kitchen door and into the coconut grove. Uncle Lono ran after me, yelling, "I'm going to get you, you cocky little runt."

I yelled back, hiding behind a coconut tree, "Try and do it. You big fat pig! You big fat pig! You big fat pig!" The chase was on and everyone in the house ran out of the kitchen to cheer. What made me maddest of all was they weren't cheering for me, they were cheering for Uncle Lono. That made me so mad, I stuck out my tongue at everybody as I ran around the house. Nancy yelled, "Get him, Uncle Lono. Get him and really give it to him." I screamed at her, "I'll get you for that, Nancy."

Running back into the coconut grove, Uncle Lono was puffing and yelling at me. Looking back, I saw he had turned red in the face and that made me laugh because he looked liked a flabby, old pig trying to run like a track star. I knew I could outrun the fat on him but dumb me - when I was looking at him, I tripped over a fallen coconut and fell. In seconds, Uncle Lono was over me. Sweating bullets, he picked me up with one arm, and right away, I felt he wasn't as flabby as I thought. A hard-muscled arm held me into his chest. He carried me to the car, knuckles rubbing my head all the way as he said, "What did you call me?"

Screaming because his knuckle rubs hurt, I blurted out, "Nothing, Uncle

Lono. Nothing. I called you a prince. A king. A prince. Nothing, Uncle Lono. Please stop hurting me. Nancy called you a big fat pig. Get her. Spank her. No, it was Marsha who called you a big fat pig. Someone did, but it wasn't me."

Uncle Lono tossed me in the back seat of Aunt Momi's station wagon and I quickly rolled up all the windows and locked the back doors as fast as I could. When I felt I was safe, I yelled at Uncle Lono that I said he was a big fat pig. "Ha! Ha! Ha!" He pretended to shake the car to pieces. As Uncle Lono kept playing with me, Aunt Momi wearily got into the driver's seat, pulled her keys out of her purse and turned on the ignition. Marigold was sitting next to her, head down and her knees pulled up to her chin. Her eyes were closed and her hands over her ears. Aunt Momi reached over, patted her arm, and gave her a kiss on the cheek. Marigold sat motionless as if no one had touched her, then she opened her eyes and focused on the clouds. Black circles ringed her eyes and she still hadn't talked since the lady told us Mother died. I was waiting for Marigold to tell me to shut up.

I whined in the back seat, "Doesn't anyone remember that my mother died? Everyone should feel sorry for me. Instead everyone keeps picking on me."

"Everyone is picking on you because you ask for it. If you'd mind me and be a good boy, nobody will pick on you. Your mother would want you to behave and do everything I tell you to do," Aunt Momi scolded as she put the car in first gear.

"Well, I'm not going to," I pouted. "From where I sit, if you do what other people tell you to do all the time, you get killed." I could have bitten my tongue. I prayed that Marigold hadn't heard me. I always hated Mondays and to make matters worse, it was raining.

We drove to the main gate at Punahou. I could see that the Army Engineers had been on the campus since nightfall because they had strewn barbed wire all over the lava rock walls, and a sentry guard stood posted at the entrance. Aunt Momi told the guard who we were, what our mission was and after he checked her driver's license, he waved her through. The campus looked like it had been bombed because the soldiers had ransacked all the buildings and pitched books, financial records, student's papers, desks, and chairs out onto the lawns. Anything that wasn't useful to the war effort, the army tossed away. Punahou faculty and administrators were running from building to building, trying to save the school's belongings, collecting them into cardboard boxes. The soldiers had stacked piles of books and papers like unlit bonfires all over the campus. I saw *Sharp Ears the Whale*, one of my favorite books, pitched at the top of one of the piles.

I spotted Mrs. Mott-Smith on the lawn, packing our schoolbooks into an old suitcase. Her hair was stringing down her face as she worked. Her nose looked longer than I remembered and she was acting skittish like a deer roaming in Hunkacha's forest, waiting to be shot by a Japanese sniper. When she saw me, I tried to look into her eyes and when she recognized me, she seemed to panic and quickly looked away. She put her head down and went back to gathering schoolbooks.

I led Aunt Momi up the stairs of Rice Hall to my mother's classroom, but the soldiers had already emptied it. We ran downstairs and looked around the grounds for anything that belonged to Mother. We were too late. A mountain wind had arrived earlier with its companion, a light rain. They had blown down from Manoa Valley and created little cyclones around the campus. One of the cyclones twirled Mother's school papers into the air and sailed them down to Waikiki beach.

Near one of the piles, Marigold found Mother's paperweight. It was one of her treasures because it was a gift from her mother, who gave it to Mother when she stayed home with poison oak. The paperweight was a glass bubble with a snowman standing in its center, all alone in a field of snow. When I shook it, fake snow fell over the forsaken snowman. Marigold brought it to me, her head down like a fighting bull, and put the snowman into my hands. She closed my hands tightly over it, turned away and walked back to the car. She got into the back seat and sat with her arms clasped around her knees, and looked at the clouds again. Aunt Momi found only two dresses that belonged to Nancy and decided that any more searching was hopeless. She drove us back to our house.

When Aunt Momi stopped at our curb, I didn't want to look down because I was afraid I'd see Mother's blood on the sidewalk. To my wonderment, it glistened clean. Mother's blood was gone, as if December 7th never happened. From the car window, I looked up at the front door and waited for Mother to walk out as if yesterday had been a bad dream. As I was waiting for Mother to appear, Marigold slammed the car door and bolted up the street. Aunt Momi called for her to come back, but Marigold kept on running, not coming back for anyone's call.

I walked up the steps to our front door and found a bottle of mayonnaise with a black ribbon tied around it. I picked up the bottle, knowing whom it was from, and threw it with all my might on the sidewalk. I almost hit Aunt Momi. She thought that I had thrown the mayonnaise jar at her and yelled at me. I yelled back that I hadn't. I told her I was a bad shot and whenever I threw anything, I never hit the person I was aiming at. I hit the person I didn't want to hit. From the top of the steps, holding Mother's paperweight in my hand, I looked down at my aunt, pursed my lips, steeled my eyes, and declared, "I hate Mr. Hamada. He's not my friend any more and from now on, Aunt Momi, I don't want anyone to touch me or kiss me. I just don't want that because I'm not going to cry because I have things to do."

"Percy!" she said, aghast.

I made two fists with my hands and sounded like Uncle Lono, growling, "I mean it. I have things to do and I mean to do them and crying isn't one of them. Do you understand me?" I was as surprised as Aunt Momi was at what I was saying. She looked at me as if I had suddenly gone off my rocker.

I had things to do and I wasn't going to tell anybody about them, not even Agnes or Gertrude. I was determined that no one, nobody, was going to stop me from doing what I was planning in my head. I had learned that when I told anybody what I was going to do and they thought it was a crazy idea, they'd always try to stop me, saying, "You can't do that! That's impossible. It's not done." Well, I wasn't going to make that mistake this time because what I had to do was too important. I was only going to tell God.

Still wearing Uncle Lono's shirt, from the front door of our house, I looked down at Aunt Momi and made another declaration, which I meant to keep, "And furthermore, Aunt Momi, I'm never going to wash my face ever again. My mother's blood is going to stay on my face forever." I stalked into the house, changed my clothes, brushed my teeth, and washed my face - by mistake. A habit is a habit. All the while Gertrude and Agnes kept watching me, not saying a word, frightened at the change in me.

Aunt Momi phoned Betsy and Jack and asked them if they would please live in the house while she got things settled at Punaluu. What she really meant was she wanted time to arrange Mother's funeral before she had to make a decision on what to do with us. Betsy and Jack would move into Mother's bedroom that afternoon.

I hadn't had breakfast. I walked into the kitchen and found Helen the Horrible baking a roast chicken. She had been at our house since dawn, cleaning up Mother's blood on the street and making our house look normal again. People in the neighborhood had left three casseroles of creamed tuna on the kitchen table. Yesterday morning, three tuna casseroles sitting on the kitchen table would have seemed heaven. Today, they reminded me of Mother. Helen the Horrible smiled when I walked in and offered me a cookie. I wished she hadn't tried to be kind.

Looking at her crossly, I grabbed one of the casseroles off the table, picked up a spoon and went out on the front porch to eat it. I ate half of it. Maybe a quarter of it. I don't know what I ate. Maybe I didn't eat it at all. I looked across the street at Walter's room, wishing he were alive because he would have understood what was going through my mind. He would have understood how sad I was inside myself and that my mind was one big jumble. I wanted to grab my brain and tear it out of my head. Walter would have understood all of that; after all, he lost his mother, too. I covered my face with my hands and thought I heard Walter's voice saying, "I do underrrstand, Perrrcy. I'm alwayyys watchhhhhing youuu." I took my hands away from my face and looked across the street. No one was there. Walter's room remained dark.

Aunt Momi became worried because Marigold was still gone. I told Aunt Momi that the only person who could bring Marigold back was Daddy. Aunt Momi phoned Kathy and learned that Daddy had been drafted in the army on December 7th and was now in charge of the entire Honolulu waterfront. Kathy was worried sick because her baby was kicking and she hadn't heard from Daddy since yesterday. Kathy's news was not going to stop my princess finding my father. Through connections in the governor's office, Aunt Momi learned that Daddy was headquartered at Pier 6 and got him on the phone. He was shocked hearing the news about Mother. Aunt Momi told me he hadn't heard and was "devastated" learning how Mother died. Then, she gave it to him with two barrels, asking why he hadn't checked on his ex-wife and children before this.

After hearing that Marigold had run away, he told Aunt Momi that he didn't care if the Japanese navy was out on the horizon, ready to invade, because he was leaving the pier and coming to find his baby. He would be up at our house in seconds. He promised Aunt Momi that he would bring Marigold home, "Not to worry."

True to his word, Daddy arrived in minutes wearing an army uniform. I directed him to where I thought he could find his baby. I had a big hunch that he would find her standing on Rocky Hill and wishing December 7th never happened. Within a half-hour, Daddy with Marigold clinging to him walked through the front door. I heard my sister tell Daddy never to leave her, "forever and ever." He promised his baby that they would always be together like bread and jelly for the rest of their lives. He sealed the bargain with a kiss. I asked Marigold where had she been and she told me to shut up. Hearing the "shut up" made me very happy because she was normal again.

Daddy asked me how I was feeling. I told him not to touch me, but I was fine. He left for the waterfront after giving Marigold his secret telephone number and promising to call us everyday. Aunt Momi drove back to her palace after seeing our household had settled.

Marigold, completely exhausted because she hadn't slept a wink the night before, went into her bedroom and took a nap. She slept until Cousin Bessie called a meeting in our house that night. Helen the Nervous went home because she told me she had a son with a bug. It was the first time Helen the Horrible had told me anything personal, much less that she had a son with a bug. She told me "bug" meant a cold.

With everyone gone, I sat in the living room, waited for Betsy to arrive and read the newspaper.

The Honolulu Advertiser

Monday morning, December 8, 1941. RAIDERS RETURN IN DAWN ATTACK.
Renewed Japanese bombing attacks on Oahu were reported as Honoluluans woke to the sound of anti-aircraft fire in a cold, drizzling dawn. Patrols were warned to be on the watch for parachutists reported in Kalihi. Brief machine gun firing was heard from several points downtown and along the waterfront as American planes soared low over the city toward the east. Warning that a party of saboteurs had been landed on northern Oahu (Punaluu) was given early Sunday afternoon by the army. The saboteurs were distinguishable by red disks on their shoulders. (All of the above was retracted in the next day's newspaper as hysterical rumors.)

CIVILIAN TOLL: 37 DEAD, MANY HURT.

DEAD - PORTUGUESE GIRL, unidentified, age 10, address unknown, female, puncture wound left temple, to morgue....

BLOOD DONORS URGENTLY NEEDED

Betsy arrived around two with her suitcases. I put down the newspaper and went to help her. After she unpacked her things in Mother's bedroom, we tacked up sheets in the living room because of the blackout law. We changed the room from light to dark in a half an hour. This was to be our living quarters after the sun went down. Betsy and I tacked the sheets up without talking. Betsy, instinctively, didn't touch me. We ate dinner while it was still light as Marigold slept. While we were eating a tuna casserole, the telephone rang. It was for me.

Hatsuko was on the line. I took the receiver from Betsy and heard Hatsuko sobbing at the other end. Her garbled words told me that she had just heard about Mother from her father, and a navy friend called and said that Charlie was missing in action. Her friend was sure Charlie had gone down on the battleship Arizona. Not believing her friend, she had visited Tripler and Queen's Hospitals but didn't find him. I told her Charlie was a smart cookie and as handsome as any sailor could be, and that he had to be alive somewhere. I swore she would find him in a movie theater eating a tuna sandwich and not to listen to her friends. She asked me how I was doing. I told her I was fine. I asked her how she was doing. She told me she was fine. For the first time in our lives, we lied to each other.

That night, after dinner, Cousin Bessie cradling Martha and absentminded Mr. Murray, who had a huge red gash across his forehead, walked down to our house and conducted an emergency neighborhood meeting. Cousin Bessie rang up the neighbors on the hill and, without asking us, set the meeting in our house. They opened up a card table next to the piano and waited for the others to join them. They paced up and down in the living room, smoking cigarettes and discussing emergency plans in case of an invasion. Five of the neighbors arrived with flashlights. Auntie Gladys and Uncle Pete were not among them. Marigold awoke from her nap and represented our family.

I sat in the dirt outside the living room window and eavesdropped. I brought eight of Helen's raisin oatmeal cookies to keep me company. Cousin Bessie called for order but everyone ignored her. She tried again and again but was ignored. Finally she hit the card table with a big stick and everyone went silent. Her first order of the meeting was the building of an air raid shelter. It was decided unanimously that the air raid shelter would be dug in our backyard. It was to be a huge shelter because it had to seat the entire neighborhood. The shelter, as outlined, would completely destroy Mother's rose garden and Daddy's fishpond. Cousin Bessie said the shelter was really for the protection of "dear, dear Deidra's children." Cousin Bessie was making me mad the way she was using "Deidra's dear, dear children" for her own ends and taking over our house. I may be only eight years old, but I saw through that old sow. She was using us as an excuse to keep from messing up her own backyard. The next logical step, she said, was to make our house the neighborhood command post. Betsy objected. Overruled.

Everyone smoked like chimneys during the meeting. The neighbors puffed on their Lucky Strikes to keep from strangling Cousin Bessie's neck because she has turned into a dictator.

I heard Marigold's voice saying to Cousin Bessie that she loved having all the action in our house and volunteered to be her sergeant-at-arms. Cousin Bessie ordered Marigold to walk around the neighborhood at night and squeal to

"Der Fuhrer" on the houses that weren't following blackout regulations. Cousin Bessie told Marigold she was the perfect choice because Marigold had a mean look, but Cousin Bessie warned her to carry a BB gun to show everyone she really meant business. Hearing Marigold's enthusiasm, I thought she had forgotten about Mother.

By the evening's end, everyone in the neighborhood was assigned a job. The worst assignments went to the people who hadn't attended. Auntie Gladys was elected to provide all the food and drinks for all future meetings and Uncle Pete and the Twins were voted to dig the air raid shelter. Cousin Bessie finally had her revenge on the hoofer from Colorado.

The bombing had turned everyone crazy. No one in the living room was making any sense. Certainly, Cousin Bessie wasn't talking sense. I guess wars did that to people. Cousin Bessie's stupidest idea of the evening was to string a bell system from our house to hers. Her logic was that if the Japanese soldiers arrived at our front door, since our house was nearest the ocean, we were to ring the bell to give her time to run for the hills with Martha.

The meeting closed after Cousin Bessie elected herself president and Mr. Murray her assistant. She named the group the WOKS, Wardens of Kapaka Street. I named them the POKS, Pigs of Kapaka Street. I would have elected Martha, the wormy old cat, to stay home because even outside I heard the cat scraping her bottom all over Mother's clean carpet. Betsy had tried her best to take Mother's place and stem the avalanche of stupid ideas from Cousin Bessie, but she was lost without Jack to back her up.

No one mentioned Mother's name.

Jack had been drafted that afternoon to protect military telephone lines from sabotage. The army generals were drafting civilian men to help protect Oahu from future enemy bombing. Everyone was nervous because short wave radio reports coming in from Wake Island, the lone outpost in the Pacific under siege, warned that the Japanese Imperial Navy was about to return to Hawaii. We were sitting ducks.

After everyone left, Marigold found me outside and whispered in the dark, "Percy, are you there?"

"Yes," I whispered back. "What are you doing out here?" she asked, coming closer to me.

"Listening."

"Come inside. They've gone."

"Why?" I asked. "Because I'm telling you to, that's why." She was trying to act like Mother.

"Why?" I asked again. Coming in closer, Marigold quizzed, "Why won't you let me touch you?"

"Because I have something to do."

"Will you tell me what it is?"

"No," I said flatly.

"Percy, do you blame me for Mother's death?" I could hear a catch in her voice when she asked that. I didn't speak for a few seconds, letting the darkness become blacker in our silence. The only sound we heard was Betsy walking back into the living room. I thought about the skull.

I broke the spell and said, "No." I spoke truthfully.

"Are you sure?"

"Yes. You didn't kill Mother. A Japanese pilot did. You loved Mother. You'd never kill her." I said that while I scraped my fingernails in the dirt pretending I was digging for a skull.

We continued sitting in the dark without speaking and listened to Betsy empty the ashtrays in the living room. Betsy finally turned out the lights, opened a window and let the cigarette smoke curl out the screen window above us. The smoke had made the living room smell like stale cigarette butts. It was a familiar smell of Mother and Daddy's cocktail parties. We recognized it and smiled to each other.

Marigold reached for me, making her fingers into pinchy little crabs, squeaking, "Tickle, tickle, tickle."

I spoke loudly, "Stop it, Marigold. Don't tickle me. I don't want to laugh."

"Okay." She stopped. Then she said, "Percy?"

"What?" I answered cautiously.

"Thank you for not blaming me. Take my hand and let's go to bed. We'll pretend that I'm not touching you, and remember what Uncle Scottie said to us, that brothers and sisters have to always be best friends. I know Mother is listening to us right now and would want us to stick together. Com'on, let's go inside." She held her hand out for me to take.

"Okay," I warned, "but remember you're not touching me."

"I know that, silly." Marigold took my hand and led me back into the house. Betsy, waiting for us, gave us each a flashlight to take to the bathroom in case we had to "wee wee" in the middle of the night.

After I used the toilet, without the flashlight, I felt my way back to bed and slipped under the covers. I asked God in my prayers to take good care of Mother in heaven and reminded Him that Mother liked green olives in her martinis. Agnes and Gertrude were lying on either side of me, not speaking a word or touching me. As I rested my head on the pillow and looked to the ceiling, I reviewed what had happened to me in the last twenty-four hours. It all seemed make-believe. A horror movie. Before I went to sleep, I thought about my secret plan.

Martial law throughout Hawaii wa

Civilian Toll
37 Dead,
Many Hurt

As many as possible of the regular workers in the surgical dressing class of the American Red Cross will report for work tomorrow as early as possible.

Following is the casualty list from the emergency hospital up until a late hour this afternoon:

DEAD

PORTUGUESE GIRL, unidentified, age 10, address unknown, female, punctured wound left temple, to morgue.

WHITE, Mrs. M. D., age unknown, 44 Dowsett Tract, female, punc-

BLOOD DONORS
URGENTLY NEEDED

An urgent call for blood to be used in transfusions has been made by Queen's Hospital.

Any person willing to donate blood is asked to make his way to the hospital and go to the fourth floor.

wound; rt. chest, treatment, dead on arrival, to morgue.

NO NAME, age 35, male, no address, dead on arrival, had initials HAD on shirt pocket, to morgue.

63

The Funeral

After the attack, when war was declared against Japan, we all played follow the leader. The leader was *The Honolulu Advertiser*. In the newspaper, we learned where and what we were to do.

The Honolulu Advertiser

PRESIDENT ROOSEVELT DELIVERED HIS SPEECH TO THE CONGRESS ON THE DECEMBER 7TH BOMBING OF PEARL HARBOR - DECLARING WAR AGAINST JAPAN THAT - "this is a date which will live in infamy!"

EDITORIAL: "DID YOU HEAR THAT . . . Every person in the Islands has listened to countless stories in the past few days that commenced with those four words - "Did you hear that!" It is safe to say that the great majority was **NOT** based on facts. If they were facts, their telling probably contributed nothing to the peace of mind of the persons listening. If you do know facts, and their recital will contribute no good community morale, **WHAT EXCUSE HAVE YOU FOR TELLING THEM?** Why not keep them to yourself?

EDITORIAL: WAR AND ITS CHANGES

At 7:55 a.m., Dec. 7, 1941, a far-reaching change struck the lives of all who lived not only in Hawaii, but all America and the world. With Japan's unprovoked attack on Honolulu and the ruthless slaying of men, women and children in our midst, two mighty war machines were added to a world war, already engaged in the greatest conflict in history.

You are going to live new lives, and there may be many more days ahead fraught with danger. You may lose friends and loved ones. The luxuries, which you have been reluctant to give up, will be denied in ever-increasing quantities. None will go hungry no matter what the emergency, but your menus may become skimpy, but with more robust foods, less frills. You're going to take this new Honolulu, this new America, in stride——-**CHIN UP IS THE BEST AMERICAN STYLE. WALK AND SAVE GASOLINE. CONSERVE FOOD. USE COMMON SENSE -** Don't stand or walk in the streets when enemy planes are overhead, although you may assume that you are beyond range of their bombs.

    START NOW! Don't delay! Start work on construction of an air raid shelter for your family, or begin building one in collaboration with your neighbors. In war, danger of bombing from the skies is ever present.

DECEMBER 11 - JAPANESE FORCES LAND IN MALAYSIA AND SIAM. LAST CONTACT WITH GUAM WAS DECEMBER 9

DECEMBER 11 - JAPANESE FORCES LAND IN LUZON, PHILLIPPINES

DECEMBER 11 - GERMANY DECLARES WAR ON AMERICA

    After that infamous Sunday, we had one ear cocked, waiting for the bombing to begin again. The adults dieted on nerves and cigarettes. Every afternoon, sitting on the front steps, I wasn't waiting for the Zeros to return; I was waiting for Mother to drive home from school with Uku in her arms. Her car remained parked in the garage.

    War made men out of boys. That's what everyone in our neighborhood said about the Twins. When Auntie Gladys and Uncle Pete went to rescue their boys at Pearl Harbor, their sons had become heroes. Their friends, the Darwins, lived on the harbor's edge in plain sight of the American fleet. When the attack began and Japanese planes started dropping bombs on American ships, the Twins grabbed hunting guns from Mr. Darwin's den, ran out on the back lawn and began shooting at the Zeros. At least three Zeros, according to Auntie Gladys, were diverted from hitting their targets because of her brave babies. The Darwins told the Navy that the Twins kept the battleship U.S.S. Pennsylvania afloat.

    After December 7th, civilians were being cited for being heroes and the Twins' names were at the top of the list. They were the youngest heroes recorded in Hawaiian history to receive a hero's award from the Navy. Because everyone told them that they were now all-American heroes, the Twins changed overnight. Instead of skulking around the neighborhood with sunken, bony chests and BB guns, they now puffed out their chests and acted like sheriffs in a John Wayne movie. Cousin Bessie asked them to take command of our neighborhood's safety and replace Mr. Murray as Cousin Bessie's assistant. Mr. Murray was demoted to managing the air raid shelter during a raid, which meant he emptied chamber pots. Cousin Bessie treated the Twins like Greek warriors. War made strange bedfellows.

    One of the most amazing changes that came over the Twins was that they treated Marigold like a real girl. One day when Roger and Marigold were dig-

ging the air raid shelter in our backyard, Roger, looking moon-eyed, told her that
she looked more beautiful than Rita Hayworth. Marigold banged him on his
head with her shovel and told him to shut up. After that resounding clank and a
goose egg on his head, Roger fell madly in love with my sister. From that day
forward, he followed her around like a lovesick puppy and became her obedient
slave.

Betsy drove Marigold and me to the award ceremony honoring our heroes.
The governor ordered the ceremony a week after the attack to boost the morale
on the island. The ceremony was held on a drizzly afternoon. The Navy built a
portable stage in front of the statue of King Kamehameha. The statue, like all
precious objects in Hawaii, was being protected with rolls of barbed wire around
it.

Watching the Twins on the stage, standing upright like soldiers, and grin-
ning like two John Waynes, I wondered if they yearned for the good old days
under the house.

I remembered that when we sat under the house, watching a pearl appear on
Roger's thing, he told us that he had gone to heaven. I wondered if heroes ever
went to that heaven again or sat under the house to explore the wonders of pearl
making. Watching the Twins shaking hands with the admiral, I saw them naked,
turning red in the face. Maybe at a certain age, heaven ran out of pearls and you
had to act like John Wayne, who never went to the bathroom. Maybe someday, I
wouldn't like Alice Faye movies. That seemed impossible.

I knew the Twins had changed when they arrested a boy for breaking a
street lamp. But the next incident really convinced me that they had gone the
way of John Wayne. I was waiting to cross a busy intersection when they happened by, and seeing me standing alone, they escorted me across the street like
an old deaf lady. I didn't care much for them after that. I liked them better when
they used to be the outlaws of the neighborhood. Being goody-two-shoes had
turned them into boring men. It turned them into Uncle Pete. Marigold said they
still poured catsup on their scrambled eggs. I thanked God that there was some
hope because I'd hate for them to go through life being boring.

Cousin Bessie spread rumors daily. Stories of brutality, women raped, children slaughtered, men tortured, were told to me in gruesome detail every time
she stopped by our house to drop something off for her WOKS organization.
Cousin Bessie, too, had become boring because her daily war stories were the
same old thing, death, death and more death. Death, especially mine at the end
of a Japanese bayonet, was her main theme. She started to call the Japanese
"Japs." I told her saying Jap was disrespectful because my best friend, Hatsuko,
was Japanese and her husband had died on the Arizona.

Being in a war, everything changed. Without Mother around, Marigold
would only take orders from Daddy. Cross-Eyed Mama and her family left for
the Mainland on the first available Pan American clipper. It was all very secret
because they left their house as if they were going grocery shopping at
Matsuda's, only they never returned home. They locked their house silent as
mice, walls still black from my fire escapade, and teary-eyed Cross-Eyed Mama
waved goodbye to her white toothpick furniture, leaving it for the barbarian

Japanese invaders to have tea on. In the bushes, Cynthia had told me on the QT that they were going to be away for the duration, which meant for a long time. I had a last peek at her tail - for free.

The people in my mother's world were booking passage on any ship or plane available out of Hawaii. They had panicked because at night, in their vivid imaginations, they saw Japanese invaders arriving with the next Lurline to kill them. "The event," as it was called, was about to happen at any moment because *The Honolulu Advertiser* printed one disaster after another. In the Far East, Hong Kong fell. Then Singapore, and we knew for certain that we were going to be next.

Because of the grim situation, Cousin Bessie had Martha fixed. "Rape, you know," she explained. You can imagine what I asked Cousin Bessie, but she snipped back that people didn't get fixed. I longed for news of Alice Faye and all the stars in Hollywood, a place where I still felt people talked sense.

Walking down to Matsuda's to buy milk, I noticed the adults on the streets running hither and thither, round in circles, trying not to look like scared Peter Rabbits. When they saw me looking at them, they scurried away and pretended like Chicken Little that "the sky wasn't falling." When old Mr. Matsuda, the grocer, put the milk into a paper bag, I noticed he kept one eye out on the horizon and one foot itching to bolt for an air raid shelter if the sirens wailed. Walking home, I just couldn't help it - I still watched the road waiting for Mother's car to drive by and rescue me, knowing all the time the car was in our garage. With all the chaos going on around me and Mother dead, I resolved to execute my plans. I had to do something to stop the curse.

Aunt Momi set Mother's funeral for Friday, December 12th at two o'clock. She reserved Central Union Church for the service. The time was set early because of the curfew law. A small reception was planned afterwards in our home. The early afternoon service gave everyone plenty of time to attend the reception and return home while it was still light. Nobody wanted to drive at night, even if they had permission.

Driving at night had become a suicidal foolishness. All car headlights were ordered painted black except for a tiny slit scraped across the center of the headlight. The slit was supposed to keep the enemy planes from bombing the Aloha Tower and to give enough light for a driver to see the road. In reality, there wasn't enough light to keep a sober driver from smacking into a lamppost, which landed the driver in the hospital with a broken leg. Terrible auto accidents were recorded in the newspaper every day, so nobody wanted to drive at night.

Aunt Mari, Cousin Dora, Aunt Ella, and Uncle Will were all coming to the funeral. They were personal friends of Governor Poindexter and General Short and received special permission to leave their islands.

Hatsuko phoned me everyday. Each day that passed, it became more certain Charlie had gone down with his ship. The day before Mother's funeral, Thursday, I whispered to her something on the phone that I didn't want anyone else to hear. After I told her what I wanted, she promised to be at the funeral with Mary Emily.

Aunt Mari insisted that Mother's funeral be an open casket affair. She was determined to keep the family tradition even if it was wartime. After the funeral, Mother was to be buried in Oahu Cemetery in Cousin Bessie's family plot. A Kauai burial was out of the question because of the war.

On the day of the funeral, I dressed in my best shirt and pants. I wanted to look especially nice for Mother. I lacquered down my hair with Vitalis. It was the same tonic Hatsuko gave me for a birthday long ago when we went to movies on Saturdays and drank free pineapple juice at the Royal Hawaiian Hotel. Betsy drove Marigold and me to the funeral in Mother's car. Aunt Momi couldn't bring us because she was in charge of arranging the flowers in the church. I carried a brown paper bag in my hand to the funeral. I wouldn't let anyone peek inside nor would I tell anyone what was in it. Betsy and Marigold could see I wasn't going to tell them and that I was determined to bring it, so they left me alone. It was one of my secret plans that I meant to carry out and no one was going to stop me. Only Hatsuko knew.

We arrived at the church a half-hour early, and already, Aunt Mari and Cousin Dora were seated in the front pew. Uncle Lono was sitting behind them, on the right side of the aisle. I walked down the aisle and sat on the left.

Aunt Ella and Uncle Will from Hilo, Kimo's parents, walked in behind us. They were about to sit with us, but Aunt Mari motioned her sister to sit with them on the right side. Marigold sat next to me on the aisle. Mother's casket was placed right in front of us. It was so close, I could see the tip of her nose peeking above white satin. Aunt Momi draped the coffin with white carnation and green maile leis. It made the church smell like old candy baked in the sun too long.

At quarter of two, Aunt Mari walked over to us and told Marigold and me to go up and visit our mother. She tugged on my shirt to make me move out. I shook my head and said I wasn't ready to go. Marigold went up, looked at Mother, ran back, and sat with me again. I knew the church was filling up from the loud sounds of people talking behind me. I whispered to Marigold that everyone was looking at the back of my head. The air in the church became hot and stuffy because the doors were kept shut, and everyone was sucking in too much air talking and not letting any out. I imagined that this air was the kind of air Mother would have to breathe when the man in the tight black suit closed the coffin over her. At that thought, the back of my neck became prickly and blood rushed up into my head. I made a great effort to breathe because I didn't want to faint like I did in the Punahou centennial show. I bit my lips, determined I was not going to act like a weak sissy.

I looked at Marigold's wristwatch, which read one fifty-five. It was time. I got up from the pew with my paper bag and walked to the coffin. I looked down at Mother. She was prettier than the last time I saw her, but she didn't look real because someone had made her up to look like Maria Montez in a Technicolor movie. Her lips were too red, but I was glad to see she looked peaceful and the bullets weren't hurting her anymore.

I whispered to her, "Mother, I wished you had finished the Hunkacha story. I'll never know the ending now." She kept her eyes closed. I reached into the paper bag and pulled out her telephone. I placed it in her hands and then turned around and motioned to Marigold to join me. Marigold came up and stood next to me and asked, "Percy, where'd you get the phone?"

"I ripped it out of Mother's room," I said plainly.

"Why, Percy?"

Looking at Mother, I said, "Well, I thought she might like to call us sometime. Wouldn't you like to have her phone us from heaven? Anyway, I gave it to her so she could keep up with the gossip."

Marigold put her arm around me and said, "That's such a good idea, Percy. But do you think she'll know our number? She never could remember it, remember?"

I said proudly, "I took care of that. Look under the receiver. See that piece of paper? I wrote out our number 98487, just in case she forgot it and God forgot it too."

Beaming, Marigold said, "You think of everything. I'm very proud of you." She put her arms around me and gave me a big squeeze.

"Really?" I asked.

"Really, I am." Her eyes glistened with tears.

"I have something else," I said, reaching into my pocket. I pulled out two shiny copper pennies and said, "Here, Marigold, you take one and I'll take the other. This is for good luck for Mother when she gets to heaven. Mother wasn't too lucky here. These pennies will make her have lots of luck in heaven and keep the curse away. Put the face of the penny up."

Marigold put her penny on Mother's right eyelid. I took the left lid because I was left-handed. We looked down and took our last look at our mother. I wasn't going to cry.

Marigold walked back to the pew and sat down like a lady. I crumpled the paper bag in my hand, walked past Aunt Mari and ran out of the church. I had done what I wanted to do and I couldn't think of another reason for me to be sitting there with all those people. I passed Daddy in the fifth row sitting with Kathy. I did notice Kathy's stomach looked bigger then a beach ball. As promised, Hatsuko, in a black dress, was waiting for me with Mary Emily in her arms and drove me home.

When we got home, I found Helen had the house all spiffed up for the reception. She had laid out sandwiches and punch on our dining room table, like Mother always did. I walked into Mother's bedroom, opened up her closet door, pulled out her favorite black velvet evening dress, and slipped it on. I walked back out into our living room and fixed myself a bourbon and water and sat down in her favorite chair. The smell of Mother was all over me. I took a cigarette out of one of her Lucky Strike packs, held it in my hand, held the drink in the other, and waited in the darkened living room for the people to come back from the funeral. I did this so they wouldn't miss Mother so much.

Hatsuko placed Mary Emily in a basket next to me and kneeled down to smooth my brow, saying, "Percy, I have to leave now. I'm going to drive out to Waialua to see Rose and I'll try to make it back to Honolulu before dark. I'm also going to try to contact my father."

I looked at my friend and sighed, saying, "Hatsuko, I'm sorry that Charlie died. I was very mean to him and I'm sorry about that." She smiled, trying to make it all right, and said, "Charlie liked you, Percy. He understood what you were going through. He knew it was hard for best friends to have someone else come into their lives. Don't you worry about that because he learned to love you like I love you." Hearing her made me feel bad inside because I should never have been mean to my best friend's friend.

She turned serious and said, "I'm going to leave Mary Emily next to you. I know while I'm away, she'll be safe with you. Helen said she'd help you feed Mary Emily and change her diapers." I grabbed her hand and murmured, "Hatsuko, you've always been my best friend. I'm glad you're with me now because Mother has gone away for good. I'm going to need you a lot."

She looked away from me, with pain on her face and said, "Percy, you know what's hard for me to bear right now? A friend of Charlie's told me yesterday that there are still men alive on the Arizona. They're trapped underwater, caught in air-tight compartments. People know the sailors are there because they can hear tapping on the sides of the ship. So far, the divers can't rescue them. I can't help thinking that Charlie is one of them. I know he is. I can't help thinking about him trying to live to see us again. He was, other than you and Mary Emily, your mother, and Marigold, the best thing that ever happened in my life. Charlie made me feel like a movie star."

She kissed me, got up off her knees and left, while Mary Emily slept at my side. Looking at my godchild, I heard the gears of Hatsuko's car grind as she put it into first and headed for Waialua. I took Mary Emily's finger and wiggled it, and hoped Hiroshi would forget Hatsuko had married a haole because she needed Rose now - like I needed my sister. Today, I wished I were all grown up.

Cars began to arrive from the funeral. Aunt Momi, Marigold and the minister were still up at the cemetery putting Mother's casket in the ground. People walked through the front door, saw me sitting in the living room wearing Mother's dress and walked right on through to the outside lanai, pretending I didn't exist. Mother's friends and cousins were all out on the back lanai, talking about what a wonderful person my mother had been and I could hear them even whispering about me.

After Marigold arrived, she was the first to come in to see me. She was surprised, not that I was in Mother's gown, but that Mary Emily was in her basket next to me.

"Where's Hatsuko?" she asked.

"She drove out to Waialua to see Rose. We have to take care of Mary Emily till she comes back," I answered.

"You smell like Mother," Marigold said, as a compliment.

"I know."

Looking down at her bare feet, she said, "Aunt Mari asked me to come in here and ask you to change clothes."

"Tell her I don't want to."

Shrugging her shoulders and giving me a punch on my arm, she smiled, "That's okay with me. Let me know what I can do for Mary Emily." Marigold picked up the baby and make cooing sounds to her. Putting her back into the basket, she turned to me and said, "Percy, I wish I left when you did. The minister didn't know Mother at all. He talked on and on about someone I never met. Call me if you need me." She sniffed the dress once more, looked sad, and sighed, "I miss Mother's smell."

"Me too," I said, smelling the sleeve of Mother's dress. As Marigold walked out, I thought she looked very pretty in her yellow dress.

Mary Emily began to cry. Hearing the baby cry, Helen rushed in, carrying a plate of sandwiches and a glass of punch. "Percy, this is for you." She handed me the plate and put the glass of punch on the table next to me.

She said, looking at the baby, "I more better take baby back to kitchen. Baby sounds hungry. Percy, I like tell you something, your mama good person to me. She keep me even when she learn I no can cook. She know I have baby to take care of. Percy, you sometimes big pest but you good boy inside. I take baby now." Helen lifted the basket and took Mary Emily back into the kitchen. Funny, Helen wasn't really that horrible after all.

As she walked out, Cousin Dora walked in. She had her hair pinned back into a tight pug. She sat down across from me, looking a prissy spinster schoolteacher. She held a lace handkerchief and used it to dab a tear or two away from her eyes. She looked at me, blinking her eyes, and spoke like a soft wind, "Percy, you don't know how sorry I am about your mother." Pausing as she pushed down her black dress over her knees, she started to cry really hard into her handkerchief and said, sobbing, "She was just dear to me. Just a dear. I'll miss her very much."

"Thank you, Cousin Dora. Don't cry. She liked you too," I said, trying to comfort her by patting her knee. Controlling herself, she continued, sniffling, "Marigold told us how wonderful you were to your mother at the end. You must feel very proud of yourself."

After she said that, I tugged up the front of Mother's dress, placing it back on my shoulders as Cousin Dora watched. She said confidentially, "You're dressing up so that your mother won't seem dead?" I nodded. "I think that's a very reasonable thing to do. It's a very nice gesture and you look so nice," she whispered.

"Thank you, Cousin Dora." She always understood me. Sitting up straighter, she made a little cough into her handkerchief and then said reluctantly, "Aunt Mari sent me in to ask when you're going to change and come out and join us."

"Thank you, Cousin Dora, but if Aunt Mari wants me to change, she should come in here and ask me herself. I'd be glad to see her - though I don't like her very much - but I don't hate her, either."

"That's a nice thing to say, dear. I'll tell Aunt Mari that you'd be glad to see her." Cousin Dora looked relieved because she had finished what she had been told to do.

"Thank you, Cousin Dora, for coming to see me." I wanted her to know that now she could go back to the reception, her mission was done.

"I think I'd better get back in there." Cousin Dora got up, looked at me, thought better of saying anything more, then was overcome with another teary outburst. She blurted out, "Percy, Aunt Mari is really not a bad person." She turned and walked out, sobbing. I closed my eyes.

"Percy!" Aunt Mari called, standing over me. "Are you asleep?" she demanded.
I opened my eyes and looked at her, and said, "Not now."

"Percy," Aunt Mari said imperiously, "do you think your mother would have
approved of the way you've acted today?" "I don't know," I said, putting the unlit
cigarette in my mouth.

"Well, I do. This is wartime. This is not the time for your silly, childish foolishness. Is this how you're going to act when the Japanese invade us? We need
men to protect us." She sounded like Uncle Sam, telling me to join the Army.

"I hadn't thought about that," I said, taking the cigarette out of my mouth.

"Well, think about it. Now, I want you to go this very minute into your room
and change into boy's clothes. Be a man." She spoke then more like a man than
my daddy ever did.

"I will when I want to," I said, putting the cigarette back in my mouth.

"Young man, just who do you think will want to raise you now with that kind
of attitude? Who wants to have such a disobedient, silly child like you staying in
their home, and wearing girl's clothes to boot and dangling a filthy cigarette in his
mouth?" she asked.

"Guess you don't! Anyway, I plan to stay right here in my own house until I
want to leave." I wasn't going to tell her any of my plans.

Raising her hands in defeat, she angrily said, "I see there's no talking to you.
But I want you to know that I and everyone else in this house are thoroughly disgusted with your behavior. Your mother would have been appalled seeing you
dressed like that. I can't believe that you had such a sweet, loving mother and
you're doing this to her memory. I'm going to have your father come in here and
give you a good talking to." She used her trump card.

"Is he here?" I asked, surprised.

"Yes, and thank God, he had the good sense to leave that coarse woman at
home. She shouldn't have been at the funeral at all. It was bad form in my book."
She had just put me and Kathy in the same keep-out-of-sight category. "She
looked big as a house." Aunt Mari said the "she" like Kathy was vermin. I wasn't
going to take the bait.

Seeing I wasn't going to reply, she continued, "You look very odd sitting
there in that dress." She shook her head and said again loudly as if I was deaf,
"Very odd indeed." She turned away from me and stomped out of the room.

People filed by the living room as they left to go home and still they wouldn't
look at me, but I looked at them. Aunt Momi rushed back and forth, leaving me
alone, because she was busy playing the hostess and was graciously blessing
everyone for coming. The Twins, holding up Auntie Gladys, who was drunk,
walked by and gave me the V for victory sign. They had to drag the hoofer from
Colorado home because she had two too many gins in memory of her friend,
"Deeder." Uncle Pete wasn't there because he now worked for the Red Cross.

Daddy walked into the living room after almost everyone had left. He sat
down on the couch opposite me and loosened his tie. The pouches under his eyes
were bigger than I had ever seen them and were colored a deep, dark purple. He
said wearily, taking off his shoes, "Well, son, we missed you out there. Your Aunt
Momi has done everything your mother would have wanted her to. The only per-

son missing out there was you."

"I was in here. I think that counted for something, don't you?" I explained.

Looking at me, perplexed, he asked, "Son, why are you wearing your mother's dress?"

I looked at him and replied, "Daddy, did you love my mother?" He was taken aback at the question and answered quickly, "I did."

"You didn't act like it, sometimes." I wanted to say he didn't act like it ever since the night he acted mean to her when she cut her hair and we ate lamb.

Looking away, thinking about those times, he replied cautiously, "I guess it looked liked that, didn't it? But I did. She was a fine woman and a wonderful mother." He took a deep breath, looked me in the eyes and said, "Percy, grown-ups sometimes just don't know how to act like grown-ups."

I looked him back in his eyes and said, "Mother once said that she should have stuck it out with you."

He laughed. "I'm glad for your mother's sake, she didn't. I'm not easy to live with." Then he fiddled with his hands.

"I'm not glad. I wish you had stayed around." I meant every word of it.

"Hmmmmm," Daddy mumbled, wiping his brow with a paper napkin.

"Daddy, would you like a drink?" I asked.

"I would very much."

"Here, take mine." I handed him the drink in my hand. "I didn't touch it. I just fixed it the way Mother liked hers." Daddy took it from me and gulped it down as if he had just walked out of the Sahara Desert at high noon.

Watching him finish the drink, I added, "Daddy, I meant it when I said I hoped your baby would be a boy. I want you to have a boy who likes football because you already have one that wears dresses and likes Alice Faye."

Looking at the glass in his hand and then at me, Daddy said, "Percy, I want you to know that I like the son who likes Alice Faye in the movies."

"Really?" I asked. "Daddy, do you like the boy who wants to be Alice Faye in the movies?"

"You bet. But I have to admit I don't understand it," he said, with a funny smile.

"Daddy, can I tell you a secret?" "Shoot, I think I can take it," he answered.

"I don't understand me, either." I said, then laughed at myself. He laughed with me. We both wished, at that moment, that the day he yelled at me sitting at the piano in this room had never happened.

He took my hand and said, "I think that's what I like best about you, Percy. You make me laugh even when I don't want to. You have a great gift for laughter, especially at yourself. I don't laugh at myself much." He said that, trying to look happy again but it wasn't easy for Daddy to look happy unless he had a drink in his hand.

"Is that a compliment, Daddy?" I asked.

"It's as close to one as I can get, son." he said and held out a hand.

"Thank you, Daddy," I replied, shaking his hand. I fiddled with the cigarette in my other hand and continued, "Daddy, I know one thing for sure. There will never be another person in my whole life, maybe forever, maybe even in heaven, like Mother was for me. Do you know why?"

"Why?" he said, sitting back on the couch, lighting a cigarette.

"Because she loved me just the way I am."

He reached for my hand again, but I pulled it away because I remembered I didn't want to be touched. He looked at me, inhaled on his cigarette and said in a low whiskey voice, "I know that, son."

"Do you want me to change clothes?" I asked.

"Why not? That would surprise the hell out of your Aunt Mari. You'd like that, wouldn't you?"

"I bet I would," I smiled.

"Me, too," he agreed. I got out of the chair, put the cigarette on the table and hiked up Mother's gown above my knees so I could walk. Then Daddy and I marched out of the living room. From behind, we must have looked like Mother and Daddy did once upon a time, when everyone was supposed to live happily ever after.

As I walked through the lanai wearing Mother's dress, Daddy walking next to me, not touching, I greeted everyone as if I had on a cowboy suit. As we walked past Aunt Mari, I let Mother's dress drag on the floor behind me for dramatic effect. I thought she was going to faint. When Daddy and I saw the disapproving look on Aunt Mari's face, we burst out laughing. I laughed hysterically all the way to my room, took off Mother's dress and hung it up in my closet.

Wearing my bunny pajamas with the back flap down and my fanny showing, I walked through the lanai again and checked on Mary Emily in the kitchen. Helen told me she'd stay until Hatsuko returned and not to worry about the baby, and to eat the supper she fixed for me and go to bed.

After I brushed my teeth, I overheard Aunt Ella say outside my room, on the lanai, "What do we do with the children?" My ears perked up at the question and I put my ear to the wall. I then heard Aunt Mari, Aunt Momi and Aunt Ella discussing the plight of the orphans. They were now referring to Marigold and me as "the orphans." We were little Orphan Annies who didn't have a Daddy Warbucks to take care of them anymore.

I heard Aunt Mari tell everyone that she had sent Marigold home with Daddy. Aunt Momi spoke up and told her aunts that she asked Daddy if she could take custody of us. I didn't hear the answer.

What they didn't know was that I had plans of my own and no one was going to stop me from carrying them out. I swore a silent oath over my mother's body that day that I was going to make everything all right again. As I kept my ear to the wall, listening to them making plans for my future, I became even more determined to carry out mine. I knew that inside of me now, I had tons of my mother's gumption and I planned to fight any roadblock the generals outside my room were going put in my way. Gertrude and Agnes taught me long ago about promises. A promise is a promise is a promise, and a promise must be kept. I planned to keep the promise I made to my mother when I stood by her coffin today.

I was going to do everything in my power to destroy the curse, so we all could live "happily ever after."

Fort and King Streets in downtown Honolulu, with Aloha Tower at end of Fort Street, 1940. Courtesy of Bishop Museum Archives, Honolulu, HI.

64

Saturday, December 13

Ever since I could remember, everybody put in their two cents on how I should handle the good and bad that comes along in life. Hatsuko said one way to keep the bad from the front door was to throw salt over my left shoulder. I tried it and it didn't work because the bad kept banging on the front door, announcing something terrible was about to happen. Hatsuko also cautioned me that the thirteenth of every month is a very unlucky day and nothing on that date can keep a curse away. She was right. I warned anybody who would listen to me to stay in bed on the thirteenth.

I loved Saturday mornings more than I did Sunday mornings because when Mother was alive, Saturdays meant a movie, togetherness, a toasted tuna sandwich and a thick chocolate shake at Dairymen's. On Saturday, December 13th, I should have taken my own advice, strapped myself in bed, locked the door, and read the newspaper.

The Honolulu Advertiser

OVER 1,000 ARRESTED IN WASHINGTON ALONE

New York, Dec 13, (UP) —-A nationwide roundup of Japanese, Germans, and Italians continued throughout the day while Atty. Gen. Francis Biddle from Washington appealed to the governors of all states to insure that measures were taken to prevent molesting of peaceful, law-abiding aliens.

Advertisement: CHUN HOON MARKET WILL NOT BE ABLE TO TAKE AND DELIVER ORDERS UNTIL FUTHER NOTICE

A number of our trucks are being used for Defense Deliveries and we are doing our part to conserve gasoline. Store Open Daily Except Sunday from 9 a.m. to 2 p.m.

AIR RAID WARNING PLANNED TODAY - Two Alarms for Noon, 3:30 p.m. At 12 noon today and at 3:30 p.m. practice air raid warnings will be broadcast over both KGU and KGMB. The method to be used will be a transcription of sirens made up of three groups of rising and falling siren sounds in sections of three blasts per group, each about five seconds in length, interposed by an announcement in line with the following: "This is a practice air raid warning. Halt all cars and everybody take shelter."

If by chance during the trial practice it should develop into a real air raid the announcer will change his announcement, stating: "This is a real air raid warning."

HEDDA HOPPER'S HOLLYWOOD Hollywood, Cal. Through these tense days, Carole Lombard has certainly kept the crew and cast on the movie *To Be or Not To Be* in a howling good humor with all her gags. When I asked her what she'd do if she caught a Japanese parachutist landing on her ranch, she said, "Let'em come; Pappy (Clark Gable) and I haven't been banging away at ducks and skeets all this year for nothing. We've put the ranch on a wartime basis, sold a couple of horses, are growing vegetables instead of alfalfa." Atta girl, Carole! And very soon too, you'll be seeing Carole and Clark stumping the country, selling Defense Bonds.

In the early morning on the 13th, Helen shook me out of a fitful sleep and shone her flashlight in my face. She told me a policeman was at the front door and was asking for me. I looked out the window and saw that it was still dark.

I asked, "What time is it, Helen?" "Four-thirty," she answered.

Sitting up in bed, I wondered out loud, "What does he want?" Helen shook her head. "Am I going to jail, Helen?" I asked worriedly.

"You better come. Policeman say he in one big hurry and he look kinda mean," she said, putting the flashlight under her chin.

It was as if she had poured a bucket of ice cubes in my bed because I shivered all over. In my bunny pajamas, the back flap down, I jumped out of bed and followed Helen. Reaching the front door, I saw a big Hawaiian policeman pacing the lanai and smoking a cigarette. He was dark as midnight and only his big white teeth showed in the shine of his flashlight. Seeing me, he beamed his flashlight into my face as he jabbed the cigarette into his mouth. He pulled a piece of paper out of his pocket, looked at it and then at me, and said, "You da kine Percy who stay live on Kapaka Street - dis house?"

"Yes, sir," I said quickly, "but I swear I didn't do it." I raised my hand like I was pledging allegiance to the American flag. "Hmmmm. You only one young kid," he said, giving his professional once-over look.

I quickly said, "I am eight years old and my mother died on December 7th, and I seek mercy for whatever crime I committed."

Looking back at his notepad, he asked, "You know one Hatsuko?"

No matter what, I was going to stick up for my friend for whatever crime she committed and replied, "She's my best friend. She didn't do it either. Helen," I added, pointing to Helen, "tell him we have Hatsuko's baby here. Don't we, Helen? Mr. Policeman, Hatsuko's out at Waialua with her sister Rose. I can give you Rose's phone number as I am sure Hatsuko is still there."

Then it suddenly dawned on me why the policeman was here. I got excited and yelped, "You found Charlie, that's it. Didn't you? I told Hatsuko that Charlie really didn't die on the Arizona. I'm right, aren't I?"

"No," he said in a matter-of-fact voice, "your friend die in car crash."

"What?" I gasped, not understanding what he had just said. He repeated, "Your friend Hatsuko die in car crash. Car go straight down Kipapa Gulch."

My mind blanked as I kept staring at him and my mouth gaped open like I had been struck dumb. I couldn't speak. I made funny sounds, gulping in air.

The policeman, sounding worried, asked, "Boy, you okay?" "Yes," I said, still gulping in air like a dying fish out of water.

Putting the notebook back into his pocket, he informed me calmly why he was here. "We need somebody to identify body. We find your name on envelope with dis address. I thought you grown-up man. Maybe Daddy come with you."

Hearing him talk in his matter-of-fact way, every emotion of love, loss, and horror churned in my stomach and shrieked to come out and scream. But I kept them stuffed in my stomach and held them down as emotional prisoners-of-war. With my eyes clamped shut, I answered, "My daddy is in the army." He looked past me and said, "Anyone else can come?" I thought about Marigold and Betsy sleeping in bed and made a decision, saying, "No, just me. I was her best friend and I want to see her. They wouldn't let me see my mother."

Helen, behind me, spoke up, "He speak truth, Officer. Percy, Hatsuko best friend. He can do it. He plenty strong boy." Whispering into my ear, she said, "Percy, no worry. I take care of Mary Emily till you get back."

With my eyes still shut, I said to the policeman, "Now, if you will excuse me, I'll put on my pants and shirt just like Hatsuko taught me to do." I opened my eyes and continued, "Policeman, Hatsuko taught me how to tie my shoes and put on my belt. I've never missed a loop in my life because of Hatsuko. She also taught me everything about movies, too. If you will excuse me, I am going to get dressed." With my flap down, fanny showing, I walked back to my bedroom, dressed in the dark, and put on my belt and missed three loops.

Keoki Apana, that was his name on the badge, drove me down to the morgue at Queen's Hospital. Driving down Beretania Street, I asked him politely not to touch me because if he touched me, I would scream. After he parked the police car under a large monkeypod tree, without touching or speaking, I followed Officer Apana into the morgue.

The morgue was a walk-in icebox that had metal doors built into its cement walls, one on top of the other. It looked like a bakery for dead people. I shivered from head to toe as soon as we entered the room. Keoki pointed to the wall and said that inside the doors were metal trays where the "dead bodies stay." I kept my mind numb as he talked because I was steeling myself against the horrible sight that was about to slide out on a tray.

A local man in a white coat rushed into the room. He was sweating all over even though the room was as cold as the inside of my icebox. The Filipino looked me over and complained to Keoki that I was too young. "I need one adult to identify one dead body, especially one like dis one. She stay banged-up because car crashed down one cliff. Rules are rules and he's one kid."

I raised my hand and told him I was Hatsuko's only relative and I was the only person who could identify her. I promised him I wouldn't faint. Keoki told the man he had no other choice and he was in "one hurry", so Keoki ordered him to pull out the body. The morgue man raised his hands, shook his head, and said to Keoki that he was responsible if anything went wrong. Keoki told him to quit yammering and hurry it up.

Reluctantly, the morgue man walked over to a middle tray and pulled it out. I watched the man as Hatsuko's body came out of the wall like a roasted turkey at Thanksgiving. They had covered her body with a white sheet. The man in the white coat started to pull back the sheet to show me her face.

I stopped him, saying, "No, Mister, don't do that. I don't want to see her face. I have known Hatsuko since I was born. She took care of me all my life. I know all about her, so pull the sheet there." I pointed to her feet. "I'll know if it's Hatsuko. Show me that."

He nodded and pulled back the sheet that covered her legs. It was Hatsuko because her toes curled into her feet. Hatsuko told me her toes bent that way because she had to wear hand-me-down shoes that were too tight for her when she was a little girl. I walked over and wiggled her right toe. Her toe was as hard as a rock. Pulling it, I pleaded, "Hatsuko, wake up. It's time to get up." Hatsuko didn't awaken because she wasn't Snow White or Sleeping Beauty anymore - she had turned to stone. I wiggled her toe again and begged, "Please, Hatsuko, wake up. Mary Emily and I need you." She wasn't hearing me any more because I knew she was now in heaven drinking hot tea with Mother and her handsome Charlie. Finally, knowing she had joined Mother, I turned away and told the man, "You can put back the sheet. It's not Hatsuko."

"You sure?" he said, surprised. I nodded, "It's Hatsuko, but not the Hatsuko I knew. The Hatsuko I knew was alive." The man pushed Hatsuko back into the wall and said, "Got it." I pressed my lips together and forced one foot in front of the other and walked out of the dead people's icebox. The man in the white coat, walking behind me, asked what I planned to do with the body. I told him my daddy would take care of Hatsuko even though he hated her creamed tuna and she had put mayonnaise all over his food.

Driving home with Keoki, he passed me a large envelope that had my name written on it and asked me why I didn't want to see Hatsuko's face. He pressed further, "If my best friend die, I stay look at her even if she all messed up."

While he was talking, I put my head out the car window, breathed in the morning air, and watched buildings fly by. I wanted to think before I answered him. So I stared at the unlit street lamps flash by as we rode along the streets of Honolulu. The light of the morning sun revealed people standing like dead bodies in doorways once hidden in the dark. The new day dawning reminded me of when I was on Maui, when the fingers of the sun streaked into the crater of Haleakala, on the day I had locked the keys in the trunk of Auntie Lulu's car. I was reminded that bad things happen to bad people. More disturbing thoughts drifted in my mind as we drove. I saw Hatsuko's frozen toe as big as the Empire State Building, looking like a giant lemon Popsicle. Gertrude whispered in my head that I was a bad person and I deserved all the sickening things that were happening to me.

Birds screeched in the banyan trees as we passed the Academy of Arts. I wanted to yell out the car window, "Shut up. Don't you know the Japanese bombed Pearl Harbor and you have to be quiet because the Japanese will hear you and come back and kill you? Be quiet, don't you know my best friend died?" The mynahs didn't listen because they were acting the same as they did yesterday and the day before that and probably how they would act tomorrow. They were the only creatures that I observed that were acting normal. I wanted to tell the birds, watch out because their mothers could die on a Sunday and their best friend could die today. A sign on a building read, "Saturday, December 13th. Now Open. We are back in business. Buy your rattan furniture here."

I turned back to the policeman and in the new morning light, his face looked like the moon bursting with empty craters. His fingers were handsome. I replied in mid-sentence, "Because, Policeman Keoki, if Hatsuko was all banged up like the man in the white suit said she was, I wanted to remember her as she was. You see, Officer Keoki, Hatsuko was a beautiful movie star. She was prettier than Alice Faye ever was. I didn't want to see her ugly."

We passed the Pawaa Theater. The marquee read, "*Blood and Sand* starring Tyrone Power and Rita Hayworth - Show times continuous starting at 12:15 a.m." Seeing it made me think of all the matinees Hatsuko and I had seen there, eating jujubes. "Officer Keoki," I frowned, "I never told Hatsuko that she was prettier than Alice Faye." I looked out the window and watched the scenery again. Rubbing my forehead, I put my head as far out of the car as I could and started to stare at the white stripe on the road. I bit my cheeks so I wouldn't cry because I had to be strong. I now had to take care of Mary Emily. That's what Mother said godfathers are supposed to do.

When the policeman reached my house, I thanked him and said, "Policeman Keoki, you would have liked Hatsuko." He reached out for my hand, making a kind gesture, and said kindly, "Call your daddy." I backed out of the car as I clutched Hatsuko's envelope to my chest and nodded. I turned and walked up the steps to my house as the police car drove away. To my surprise, I found two bottles of mayonnaise leaning against the front door. Two black ribbons were tied around them. The mayonnaise bottles made my house a Buddhist temple for the dead. I reached down and picked up the bottles, looked at them and carried them back to my bedroom, then laid them carefully on my pillow.

I saw that Marigold and Betsy were still asleep because their bedroom doors were closed. I tiptoed into the living room and found Helen cuddled up on the couch with Mary Emily. They were drooling together. Looking at them, so content in their slobbering, I wondered if Helen would raise Mary Emily with her son. They could share bugs together. As I watched Helen cuddle Mary Emily, I wondered how I could ever have thought Helen was horrible.

Back at the kitchen table, I made an egg salad and mayonnaise sandwich while I opened Hatsuko's envelope. In it, I found Mary Emily's birth certificate and a list of instructions. In a small envelope folded in half was Hatsuko's birth certificate and her marriage license. On the front of a smaller envelope in Hatsuko's tiny writing, was written, "I trust you, Percy, to do the right thing. I love you, Percy. I'll miss you." Underneath was written Rose's Waialua phone number. I caressed the envelopes all over my face, looked at them again, then rubbed them under my nose, smelled them, and kissed them. I wanted Hatsuko all over me because the envelopes were all that I had left of my best friend.

While everyone was still asleep, I phoned Rose and told her what had happened. She burst into tears as she told me that Hatsuko had driven out to Waialua the day before and begged her and Hiroshi to adopt Mary Emily. Hiroshi stormed out of the house yelling like a samurai that he was going to divorce Rose if she took in that "goddamned haole kid." Hatsuko fled in tears. Before Rose hung up, she asked if I thought she and Hiroshi were to blame for Hatsuko's death. I didn't know what to say, so I hung up.

When Marigold got out of bed and came into the kitchen, I told her everything that had happened. She was furious and stormed around the kitchen table, scolding me. When she calmed down, I reminded her that she had been up most of the night guarding our neighborhood and that she needed her sleep to protect our house, and anyway, I wanted to do it by myself. I asked her for Daddy's secret phone number. Marigold, a born general like Aunt Mari, immediately took over. She flat out said that she was calling Daddy and that Hatsuko was her friend, too. Older sisters have a certain way of taking over their baby brother's problems.

When Marigold left to brush her teeth, I phoned the hospital and asked to speak to the man in the white suit about Hatsuko. After a long wait, someone came back on the phone whom I didn't think was the man in the white suit, and he told me a man had made arrangements and Hatsuko's body had gone to a funeral parlor. I asked him what funeral parlor and who was the person who arranged it. The man told me he was too busy and, for God's sake, didn't I know we were at war. He slammed the phone down in my ear.

After Marigold informed Daddy about Hatsuko, he made inquiries but even Daddy didn't have enough strings to pull to find out what happened to Hatsuko's body.

I figured that Hatsuko had gone to be with Charlie. Either they were in heaven having tea with Mother or she was down on the Arizona helping Charlie breathe. At least, I knew where Mother's body was buried and Marigold promised that one day we would visit her and take her flowers.

Marigold phoned Daddy every afternoon and asked when we were going to move in with him and Kathy. Daddy answered saying "soon," but he said in a worried voice that Kathy was very ill because my new sister or brother was due in days.

By ten that morning, I thought everything bad that God had planned for me on the 13th of December was now over. I sat at the kitchen table and tried to empty out. Looking at my hands, I couldn't see my veins. I reasoned that I couldn't see my veins because my blood had evaporated out of my body. I was now an empty shell, a body without blood. I started to creep around the kitchen acting like Frankenstein. After I walked around the table three times, I sat down and ate a tuna sandwich.

By 10:30, everyone in the house awakened. Mary Emily had her breakfast at lunchtime. Marigold revealed, slurping her soup, that our relatives were having a meeting in our living room that afternoon. They were to decide where the orphans were going to live and with whom. Aunt Mari had called the meeting because she had to return to Kauai on a military transport that night. As Marigold wolfed down a piece of apple pie, she told me that those old so-and-so's can go to hell and do all the planning they want, but she was moving in with Daddy and I was to follow right behind her. I didn't say anything because I had my own plans and I had them stuffed down in my stomach with my second helping of apple pie.

Helen had to go home after lunch. Her son still had the bug. Betsy said she was going to the Academy of Arts, as she had volunteered to wrap and store priceless paintings in their basement. Marigold, the neighborhood organizer, had called a meeting after lunch up at the Twins' house to schedule next week's night shift. Everyone kept busy. Cousin Bessie lectured us, "Busy minds keep scary thoughts from entering the front door." I told her it was too late for me because I had opened the door and the goblins were eating up my brain.

Helen patted me on the head as she helped me carry Mary Emily into my bedroom. I promised by crossing my heart and hoping to die that I would take good care of the baby while she was gone. I said, proudly, "Hatsuko took care of me, Helen, so I know how to take care of babies. I can take care of anybody's baby now." Agnes and Gertrude rudely jumped into the window seat because they hated babies. Like all spinsters, except for Cousin Dora, they didn't have an ounce of mothering affection in them.

They did watch us, holding their noses, as Helen taught me to change Mary Emily's diapers. On my second try, I wiped, cleaned, powdered, folded, and safety pinned the diaper on my goddaughter like a mother. I had covered all the important parts in a minute. Helen informed me that when Betsy came home from the art academy, she would help me feed the baby. I told her with a lot of misplaced confidence that I could feed the baby by myself and demonstrated. Playing doctor, I said, "You heat the milk, shake a little of it on your arm to see if it is just the right temperature, and then stick the nozzle into the baby's mouth." Helen looked surprised at my demonstration. I snorted modestly, "Gosh, Helen, I've seen hundreds of Irene Dunne and Cary Grant movies."

After Helen left the room, I sat on my bed and stared into Mary Emily's pretty brown eyes, and thought and thought, "What am I going to do with you, my little goddaughter? You just don't happen to fit in with my plans." I picked her up and we lay down for a nap like I did with Uku as I heard the relatives begin to arrive for the meeting. I stayed in my room but had my ear to the wall so I could hear their mumbling in the living room. Aunt Momi raised her voice about five times. After awhile, when it was quiet and the mumbling had stopped, I heard a knock on my door. A voice called, "Percy, are you in there, darling?" It was Aunt Ella.

I got out of bed and opened the door. Standing outside my room were Aunt Ella and Uncle Will. They stood straight as Christmas trees all covered in snow. They had turned completely white-haired since my Christmas visit last December. They now looked liked the real Mr. and Mrs. Santa Claus who lived in the North Pole with their reindeer. Aunt Ella spoke first, "Percy, would you come out on the lanai for a minute? Your Uncle Will and I would like to speak to you." "Yes, Percy," Uncle Will said behind her, "Aunt Ella and I have something very important to say to you."

Putting on my shorts, I replied, "I only have a minute because I have to watch the baby. Helen had to go home because she has to take care of her son's bug."

Taking my hand, leading me out of the bedroom, Aunt Ella nodded, "We understand that, child, and we too have to leave for Hilo this evening. So there isn't much time to speak. A military plane is flying us home after dark." As Aunt Ella spoke, Uncle Will looked at his gold pocket watch to check the time and then at me.

"Dear," Aunt Ella said kindly, "sit down. In fact, let's all of us sit down. This has been a tiring and emotional time for all of us." We sat down together. I looked out at Mother's garden where a mound of dirt had replaced her roses. Uncle Pete, the Twins and Marigold had finished digging the air raid shelter yesterday and they planned to roof it over with tin sheets on Monday. Aunt Ella, Uncle Will and I looked out at the large hole in front of us. I imagined the hole as a huge grave, large enough to bury all of Mother's relatives still talking in the living room, and I'd most definitely put Aunt Mari in first.

"As I said, this is a very important matter," Aunt Ella said as I was laying out Aunt Mari in the hole. "Are you paying attention, Percy?" Aunt Ella broke into my funeral thoughts. Looking at her, jolted out of my daydream, I muttered, "I was thinking that air raid shelter looks like a grave."

Aunt Ella sliced my morbid thoughts away, saying, "That is precisely why it is important that you hear us now. Uncle Will and I and Aunt Mari feel that it would be good for you to get away from here. Uncle Will and I want to take you back with us to Hilo. We want to raise you as our little boy. We have missed Kimo so much that we need another little boy to take his place." I frowned at the thought.

Aunt Ella continued, "Before you say anything or give us an answer, I would like to tell you how sorry I am for what I said at Christmas."

I looked at her quizzically and asked, "You mean about Santa Claus?"

"Yes. I am so ashamed of myself," she sighed. "I don't know what came over me. I told Kimo what I had done and he became very angry with me. He wouldn't speak to me for days."

Uncle Will, taking her hand in his hand, consoled her, "Now, now, Ella. You are too hard on yourself." Uncle Will kissed her hand, and I thought, postmasters who send out letters to other people to read have to be kind men. We all drew in a breath and let Aunt Ella's words sink in.

I looked down at my bare feet and thought about an answer for Aunt Ella. All I could think about was that my feet were covered in black mud. They looked like I was living in a pigsty. Cousin Rose and Cousin Nigel would be very ashamed of me if they saw my feet now. They were so dirty because yesterday, I had tramped though the dirt mound in the backyard, trying to rescue Mother's roses. The roses I found alive, I planted right under my bedroom window, at the very spot where I had played with matches. Further inspection of my feet showed that I forgot to cut my toenails. Smelling myself, I remembered I didn't take a bath last night. With that thought, I moved away from Aunt Ella and I hid my feet from her by curling my toes inward like Hatsuko's toes did in the morgue.

Suddenly, I replied, sincerely and seriously, "Aunt Ella and Uncle Will, I want to thank you for asking me to come live with you, and I have thought a lot about what you said to me about Santa Claus, Aunt Ella. But you were right to tell me that there is no Santa Claus - because there isn't one. There never was. Aunt Ella, I think God made you say that to me because He knew what was going to happen to me, and He didn't want me to be a baby anymore." I took in a deep breath and leaned back into the sofa pillows and rubbed my head because now it hurt. I continued, "I have to admit I liked being a baby. I liked being rocked in my mother's arms and having her do everything for me. Hatsuko babied me, too. I was born a baby and I wanted to stay a baby all my life - just like you, Aunt Ella." Aunt Ella started to speak. I shook my head. "No, Aunt Ella, you were right and Kimo in heaven knows it too, now. God told him why you did it and he understands now. Just like I do."

"Do you think so, Percy?" Aunt Ella reached for my hands so I quickly sat on them. Tears were welling up in her eyes, so, trying to make her feel better, I said, "Kimo was one of my best friends and I know he really loved you and me and Uncle Will very much. I now understand how much it hurts to lose someone, Aunt Ella. I really understand it."

"Won't you come home with us, Percy?" Aunt Ella asked, squeezing her hands together till her knuckles turned white.

"No, thank you, because I've made other plans which I can't tell you about right now because they haven't happened yet. But I know they will happen because I pray to God to make them happen everyday."

Aunt Ella unclasped her hands and said, "Oh, I'm so sorry. Uncle Will and I were so counting on raising you. We knew how fond Kimo was of you." She started to cry, "Oh, Percy, I was really counting on taking you home. I wanted another child to take care of." She wailed when she said, "I wanted to try again."

I know Kimo whispered into my ear because I heard his voice as clearly as if he was sitting next to me. It came to me in a flash. I jumped up and said, "Aunt Ella and Uncle Will, you can have your wish. Do you remember the name of the child that Kimo wanted to have, the little girl's name?"

Uncle Will said, "Mary Emily. Every since I can remember he was always saying that he wanted a little Mary Emily for a sister, which we never gave him."

I shrieked, "Well, she's here right now for you to take home instead of me."

"What do you mean?" Aunt Ella said, looking perplexed.

"Hatsuko's baby." I told them the whole story and how little Mary Emily had no home or mother or father. Immediately, Aunt Ella put a stop to the idea, saying, "Will, we're too old to raise a little baby. So we won't go any further into this."

I pleaded, "Please come into my bedroom and see her. I know she belongs to you and Uncle Will. I just know it. Kimo wants you to have her. He just told me so." They stood up, looked at each other, saying without words that I had just gone crazy, and were about to leave. I picked up a broom that Helen had left on the lanai floor and I waved them into my bedroom. They kept on protesting as I said, "Please go in." The broom in my hand helped to persuade them, so reluctantly they walked into the bedroom because they didn't trust a madman with a swinging broom.

When we entered the bedroom, Mary Emily had awakened from her nap and thank goodness, she looked like a movie star. I made them go over and take a good look at her. God or Kimo was a wonderful director because He had Mary Emily reach out her little hand towards Aunt Ella. I would swear on a stack of angels that I heard Mary Emily say, "Mama." Uncle Will thought he heard it, too, and said in amazement, "Did you hear that, Ella? The baby called you Mama."

Aunt Emily turned away and started to walk out the door, muttering, "I'm just too old to start this again, Will, I mean it. This is a little human being we'd be raising - not a puppy dog you can put in a dog house whenever it became troublesome."

"I know that, Ella, but I kinda like the idea of raising a little girl. I always wanted to," he said, smiling at the baby. Turning back from the door and coming into the room again, trying to put sense into his head, Aunt Ella said, "She's half Japanese, Will. What will people say?"

With a big grin on his face, Uncle Will put his arm around her and said, "Ella, that's the best part of her. From what I hear from Percy right now, Hatsuko was a pretty special person. I think we would be pretty lucky people to have her baby. Look at her, for God's sake. She has no home now, no mother, no father, and we have so much to give her."

I knew Mary Emily was going to grow up to be another Alice Faye because her timing kept on being perfect. Mary Emily again said, "Mama." Agnes said she was burping up gas. I knew she said Mama and we all heard it except jealous old Agnes who hadn't taken to Mary Emily. Uncle Will nudged Aunt Ella and asked, "Why don't you pick her up; she's calling for her mama."

Aunt Ella reached over and took Mary Emily out of her basket, and held her up in front of herself and said, "Young lady, if you think you can win me over by playing these tricks, well, it won't work. Young lady, I can't be raising a baby again. I'd be a crazy woman to do it and a Japanese baby at that. Now, don't look at me with those pretty brown eyes, Miss Mary Emily, because I'm not the pushover you, Will and Percy think I am." They kept staring at each other and making each other's acquaintance and, I'd swear to it - Mary Emily winked an eye at Aunt Ella and smiled just like Ann Sheridan, Hatsuko's favorite movie star. Aunt Emily melted when she saw the smile and then and there, she drew the baby to her chest and rested the baby's head on her shoulder, next to her cheek. Aunt Emily began to sing a lullaby and patted the baby's back. They fit together just like bread and jelly.

Uncle Will beamed as Aunt Ella held Mary Emily. His smile was the same smile Charlie used when he saw Hatsuko and Mary Emily lying together in the hospital bed. It was the exact same look, I'd swear to it. Both Uncle Will and Aunt Ella grew taller than any tree in Hunkacha's forest in those few minutes with Mary Emily in Aunt Ella's arms, and all the snow disappeared from their branches and heads. They now bloomed as vigorously as the roses that once grew in Mother's garden.

Aunt Ella and Uncle Will went into immediate action. They wanted to claim guardianship of Mary Emily before they left for Hilo. With all the proper documents in Hatsuko's envelopes, and this being wartime, all they needed was the military governor's official permission to let them take the baby to the Big Island. Everyone knew that martial law, now the rule in Hawaii, meant that whatever the military governor decreed became a done deed, so they phoned his office. Being that Uncle Will worked for the government, all they had to do was to sign papers in the governor's office. I reminded Uncle Will and Aunt Ella that Marigold and I were Mary Emily's godparents if anything went wrong, so there was nothing to worry about. Aunt Ella kept saying back to me, "I hope I know what I am doing. It's so fast, Percy." But with another look at Mary Emily smiling like Ann Sheridan, all her doubts vanished. Aunt Mari, hearing the news, wanted to commit her sister into the Kaneohe Mental Hospital.

I kissed Aunt Ella goodbye and whispered to her that there really was a Santa Claus after all, and Mary Emily had found Santa and his wife living in Hilo. She cried as I added, "Please promise to tell Mary Emily when she grows up that her mother was a real movie star." Aunt Ella wanted to hold me but I told her I wasn't touchable right now. I thanked Uncle Will for wanting me and shook his hand. I told him shaking hands didn't count as touching because, when gentlemen shook hands with other gentlemen, they acted like they weren't touching each other. As they drove away, I yelled after them, "God makes everything happen in one day, the good and the bad."

I kept Hatsuko's birth certificate and marriage license with me and laid them next to Mother's paperweight, the snowman standing alone in a glass bubble, and Mr. Hamada's bottles of mayonnaise. When I died, I said to myself, the collection would belong to Mary Emily.

Aunt Mari got into the swing of things and wanted to copy her sister. She was not to be outdone by anyone. She told Aunt Momi that she was going to adopt Marigold and leave all her money to my sister. Aunt Momi wouldn't hear of it and after Marigold heard about it, she clenched her fists and said adamantly, she was not going to live with anybody but her daddy. Hearing that, Aunt Mari left our house steaming like a choo choo train, as she said no one had refused her anything in her whole life. We watched from the porch as Aunt Mari behind the wheel and Cousin Dora at her side drove away on their orange broom.

Marigold, a cigarette dangling out of her mouth, scratched her behind, let out a whistle and said, "Boy, I sure was on some fast trip. I went from rags to riches to rags again." Marigold knew she had just been cut out of Aunt Mari's will. As soon as Aunt Mari left, everyone went home. The meeting was not successful as Marigold and I were still cast adrift, bobbing up and down in a stormy sea without Mother. Aunt Momi told us not to worry as she left for Punaluu and the problems at home that awaited her. What Aunt Momi didn't understand was that we weren't worried in the slightest.

Helen came back to our house mid-afternoon. Her son was well again and "bug-less" because a neighbor had taken care of him by giving him a big dose of milk of magnesia. I told Helen I never wanted that bug. She was also relieved to hear that Mary Emily was going to be adopted because having to take care of two children with bugs might have put her in a bad mood again. Since December 7th, Helen, in my mind, had become a great big Technicolor movie star.

The afternoon newspaper, *The Star Bulletin*, was delivered early. The headline read in big bold capital letters that the most infamous Japanese spy of the war had been captured in the late morning hours. He stupidly revealed himself at a Buddhist temple. He was now being kept in secret seclusion somewhere on the island. The army was going to transport him under heavy guard to Sand Island, the newly erected prison for war criminals. It was rumored in the paper that the transfer was to be that afternoon. The trial for treason would be set at a later date. His temporary place of imprisonment was being kept a dark secret because the newspaper said the spy was a slippery, dangerous character. It had to be Mr. Hamada.

I ran up to Cousin Bessie's house because she knew everything about everybody - more than the FBI, more than President Roosevelt and, this I never told anyone though everyone accused me of saying it, more than God. I was joking when I said that because God, I hoped, knew more than Cousin Bessie.

I knocked on her front door and heard a muffled, faint "Come on in." I walked in and found Cousin Bessie on her hands and knees with Martha beside her. Martha was rubbing her cat fanny all over maps that Cousin Bessie had spread all over the living room floor. Cousin Bessie, with a red pencil in hand, was poring over the maps and scratching them up. She told me right away that she was trying to out-smart the evil General Tojo and was going to figure out on what Oahu beaches he was planning to land his troops.

I got right to the point and said, "Cousin Bessie, they caught the biggest spy in all Hawaii this morning." She said nonchalantly, "Oh, I know that." She wasn't pay-ing attention to what I was saying, so I said quickly, before she could think, "Where are they keeping him?"

She hummed, while scratching lines on the map, "Punahou School. On the stage at Dillingham Hall." Before she could think, I zapped, "When are they going to move him to Sand Island?" She zapped back, "This afternoon at five-thirty."

"What gate?" I asked. "The main gate," she answered.

I said, sounding like the FBI, "Cousin Bessie, you're under arrest. You just told me three big military secrets. Ha! Ha! Ha! You're going to prison and I'm going to send you there."

"Whaaaaaat?" she screamed. I laughed before she could get upset with me, say-ing, "Just kidding. But thank you for the information."

I started for the front door as she came out of her fog and stood up, yelling at me, "Percy! Percy, please don't you dare tell anyone what I told you. I'd be sent to prison for telling you that information. You caught me off guard. I wasn't paying any attention to you."

I smiled like her cat, Martha, "Cousin Bessie, you're a terrible spy because you blab everything. But I won't tell on you because if you go to jail, I'll never hear any more news. What time is it?" Annoyed, she pointed to the grandfather clock nearby. "Look up there, you miserable little boy. Can't you see for yourself, it's almost five."

I started to leave, mumbling to myself, "I have enough time."

She stopped me at the door by saying, "Percy, did you hear about Mr. McLaine?"

I stopped and turned to her, scared to hear what she was about to tell me, and mumbled, "No, I haven't seen him since he took us to the hospital. What happened to him? Did he die, too?"

"No, his relatives on the Mainland made him leave Hawaii. He's gone. It was all very secret," she said, pleased that she had news that I didn't know.

"No wonder I didn't see him at the funeral. Did he take Fluffy with him?" I asked.

"No," she said, looking away, going back to her maps.

"Where is Fluffy?" I asked.

"I was sworn not to tell you," she said, kneeling down on the carpet and re-arranging her maps. "Who told you to do that?" I said, standing over her.

"Everyone, and I never reveal my sources. Anyway, I swore I wouldn't tell you." She picked up a red pencil and waved it at me.

"Don't wave that pencil at me. Okay, what happened to Fluffy? You tell me or I'll phone the FBI right now and tell them what you just told me," I said in my most threatening voice.

"You're a blackmailer, Percy. I'm shocked at you." I kept looking at her like I meant what I just said. It didn't take her a minute to change her mind, so she 'fessed up, sighing, "Oh well, you might as well know, Mr. McLaine had that mangy old dog put to sleep."

"He killed Fluffy? He murdered Fluffy?" I said, not believing my ears.

Trying to calm me, she said, gently, "It was a very kind thing to do." My eyes started blinking fast. "No, it wasn't," I said vehemently, "I would have taken care of Fluffy." It was another stab to my heart.

She changed the subject to throw me off and reminded me, "Why did you want to know what time it was?"

"Oh, I forgot but I've got to go." I ran from her house like Cinderella, down the hill, and headed for the front gate of Punahou School, all the time thinking about Fluffy - my little Bullet, now having tea with Mother, Hatsuko and Charlie. I couldn't stand to have any more people dying on me. I had to stop the curse from killing the people I loved.

I arrived at the Punahou gate, panting. As I stood by the entrance, I hoped I hadn't missed Mr. Hamada. I knew the truck would have to stop to be checked through and it would at least give me a moment to see my spy friend. The guard at the gate and I were the only people standing around and he stared suspiciously at me. Seeing I was little and fat wiped any thought of danger from his mind.

In the distance, I heard the truck coming. It neared the gate. Suddenly, it appeared and stopped. The guard stopped the truck and looked at the driver's papers. The truck was an old Ford, camouflaged in green and brown. The back of the truck was open and men were standing up, holding onto the sides and smoking cigarettes. They were all Japanese except for a baldheaded haole man and a blonde lady. The haole man must have been a German spy because all German spies in the movies were baldheaded, and the woman was the same lady I saw drinking champagne at the Kewalo Inn.

Looking past them, I saw Mr. Hamada standing at the very back. I called out, "Mr. Hamada." He didn't move. That's when I realized for the first time that Mr. Hamada wasn't his real name. I yelled out, "It's me, Percy."

He raised his head and looked startled. I guess he was surprised to see that I was a better spy than he was and that I had found out when he was going to be transferred to Sand Island. He put his finger to his lips and shook his head and then looked at the guard. He then did something that really surprised me - he put his hands together and bowed to me as tears ran down his cheeks. Since December 7th, everyone cried, except me.

I put my hands together and bowed back. I mouthed carefully so he could understand me, "You are still my friend." He understood what I had said and closed his eyes and scrunched his face. I thought he had to go number two. The truck moved out with a jolt and rumbled down Punahou Street. Mr. Hamada kept standing in the back of the truck with his eyes closed. I watched him until the driver turned right on Wilder Avenue and disappeared.

The Hawaiian Islands turn dark quickly in December. It rains, too. I was soaked when I got home and my street was as black as a cave without a dragon's breath to light it, but a star twinkled here and there up in the sky, showing me where Mother now lived. I kept saying to myself as I walked home, "A friend is a friend is a friend, and no matter what Mr. Hamada did, he will always be my friend and I don't want him to die."

Betsy and Helen were on the porch, sitting in the dark, waiting for me to come home. They looked worried. It was nice to have someone still worry about you. As I climbed the steps to join them, I told them I was out saying goodbye to a friend. I asked about Mary Emily. They said she was gone. Aunt Ella and Uncle Will had taken her back to Hilo. Now, my house felt as empty as I did inside my head. I told them I didn't feel like eating, not even a mayonnaise sandwich. They thought I was coming down with Helen's son's bug. I told them that I was just feeling empty and nothing could fill me up.

Lying in bed, looking up at the ceiling, I thought December 13th was a day I would never forget even if I lived to be a thousand years old. From the time I wiggled Hatsuko's toes, shook Mary Emily's finger, made Aunt Ella cry, and waved goodbye to Mr. Hamada, God had dished it out. I should have stayed in bed and slept the day away.

When Betsy walked into my bedroom carrying a glass of Ovaltine, even in the dark, I could see she held a yellow telegram in her hand. It had arrived in the afternoon. She said she forgot to tell me about it. Betsy showed me that it was addressed to both Marigold and myself and suggested we wait for Marigold to finish making her nightly rounds before we read it. I told her that was an excellent suggestion as I was already in big trouble with Marigold for not taking her with me to see Hatsuko.

"Betsy," I said, hugging myself, "Mother would have thanked you for everything you're doing for us. I hope you will forget what a brat I was." She looked at me, thinking back to all the breakfasts where I had tortured her.

"Betsy?" I said again. I could see she was about to cry and she said quickly, "What? Make it snappy. I have to help Helen." She made that up about having to help Helen. Wanting her to forget every bratty thing Marigold and I did to her, I said, "You're going to be a great mom." She handed me the Ovaltine and left.

I knew that telegram had to come. Now I had to think of all the things I had to do to carry out the plan. In the midst of thinking, I fell asleep from the exhaustion of the day with Agnes and Gertrude beside me. I dreamed of Kimo in his plane under the English Channel, trying to get out of his cockpit. This time I had the key and unlocked it. Kimo thanked me for taking care of Mary Emily. We swam to the surface together. Mary Emily, Uncle Will and Aunt Ella, Mother, Hatsuko, Walter, and Charlie were waiting for us. They lifted us into the lifeboat. Fluffy and Uku licked my face and woke me up.

I walked out of the bedroom, and Marigold still hadn't come home from making her rounds. I went back to bed to wait for her, asking God to do away with the number thirteen. I practiced counting - "ten, eleven, twelve, fourteen." After I did that about fifty times so God would hear me, I asked, "God, don't let everything happen to me all in one day - please, not ever again. If You do let only good things happen to me and not let anyone else die on me, I'll give up seeing Alice Faye movies for a whole month."

God is deaf.

65

"The Days Dwindle Down to a Precious Few"

The military governor, the army, the navy, the announcers on the radio, and especially *The Honolulu Advertiser* kept repeating to the citizens of Hawaii to have courage. Everyday, from the insistent news of war, it seemed that on any day our number might be up and that the Japanese fleet would be out on the horizon ready to land its mighty forces on Waikiki Beach.

The Honolulu Advertiser

DEC. 22 - A MAJOR JAPANESE INVASION OF THE PHILIPPINES BEGINS.
DEC. 23 - WAKE ISLAND FALLS TO THE JAPANESE.
DEC. 25 - HONG KONG FALLS TO THE JAPANESE.

BLACKOUT BREVITIES

Black oilcloth has been reserved for hospitals. The thickness of light colored oilcloth is just as opaque. So-called window shades, of course, are not opaque to light.

It is not unneighborly to report your neighbors if they are careless in observing blackout regulations. Remember it is for their own safety as well as that of the entire island. Tell them first if you notice violations; if they refuse to comply, telephone 2948. But **DO NOT TAKE THE LAW INTO YOUR OWN HANDS.**

CIGARETTES and matches are the cause of many violations. We sat on the porch Tuesday night, and within an hour saw five houses light up all windows when a single match was struck. A deep puff on a cigarette is sufficient to throw a light for many miles. Admittedly, a cigarette is a comfort at times for tension, but surely we can exercise enough self-control to refrain from smoking after dark.

HAWAII THEATRE. Continuous from 10 to 4
SOUTH OF TAHITI staring Brain Donlevy, Broderick Crawford, Andy Devine and luscious **MARIA MONTEZ**, "A Sarong-Clad Goddess of Love!"

WARNING ON NIGHT DRIVING: 1) Tail lights must be painted blue/black or covered the same as the headlights. 2) Proceed to and from your home and work by the most direct route. 3) Do not travel over 20 miles per hour during dark hours. 4) In event of air raid alarm, pull to the side of the road, turn off lights, stay in your car and await the all clear signal - only special emergency cases are excepted and may proceed. 5) If you follow these instructions, you will save time and trouble; no one operating a car properly will be molested.

AUTHORIZATION TO OPEN SOME SCHOOLS IS GRANTED

Authorization for the opening of certain private schools in neighborhood classes has been granted by the office of the military governor. Authorities of Punahou School have announced that limited classes will be organized on an informal basis. These will assemble in private homes and other designated meeting places to be announced by school heads.

My life now traveled at the speed of Superman because everything around me was whirling like an out of control merry-go-round. Cousin Bessie had the job of a lifetime that made her a star. The military governor assigned her to be Director of Censorship. That meant she and her staff were to read every piece of mail that left the Hawaiian Islands. Cousin Bessie was well qualified because she was a wizard at steaming open letters and I remembered that Grandma had been her star pupil. With a staff of Honolulu busybodies, scissors in hand, they pruned from letters any information that could assist an enemy invasion. The military governor instructed "the girls" that weather conditions were at the top of his list to cut out and mentioning a volcanic eruption was a huge no-no. Ship movements in and out of Pearl Harbor written in a letter had the FBI breaking down doors in the middle of the night and many letters that left the Islands, after Cousin Bessie and her crew butchered them, looked like Irish lace doilies.

Actually, Cousin Bessie and her girls were more interested in scandals - who was pregnant, who drank too much, who slept together, and who gave parties that they weren't invited to. Cousin Bessie's popularity soared because supposedly she now had secret files on all her friends and enemies. It was no rumor because she showed me stacks of green file boxes piled up on her bookcase. What was contained inside those little green boxes struck more fear into the hearts of Honoluluans than the attack on Pearl Harbor. Filed in alphabetical order, the cards contained mounds of dirt that best lay covered up. Keeping my ear cocked to grown-up talk, I made myself Cousin Bessie's right arm, indispensable, hoping to keep my name out of her little green box. Because I repeated everything I overheard to Miss Snoop, word for word, she swore on a stack of Bibles that none of my personal dirt would ever enter her files. She lied.

To her face, I called her the Queen of the Dirt. The title pleased her so much that one afternoon she let me rummage through a file box. Boy, did I find out a lot of dirt on the Twins that even I didn't know. Because everyone began to fear Cousin Bessie and the little green boxes, they started to write their letters in code. Some of the codes were so complicated, they baffled the best Japanese and American cryptographers. Friends and relatives on the Mainland were even more baffled after receiving the letters from Hawaii, and thought a Japanese virus had attacked our brains. I kept the Queen of the Dirt at arm's length because she could turn into a raging monster in the flick of an eyelash, and I wasn't about to let her spoil any of my secret plans. Therefore, I never told her about the contents of the yellow telegram.

Marigold, dangling a dirty old cigarette from her mouth, clumped into the living room after making her rounds on December 13th and fell exhausted on the couch. She had started wearing Army boots two sizes bigger than her feet after the war started, and that made her feet clump whenever she walked. Hearing she was home, Betsy gathered us together and read the telegram. It was an invitation from Nelda and Louisa, Mother's cousins from Baltimore, Maryland. It read:

Marigold and Percy. Stop. Devastated to hear news. Stop. Come to us. Stop. Safe haven. Stop. Lovely attic. Stop. Write when arrive on Mainland. Stop. Love, Nelda and Louisa. Stop.

Marigold yanked the soggy cigarette out of her mouth and announced, "Stop. I'm not leaving. Stop. I'm staying with Daddy. Stop. Stop. STOP."

Tugging up my pajama bottoms, taking in a deep breath, I turned to Marigold and Betsy and declared, "Stop. I'm leaving. Stop. I'm going to Baltimore. Stop. Stop. Stop. STOP. And you can't stop me. STOP."

Marigold jumped off the couch and yelled, "STOOOOOP, Percy. You're a big chicken. How can you be afraid of puny little men with bayonets?" As she said that she acted like a Japanese soldier stabbing me. I ignored her by looking down at my old Coke and ink stain on the carpet.

Finishing her stabbing routine, Marigold gave me a Bela Lugosi look and snarled, "Are you listening to me? You're a chicken, aren't you?" I stepped back, raised my head and planted my hands on my hips, looked straight into her eyes and swore, "I am not chicken, Marigold. I made a promise to Mother and I plan to keep it. I'm going to the Mainland not because I'm scared to stay here, but because I made up my mind last Sunday that I was going away. I've just been waiting for an invitation."

Marigold, clumping down on her boots, screamed, "You're not going."

"Yes, I am," I screamed back. "Tomorrow, I'm going to call Aunt Momi and Daddy and tell them to put me on the next boat to San Francisco. I'm leaving. You betchum, Red Ryder, I'm leaving. And neither you nor anyone else is going to stop me. For your information, I'm doing it for you."

Marigold stamped on the carpet like a Russian dancer and asked, "For me? You're nuts. Why didn't you tell me before this that you wanted to leave?"

"Because I knew you'd say I'm nuts." Standing tall like Cousin Nigel taught me to, I said, "Marigold and Betsy, I'm not going to change my mind. I'll come back when I become a rich movie star."

"You're crazy as a coot. Daddy won't let you go alone," Marigold snipped, throwing herself down on the couch. Walking in circles in front of her, I muttered, "I'm not crazy and I'm going to ask Aunt Momi to take me."

"What did you promise Mother?" Marigold asked, putting the dirty cigarette back in her mouth "I'm not going to tell you," I said. Turning to Betsy, I asked, "Will you help me?"

Betsy, not taking sides, answered, "I'll help both of you. But Percy, you need to think carefully about what's the best thing to do."

"Thank you, Betsy. The best thing to do is for Marigold to stay here with Daddy. That's certain. Marigold, I want you with Daddy. I mean it. I belong in Baltimore with Auntie Nelda and Auntie Louisa," I said, with a finality that surprised me. Clapping my hands together, I continued, "Now that's settled, I'm going back to bed."

Marigold, throwing the old cigarette out of her mouth and shoving a fresh one in, mumbled, "You watch out, Percy. Daddy won't let you go to Baltimore." I answered, heading for bed, "You watch out, Marigold, I'll bet you five cents he will." I held out my finger and crooked it. Marigold got up and crooked hers around mine and we pulled together, making the bet final. I would have bet her a hundred million dollars that Daddy was going to let me go. I walked into the dark bedroom and felt my way back to my bed, knowing my plan was going to work.

After I announced that I was going to live with Nelda and Louisa, Daddy and Aunt Momi seemed relieved that one bother was out of the way. They said I had made a wise decision. Marigold paid her debt and gave me five pennies out of her piggy bank. I told Daddy I wanted him to book me on a ship to San Francisco right away. I made it very clear I only wanted to go to San Francisco, and Aunt Momi, without much urging, volunteered to escort me. Being in charge of the harbor, Daddy promised Aunt Momi that he'd find passage for her and her children out of Hawaii after she returned from getting me on a train for the East Coast.

After I was settled, Aunt Momi planned a quick turnaround because she was in the midst of an emotional court case. Aunt Momi was suing Uncle Hans to win full custody of her son. Her ex was fighting her tooth and nail to keep their son on Kauai. Aunt Momi wanted her baby with her and away from Uncle Hans, the German, and as far away as she could get him from the Japanese invasion that Cousin Bessie predicted would happen in May. The trial judge wasn't going to make the final decision until the end of March. There was another reason Aunt Momi wanted to escort me to San Francisco. The day after Mother's funeral, Uncle Lono had joined the Merchant Marines and was stationed in the city that I heard you entered under a gate of gold.

Marigold phoned Daddy twice a day and asked him when she should pack up her things and move down to live with him and Kathy. Everyday, he gave her the same old excuse, "Soon, baby, soon. But right now, Kathy is terribly sick."

While Marigold was waiting to move to Daddy's, I began to act normal, pretending that I wasn't leaving Hawaii. I was no fool because hundreds of signs were tacked all over Honolulu warning, "Loose Lips Sink Big Ships." I was going to do everything possible to keep my mouth buttoned up so as not to alert a Japanese submarine that I was crossing the Pacific for San Francisco. With that in mind, I decided to become invisible, too, and play follow the leader. I stopped wearing dresses, singing Alice Faye songs, telling dirty jokes, and poop-da-pooping in public. I copied all the normal things that everyone else was doing around me. I was trying to act like Tyrone Power, not Alice Faye. I did everything possible, dropping big hints, to make Cousin Bessie believe that I was hanging around Hawaii for the duration because her big lips would certainly sink my ship. Daddy advised that it might take a couple of months before he could book passage for me, especially on a ship sailing for San Francisco. Most of the ships were booked solid until June, and most of them sailed for Los Angeles. The terrifying news of daily Japanese conquests had driven civilian evacuations into second gear. Marigold didn't believe I was going and was dead sure that after the New Year, I was going to change my mind.

As part of acting like a normal person, I made myself stand in lines patiently like a Buddhist monk because after December 7th, everyone stood in long lines all the time for everything. I was on my two feet for hours in a long line at the Masonic meeting hall, waiting to be issued a gas mask and an identification card. As I waited, I hummed "The Battle Hymn of the Republic" trying to act normal, invisible and patriotic.

By order of the military governor, public schools were shut, and he had the public school teachers take charge of handing out gas masks and identification cards. The teacher who gave me my gas mask looked like Jesus. He said he taught wood shop at Farrington High School. As soon as he put "the mask of suffocating death" over my head to check the fit, I ripped it off because it smelled ooogy inside, being made of canvas soaked in formaldehyde, and I couldn't breathe. In the gas mask, I felt I was being buried alive in its own puke. Harried, not wanting to fool with me because there were a hundred little children behind me, he shoved the mask in a canvas case, slung it over my shoulder and warned, "Carry it everywhere. It's the law." I promised him that I would and that he could trust me to follow the law to the letter, and I raised my fingers and gave him the Boy Scout trustworthy salute. I never belonged to the Boy Scouts but I knew how to do it because Mickey Rooney did it in the movies.

Trying to stay normal and invisible, I replied sweetly, "It fit perfectly, sir. So perfect that I could smell my poopy bad breath. Confidentially, don't tell Tojo this, but my bad breath smells worse than poison gas. My breath is going to be America's best secret weapon. Anyway, that's what my sister tells me all the time." I thought I replied very normally, but he gave me a weird look and shoved me into the next line. When I got home, I tossed the gas mask under my bed for the duration.

In the next line, an old lady sat behind a metal desk. She had blue hair pushed up into a swirl of curls with an orchid pinned to hold it up. She looked like a blueberry muffin with a fat cherry for a nose; she taught poetry at McKinley High School. Her responsibility was to fingerprint me and make me fill in all the blanks for an identification card. In a horsy voice, she neighed, "Everyone in Hawaii has tah carry a card, deah, and you must nevah, nevah lose it." Her fingers were strong as Hercules' as she rolled and pressed my fingers back and forth over a black inkpad. The horsy-laugh lady informed me that the card would help the Red Cross identify my body if a bomb blew me to smithereens. Talking a blue streak, her eyes glowing like hot coals, she told me in minute detail how all my body parts would look splattered all over the ground. (She was from the Scottish highlands where I guessed, those things happen all the time.)

Wiping ink off my fingers, she gurgled, "I've never trusted fat people, deah." She thrust a bony finger into my belly and continued, "Ya eat too much, laddie. They'll be a lot to splatter if the Japanese bomb gets you. You'll cause a big mess. You shure a sight. So carry ya card next tah yah heart. Your mother must spoil ya a lot, laddie."

I smiled at her, and without saying a word, continuing to act normal, I gave her a loud poop-da-poop farewell when I left. I couldn't help it. I always got gassy around rude people.

Betsy and I lined up for gas coupons, butter, mayonnaise, chocolate, nylon stockings, eggs, all the basic essentials we once took for granted. If I saw two people forming a line, I would automatically hop in that line, praying that a case of mayonnaise waited at the other end. Movies were more popular than ever and long lines formed by ten in the morning because everyone wanted to be distracted from the war news. In the movies, for an hour and a half, we stopped hearing the drums of war that were beating in our heads, drums that pounded that death and destruction loomed out on the horizon where the sun rose. Most of us imagined a hundred-foot tidal wave of Japanese armies coming in on the tide and crashing on our beaches, killing everyone in sight. As I watched Betty Grable, looking as pretty as the top of a See's candy box, sing, "Cuddle Up A Little Closer, Lovey Mine," my ears were on alert, waiting for the sirens to blow. When the movie projectors shut off at six because we had to be home before dark, the drums of war began beating in our heads all over again.

In Hawaii, we weren't rationed for anything except gasoline and liquor. Ten gallons of gas a month was our allotment. To buy booze, you had to be over twenty-one and the permit was good for only six weeks. With a permit you were able to purchase four bottles of wine a week, or a quart of hard liquor or a case of beer. For the really serious drinkers, it motivated them "to get the hell out of Hawaii." Whiskey that was made in Hawaii was colored water mixed with watered-down alcohol. It made Uncle Pete puke. Uncle Pete, after a horrendous hangover, wanted me to forge my name on an alcohol permit so he could have double the allotment. I told him I wasn't twenty-one and he wasn't acting very normal. I declined to sign on his dotted line.

The Coca-Cola Company and Dairymen's both instituted a policy, "no bottle, no product." In other words, for every bottle of Coca-Cola or milk you bought, you had to turn in an empty bottle. You were really in the soup if you lost or broke a bottle. I was in the soup once when I broke an empty milk bottle while running to answer the telephone.

The reason we weren't rationed like the people on the Mainland was because there wasn't much to ration in Hawaii. The best brands of tinned food and fresh produce imported from the Mainland were gone from the grocery shelves because the ships coming to Hawaii now carried troops and supplies for the war effort. Tourists and artichokes were things of the past. Our grocery shelves were emptied of fresh fruit within a week after the bombing. Newspapers and announcers on the radio begged everyone not to become a hoarder. But everyone was like God; the words in the newspapers and voices on the radio fell on deaf ears.

If you were smart, you made new friends in the armed services because they could buy from the PX juicy porterhouse steaks, tubs of mayonnaise and gallons of gas. The Cookes, Judds, Dillinghams, Kealohas, Auntie Gladys, and Cousin Bessie dropped old friends and entertained generals, ensigns and colonels. After Cousin Bessie's first dinner party with an admiral, she could drive her Packard to one end of the island and back. After her second dinner, when she entertained a colonel, she and Martha dined on steaks for weeks. When a lonely, dried up lamb chop showed up on our dinner table, I treated it like a rare ruby from India, canned chipped beef like an amethyst from Brazil and New Zealand butter, a yellow topaz from Guatemala, and a jar of Best Foods mayonnaise was the Hope Diamond. We didn't starve because we still had cases of tuna fish stored in Grandma's shower and I never tired of Coral tuna fish fresh out of a can, swimming in oil, mixed in with Campbell's cream of mushroom soup. I considered a tuna casserole an emerald brooch.

Always on the lookout for any food sighting, I overhead Auntie Gladys tell Cousin Bessie that down on Hotel Street, fresh Waimanalo eggs were being sold - cheap. I leaped in the air and ran for home, shouting the news to Betsy and I pleaded with her on my knees to use some of our gas allotment and drive us down to Hotel Street. I told her I was aching for an egg salad sandwich. It didn't take much effort to convince Betsy to take me because she longed for a tomato omelet.

We hopped into Mother's car and drove to Hotel Street in search for the Chinese store that was selling fresh eggs. As her trusted copilot, ever alert, I spied a long line of people near a sign painted in Chinese lettering. I interpreted the sign to Betsy as reading: "Fresh eggs from Waimanalo." Seeing a long line had already formed, Betsy, too, was convinced it had to be the store. She drove like a mad woman around the block, looking for a parking space. After the third try, I told her I'd get out, get in line, and for her to find a parking spot on either Fort or Bethel Street just like Mother used to do. So I jumped out of the car, ran to the line and squeezed in behind an old *mama-san* Japanese lady, who didn't speak English. The line was moving at a snail's pace, so when Betsy appeared down the street, and I waved madly to show her where I was standing, I hadn't moved an inch since I left her. Everyone in line hooted, hollered and whistled as she elbowed her way in front of me. I told Betsy they were jeering because they were bad sports and thought she had cut in line. Looking around, she asked, "Percy, are you sure this is the egg line?"

"I'm pretty sure. Why?" I asked, looking at the people standing in front of me. She whispered, "They're mostly servicemen." "I bet they're aching for an egg salad sandwich too," I answered, not taking into account that the servicemen were leering at Betsy.

Betsy kept on insisting, "Percy, I'm sure we're in the wrong line." I gave her my "I'm right" look and spoke to her like Marigold did when Marigold thought she was dead right, "No, Betsy, we are not in the wrong line." The soldier behind me snickered to the fellow behind him when he heard me say that. I gave the GI a dirty look. He looked sixteen, was pimply-faced and acted as if he had to go to the bathroom.

Across the street, Uncle Kanaka, Daddy's best friend with the big reputation, was driving past in his car. When I saw him in his car across the street, I waved my hands up and down wildly and yelled, "Uncle Kanaka, Uncle Kanaka." After he saw us, he began honking his horn and acted like a madman being attacked by a Frankenstein monster. He stopped his car in the middle of the road and made more funny faces. His antics were holding up the traffic behind him. Betsy turned me away from his funny goings-on and told me to ignore him because he was acting like a silly, old fool and embarrassing her.

Seeing we were ignoring him, he swerved his car, made a U-turn and parked it on the curb next to us, one wheel up on the sidewalk. He flew out of the car and pointed his hand down the street, whispering something into Betsy's ear. Immediately, Betsy clutched her breast like she was having a heart attack, turned white, and gasped, "I'm going to die right now." Uncle Kanaka jumped back into his car and yelled at me, "Hi, Percy. Your time will come." He made another U-turn and zoomed off.

Betsy grabbed my hand to leave and also tried to get mama-san to come with us. But mama-san wouldn't budge and from the fierce look in her face, she said without words that she knew a fresh egg line when she saw one and remained an immovable mountain. After Betsy gave up, we streaked like roadrunners down the sidewalk for the car. As we passed the uniformed guys standing in line, they pleaded with Betsy to stay, hooting, "Baby, don't leave us now. Come to me, my melancholy baby. Boy, oh boy, baby, you're as sweet as they come. Come to me, honey. Rosie, you are my posy." Their catcalls made Betsy run faster.

Puffing behind her, I yelled, "Betsy, why are we running so fast?" Betsy stopped and grabbed me by the shoulders, wheeled me around, gritting her teeth, and snarled, "Look down there." She pointed to a sign above a door where the line of people was headed that read: "Rosie's Girls - Lots of Them. All of Them Movie Stars. Hedy Lamarr look-a-likes in from Hollywood." Underneath in pretty blue letters was "Hot Showers Included."

"Look what you've done to me, Percy. My reputation is completely ruined," she said, then put her hands to her face and burst into tears. Trying to console her by being my new normal self, I put my fingers on her cheeks, wiped away the tears and said as sincerely as Jimmy Stewart talked in the movies, "I bet Rosie sells eggs, too." She stopped crying, took her hands from her face and yelled at me, "How stupid can you be." We started running again.

A war sure shatters people's nerves.

Trying to keep up with her, I said to myself as I looked back at the sign again, "I'm not going to talk ever again because even trying to be normal and nice, everyone still hurts my feelings." I made myself turn invisible again.

At the end of the line of GI's, I stopped, waved and gave them my V for victory sign. They cheered. I wanted to hold back for an encore but seeing me, Betsy ran back, yanked me away and hissed like a cobra spitting venom, "Stop that. I'll never live this down, Percy. And it's all your fault."

On the next block, we saw a sign reading, "Fresh Waimanalo Eggs For Sale." There were only ten people standing in that line. I said to Betsy that taking a bath with Hedy Lamarr must be better than eating an egg salad sandwich.

Driving home with Betsy, I began to sing loudly,
"Oh, Johnny,
Oh, Johnny,
How you can love.
Oh, Johnny, Oh, Johnny,
Heaven's above.
You made my sad heart jump for joy..."

Betsy stomped on the brake, screeched to a halt in the middle of the street and screamed, "Percy, that's enough. Enough. Really enough. I can't stand that song, or you, or you singing it. Do you understand me? Stop it and behave yourself. Don't you realize I'm doing you a big favor just sticking around your house? I don't think you understand or appreciate what I am doing for you." When she finished yelling at me, she took in a deep breath and collapsed her head onto the steering wheel and started to cry.

Cars behind us honked, wanting us to get out of the way. Lifting her head, wiping away her tears, Betsy shifted the car into first gear, gave a left-hand signal, and turned the corner. While driving home, I looked ahead, being normal, invisible, and pretended I wasn't in the car. I said, with my lower lip sticking out and trying to hold back tears, "You won't have to put up with me for much longer, Betsy. I'm glad I'm leaving. Everyone isn't normal or nice to me anymore. I guess Mother being dead, Hatsuko dead, there's nobody around anymore to like me." I said that while we were driving past a park where rolls of barbed wire were being stored beside a jungle gym.

Betsy reached out her hand to call a truce. I pushed myself away from her and sat stiff-bodied pressed into the handle of the car door. I wanted the car door to spring open and I'd fly out of the car like Superman. For the rest of the ride, we drove in silence. I spoke first as we zoomed up our driveway and said, "It was nice of Uncle Kanaka to warn us." Betsy looked relieved that I had broken the ice and answered confidentially, trying to make like we were normal again, "Uncle Kanaka is in big trouble. His wife divorced him. She took everything he's got. He's so broke now that he had to sell his house. Now, I hear she's going to marry some big shot in the army." I thought back to Daddy and Kathy's wedding day and told Betsy what Kanaka's peanut butter lady had said to me. I remembered that someday she promised to get back at Kanaka for saying she could really spread 'em.

Relaxed, forgetting that I had hurt feelings, I sighed, "She got her revenge, didn't she?" Betsy, trying to smile like Mother, said in lady-like fashion, "Percy, please don't talk dirty like that and please let's not say anything to anybody about what happened today, especially not to Jack."

It was too late because Uncle Kanaka had spread the story like peanut butter on Love's bread. By cocktail time, everyone in Hawaii heard the story and by five that afternoon, everyone from the serious cribbage players at the Pacific Club to the KP workers at Schofield Barracks had heard Betsy and I had stood in line at Rosie's. The story changed by the time it came back to me the first time; we had not only stood in line but I had taken a bath with Rosie. A week later, a B-52 bomber crew at Wheeler Field named their plane after Betsy. Under the cockpit was painted, along with Betsy's name, a beautiful brunette in a bathing suit. The war had turned Betsy into a Warner Brothers starlet like Ann Sheridan. Jack brought home a photograph of the plane to Betsy. She could have died. I would have been jumping for joy if someone named a plane after me. The last time I heard the "egg" story was from Cousin Bessie and my name was left out altogether. I guess I was acting so normal and being so invisible now, I had become forgettable. The great tragedy of the whole story was, I had lost out on an egg salad sandwich.

After December 7th, since our campus had been taken over by the army engineers, our school days came to a halt. By the third week in December, parents wanting children "out from under" got together with other parents, and some volunteered their homes so that our education could continue. That meant that different teachers would teach us in a haphazard fashion, but they thought it was better than having children wandering the streets getting into trouble. The Territorial Government also donated a community hall so that Punahou could teach the upper grades and hopefully graduate the senior class. My new classroom was now on top of our hill in a well-known doctor's home. We met from eight to noon.

On the first Monday, in two hours, we completely destroyed a fabulously decorated living room. By twelve, the house looked like a Saturday morning sale at the Salvation Army with crayons, poster paint, ripped clothes, and scrap paper strewn and smashed on the living room carpet and furniture. Two tic-tac-toe games, in indelible black ink, were written on the lady of the house's antique Chinese wallpaper. By the second day, the lady of the house was under the covers having a nervous breakdown. We were forced to move our class to a nearby city park and play tag. In a day, we were forgiven, and our next class was held in the home of the Honolulu Chief of Detectives.

After school one day, the air raid sirens sounded. Thinking the Japanese planes were coming back, I ran for home but avoided our air raid shelter because last week, Marigold had found a pair of centipedes crawling along the benches and the day before that, she destroyed a hornet's nest near the entrance. No one was at home when I ran through the front door, so I sat in Mother's chair in the living room and waited for a bomb to explode over my head. Clasping the sides of her chair, I moaned to myself that I didn't mind so much being bombed, but it would have been comforting to die with someone holding my hand.

Waiting for the planes and a bomb to drop on the house, I started to think about all the things that had happened to me since the war began. I realized that everyone I cared about had died from the curse and had gone to heaven except Helen the wonderful. She was alive, but had left without saying goodbye because Daddy couldn't pay her salary anymore. Daddy did help her find a new job and from what I heard she made the big time. She now worked for an admiral who didn't have children.

Marigold, now the cook, was shaking a can of Campbell's cream of mushroom soup into a saucepan for dinner as she explained that since Mother died, we had only a little insurance money to live on. The insurance money hadn't arrived yet because it had to come from a faraway place called Hartford, Connecticut. She further explained that except for a few dollars donated by Mother's family and some money from Daddy, we had very little money to live on. Marigold warned, "Percy, this means no more buying toys or going to the movies or you'll end us up in the poor house. We are very lucky just to have a roof over our heads." Marigold now sounded like a grown-up. She also added that Daddy's salary had been cut in half since the Army drafted him and, being that we were "poor as church mice," that was the real reason Daddy was letting me go to Baltimore. After I heard all that bad news from Marigold, and knowing God needed a hearing aid, it made my plan all the more important. My goal was to become Prince Lancelot and find the Holy Grail.

Waiting to hear the whistle that a bomb makes when it falls on you, I kept my mind occupied thinking about other things. I made a mental list of fourteen things that had changed since Mother died and Hatsuko, Mary Emily and Helen had gone away. Betsy worked at the Academy of Arts from nine to four: that was **one**. Jack was forced to bunk at Schofield Barracks and that made Betsy grumpy: **two**. Uncle Pete, Auntie Gladys and the Twins were busy with the war effort and didn't bother with me anymore: **three**. Cousin Bessie was cutting up people's letters: **four**. Mr. McLaine was on the Mainland: **five.** Daddy and Kathy were having a baby: **six**.

I paused while I added up my list so far and then counted further, making some of the things up. Daisy and Neal must have flown the coop to Timbuktu with Mina riding on their mother's polo ponies because we lost contact: **seven**. Everyone else was dead or with Cross-Eyed Mama and her family: **eight, nine, ten,** and **eleven**. (I counted Fluffy and Kimo in that number). Agnes and Gertrude disappeared from my window seat the night before last: **twelve** and **thirteen**. Since thirteen was a bad luck number, I rounded out the list to **fourteen** things.

After I had made out my list, sitting in the living room, waiting to die, I knew I was the only person left on earth acting normal because everyone else around me was not acting normal. And with only Cousin Bessie left to talk to and she was crazy, pretty soon I wasn't going to be normal, too. Everyday, I went up to her house and bothered her to tell me about ships leaving and arriving down at Daddy's piers. Under sworn secrecy, she told me every ship that docked and at what pier. Daddy was an army officer so he wouldn't have told me anything secret because he had taken an oath. It was settled in my mind that I was to wait patiently for my ship to come in.

The sirens wailed and the air raid was over. After the all clear signal, I lumbered into the kitchen and vowed to eat only one slice of bread with a glass of water. I was saving money. Since no one was watching, I cheated; I spread two tiny spoonfuls of mayonnaise over the bread.

God did it again! Everything happened on Christmas day. Jack came home from Schofield Barracks and brought us our Christmas dinner - a turkey with all the fixings. That afternoon, we dined like kings. We ate emeralds, rubies and diamonds.

Betsy found two wrapped Christmas presents hidden in Mother's closet that Mother must have bought after Thanksgiving. Marigold unwrapped a blue Swiss organdy dress from McInerny's and I opened a cardboard box from Kress store that had a medieval castle with tin soldiers wrapped in tissue paper. The castle had a drawbridge that went up and down like the real ones in France. Opening Mother's present in a house without Mother and a Christmas tree, it was a Thursday in July, I was on Kauai and Mother was in Tahiti.

I presented Betsy with my koala bear and Jack, the radio Daddy gave me for my birthday for their presents. For Marigold, I wrapped in old newspapers all my Oz books. Marigold gave me money for three movies with a little left over to buy a box of Cracker Jacks. She earned the money cleaning up the doctor's living room on the hill after my class destroyed it. Daddy called midday and said he wouldn't be able to see us and wished us Merry Christmas, and then he said in the next breath that Kathy had her baby. It was a boy and they named him Nathan Ward after one of Daddy's American Revolutionary ancestors. They were going to nickname him Nate. After I congratulated and wished Daddy Merry Christmas, I told him Nate sounded like he was going to be a football player.

After we hung up, Marigold looked as if she had lost her best friend and sat in Mother's chair for the rest of the afternoon, holding the blue organdy dress to her face, smelling it. Betsy and Jack went for a drive in Mother's car and they asked me to join them, but I declined because I knew they didn't mean it just from the way they were looking at each other. Wandering out on the front porch, I found a telegram sticking out from under our doormat. I ripped it open and read:

Santa Barbara, California.
Your great grandmother Liza died today. Stop. Burying right away - my girls cemetery. Stop. Never recovered Dec 7th. Stop. Deidra's death. Stop. Merry Christmas. Stop. Sally Stanford. Stop.

I stuffed the telegram in my pocket as I heard the telephone ring. It was Aunt Momi on the other end wishing us Merry Christmas. She had already used up her monthly gas allotment and was stuck in Punaluu, so she said our Christmas presents would have to wait. Marigold wouldn't speak to her because she was being sad in Mother's chair. Hearing Aunt Momi's voice on the telephone made me sad, too, missing my mother even more. After Daddy and Aunt Momi called, no one else phoned. The room in our house darkened in the afternoon sun. Only shadows of palm trees flickered on the walls. I was living in a house without light.

The afternoon paper thumped against the front door. Picking it up, in bold headlines, I read, **"JAPANESE SPY ESCAPES SAND ISLAND."** The article said that this spy was a dangerous man and the army was ordered to shoot him on sight. I smiled because I knew they couldn't keep a smart spy cooped up.

Marigold, in Mother's chair, was still smothering the Christmas dress all over her face, so trying to cheer her up, I told her I'd treat her to a movie with her Christmas money. She told me to go away and please leave her alone. With nobody to talk to, I walked down to the Pawaa Theater, used Marigold's money and saw the three o'clock matinee starring Tyrone Power and Betty Grable in *A Yank in the R.A.F.* The billboard read "A Story of Brave Men Who Fly High and Fight Hard."

The day after Christmas, I found a big box of groceries sitting on our kitchen table. I peered inside and pulled out fresh eggs, a quart of milk, New Zealand butter, a ham, canned fruit, canned tuna, lettuce, tomatoes, two oranges, and wrapped together, three bottles of mayonnaise. The word was out, even in Tokyo, that we had become poor. I had to admit that old Mr. Hamada had to be the best spy in the world.

When Betsy and Marigold came into the kitchen, I showed them what Santa Claus brought us. Marigold guessed it was Daddy. Betsy was certain it was Jack, but I smiled because little did they know, this year, Santa Claus was a Japanese spy.

After Marigold ate an orange and cornflakes, I pulled out the telegram about Grandma from my pocket. After she read it, she spent the rest of the day back in Mother's chair, covering her face with the blue organdy dress.

On New Year's Eve day, Daddy picked us up and took us to meet Nate, my new half-brother. Marigold had packed all her belongings into one suitcase. She had made up her mind that on New Year's Eve, she was moving in with Kathy, Nate and Daddy, no matter what Daddy said. Looking into Marigold's eyes, Daddy saw that standing before him was a mountain he couldn't move, so he agreed to Marigold's plan. After all, they were two peas in a pod. From the weary look in his eyes, I saw he didn't mean a word of it. Marigold gave me her brass knuckles as a farewell present to protect myself against "the bloodthirsty Japanese soldiers."

At Daddy's house, Kathy looked very pretty lying in bed with a red ribbon tied in her hair, holding a red, wrinkled little baby in her arms. I shook the baby's finger, then said all the right things normal people say to a future football star, "Gee, you look big for a baby." After the audience with Kathy, I kissed Marigold goodbye and she told me to call her if I needed anything. She reminded me to phone Mr. Murray and tell him that he had to take over her job walking the neighborhood at night.

When I left with Daddy, Marigold looked as happy as if Mother were still alive and I could see she was going to be a big help to Kathy. She had already started to organize the baby's feeding schedule over Kathy's protests and told Daddy that she was going to cook all his meals, clean his house, shine his shoes, fix his drinks, and read the newspaper to him as soon as he got home from work. She was going to love Daddy to death.

Driving me home, I asked Daddy, "Was I red and ugly as a little baby, Daddy?"

"No, son, you were a very pretty little baby," he said, smiling at me.

I replied, beaming, "I just knew that, Daddy. I just knew it. I knew I had to be a pretty baby because I wasn't fat then."

Daddy turned serious, telling me, "Percy, you mustn't get your hopes up too high about leaving because all the ships are booked through the summer. I don't know when I can get you and Aunt Momi to the Mainland. It will have to be on a ship we're not expecting." I asked quizzically, "Is everybody leaving because the Japanese are coming soon?"

"Important people are worried that they are, son," he answered. Trying to make Daddy feel better, I said like Tyrone Power, "Don't worry, Daddy, I'm praying to God, but I have to tell you, Daddy, God is hard of hearing." I frowned, but somehow knew in my heart that everything was going to turn out all right.

Daddy smiled and tousled my hair, saying, "Well, if you get through to God, stick in a good word for me, will you?" I patted him on the back and replied, "I have already done that, Daddy, a long time ago."

After Daddy dropped me off, I walked into a darkened house. Everyone was gone. Betsy and Jack had gone to a party. Agnes and Gertrude had really gone away because it had been weeks since I had heard them in my head and the toy box was empty. I told God, if he was listening, that with all the bad things going on in my life and everyone leaving me, I was going to buy him an ear trumpet for the New Year so He could start answering my prayers.

Getting under the covers, I told myself that my New Year's resolution was going to be to find *IT* in San Francisco and make all the troubles go away. Being home alone, in bed, I wished myself a happy 1942. A house creaks when there is no one living in it but me. There were no Chinese fireworks for New Year's this year.

66

January 1942

I was catching colds in the New Year and *The Honolulu Advertiser* explained why.

The Honolulu Advertiser

BLACKOUTS MAY BE BLAMED FOR MANY COLDS

Reports to the board of health for the month show a sizable increase in number of lobar pneumonia, flu, and common colds cases. "The blackout could be responsible for the new cases, we are investigating," said Dr. James R. Enright, bureau of communicable diseases, board of health, yesterday. Lack of proper ventilation in blacked out rooms is likely to cause common colds and other upper respiratory ailments, Dr. Enright said.

8 P.M. CURFEW IN EFFECT FOR PEDESTRIANS

All pedestrians except enemy aliens will get a break from blackout routine under an order by the military governor yesterday establishing an 8 p.m. curfew. Beginning tonight, pedestrians, except enemy aliens, will be allowed on the streets until that time, providing they strictly observe blackout regulations.

CAROLE LOMBARD, MOVIE ACTRESS AND WIFE OF CLARK GABLE, AND 21 OTHERS FOUND DEAD IN NEVADA AIR CRASH. BADLY BURNED BODIES ARE NOT YET IDENTIFIED; PLANE HIT MOUNTAIN.

GAS MASKS: Gas masks issued by the Chemical Warfare Service to civilian personnel remain the property of the United States Government and are lent only for the duration of the war. These masks must receive proper care. All mask recipients will observe the following rules and regulations:

Keep mask within reach.

When carrying the mask, it will be worn with strap over the shoulder opposite the carrier as instructed.

Painting and cutting fabric is forbidden.

Every person shall place a paper or card with his or her name and address plainly written thereon within the carrier. Besides the identification paper, nothing else shall be carried in the Gas Mask Carrier.

When the mask is removed from your person, it will be hung or laid in such a place that the movement or acts of yourself or others will not damage it.

Do not drop, kick, throw, or otherwise mistreat or mishandle the mask or carrier.

After we moved our temporary classroom three more times, I quit going to school. I went to the teacher, whose name I never remembered because we changed teachers every week, and told a big fib. Piling my books on her desk, I whispered to her, "Mrs. Lady, this is my last day because I'm leaving for the Mainland tomorrow. Please don't tell anyone because it's a big military secret. I'm going on a Navy destroyer." She hid her face behind a grade book and whispered with her skinny lips like a conspirator, "Really; don't get torpedoed." I put my fingers to my lips and warned, "Shhhhhhhh, loose skinny lips sink big ships." Looking back at the teacher as she waved goodbye, I didn't realize until that very moment she looked like a giraffe.

From that day on, I went to the movies. Daddy sent me money to buy food and other incidentals such as having my dirty laundry washed by a Chinese lady on King Street. Betsy would give me Daddy's money on Monday mornings and it was enough money to see one movie a day if I didn't wash my clothes, so all my dirty underwear was hidden under my bed. From Monday through Sunday, I sat through the same movie from ten in the morning until the movie operator turned off the projector at night. No one missed me because nobody was at home anymore. Betsy was working. I made myself look like everyone else on the streets of Honolulu by carrying a gas mask over my shoulder.

At the Princess Theater, they showed a revival of *Bringing Up Baby* with Katharine Hepburn and Cary Grant. I laughed so hard when Cary Grant dressed up as a lady, I wet my pants. By the third showing, when the tiger chased Katharine Hepburn and Cary Grant into the jail, I had dried out but my pee perfumed the theater. After that accident, I carried an old copy of *Life* magazine to put in front of me to hide any further embarrassment.

Everyone in downtown Honolulu, I noticed, ran lickety-split from building to building. No one looked at me or even questioned what a little boy was doing walking alone on the sidewalks in wartime Honolulu. I figured it was because the once happy-go-lucky people on Oahu kept their eyes always looking upward in case the Japanese Zeros were flying back through the clouds.

Finishing my first week away from school, I walked home from the Pawaa Theater, red eyed because I had sat through five showings of Bette Davis's *All This, and Heaven Too*. To my surprise, I found Marigold sitting on the front steps with her suitcase beside her.

"Oh, oh," I thought, "something's definitely wrong." I walked cautiously up to her and asked, "What are you doing home?" She didn't answer and kept her eyes staring at her bare feet. A dark, black rain cloud was hanging over her head. Then all of a sudden, the thundercloud burst and Marigold jerked her head up and raged, "They don't want me." She then held her head in her hands and wailed as if her world had come to an end.

"What do you mean they don't want you?" I asked. Her voice muffled, she sobbed away, saying, "I'm in the way. Daddy loves Nate best now."

I sat down next to her and patted her head, trying to console her, saying, "Daddy loves you best, Marigold. Nate's a boy. I know Daddy loves you best because he told me so. You're his best girl. He'll never love Nate like he loves you."

She looked at me with tears falling like little raindrops from her eyes, and wailed again, "He loves Nate more. Anyway, Percy, I promised Mother I'd take care of you."

I was taken aback and asked, "When did you say that to Mother?" She replied, "When we took her to the hospital in Mr. McLaine's car."

I protested, "I didn't hear her say that and anyway, I can take care of myself." Marigold yammered back, "No, you can't, and I've come home to take care of you." Sniffing my clothes, then holding her nose, she yelped, "Whew! When did you take a bath last?" "I forget," I answered truthfully.

"You stink." With that remark, Marigold got up and stood over me in her General Douglas MacArthur stance and with her old, forceful Marigold tone of voice and a familiar feverish look in her eyes, she announced, "I'm home and you're going to shape up. Get inside. You're gonna take a bath right now. I phoned Aunt Momi from Daddy's and told her that I am going with you to Baltimore. You need me."

I sensed she had turned me into one of her projects, right after scanning the skies for Japanese planes, so I surrendered easily. I wearily got up, because I knew I couldn't fight back and realized because she sounded so determined, my freedom had just flown away. I wanted to shout out to the world like Patrick Henry did, "Give me Liberty or give me Death." I knew the answer back was - deeeeeeeeeeeeeath.

Hoping to change her mind, I pleaded, "Marigold, I promise, you don't need to take care of me. You need to stay with Daddy. Mother in heaven will know you didn't break your promise." In the panic over losing my freedom, I looked up to heaven and begged, "Mother, please tell Marigold that I can take care of myself. Use your phone right now and tell Marigold that you didn't mean it." Of course, the phone didn't ring because Mother was deaf like God or had lost our number. From the way things were going right now, most of the people in heaven needed a fresh supply of hearing aids.

After I made my appeal to Mother, I saw what a mean look Marigold could make if you crossed her because her eyes were shooting poison darts into my eyes. She hissed, "You don't get it, do you? You just don't get it. You're the stupidest brother in the whole world. Percy, for one minute, for just one minute, can't you think about anybody else but Percy? For just one little minute, why don't you stop and look around and see that there are other people living in this world besides you."

"Like who?" I asked.

She gulped, "Me. ME!" Marigold looked to Mother in heaven and pleaded,

"Please, Mother, please phone and tell Percy to think about someone else other than Percy." Marigold was huffing and puffing, breathing hard like a bull as she spat at me, "Percy, maybe, just maybe - now think hard on this - just maybe, little brother, I might need someone to take care of me." With that she picked up her suitcase, whipped herself around, walked into the house, and slammed the door. Hearing the door slam, I knew for sure, Marigold had come home for good.

Later, soaking in the sunken bathtub, lathered all over with Palmolive soap, I washed away the two-week stink. I stayed too long in the hot water because when I got out of the tub, I looked as old and wrinkly as Mr. McLaine. Ever since Mother had died, I felt as old as Mr. McLaine.

Betsy was ever grateful that Marigold had come home to help take care of me. They hugged a lot and for the first time in a long time, I sat down at our dinner table and had a home-cooked meal. Marigold cooked it. I ate two hot dogs with pickle relish and a slice of leftover ham from Mr. Hamada's package. By now, the ham had turned green around the edges. With Marigold back as the cook, I ate a lot of green ham and pickle relish because she hated vegetables, mayonnaise and tuna fish.

I pretended to go to school every day and made a big production of waving goodbye to my sister, then headed for a movie theater. As soon as Marigold got back into the swing of things and thought I was under control, she happily demoted me way down on her "busy" list of things to do. She spent her days, after school, perched on top of Rocky Hill, binoculars in hand, watching the sky for enemy planes, and at night was back walking the neighborhood, trying to forget about Daddy and Nate.

Everyday, Daddy called the house but Marigold wouldn't speak to him. I pleaded with him to come get Marigold because he had broken her heart. Daddy sounded sad when he responded, "It won't work out, son. Our house is too small."

I inquired, "Doesn't Kathy like Marigold, Daddy?" He answered, "It's not that, Percy. Marigold wants to take over Nate and me, but Kathy is my wife and the baby's mother. Anyway, Percy, Marigold will get over it."

I hated it when grownups said to me that I would get over it. It was very annoying to hear because I always felt dismissed for other things. Feeling annoyed all over, I said back to my father, "You know something, Daddy?" "What Percy?" he asked, tentatively.

I said, "Movies are better than life, Daddy." "How's that?" he asked.

I explained very carefully, "A movie ends in two hours because the story is over, the mystery has been solved or everyone is happy at the end and kissed and made up, anyway, most of the time. I go home and know the next day I get another chance to see an even better movie. And even if the movie was a sad Bette Davis movie, I always know there's going to be a new and better and happier movie just around the corner. Daddy, I wish life was like that. You see, movies make life look wonderful because most of the time they end happily. It seems in my life, there's not much happiness that I can see coming around my corner. I just gotta stick it out because there are no second features, no second chances, in real life. That's what I'm trying to do, Daddy, stick it out, and so is Marigold."

Daddy yawned and mumbled, "Gotta go, Percy. We're changing shifts." He hung up.

Everything in Hawaii turned gray after the attack. The people, the mountains, the Lurline, moods - everything was now colored gray. We lost color because we were hiding from an enemy that wanted to kill us out on the horizon. Riding the bus into Waikiki, I pulled the bell cord, the bus stopped, and I stepped off onto the sidewalk. I landed right across the street from the gray Waikiki Theater. Crossing the street, I bumped into hordes of servicemen wearing khakis and sailor whites looking gray in the face. They were wandering up and down Kalakaua Avenue looking for a Hawaii that had once been advertised in *Life* magazine in bright colors. The servicemen now sat on the beach surrounded by coils of gray barbed wire that had replaced the pretty sunbathing girls from the Mainland. Clothing stores next to the theater that once displayed colorful Aloha shirts had shut their doors for the duration and covered their windows with gray sheets. The hula girls at the Kodak show packed up their green cellophane skirts in gray boxes and were hoeing weeds in the sugar cane fields. The worst change of all was that the free pineapple juice no longer poured into paper cups in the lobby of the Royal Hawaiian Hotel, just gray water came out. Everything in Hawaii turned colorless. I was now living in a black and white movie.

Walking into the Waikiki Theater, I dodged rolls of barbed wire stashed here and there because the manager didn't want an invading Japanese soldier getting into the movie without paying for his ticket. Today's movie advertised:

SOUTH OF PANAMA: Virginia Dale, Roger Pryor and Lionel Royce. "She is just a Latin from Manhattan but there's revolution in her eyes. One night a glamorous blonde, the next a Latin brunette. But when her boy friend doesn't know the difference and woos both of her...BINGO! A Million Thrills - with a Nation's life at Stake.

2nd Hit! **A SHOT IN THE DARK:** Wm. Lundigan, Nan Wynn, Ricardo Cortez, Regis Toomey, and Maris Wrixon. "Trapped by a Killer in a Night Club..."

Waikiki Theater was reduced to showing second run movie fillers because gray guns and ammunition took priority over shipping out Technicolor motion pictures to the Hawaiian Islands. Dozens of film canisters of MGM dramas and Alice Faye musicals lay piled up on the docks in Los Angeles. Sitting in the third row, anticipating the Latin Babe from Manhattan, I prayed out loud, "God, you can kill me, bomb me, shoot me but just let me see one more movie on the screen. Thank you, God." I prayed that prayer everyday before the lights went out and would have been very cross with God if he had dropped a bomb on me before I saw how the movie ended. I sighed as I looked around the theater because the war had taken over in here. Mr. Sautelle's organ was covered with a gray sheet and the electric rainbow wasn't lit up in all its beautiful colors. Looking up at the ceiling, there wasn't a fake cloud rolling around on a fake blue sky and not one fake star twinkled down on me. For the first time, I could see the cement walls of the theater.

The jig was up. Walking home from the Waikiki Theater, singing "She's A Latin from Manhattan," I spied Marigold pacing up and down on our front porch, storming like a Nazi Gestapo. With one eye closed and squinting with the other eye, I swore there was steam coming out of her ears. She was mad about something and I hoped it wasn't about me. Watching her clump her boots across the porch, without her seeing me, I thought of writing to Madame Pele, the fire goddess, telling her to take lessons from Marigold on how to act really mad because Marigold had Madame Pele beat in that department.

"Hi," I shouted and waved from across the street. I wanted to be out of shooting range and was testing the waters to see if she was mad at me. Marigold stopped pacing on hearing my voice, stood at attention and looked at me. Her Superman rays shot out, stinging my eyes, as she stared at me without saying a word. I straightened up my backbone, pushed my shoulders back and walked over to her like a Cousin Nigel soldier and gave her my sweetest, my most innocent look and smiled with all my front teeth.

"WHERE HAVE YOU BEEN?" Pele's sister bellowed from the porch. Boy, I thought, she missed her calling because she could really heat up a volcano. I answered innocently, "At school."

"You're lying," she screamed. Another thought: Bette Davis could sure take angry acting lessons from Marigold. "No, I'm not," I said hotly.

She screamed again, "Yes, you are. Punahou called and said you left on a submarine."

I gasped, "Where did they hear such a horrible thing?" "Peeeercy," Marigold screeched.

Looking at the ground, wiping my nose, keeping my distance, I said, making a minor concession, "Well, it might have slipped out something like that. I don't remember good anymore. But I never said I was leaving on a submarine."

Not letting me off the hook, she asked pointedly, "Where have you been?"

I raised my hands into the air as if I was in the midst of a stagecoach hold-up and drawled like Scarlett O'Hara in *Gone With the Wind*, "I've been attendin' the school of life, my darhling." Not taking to my southern accent, she snarled, "Don't you darling me. You've been going to the movies, haven't you?"

I danced around the sidewalk and said, "You might say that." Turning dramatic again, I picked a branch off a hibiscus bush and walked up to her and presented it to her as a peace offering. I continued drawling, "Dahling, I get moah learning goin' to movies than read'n some dumb stories about a train that couldn't get up a hill or something even dumber like Spot run'n aftah a red ball because, today, I learned something more important. Latin girls weah wigs to fool men to marra them."

"You're going to school tomorrow with or without a wig," she roared. Clumping down the stairs in her boots like Grandma, she grabbed the branch out of my hand, conked me over the head with it, then walked into the house and slammed the front door - of course. I thought we had the strongest house in the neighborhood because everyday, it took a terrible beating when Marigold slammed its doors. Three Little Pigs could have moved into our house because no wolf could have blown a house down which withstood Marigold's hurricane moods.

Lowering myself into the bathtub later, I became depressed because my movie days were now over. There was only one good thing I could say about Marigold being home; I no longer smelled like a bathroom at a beach park.

Punahou School had phoned our house to inquire on my whereabouts because it was rumored that I had gone to the Mainland on a submarine. The giraffe lady teacher who spread the rumor had been nibbling on the treetops because I had made it perfectly clear I was leaving on a Navy destroyer. Nobody got anything right any more and I would never have said I was leaving on something so preposterous as a submarine.

Punahou had rented the Teachers College buildings across the street from the University of Hawaii for their new temporary campus and before moving in, the administration was checking on students who hadn't left the Islands. Now that Punahou had a campus again, they said our education was to continue on as if the battleship Arizona had never sunk in Pearl Harbor. This meant I was going to be reunited with my classmates and Mrs. Mott-Smith.

The next day, after I was caught going to the movies, Marigold combed my hair, poked the dirt out of my ears, dressed me, brushed me off like a horse, and followed me to school to make sure I didn't head for the Hawaii Theatre. I had on my first clean clothes in weeks because Marigold had also discovered the pile of dirty clothes under my bed. That night, Betsy washed and ironed most of them. So I went to school with clean underwear and cut toenails. Inspecting me before I left, they lied, saying that I looked handsome, but I now smelled presentable.

I fixed my own lunch, two tomato and mayonnaise sandwiches wrapped in wax paper stuffed in a paper bag. With the paper bag in one hand and gas mask slung over my shoulder, I strolled to school barefooted, with Marigold stalking behind me like a prison guard. Walking towards the new campus, I felt Mr. Hamada's presence had gone away. Marigold stopped following me midway because she had to veer off to get to her own classroom on time.

I arrived and met a teacher at the entrance who was checking students off on her clipboard. She directed me to a bulletin board to find out where my third-grade class was now being held. As I walked past her, she made a big production of checking me off as present and alive. Trudging down to the bulletin board, my classmates were standing around it, gossiping. As I walked past them, they looked at me cock-eyed. When I caught them staring at me, I saw the look of "poor Percy" in their eyes and heard them whispering, "Percy's mother died. Japanese bullets. Poor thing. Isn't that awful...What do I say to him? Just act normal. Tell him he's fat. My mother says they have no money now. I bet Percy lives on worms."

I got in line to look at the bulletin board and ignored their whispering, and hummed "After the Ball." Waiting in line, I felt something brush past my pant leg. I looked down and saw the tomato sandwiches had leaked out of the paper bag and lay on the cement walkway. The gooey, red guts were spread all over the gray cement. The boy behind me, not seeing the sandwiches on the cement floor, stepped on them and squished them through his toes. As I watched, I wanted to run away to the movies and live a happy life again. Wigay saw what had happened, ran over, and pulled me out of line as a teacher quickly washed off the boy's foot and another teacher scooped up my lunch and threw it into the trash bin. In a minute, the evidence of the accident had gone - like it never happened. It was just like my mother's blood on the sidewalk, washed away like it never happened - like she had never died. But it did happen.

Wigay gently moved me past the staring people and said in a kind voice, "Percy, you'll share my lunch with me. I made much too much and anyway, I'm not really very hungry." As she tried to take my hand, I shoved my hands into my pockets, still not wanting to be touched. I laughed as I said, "Wigay, I'm not hungry. Anyway, I hate tomato and mayonnaise sandwiches. That's all our maid fixes for me, nowadays. I'm going to have to tell her to make me a steak sandwich tomorrow. For today, I'm going to act like Scarlett O'Hara and only think about tomorrow and be a good sport." Snapping my fingers like Carmen Miranda, I chortled, "Let's forget about my old lunch, Wigay. Anyway, my mother said I have to lose weight if I'm going to be a star in the movies."

"Percy," Wigay said, looking at me with goo-goo eyes, "you're just the best sport I know." A tear fell out of her eye. I looked away so a tear wouldn't fall out of mine. I walked ahead so I wouldn't cry.

She ran past me and called, "Follow me, I know where Mrs. Mott-Smith's room is." Coming back to me, she said, "Isn't it fun to be back at school and for us to be together again? It's just like normal." She stopped and turned to me, wiping her eyes, and mumbled, "I've missed you." I could tell she wanted to ask me about my mother because she kept her eyes on the ground. As we walked along the corridors, out on the lawns between buildings, Wigay pointed to zigzag trenches that the senior boys dug for us to hide in when the Japanese dropped their poison gas bombs. Our classroom was in the last building, three rooms down, making our class the last to get into the trenches.

Mrs. Mott-Smith was seated at her desk when we walked in. She was correcting old spelling papers. Without looking up, she said, "Welcome, children. Percy, you sit in your same seat and, Wigay, I want you now to sit next to Percy." Mrs. Mott-Smith's gesture made me love her long nose even more.

At eight o'clock, when the first bell rang, all the seats in the class were filled before you could say "Jack Robin." At roll call, we were counted all present and accounted for; nobody in our class had died or had even evacuated to the Mainland. With words and touches, everyone acted extra kind to me. Even Booby the Bully put an apple on my desk and blushed when he said, "Heard what happened out there. Mother gave me two apples. I can only eat one." He lay the apple on the desk and said he lost a tooth in a fight when the Japanese were bombing Pearl Harbor.

I hated that everyone was being kind to me because it made me feel uncomfortable. They turned me into a sad, purple striped hippopotamus that needed to be petted. I liked it better when they treated me like a fat boy.

After the tardy bell rang, Mrs. Mott-Smith stood up and looked around the room. For the first time, I saw into her eyes. The war had made them look old and sad and folds in her face hung down like a melted candle. She said, wearily, "Welcome back, children. I'm glad to see all of you. We have lots of catching up to do because we've missed so many days. So this semester, we'll all have to buckle down and do our best, won't we? The first order of the day, we're going to practice getting into the air raid trenches. In a few minutes the bell will ring many short bursts, and when you hear the bell, stand up and take your gas masks with you and walk to the trenches. The first row will march out first, then the second row, and so forth. Walk quickly and don't run. We don't want any accidents, do we?"

Short bells began to ring. We stood up and marched out in perfect order and climbed down into the zigzagged trenches. At Mrs. Mott-Smith's hand signal, we crouched on the muddy ground like we were going number two. I poop-da-pooped as everyone put on their gas masks.

Before the lunch bell rang, I whispered to Wigay that if she wouldn't mind I just had to take her up on her lunch offer because I was about to faint. She nodded and smiled like Snow White and at lunch gave me all of her sandwiches. After we ate, Mrs. Mott-Smith read three poems by Longfellow, and then assigned us to write our own poem. "Anything that comes to mind." So we spent the rest of the afternoon writing poems. Fifteen minutes before the dismissal bell rang, Mrs. Mott-Smith asked if anyone in the class would like to read their poem to the class. Dressed in pink ruffles, Peggy yelled, waving her hand back and forth like a palm tree in a gale. "Me. Me. Me, Mrs. Mott-Smith."

"All right, Peggy, stand up please," Mrs. Mott Smith said slowly, trying to calm Peggy's enthusiasm.

Peggy stood next to her desk and smoothed the ruffles on her pink dress. (Peggy was the drip that bit a lizard in half in her watercress sandwich.) The little darling pursed her lips out like a guppy, blinked her merry eyes, and said in a sickening sweet pink cotton-candy voice, "I think that my poem is just the most perfect one to read for today. It is dedicated to Percy." She cleared her throat and began:

"Percy's mother is dead,
It hasn't gone to his head.
He's just the same, fat and plain,
And oh so full of gas.
Oh, alas,
If he wants his fame,
He must change his name
Because Percy sounds too pursy."

The classroom went silent as I sat listening to the birds chirp outside. Miss Pink Cotton Candy continued at her peril, "I hate your name, Percy, so I'm going to call you 'Pumpkin' from now on because you are shaped like one and it makes you all the more darling. Isn't that the sweetest poem you've ever heard, Pumpkin?" After she finished, I thought, "Isn't it funny, Pumpkin was the same name they teased my mother with when she was a little fat girl."

The class shook their heads in disbelief after hearing Peggy. They put their heads down on the desks, stuffed wads of paper in their mouths and held their stomachs to keep from breaking out into shrieks of laughter. I stood up and faced Peggy and, imitating her cotton candy voice, said, "Pink, Piggy Peggy, that was the best poem I've ever heard. Thank you so very much. And Miss Pink Piggy Peggy, you know what, I don't like your name too - it smells just like mine. So from now on, I'm going to call you 'Snot.' Snot is a fine name for you because you have the runniest mouth in the whole wide world. Snot, I want to thank you for the poem and now, I wrote a poem for you. I just made it up.

"Peggy's name is Snot
It's better than to be named Spot,
For Spot is a dog's name
And Peggy's S'not."

I sat down. Everyone clapped. Peggy, not knowing what to do, clapped the loudest. Mrs. Mott-Smith, flummoxed, dismissed us for the day without adding another word. I waited until everyone left and walked up to Mrs. Mott-Smith's desk and stood still as a statue. I waited for her to look at me.

She finally looked up and said, "Yes, Percy?" I put my hand on her desk and asked, "Mrs. Mott-Smith, I want to ask you a favor."

"What is it, Percy?" she said with concern.

"I need your help. I don't want to come back to school again. It's not the same for me anymore and anyway, I'm leaving with my Aunt Momi and Marigold for the Mainland. Please give me some books to read at home and I promise you I'll read them. I'll do the work. It's just that coming back to school makes me feel like running away from here. I'm just not ready to come back. Please."

"I don't think I can do that," she said, opening up her drawer. She took out a pencil and closed the drawer. I looked her in the eye and said, "If you do let me skip school, I'll keep your secret."

She dropped the pencil and faced me. "My secret? Percy, what do you think my secret is?"

I watched her pick up the pencil again and fiddle with it as I said, "Your secret is that you miss my mother very much." She put the pencil down very carefully on the desk and asked, "How do you know that, Percy?"

I said, "Because you can't look me in the face. Every time you look at me, you see my mother and you turn away from me." After I said that, we listened to the clock ticking on the wall.

Breaking the silence, she said, "Percy, I'll tell you what. You call in sick and I'll cover for you. But I am going to drop by your home with schoolwork and you must promise me you'll do the work I bring you. Your mother would be very unhappy with you and with me if you turned out to be an ignorant little boy. Every week, I'll come to your house and collect the homework and then, maybe in a little while..." She paused, picking up the pencil again and repeated the same four words again, continuing the unfinished sentence, "in a little while, you'll feel like coming back to school again."

I smiled and took the pencil out of her hand and said, "One more thing, Mrs. Mott-Smith." "Yes?" she answered. I looked away and said, "Tomorrow, promise me, you'll tell Peggy that I don't think her name is Snot. Tell her Pumpkin told you to tell her that and tell her that she was the only one who acted normal to me."

Mrs. Mott-Smith took my hand and held it. I closed my eyes as she held my hand and pretended she wasn't touching me. I told Mrs. Mott-Smith that she had the most beautiful nose in the world. She never told Daddy or Marigold or anyone about our secret pact.

Happily, every morning, I pretended to walk to school, and when Marigold was out of sight, I ran back home and called in sick. I then mounted the bus and saw only two movies because I had to be home before Marigold got back from school. On those days playing hookey from school, sitting in a darkened movie theater, I learned English, history, and the worldly affairs of love and hate from the best teachers in Hollywood: Carole Lombard, now dead, Clark Gable, Jack Benny, Bob Hope, Gary Cooper, Bette Davis, Maria Montez, Cary Grant, and of course, Alice Faye.

67

The Story's End

Aunt Momi called for an emergency meeting at our house. We hadn't seen much of her in January because she had been running at top speed trying to conclude her court case and tie up the loose ends in case we suddenly left on a ship. Her daughters were living with Uncle Hans's relatives up on Makiki Heights because she had closed the palace at Punaluu.

At four o'clock in the afternoon, she, Marigold and I sat in the living room for a serious powwow. In a husky voice, she gave us the facts of life, "Kids, I have a feeling that when we leave it's going to be fast, so we need to prepare ourselves and not get caught off guard. Time is fleeting, jolljamit. There are a couple of things I need your permission to do. First of all, I want to sell this house so you kids can have some money to live on. I've got some feelers out and though we're in a war, this house was designed by Ossipoff and a famous artist lived here before you all did, so it is well known to have character and I'm sure somebody will buy it. Is it okay for me to sell this house?"

We slumped down on the couch as Marigold nodded for us. I hated the thought of losing my sunken bathtub forever. Aunt Momi continued, puffing on a cigarette, "Next, once the house is sold, I'll put all your mother's valuable things like the dining room table, paintings and silver in storage and sell the rest of the stuff or we'll give it away. Is that okay?" Again, we nodded numbly. I was losing my childhood almost before my childhood had begun.

Relieved that we hadn't thrown a tantrum, she smiled and said sadly, "Good. If there is anything you want to keep special, let me know. I'm sorry to have to do this to you kids, but it's the only way I can see that you'll have some money to live on. Your father is strapped financially because of the new baby and I've cleared all this with him. Everything okay so far?"

I wished she would leave and disappear. Why wasn't my life like a movie that had a happy ending?

Not disappearing like I wanted her to, Aunt Momi gave us one last instruction, "Now, the last thing we need to do. I want you to pack a suitcase with things you want to take to the Mainland. We can only take one large suitcase apiece. Pack something warm because it's going to be cold in San Francisco and probably snowing in Baltimore. I'm going to leave the packing up to you, Marigold. Check on Percy or I'm afraid we'll arrive in San Francisco with a suitcase filled with jolljamit egg salad sandwiches." She wasn't far from wrong.

"Is there anything else?" she said, tapping her feet. Aunt Momi spoke like her car was running outside and she was impatient to fly away to do something more important. I raised my hand. "Yes, Percy," she said, in an edgy voice.

I decided that now was the time to reveal what I planned to do. I said loudly, "I need your help. Your help too, Marigold. There is a big reason that I want to go to the Mainland and I might as well tell what it is now."

"Yes, Percy?" Aunt Momi said again, crossing her legs and leaning toward me. I said in a conspiratorial tone, "I want to find and bring back the skull Grandma took away from Kapake. Last summer, Mother told me about the curse and made me promise that I would bring it back home. The curse is the real reason Mother died and why we have to sell our house and everything is going so bad for all of us. I know if we re-bury the skull back in the sand dune - nothing bad can ever happen to us again. You see, Aunt Momi and Marigold, we are a cursed family. I always knew it. And because we are cursed, other people around us die, like Hatsuko." I looked at both of them to see if I could see any disbelief in their faces and added, "I really know it's true. Promise."

Aunt Momi uncrossed her legs and answered quickly, "Percy, you're absolutely right, jolljamit, and when we get to San Francisco, we'll find that old Dr. Prescott and get that skull back. I'm amazed I can still remember the dentist's name. I promise you, we'll get it and I'll bring it back here and get it buried. I told Mama that she shouldn't have taken it. It has just been plain bad luck for all of us, but now we can change all that." She got up, pushing her hair up from the back of her neck, and sighed, "Kids, I've got a thousand things to do. I'm glad we are all in agreement and we'll take care of that funny old skull."

I hoped Aunt Momi wasn't humoring me and believed what I had just said because I was serious. You can never tell about adults if they take kids seriously. I could see Marigold believed me because she said enthusiastically, "I sure know a lot about bad luck. I've known the story about the skull for a long time and I'll help you, Percy, bring it back and then maybe, Daddy, you and me can live together again like we used to. We'll do it."

Having that out of my stomach, I felt relieved and looked at Aunt Momi and Marigold as they were nodding to each other in agreement. I smiled to them because we were now going to be the Three Musketeers and just like in the movies, maybe live "happily ever after." And if they let me down, I would still do it myself.

As Aunt Momi was going out the door, she turned back to us and added that we should give Betsy and Jack Mother's car for taking care of us. I piped up, "That's a very good idea, Aunt Momi, because maybe Betsy will change her mind about having babies. We were very bad to her when she first came to live with us. Remember, Marigold?"

Marigold, next to me, said, "Don't worry, Percy. Betsy is going to have a baby." That puzzled me and I asked, "When did she have time to do that, Marigold?" Marigold gave me a knowing look as a light bulb lit above my head. I got it; Betsy was under a house with Jack when the Japanese bombed Pearl Harbor. Aunt Momi blew kisses and flew from our home in her car to scatter more gold dust, as princesses should do.

Since time was flying, like Aunt Momi said, and a sense of urgency was in the air, I asked Marigold to take me to the Oahu Cemetery to visit Mother's grave. I said, pleading, "This may be for the last time, Marigold, before our ship comes in."

Marigold agreed and we rode the bus to the cemetery. Getting off the bus, Marigold walked me around masses of tombstones, hunting for Mother's grave. A fresh mound of dirt marked the spot where she lay. There was still no permanent marker. When we reached the grave, Marigold sat down and began to cry. She put her face down into the dirt. I walked over to a plumeria tree and broke off a small branch, and stuck it into the mound. The yellow, scented flowers gave Mother's grave color. I sat across from Marigold and watched her cry, as I played with the dirt. Marigold looked over at me as she wiped specks of dirt from her face and asked, "Percy, why don't you cry?"

I answered, "I don't know why. Why do you cry?"

"I cry because I'm sad. Aren't you sad?" she answered.

"I'm sad all the time, Marigold, but everything stays stuck down in my stomach." I shook my head and wondered to myself, what was I going to do with all the tears tangled in my stomach?

Marigold continued, explaining, "Crying makes me feel better. I wish you could cry. You didn't even cry when we heard that Grandma died." She looked at me for an explanation.

I tried to spell it out, saying, "For me, Grandma died when she left Hawaii. When people leave me and go away, they die. Daddy died when he left our house. When he'd take us to the beach, he'd come back to life for a little bit but when he drove away again, he died." I sighed and picked a flower off the branch and laid it on the grave. I persisted, explaining how I was feeling, "When people go away, Marigold, you can't see them, hear them, smell them, or lick them. Marigold, I wish I had been born a dog. Have you ever wanted to be a dog?"

Marigold, turning what I said into a funny joke, barked, "Bow wow, Percy." Sniffing like a dog, I growled back, "If I were a dog, I'd lick people all over."

"Oooooo. Who would you want to lick?" Marigold said, looking disgusted at the thought. Sticking out my tongue, making licking movements, panting like a dog, I said, "I dunno. I don't want to lick you."

"I wouldn't let you lick me," she said, looking like she wanted to upchuck on me. I continued, pondering the thought, "I can't think of anybody I'd like to lick right now. I just know I'd like to lick someone." Marigold rolled her eyes to the sky and yelped, "You're crazy, Percy." I said back to her, in a matter-of-fact way, "I know that."

Marigold put a plumeria flower on the grave and asked, "I keep wondering, is there a God? You can't see Him or lick Him."

Thinking back to when I was sick with pneumonia, having a hard time breathing in the dark of night, I answered, "God is different, Marigold. I don't know why He is but He is. When I was sick at night, I thought I heard Him talking to me. I don't hear God anymore. I hear Walter's voice." Shaking her head, sprinkling a little dirt in her hand, Marigold looked at me and said, "Percy, I don't think I'll ever understand you."

I then made a request, "Marigold, since we are going away for a long time, let's do what Mother did on the nights before we left on a trip. I was thinking about this last night in the bathtub. Let's you and me finish the Hunkacha story."

Turning away, she answered softly, "I don't want to." "Please Marigold," I persisted, "I want to know the end of the story."

Wiping the dirt off her jeans, deciding to humor her baby brother, she sighed, "Okay, but you first. Then when you get tired, I'll continue." My eyes lit up because I remembered exactly where we had left Little Johnny and Patty in the story. They had the blue pearls in their hands because Little Johnny brought them back from the middle of the lake and Hunkacha, the beast, knew Johnny had taken the pearls and was chasing them. He was going to eat them up.

I began, "By the side of the lake, Little Johnny and Patty could hear Hunkacha snorting red fire and yelling out loud that he was going to kill Little Johnny first because he stole the blue pearls, and then kill Patty. Little Johnny got real scared and said to Patty, 'You go one way into the forest and I'll go the other way. That will confuse Hunkacha and then one of us can be safe from the monster.' Another roar from Hunkacha, who was coming behind them, made them run and take different paths into the forest. Little Johnny, running for his father's house, ran as fast as his little legs could carry him. There were lots of sharp rocks on his path because he had lied a lot going through the forest, so he fell down lots of times. His knees got all bloody from his falls and he got real scared because he could hear Hunkacha breathing down his neck, yelling his own monster name as he ran, 'Hunkacha, Hunkacha, Hunkacha.'"

"My turn," Marigold butted in, now excited, and took over the story. "Patty, holding (Marigold made a big fist) her blue pearl in her hands, could hear Hunkacha was right behind Little Johnny and knew she had to do something because if she didn't, Hunkacha was going to eat up her little brother. Patty was a smart cookie and made a trap by stringing two vines across the path to trip Hunkacha. She yelled, 'Hey, Hunkacha, come over here, you big chicken.' When Hunkacha heard Patty calling him a big chicken, he ran over to Patty's trail, tripped on the vines and broke his head. His head opened like a raw egg in a frying pan and splattered all over the ground and he died."

"Me, now," I said, interrupting, talking fast like I was Little Johnny running from Hunkacha. "Because Patty saved Little Johnny's life, he ran back to his father's house safe and sound and Patty was right behind him. They were both safe and sound. But when they got home..." We knew what to say next and said it together, "their father had died and they were now all alone."

Marigold continued the story again slowly, thinking carefully what she wanted to say next, and whispering like Mother did when she wanted to hold our attention for an important part of the story, "The children looked at the pearls in their hands and started to rub them to create magic. The pearls then glowed as a voice came down from heaven and said that the pearls would lead them out of the forest, away from all the bad things in the world, and would keep them safe for all their lives, but first they had to make a big decision. How were they going to travel? On different paths? Or together? Do you know what their decision was, Percy?"

"What?" I asked excitedly. Marigold, in her John Wayne voice, announced, "Pardner, they decided to take the same path together. So side by side, together, for the rest of their lives - just like Uncle Scottie told us to do - they traveled together, so together they would find all their happiness and all the golden castles that awaited them outside of Hunkacha's forest." Marigold told the rest of the story to herself, "Yea, that's how the story ends - they are going to travel together as best friends for the rest of their lives. The end." Finishing the story, and laying another plumeria flower on Mother's grave, she looked at me and said, "That's how Mother would have wanted us to end the story."

I reached into my pocket and pulled out two marbles, one that was clear blue and the other with lots of different colors in it and said, "That's exactly how Mother would have ended it. Here, I brought these from home." I handed Marigold the bright blue one and kept the ugly one for myself, saying, "Let's pretend these are the pearls and leave them for Mother so she can have lots of luck until we bring the skull back."

"Percy," Marigold exclaimed, "you have the best imagination."

"No, Marigold," I replied, trying to be like Little Johnny, "I think you have the best imagination because you ended the story just right. Let's shake hands and travel like Patty and Little Johnny together for the rest of our lives together. Let's shake." I reached my hand over Mother's grave, reminding Marigold that even though we were shaking hands, we weren't touching. After we shook hands, I dug a little hole into the grave with my finger and put my marble in it and Marigold followed, placing her marble next to mine. Together, we covered dirt over the little hole.

When we finished, a yellow plumeria fell off its branch and landed on the grave, making three flowers lying side by side on top of the grave. That was the last time we ever told the Hunkacha story as a family. We climbed back on the bus and went home, leaving Mother resting in the Oahu Cemetery with our "pearls."

A few days later, I had an urgent message to see Cousin Bessie. Walking into her house, she yelled at me as she was pulling a fur ball out of Martha's ear, "Eureka, Percy, your ship is coming in." I said to her crossly, trying to pretend I didn't understand what she meant, "What do you mean, my ship, Cousin Bessie?" Teasing me, putting Martha down on the carpet, she scolded, "Don't play Mr. Mysterious with me, Mr. Percy, you little sneak. I know you and Marigold are going to Baltimore." It struck me right away: of course, she read Aunt Momi's letters to Uncle Lono.

I told the Queen of the Dirt, "You sure get the scoops all right." Getting excited, I asked, "When does the ship come in?" "In a couple of weeks," she answered. "It's top secret so it's hard to know anything for sure but it's a big ship with four stacks. They are going to form a big convoy, making the Lurline the lead ship, and it is going to take as many civilians out of Hawaii as they can. The ship is coming all the way from Australia because it has been carrying British troops from England to Australia."

"Do you think I'll be on it?" I asked, worriedly. Cousin Bessie, wiping my fears away, said, "Your daddy is such an important man on the waterfront, so it's certain, Percy, you'll be on the ship." I breathed a sigh of relief and sat down and stroked Martha, saying, "Thank you for telling me, Cousin Bessie; that will give me time to get ready."

"Percy, I have something for you." She walked over to her card boxes and pulled a card out from one of her files. She handed it to me and said, "This is a goodbye present." Cousin Bessie had a card on me all the time. I looked at the card and read: (The first part of it was typed.)

Percy.
Fat.
Wears his mother's dresses.
Big gossip.
Saved Walter McLaine's life.
Likes me.
(The rest was handwritten.) Leaving on the Aquitania. He has been my best friend since he turned eight. He listens to me and never tells on me. I will miss him. He is a true friend and a true friend is hard to find.

After I read the card, I looked at Cousin Bessie and that old snoop blushed. Watching her turning red, she turned beautiful right in front of my eyes. I put the card into my pocket and announced, "You forgot one thing, Cousin Bessie."

"What's that?" she asked. I answered, "You should have to put on this card that I thought Martha and Darlene are the best darn cats in the whole wide world. Even though they had worms sticking out their behinds and made me sneeze all the time, I've always loved them and you - worms and all."

"That's a very nice thing to say to me, Percy." I thought she was going to cry.

"Cousin Bessie," I said, looking at her quizzically, then asked a question that I had been holding back for a long time, "I've been meaning to ask you, whatever happened to Pamey?" Taking in a deep breath while looking at one of the letters she was cutting up, she said quietly, "That little darling is just like her mother. She's turned stark raving mad. I had to put her in a private rest home up on Wilhelmina Rise."

I shook my head and said, "I'm sorry about that, Cousin Bessie. You must miss her a lot." I paused and thought for a minute as I watched Martha scoot her fanny across the rug, that craziness runs in our family. I broke the silence and said, "That's really very interesting. Doesn't it seem forever ago when Pamey let go of the brake and she and Nana went down the driveway into Cross-Eyed Mama's backyard? Nana was the first dead person I ever saw in my life and Daddy still lived in our house. That was a long time ago, wasn't it?" I looked around the living room trying to take it all in - the fireplace, the file boxes on the bookcase, old Cousin Bessie, and wormy Martha. I wanted to press them into my memory forever.

I had another question that I had been dying to ask ever since I started getting into trouble with Cross-Eyed Mama. I asked, "Cousin Bessie, tell me the truth, did anyone ever want to put me away like Pamey?" Looking up at me, putting down the letter, she said without hesitation, "There was talk of it, Percy."

That night, I packed my suitcase to leave on a four-stack ship. The first thing I packed was Mother's black velvet gown, then her paperweight, and then her wedding picture. Hatsuko's birth certificate came next with Cousin Nigel's book, *David Copperfield*, Walter's train engine, a Lana Turner coloring book and crayolas, a picture of Alice Faye and her letter, Grandma's gold watch, Cousin Bessie's card, and Mr. Hamada's two bottles of mayonnaise. I carefully packed them around the black velvet gown. I then added clothes. Underwear, handkerchiefs, and some socks had to be left behind in the bureau drawer because I had filled up the suitcase. I laid Marigold's brass knuckles wrapped in tissue paper outside her bedroom door for her to pack.

As I sat in bed, looking at my bulging suitcase with my take-a-ways, I thanked God for finally hearing me and told him that I was glad he bought himself a hearing aid. After I finished saying my prayers, I found Agnes and Gertrude sleeping next to me, wearing kimonos, curled up into little balls. They now looked Japanese.

HMS Aquitania, approximately 1940. From [Ocean Liners of the Past, Aquitania, reprint from "The Shipbuilders", PSL London 1971].

68

"The Ball is Over"

On February 20th, before I left for the ship, I wrote two letters in my own secret code.

> Dear Alice Faye,
>   I am leaving for the moon on Buck Roger's four-stacked rocket ship.
>   I hope someday when I am in Hollywood you can have lunch with me at the Brown Derby because you are my favorite movie actress. My sister, Marigold, helped me with my spelling and this letter - that's why it's perfect.
>   Your fan,
>   Percy
>   P.S. Cousin Bessie, if you are reading this letter, I never told Alice Faye I was leaving on the Aquitania, on Friday, February 20th at 5 p.m.

My next letter to Hilo was shorter.

> Dear Mary Emily,
>   I am leaving with Babar the Elephant in a balloon for the snow.
>   Remember Marigold and I are still your godparents.
>   Marry my friend Kaina. Love to Uncle Will and Aunt Ella.
>   Love to you from us who are going far away with Babar,
>   Percy and Marigold.

Marigold made me write my letter to Alice Faye over three times. When I sealed and stuck the postage stamps on the letters, I ran up to Cousin Bessie's house and slipped them under her door so Mrs. Snoop could cut holes in them to her heart's content.

Daddy had phoned on Monday and told me that Aunt Momi sold our house to a Japanese dentist and that we were leaving on the Aquitania. He warned me to button up my lips because this piece of news was a top military secret. I could have told him the news wasn't so top or secret because Cousin Bessie had spread it all over Honolulu. He further instructed that Marigold and I were to be packed by Thursday and ready to leave on Friday. Marigold still wasn't speaking to Daddy.

On the day we left, I had unpacked and repacked my suitcase five times before lunch. I stuffed everything in it but my underwear. When it came to a choice between a carton of Hershey candy bars and underwear, the underwear lost. Aunt Momi phoned after breakfast and asked Betsy to drive us to the pier as she was running late. I told her, "What's new." Betsy agreed as Aunt Momi informed her the Army MP's wouldn't allow her out of the car at the dock and she shouldn't count on seeing us off. She instructed again that we must be at the pier by two-thirty with only one suitcase apiece. Each suitcase must be tagged in ink with our names on it and Aunt Momi told Betsy she'd meet us inside the pier.

After breakfast, I searched for Agnes and Gertrude. I had told them the night before they had to be packed by lunchtime. I found them sleeping under my bed, and on all fours, I ordered, "Wake up, lazybones, get out of there." Really annoyed, I continued, "Agnes, Gertrude, why aren't you packed?" They crawled out from under the bed, rubbing their eyes, as Gertrude wrapped her kimono around herself and said, "Percy, we aren't going with you."

"You're what?" I answered, incredulously. Agnes quickly confirmed what Gertrude had just said, speaking in a Japanese accent, "We not going."

I yelled, "Yes, you are. You are not going to leave me like everyone else has done. Pack your things right now and I don't want to hear any more stupid things like that out of your mouth."

Gertrude looked at her nails and yawned, "Now, Percy dear, calm yourself. You're not going to get anywhere by shouting at us. Please sit, dear. NOW!" I sat on my suitcase. I hated it when she called me "dear." Gertrude continued in a soft, soothing voice, "Percy, dear, you haven't needed us for a long time. You certainly don't listen to us any more. We think it's time you were on your own and put us behind you. Someone else is bound to come along to guide you, but the way you've been acting lately, you're about to forget all about us like all grown-ups do." Agnes, with a tear in her eye, sniffled, "Yes, we do think that. You're just going to forget all about us."

I cried, "I won't ever forget you. How could I? You're my guardian angels."

They looked at each other as if I had dropped a stink bomb on them. Gertrude, flustered, asked, "How did you know that?"

"Because you're always with me," I said knowingly. "You came to me when I needed you and I still need you. You can't leave me now because my life is going bad right now and remember, I could be torpedoed at sea. Gertrude, I am a cursed boy."

Sounding like Mrs. Mott-Smith, very "teacherish," Gertrude began scolding me, "Oh, Percy, stop that nonsense. There are no such things as curses unless you believe them and make them so. All you have to do to break a curse is to change your mind about them. It's that simple. Tell all those bad voices inside you to go away. Just say to them, 'I don't believe in curses and be gone.' Believe what I'm saying and all the bad curses running around in your mind will fly away. It's time you made that little mind of yours strong and made something of yourself. You can't rely on us anymore and you know that and anyway, you're acting like a big Mr. Smarty-Pants all the time. You hardly remember to pull us out of the window seat."

"But Gertrude," I pleaded. "Don't you 'but Gertrude' me," Gertrude answered.

"Agneeeeees!" I said, making my eyes like a beagle begging for food. She snorted back, "Don't give me that face. You're not going to get around me, playing a sad puppy dog. I stand behind Gertrude. Anyway, we've been called somewhere else."

"Where?" I demanded. Agnes, playing a coy geisha, continued, "We can't tell you that because it's a big military secret. We're doing our war bit for President Roosevelt. It's very hush hush, Percy. Now be a big boy and get on that ship and be off. Let's say our goodbyes right now." She waved her hand and said, "Bye. bye."

Gertrude waved too and also said, "Bye, bye, Percy. We are going to leave you now. Someday, I promise you, you will forget all about us."

I sat on my suitcase and looked at them, holding my stomach, trying not to cry. "Cat got your tongue, Percy? Aren't you going to be polite and say goodbye to us?" Gertrude asked.

I turned my back on them and snorted, "I'm not going to say anything and I'll be glad you're gone and not going to sleep in my bed anymore. Anyway, you both stink and snore. Go away. See if I care." I turned back to them and gave them my puppy dog look again, hoping I'd make them change their minds.

Sighing, Gertrude said, "Okay, Percy, if that's the way you feel about us, we're going now. But someday, you'll realize we did it for your own good." I whined, "That expression 'for your own good' is right behind 'you'll get over it' as my most hated things people say to me." My lower lip began to stick out a mile.

Gertrude raised her hand and called to Agnes, "Okay, Agnes, count one." "One, Gertrude dear," Agnes counted loudly. Gertrude turned to me as she said, "Two." They held hands, twirled around, counted three, and disappeared. They had either gone on a spy mission with Mr. Hamada or were having tea with Mother. But no matter where they went, they were in that awful place - beyond my reach, where I couldn't smell them anymore.

With the girls gone, I went to the window seat, pulled out my old smelly teddy bear, opened my suitcase, took out a pair of pants, and shoved the bear right under Mother's dress. After all, I needed someone to sleep with me.

Betsy backed Mother's car out of the garage as I slammed the front door and Marigold locked it. At the click of the lock, we looked at each other and knew our childhood had ended. Suitcases in hand, we got into the car.

It was a hot, humid Friday afternoon, a day when the old people in Manoa Valley prayed for rain. Marigold slid into the front seat as I sprawled out in the back. We drove through the streets of Honolulu without speaking, keeping our thoughts way down inside ourselves.

I put my head out the car window and watched the scenery go by. When we passed the statue of King Kamehameha, it was alone and deserted. The king now seemed as foreign as a Buddha statue in New York City and as out of place with the barbed wire and army tanks surrounding it. The guns on the tanks were pointed toward the Hawaiian palace across the street.

As Betsy drove in silence, I kept searching for familiar landmarks to say a last goodbye. Nothing was familiar. In front of the Young Hotel Coffee Shop, buck privates with vacant eyes now stood at attention. Other soldiers, in pairs, meandered down Fort Street, rifles slung over their shoulders, looking into empty store windows. They kicked scraps of paper lying in the gutters, pointed their guns at them and pretended to kill them.

I saw Honolulu, my long ago fairyland kingdom once inhabited with exotic people and Kress Store, once filled with candy and Japanese toy boats, had now become a deserted forest of concrete. Little Johnny and Patty, Hansel and Gretel and Little Red Riding Hood no longer lived in this forest. Now, invisible trolls and mean witches hid in the afternoon shadows and were ready to take over when the Japanese soldiers landed on the beach at Waikiki. Liberty House had turned into Hunkacha's castle and Hunkacha was inside, hiding under a counter, waiting to pounce on Little Johnny and Patty and eat them for breakfast.

I closed my eyes and saw Hatsuko and me walking into Liberty House to smell the Christmas tree while Mother was in the ladies department wearing a white orchid in her hair, buying a girdle.

As we drove to the pier, I caught my first glimpse of the Aquitania. It was the biggest ship I had ever seen. It was at least three football fields long, a gray Noah's ark with four tall smokestacks billowing black smoke. Betsy drove us to the entrance of the pier and nosed in behind a long line of cars. Three Army MP's were directing traffic, and I could see that at the end of the line, people were hustled out of their cars, suitcases in hand, and directed hurriedly by the soldiers onto the pier.

I looked for the lei sellers standing against the wall of the pier but they had vanished and left none of their sweet flower fragrances behind. Instead, the smell of diesel fuel permeated the air, making my eyes sting. Loud noises boomed everywhere. Clanging metal hitting metal, whistles and shouting had replaced the call of "Aloha." The legendary land of love had flown away with Agnes and Gertrude.

When we reached the end of the line, Betsy stopped the car as jitneys zoomed and shifted gears around us. An MP came to her window and ordered, "Ma'am, unload your passengers and get on your way." He opened the car doors and pulled us out with our suitcases. Tapping his rifle on top of the car, he ordered, "On your way, Ma'am." Betsy looked back at us with red eyes, but before she could say anything, the MP spoke again, "Now, Ma'am." Betsy looked ahead, shrugged her shoulders, and drove from the pier without saying goodbye. We watched her disappear up the street.

At the MP's urging, we dragged our suitcases into the pier's warehouse. As we walked, the pesky jitneys came at us, barely missing us, then circled around us in a jitterbug dance of death. Pretty soon, because there was so much noise, confusion, and people running at us, and not seeing Aunt Momi, I yelled to Marigold, "Stop, I can't go any farther." Marigold pushed her suitcase over to me and instructed,

"Percy, you watch the suitcases. I'll find Aunt Momi." I sat on the suitcases and watched Marigold disappear in the crowd.

I looked around. People kept arriving in Fords, trucks, taxis, and limousines. The vehicles spit out people of all kinds and shapes and they ran past me as if Hitler and Tojo were shooting at their behinds. Looking outside, I peered up at the Aloha Tower, the tallest building in Hawaii. It too had changed its clothes. Once a tower that stood tall to greet tourists as a light of Hawaiian hospitality, it now watched over Honolulu sadly camouflaged in swirls of green, gray, and brown. Its new look was to keep it from being blasted to smithereens by a Japanese battleship.

"I found her," yelled Marigold, towing Aunt Momi through the crowds. A beet-faced soldier followed them. Aunt Momi was dressed all in white and had a large, white Panama hat covering half her face. She pushed the soldier towards me, instructing, "Percy, get off the suitcases and let this young man take the bags." Ordering him like a princess, she said, "See that these bags have been tagged properly and get them into our stateroom. The major is their father and these suitcases take priority."

"Yes, Ma'am," the soldier replied, saluted, and checked our tags. He then picked up the suitcases and disappeared into the crowd.

Aunt Momi handed us each an identification card and instructed, "Here, pin these to your shirt. These purple cards will get us aboard the ship. Don't lose yours, Percy, or you'll be left behind." I was all thumbs pinning the card and made a mess of it. Frustrated by watching me and anxious to get on our way, Aunt Momi yelped, "Percy, you got yours upside down. Never mind. Take my hand and let me get us through this crowd. Your daddy is waiting for us at the gangplank." She muscled her way through the crowd, cutting through every line until we reached the gangplank. A man in an officer's uniform was checking the purple identification cards and permitting passengers, one by one, to walk up the gangplank. I watched a bearded man being carried up by two soldiers because he was so old.

I spied Daddy first. He was standing by a cement post, dressed in a major's uniform, handing out papers to a private who was sweating buckets next to him. I yelled, "Daddy, we're over here." Once he saw me, he shoved the papers into the private's hands and rushed over to us. Seeing Daddy coming, Marigold hid behind Aunt Momi.

When my father stood in front of me, I said, "Hi, Daddy." "Hi, yourself, Percy," he answered, saluting me. Trying to see Marigold hiding behind Aunt Momi, he said, "You haven't got much time, kids. Here, I brought you a present, Percy. It's a little something you can use when you get to San Francisco." He pulled an envelope out of his jacket and gave it to me. In my hand, it felt like dollar bills. I put the envelope into my pants pocket and said, putting my hand out to shake his, "Thank you, Daddy, for the present." He took my hand and squeezed it, saying, "Goodbye, Son. Take care of your Aunt Momi and your sister."

"I will, Daddy, and will you say goodbye to Kathy and Nate for me." Feeling the money in my pocket, I added, "Daddy, I'm really glad you have a football son, now."

He kneeled down, took my hands and looked me in the eye, and said, "I want you to remember, I will always be very proud of my son Percy." I looked at him as he got up and nodded. We parted our hands, and without another word, I turned and walked over to the gangplank because I was ready to climb aboard the ship and bring the skull back to Hawaii and make everyone happy again. I was determined to make Daddy proud of me.

I watched from the gangplank as Aunt Momi, with Marigold still behind her, gave Daddy a kiss on the cheek, saying, "Thank you, Dick." She pushed back a strand of hair that had fallen onto her face and continued, "I'll be back on the next ship. Please check to see that I have reservations to leave with my children right away. That son-of-a-bitch Hans had better let me take my son with me or else he'll wish he had never been born with balls. He's being a real bastard to me."

Daddy took her hand and said, "Thanks for taking the kids, Momi. I know this is the way Deidra would have wanted it."

Aunt Momi reached around and brought Marigold in front of her and said, "Here's someone who wants to say goodbye to you, Dick." Daddy and Marigold faced each other as Daddy got on his haunches and took her into his arms. In Daddy's arms, Marigold quivered all over as if she was freezing to death and then grabbed Daddy with all her might and held him so tight, I thought her arms would break apart. I couldn't hear what they were saying and I didn't want to. Aunt Momi joined me and we held hands, watching them love one another.

The ship's whistle blew and I jumped a mile at the sound. Daddy stood up and nodded for Aunt Momi to take Marigold. Aunt Momi took Marigold by the shoulders and tried to lead her to the gangplank, but Marigold kept on clinging to Daddy. He had to pry her hands away and then helped Aunt Momi lead her to where I was standing. Aunt Momi held Marigold and said, "Say one more goodbye to your father. Percy and I will wait for you at the top of the gangplank." Then Aunt Momi put on her dark glasses, took my hand, and after the man checked our identification cards, she led me up the gangplank.

From the top, we watched Marigold clinging to Daddy's neck as he rocked her back and forth. The soldier with the papers in his hands interrupted Daddy. Daddy then took Marigold's arms away from his neck, gently turned her away and gave her a slight push up the gangplank. Marigold started to climb. Slowly, hand over hand, heaving herself up along the railing, tears streaming down her face, she chanted, "I'm nobody's baby now. I'm nobody's baby now." When she reached us, she stopped chanting.

The purser of the ship inspected our cards and shouted to a big red-headed man in back of him, "These are yours, Johnny." "Righto, mate," was the cry back. A sailor bounded in front of us in two leaps. He had a red nose, red hair and red cheeks and was full of pep. He acted like he had stepped out of a Fred Astaire and Ginger Rogers musical because he acted so British. He looked familiar and I was sure we had met before.

Cheerily, he said, "Hello Madam, children. My name is Johnny and I'm going to watch over you during this entire journey. I'm now going to show you to your quarters. Excuse me, Madam, may I see your pass before we proceed?" Aunt Momi presented her purple pass. After he inspected it, he said, "Ah, Cabin 305 on Boat Deck. Lovely quarters." He handed the purple pass back to Aunt Momi and asked, "Shall we be off?"

He made a quick appraisal of me and warned, "Young master, don't get lost." I loved hearing him because he sounded just like Cousin Nigel. I answered him in my best Powderhurst accent, "Tally ho, Johnny. I never get lost, old chappie." Aunt Momi tapped me on the head, warning, "Be polite, Percy. I hear the captain of this ship throws fresh little boys overboard to the sharks."

"That's all right, Madam," Johnny said. "He has a very good accent." After Johnny said that I stuck out my tongue at Aunt Momi and gave Marigold my best "smarty" fresh, little boy smile. Marigold punched me.

We followed him, filing one behind the other down corridors, upstairs, downstairs, passing passengers looking confused because they were not lucky enough to have a guide like Johnny. Walking behind Marigold, I pulled a Kleenex out of my pocket and called to her because I could hear she was crying. I called out, "Here!" I punched her back holding the Kleenex in my hand and said, "Here" again.

She snapped, "Stop it, Percy."

I persisted, "Turn around." She snarled, "Percy, don't bother me."

"I have some Kleenex," I persevered. "It's probably dirty," she said, menacingly.

Still trying to cheer her up as we walked, I kept yammering away, "It's s'not. Just joking, Marigold. Cross my heart and hope to die. Take it." Marigold turned around, snatched the tissue out of my hand and blew her nose, saying, "Thank you." She sniffled some more as we ran to catch up with Johnny.

Johnny must have never learned the word "walk" because he loped along on long legs like a gazelle running from lions in Africa. As we ran, I kept on trying to make Marigold feel better by making sinister sounds and making my fingers into little crab pinchers crawling on her back just like she did with me at the beach. "Pinchy, pinchy, pinchy," I called out.

"Stop that, Percy," Marigold snapped again. "I mean it. I'm not in a good mood." Well, at least she was talking and thank God, there were no doors in the hallways for her to slam. Going up a long flight of stairs, I stopped playing "pinchy" and called out, "Dopey calling Grumpy. Come in, Grumpy. Is Grumpy there? Hello, Grumpy. Grumpy, this is Dopey. Is Grumpy too grumpy to laugh at Dopey?"

Marigold stopped at the top of the stairs, turned around with Pele's fire in her eyes and exploded, yelling, "I MEAN IT." I was so taken aback by her blast, I stopped and fell backwards into a fat lady with a very large bosom who was right behind me on the stairs. Marigold laughed at the sight of me in the lady's bosom and I laughed too because the fat lady's bosom felt like a lumpy mattress.

The fat lady didn't laugh as I pulled myself away from her. I apologized right away, saying, "I'm sorry." The fat lady threw me from her, dusted off her bosom, and scolded, "Little boys should watch where they're going, especially fat little boys." She said the word "fat" like I had a terrible disease.

I put my hands on my hips, stood on the top step and snipped at her like Bette Davis, "I am not fat." I spit the word fat at her like a rocket. Then I smiled sweetly and said, "I'm pleasingly plump."

The fat lady squealed, "Why do I have to put up with such rudeness? Don't you know we're in a war, you brat? Out of my way." She sniffed the air as her gigantic bosom heaved up and down and tried to move past me. I stood my ground, but she pushed me away with her fat arm, howling, "Out of my way, little fat boy. You certainly have no respect for your elders. Your mother must be a terrible mother."

At that, Marigold went nose to nose with her and cursed, "Damn it, don't you talk about our mother that way. It wasn't his fault. It was mine." Marigold was still nose to nose with the fat lady when the dragon threatened, "Let me pass, or I'll scream for the captain." Immediately, Marigold and I pressed ourselves against the wall as much as we could to let the fat lady get by. As she stormed past us, she pressed me so hard into the wall, I thought my eyeballs were going to pop out of their sockets. Her dirty looks and sashaying rear end made us giggle. I held my nose because she smelled like the locker room at the Honolulu YMCA. Seeing me holding my nose, she slapped me on the head with her purse.

As soon as she disappeared, Johnny was back looking for us and said, annoyed, "I thought you chaps didn't get lost." "We didn't," Marigold said in our defense, "we got held up by a fat old tugboat."

Johnny laughed, "I saw her and methinks she could have held up the entire English fleet. You're right, Miss, she was a fat old tugboat." For the first time that day, I saw a smile in my sister's eyes. I thought to myself, this man could even charm Madame Pele from erupting.

Arriving at the cabin, Johnny unlocked and opened the door to our suite. Aunt Momi gasped with relief as she took off her dark glasses and looked into our cabin. It was fit for a princess, large and decorated in royal blue. It even had an outside porthole. Aunt Momi, walking in first, took off her hat and threw it on a bed, saying, "Your father has done very well for you, kids."

Johnny opened up the closet doors and pulled out three gray life jackets and instructed, "You have to wear these at all times when you leave the cabin. Your luggage should be here shortly. I'll be back after we set sail to tell you about dining hours and any information you might need. Have to go now because I have other passengers to board. Any questions?" I raised my hand. Aunt Momi pulled my hand down and ordered, "Let the man go."

She reached into her purse and took out some dollar bills to give to Johnny. These dollar bills were different from the old American ones because they had "Hawaii" stamped in black on one side of them. They were made special for the Territory so that the Japanese couldn't use them to buy anything on the Mainland. Johnny waved the dollar bills away and said, "This is wartime, Ma'am. I can't take tips."

Looking down at me, he asked, "Young man, what's your name?" "Percy," I said, making a face. "I know it's a terrible name."

"Percy!" he exclaimed, "that's not a terrible name. That's me favorite name. You know, young lad, you're named after a great hero, the Scarlet Pimpernel, Sir Percy Blakeney. He is a great storybook hero who saved many people from being guillotined in the French Revolution." He repeated it again because I had a look of disbelief on my face, "A great hero, young lad. Believe me and you must say that name proudly."

"I guess so," I replied, in disbelief. Johnny struck a pose like a Shakespearean actor, put his hand in his tunic, and spoke in a deep voice, "This is what they say about that hero whom they never caught because he was so clever and brave: 'We seek him here, We seek him there, Those Frenchies seek him everywhere. Is he in heaven? Is he in hell? That damned elusive Pimpernel?' Young lad, you must be proud to wear that name." When he finished speaking, I clapped my hands.

"Well, take care of the ladies, young Percy, and remember you have a heroic name and you must act like a hero now." Johnny handed the cabin key to Aunt Momi, saying, "Here's your key, Ma'am."

I spoke out, "Don't call her ma'am, Johnny, call her Princess because she's a real genuine Hawaiian princess." He then bowed low to Aunt Momi and Marigold and said, like a prince himself, "I guess I'm going have to take good care of two Hawaiian princesses and one hero. Don't forget your cabin number if by chance you get lost, Sir Percy." He winked at me as he closed the cabin door. I said to myself, I would share my mayonnaise with that man any day.

Aunt Momi chortled, "Boy, that's some character." Marigold, still looking sad, walked over to the porthole to see if she could find Daddy standing on the pier. Aunt Momi, dumping out the contents of her purse on the bed, said, "That reminds me of something, Percy." She was looking for her key ring to attach the cabin key to as she continued, "Your mother was reading *The Scarlet Pimpernel* just before you were born, and that's why she named you Percy. She wanted you to be the hero in the family."

I squealed, "Why didn't she tell me about that? Why didn't anybody tell me that I had been named after a hero?"

Attaching the cabin key to a ring of keys, Aunt Momi shrugged her shoulders, "I guess she forgot." Looking at her, I said, "She shouldn't have forgotten because until now, I've always hated my name because it sounded like a sissy name. I guess I should be glad she didn't name me Scarlet or the Pimpernel because at school, they would have called me the red pimple. Aunt Momi, I always thought I had a sissy name because I was born a sissy. I can't believe it, I just can't believe it. I was born a hero."

Aunt Momi shook her head and stood, saying, "Percy, where in heaven's name do you come up with these ideas? You're different, all right. You're as different as purple rain falling on a red pimple." Looking at Marigold and Aunt Momi, I brandished an imaginary sword in the air and shouted, "From now on you have to call me Sir Percy because now I'm a hero. On guard, everybody." I thrust my imaginary sword at Marigold.

Hearing me, she turned away from the porthole, walked over and pressed her shoe hard on my shoe and warned, "Sir Percy, if you keep up that accent and play-acting like a hero, I'm going to throw up all over you, Siiiir Percy." I put my imaginary sword down and went looking for a mirror to see if I could find a hero in my face. Marigold still looked sad, like a princess in a dungeon waiting to be executed.

I scanned the suite and saw it had two single beds and a canvas cot set up next to a marble floor heater. Aunt Momi had her purse and hat on one bed and Marigold now sat on the other. I looked longingly at the two comfy beds that were just perfect for Princess Elizabeth and Princess Margaret Rose to sleep in. The beds even had the ship's insignia sewn in yellow on the royal blue bedspreads. Aunt Momi, seeing my longing look, pointed to the cot and ordered, "That's yours."

The canvas army cot had a thin green blanket spread lightly over it and on the blanket was stamped in black, "Property of the British Army." I pointed to the cot and complained, "There are a lot of white things crawling on that pillow, Aunt Momi. You take it." Aunt Momi immediately squashed my complaint, saying, "It's your imagination. We'll just have to make do."

I mumbled back to her, "You mean I have to make do." I walked over and sat down on the cot and bounced up and down without even trying. The other adult saying I hated was "It's your imagination and you'll just have to make do." Don't adults ever realize that children don't like to be good sports all the time?

There was a knock on our door and it was Johnny again. This time he was puffing hard and both his armpits were circled wet. He and a steward lugged in our suitcases and set them on the beds. The ship's whistle blew three long blasts as Johnny straightened my suitcase on the cot. He remarked, "You all ought to come up on deck before we sail. It's pretty exciting out there. Latecomers are still coming on board."

I turned to Marigold and said, "Marigold, maybe we can find Daddy." Johnny interrupted, "Don't forget to put on your life jacket, Sir Percy. Ma'am, if it's all right with you, the steward here would be most grateful for a tip. This is special." Aunt Momi reached into her purse and pulled out three one-dollar bills. The steward took the money and left smiling.

Johnny whispered so the steward wouldn't hear him, "Thank you, Ma'am. My boys are working very hard today and doing that makes my job a little easier. We have to make exceptions to keep morale up. But let's keep it our little secret, shall we? I wouldn't want to get the boy in trouble and he just got married." Aunt Momi said she understood. As Johnny left, he gave me a salute, saying, "See you on deck, Sir Percy." He didn't look like Tyrone Power, but he dazzled me.

"Aunt Momi," Marigold pleaded, pulling on Aunt Momi's arm, "let's go on deck and see if we can find Daddy." Aunt Momi grabbed her purse off the bed and said, "All right, kids, but Percy, go to the bathroom first." Mother must have been calling in from heaven.

I opened the bathroom door and saw it was the best room on the ship. The room was almost as large as the stateroom and all the faucets were made of gold. There was a huge porcelain bathtub standing in it, large enough to hold a birthday party for five of my best friends. A sign hung from one of the faucets, ordering, "Please do not use the bathtub. Water is rationed." Disappointed, I had to hoist myself up onto the toilet because it stood very high off the floor. Sitting on it, I felt like I was on the throne in King Midas' castle. As I sat there and did my stuff, it was the first time on board that I missed Mother and Hatsuko. I remembered all the times Mother drove down our driveway and smashed into the kitchen wall and I pooped. They would have loved this bathroom.

When I was fully successful, I pulled the chain and walked back in the stateroom, opened my suitcase and pulled out a bottle of mayonnaise. Aunt Momi, wearing her bulky life jacket over her dress, asked, "What in the hell are you going to do with that?" As she put a life jacket over me, I answered, "I am going to find the kitchen and put this in the icebox."

"Percy," she said, sounding a little exasperated, "put that away."

"Please, Aunt Momi," I pleaded.

"Oh, all right," she sighed, tying the strings of the life jacket around my chest.

Marigold, at the door, called, "Hurry up, slowpokes. I'll never see Daddy if you don't hurry." I pulled on Aunt Momi's hand and asked, "Aunt Momi, doesn't Marigold have to go, too?" Marigold snapped, "Percy, I am a grown-up and grown-ups can hold it. Come on."

I hated it when an older sister tells her little brother that she didn't have to do something because she was all grown up, like taking naps I wanted to say to her, as if being a grown-up was anything special, but I didn't because today Marigold might have killed me.

Aunt Momi, her purse under her arm and hat on her head, locked the cabin door as she warned me to remember the cabin number. Of course, I didn't listen to her because I was concentrating on tying the last string on my life jacket. I wasn't about to drown in a sea of sharks. I followed them down the passageway but I had a hard time maneuvering over the metal sills that separated one section of the ship's interior from the other. My fat life jacket, my fat short legs, my fat stomach, and a fat bottle of mayonnaise that I carried under my arm made going over the sills a hurdling obstacle course. I held up the passengers trying to get by me as I desperately tried to throw myself over the sills. In frustration, men behind me picked me up and tossed me over to the other side.

Once on deck, Marigold ran to the railing while Aunt Momi and I stood on either side of her. She yelled to us, "Everyone look for Daddy." Marigold began scanning the pier below looking for his familiar figure.

I peered through the bottom rungs of the railing and found we were at least seven stories above the pier and everybody below ran around looking like ants. "Whoa," I said holding tight to the rail. With a sudden move of the ship, I might fall through the railings and scream past all seven stories. I imagined I saw blood and guts splattered all over the cement pier. I hated heights and my hands began to sweat. I told myself it was the old Percy talking, not the Scarlet Pimpernel. So trying to be like the Scarlet Pimpernel, I breathed hard and began to search for Daddy.

Looking down, I realized more familiar sights were gone. People on the wharf were not waving up to us and shouting aloha and across the way, on the second story balcony of the pier, the Royal Hawaiian band had disappeared. No one was playing one, two, three oompapa beats to Hawaiian songs. The customary thousand multicolored streamers floating in the air had vanished. More disappointingly, golden Hawaiian boys weren't diving in the murky waters for copper coins. Poof, like when Daddy disappeared from our house, the familiar had suddenly changed.

Now soldiers with rifles marched up and down on the pier, menacing civilians who strayed out of a long line and a continuous stream of bent over, pinch-faced refugees climbed single file up the gangplank. They looked like the people in newsreels fleeing the Germans in Poland.

Suddenly, I rubbed my eyes twice and couldn't believe my good fortune because Auntie Sissy was walking up the gangplank with Daisy and Neal in front of her. They looked pretty strange because Auntie Sissy was carrying a polo mallet and was waving it in the air like a madwoman. The polo mallet kept all the attention on her as Daisy and Neal climbed ahead with a brown horse blanket covering them. They looked very odd indeed, and I saw what it was. Boy, was I a good spy. In between Neal and Daisy, spiky black hair was sticking out of the blanket. Immediately, I knew they were smuggling Mina aboard.

Boy, this trip was going to be an adventure. I was going to have to find Mina a comfortable lifeboat to hide in just like Bobby Breen did in the movie *Hawaii Calls*. I waved and yelled down at them, but they didn't hear me because they were concentrating on getting Mina aboard. They weren't looking at anyone but the man at the top of the gangplank who was checking the passengers on. When Auntie Sissy reached him, she put her polo mallet into the purser's face and kept it there until he had checked their tickets. With her free hand, Auntie Sissy shoved her kids past him, with Mina's hair sticking out even further.

Behind Auntie Sissy, five people back, walked the Twins with Auntie Gladys. Uncle Pete staggered behind them. He was carrying a huge paper sack in his hand and I was sure that inside the sack were his favorite bottles of scotch. He loved his bottles of scotch as much as I loved my bottles of mayonnaise and probably more than he loved the Twins. More than once I saw him kiss his bottle of scotch. Seeing him reminded me to hold onto my bottle of mayonnaise tightly because I didn't want to let it fall through the railing and hit someone on the head.

At the end of the line, Cousin Rose, Cousin Nigel and Tom were being escorted aboard by one of the British officers. He treated them like English royalty. It seemed like everyone I knew was leaving Hawaii today except the two tough, old birds, Cousin Bessie and Aunt Mari. I bet if old Tojo knew those witches were left behind, he'd call off the invasion.

It felt like I was leaving on a Noah's ark because every kind of human being had boarded the ship. Even the handsome older Hawaiian lady, who wore purple orchids on top of her white hair and walked around downtown Honolulu, had walked up the gangplank using a cane like a queen. It was if Queen Liliuokalani, who wrote "Aloha Oe," was fleeing the terrible Japanese storm that threatened to destroy her kingdom. She was the last passenger to board the ship. Since most of the people in my world who survived the attack at Pearl Harbor had entered the ark, I knew this trip was going to become a great new adventure; that is, if we weren't torpedoed at sea.

Men on the dock began shouting final orders for departure. They screamed at each other with unintelligible words above the din of the engines revving up somewhere in the bowels of the ship. The beat, beat, beat of shoes pattered behind me as crew members ran from one end of the ship to the other, unfastening ropes and bringing up from the harbor water, the chain and anchor. Bilge water started to gurgle out of the ark's belly holes, making sounds like one of Noah's animals was throwing up.

"There he is," Marigold screamed, pointing down to Daddy. He stood framed against a gray cement wall with both his hands cupped over his eyes, searching for us. Daddy saw Marigold waving and began waving at us, and we waved back. I stood next to the railing, staring down at him as he kept staring up at us, waving. Uncomfortable thoughts were aching to come up from my stomach as I looked down at him, but I held them back by watching other passengers next to me who were crying. Marigold leaned over the railing as far as she could, letting her little arms flail up and down and drinking in the sight of her father. She kept yelling to him that he was the one that she loved best in the whole wide world as tears poured down her cheeks. I don't think he heard her or saw the tears and for that reason, I couldn't look at Marigold.

Men in brown shirts and blue pants pulled away the gangplank. The ship's whistle blasted four times. The blasts were so loud and scary I almost dropped my bottle of mayonnaise over the railing.

Looking past the bow of the ship, I saw the newly gray-painted Lurline steaming out of the harbor. She was taking the lead and six more ships followed behind her. Cousin Bessie told me that this convoy planned to zigzag its way to San Francisco to keep from being torpedoed by Japanese submarines. She said we were going to be the last ship to exit the harbor, the eighth ship.

A final woeful whistle blew, louder and more deafening that time, waking up all the mynah birds in the trees. The gangplank now rested on the pier and all ropes were untied, cutting the ark's umbilical cord. With a forceful thrust, the gray ark detached herself from her berth, and we followed the Lurline and the other ships out into an ocean of dark blue. I stared back at Daddy still standing on the pier. He was becoming smaller and smaller. Seeing him fade from sight, it finally hit me that I was leaving my home, my Hawaii, my daddy...maybe, forever.

Next to me, Marigold gave a last fierce wave, trying to make her arms fly into his. Daddy raised his right hand like a baseball outfielder and pretended to catch her arms into his as the engines roared and the ship's propellers churned white foam from its stern. Our Noah's ark began to navigate with the help of a tug toward the narrow channel. We all waved a last goodbye to Daddy who had disappeared from the pier.

Marigold turned to Aunt Momi, and scrunched her face and railed, "I hate you, Aunt Momi. I hate the Japanese. I hate Percy. I hate Daddy. I hate Hawaii, and I hate Mother most of all for leaving me." Aunt Momi kissed the top of Marigold's head and whispered, "I hate your mother, too, for leaving us." Marigold looked into Aunt Momi's eyes and gasped, "You do? Oh, Aunt Momi, thank you for saying that." Then Aunt Momi crushed Marigold to herself and for once, Marigold didn't resist. For that moment, Marigold became Aunt Momi's baby. Aunt Momi released her, opened her purse, took out her dark glasses, covered her eyes, and said, "You know what, Marigold, honey?"

"What, Aunt Momi?"

"I need a drink." Taking Marigold's hand tenderly, they headed toward the bow of the ship to look out at the horizon. As they walked away from Daddy and Hawaii, each lost in their own broken dreams, I thought of the ending of *Modern Times* when Charlie Chaplin and Paulette Goddard, holding hands, walked into

an afternoon sun as Chaplin's song, "Smile" played in the background.
"Smile when your heart is breaking,
Smile though your heart is aching..."

Watching them, walking and holding hands, I knew I would love them forever - for as long as they lived and for as long as I lived. I looked back to where Daddy stood and gave a final wave to the Aloha Tower as it too was fading from sight. I waved with my left hand hoping that one day, Daddy would be there standing, looking up, reaching out, and catching my left hand in his.

As the ark left the calm, green harbor water, it now plowed into large black waves, colossal rollers coming in from a hurricane raging out at sea. It was the same rough winter seas that Grandma told tales about. The skies ahead had turned brown and thunder, lightning and heavy rain were promised beyond the line of ships. Foamy white spray began cascading over the bow and I began to taste salt on my lips.

The white spray became ostrich feathers on Alice Faye's hat and I imagined handsome men in tails and beautiful women in satin gowns waltzing in a huge ballroom with Alice Faye standing at the top of a towering staircase dressed in Mother's long, black velvet gown, singing:
"After the ball is over,
After the break of dawn,
After the dancers leaving,
After the song is gone.
Many the hearts are breaking,
If you should leave them all,
Many the hearts that are breaking
After the ball."

My ball was over and tonight Marigold was going to be seasick.

69

Better than Mayonnaise

I walked into the ark with the mayonnaise bottle and went to find the galley. Perhaps on my way, I'd be lucky enough to run into Daisy and Neal - and that stowaway Mina. Strolling down the corridor singing "After the Ball," I kept bumping into passengers because the ship began to roll back and forth. I once again pretended I was strolling down the lobby of the Royal Hawaiian Hotel holding Hatsuko's hand and looking for movie stars.

As I walked, mirrors on both walls reflected me - then other images replaced mine. Kimo was in a lifeboat with Grandma as captain. Fluffy was licking my face. Walter was playing with his train. Uku, Kaina, Mary Emily, Uncle Will, and Aunt Ella were under a Christmas tree opening presents. Mr. Hamada was spying. Uncle Lono was lying next to me on the grass as Gertrude and Agnes were sticking out their tongues at us. Charlie was underwater in the Arizona calling for help and Hatsuko was making me an egg salad sandwich. Mother, last of all, was wearing her black gown and holding up a skull. Everyone had their eyes closed.

I stopped and looked into one of the mirrors and saw me staring back at me. I saw I was still fat-faced and didn't detect one handsome Tyrone Power feature. But I liked my name and said "Percy" to myself and then made all kinds of funny faces to the person reflected in the mirror.

I moved away from the mirror to search for an icebox and realized I was lost. Every corridor looked the same and I forgot the cabin number. I wasn't scared because Marigold and Aunt Momi would find me before we reached San Francisco because I'd look for them if they were lost.

I stopped and looked into another mirror and studied my profile. Sticking out my chin, squinting my eyes, curling up one side of my mouth, I detected a hero. There was the beginning look of a Scarlet Pimpernel.

A large hand descended on my shoulder, startling me, as a voice boomed out, "I believe I have found the Scarlet Pimpernel. Sir Percy, I presume." I turned around and I was amazed to see Johnny. I asked, "Where did you come from?"

He put his face down to mine and said, "Young lad, I've been looking all over for you. The princess and your sister have been worried about you because they thought you might have fallen overboard. But your aunt did say that you might be headed for the galley. They didn't want to lose you so early in the trip."

"They've been worried about me?" I said, surprised. Acting like the Scarlet

Pimpernel, I puffed out my chest and boasted, "I can take care of myself, Johnny."

"I think you can, too, Sir Percy. I believe I can help find what you're looking for."

I explained, "I was looking for an icebox for my mayonnaise." I showed Johnny the bottle of mayonnaise. Putting his arm around my shoulder, he said, "That's a fine bottle of mayonnaise if I ever I saw one. Let's go find a home for it right now."

I frowned and held back. "What's troubling you, mate?" he asked. "I don't know," I sighed, "I wish my mother was here with me."

"Where is she?" he asked. I answered, not looking at him, "She's in heaven with Hatsuko and Fluffy and everyone else I know. Don't come too near me, Johnny, because everyone who knows me dies. I am a cursed boy."

He smiled and said, "I don't believe in curses, mate, and your mother must be pretty happy up there with all that good company that's died on you." "I hope so," I answered.

Taking me by the shoulders, he looked me straight in the face and said, "Here, boy, I think what you need right now is a good old-fashioned hug."

I pulled away and said, "No, Johnny, I don't like to be touched."

He held my shoulders tight and cocked his head, and said, "You don't, do you? Well, I've never let a little thing like that bother me because when I see a young hero who looks like he needs a big hug - he gets one. Come here, lad."

"Please, Johnny, don't," I pleaded, pulling away from him.

He reached out his two big, burly arms and brought me toward him. When I felt his chest, I blasted a sound louder then any ship's whistle I ever heard. I wailed like three werewolves and all the secrets and tears that I had been holding in my stomach came crying out. Out of my Pandora's box flew: Daddy's disappearance, the dresses I wore, Kimo and Walter's deaths, Agnes and Gertrude, the secret under the house, Mr. Hamada, Uku and his fleas, Kaina up on the hill, Aunt Mari's enema, Uncle Lono killing his wife with a plate, my terrible jealousy about Charlie, being fat, hating my name, Hatsuko's frozen toe, Mary Emily, Mother's ruby red lips in the coffin, and the curse. More and more things gushed out as Johnny sat me gently down next to the wall. Breathing hard, I kept on telling him everything that I had stuffed away, sounding like a ship's engine churning.

I stopped as suddenly as I had begun. I had emptied out all the bilge water from my ship. Johnny sat down next to me and I started to cry. People passing us pretended I wasn't there.

Johnny took my hand and asked, "Are you finished, mate?" I answered, still crying, looking at my hands' shaking, "I think so, Johnny but I don't feel so good now." I laid my head on his lap as he stroked my head and said, "You'll be all right. You had a lot to get out, Sir Percy. A little person can only hold so much in him without it having to get out sometime."

After I finished crying, I lifted my head up and asked, "Johnny, would you mind holding the mayonnaise bottle? I'm a little shaky right now." He nodded, saying, "You trust me with that?"

I handed him the bottle and curled up next to him, saying, "Mother used to tell us a story about a terrible monster named Hunkacha. The little boy in the story was named Johnny. Isn't that funny because your name is Johnny, too. He was a nice boy. I always wanted to be brave as Johnny and tell the truth."

He answered, stroking my head, "Johnny is a common name, lad, but I'm glad to hear that your Johnny was a nice boy. You know, Sir Percy, I wouldn't let another day go by without having a hug and getting out the bad stuff. I'd say a hug a day for Sir Percy, wouldn't you?"

I said, closing my eyes, "I guess so, but my family doesn't touch." He laughed, tapping his finger on my head, "We can change that, can't we?"

"I guess so." I looked up at him. "Will you give me a hug a day?"

"I'll do me best," he said, patting my back. I put my head back down on his lap as he stroked my head, saying, "Young Percy, I want you to know about the Scarlet Pimpernel. Everyone thought he was a sissy because he acted like one but he wasn't. He acted that way because it helped save the lives of Frenchmen from being guillotined. Heroes never tell anyone they are heroes."

"That's me, Johnny. I'm the Scarlet Pimpernel but don't tell anyone."

"I promise." He asked again, "You sure you want me to hold this bottle of mayonnaise?"

I took my head off his lap. "Yes, I trust you." Taking a deep breath, I asked a big question, "Johnny, have we met before? I don't think we're strangers."

"It might have happened."

Sitting up, I said, "I'm ready to go back."

"If you're feeling fit, let's go."

"I am." I got up off the floor and helped Johnny up because he had to struggle to get on his feet, being a big man.

Once standing, I said, "Johnny, may I ask you another personal question?" He answered, "My dad said they're the only questions worth asking. Shoot away, lad."

"Are you an angel?" I inquired. He laughed, "My mates don't think so." I asked further, "Do you know who Alice Faye is?" He looked at me as if I had read his mind and answered, "That's me favorite actress, Sir Percy." I hit his arm and said, "No! You're fooling me now."

"Honest to God," he said back. "That blonde beauty is me favorite movie actress. I know everything about her. Her real name is Alice Jeanne Leppert. She was born May 5, 1912 in New York City. She is married to Phil Harris, which I think is the biggest damn crime in the world because she should have married me. Her first movie was *George White's Scandals* and her father was a fireman."

"No, Johnny," I corrected, "he was a policeman." Slapping his forehead, he replied, "Of course, you're right. That he was. He was a policeman in New York City."

"What is your all-time favorite Alice Faye musical?" I asked. I knew it before he said without hesitation, *"Lillian Russell."*

I was in shock because no man I had ever asked about Alice Faye had ever said that to me. "Me, too," I said, giving Johnny a punch on the arm like the heroes did in the movies. He reached his hand out and grabbed mine. "Take my hand and let's go hunt for that icebox. It's nice having a friend who likes my Alice Faye as much as I do."

I looked at his gigantic arms with red hair all over them and remarked,

"Johnny, I used to think that red was a bad color because my Aunt Mari wore a red wig and the person that took my daddy away wore red all the time. I think I have been looking through a telescope from the wrong end. Do you think that's possible, Johnny?"

Putting his hand holding the mayonnaise jar around my shoulder, he said, "Sir Percy, at one time or another, we all look through the telescope from the wrong direction. It's just being human, Sir Percy."

"Don't you think that's a curious thing, Johnny?" I asked.

"Yes. At times, I'd say life is curious."

As we walked down the passageway, he remarked, "Sir Percy, before we turn the corner, I want you to know that nobody ever leaves you unless you want them to. Your mother and all your chums in heaven will always be with you, protecting you, helping you, loving you for the rest of your life if you will believe that and let them.

"I do, Johnny. I do." I stopped walking and held Johnny back, saying, "Johnny, I have something important to say, and I can't walk and say it." He stopped and looked at me. Taking a deep breath, I said, "I have another bottle of mayonnaise left in my suitcase and I would be very pleased if you would accept it as a gift."

Johnny beamed and said, "Thank you, young Percy. I will receive it with great pleasure. I couldn't think of anything better to have in the whole wide world. You have all the makings for a Scarlet Pimpernel hero. He was a spy, he wore ladies' clothes as a disguise, he was smart, he had honor, he was brave, and he knew how to keep secrets. But most of all he was generous to his friends and I want to tell you, Percy, that Best Foods mayonnaise put on anything is my favorite dish."

I held Johnny's hand in mine and said, "I knew you were going to say that. I just knew it. I also know Mother sent you to me. You're going to be my new friend for life - anyway for as long as you live and for as long as I live. I also know that you will help me hide my friend Mina in a lifeboat just as I know I will bring back the skull to Kapake, bury it and make the curse go away. And I know that one day soon I will become a famous actor who is a famous spy, take Alice Faye for lunch at the Brown Derby and become a millionaire like Mr. Dillingham. I also know for certain that Marigold will marry John Wayne and Aunt Momi will get her son back. I also know that around my corner, only good things are waiting for me because I just found out that I was born a hero. My mother named me Percy so I could fight all the curses and all the bad Hunkachas that come at me in the world. And, now that reminds me, I remember where we met before."

Johnny looked at me and smiled, "I remember, too." Then Johnny and I turned left at the next corner and walked smack into the ship's galley. For the first time since the Japanese bombed Pearl Harbor, something wonderful was waiting for me. I looked right at it. It was the icebox for my Best Foods mayonnaise.

Epilogue – A Dream

I had a dream on the first night out at sea sailing on the Aquitania. The dream is as vivid today as it was the night I dreamt it.

A Japanese submarine was submerged in the middle of the Pacific. The captain of the submarine ordered, "Periscope up." The periscope rose to the surface as the captain looked through it. He saw a convoy of ships, eight of them zigzagging in front of him, the biggest ship being a big four-stacker. He turned to a man in a black suit behind him and said in Japanese, "We get plenty big fish to kill tonight." The captain over his intercom ordered his men, "Get torpedoes ready."

The man behind him commanded, "Move aside. Let me see." The captain moved away as the man in the suit looked through the periscope. He said to the captain, "Ah, just as I thought, the Aquitania. She's a beautiful ship." The captain smiled and said, "She make big splash when she goes down."

Taking over the periscope, the captain bellowed into the intercom, "Men, torpedoes ready?" A reply came faintly back over the intercom, "Yes, Captain. Torpedoes ready."

The man in the dark suit suddenly heard a loud buzz in his ears. It almost deafened him. He ordered, "Captain, stop. We not torpedo these ships. They only carry old men, women, children, and small boy of eight. That boy on the Aquitania is my best friend. One day after the war, you will hear he has done great things. He is a great hero just like the Scarlett Pimpernel. Save your torpedoes for battleships and aircraft carriers. We not torpedo my best friend. Captain, stop your orders right now. At once."

"But..." stammered the captain.

"Captain Ishida, I outrank you. Command your men to stop. We get bigger fish to sashimi near Midway." The captain lowered the periscope, locked it in place and ordered the men in the torpedo room to cease action. The navigator set a new course to the East and the submarine headed for bigger fish.

Mr. Hamada looked pleased.

Sitting on the captain's desk, right behind Mr. Hamada, were two little invisible Japanese mama-sans. One was named Agnes-San and the other Gertrude-San. They watched as the man in the black suit and the captain continued to talk while the mama-sans ate bowls of rice using chopsticks and sipped strong black tea. The girls were dressed in formal crimson-colored kimonos that had the Emperor's yellow chrysanthemums printed all over. Agnes, clicking her chopsticks, said, "Whew, that was a close call, Gertrude. Glad you buzzed into his ear."

Taking a sip of tea, Gertrude informed Agnes, "I told you we had to leave Percy because we have to follow Mr. Hamada to see that he does all the right things. When the war is over, he'll thank us for it because he and Percy will be friends again."

"Gertrude, how do you think Percy is doing right now?" Agnes asked.

Gertrude replied, "He's doing just fine. Kimo and Walter check on him all the time. But that Mr. Percy has turned into a little know-it-all. He has become an annoying little smarty-pants pest because he thinks he knows everything." Gertrude, sticking a chopstick in her hair, sniffed, "That little smarty-pants doesn't know everything by a long shot."

"Like what?" Agnes asked.

Gertrude, speaking like a Miss Smarty-Pants herself, said to Agnes, "It's something even you don't know." Agnes began to get upset and pounded her chopsticks on the table, whining, "I hate it when you keep secrets from me, Gertrude. What is it? If you don't tell me, I'll stick one of these chopsticks up your nose."

Before Agnes could do that, Gertrude hit her on the head with a chopstick and warned, "Don't you threaten me, Mama-San, or you won't get a second bowl of rice." Then Gertrude made her eyes into inscrutable Japanese eyes and told a secret she had been holding ever since God gave Hatsuko to Percy. She said, "Mr. Hamada, standing over there, was Hatsuko's father."

"No," squealed Agnes with surprise.

"Yes," Gertrude said, nodding like a wise Buddha.

At the shock of hearing that piece of news, Agnes spilled shoyu on the floor, then complained, "Darn it, I wish there was some mayonnaise around here for my rice. I hate shoyu."

"You're a mess, Agnes," Gertrude said, wiping up the shoyu off the floor. "Look at what you've done. You've been around Percy too long."

Ignoring Gertrude, putting another a big mouthful of rice into her mouth, Agnes asked, "Gertrude, what do you think Percy would have said if he knew Mr. Hamada was Hatsuko's father?"

"Let me think," said Gertrude, pondering the question while pulling the chopstick out of her hair. She pointed it at Agnes, thought for another minute, then she put the chopstick back in her hair and finally said, "Percy would have said that life and heaven get curiouser... and curiouser."

In *The Honolulu Advertiser*, on the night of Percy's dream, Friday, February 20th, the paper noted that the Technicolor musical, *That Night in Rio*, starring Alice Faye, Don Ameche, and Carmen Miranda, played to packed houses at the Waikiki Theater. In the Piggly Wiggly market on Nuuanu Street, Best Foods mayonnaise was on sale at 43 cents a quart.